MW01482028

The Messenger from Myris Dar

BOOK ONE OF THE STONE GUARDIANS

A Novel by Kindrie Grove

Kindrie Grove Studios Inc.
© Kindrie Grove Studios Inc. 2016

Kindrie Grove Studios Inc.
Box 234, 113- 437 Martin Street
Penticton, BC, V2A 5L1
Canada

Story and illustrations © Kindrie Grove 2016
All rights reserved. No part of this publication may be reproduced without prior written permission from the author.

First published in Canada, 2016
Paperback Book Version published in 2018
The Messenger from Myris Dar
ISBN – 9781549945472

Author: Kindrie Grove
Front cover art and map illustration:
Kindrie Grove

This book is dedicated to all those who choose to find light in the darkness.

Acknowledgments

This project began almost 12 years ago with a scene that came to my mind and would not leave. I began to write, thinking that it would free me to move on. Little did I know what a torrent of storytelling it would release. The book began to write itself, and I read it as it was written. The initial bones of the tale came through incredibly quickly with characters so powerfully real for me that I lived and breathed with them.

Then began the slow task of turning the telling of the story into a well written adventure that could be shared with the world. From then on, the work on the manuscript happened in short moments snatched from a busy family life and career as a professional artist.

As I neared the end of the incremental editing process, the images and spirit of the characters began to arrive as sculptures and paintings. Thus was born the *Legend Collection* – works of art that explore the archetypal essence of my book as well as other mythologies. This series of works is on-going as is the writing now of the second book of the Stone Guardians series. It is my hope that you enjoy the characters and story as much as I have enjoyed writing it!

Many wonderful people have helped to make this book a reality and I wish to express my sincere thanks for their input and support:

Initial story edits by Jerrica Cleland-Hura were immensely helpful. The first readers of the early manuscript offered great feedback – Michael Bezener, DJ Cleland-Hura, Wendy Grove, Barbara Tomes and Heather Campbell. Thank you all for your comments! I wish to thank Dawn Renaud for her great advice which made me a better writer. To Aurora Renée Matheson who helped me understand the importance of the Legend Collection's link with the books. Lastly, to my husband Michael, for his unfailing support of my writing and the belief that it should be published. It has meant so much to me.

Table of Contents

Map of Eryos

ERYOS
Great Timor Mountains
Northern Sea
N
Tyrn
Pellaris
Tabor
Pellar
Krang
Rith City
Tyrn R.
Pellar R.
Lok Myrr Fortress
Boglands
Klyssen
Balor
The Wilds
Wyborn
Ren Mountains
Lor Hoth
Lor Danith
Ren
Dan Tynell
Dencior
Ren Tarner
Black Hills
Southern Eryos Ocean
Myris Dar

Prologue

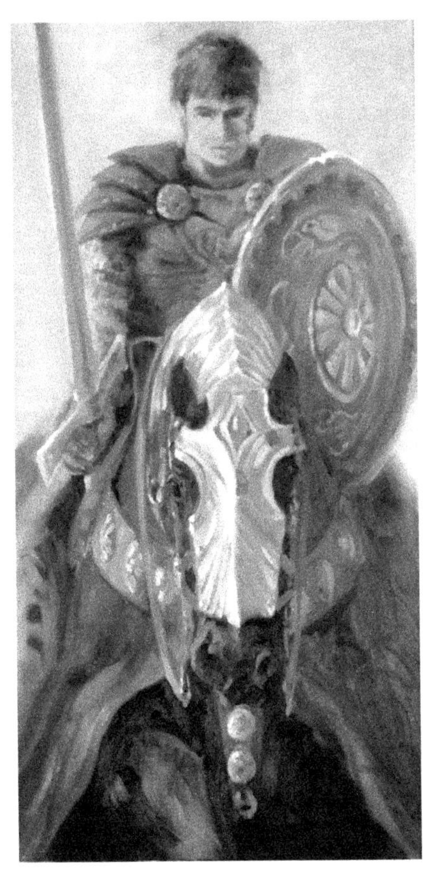

The Summoner

Light seeped into the darkness. It grew from a faint pinpoint with a sickly, green glow – slowly pulsing. It expanded outward, pushing the blackness back. The pulsing was arrhythmic, thudding like a diseased heart. Vibrations stirred the cool night air.

The glow revealed a figure in a dark hooded cloak holding a long staff high with a gnarled hand. The glowing green light was emanating from the tip of the staff.

A second light burst into the space before the figure. It exploded into the night, a blinding, dazzling white with a thunderous crack, rolling and echoing in the unseen distance. The shockwave whipped up the figure's cloak.

The second light pulsed differently from the staff tip. Its rhythm was solid and constant. With each beat, it expanded outward until it dwarfed the figure. It appeared as a thin vertical slash, an illuminated disk. From the front it was like a sun, too bright to look into. Light rays scattered outward, crackling and sizzling through the air.

Despite the blinding glare, the face of the figure remained in shadow within the deep hood. Only the creases and folds of the cloak were thrust into clarity.

The figure stood like stone, waiting, summoning.

Soon a shape began to take form within the circle of light. Flickers and shimmers coalesced into the dark mass of a monstrous figure. It erupted from the centre violently, head thrown back as an agonized howl died in its throat.

Grudgingly, a deceptive calm descended upon the creature – a constrained stillness. It strode out into the darkness to stop in front of the one who had summoned it.

The Summoner looked up, for the creature before it towered. The beast ponderously bowed its enormous head in response to the command and turned to stand facing the portal.

As it turned, its features were exposed to the unforgiving brilliance. A great head, sporting a spiky crest of stiff fur swivelled to watch as more movement stirred from the other side.

Another huge figure exploded forth.

The second creature, arriving in torment like the first, accepted its orders from the Summoner and turned to wait as well.

And so it began – more and more of the huge beings emerged through, sometimes in twos and threes, howling in unison. Their ranks grew, merging into the shadow.

They were enormous, with wide shoulders jutting with spikes that traveled the length of the arms to end in sharp, clawed hands. They wore no clothing and with each pulse of light, their muscular forms and sinewy movement was illuminated. The glare reflected off their jet-black skin, glittering on scales. Long ivory fangs gleamed when they opened their mouths. When the huge heads turned to watch the next of their kin arrive, thick corded muscles flexed down their necks.

There was a formidable beauty about the creatures. Yet for all their grace a harrowed stiffness settled upon them as they arrived, hunching their erect bodies.

The creatures came to the Summoner, ripped from their own lands, escorted by the dying sound of a roar they had begun on the other side. By the time the last of the terrible sound left their throats, their transformation was complete.

Time eked by and the length of the night slowly passed. And still more came, swelling the throng of black bodies, standing shoulder to shoulder, rank upon rank.

Finally, when so many of the great beings had gathered that they spread out into the darkness where only the imagination held sway, the hooded figure lowered the staff. The greenish glow from the tip faded. In response, the portal of light flashed outward – streaks knifing out across the blackness then collapsing back with a great crack, leaving a burning after-image and a ringing in the air.

Blackness engulfed the scene, then was beaten back as the staff flared once more, lighting the towering bodies closest. Stone-still they stood, a forest of huge black trunks.

The Summoner reached up a pale, bony hand and cast back the hood. Green light glistened on his bald head as he turned to survey the ranks. The figure swept out a hand with fingers splayed and spoke.

A harsh guttural sound of an odd language, accented with strange clicks and burrs, echoed out over the sea of waiting creatures. Wind stirred the figure's cloak, lifting the hem to reveal blood red robes beneath and swirling the strange sounds into the night.

As the last of the speech died away it had reached every ear, made every command clear.

The immense beasts began to stir, slowly at first, then more and more quickly as the innumerable host fragmented and broke apart and the last of the creatures disappeared silently into the night.

The creatures had been brought through. The Summoner sagged in exhaustion but a flash of teeth gleamed in a twisted smile. A price had been paid this night in excruciating pain and mortal weariness, but the Summoner was pleased even as the lassitude washed through him.

He had waited almost a thousand years for this; it marked the beginning of the end game, of events carefully planned and long anticipated. He would not be able to bring more of the creatures through this way again – would have to rely on his more conventional methods, but it would be enough. He slowly pulled himself upright with the help of his staff. As he took a step to leave, his mind was already turned to the next tasks.

Part I

A Light in the Dark

Therial Lan Morian sat quietly waiting. Her ancient bones ached keenly from the cold of the stone floor and her ropy back muscles had stiffened in protest. It used to be she could wait like this for days, moving only occasionally as her bodily functions demanded.

She could sense the others in the room with her always, knew exactly where they sat and when their breathing or concentration faltered. When the sight took her, though, she would not be able to feel anything of this world. She would be lifted up, away from her aching bones and the inadequacy of her withered lungs, away from the perpetual shadows, and she would be able to *see*. Colour and light, the unbearable beauty of Erys's world would unfold in a swirling, spinning deluge of imagery.

The calling of sight was Therial's one true joy and she endured the darkness of her days living for the visions. As a child, she had been quite content, never knowing what she lacked. But when she turned thirteen, the inner sight found her, and she finally understood what she was living without. She had languished for months, devastated by the knowledge that she should live her life bereft of eyesight.

Her mother had gone to the Seers in hopes that a place for her daughter could be found, where she could live happily among others like herself. Not all the Seers of Danum were blind but many were. The gift of inner sight, it seemed, came often to those who were not whole. And so she had found a purpose for her life – to be a vessel for the light of Erys, waiting always for the wonder of visions to shed light on her darkness.

It was coming now. Therial could feel it, like a faint breeze that stirred the stillness, ruffling the hair on her head. It always came with sound as though a distant storm approached, growing in volume as it came. When it hit, it was with full force and Therial was continually surprised not to find herself flat on her back afterwards.

Light suddenly blazed into her blackness and she turned her head instinctively to ease the brightness. She saw stars, a wide bright spangle that studded the heavens and glittered like jewels in the dark. She was floating and she felt coldness unlike any she could have imagined. The bright light came from the moons, but Raelys and Bashelar were not in their own space. Bashelar's smaller reddish surface barely peeked out from behind her larger sister.

Before Therial could wonder, sound crashed into the peaceful space. Screams and curses, animal growls and men's voices swirled around her, clashing metal. A dizzying spiral of movement. She could still see the moons but she was looking up at them from the ground.

A black streak hurtled passed her with an animal scream and a battle solidified. Before she could make out the details she was above once more, looking down on a great city perched on the edge of high sea cliffs. The city was about to be swallowed by a mammoth black tide but the wave came from the land not the ocean. She did not recognize the place but she knew with certainty that the city must not fall.

And then she was hurtling through space with only the moons for company until she felt it – a nameless dread welling up. It rose from the blackness beneath her and she could taste the wrongness of it in the back of her throat. It was older than time itself. It existed outside of the endless march of days, forever just under the surface, awaiting the call. Then it would be pulled into this world along with the doom it harboured.

It took a moment for Therial to realize the darkness she saw was her own. Hoping to steady herself, she took as deep a breath as her scarred lungs would allow. She reached up and wiped away some of the sweat on her wrinkled brow with a shaking hand.

Ignoring the pain that darted through her neck, she turned her head to the others, opening her eyes. Her voice came out in a hoarse whisper that had as much to do with what she had seen as the dryness in her throat. "The time has come."

Leave-taking

The blue water of the Eryos Ocean was pure and deep. A wind blew from the northwest. Northern winds were a rare occurrence but seemed fitting for their departure, bringing the faintest scent of the unknown continent they were to sail for. Rowan looked away from the surging swells that rolled under the dock and studied the rocky shore of the bay. The wind caught a few loose strands of her hair, tugging them free of her long braid.

Her small party stood on the shore, going once more through last minute packing and organization. She could hear their excited voices now and then. Their horses stood in a milling group beyond and Rowan made out the grey flashes of her big stallion.

Her mother and brother had seen her off from the city earlier this morning but she had not wanted them to come to the port, needed time to herself before they were to embark on the foreign ship. Her cousin Dell was off to the side, perched upon a huge boulder rooted in the churning surf. Like her, he needed to be alone for a last farewell to their island home. Most of their small party had said their good-byes back in the city, except for Lesiana, inseparable from her husband until absolutely necessary.

Rowan turned her back on the rising volcanic hills of the island to face the sparkling ocean again. After the banquet last night with its fanfare and revelry, the morning was quietly portentous. She flexed her hands into fists and relaxed, exhaling. The sense of the gravity for their mission would not leave her. Myrians were very supportive of sending aid to the mainland, even when they knew little of its people, but Rowan suspected that many of the Islanders did not completely understand the nature of the mission they had voted to send to Eryos.

She had woken long before dawn to sit, awaiting the soft glow of the rising sun as it filtered through the open fretwork of her room. She had been suddenly afraid she would never again see the sun rise over the land of Myris Dar.

When she and Dell had spoken last with the Seers, they had been cautioned that their small party would face hardship in the distant lands and that strength of heart would succeed at times where strength of arms failed. In typical fashion, the Seers had given no details or further help beyond the vague, cryptic warning.

Rowan shook her head and sighed, glancing to the side at the rising shoulders of the bay. The green of the spring grass had faded to the customary golden hues of summer. Only the olive trees and terraced gardens retained their verdant colour.

Seabirds called from overhead, their long narrow wings suspending them on the strong wind, floating in place with only a ruffle of feathers to attest to the effort. Rowan watched wistfully as they spied fish and folded their wings to plummet headfirst into the sea.

The smooth round head of a cellion popped up above the rolling surface, its liquid brown eyes regarding Rowan with curiosity before it slid beneath the waves, oscillating one of its flippers as if in farewell.

She reached up and adjusted the baldric that carried her sword strapped to her back and caught sight of the intricately tooled leather of the new vembraces her brother Andin had given her last night. She smiled; he had made them for her himself and been so proud to see her wearing them this morning.

Rowan looked to the edge of the bay as movement caught her eye. Three ships hove into view around the tip of the headland. They were making good time in the strong wind. The two smaller, sleeker ships were Myrian, their narrow prows slicing through the waves with precision.

The larger ship was foreign; its many coloured pinions and square sails belled out in the breeze and its wide beam sitting low in the swells. It was flanked by the two Myrian ships — escorts to shadow it into the bay. A merchant ship from beyond the land of Eryos had been easy to acquire passage upon. The Westerners from beyond Eryos and the high mountain barrier that separated it from the rest of the continent were staunch seafarers who explored the waters of the known world to its limits. They brought spice and copper and extraordinary woven goods to the few active ports in Eryos and in turn filled their holds with the rare blue-glazed Stoneman pottery and bales of wool and other trade goods.

Myris Dar was a frequent stop along their trade routes, though it was rare for the merchant ships to be granted permission to land. They were usually met out at sea by the Myrian patrol ships that could easily outrun the larger, more cumbersome vessels to prevent a daring captain from getting through to land ashore. Many battles had been fought several leagues offshore to keep the Western Pirates from sailing off with a ship hold's worth of Myrian plunder.

Rowan could just make out the distant forms of sailors as they scurried over the decks to reef in the multitude of canvas sheets. She had fought and killed men like these who had broken through the Myrian patrol ships to land on Myris Dar. There was often little difference between merchants and pirates and she had battled alongside other Myrians to keep their island sovereign and safe from such raiders.

The island of Myris Dar was almost completely forgotten by the people of Eryos, who had not plied the deep oceans to the south of the mainland for centuries. Even if they had heard of the island from western traders, they would be incapable of reaching Myris Dar in their small fishing boats and sloops.

The kingdoms of Eryos had not been able to look beyond their own borders to the wider world since the vast empires that had flourished hundreds of years ago had crumbled to leave only scattered tribes and a chaotic quest for power. From the little she knew of Eryos, it was only just beginning to rise above the age of darkness and turmoil that had swallowed it after the fall of the twin empires. And she and her companions were about to journey into the heart of that struggling, unsettled land, with little idea of what they had to do once they arrived to fulfill their mission.

Rowan looked critically at the large ship as it came about and began to head towards the small port. It had been given permission to land only long enough to accept its cargo, and then it was to sail out on the same tide that brought it in.

The ship's high deck had a convex camber to it and the hull's wooden planks were smooth and free of barnacles. The three masts rising from the centre line of the deck were thick and tapered gracefully to the tops. The middle mast ended in a high crow's nest, with a sailor posted there for lookout.

There would be more than enough room for the small party of warriors, their horses and the gear they would need for the weeks long journey across the Eryos Ocean to the mainland port city of Dendor in Lor Danith. From there Rowan and her party would head into the unknown in search of a city built on high sea cliffs.

Rowan's gaze slid past the large ship to the sky and ocean beyond in the northwest. Dark thunderclouds were gathering on the horizon in deep grays and purples. She saw a brief flash of white lightening and distant thunder rolled across the swelling waves toward her. Myris Dar experienced little rain during the hot, dry summer. She wondered whether the Seers would note the approaching storm as a sign of things to come.

She looked again at the ship. It would not be long before it pulled up beside the pier. Rowan turned away from it and the ocean and walked across the heavy wooden planks towards her companions.

There was much work to be done yet before they set sail for Eryos.

A Chance Encounter

As he crept towards the campsite, Torrin studied the lonely figure huddled over the small fire. The flames of the fire were well concealed. Only the light it cast upon the figure hunched over it betrayed it. A larger pale form, highlighted against the deeper surrounding shadow, shifted beyond the camp – a horse.

Despite the lateness of the season, the night air was still warm and although this was one of the most beautiful places to be traveling, it was also an extremely dangerous one.

Torrin crouched down and waited, as he knew the others were also doing. The scent of earth and dead leaves rose from the forest floor and he breathed it in deeply. Arynilas appeared suddenly at his side, motioning that all was clear.

Torrin had long since become used to the silence of the Tynithian. He could almost always hear the approach of men like his own kin but a Tynithian was something completely different. The stealth of the Twilight People was legendary, their tracking skills unparalleled. Torrin believed it had to do with the shape shifting abilities of the slight, nimble race. They all had the ability to assume animal form and the instinctual intelligence they gained from that talent was uncanny.

Torrin had heard stories of Tynithians who renounced their human-like forms entirely, living out their extremely long lives in animal shape. As a race, they were very different from humans. Their eyes were tilted and jewel-like in color and their skin was an almost metallic copper tone. They also lived to be thousands of years old.

It was Arynilas who had first seen the faint glimmer through the trees that marked the camp. While Arynilas had crept close to the campsite to investigate further, Torrin, his brother Nathel and their two other companions, Dalemar and Borlin, had waited in the shadows. When the Tynithian had returned, with the news that there appeared to be only one occupant, they had tethered the horses and begun to cautiously move toward the light of the small fire.

The camp and its single occupant were cause for more than a little curiosity. Torrin and his companions had believed they were the only ones able to move through these rugged lands. He glanced up at the stars, marking them. Only half an hour had passed since the discovery of the stranger. Torrin looked ahead to the campsite and the lone figure, questions filling his mind. When he glanced back to Arynilas, the Tynithian had already disappeared, moving on to signal the others that all was safe.

Dalemar had sensed no magic in the stranger, which meant they would not be surprising a Rith who could wield deadly fire. Dalemar, a young Rith himself, a magic wielder, had stood silently with his eyes closed, casting out for the signs of a fellow Rith. He had sensed nothing.

Torrin stood and began to walk towards the campsite. It was time to solve this mystery. It was important to know how this stranger had traveled so far into this forbidden territory, avoiding the death that claimed so many others. "Ho the camp!" he called. Torrin watched closely as the figure rose smoothly, reaching swiftly to the sword over his right shoulder.

"We are friends and mean you no harm. We simply wish to share your fire for a while," Torrin called quickly. The figure hesitated but did not lower his hand from the weapon. He was cloaked and hooded such that Torrin could not make out a face in the darkness.

"What do you want?" came a soft reply. It was almost a whisper and there was a hint of a strange accent.

"We were passing by, looking for a suitable rest site and saw your fire. We have food if you have not already eaten. We would share it with you."

"How many is 'we'?"

"There are five of us. It is safer to be with a few than with none, don't you think?"

The figure dropped his hand slowly and looked around at the shadows. He stumbled and caught himself, standing upright again. He reached reflexively to his left shoulder. The man was wounded.

"I do not trust strangers to share my camp." Again a quiet reply and the unfamiliar accent.

Torrin resumed walking towards the fire. "You look like you are injured. My brother is a healer. He could take a look at your wound." He stopped three paces from the stranger to avoid causing alarm, though from what he could see of him in the darkness this stranger did not appear to be intimidated, despite his condition.

Torrin had learned long ago how to use his large size to his advantage. He was bigger than the average man, especially the smaller southern people. He was tall and broad of shoulder and his dark hair and eyebrows over an intense blue gaze naturally lent to the stern impression he made. He had used those attributes often to intimidate when he chose, but it also meant he was aware of the fear he could cause unintentionally.

The stranger was smaller than he looked from a distance, perhaps a Lor Danion, though the accent did not fit. The face was still in shadow but as Torrin studied the stranger he caught a glimmer of pale hair within — a plaited braid that disappeared into the darkness of the hood. The people of Lor Danith were almost always dark haired. Torrin supposed he could be a Tynithian; the size would be about right.

Torrin frowned in puzzlement. A long cloak covered most of the stranger but he was well dressed, if a little differently from the styles he was accustomed to. He wore a leather breastplate, intricately tooled with unrecognizable designs; leather vembraces with similar decoration covered the forearms. The cloak was too warm for the balmy weather and Torrin suspected it was worn more for concealment. Shin guards of the same tooled leather were strapped over leather boots with soft soles made for gripping and balancing as well as treading quietly.

Torrin observed the fine boned hands, one of which was resting comfortably on the hilt of an intricately wrought dagger sheathed at the belt. He saw the delicate fingertips and his eyes widened in sudden realization – even Tynithian hands were not that slim, at least not male ones.

"A woman!" exclaimed Borlin in surprise. The short, burly Stoneman had just come into the firelight from the right and was peering at the stranger intently. The stranger assumed an air of ready tension, hooded head turned quickly to the new voice. Torrin could now see the smooth features of her face. He wondered again if she was a Tynithian; the finely arched eyebrows and high cheekbones certainly could belong to a Tynithian. But when she moved her head to look at the rest of

Torrin's companions as they moved into the light, he caught a glimpse of her eyes. Human eyes. Torrin could sense her unease as the rest of his companions gathered around them.

He pitched his voice low, speaking gently. "Please, do not fear us; we mean you no harm. Your honour is safe among us."

She cast her hood back then and turned to look at Torrin, a dangerous glint in her eyes. She wasn't afraid, only ready for whatever may come.

The thought struck him with intense incongruity. His experience offered him an opinion of what to expect from a woman but his instincts told him to ignore that opinion, in fact they screamed at him to be wary. This woman was not helpless. Far from it, judging by the way she held her ground — confident and steady.

She stood looking at Torrin, ignoring the rest of his companions, who had stopped now to watch the encounter unfold. A log on the fire popped suddenly, sending up a spray of sparks into the darkness. The woman barely responded to the noise, her gaze evenly on his. There was a challenge there.

Torrin searched for a way to dispel the tension. He lifted his hands, palms outward. "Upon my honour, we are no threat to you," he said softly.

The defiance in her gaze was replaced by pain and she reached again for her left shoulder with a sharp intake of breath. She swayed on her feet and her knees buckled, eyes closing as consciousness fled.

Torrin jumped forward, reaching out reflexively to catch her. A dark stain had spread through the shirt under the leather breastplate she wore.

"Nathel!" As Torrin lowered the woman to the ground, his brother came forward and knelt on the other side, swiftly unrolling a soft leather packet he took from his satchel. He unbuckled her breastplate and pulled the neck of her shirt up to see the wound, sucking air through clenched teeth as he did. "An arrow wound." He brought his face closer to see better in the dark. "It looks like she has removed the point and applied a poultice but the wound still bleeds. It looks as though infection has set in. The wound is a few days old, I'd say. Boil some water for tea. I must staunch the flow."

Borlin went striding off to get the horses and gear, and the Tynithian, Arynilas, went to calm the woman's restless animal, tethered nearby.

Nathel shook his head, frowning. Firelight caught his close-cropped hair, gilding its sandy color to gold. "It doesn't look like she has taken the time to let the wound heal properly. It looks to have been broken open more than once." Nathel looked at Torrin. "How do you suppose she made it this far in without catching the sickness?"

Torrin shook his head in silence, running a hand through his short dark hair. He had no idea.

The woman groaned in pain and the questions in Nathel's face dissolved into concern for the wounded. He pulled out a clean rag and unstopped his water skin, soaked the cloth and began to clean her wound.

Torrin found himself staring down at her. She was completely unconscious now. What would a woman be doing alone in the Wilds? She was well-armed and provisioned by the look of her camp, but this was a very dangerous place to travel. The Wilds were a no-man's land, one of a few places in the Land of Eryos where darkness and mystery still held sway. The contested boarders of Klyssen, Lor Danith, Ren and Tabor drew together into a tangled knot in this densely forested region.

Of the seven Kingdoms of Eryos, it was one of a few forbidding places where terror kept most out. Each of the four kingdoms that bordered the Wilds claimed some or all of it but none were willing to defend their stake.

The land was almost impossible to defend in any case — hilly, heavily treed and rugged. Armies had entered the dense vastness, intent on claiming land, but of those that entered the Wilds, few returned. Those that did came out covered in terrible weeping rashes and bloody boils, babbling incoherently about ghost lights and evil Tynithian magic. Most survivors eventually healed from their wounds, but few recovered their sanity.

Torrin and his companions had often come across rusted swords and shields, buckles and half-buried breastplates, the bodies of the warriors they had belonged to long since decomposed and absorbed into the moss covered ground. Graveyards for those swallowed by the Wilds and never heard from again.

But Nathel had discovered the truth about what the ignorant called "Tynithian magic." It was true that Tynithians had once dwelled in the Wilds, but that was centuries ago. The only magic they had left behind was the wonder of what little remained of their dwellings. It wasn't until Nathel had solved the mystery that Arynilas had admitted knowing the secret of the Wilds defence. He had kept silent for his people's sake and their pledge to keep the Wilds safe from human axes and colonization. The Tynithian had sworn Nathel and the rest of the companions to secrecy about the source of the magic — a delicate, creeping vine found throughout most of the forest, climbing up trees and over stones. It had tiny sky blue flowers that attracted bees and butterflies, the only creatures that seemed to be immune to its toxic oil. It was this unassuming plant, with its invisible defence, that had kept men and their armies or their logging expeditions from making forays into the Wilds since the Tynithians with their slowly shrinking population had abandoned it and their role of protecting the woodlands.

As a healer trained in herb lore, Nathel had thought the rashes and madness people told of to be more likely a result of exposure to poisonous plants. He had carefully taken samples of plants from along the edge of the Wilds and, without touching any of them directly, rubbed them into a fresh hide. It had not taken him long to link the violent reaction with the small vine.

It seemed an absurdity that no one had discovered the truth about the magic before now, but it suited Torrin and his companions well. They had thus learned to identify the plant and how to avoid it and the sickness it carried. It meant that they and they alone could navigate the beautifully rugged country unharmed, a great advantage when the roads that bypassed the Wilds were rife with thieves and brigands.

"Perhaps I can be of assistance?" It was Dalemar. The young Rith knelt at the woman's head and tentatively placed his hands on either side of her temples. A moment passed and then she thrashed suddenly, knocking Nathel's hands away as he tended the shoulder. When she stilled, she appeared to be sleeping peacefully. "There, hopefully that will help."

Nathel drew back after wiping at the wound to discover the bleeding stopped and the wound almost healed over. He looked across at Dalemar, a grin on his face. "You've been keeping secrets from us, Dalemar. Small skill indeed!" He turned to look at Torrin. "Our fledgling Rith has surprised us again, Tor. Soon you will have no need for me at all." He chuckled to himself while shaking his head at Dalemar.

"Nonsense," scoffed the Rith, his long, pale blond hair caught the dim light as he shook his head. A smile transformed the smooth lines of his normally thoughtful face. He flipped his hair over his shoulder, exposing a slightly pointed ear, and bent down to look closely at the woman's wound. "My powers are inconsistent at best. I was lucky Nathel. It will be quite a while before I can surpass your skills as a healer." He patted Nathel's shoulder consolingly, which made the big man laugh all the more.

"Never fear, brother, we will always need the use of your sword arm," said Torrin quietly. Nathel grinned up at his brother before turning his attention back to his patient. Torrin sometimes thought the healing and tending of the sick or wounded was the only thing his younger brother took seriously.

Borlin came back then to the campsite with their animals, and the stocky Stoneman set about cooking them all a meal. Torrin and Arynilas unsaddled and cared for the horses and began to set a camp.

The water boiled and Nathel brewed a bitter tea from his precious stash of winoth root. Torrin knew the tea well; his brother had fed it to him on numerous occasions when he had lost blood to a deeper wound. It tasted fouler than copper tainted water but it worked, helping the body to replenish the blood that was lost. Torrin had seen men treated with the root recuperate days before those not dosed.

Borlin helped Nathel pour the tea into the woman's mouth, spoonful by spoonful. She swallowed reflexively but did not wake. Nathel mixed a poultice to apply to the wound to help draw out the infection, and covered her with a thick blanket before joining the companions in their evening meal.

Of Eryos and the Stranger

"How is she?"

Nathel looked up at Torrin from where he was checking his patient. "She will be fine. Thanks to Dalemar the wound is mostly healed and the winoth tea will help her regain her strength." He smiled mischievously. "Lucky for her she was asleep when we gave it to her." Nathel knew how horrible the brew was that he gleefully forced on them now and again; he'd had to take it himself on more than one occasion.

"What do you make of her, Nathel?" Torrin crouched down beside his brother.

Nathel shook his head. "I don't know. It is a strange thing. Why would she be alone out here, wounded like this? And the leather armour she wears." He reached out to trace a finger along the flowing, tooled design of the leather breastplate he had removed. "I've never seen its like, and we've seen a lot of war trappings, you and I. And a woman, no less, wearing leggings instead of skirts! Do you reckon she knows how to use that sword?"

Torrin glanced at the woman's face. "Something tells me she knows." He looked back at the breastplate. "I don't recognize the designs either." He picked up the sword and baldric Nathel had also removed and slowly slid the lightweight blade from its leather scabbard.

It was single edged, ever so slightly curved, and the balance was superb. A pattern similar to the breastplate was inscribed down the blade from guard to tip. As Torrin tilted the blade, the etched lines caught and reflected the firelight, shifting and glittering across surface. Soft leather was wrapped around the hilt to absorb sweat and prevent the grip from slipping. It was a beautiful thing. There was a sense of strength and power emanating from it. The longer he held it the more certain he became of the feeling – this was a deadly weapon and the grace and beauty of its form only served to heighten that impression.

Something about the sword caught his attention and he looked more closely at the inscribed blade. It wasn't just purely design but a curling script of some kind. He had no idea what it said.

He reluctantly slid the weapon back into its scabbard and laid it aside. His palm and fingertips tingled when the cool metal no longer touched his skin. The dagger he had noticed earlier, now buried under cloak and blanket, had looked to be a similar weapon. "Her features are almost more Tynithian than human," he said.

"Not so," Arynilas said from behind, and the brothers turned to look at him. "Although she does in some ways resemble Tynithians, she has many differences. Her eyes of course do not tilt and she is too tall for a Tynithian." Torrin nodded, she was indeed tall for a woman, the top of her head was level with his nose; most women barely reached his shoulders. It was one of the reasons he had first mistaken her for a man.

Arynilas pointed to the breastplate they had been examining with his slim hand. "Her weapons and features remind me of a people I learned of from my grandsire. He traveled the Eryos Ocean for many seasons and had once met an Island people he called Myrians. He said they were unlike the rest of the races of men, and were renowned for their swordsmen and women. He recalled their artistry to be unparalleled by any other humans."

"Myrian?" Torrin exchanged glances with his brother, who shared his perplexed expression. "We've never heard of this Myrian place."

Arynilas shook his head, glossy black hair swinging. "I would be surprised if you had. It is located deep in the Southern Eryos Ocean. I believe the island is called Myris Dar. My grandsire spent a long time among them. Long in human terms." Kneeling smoothly, he looked at the leatherwork. "Though they have not been heard from here in Eryos for centuries, it would be my guess that she is Myrian. As to what she is doing here, only she will be able to answer that question.

"My grandsire said the Myrians fiercely protect their isolation, permitting only limited trade and even that is done at sea. They will rarely allow a foreign ship to dock in their harbours. For one to be traveling here is indeed exceptional."

As the Tynithian left them, the brothers shared a look and Torrin glanced back down at the sleeping woman. "Go and get some sleep Nathel. I have first watch and will wake you if your patient needs you."

Nathel nodded agreement and stood up to stretch before walking to his sleeping roll next to the dying fire. Dalemar and Borlin were already snoring softly, indistinct humps covered in blankets. It had been a long day of travel for them and the discovery of the strange women had made it longer.

Torrin looked again at the woman; she would most likely sleep for some time. Aside from her slightly outlandish features and clothes, she looked not unlike other women he had met. He studied her slim nose and arched eyebrows, the smooth curve of her cheek and jaw, the slim neck and long, golden hair twisted into a braid – a vision of repose.

Their first encounter with her had left a very different impression, one that had surprised him. He remembered the defiant gaze, the confident stance and the fierce look of independence. He wanted her to wake up. Torrin looked forward to meeting this woman again.

He shook himself and turned to take up his position for watch, away from the firelight so that his eyes might adjust to the darkness. Now that they knew other people could travel the Wilds as well, greater vigilance was required.

The original mystery they had come to investigate had only led to more confounding questions — a woman from a forgotten place, carrying a deadly sword and dressed as a warrior. He and his companions had traveled the length of Eryos, from the Black Hills and Ren Tarnor in the south to Pellaris and Tyrn in the north. Never had they seen a female warrior. As diverse as the seven kingdoms of Eryos were, one thing was consistent – men waged war, not women.

Torrin looked back at the bundle of blankets lit dimly by the fire's embers. He shook his head; they could not leave her to whatever strange fate she followed alone, not here, nor could the companions afford the time to delay here to tend to her wounds. They would have to take her into Klyssen to the nearest town along their route.

These days, even a fortified town was no guarantee of safety. Sightings of the strange groups of creatures they had seen occasionally throughout the last weeks of their journey were increasing. They had no idea what the frightening creatures were or where they had come from but the situation was very alarming. The terrifying beasts moved about in trietons, ragged groups of 30 that spread fear and death in their wake. If the huge creatures were already this widespread, then it did not bode well for the kingdoms of Eryos. As Torrin and his companions traveled steadily north, the creatures were becoming more prevalent.

They had learned that folk were calling the frightening beasts Raken, a name taken from the old Empire legends of Roon the hunter and the beast that he was forever pitted against. Roon and the Raken could be seen battling in the heavens among the stars, low on the western horizon in winter. But the villagers they questioned had seen creatures made of flesh and bone, born into the world from fireside tales to reap fear and death.

Torrin and his companions had encountered a few of the beasts traveling as scouts singly and in pairs. They had learned quickly that it was better to avoid the huge, black creatures than to engage them. The beasts were savage in battle, and not to be taken lightly, their speed and size making up for the lack of skill they demonstrated with weapons.

The creatures seemed more comfortable with their claws and sharp teeth than with the various weapons they carried. As a warrior, Torrin found it strange for troops to handicap themselves needlessly. It was odd but he welcomed their choice. He had a feeling these creatures would make far more frightening opponents if they discarded their weapons. He and his companions had seen them use scimitars, clubs, spears, maces, flails and even bows, but there was little skill or finesse, only strength and speed and overwhelming size.

A battle with a handful of the creatures at close range with even odds was one thing, but engaging them while outnumbered was very unwise. The Raken could be beaten by skilled swordplay, but they were more than a match for a veteran soldier if they breached his guard and got in close.

Torrin and his companions had discovered five ravaged villages so far. The inhabitants were dead, ripped apart and left to rot in the hot sun. It was a vision of horror, especially in the height of summer. The memory of those terrible places, where death had stalked the streets, lay heavily on all the companions. The scenes were made all the more horrifying by the lack of destruction; no buildings were damaged, nothing was stolen or looted. There were no piles of possessions pulled from the houses and scattered across the windy streets, picked clean by rough hands; not a fence rail or curtain was out of place. Only the living had been brutally killed, eviscerated, and left to stain the silent streets.

They had known to avoid slaughtered towns by the stench that was carried on the wind as they approached. It was always the same, like a signpost, a message. Not a soul was left living. Torrin and his companions couldn't spare the time to stop and bury the dead. They took to passing by such towns, knowing from experience they would find no survivors.

The tales of these slaughters had spread through the countryside like wild fire, inciting panic and fear among farmers and townspeople. The murdered towns became places of evil that surrounding farmers wouldn't approach even to bury friends and relatives.

Superstitions. Most rural folk were prisoners to their superstitions – Lor Danions especially. Torrin supposed he couldn't blame them. He had faced the creatures in battle and knew they were mortal, but that still didn't stop the hair from rising on the back of his neck each time he saw one of them. He could well imagine how a defenceless farmer would feel with nothing but the thin walls of his house to protect him and his family.

The attacks on the towns and villages were random with no apparent reason as to why a particular place was taken. There would be two villages in close proximity slaughtered and the next left alone, then the one after that taken again. It made no sense. Torrin could find no patterns, nothing at all to explain why. In the end they had to assume the simplest answer – fear. The attacks were meant to instil fear. And it was working.

Until they entered the Wilds, they had been met with suspicion and fear by everyone they encountered. The only people who seemed unaffected were the bands of thieves roaming with increasing brazenness. They fed on the growing climate of terror, taking advantage of people already paralyzed by the horror of the Raken assaults.

How far had this Raken invasion spread since the companions received the summons from Pellar? It was now nearly two months since King Cerebus of Pellar had issued his call for help. Much could have happened since and Torrin had no idea what they would find when they reached the northern kingdom.

Pellar was the most powerful of the seven kingdoms in the land of Eryos, and Torrin had a hard time believing it might fall. The fact that Cerebus had even issued a summons meant his kingdom was in great peril.

Torrin sensed the invading Raken were intent on taking all of Eryos, and that they had attacked Pellar first to gain the greatest foothold. The other kingdoms would fall easily afterward.

Only Pellar had any rapport with the other six kingdoms of Eryos. Cerebus was the one king who had made attempts at developing ties of goodwill. Pellar's two warring neighbours to the south and west, Klyssen and Tabor, were entrenched in strife hundreds of years old. Border squabbles and enmity, so ancient the root causes were long forgotten, had reduced the trade between the two countries to a bare trickle. Ren, to the south of Tabor, was caught up in a ruinous civil war; merchant trains foolish enough to venture into its lawless territory were quickly looted and destroyed. As a result, most trade was routed through Pellar, filling its coffers and reinforcing its status as the most powerful kingdom in Eryos.

The great city of Pellaris, boasting the largest of only three main ports on the whole continent, welcomed many ships from Tabor and further west beyond the Timor Mountains. After a sizeable port tax, goods moved in a constant stream south from Pellaris into Klyssen and down into Ren and Lor Danith. Smuggling became a second profession for traders who brought embargoed Taborian goods into Klyssen. Wine, cheese and drenic, a strong, hot drink brewed from the leaves of a plant found only in Tabor's coastal bogs, were much sought after even in Klyssen, Tabor's bitterest enemy.

Further to the south, below Klyssen, the lawless land of Ren seethed in unchecked turmoil. Almost everything was in short supply in Ren but only traders with heavily armed escorts could safely navigate the gauntlet of thieves to make some coin in the unstable landscape. It could be quite profitable for those who could get goods into the country and then get the profits back out again without loosing their heads in the process. Few were willing to take the chance.

Between Ren and the Eryos Ocean, Lor Danith received trickles of wealth from the northern kingdoms and sent back wool in return. If Pellar was caught in a war with these Raken, the stable trade routes would falter.

The rest of the kingdoms in Eryos were even less stable than Klyssen and Tabor. Alliances and power shifted frequently, keeping lands that once were rich with great civilizations unstable and weak. Diplomacy was not a well-practiced art in Eryos and most kingdoms were insular and suspicious. Attempts at peaceful resolution of disputes almost always failed and the way of the sword inevitably settled all.

Violence ruled and kings warily watched each other for the slightest tipping in the scales of power, taking swift advantage of any weakness. It had been that way for centuries after the fall of the Kathornin and Trillian empires. With the collapse of the structures of government, all peace and prosperity was swept away in a tide of lawless chaos. Out of that miasma the seven separate kingdoms grew from tribal states and small fiefdoms to become what is now Eryos.

Torrin believed the only reason that Pellar had been successful in keeping good relations with the shifting powers of the surrounding countries was because it was too powerful for any of the other six kingdoms to overthrow.

Eryos had been conflict ridden for generations. Small, localized wars raged and faded like wind-whipped grass fires. The goddess Erys knew how many lives had been spent over the last five hundred years in the name of greed and petty bickering. The memory of the dead added fuel to new conflict and plunged more and more men into bloody battle.

There was always a war that needed fighting. There was plenty of work for a mercenary, and if you were good, your reputation ensured you were well paid for your work.

During his travels through Eryos, Torrin had heard many stories — if there was one thing fighting men loved to do, it was to tell stories — of the grand empires of the golden past. Trillian had been a vast empire that covered the territories of present day Ren and Lor Danith. The empire was fabled to have cities with lofty architecture, where the red gold from the mines of the great Timor Mountains to the west flowed freely, paving even the streets it was said, though Torrin knew embellishment when he heard it. But the wealth of the mountain mines eventually ran dry and what was once bright and fair had slipped into decay.

Ruins of those great cities were all that remained now, worn down and mostly buried, forgotten along with the names of their emperors, names whispered only by the wind whistling through the eroded stones.

The ruins could be found throughout Ren and Lor Danith. Torrin and his companions had camped or ridden through the remains of high columns and towers, the crumbling stones covered in centuries of lichen and moss – homes now only for the nesting birds and small animals. Some ruins were bare hints of their former stature and only those who knew where to look could find the worn stone foundations of the ancient buildings peeking through the ground.

Pellar was the only kingdom that had retained some glory of former Kathornin, a powerful empire that historically covered present day Pellar, Tabor and Klyssen, though Torrin had heard tell that Pellar was but a pale reflection of that great empire. The city of Pellaris was built on a grand scale with libraries and courthouses and great open squares with plunging fountains and the great fortress of Pellar overlooking it all.

Klyssen was a land of open grassland and steppes where the great horse herds of the clansmen ranged. Torrin had met and fought alongside the men of Klyssen; they were fierce horsemen and honourable in spirit, but they also had a nomadic history, traditionally moving with their horses to summer and winter grazing grounds. Klyssen had only a few permanent towns and cities populated with people who had turned away from the ancient ways of the horse to plow under the fertile soil and plant crops. Klyssen's capital city of Wyborn was a quarter of the size of Pellaris and it lacked the sense of permanence and timelessness that had settled over Pellaris. Despite Klyssen's considerable coastline, it had few ports. It was content, it seemed, to rely on the overland trade from Pellar and Lor Danith.

Tabor had the potential for greatness, but its capital city of Tyrn on the North coast was so bound up in political intrigue and maneuvering that its monarch had never been able to look beyond his own borders to the rest of Eryos. Torrin's father had taught him long ago that politics — especially in a climate of corruption — would hobble a land as completely as civil war.

Ren covered the greatest territory south of Tabor; it lay between Lor Danith and the great wall of the Timor Mountains.

The Tynithian homeland of Dan Tynell nestled in the northwest corner of Ren against the high mountains, but the strife from within Ren rarely troubled the Twilight People.

The Lor Danith–Ren border was a stretch of land that had to be crossed in force. In Ren itself, might ruled and the weak were preyed upon without pity. The southernmost border of Ren was an ever-changing line that ended somewhere in the shoulders of the Black Hills, where fierce Stoneman pride and cunning kept the Ren warlords from taking advantage.

Torrin and his companions had intimate knowledge of Ren. The Ren Wars had earned them a fair amount of gold and a widely known reputation. Thaius the Great, one of Ren's self-styled rulers, had treated them well in return for their loyalty. Thaius had been the only warlord with the potential to unify Ren. Before he died with an assassin's arrow in his throat, he had managed to gain control of over three-quarters of the country. With his death, any hope for a united Ren had died also.

To the east of Ren, the lands of Lor Danith and its island neighbour, Lor Hath, had long ago turned their faces to the sea, shunning the rest of Eryos for the ocean's bounty. The two realms had grown slowly and of necessity from small villages and fiefdoms ruled by chiefs to a more centralized form of leadership where stewards kept watch on the sovereignty of the country's borders. The Lor Danions were a quiet people who were suspicious of outsiders; they kept to themselves and discouraged foreign trade above the bare minimum. The constant need for vigilance along Ren's border kept the realm poor and down-trodden – a land of sheep farmers and fishermen with a ragtag militia that barely kept the bickering Ren warlords at bay.

Only King Cerebus of Pellar had a chance of uniting the kingdoms to stand against a common threat. Only Pellar was strong enough to make the other kingdoms of Eryos listen; perhaps even the forbidding land of Krang, to the north east, in its mountainous isolation would take notice.

These Raken were just such a threat, one that Torrin feared could tear Eryos apart if they were not stopped. Erys only knew where they were coming from. In all his days Torrin had not seen their like.

In the back of his mind a thought uncoiled like a spring, bringing with it a cold dread. Perhaps these creatures were not from Eryos at all. The Timor Mountains existed like a great barrier between Eryos and the shadowed west. Perhaps these creatures were traveling across somehow. The range ran north and south, parallel to the Eryos Ocean with Eryos trapped between and isolated from the rest of the world. Little was known about the realms that lie beyond the Timor Mountains and if the Raken were in fact coming from the west…

Torrin sighed and shook his head. There was nowhere for a large force to cross the mountains — no supply routes, nowhere to get horses and wagons through. Only the odd intrepid mountaineer had ever ventured up into those intimidating heights. The mountains were said to be impassable and those who attempted crossings returned in weary defeat or were never heard from again.

Torrin knew the height of the Timors was a killing factor for anyone attempting to climb. Weather became the enemy as much as the sheer cliffs and deadly falls. It was also said that mountain ghosts sucked the air from the sky at the top of the peaks, making it almost impossible to breathe.

A quiet rustle brought Torrin out of his thoughts. He trained all his senses toward the sound and waited. There was only a sliver of moon and starlight to see by; the second moon would not rise for another hour yet. He silently drew his sword from its scabbard. Staring hard at the surrounding trees, Torrin strained to see through the darkness. He stalked slowly toward the source of the sound, stepping silently through the grass. The minutes slid past. Torrin heard nothing more and began to relax. An animal perhaps.

As the stars wheeled overhead and the first moon glided through the sky, Torrin stood watch for his companions. When the time came to wake Arynilas for his turn, Torrin found the Tynithian already walking toward him. In the light from the second moon, newly risen, he saw Arynilas pause to look down at the sleeping woman.

Torrin moved into the campsite and Arynilas nodded to him. “All quiet?” the Tynithian asked.

Torrin thought of the sound he had heard earlier and dismissed it. “All quiet.”

Arynilas nodded again and walked silently out to take up watch and Torrin fell wearily into his blankets. As he slid quickly into sleep, his thoughts turned to the west and the shadows therein.

Torrin woke to the sound of Nathel's curses. He opened his eyes and looked around the camp in the pale dawn light. Bringing his rough fingertips to his eyes, he attempted to rub away the remaining sleep. Borlin was still snoring under his blankets and Dalemar's slim frame in his long green coat stood bent over the woman, his back to Torrin. Nathel was crouched on the other side of her, muttering now under his breath, his hand on her brow.

Torrin sat up and saw Arynilas moving among the horses, offering them water from a bucket. Their nostrils curled with frosted breath in the cold morning air.

Reaching for his boots, Torrin threw his blankets aside. The insides of his boots were freezing. He stood and stretched his shoulders and back. He was not looking forward to traveling in the cold weather. There was still time before the snow flew, but chilly mornings like this one reminded him that it wouldn't be long before winter set in, transforming the world to grays and whites.

He nudged Borlin with the toe of his boot and was rewarded with a groan. The southern Stoneman was usually the first of the companions to rise, puttering around the fire and steeping hot tea for everyone. It was a testament to the long hours of travel the previous day that Borlin still slept.

Torrin knelt in front of the cold fire, pulling some unburned wood from the black ashes and grabbing a fistful of dried grass he found next to him. He placed it under the wood and drew his firestones from a small pouch at his belt. It took a few quick strikes for a large spark to land in the grass and a thin wisp of smoke began curling upward. Torrin blew on the infant fire and glanced to where his brother and Dalemar were tending the woman. It didn't look as though she had moved during the night.

"Here! Get away from me fire!" Borlin's gruff voice sounded behind Torrin, and he turned to see the Stoneman looking crossly down at him with his broad hands on his hips.

Torrin rose to his feet and was now looking down at Borlin. "You're welcome," he said with a snort. "If you don't want anyone else doing the cooking, then you should get up to do it before someone else has to."

Borlin barked a short laugh. "Ye! Cook? Sweet Erys, save us from that day!" He tilted his head up and jutted his short, red-bearded chin forward, brown eyes challenging. His thick, rusty eyebrows drew down into a scowl, and he made an expressive shooing gesture with a beefy hand.

Torrin shook his head and turned away, a smile pulling at the corners of his mouth. The five of them had been together for almost four years and Torrin could count on one hand the number of times that Borlin had let anyone else do the cooking. The stocky Stoneman took great pride in his culinary skills. Borlin's southern people traded in rare spice found only in the Black Hills and their recipes, highly prized throughout Eryos, were almost considered a form of currency. Torrin had no trouble relinquishing cooking duty, though he could fend for himself if he had to.

When he reached Nathel and Dalemar, his brother was ringing out a wet cloth and placing it over the woman's forehead. Torrin frowned. "What is it?"

"Fever has her," replied Nathel. "The wound's infection was not drawn out last night as I had hoped. It is now in her blood and her body is trying to fight it."

Torrin crouched down and reached out to touch the smooth skin of the woman's cheek. It was burning. "Will she survive?"

Nathel sat back on his heels after examining the arrow wound. He frowned slightly. "With careful tending she will."

"Perhaps I should try to heal her again?" said Dalemar.

Nathel raised his blond eyebrows, his pale blue eyes looking at the Rith. "It couldn't hurt."

Torrin moved back out of the way and Dalemar knelt as he had the previous night and placed his hands on the sides of her head. The Rith closed his eyes and took a deep breath. After a while Dalemar dropped his hands and sighed, shaking his head. A deep frown marred his smooth brow. "Nothing."

"It will come, Dalemar. You just need to give it time," said Torrin. "What you did last night proves it is there."

The Rith sighed. "I am tired of giving it time. At this rate I will still be trying to summon a fire when I am five hundred," he said the words softly but they were tinged with bitterness. Dalemar's innate abilities as a Rith were slow to manifest, and his use of them was frustratingly inconsistent.

Torrin shared a look with his brother and Nathel wisely changed the subject. "It will be difficult to move her like this."

Torrin shook his head. "We can't afford to stay here and let her recover — our time is too short. Can you carry her in front of you as we ride?"

Nathel nodded. "If I have to. But I will need to stop frequently to tend her."

"That's fine."

Arynilas appeared behind them. He studied their sleeping guest for a moment, then turned his sapphire eyes to Nathel. "She is very strong. Do not fear for her. She will wake when she is ready."

"How do you know?" Nathel looked up at the Tynithian.

Arynilas cocked his head, the refined lines of his face drawing into a mysterious smile. "It is there, for anyone to see."

The Elusive Stalker

Once the sun had risen, it dispelled the cold of the morning and warmed the air considerably. The sky was clear and the orange and yellow of the turning leaves contrasted against deep blue. The five companions rode through the forest, winding through dense trees in single file and keeping careful watch for the poisonous vine. If it crawled across a pathway they needed to take, they had to clear it from the ground with a pole. It made for slow travel, but it was still faster than the long way around the Wilds. At this time of year, the vine was easy to spot as its summer-green leaves turned early to bright crimson.

Torrin could see Arynilas ahead of himself and Dalemar through the dappled sunlight as the slight Tynithian scouted. Late-hatching insects buzzed lazily through the warm air around them.

Torrin heard a moan and swivelled in his saddle. Nathel was riding behind him with the woman seated sideways in front of him like a child. She was swathed in a blanket. All Torrin could see was her face. Still asleep, she twisted restlessly in Nathel's arms, muttering in her fever. Torrin couldn't understand what she was saying.

His brother looked up at him, his face pained. "I need to stop for a while."

Torrin nodded and issued a short whistle, signalling to Arynilas at the head of the column to stop. They pulled their horses up and dismounted.

Borlin, who brought up the rear, had the woman's big grey stallion tethered to his saddle. The horse tossed his head and snorted with impatience. It was a lovely animal, with a deep chest for stamina and strong, well-formed legs for speed.

Torrin took the woman from Nathel and placed her gently on the ground while Nathel dismounted. She was scalding hot. Torrin could feel the heat even through the blankets, but her face was dry. She tossed her head, mumbling, the words garbled and incoherent.

As Nathel began to unwrap the blankets from around her, she opened her eyes suddenly and their piercing gaze pinned Torrin. They were the brightest green eyes he had ever seen.

She looked around at them, her expression glazed. Torrin knew that look well. It wasn't them she was seeing, but something else entirely. Pain washed over her features, arched eyebrows pulling together in a frown. Her lips parted. Even, white teeth flashed in a sudden grimace.

"Dell?" she asked, her voice quavered but then grew in intensity. "Where are you?" There was barely controlled desperation in her tone; anguish and despair rang clear in her words and Torrin's chest contracted in response. "Sweet Erys!" she cried. "There are too many, we can't fight this many. It is folly! Dell… We must find a way through. It cannot end here! Please Erys, not like this. Dell! Lesiana! Trevis!. . . *No*!" The last was shouted into the clear midday air, echoing through the trees and startling a flock of blackbirds from their roost. Then her eyes closed and she was still.

Nathel placed a cool cloth on her forehead and looked meaningfully at Torrin. They both understood what they just witnessed. The question was whether the arrow wound in her shoulder had come from that battle.

Torrin thought about the names of people she had called out. They were not names he had ever heard before in his travels through Eryos. Were they her friends, family, a husband or brothers and sister?

Torrin felt a light tap on his shoulder. He turned to find Arynilas standing behind him. The expression in the Tynithian's face warned him that something was wrong.

His mind stilled as he rose to his feet. "What is it?"

"We are being followed." Arynilas's calm voice betrayed no alarm.

Torrin glanced around at the surrounding trees. "Any idea who or what it is?" he asked.

Arynilas frowned. "Yes, but it is not behaving as I would have thought. It is keeping far enough away to avoid detection and it is very good at keeping itself concealed. I have been able to see only glimpses of it."

Torrin knew the answer to his next question before he asked it. His hackles rose as he spoke. "What have you seen?"

"It is very large and pure black," said the Tynithian.

Torrin nodded, and took an involuntary glance behind him. They were being stalked by Raken. "Are you certain there is only one?"

"I am certain, yes."

Nathel looked up from tending the woman. "Could you kill it with an arrow?"

Arynilas shook his head. "The creature keeps just out of range."

Torrin clenched his fists in frustration and felt a growing measure of dread.

Dalemar was frowning in concentration. "It does not fit with what we know of the Raken, if that is indeed what the creature is. They do not skulk and avoid confrontation, and we have never seen just one alone before."

No one had an answer. Borlin patted his short sword. "Just let the beastie try somethin."

Torrin rubbed his brow. "It is of little threat to five of us, provided that it does not catch us unaware and more of its kin don't join it," he said. "We know how fast these creatures are. It would do us little good to try hunting it down, especially in these dense trees. I can see no other alternative but to keep moving and be on our guard."

The rest of the companions nodded their agreement and Torrin looked down at his brother who was slowly administering water to the woman. "Are you ready to move?"

Nathel sighed. "If we must."

Borlin reached down to help Nathel with his patient. She was deeply unconscious now, limp and relaxed. Her peaceful face belied the terror and intense pain from moments ago. Torrin could still see those impossible green eyes.

An Uninvited Guest

Torrin watched as the second moon of Eryos rose slowly in the sky. Bashelar was redder and smaller than Raelys. She was shy and rose into the night sky only after her larger sister was high in the heavens.

It was said that the twin moons were once sisters to the goddess Erys but that the sun god, Raithyn, wanting Erys for himself and refusing to share her with her sisters, had transformed Raelys and Bashelar into barren moons. Angered and broken-hearted, Erys had shunned Raithyn for his treachery, creating the world and the lands of Eryos to hide herself from his searching light. In her sorrow for the loss of her sisters, she created the Tynithians, the other races and all the creatures of Eryos to keep her company. Raithyn became so enraged at her rejection that his light blazed, burning so brightly that none of the creatures upon Eryos could look upon him without suffering blindness.

It was an ancient tale, a story Torrin had been told as a child. But the bitterness of life had scoured away any faith he may have had in the world of gods and goddesses. Let the Priests of Erys believe what they liked. To Torrin they were only the sun and moons, nothing more. He relied on his sword.

Torrin shifted his weight and scanned the shadows before him. He and Borlin were standing second watch together, each of them on opposite sides of the small camp. It was almost time to wake Arynilas and Nathel for their turn. It had been a slow day with frequent stops made to tend to the injured woman. Arynilas had only seen their stalker once more during the afternoon, a black shadow hiding from the light. Try as they had, Torrin and the rest of the companions had not been able to detect the creature.

He scanned the surrounding shapes of trees again, straining for the slightest sound. He heard a faint rustle. It brought to mind the sound he heard last night on watch. But this time it came from behind him in the camp.

His stomach clenched and his hackles rose. The sleeping companions could have made the sound — someone turning over or pulling a blanket across the dry grass. But Torrin dismissed the notion. His instincts told him otherwise.

He grasped the hilt of his sword, testing it in the scabbard as he turned his head to look back at the camp. What he saw there caused him to tighten his grip on his sword and draw a sudden breath.

A great, black, monstrous shape was bent low over the woman. Torrin could just make out the jutting crest on the creature's head and back in the pale moonlight. It had its huge arm extended and was reaching towards the woman's face.

Torrin yanked his sword free of its scabbard, the metallic ring mingling with the warning he shouted to the others.

Borlin spun around and cursed loudly. He tugged his sword free and began to run towards the intruder. Torrin himself was already halfway towards the creature.

It reared up to its full height and Torrin almost stumbled in amazement at its size. It was enormous. It was even bigger than the Raken they had fought before entering the Wilds. Torrin doubted he stood as high as its black scaled chest. He clamped his teeth shut and hefted his broadsword.

The huge creature spun, lightning quick, and launched itself into the darkness of the surrounding trees. Torrin stopped when he reached the woman. Dalemar, Nathel and Arynilas were all up and out of their blankets. Except for the Rith, they had weapons in hand.

Torrin turned to Arynilas. "Can you see it?"

"No, it has already disappeared. It is much faster than the other Raken we have encountered."

"What was it doing?" asked Nathel.

Torrin shook his head; the same question had been on his mind. "I don't know but it was interested in her."

They all looked down at the woman on the ground. Nathel bent close to inspect her. "She appears to be fine. The creature must not have had time to hurt her."

"What makes you so sure it wanted to hurt her?" Arynilas asked quietly.

Torrin and the others turned to look at the Tynithian. It was difficult to see his expression in the dark.

They knew next to nothing about these Raken creatures; they could not discount anything. "He's right," said Torrin. "It had time to kill her or even to abduct her if that had been its intent."

He hissed in anger. "It got right into the camp before we detected it. It was almost as quiet as you are, Arynilas."

"Did you see how big it was?" asked Dalemar.

"Aye, it was far bigger than any Raken we 'ave seen so far," stated Borlin.

"Yes, but it was definitely Raken. I saw that much," said Nathel from where he was checking the woman.

"Aye, that it was lad. That it was," echoed Borlin.

The remainder of the night passed tensely. The companions slept little for fear of the creature stealing into the camp again. Torrin was angry with himself for allowing it to get passed his watch. The way the huge creature moved, he knew it could have hurt the injured woman if it had wanted to. There were now even more questions he wanted to ask their new traveling companion.

The next morning Nathel found that the woman's fever had passed and she was sleeping restfully. He dosed her again with winoth root and Borlin made a fine gruel that they were able to feed her carefully with a spoon.

Nathel's compassion for the sick and injured never ceased to amaze Torrin. His brother would attach himself to complete strangers who needed healing, exhausting himself to bring them back to health. Torrin was often struck by the irony that his brother's other great talent lay in inflicting with his sword some of the same injuries that he strove to cure.

Nathel had never taken to the sword as completely as Torrin had. His skill was still impressive, and he used his weapons with a calm efficiency born of necessity, but Torrin suspected that his brother experienced none of the cathartic release that Torrin had always felt when his sword was in his hands.

Nathel was a clown and a rascal at heart whose ability to heal others had as much to do with his jokes and laughter than his herbs and medic's skill. But despite his younger brother's pranks and Torrin's frequent urge to throttle him, Nathel was absolutely loyal. An unshakable bond held them together that went beyond the love of brothers. Nathel had been the only one able to bring Torrin back from where he had been lost seven years ago. At the time, the last thing Torrin had wanted was to be found, but Nathel had refused to give up; refused to allow his older brother to disappear forever into his own private oblivion. They never spoke of it, but Torrin would be dead if not for Nathel.

The companions traveled slowly through the trees and rock-strewn gullies of the Wilds as the sun slid across the sky. The day was bright and clear. They were entering a more rugged section of the Wilds. Craggy tors of exposed rock covered with twisted trees rose to either side as they moved through the narrow clefts. The occasional rockslide sounded above as small game flushed from hiding at their passage.

Hawks circled above – a pair that Torrin had been watching for over an hour. Their speeding shadows swept over the sunlit ground around them, reaching a jutting cliff wall and racing up its rough surface at a sharp angle. Torrin relaxed in his saddle and sighed. He loved the quiet peace of the Wilds and he could well understand why the Tynithian race once chose to dwell in its guarded forests.

The woman in their midst had slept quietly all day, her exhausted body trying to recuperate through sleep. Nathel still rode with her in his arms. He expected her to wake soon and they all anticipated the meeting. Torrin frowned, pulled from his reverie. He was impatient to have his questions answered and he was lying to himself if the thought of seeing those green eyes again was not part of the reason he wanted her to wake.

A piercing howl erupted from the woods to their right.

Torrin reached for his sword and looked to Arynilas. The Tynithian was scanning the surrounding forest with bow drawn and a golden fletched arrow nocked. He glanced over at Torrin, shaking his head.

The howl ripped through the air again, closer this time. The horses twitched their ears and Torrin's young stallion spooked to the left.

Torrin thought he could hear the faint echo of returning howls, pitched higher, in the far distance. He glanced around at the terrain, assessing it as he pressed his knee to the side of his horse and shifted his weight to move it back to the path. They were in a small clearing surrounded by the denser forest. A rocky hill rose on their left, its top covered with trees and moss. Aside from the hill there was little hope of defending the clearing if they were outnumbered.

Again the howl erupted but it was behind them now. “Let’s move!” called Torrin. The companions spurred their horses forward and plunged into the trees. When they heard the howl again, it was further behind them, much further than they had moved in the short time since hearing it last – it was traveling away from them.

Torrin pulled his horse up to maneuver around a large patch of the poisonous blue-flowered vine. He slowed to a trot. The horses were excited by the howls, and Torrin reached down to soothe his big black mount.

They heard the howl again, along with its answering echoes, further away still. If Torrin had to make a guess, he would say that the Raken they had heard first was the one that had been following them. He shook his head, running a hand through his short dark hair, frowning. It made no sense.

“What is going on?” Nathel put voice to the question.

“Is it just me, or did the closer Raken lead the others away?” asked Dalemar.

“It is not just you, Rith. I also believe that is what happened,” said Arynilas.

“Let’s keep moving. The more distance we put between ourselves and the Raken the better,” said Torrin. “We know how fast these creatures can move.”

They began to move once again through the trees. By unspoken agreement Arynilas fell behind to take up the rear and keep watch on the path behind.

As always the Tynithian’s demeanour was unruffled. Torrin wondered if it was because Arynilas was so much older than the rest of them or whether his calm, like his keen senses of sight and hearing, was a trait shared by all his people. Torrin had seen other Tynithians but Arynilas was the only one he had ever gotten to know.

They traveled steadily throughout the rest of the afternoon, picking their way slowly through the difficult terrain. They heard no more sign of pursuit. Near the end of the day they passed a small vale with a rising stone cliff. A cleft cut into the rock face at the top of a small hillock. It was a defensible place to camp but the need to replenish their water outweighed other considerations. Torrin was loath to leave the place behind but the horses hadn't had a proper drink for over a day.

A few leagues further they came across a small clearing with a tumbling creek falling out of the hills to the west. The sun was setting as they set up a small camp in the lee of a hillside. Borlin lit a small fire, concealed by boulders, and proceeded to prepare a meal. Nathel saw to his patient as Dalemar rifled through his saddlebags in search of a book which, once found, he reluctantly set aside to gather firewood. Arynilas and Torrin took the horses to the creek for water. The thirsty animals drank deeply for a long time.

Torrin stood listening as they sucked water in, puzzling over the events of the day. He sighed and wiped a hand over his face, feeling his whiskers. Time to shave. In the warm weather, Torrin hated having a beard. Sweat trickled through it and it became unbearably hot and itchy. He glanced at Arynilas, who was loosening cinches and undoing tack. He sometimes envied the Tynithian his smooth-skinned, hairless face.

"What do you make of today, my friend?" asked Torrin.

Arynilas turned to face him, one arching brow raised. "I believe the answers lie with our lovely guest. The large Raken following us is linked to her somehow." The horses were almost finished drinking. Arynilas reached for the nearest waterskin and knelt lightly to refill it upstream from the horses.

Torrin took his own waterskin from his saddle horn, uncorked it and crouched down to refill it with cold, clear water.

Arynilas had the right of it. There was something strange going on and it was tied to the woman. He glanced back toward the camp. The sun had set now, casting an orange glow in the west. Borlin's fire was well concealed and created little smoke. In Torrin's experience most mysteries had simple explanations but somehow he doubted that was the case here.

When they returned to the small camp, they found Dalemar attempting to read in the failing light. Torrin looked closely at him. The Rith was slowly losing his confidence. His skills in magic wielding had not improved in quite some time and his failures were leaving their mark. Unlike the rest of his race, his progress in developing was slow. He was still trying to learn things that much younger Riths had already mastered. Dalemar had vast potential for a Rith; they all knew it. Each had witnessed his power on occasions when he was able to access it, but sometimes it seemed as though the young Rith, usually positive, was fighting to keep despair at bay. Torrin had no idea how to help him. He knew little about Dalemar's power, except that it was different from that of other Riths. There was no one the young Rith could turn to for advice. Although the companions could offer him their support and friendship, none of them had magical abilities except for Arynilas, and his magic, linked only to his shape shifting, had nothing in common with Rith magic.

Torrin searched through his saddlebags for his cleaning cloth and sat down beside the small fire to clean and oil his sword. The blade hadn't been used in a while but force of habit kept it cleaned and oiled daily. He glanced across to Nathel who was checking the woman's wound.

"How is she doing?" asked Torrin.

Nathel looked up, a grin on his face. "The next time she has to take a dose of winoth root, she will be awake to savour its lovely flavour."

Torrin chuckled and eyed the woman's sword where it lay next to her, strapped to her saddlebags. "Just make sure she can't reach that blade when you give her the tea, or you take the chance of losing your life."

Torrin looked up as Borlin handed him a hot cup of tea. He put aside his cleaning cloth and accepted the drink, thanking the Stoneman.

"This brew won't get me 'ead sliced off. I'm fairly certain the lass 'll prefer mine to yours, Nathel," said Borlin.

Nathel's blond eyebrows rose in mock surprise, his boyish face completely guileless. "You don't like my special tea? How ungrateful of you, considering it's done such wonders for you in the past."

Borlin scowled. "Ye 'ave nerve, lad. I'll say that for ye."

Nathel echoed Torrin's chuckle. "There will be plenty left over once the woman has had her share, Borlin. You are welcome to it; I know what refined tastes you Stonemen have."

Borlin turned his back on the insult with a growl and went back to his pot on the fire.

"One day you will receive the flat of his sword over your head, Nathel," said Dalemar without looking up from his book. He had his long hair tucked behind one pointed ear and the rest of the pale strands fell like a screen on the other side of his head, pooling on the page of his book. He wore a slight smile and had one slim eyebrow arched upward. “Ah, thank you Borlin.” The Rith reached up to receive the proffered cup, his index finger marking his place in the book as he closed it. Torrin rethought his earlier assessment of the Rith’s spirits.

Arynilas appeared and took tea also. He lowered himself smoothly onto his customary cross-legged position. Taking a sip, his tilted eyes wandered over the group. His black hair was pulled off his face in its usual manner, the top half tied behind his head to fall in with the rest. The Tynithian rarely spoke unless he had something significant to say.

“Hey! Don’t I get one too?” asked Nathel.

Borlin ignored him completely and Nathel rose to his feet, dusting his hands on his thighs and sighing theatrically as he went to pour himself a cup.

Torrin sighed with exasperation; his brother would forever be fourteen years old. He glanced over to the sleeping woman. Her face was turned towards them as though listening to the conversation but he could see her chest rise and fall slowly in sleep. Why would a huge Raken be interested in her? The creature had not looked as though it was about to hurt her — quite the opposite, it had looked as though it was about to gently touch her face. Implausible, he knew, but the impression would not leave him.

New Friends

Torrin took first watch. He had sent Borlin to his blankets halfway through their watch when it was clear the Stoneman was having great difficulty staying awake. They all were tired from keeping double watch for two days. They had seen nothing of the strange Raken visitor since the howls in the forest that day.

Torrin glanced up to the stars. His watch was half over now and Bashelar was just beginning to rise over the treetops. The night had remained warm and bats were flitting overhead – black against the moon and starlight.

A sound behind him made him turn to look back at the camp. His companions were indistinct humps in the darkness. The sound had come from the woman.

Torrin watched as she stirred from sleep. She sat up and looked quickly around. Flexing her shoulder, she gave a soft exclamation, feeling the arrow wound with her fingertips. She looked again carefully at the sleeping forms of his friends.

Finding her sword and breastplate among her belongings beside her, she put them on, slipping the baldric over her head and settling it across her chest; each motion fluid and effortless. She stood, unsteady on her feet. He began to call out but stopped himself when she slipped silently away from his companions. She moved through the darkness and he saw her shadow stop at the big grey horse. The animal nickered softly and Torrin thought he could make out a few murmured words. Then she left the horse and moved on into the trees at the edge of the small clearing.

He watched and waited, but it was several minutes before he detected a shadow moving back out of the trees. She had come back out into the clearing nearer to him, fifty paces or so from where she had entered. This was a surprise.

She stopped when she realized that he was there. Bashelar, the second moon had risen now and Torrin could see her clearly.

She watched him warily.

"How are you feeling?" he asked quietly.

She inclined her head and touched her shoulder. "I should thank your healer. He has done a remarkable job. I have never seen a wound heal so fast."

Torrin glanced back at his sleeping companions. "You must thank two of my friends. My brother Nathel has tended you and Rith Dalemar preformed a surprising trick of his own."

Her gaze turned shrewd. "Three men, a Rith, and a Tynithian. You keep interesting company."

Torrin extended his hand out toward her. "My name is Torrin. I am glad we were able to aid you."

She stepped forward and grasped his hand. Hers was slim and lost in his, but her grip was firm and he could feel sword calluses on her palm. "I thank you, Torrin, for your aid. My name is Rowan."

She released his hand and looked toward the camp. "I am afraid you and your friends will come to regret your generosity. You must go your own way come dawn."

Torrin raised his eyebrows, surprised by her forthrightness. "Why?"

She looked up at him, asking instead a question of her own. "How long have I been unconscious?"

"Two days."

She drew in her breath and let it out slowly, looking around at the surrounding trees. "That long? You and your companions tended me for that long? We are no longer in the place where I first met you. You have been traveling with me?"

Torrin nodded. "My brother takes his calling as healer seriously, if nothing else. You haven't answered my question."

"Which direction?"

Torrin frowned. "What?"

"Which direction have you been traveling?" She asked, suddenly anxious.

"North."

She relaxed with a small exhalation of breath. Torrin leaned forward, looking down at her. "Now answer my question."

She paused as if deciding something, sighed and shook her head. Starlight gleamed in her pale hair and reflected from the silver pommel of the sword over her shoulder. "You will be in danger as long as you remain close to me."

"We are quite used to danger," he said. "Speak plainly."

"I am hunted." It was a quiet statement of fact and Torrin could detect only resignation, as if it had been a long association.

"Surely six together are better than one alone." He did not say one woman alone. She had obviously survived somehow on her own for quite some time.

A brief, wry, smile appeared on her face as if she had heard his unspoken thought. "I cannot ask it of you. Too many have died already."

She began to step past him back to the camp, but he stopped her, circling his hand about her arm. "Who hunts you?"

She stilled and Torrin realized she was tensing, ready to act. He released his grip and stepped away but in front of her again to wait for an answer.

She frowned. "Why are the men of Eryos so stubborn? Have you never seen a woman who can fend for herself?" She looked hard at him for a moment. "I am being tracked by a trieton of Raken."

Torrin's stomach clenched, a cold prickle ran across his scalp. "A full trieton?"

She nodded in the dark.

"For how long?"

"For about a month. Ever since I set foot in this land."

"These Raken, they have tracked you into the Wilds?"

She cocked her head. "By 'Wilds,' do you refer to this forested region?"

"Yes."

She nodded, looking around at the trees. "I believe they are not far behind me."

"Then it was you they were after, not us." Torrin said quietly.

She looked sharply up at him. "You've been attacked by Raken?"

Torrin shook his head. "No. We heard a large group of them today behind us, but a very large one has been following us. It came right into our camp last night, but escaped when the alarm was raised."

She nodded her head thoughtfully but offered no explanation. If she had one, she was keeping it to herself.

Another thought struck Torrin suddenly and he wondered how he had missed it. "They must be immune to the plant," he said, more to himself.

She frowned. "What plant? Do you speak of Erys' Bane?"

"Erys' Bane?"

"The vine that grows through this forest," she gestured vaguely around them. "It is very poisonous."

Torrin nodded. "We do not know it by that name, but yes…how did you learn of it?"

"Where I come from there is a very similar vine — different coloured flowers but the leaves are identical. It is found high on the slopes of some volcanoes."

"And where have you come from?"

She shook her head, dismissing the question. "I am from a place long forgotten to this land and its people."

"You are Myrian."

Her eyes widened in surprise. "I did not think any here knew of us."

"Arynilas knows of your people," Torrin replied.

"The Tynithian?"

"Yes."

A flash of white teeth in the moonlight – he took it for a smile. "You are not like any of the people I have met here," said Rowan.

"I would be surprised if you *had* met anyone like us. We are an unusual group. The races of Eryos do not share company." He glanced up at the stars, then looked back at the woman, Rowan. He couldn't see the green of her eyes in the darkness but he remembered it well. She was very weak, though trying hard not to show it. She reminded him of some of the young soldiers he'd had under his command in Ren – stubbornly refusing to show weariness and pain.

He supposed he could wait for morning to satisfy his remaining questions. She needed rest. "Come, it is time for me to wake Arynilas for his watch. You should get some sleep to rebuild your strength. We will speak of this further in the morning."

Rowan went to sleep feeling vaguely like a chastised child. The big dark haired swordsman had somehow assumed command of something that was none of his concern. She thought briefly of stealing away in the night, but they had set watch and would see her before she had gone two steps. She doubted she had the strength to do anything on her own at the moment anyway. The short walk in the trees and the time she spent standing talking to Torrin had drained her.

Besides, it was very comforting to be surrounded by people again. It had been so long since she had felt safe, without being constantly on her guard. She had no illusions about these people. She knew nothing about them, where they were going, or why such a motley group traveled together. They seemed easy with one another though, a rapport only gained through long hours spent together in friendship.

She had been in bad shape when she had first met them and her pride still smarted. In her weakened state she would have been in trouble if they had been hostile. When the strangers had finally shown themselves, minutes past when she had first begun to detect them, one glance had revealed how well armed they were.

She couldn't believe they had spent two and a half days tending her while she was unconscious. Given what she had so far encountered in this land, she would have expected to be robbed and left for dead. Instead this strange group of companions had gone to the trouble of caring not only for her, but her horse as well, taking them along as they traveled.

She knew only that she didn't want to repay their unexpected kindness by getting them all killed. Hathunor made a fine traveling companion, despite his ferocious appearance. And he was able to detect his people far before she or her big horse Roanus could.

Her huge companion had been waiting for her in the trees at the edge of the clearing when she finally woke from the fever. He had been very worried about her but knew that the people she was with were able to care for her better than he could. When she walked out into the forest in the hopes of finding him, his huge form had materialized out of the dark shadows and he had gently scooped her up into his massive arms. She assured him that she was safe and in no danger but asked him to stay out of sight until she was sure the strangers wouldn't try to kill him.

She had originally sent the great Raken into the trees to ensure his safety when he had first heard the approaching men.

The last thing she wanted was a misunderstanding. The Tynithian, Arynilas, looked very adept with his beautiful re-curved bow, and the two big swordsmen were obviously formidable. She had persuaded Hathunor to wait until morning, until she'd had a chance to explain his presence to the strangers. But she never woke the next morning. Hathunor had been following as closely as he dared for the past two days.

She still puzzled over the huge Raken and why he was able to resist the power that controlled his kin. The night she had found him bound, surrounded by Raken, was still vivid in her memory.

She had been surprised at how much bigger he was than the others. Even doubled over and tied, she was aware of his enormous stature. Her mind had screamed at her to quickly leave the scene she'd stumbled upon within the small copse of trees. It had looked a likely place to camp but she had almost walked into the midst of a group of Raken milling about the clearing. They were not the ones hunting her. She knew she was ahead of the Trieton tracking her. This group was different, smaller.

Before silently retreating, she looked again at the huge Raken on the ground – something made her hesitate. To her dying day she would not understand what it was that made her stay. Some inner guidance, she supposed.

The bound Raken was torn, bleeding from a multitude of cuts and scratches. Dead Raken were on the ground – a testament to the battle. Things were about to end badly for the captive. As the drama unfolded it became clear that the huge Raken was about to be executed.

From her hiding place, Rowan had inexplicably wanted to help him. The captive Raken seemed different from the others: more alive, more intelligent, and gentler somehow. She had wondered wildly at the time why she would ever ascribe those particular attributes to a Raken, but they fit.

As she watched, the urge to help the huge captive took hold of her. She looked back with amazement now at her actions – she couldn't explain it. Since the horrible day in Dendor, just after she arrived in Eryos, she had been running from the Raken, always only a step ahead of the huge beasts. But the day she met Hathunor she did the exact opposite – she attacked *them.*

The momentary surprise caused by her charge gave her the time she needed to free the captive. Rowan had darted among the giant black bodies, her sword humming. The rescue was successful, mainly because of the great beast she had freed. Slick with blood, huge taloned hands rending, the freed Raken had balanced the odds considerably.

Standing in the aftermath, bloody sword in hand, stunned at her own actions, Rowan stared up at the creature she had risked her life to save. Then the Raken had stepped towards her, a snarl on its monstrous face. Rowan had raised her sword and stepped back. The Raken, appearing confused by her reaction, lost its snarl and tentatively reached out one huge hand, palm open.

She remembered well the first time she had touched Hathunor. His giant hand had engulfed her own, the touch as gentle as a child's. The snarl reappeared and Rowan realized it wasn't a snarl but a smile. She'd found an unbelievably gentle soul in the body of a ferocious monster.

Hathunor was the primary reason she had been able to survive so long and stay ahead of the Raken trieton pursuing her. He guided her unerringly past Raken patrols and kept watch when exhaustion overcame her. He became a friend in a dangerous and otherwise friendless place.

Her mission depended on stealth and speed and, despite Hathunor's aid, she feared the Raken were closing in again. The arrow wound she sustained a week ago before entering this wilderness had caused her to lose precious time. She had been attacked by bandits on the road wanting to steal her horse — a trieton of Raken wasn't enough to contend with, it seemed. She had to be wary of the people of Eryos also.

She felt her shoulder again, the almost healed wound was still tender but nothing compared to the wrenching pain that gripped her two days ago. She shook her head in amazement. It would have taken two weeks, keeping very still, for it to heal as much on its own. She whispered quiet thanks to the sleeping Rith and the healer, and to the big swordsman who so far had helped her without asking for anything in return.

With her mind turning over the best way to separate herself from her new companions, the weariness in Rowan's body slowly asserted itself, and she fell asleep.

A Desperate Battle

Rowan awoke to the sound of a very distinctive howl. It was Hathunor. His voice was like the peal of a deep clear bell compared with the mindless snarls of the Raken trieton. Rowan was on her feet in an instant. The five companions around her were up also. Torrin already had a great sword in his hand and the Tynithian, Arynilas, had an arrow nocked and drawn as he scanned the trees in the direction of Hathunor's warning call. The Stoneman carried a short sword and round buckler and the other large man, whom she took to be Nathel, the healer, had a sword and round shield. The only member of the five that was without a weapon was the one she assumed to be the Rith, Dalemar.

Rowan walked quickly to Torrin. He glanced down at her and then went back to scanning the trees. "Your hunting party has arrived," he said grimly.

Rowan took an anxious breath. "We still have a few minutes before they get here. You should leave now. You won't have time to take your gear but at least you will have your lives. They will only follow my scent."

Torrin dropped his gaze to look at her, an inscrutable expression in his eyes.

The other big swordsman stepped forward. "I didn't spend two and a half days healing you, just so you could go off and get yourself killed!"

Rowan turned to him. "There is almost a full trieton of Raken out there. Six are better than one but it is still no contest. We will be overrun."

The healer's eyes widened. "A trieton! You have a trieton chasing —"

Rowan cut him off with a wave of her hand, ignoring his look of surprise. She focused on Torrin. "Please, I cannot let you be killed in return for your kindness."

Torrin was silent for a moment, searching her face, then he shook his head. "I will not leave you to be hunted down and killed."

Rowan growled under her breath. "Then let us fly together; at the least we can find a more defensible spot to make a stand. If we survive, we can come back for the gear."

Torrin glanced at the others and received nods in return. The five suddenly launched into action. Two went to get the horses; the other three grabbed the remaining weapons and the few packs that they could carry. There was no time to properly saddle the horses.

Rowan raised her fingers to her lips and blew a short whistle blast. Roanus came hurtling towards her and slid to a stop, his lead rope whipping around his neck like a snake. She threw one of her saddlebags across his withers and then jumped up, swinging a leg over to gain a seat on his broad back. Around her the five companions were mounting as well. A silent look passed between Torrin and Arynilas, an unspoken question in the big swordsman's eyes.

The Tynithian nodded and amid the chaos, Torrin said to Rowan. "There is a cleft in a rock face a few leagues back that we passed yesterday. It is defensible."

"Lead the way." Rowan pressed her heels to the sides of her horse, launching him after the others as they fled into the grey early morning light, the howls of a Raken trieton in pursuit.

It had been a while since Rowan had been up on Roanus without a saddle and the powerful muscles of her big horse surged under her. She had not nearly recovered all her strength and her limbs shook as she clung to his back. They raced single file through the trees, back the way the five had come the previous day. Rowan found herself led by Borlin and Dalemar, and followed by Nathel and Torrin with Arynilas as rearguard, an arrow nocked and ready to send at approaching foe.

Branches and tree limbs flashed past. *Hathunor, I hoping you are safe, my friend.* She had to duck suddenly as a heavy branch loomed ahead. She raced under it, shouting a warning back to the others. The thunder of their passage shook the forest around them while the gentle morning light filtering through the canopy to mock their dire circumstances.

They finally exploded into a clearing. It was partially circled by a cliff, rearing upwards some 40 paces, forming a small amphitheatre; a gentle slope rose up against the cliff with a flat top. At the top of the slope a notch in the cliff funnelled back into a tight crevice. They galloped to the top, dismounted and sent the horses to the back of the cleft. The animals milled in fear but stayed near the rock face.

The companions spread out in a semi-circle to defend the hill top. Arynilas stood to the left where he would be unhindered by the fighting, commanding a good view of the rising slope below to aim his arrows. The short Stoneman stood clear of the Tynithian and slightly forward. He was balanced on the balls of his feet, lightly tapping his short sword against the bronze edge of his round targe. Rowan thought she could hear the burly fellow muttering under his breath. She was near the center of the semi-circle between Torrin and Nathel, flanked by the two large men. Dalemar stood to Nathel's right, the Rith's eyes closed in concentration. There was enough space to fight, but not enough room for the enemy to get through and attack from the rear.

The sounds of Raken increased through the surrounding trees. Rowan expected to see their huge dark forms come hurtling into the clearing at any moment.

So it was finally time to stand and fight. These Raken had pursued her since her arrival in Eryos. She almost welcomed the battle; either way it would end the constant running.

Nathel looked over, noticing her. "You should stand back. I'll not let you stay where you will be re-injured. You will be safer with the horses. I suggest you make your way back there now." His tone was polite but dismissive.

"I will do well enough here, thank you," Rowan said.

The healer-swordsman frowned, then looked past her to his brother. "Tor."

Torrin glanced at his brother, then at her. "He is right. Please get to where you will not be hurt."

Rowan would have laughed if she had not been so tightly wound. There was no time for this. She looked him in the eye. "I will guard your back if you will guard mine."

Torrin's eyes widened in surprise. They were a deep blue she noticed, contrasting with his dark hair and brows. It must have been her calm tone of voice he reacted to; her words had been unimpressive — a simple soldier's oath.

Heart pounding, Rowan reached up and pulled her sword free of its baldric. She raised the blade to her forehead and whispered the words: "Dyrn Mithian Irnis Mor Lanyar." The sword began to hum softly in response and she felt its power spread through her arm, lending her strength. Torrin and Nathel were both staring at the sword in wonder, but there was no time to question.

Below them the Raken erupted from the trees. They spotted their quarry and a collective howl echoed from the rock cliff.

Rowan drew her long dagger as well. She pulled in a deep breath – noting the pain in her shoulder. Familiar words came unbidden and Rowan whispered them. The words calmed her, helped to focus her mind. "*On this day when blood is to be shed, let this sword be true, let this arm be strong in the defence of my land, my people and myself. On this day when blood is to be shed...*"

Time slowed. As the Raken came, the ground began to shake. A horse squealed in fear; a golden arrow flashed from the left. One of the Raken to the fore suddenly slumped and rolled back, colliding with another from behind. The howling changed in pitch as more arrows rained down into the swarming Raken.

Rowan turned, watching in amazement as the Tynithian nocked and fired so fluidly that she had trouble following his movements. She turned back to face the advancing Raken just in time to see a blast of brilliant blue light explode into them and from the right, sent from Dalemar's outstretched hand. The huge creatures scattered around their dying brethren but continued to charge.

The first huge beast to reach them hurled into Torrin, a black streak. The big swordsman grunted under the power of the charge. He stepped sideways, twisting, letting the Raken's momentum take it past him, then drove his sword through the beast's back. The Raken dropped with a bellow.

A dark, scaled body came at Rowan. She waited. Its heavy club whistled through the air, descending toward her head; she dodged the arc of the weapon, dropping low. Parrying upward with her dagger, she severed the Raken's wrist tendons. Then, with a sweep of her right arm, Rowan sliced her sword down into the creature's chest. It screamed and crumpled forward.

As she jumped back to avoid its fall, the next huge body was upon her, its studded club swinging down. She lunged forward, closing the distance before it could strike. The sword's hum amplified – as the hum increased, so too did the blade's sharpness. It would soon cut through skin and bone and leather like butter.

Rowan caught brief glimpses of the companions battling around her. Torrin's great broadsword scattered the light, glinting red in the rays of the morning sun. Arrows flew through the air, golden fletching gleaming like birds; Raken dropped like stones as the deadly missiles struck.

Peripherally, she saw more blue fire streak out from Dalemar. The fire sent several Raken flying backward, tumbling down the hill.

The Stoneman, flailing about, roared incoherently, using both short sword and targe as weapons.

Another wave of Raken reached the hilltop. Rowan was crushed against Torrin; the big warrior engaged with a foe to his left. A Raken sword sped towards his exposed side but Rowan's sword was faster, deflecting the blow. The force of impact shivered up her arm, numbing her fingers. She stepped forward with her dagger to slice the creature's throat. As it went down another beast lunged forward, black scales absorbing the light. Rowan sidestepped quickly. The creature spun, following her movement, and Torrin killed it from behind.

The howls were deafening. The clash of steel, grunts of bodies colliding filled the air.

"Ware, Rowan!" Torrin shouted. She turned to see a black beast flying at her. Her sword and dagger came up in a cross, blocking the Raken's swing. As its cudgel hit the slot made by her crossed weapons, she twisted, sweeping it down to the side; then she sliced upward. The Raken roared in pain, it's dying screams adding to the din.

An arrow sped through air over her head to bury itself in the eye of an attacking Raken. The impact pitched the creature away from Rowan and back down the slope. Arynilas had already taken aim at another target. The Tynithian stood calmly amid the turmoil – only a few shafts remained in his quiver.

Movement caught the edge of her vision. Raken had broken through and were coming from behind. Her big stallion reared high into the air, hooves flailing and teeth bared.

"Arynilas!" The Tynithian turned as she pointed at three Raken behind them; and within seconds his arrows halted their advance.

Rowans' left arm was tiring. Her wound throbbed and she felt the warm wetness of blood sliding across her skin and down her arm.

She looked out over the clearing, her heart sinking. *Too many*. The five companions were fighting courageously, but being pushed back step by step. Soon they would have no room to move.

Arynilas fired his last arrow; he drew twin short swords, slicing deftly around him. The tall brothers fought back-to-back, and the Rith sent short bursts of blue flame at individual targets. As each Raken fell, its space was immediately filled.

Rowan ducked under a sweeping enemy blade, her sword and dagger slicing into the Raken almost in unison. She landed a kick in its body, sending it stumbling backward.

A great roar echoed suddenly from down at the bottom of the hill. She turned, hope welling as Hathunor smashed into the back of the smaller Raken. They scattered in surprise, turning to meet him as he attacked with a crazed ferocity. Half of the Raken on the hill turned back to meet the new threat, and the companions renewed their attack from above.

Rowan took a glancing blow to the back. She stumbled forward, spinning around. A club-wielding Raken snarled at her, rows of sharp ivory teeth glinting. The beast jumped forward, its club descending. Rowan dodged the studded weapon and stepped in as soon as it cleared her, slicing with her humming sword.

Another Raken lunged. She tried desperately to parry its attack. A hand clamped around her left arm and yanked her back out of the weapon's range. The pain in her shoulder burst like fire and her vision swam. As it cleared, she turned to see Torrin stepping forward to meet the creature. Nathel closed from the other side – a human wall, giving her a rest. She stepped up behind them, protecting their backs.

Roaring, the Stoneman shoved a Raken down the slope to land on others. Rowan caught glimpses of Hathunor down at the bottom of the hill – his shaggy crest, a raised arm, bloodied claws.

He was almost completely surrounded by his smaller kin, but a growing number of bodies were piling at his feet.

The last of the fighting was fierce, but the battle ended quickly soon after. The last beast stood amid the bodies of its comrades, its huge head swivelling as it appraised the companions. Its red eyes fastened on Rowan. Snarling, it leaped at her. Torrin's broadsword found it first, and the Raken threw back its head in a pain-filled howl. Entwined with this last utterance was a human scream that chilled Rowan's blood. The menacing light faded from the Raken's red gaze as it slid from Torrin's blade and collapsed to the ground.

Silence enveloped the hilltop. Rowan became aware of the breathing of her companions; her own ragged gasps. She sank wearily to her knees, soaked with sweat and blood, her left arm completely numb and useless. It was all she could do just to unclench the hand that grasped her blood-covered dagger. She whispered to her sword, and its humming ceased.

"It is the creature that has been following us," said Arynilas. Rowan looked up and saw the Tynithian stoop to pull one of his arrows from a black scaled body, calmly fit it to his bow and aim down the hill at Hathunor.

She struggled to her feet. "No! Hold Arynilas! Hold!" She stepped between the Tynithian's drawn bow and her friend.

Torrin moved towards her with a fierce scowl above piercing blue eyes. He raised his gore-covered sword to point down the hill. "It's the same Raken that came into our camp! If you know why it would help us, speak quickly. You know why it's been following us, don't you? Tell us why we should spare it."

Rowan frowned up at him, standing her ground. "He is no threat to you. He's my friend. He was the one that warned us this morning."

"He?"

"Do you think the Raken would have given themselves away like that? They have been tracking me for a long time. They do not howl until they have spotted their quarry." Rowan looked down the hill at her large friend. "He warned us they were coming, gave us the extra time we needed."

The rest of the companions gathered to look down at Hathunor. "He did help us fight them off," said Dalemar.

Hathunor stood at the bottom of the hill watching them warily.

Rowan looked back at Torrin to find him studying her intently. She struggled to pull herself up to her full height, tightening the grip on her sword.

"He is my friend," she said, "and if you wish to harm him, then you must go through me."

Torrin sighed, nodding and Arynilas lowered his bow. Rowan turned to look down at Hathunor. She waved to him and he turned, loping back into the trees.

"Where is he going?" Torrin was standing beside her now.

"He is going to scout for any remaining Raken." Torrin raised his eyebrows in question and Rowan explained. "His senses are keener than ours and he can track and hear his own people better than we can. He will warn us before they get too close." She was weary beyond belief, and the throbbing pain in her shoulder was sapping what little strength she had left.

The big swordsman looked down at her, shaking his head. Then turned to his brother. "More surprises, hey Nathel?" A chuckle was the only reply.

She began to sit down before her legs gave way entirely. Torrin helped ease her down. He probed her left shoulder. Rowan winced.

"Nathel!" Torrin called. "The wound has reopened."

Nathel was there quickly, reaching for his healer's satchel.

Rowan tried to wave them away but they ignored her. Torrin told her to keep still; she gave up. He shifted his attention away from her shoulder to look her in the eye.

"Tell me about your – friend. How long have you known him?"

"About three weeks. He —"

"He's a great bloody Raken!" exclaimed Nathel to her shoulder.

Rowan tried to ignore the pain as he worked on her. "I rescued him from a group of Raken that were going to kill him."

"What in the name of Erys would possess you to do such a thing?" asked Torrin in awe.

Nathel looked up at her from his work on her wound, his pale blue eyes full of disbelief.

Rowan shrugged; it was not something she could easily explain. "He has been a good friend to me since. They are quite interesting creatures actually – intelligent, resourceful and fiercely loyal. It takes a little to get passed his appearance, but once I did, I found him to have an engaging personality."

Torrin shook his head and shared a glance with his brothers. "We're talking about the Raken, the same bloodthirsty, mindless monsters that we just fought? Slaughtering entire towns, leaving people to rot in the sun? The same creatures that have been hunting you for a month?" protested Torrin.

The short Stoneman shook his head, staring at her with disbelief. "A month? Ye 'ave been hunted by a trieton for a month?"

"The Raken are not the terrible monsters they appear to be," said Rowan.

Torrin snorted. "You'll forgive us our scepticism. We've encountered Raken before this, seen first hand the carnage they wreak. They are savage and remorseless."

"The Raken that we know here in Eryos are not the people Hathunor describes," she insisted

"Hathunor? It has a name?" Torrin asked in surprise.

Rowan nodded. "Hathunor says the Raken come from a far distant land. They have been brought here against their will, and somehow forced to do these terrible things."

"How do you know all this?"

"Everything I know about the Raken, I have learned from Hathunor," said Rowan wearily.

Torrin frowned, his blue eyes intense as he considered her. The morning sun lit his features, creating shadows along the planes of his face. "Why are the Raken hunting you? We have seen nothing from them so far but random slaughter. What would make them track you for a month and die in the attempt to kill you?"

Rowan sighed. "It is a very long story." She held her breath as Nathel applied pressure to her shoulder to bind it tightly.

Dalemar sat down beside them, looking at Rowan curiously with pale grey eyes. "Your friend, Hathunor? He believes his kin are being controlled somehow?"

"That is the only way they would be doing the things they are," she replied.

Dalemar turned to look at Torrin, the tip of his pointed ear peeking out from his pale hair. "When the last Raken died, there was another… presence with it. I felt it only briefly and I cannot be certain of what it was but I believe the death of the Raken caused it considerable pain."

Rowan remembered the unholy scream that had combined with the Raken's howl.

"I also felt something," Arynilas said. "It fled when the beast died," The Tynithian narrowed his sapphire eyes. "It felt similar to the sense of another Tynithian's true self, but it was powerful and –" Arynilas tilted his head, looking at Torrin. "Wrong, evil – it was focused on the Myrian."

Rowan stared up into Arynilas's jewel-like eyes as she registered what he said. The Twilight People were said to live for hundreds of years, accumulating great wisdom. She knew something uncanny must have driven the Raken to pursue her for so long, given Hathunor's bafflement over the behaviour of his kin. She could only assume that it was somehow tied to her mission.

She shrugged her good shoulder, realizing they were all looking at her. Even Nathel had stopped his ministrations, staring.

"It is apparent we have much to discuss," Torrin said quietly. "And it would seem our fates might be more closely linked than we realize. Let us leave this place and hope the gear we left behind is unspoiled. Now is not the time for discussion." His blue eyes locked with hers, an intensity in them that belied his calm expression.

They split up to retrieve their horses and weapons. Only Nathel and the Stoneman remained with Rowan. The Stoneman leaned down and held out a broad, blood-stained hand. "I am Borlin. 'Tis a pleasure to meet ye, lass. Would ye give me the honour of cleaning yer sword for ye?" His voice was low and gruff but it carried a musical lilt, and his face sported deep laugh lines.

Rowan reached out and grasped his rough palm, smiling. "It is a pleasure to meet you as well, Borlin. As to my blade I thank you, but it is a task that I am well used to; you need not bother yourself."

The Stoneman released her hand and held his out to receive the weapon. "'Tis no bother lass, but an honour." His amber brown eyes were completely serious but there was a lurking sorrow that seemed at odds with his friendly manner.

Rowan nodded and held out her sword, certain that Borlin would take no other answer. He bowed his head to her and turned back to their sparse gear with her sword in hand.

Nathel looked up from her shoulder. "That was one of the highest praises anyone could ever expect from a Black Hills Stoneman."

Rowan raised her eyebrows. "But I've done nothing to warrant such praise. In fact, it was my pursuers that you chose to fight today. You would not have had the trouble were it not for me."

"True," said Torrin, leading her big grey horse towards them. "but you accorded yourself well in battle and to a Stoneman, that is the most important thing. We have all taken note of your skill with a sword."

"Where I come from, skill in battle is second nature, for both men and woman," she said.

He stopped, looking down at her. "You are a long way from home, Rowan."

Nathel, having finished binding her wound, tucked away his healer's satchel and offered her his hand. "In case you had not already discovered, I am Nathel, Torrin's younger and better looking brother." He winked at her and an infectious smile spread across his face. He exuded an light-hearted charm, very different from Torrin's dark intensity. In fact, the only similarity between the brothers was their size and build. Even the color of their hair was opposite, Nathel's fair and Torrin's dark. Their eyes were the same blue, though Nathel's were paler. He looked to be five or so years younger than Torrin. They were clean-shaven with close-cropped hair. Both of their breastplates were embellished with identical crests – an eagle with outstretched wings over a round shield.

As she took Nathel's hand in greeting, the rest of the companions gathered around and Rowan was properly introduced to Dalemar and Arynilas as well. Dalemar she found open and friendly. Arynilas was almost as inscrutable as Torrin, but he took her hand respectfully and bowed his dark head to her.

Nathel helped her to her feet and gave her a boost up onto Roanus. As the others mounted up, Rowan surveyed the carnage littering the hilltop. The dead faces of the Raken now looked much like Hathunor and her chest ached for the loss of so many lives.

They retraced the route of their wild flight through the woods and came eventually to the previous night's camp. It was lucky that their path had very little Erys' Bane and they had been able to avoid running through it. Their gear was as it had been left during their hurried departure, although some things were trampled as if the Raken had charged through the site without stopping.

They took the time to make a hot meal after packing up the gear and making ready to leave. Nathel tended to the cuts and wounds taken in the fighting.

Finally, Torrin set his cup aside. "Now, please tell us Rowan, how did you come to be here in the Wilds, alone save for the unlikely companionship of an enormous Raken, with a trieton of the beasts hunting you down?"

The Messenger

Torrin waited with the others for the answers to all his questions.

Rowan flipped her long braid over her shoulder and took a deep breath. She began haltingly, but then continued with more confidence. “My name is Rowan Mor Lanyar – I have traveled to Eryos from my homeland of Myris Dar. I am a messenger and an emissary for my people and I bear a warning for this land. I am on my way north following the only clue I have to deliver that message. I search for a city, a grand city that sits on the northern edge of Eryos with its back to the sea and high cliffs that plunge into the waters of the ocean. That city must not fall in the struggle that is to come.”

“This city you seek,” Torrin interrupted, his pulse quickening. “What is its name?”

“I know this city only as Kathorn, but that name is thousands of years old and those I have ventured to ask about it have not recognized it. I fear the city may have been lost centuries ago.”

Torrin glanced at his friends; only Arynilas was unreadable. The others shared his amazement. There could be no mistaking the description. Rowan was searching for Pellaris. What were the odds that they should meet someone out here in the wilderness, duty bound like them to reach Cerebus in Pellaris? Torrin focused his attention back on Rowan as she continued, noting again the strange accent in her speech.

“The land I come from is an isolated island lying deep in the southern Ocean. We have been cut off from the rest of Eryos for centuries, but our knowledge of the rest of the world is ever present to the Seers of Danum. They are a small group of holy men and women who have made it their responsibility to guard against the return of the Wyoraith.”

Torrin frowned. “The Wyoraith?” Rowan turned to gaze at him. But before she could speak, Dalemar supplied the answer.

“The Wyoraith is a very powerful force of evil. Rithkind legend has it that the Wyoraith, in seeking to control the free worlds, will ultimately destroy them all. Most of the Riths in Eryos scoff at such a tale, it is told now only to frighten children into obeying their mothers. I had not realized that men still knew of the legend."

Rowan nodded. "We have been isolated for a very long time. The legend is still very much alive among my people, but the Seers know a slightly different tale. They believe the Wyoraith is not an entity unto itself, but a tool. An immensely powerful tool – a force of magic that could destroy the world if someone with ill intent learns to control it. The legend of evil comes from past intent to use the Wyoraith for harm. The Seers of Danum have prophesied the returning of the Wyoraith for centuries, but there was never any clue as to when it might happen. Until now.

"I was part of a small company that set out from Myris Dar by ship and sailed to the port city of Dendor. We were to make for this northern city to warn its king or steward. We traveled the Eryos Ocean for weeks, but when we reached Dendor, the Raken were waiting for us. They ambushed us along the road only an hour inland from the city. I have no explanation for how they knew we would be there or why they were trying to kill us. I can only assume that they were sent to keep the message from reaching Kathorn. We lost most of our small company. The Raken killed and dragged them away. My cousin Dell and I were the only ones to escape the ambush. Dell died a week later from his wounds." She paused, her face reflecting her despair.

Torrin flicked his eyes to his brother. This then was the memory they had witnessed while Rowan was in the clutches of fever.

"I have been hunted ever since. Hathunor is the only reason I have made it this far," she finished with a resigned tone.

Torrin stirred and sat forward. "The city you describe can be none other than Pellaris, the capital of Pellar."

Rowan's green eyes widened and he thought she might have sighed in relief. "How far is it from here?"

Torrin scratched his whiskers. "It is far – four weeks journey at least."

"If you had to get to Pellaris in haste, why not sail north around Krang? I imagine that the storm season would not have been in full force at the time of your sailing. Your ship likely would have made it through and it would be easier than traveling over land," asked Nathel.

"We had acquired passage on a trading ship, and that was as far as the captain was willing to take us. Also, the Seers of Danum were adamant that we sail to the port of Dendor and then travel north overland. I have no idea why and the Seers would give no answer when asked to explain themselves," said Rowan.

"Why Pellaris, and why now?" asked Dalemar.

"The Seers foresaw a great attack on a grand city of stone perched upon high sea cliffs while Bashelar hides in the shadow of her older sister. The Wyoraith will arise on the night that Bashelar is eclipsed, and with the attack will come darkness to last an age. Also — and perhaps the most important reason — it is where the last slayer of the Wyoraith was found."

"Slayer of the Wyoraith?" Nathel asked.

Rowan nodded. "Perhaps a thousand years ago, no one knows for sure, a man was born in the ancient city of Kathorn. He grew up to become the Slayer of the Wyoraith. History has not recorded his name and the Seers know only that he was descended from a Slayer before him. The Seers believe a new Slayer will be found in Kathorn —Pellaris — though I do not know where.

"The Seers tell that if the world is to prevent the summoning of the Wyoraith for evil purpose, then the one who seeks to control it must be stopped. However, if the Wyoraith is successfully brought forth into this world and harnessed, its master will become invincible and Eryos will fall and be destroyed. This Slayer is charged with protecting the Wyoraith from that evil intent.

"The Seers deemed it time for Myris Dar to rejoin the rest of Eryos. To that end, my small party was sent to re-establish contact with the kingdoms of Eryos, principally the kingdom that was once part of the Kathornin Empire, which from what you tell me is Pellar. But I am now the only one left of that party." Rowan finished, her gaze downcast as she stared into the fire.

Torrin shifted on the log and looked around the circle of his companions, studying their grave faces. As he met the eyes of each one, he received a nod to the unspoken question.

They had been traveling to answer the summons from King Cerebus, unsure of what role they would play in turning back the invasion of Raken, if indeed they would reach Pellaris in time to help at all. If what Rowan told them was true and the Raken attacks foretold the unleashing of an even greater doom —

the Wyoraith — upon the world, then King Cerebus, Pellar and all of Eryos were in grave danger.

If they did not reach Pellaris in time to warn King Cerebus, he might not be able to act. As to the rest, Torrin hoped the answer to this mystery of the Wyoraith lay somewhere within the northern capital.

He studied at the woman Erys had placed in their path and wondered again at the impossibility of it. The fact that she had survived thus far spoke volumes about her character, but he believed she needed help to complete her mission. The journey to Pellaris was long and hard, even without Raken trietons tracking her.

He also knew his friends and not one of them would leave a woman to fend for herself, regardless of the skill she had with a blade and the aid she seemed to command from a renegade Raken beast.

Torrin picked up his broad sword, from where it rested beside him after cleaning. He slid the blade into its scabbard with a metal hiss and looked Rowan in the eye. “We will see you safely to Pellaris.”

She looked around at the others and began to shake her head, but Torrin held up his hand to stall her.

“We were on our way there before we came across you, to answer a summons from King Cerebus. Our destinations are the same. The Raken patrols are increasing. It would be foolish for us not to travel together.”

After a short pause, Rowan agreed. “I would be honoured to travel with you then, but I have one condition.”

Torrin almost smiled. Why was he not surprised? This woman was quite unlike any he had ever met. “And what would that be?”

“Hathunor. He must come with me.”

Torrin narrowed his eyes; he had been expecting the request. “He may come with us. Who knows, we might learn a great deal from him about his kind. But heed my words – if he betrays us in any way, I will kill him.”

Rowan gazed silently at him and Torrin was struck again by the green of her eyes. He had the distinct impression that she was sizing him up, looking for weaknesses. He was surprised to find it made him uneasy.

"So be it," she replied finally.

Dalemar cleared his throat and Torrin pulled his gaze from Rowan's challenging stare.

The Rith's smooth brow was furrowed. "I think the eclipse of Bashelar will occur this fall. I cannot be totally accurate without the proper charts. If it is true and the summoning of the Wyoraith is coming, then we may not have much time."

Torrin suppressed a sudden shiver and rose to his feet. "Then let us be away. We still have a fair afternoon for travel and should be able to make good distance."

Hathunor

Rowan mounted her big grey horse and rode to the edge of the trees. The others waited at the campsite for her. She sat astride Roanus for a minute or so, waiting. Her shoulder still throbbed but the bleeding had stopped. From the corner of her eye she glimpsed a large, dark form emerge from the trees to her left. She turned as Hathunor strode toward her.

"Hello, my friend, are you well?" she asked.

"Well," came the reply from deep in the throat, like heavy stones grinding together. As he approached, his glowing red eyes turned from her to look warily at the group behind her.

"They are good people, Hathunor, and will not harm you. They have offered to help me get to Kathorn. They know it as Pellaris and they were heading there when they found us."

The red eyes focused back on Rowan, and the heavy brow ridges above them drew down in concentration as Hathunor translated her speech. Rowan had abandoned attempts at trying to understand his language. The clicks and burrs of his speech were unpronounceable, with no relation to any other language she had heard. Hathunor, though, was learning the common tongue of Eryos quickly, a testament to his intelligence. "No harm?"

Rowan nodded

"No harm Rowan?" The frown on Hathunor's face turned into a snarl and the image of the attacking Raken from the morning flashed through her mind. Hathunor's black-scaled face was surprisingly mobile; she didn't think she'd seen his full range of expression yet. As his brief snarl faded, the smooth scales of his skin glittered in the sun.

"They have aided me greatly, Hathunor. Look, my wound is almost healed." She pulled back part of the bandage that Nathel had applied to stop the renewed bleeding.

Hathunor peered at her shoulder and an expression that Rowan recognized as a smile spread across his frightening face. He nodded once and his huge, clawed hand came up to touch her arm gently. "Hathunor not want Rowan hurt."

Rowan covered the giant hand with her own. His scaled skin was warm and soft like fine leather. "Come and meet our new friends, though it sounds as though you have already met them, judging by the alarm you caused the other night."

A sound like gravel sliding downhill welled from Hathunor's throat. His red eyes gleamed with humour and his lips pulled back to reveal sharp ivory teeth.

The light breeze rustled his furred crest, beginning at the top of his forehead running down his broad back. It was the only part of him other than his red eyes that wasn't black. Glowing a warm chestnut in the sun, the hairs of the crest were coarse, like a horse's mane that didn't grow long enough to fall down. His wide shoulders sported spiny ridges and knobs that protected the shoulder joints. The muscles of his arms were huge. When they flexed, tendons and sinew stood out under the smooth scales. His hip girdle was also protected by bony protrusions and the scales broadened over his belly. His legs were long and muscled like his tree-trunk arms and his lower legs had another joint above the ankle, which gave him a hock below the knee. He walked on his toes, which had long curving claws.

Rowan turned her horse and they began to walk back to the others. The huge Raken pacing beside her was taller than she was sitting on Roanus.

When they reached the campsite, Rowan introduced Hathunor to the five companions. As each was named, he brought a huge fist to his dark, scaled chest and bowed his massive head. He received tentative nods in return. Then Hathunor spread his arms wide, and stated in his deep, gravel voice. "You help Rowan, you Hathunor's friend."

Torrin shook his head in wonder, a slow, reluctant smile spreading across his face. "You are welcome, Hathunor."

Rowan smiled at the expressions of disbelief and wonder on the faces of such self-possessed men.

As the sun reached its zenith and began to descend through a clear early autumn sky, the group of seven left the abandoned campsite and made their way north through the surrounding trees. They rode at a steady pace for the rest of the afternoon, each turned inward – the addition of two new members to the group had changed the dynamics within the companionship considerably. None of the companions completely trusted the huge

Raken in their midst and Rowan was the mirror opposite of the women of Eryos.

Rowan pressed her heal against Roanus, shifting him around a fallen log. She glanced at the men riding ahead of her – they were wary, uneasy. She turned to Hathunor, striding beside her. "Will you scout ahead, my friend?"

He nodded and flashed her a knowing smile full of sharp teeth, then loped ahead to disappear into the trees.

The others watched him go but then their attention switched to her. She shook her head in amusement as she caught them looking at her. Arynilas seemed to be the only one unruffled by her presence. It was not the first time she had received such attention in Eryos, and it probably wouldn't be the last.

When she and her small company had landed in Dendor, happy to be off the ship and spending the night at a portside inn, they had been openly stared at. She and the two other women in their party had received the most scrutiny. Rowan thought at first it was because their clothing and appearance was foreign but as they had walked through the narrow streets of the city, she had become increasingly aware that the women of Dendor didn't carry swords. Upon leaving the city, she had received the exact same reaction from the farmers and villagers in the rest of Lor Danith.

She supposed now was no different. These companions, with the exception of Arynilas, had probably never seen a female warrior. Some local Lor Danion men had even gone out of their way to have sport with her, interpreting her clothes and openly carried weapon as a challenge of sorts. It had infuriated her – a needless waste of energy and time. She'd had to defend herself from such challenges, trying to defeat her opponents without killing or wounding them seriously. One fool had been so enraged at his defeat by a woman that he had sent his three friends after her as well. He had succeeded only in getting them all injured.

The women she had met had been coldly disapproving, a reaction that had puzzled her considerably. How could people be so closed and unfriendly? When Myrians met strangers, they treated them with respect and interest. Travelers were always offered food and water, even lodging. Rowan supposed it was foolish of her to have expected the same on the mainland. She had thought about it often and had come to the conclusion that Myrians, with their well-practiced martial skills, were simply not afraid of strangers. If you couldn't defend yourself, it would be natural to feel uncomfortable, even afraid, around people that you didn't know and trust.

The only people Rowan had met so far who were curious and friendly had been young girls and boys in Lor Danith but she was rarely given the opportunity to enjoy their company. Parents would snatch their children away, scowling at her when they realized she was the person their children were grinning at.

Her clothes had bothered people as much as her sword. She was spat at, named as a whore for showing her legs, even though they were covered in her leather leggings. Men propositioned her frequently, assuming she was selling herself. Despite the hot summer season, she had purchased a long cloak to hide her legs and some of her weaponry. She had rejected the idea of buying a dress to blend in, refusing to handicap herself with the impractical ground-length skirts fashionable in Lor Danith. Besides, it was impossible to hide the sword pommel over her shoulder, even if she had dressed as other women.

In the end, she had taken to staying away from settlements. Her demeanour had changed by necessity, her open-minded curiosity curbed, becoming aloof and solitary. For her own safety and others, she had kept contact with people to a minimum.

Rowan frowned. This was not the way it was supposed to have been. The journey through Eryos should have been shared with her fellow Myrians. She had looked forward with excitement to meeting new cultures and races. Instead she had been running for her life – unfriendly faces everywhere she turned.

She studied the five companions; they seemed surprisingly accepting of her. As a group, they were themselves unique. Rowan had not seen Tynithians or Riths until now in Eryos. It had been her secret hope that she might meet the fabled races.

Myris Dar was closed to most foreign people but Tynithians, who travel the oceans often, had always been welcome on the protected isle. Rowan had been taught early on that the Twilight People inspired the artistry Myrians strove to incorporate into every aspect of life. Although Rowan had seen a few Tynithian visitors to Myris Dar during her lifetime, she could not claim to have known any.

She looked at Arynilas, riding ahead. She had been surprised by his small size. She could almost look him directly in his wise, timeless eyes, yet he looked no older than she did. She had to keep reminding herself that he was likely hundreds of years old. The tilt to his sapphire eyes and the refined bone structure of his features were easy to mark as Tynithian and his onyx-black hair and dark arching eyebrows gave him a striking appearance. His clothing was mostly soft leather — greens and browns — and he had the most unnerving ability to blend into the surrounding landscape. Even with his dark hair she found herself surprised to suddenly see him move from an unexpected place. His movements were quick and fluid and Rowan suspected that his athletic abilities far outstripped those of the others. She knew Tynithians were shape shifters, and she was curious about Arynilas's animal form.

Legends told that the Tynithians were named the Twilight People because Erys created them during the first night of her self-imposed exile in Eryos to hide from Raithyn. To amuse her, the Tynithians had formed themselves into animals, keeping her sorrow at bay.

Rowan watched her companions as much as they studied her, taking in their features and dress, weapons, voices and movements. Her shoulder still throbbed and she absently rubbed the surrounding muscle to ease the ache; massaging an injury shortened the time it took to heal. She concentrated her attention back on the other companions to take her mind off the pain.

Stonemen rarely traveled the oceans so their reputation was gleaned from stories and rumour alone. Even though the stocky men seldom traveled the seas, their trade goods did. Rowan's family owned a rare Stoneman blue glazed pottery urn. It was her favourite thing in her mother's kitchen. The blue glaze was a secret known only to the Stonemen and it was one of the most sought after items on the rare trade ships allowed into Myrian waters. Stonemen were exceptional stone carvers as well. They had quite literally built the stone city of the Riths, modeling it after their own stone forts and towns perched in the heights of the Black Hills.

Of the Stonemen themselves, Rowan knew very little. Borlin was almost the complete opposite of Arynilas. Where the Tynithian was slim and graceful, Borlin was broad and stocky. His square face with its straight nose and bristly red beard exuded stubborn resilience. His soft brown eyes were kind and apt to twinkle and she enjoyed listening to his lilting voice. He was quick to laugh and bantered constantly with Nathel.

The sadness she had glimpsed in his eyes earlier was a puzzle and she wondered what his story was.

He stood almost a head shorter than she did but was more than twice as wide. Rowan was willing to wager that Borlin was stronger than both Torrin and Nathel combined. The Stoneman's bones were thick and his hands resembled those of a blacksmith. His clothes consisted of worn brown leathers and silver buckles. Under his leather vest and jacket, he wore a creamy shirt that peeked out from the darker colors, giving him a dapper look. She looked forward to getting to know him better.

Riths were a race Rowan knew almost nothing about. Her great grandfather was said to have known a great Rith but no one in her family had been able to tell her anything more. As a child she had heard wondrous tales of the Rith city high on the slopes of the great Timor Mountains — a city carved from the living stone, where magic was used to do all the chores she had to complete by hand. She had never really believed the stories she had been told but seeing the way Dalemar had fought with Rith fire this morning had made her rethink her scepticism. She understood now why he didn't carry a weapon.

Dalemar, riding directly ahead of her, was medium height and slim. He wore a long, green leather coat that was split in the back for riding and his pale blond hair lay loosely down his back. He kept his hair pulled back off his smooth face and she could see his pointed ears when he turned his head. His features fell somewhere between Tynithians and men. He was larger boned than Arynilas and his eyes didn't tilt upwards, but Rowan thought he resembled Tynithians more than men. He had beautiful pale grey eyes and blond eyebrows, which were his most expressive feature, moving constantly as he spoke. His saddlebags appeared to be stuffed with books, which he sometimes read as he rode. He was friendly and open and Rowan had taken an instant liking to him.

Then there were Torrin and Nathel – so different from the small, olive-skinned, dark eyed people of Lor Danith she had encountered. They were tall with broad shoulders, fair skin and blue eyes. Nathel in particular looked northern. His short, sandy hair was curly, and his pale blue eyes, under their blond brows, held laughter more than anything else. Rowan drew in a sharp breath as a wave of homesickness washed over her. He reminded her strikingly of her younger brother Andin.

They were an impressive pair with straight noses, high cheekbones and similar builds. Their large hands were almost identical — the same knuckles, thumbs and fingertips.

But the similarity ended there. Where Nathel was open and gregarious with a ready wit and a smile, Torrin was closed and reserved. His dark brows and intense blue eyes were intimidating. He was friendly enough she supposed but seemed to offer nothing of himself to anyone.

He was a natural leader, a man who could put thought into action in an instant but aware enough of others to look for direction when he knew they could give it. It was a puzzle to find a Tynithian and a Rith following a man. She got the impression that Dalemar was quite young. Arynilas must possess by far the greatest experience among them, and yet he looked to Torrin for direction.

Rowan studied him as he rode ahead of her on his big black horse. There were strong, quick currents beneath Torrin's calm surface – of that she was certain.

Judging from the way the five companions interacted, they had been traveling together for a long time. The battle this morning had revealed this, if nothing else. An unspoken unity, the ability to anticipate each other's needs and act accordingly, these were traits of some of the longest acquainted and renowned fighting units on Myris Dar.

These people were very good fighters, each showing an ease and expertise with his chosen weapon. They knew each other's minds as well – had not even discussed the decision to see her to Pellaris this morning.

They were a tight-knit group of mercenaries, judging from the lack of uniform or resemblance. Aside from the brothers, they most assuredly all came from different lands. There was an interesting story to be told here and she looked forward to hearing it.

Getting Acquainted

When the sun began to set, they made a sparse camp in a small clearing with a fast-flowing stream cutting through it. After the horses were watered and cared for, the companions gathered around a small fire to eat a hot meal.

Rowan spread her sleeping roll down in front of a downed log by the fire. She scanned the surrounding trees, wondering what had become of Hathunor. Then she spotted him at the creek, crouched low to drink his fill and wash his limbs. The companions eyed him as he moved among them toward Rowan. He nodded to each and in return was rewarded by tentative acknowledgments. Rowan smiled, it wouldn't take long for them to begin to see him as she did.

Hathunor settled down in front of where she sat with a bowl of remarkably good stew in her hands. "Hathunor sense no others."

Rowan could feel the low rumble of his voice vibrate through her chest. She looked up at him. "You must be hungry my friend; come, have some food."

Borlin, who had prepared the meal, brought over a steaming bowl and held it out to Hathunor. "I don't know what ye eat but ye are welcome to our fare," he said gruffly.

Hathunor rose quickly to his feet and Borlin stepped back, craning his neck to look up at the Raken. Hathunor accepted the food carefully and bowed his enormous head, rumbling a distinct thank you before dropping to sit next to Rowan.

Borlin blinked in surprise before shaking his head and returning to the fire.

Rowan grinned in delight. No, it wouldn't take long at all.

The sun set and cool evening air stirred as twilight descended over the clearing. Hathunor left them again after he had eaten, his black form disappearing quickly into the gathering gloom. Rowan took out a rag from her saddlebags and began to oil her sword.

Torrin approached and sat down next to her. "How is your shoulder?" he asked as he settled himself. His face conveyed nothing but polite concern.

She inclined her head. "It is well, thanks to your brother and Dalemar."

He watched silently as she worked the soft oily rag over her blade.

She knew there were questions they both wanted to ask. Torrin seemed content to wait so she spoke hers first. "Tell me about your companions? How is it such a diverse group travels together?"

Torrin cocked his head, shrugging one shoulder. "We have been together for a while. I suppose we take for granted the mix of our races. We are well known in certain circles and are rarely asked about how we all met."

"You are a mercenary company." It was not a question and Torrin glanced at her before nodding.

Rowan pointed her chin towards Dalemar who sat across the fire from them. "I have never met a Rith. Do they not always carry a staff?"

"Yes," replied Torrin, "but Dalemar is not much like other Riths."

"How so?"

"His potential is thought by some to be boundless, that he might one day be the most powerful Rith in a thousand years. But only if he can learn to master his gifts."

Rowan's eyebrows shot up and she looked at the Rith, who was buried in a leather bound book, his smooth brow furrowed in concentration. His face was difficult to see in the growing darkness. He looked much like a young man of twenty-five, but Rowan knew Riths, like Tynithians, could live to be several hundred years old. They were said to wear long flowing robes. Dalemar, however, wore clothing much the same as the others with the exception of his long dark green coat. Having never in fact seen a Rith before, Rowan wondered if what little she knew of them was correct. "Why doesn't he use a staff?"

Torrin looked across at the Rith. "At a very young age he discovered that he could channel his power directly without the aide of a focus."

"A focus? Like the staff?"

"Yes. Riths use an object of some kind to focus their power. It is quite often a staff but doesn't have to be. It is a way to train young Riths to control their magical abilities when they begin to manifest. Otherwise a young Rith can become dangerous and unpredictable. Terrible accidents have happened in the past, or so Dalemar has told me, where young Riths trying to control their newfound powers have killed themselves as well as those around them. Strict laws were passed long ago to protect against such use of power without the aid of a focus to control a Rith's magic. The focus acts like a sort of buffer to diffuse the potency of the magic. Once young Riths master their new powers, the use of a focus is no longer needed, but most find it has become an integral part of the process by then. The Council of Riths has not tried to change the practice because it helps to regulate the use of magic."

Rowan eyed her blade critically, then resumed polishing. "But all Riths can wield magic without a focus?"

"Yes, but Rithkind lives in a densely populated city in the Timor Mountains. They have regulated the use of magic by necessity to keep order. Dalemar's innate ability to channel magic without a focus was essentially breaking the Rith laws of magic use. It frightened the council of Riths. Others didn't approve of a non-traditional approach."

Torrin leaned forward to add another few branches to the fire. "Dalemar was forced to use a focus object. As a result, his progress stopped. He became frustrated and decided to strike out on his own, believing that he could learn better on his own terms. He left the Rith city of Tirynus and spent a long time traveling from one outside group of Riths to another, looking for someone who could teach him. He found only frustration.

"All those who had been willing to teach him had no idea how to instruct him without the use of a focus. He wandered aimlessly for a long time, learning his craft through trial and error. We found him sheltering in a ruined fort during a winter storm. He was in poor shape. Nathel cared for him and convinced him to join us and we have enjoyed his company since. He is older than any of us save Arynilas, but still young for a Rith."

Rowan looked across at Dalemar. He had lit a pipe and was squinting at his book through a wreath of smoke.

"Tell me of the rest of your companions; where did you meet them?" Rowan finished with her sword, re-sheathed it and took up her dagger to repeat the process.

Torrin stared at the fire. "We've been together a long time – been through enough to know each other very well. Nathel and I met Arynilas in the Ren wars. He was fighting with a company of Tynithians that was slaughtered by a Ren ambush. Arynilas was the last one left alive when we came across him. He had the entire squad of enemy pinned down behind a rock outcrop with his bow. A single warrior against twenty-five." Torrin shook his head in admiration, lost in the memory.

Rowan found the slight Tynithian speaking quietly to Nathel while fletching arrows for his bow, his nimble fingers working with speed.

"I have little knowledge of the rest of Eryos, but I thought Tynithians didn't concern themselves in the affairs of men. Yet you met him in a war, where his company was fighting men?"

"It is rare, but sometimes if circumstances warrant, they will come out of Dan Tynell. Tynithians are fierce in the defence of their forest realm. The whole of southern Eryos was embroiled in the fighting. The Ren warlords sought to take new territory and they expanded outward like raging floodwaters. They even tried to take the Black Hills but it was a mistake that marked the beginning of their downfall. It is less than wise to anger Stonemen."

Rowan glanced over at the Stoneman. "And Borlin?"

Torrin clasped his hands in front of him with his elbows on his knees. "We met Borlin in the same wars. Stonemen are ferocious fighters, and the small company he was with during the three years the wars lasted became quite renowned. Borlin's sire is the lord of Drenwin, which lies in the eastern portion of the Black Hills." Torrin pointed vaguely towards the south. "His father arranged a marriage for Borlin, a tradition common among Stonemen, but Borlin had already found his partner. Unfortunately, his father vehemently disapproved of the match, for his chosen was a Lor Danion woman. They ordered him home, but he refused. His sire declared Borlin an oath-breaker and banished him from Drenwin. Nathel, Arynilas and I found ourselves campaigning with him to keep the Warlords contained inside the borders of Ren. We fought for Lor Danith mostly, hired to train and help their militia. When the outward expansion of the Ren Wars was halted, chaos ensued as the coalition of warlords disintegrated and turned upon each other. We worked for a time for one warlord who it seemed would be able to bring peace to

Ren, gathering all the tribes under a single banner. But it was not to be."

Rowan looked at the broad-shouldered Stoneman as he tended to the horses. She turned back to Torrin, who was staring into the fire again. "Borlin's chosen, what happened to her?"

Torrin sighed, and turned to look at her. "She died of the plague. Erys took her not six months after they pledged to each other."

Rowan shivered in understanding – Borlin had lost his people and his love. She felt Torrin watching her and turned to meet his gaze. "And what of you and Nathel? You are not from the south. How is it you both ended up fighting in Ren?"

Torrin shook his head and his expression changed, becoming guarded and cool. His answer, when it came, was dismissive. "We were young and blinded by the glory of adventure." He nodded toward her sword on the ground. "Tell me about your humming sword. It is a beautiful weapon."

Rowan halted the rag upon the blade of her dagger – she had long since finished cleaning it. Picking up the sword in its tooled scabbard, she handed it to Torrin. He took it gently from her and pulled it clear of the leather. It looked like a toy in his large hands.

"It is a spell sword," she said.

Torrin looked at her, raised his eyebrows, then looked down at the weapon. "It has a magical spell set upon it?"

"In a sense," Rowan replied. "It is an art form that is lost to my people now, but from what I understand, the spell is bound to a spell sword in the forging of it, and will last as long as the sword does. It is an ordinary sword until the spell words are spoken. As the humming increases, so does the sharpness. The humming creates an edge keener than anything known. This sword has been in my family for generations, passed down from mother to daughter."

Torrin looked up again from his examination. "It was made specifically for a woman?"

Rowan nodded. "Indeed. On Myris Dar both men and women are trained to the sword from a very young age. We are also trained in hand-to-hand fighting. The sword comes first, though, because the fundamental forms are the same for both. In my homeland, men use swords not unlike your great broadsword in size, but they are slightly curved and only single edged. A woman's sword must be balanced for her because she often has less size and strength than a man. What women lack in strength and size, they quite often make up for in speed and agility. Girls are taught a different form of fighting that emphasizes redirection of force instead of meeting it blow for blow. Thus woman can fight men in battle without being at a disadvantage."

Torrin nodded in understanding. "Your people must be formidable fighters if everyone can handle a sword as you can."

Rowan shook her head. "Not all Myrians can fight with equal skill, but all are trained to some extent. I am one of a few Myrians chosen to follow the way of the sword to its highest level."

"There are different levels?"

She tucked away her rag. "Yes, there are many different forms taught, and many different masters to teach them. I have trained under twenty masters. Each taught a different form with a different weapon. I stayed with some masters for up to two years at a time, others for a few weeks. Different people have different abilities. To place a sword in the hands of a student who has the potential to become a master archer, and force her or him to develop sword fighting skills instead, does not make for a satisfied warrior — or a great warrior who has reached their full potential.

"It is like Dalemar and his unique ability," continued Rowan. "On Myris Dar, unique abilities are fostered and developed. A student who shows aptitude for spear or bow is encouraged to follow that training as far as they are willing. That is not to say such a student would be trained only in the spear or bow to the exclusion of all else, but that weapon is certainly what the student would focus upon."

"You are versed in more than the sword?" Torrin glanced at the dagger still in her hand.

"Certainly; I have trained in most weapons, and many weaponless forms as well. I can use almost any weapon on hand if I need to." She eyed the long pommel of his heavy broadsword. "Providing, that is, that I can lift it," she amended with a grin.

Torrin rubbed his chin. "But the sword is your first choice?"

"Yes, sword and dagger are what I like the best."

"Hmm, I saw how you used your sword and dagger today. Your technique has similarities to the way Arynilas uses his two blades."

She nodded. Having noted the Tynithian's fighting style. "I have many questions for him and hope for the opportunity to ask."

As Torrin began to slide her sword back into its sheath, he stopped and studied it again. He traced a thick finger down the incised script on the blade. "This writing – what does it mean?"

Rowan was impressed. Most people, even Myrians, mistook the flowing script for pure design. "It is an ancient form of Myrian, a text no longer used today. It scribes the name of Mor Lanyar. My mother's name, my name."

Torrin looked up at her in surprise. "You do not take your father's name?"

Rowan swallowed back a surge of familiar grief at the mention of her father. She shook her head. "Girls take their mother's name and boys their father's."

"And is your dagger also magical?"

Rowan reversed her grip on it and handed it to him hilt first. "No, it only looks the same. It was commissioned by my mother as a gift for me when my training was complete. But although my formal training is finished, I will never stop being a student. I look forward to learning more here in Eryos."

"How old are you, Rowan?" His question caught her off guard. She turned and regarded him silently for a moment.

"I am six and twenty. Why do you ask?"

Torrin's eyes widened. "You are older than Nathel. The same age as —" Rowan waited but he did not finish. He handed the dagger back to her and turned back to the fire, his face unreadable.

She assumed the conversation had been concluded. Torrin seemed suddenly withdrawn, absorbed in his own thoughts.

"Your Raken friend," he said suddenly. "What makes you so sure you can trust him?"

"What makes you so sure you can trust Borlin, or Arynilas?" Rowan replied. "I have known Hathunor for a while now. There is no deceit in him."

"Why does he keep leaving?" asked Torrin. "It is odd."

"To be honest, he is staying out of sight so that you and your friends are not disturbed by his presence. He is probably somewhere close by keeping an eye on me."

Torrin looked at her incredulously, and then glanced around at the surrounding trees. "He is very protective of you, isn't he?"

Almost as though he had been listening to their conversation, Hathunor appeared out of the surrounding dark. He sank to his haunches on her other side. "Hathunor no leave Rowan now," he rumbled.

Torrin eyed him and then looked intently at Rowan. Hathunor was far more intelligent than his appearance suggested and his simple speech only lent to the false impression that he was slow-witted — something Torrin was grasping.

The rest of the companions looked up from what they were doing to watch Hathunor as he settled himself comfortably. He returned their gazes steadily.

Dalemar closed his book with a snap and rose to cross to the other side of the fire where he sat down next to Hathunor. He looked up at him. "Tell us about yourself, Hathunor. How long have you been in Eryos?"

The huge Raken cocked his head slightly. "Hathunor is here thirty-three moons."

Dalemar's eyebrows rose. "You have a remarkable grasp of our language for such a short time."

"Rowan teach Hathunor," rumbled the Raken.

Rowan chuckled. "What he fails to say is that I was hopeless at learning his language, so he has learned mine instead."

"You certainly gave us all a start the other night," said Torrin. "We took you for an enemy."

Hathunor flashed Torrin a grimace. "Hathunor guard Rowan. Worried."

"I had asked him to keep out of sight until I could explain his presence to you all," said Rowan, "but I never got the chance, so he stayed as close as he could."

Dalemar looked back up at the giant Raken. "He might have succeeded in remaining undetected were it not for Arynilas and his keen sight."

"Rowan said you can detect your Raken kin," said Torrin. "How is that possible?"

The rest of the companions gathered closer to hear the conversation.

Hathunor reached up and tapped the side of his head. "Hear them."

"How close can they get before you hear them?" Torrin asked.

Hathunor's ridged brows drew together and a deep grunt escaped his throat. "Soon enough to run. Hathunor hear better than little brothers."

"Will they keep coming after Rowan?" asked Nathel.

Hathunor growled. "Little brothers not follow hearts," he shook his head sadly. "Hathunor think Little brothers keep coming."

"So whatever hunts the Messenger will not stop," said Arynilas quietly.

Rowan turned to look at the Tynithian; the title surprised her. "I have been tracked for far too long for whatever or whoever controls the Raken to stop now. I do not believe this morning's fight was the end of it. I fear we have only earned a respite."

"Then the question we must ask is how long it will take them to find you again," said Torrin grimly.

A cool wind blew through their campsite, causing the flames of the fire to gutter. A log collapsed in a swirl of sparks.

Rowan shivered. Suddenly, she felt very tired. Weeks of pushing herself to the limit had brought her no closer to her goal. She missed Lesiana and Dell, and dreaded having to tell Aunt Dea and Uncle Therious of her cousin's death. Dell had been their only son.

Nathel was looking closely at her. "You need to rest, Rowan, it will be a while before you are fully recovered. You must not overtax yourself."

Rowan sighed and nodded as she put away her dagger. "Wake me when it is my turn to stand watch."

Torrin shook his head. "You will not stand watch until your shoulder is fully healed." Rowan began to protest, but one look at Torrin's face in the firelight told her she would not get far. "If it is to heal quickly, you will need all the rest you can get," he finished.

Rowan frowned. She sincerely hoped her shoulder would heal swiftly because she wouldn't stand for being told what to do for much longer. She pulled her blanket over herself. “As you say. Good night then.”

“Good night Rowan,” came the quiet replies of her new companions.

Hathunor was already curling his bulk up for sleep and Nathel, Borlin and Dalemar were pulling out their sleeping roles. The last thing she saw before closing her eyes was Torrin’s broad back as he strode out into the darkness to stand guard.

Lok Myrr and the Master

Sol hurried through the cold stone corridor, trying to calm his growing fear. The lantern shook in his hand, its feeble light swallowed by the dark spaces between the guttering wall sconces. At the end of the corridor, a great iron-clad door loomed out of the shadows with two huge Raken standing guard. Their frightening red eyes froze Sol's feet. He tried to speak, but only a squeak emerged. Sol cleared his throat and began again. "Master Miroth wishes to see me." His voice sounded small in his own ears.

The guards moved to the sides of the door and shifted their attention beyond him. Sol let out his breath, relieved to no longer be the focus of their intense red gaze. He proceeded to the huge door and pushed. It swung smoothly and silently on its great hinges.

The room beyond was in stark contrast to the bare corridor outside. The marble floors were covered in layers of rich red carpets. Intricate tapestries hung on the walls, covering the crude stones, and comfortable chairs and small tables were arranged around a crackling fire. But instead of soothing Sol's fear, the warm atmosphere only served to heighten it.

He made for another ornately carved door on the far side of the room. He knocked quietly and the door swung inward of its own accord. Sol shuttered in the cloying warmth. This room was just as lushly appointed, but made for work, not pleasure. It was lit only by the fire in the hearth and a single candle burning on a huge wooden table. It was afternoon, but the room's only window was shuttered and sealed against the light and the cool mountain air. The surface of the table was covered with all manner of things, many of which Sol couldn't identify. Scrolls and books were everywhere, even stacked on the floor around the ornately carved lions' feet of the table legs.

Sol's attention wasn't on the table. His eyes were riveted to the shadows behind it, where a figure sat in a huge throne-like chair. Sol bowed his head deferentially and awaited his master's attention.

"Have they found the Myrian?" The voice from the shadows was dry and raspy. Master Miroth had been angry for two days now, ever since Sol had found him on the floor of his study unconscious and with blood seeping from his nose and ears. Sol had been panicked, alternately hoping and fearing that the Master would never wake up.

"I, I think…." Pain lanced through Sol's head. He dropped to his knees, trying desperately to draw breath. All thought vanished and he forgot himself. Only pain existed. It drilled into his ears, drove spikes deep into his skull. His eyes burned and he feared his head might burst. Splinters of pain shot from the top of his head, down his back, traveling through his limbs to curl his fingers and toes in spasms of agony. He barely registered a thin wail, his own, as the world blackened toward oblivion.

The pain left as suddenly as it had come, leaving Sol shaking, face down on the floor, retching out the meagre contents of his stomach. Throat burning, he wiped quickly at his face and scrambled unsteadily to his feet.

"You are not here to think, child. You are here to carry out my orders." The Master had not raised his voice but the sound reverberated around the room, rustling through every corner, around the stacks of books and scrolls. "If you cannot do these simple tasks for me, I will find someone who can."

Sol had no trouble understanding what that meant, yet it seemed unlikely there was anyone in the fortress who could replace him. He had been the only possible replacement for old Darion: it was logical to replace the assistant with the assistant's servant boy. Old Darion had been in his nineties, older than any one Sol had ever known, excepting of course the Master. Darion had been the Master's assistant for most of his life and had told Sol stories of traveling to the ends of the known world with Master Miroth, even beyond the great Timor Mountains – though Sol suspected that that wasn't even possible.

Sol had only been at Lok Myrr for four years and he was still cleaning Darion's workroom and turning down the old man's sheets to put the warming stone under the blankets when Darion died. Sol felt grievously out of his depth; he often imagined himself as a tiny fly caught in the sticky strands of Master Miroth's great web. If he struggled too much, he would attract attention from the spider and get eaten.

Now the Master expected Sol to perform the same tasks that Darion had. Unfortunately, the Master was less than pleased with Sol's abilities. Sol felt very unfairly judged, but speaking out against his mistreatment was inviting the worst punishment.

"I ask you again, boy, has the Myrian been located yet?"

Sol wrenched his wandering thoughts back to the soft, frightening voice. "Forgive me Master, but she has not been found again. The new Raken you sent are still traveling to where she escaped." Sol rubbed his sweating palms against his frayed pants, waiting for the pain to start once more.

Initially Sol was very pleased to be able to relay the messages brought in by the Raken runners, but he increasingly feared his master's reaction to the news. Oh, the Master was perfectly capable of finding things out for himself, Sol was almost certain. But Sol was also the only one in the fortress who knew how taxing it was for the Master to use his special powers to get that information. Sol had no idea how the Master's magic worked but he saw first hand how weak the Master was afterwards.

The rasping voice shuddered with suppressed anger. "A full trieton lost. It will take time to get another one that close again." Sol blinked in confusion, unsure if the Master was speaking to him. He began to tremble as the silence stretched. Then the Master continued softly from the darkness behind the table. "She was extremely lucky. If it were not for her tame beast, I wouldn't be wasting this precious time. I would very much like to know what that beast is doing here." The Master looked up suddenly, and Sol backed up a step before he could still his feet.

Sol still didn't know what had caused the Master to become so ill two days ago, but he was willing to bet old Darrion's shoes that it had something to do with this Myrian. Sol was curious about the Myrian. If the master was that interested in her then she had to be very important.

The Master leaned forward into the light and Sol struggled not to recoil at the sight of the grizzled, bald head. Bags of loose flesh hung from the skeletal bones of the Master's face. But it was the eyes that frightened him the most. They bore into him mercilessly and Sol felt as though they were sifting through the very essence of his soul.

"What news is there of the King and his army? Are my Raken in place yet?"

Sol swallowed and shifted from foot to foot. "King Cerebus and his allies are fleeing to Pellaris. The Raken will be in position soon Master."

"Good," came a dry chuckle from the withered throat. Miroth's intense gaze focused on Sol once more, and he cowered back. "Is there anything else?"

"No Master, nothing," squeaked Sol.

"Then get out of my sight. I need to think." The words were stated quietly, but they cracked like a whip inside Sol's head.

Sol skittered backward, head bent, trying in vain to control his trembling limbs. He all but ran through the outer sitting room to the cold corridor beyond.

Bathtubs and Preconceptions

As the days passed, the company traveled north through the rugged woodlands of the Wilds. The trees were clad in bright colors and they had to weave their way carefully to avoid any patches of the plant Rowan knew as Erys's Bane.

Torrin shaded his eyes from the bright sun as they moved through a small clearing. Nathel was ahead of him, riding next to Rowan. They were deep in discussion, Nathel asking her questions about Erys's Bane.

"Are there any remedies for its poison?"

Rowan shook her head. "I am sorry. I know little of plant lore. The only remedy I've heard of is a root which, when crushed and applied to the affected areas, soothe the blisters somewhat."

Nathel nodded. "What does it look like?"

Torrin scanned the trees ahead, only half listening. Hathunor had disappeared a while ago and not been back.

"It sounds like tabica root," said Nathel after Rowan's description. "We know it well; it was my first thought for treatment." Nathel shook his head. "I've found no way to cure the madness."

Movement to the right caught Torrin's attention – a sandy coloured rabbit darted from cover, chased by a small fox. The quarry escaped and the fox stopped to watch them before trotting back into the trees. The bird song was muted; many had flown further south for the winter. Arynilas had brought down a few of the tiny deer they flushed out of hiding with his bow. The fresh meat allowed them to save their dry provisions for the days ahead. They would soon reach the vast plains of Klyssen. The journey across would be long. In the endless sea of grass, game would have ample time to distance itself from hunters.

Torrin rubbed the back of his neck and looked up at the cloudless sky. It would take about a month to reach Pellaris. The plains of Klyssen would take almost two weeks to cross with the open grassland offering little cover. Torrin frowned and resumed his scan of the trees. He was very disturbed by the possibility of Raken tracking them across the open plains of Klyssen. Speed would be their only defence.

The twisting marshland beyond that marked the boarder between Klyssen and Pellar would offer more cover, but they would be much slowed. The marshes, a distance of only ten leagues in width, would take them almost a week to traverse. Once they were free of the Boglands, travel would become swift again. The rolling parkland of Pellar, which surrounded the city of Pellaris itself, would offer good cover with enough open land for movement.

In Klyssen there were villages and walled towns where they could stay along the way to replenish supplies. He glanced ahead to where Rowan rode on her big grey, her long braid hanging down her back. It was taking some getting use to having a woman among them. He had noticed the others also having trouble adjusting. They would automatically do things for her, assuming that she would need help or didn't know. If she began to light the fire for the camp, Nathel would take the flint from her hands, telling her to rest; Borlin would hasten to lift her saddle before she could get her hands on it. And Torrin caught himself once taking the leather punch from her hand to mend her armour for her, assuming that she didn't know how. She had thanked him for his offer but firmly taken the tool back and resumed her work, obviously more than capable. Torrin told himself it was because she was still wounded but he had to admit that perhaps it was just an excuse to justify previously unchallenged customs.

The companions were torn. She was obviously a skilled warrior and they had all seen what she could do with a sword but she was also a woman and women needed protecting, didn't they? They needed men to do certain things for them. Arynilas and Dalemar watched the antics with growing amusement.

Torrin exhaled and shook his head. Rowan seemed remarkably unruffled by it all. He had a feeling she was getting frustrated with them but she hadn't uttered a sharp word.

He cast a quick glance over the rest of his company. The five companions had been in the Wilds for quite a while; they were all in need of a real bed and a good scrubbing.

A faint smile pulled at his mouth. He could still hear Emma scolding him for not procuring baths for her and the girls during a stop at the Balor Inn. Even the name of the innkeeper was burned into his memory. Mr. Trotle — a remarkably tall, thin man who defied the stereotype of an innkeeper. The smile faded abruptly from Torrin's face. It was the last times he had seen his wife and daughters alive.

An ache rose in his chest. It had been so long since that terrible day, but the pain of the memory was still strong and fresh. He expected it would always be that way – had given up hope of ever moving beyond it.

Nathel's knee nudged Torrin's as he drew his mount closer. "Was that a smile I just saw, Tor? I though you had forgotten your face could make one of those. What were you thinking about?"

Torrin awoke from his musing and looked across at his brother. "Bathtubs."

Nathel looked at him quizzically then scratched the few day's growth of beard on his face. He shrugged and changed the subject. "I am looking forward to going back to Pellar, even though the circumstances of our return are dire. Still it will be good to walk the land of our people again. It has been a long time since we last saw it."

Torrin frowned and shook his head. "There is nothing left for me in Pellar, Nathel. I answer the summons out of duty and loyalty only, nothing more."

"Perhaps it is time to look for something more, Tor."

Torrin glanced at his brother in surprise, but Nathel was busy looking for something to eat in his saddlebags. Torrin sighed and looked ahead, his eyes catching on a long golden braid shining in the late afternoon sun.

The Black Fox

Rowan sat on a fallen tree trunk in the dusk light, resting after the long ride. The small clearing they had chosen for the night had stunned them with a display of amazing color — yellow fire had blazed around them as the sun had touched the turning leaves of the treetops before sinking beyond the horizon.

Pulling her dagger from its sheath, she rooted through her saddlebags for a cleaning rag and oil. Borlin, as usual, was making the evening meal. Dalemar was seated on the ground across from her, pipe clenched between his teeth and his nose in a book. Arynilas sat beside him fashioning arrows. Torrin lay stretched out and propped on one elbow, a cup of tea in his hand and his eyes fastened on the fire.

Nathel strode across to Rowan from the tethered horses, his healing satchel in hand. He stood before her unlacing the leather ties. "I need to have a look at that shoulder."

"It is fine, Nathel. I do not need you to look at it. It heals well and there is only a little soreness and stiffness. You have done a fine job with it, I thank you." Rowan soaked some oil through the cloth and began to rub her blade.

Nathel frowned down at her and began to argue, but Borlin cut him off. "Oh, ahes'n three 'orned goat's blood, Nathel! Leave the lass alone! Here ye are, Luv, a nice 'ot cuppa tea." Borlin moved toward her, blowing on the contents of the cup in his hands.

Nathel's frown deepened and he turned on the Stoneman, looking down at him. "I've a sense that my healing is a tad more important than your tea, Borlin!"

Borlin growled, his ruddy face flushing deeper in anger.

Rowan couldn't help herself. She snorted loudly in amusement. The two turned to look at her in surprise, and suddenly irritation got the better of her. She drove her dagger into the ground and threw her cleaning rag down in disgust. Standing, she faced them. "It's comforting to know that you both care, but enough is enough!"

Borlin stared in stunned silence, but Nathel opened his mouth. She cut him off before he could speak. "Have you two stopped to listen to yourselves? Sweet Erys! You sound like a pair of mother hens clucking over a chick!"

Rowan heard Torrin's dry chuckle and turned to look at him, her scowl deepening. "You are not much better!"

His eyebrows lifted, but at least he had the decency to stop laughing.

"You three act as though I'm capable of little more than riding a horse!"

She looked back up at Nathel and took a step towards him. He leaned away from her, a wary look on his face. "I am perfectly able to light a fire; in fact, I've had a lot of practice at it, and I can also carry a bucket!" She turned to confront Borlin. "I'm also very good at saddling my own horse. I'm taller than you are for Erys's sake!" Then she scowled at Torrin, "And you! I am hardly a useless maiden incapable of lifting my own saddlebags, mending my armour or making decisions."

Rowan took a deep breath. She held her hands out toward them, making them into fists. "If these hands are capable of wielding a sword in battle, do you really believe that they wouldn't also be capable of helping with camp chores?" She dropped her hands to her side and looked them in the eyes. "I know women have a different role here but I'm not from this land. I do not always need or want your help. I ask you to respect that."

Finished, she looked around at the faces of her companions. Nathel was frowning down at the satchel in his hands. Borlin was looking sheepishly at the ground, his toe tracing a line in the dirt. Dalemar sat watching her, his pipe halfway to his mouth, book forgotten. Torrin watched her too, an off-kilter cup still in hand. Only Arynilas seemed uninterested in what had just been said. His fingers and attention were still on his arrows but a slight smile had slipped onto his face.

The frustration that had been welling up over the last few days was suddenly spent, and Rowan struggled not to laugh at their ridiculous expressions. She sighed, she couldn't expect them to change a lifetime of habit in little more than a week, but it was about time they began to try. She turned away and leaned down to retrieve her dagger.

She heard Nathel step up behind her. "I still want to look at that shoulder."

Rowan shook her head in submission. If there was one thing the brothers had in common besides their size, it was stubbornness. She turned to look up at him. "Very well, but it is no longer necessary."

"We'll see." With a boyish smirk he began to unwrap his satchel.

Rowan caught sight of Borlin, still standing with her tea in hand. "Borlin, how about that cup of tea? You'll not keep it hot by staring at it."

The Stoneman chuckled, stepping forward.

"Thank you, my friend," she said.

Borlin winked, handing her the cup.

Once Nathel had seen to her shoulder, Rowan settled down against the log to enjoy her tea. The companions were quiet tonight – her outburst most likely had something to do with their mood. Hathunor lay a few feet from her, his bulk curled up and his red eyes closed. The image of a content cat sprang to mind and Rowan smiled at the incongruous impression.

Arynilas had left the camp a short time before and slipped silently into the darkness. It had taken Rowan a while to notice his absence. Her eyes were beginning to close and she tried to summon the energy to pull out her bedroll. As she sat in half sleep, a movement caught her attention. Forcing her eyes to open wider, she turned to see a large black fox trotting into the camp. Rowan looked around at her companions. Torrin was the only one still awake.

The fox trotted across to Rowan and sat on its haunches before her, its pink tongue lolling and its large ears pricked forward. Rowan kept still to avoid frightening the visitor away. The black fox looked her directly in the eyes, then jumped and spun in the air, bushy tail wagging. It raced out of the camp, rolling its head at Torrin on its way past. As its black fur blended into the surrounding shadow, Rowan was left wondering if she had actually experienced the strange encounter.

She looked over at Torrin. He was watching her expectantly.

Rowan turned again to where the fox had vanished, and noticed Arynilas's bow and long knives leaning against the stone he had occupied earlier. She drew in a sudden breath and looked at Torrin with wide eyes. "Arynilas –"

Torrin nodded. "You are fortunate. He does not reveal his other self lightly."

Rowan peered into the darkness around the camp. Now that she knew, she found it hard to believe that she had not recognized him. The fox was as much Arynilas as the form she normally saw. She turned back to Torrin, questions crowding her mind. She was no longer tired.

"Does he change often?" she asked.

Torrin shook his head and looked up at the full moon of Bashelar overhead. "The moons call to him. The Twilight People worship the moons for Erys. They honour her sisters with their animal form to remind Raelys and Bashelar that Erys is not alone here in Eryos."

The solemn response quelled her remaining questions. Rowan looked up at the red moon in its fullness. Its light was bright and clear against the starlight. Raelys was just a glimmer of light low in the sky, hidden by the treetops.

A strange glow began to wink in the trees. Rowan frowned and looked harder. "Torrin, what is that?"

Torrin followed her out stretched hand. "That is as much responsible for keeping people out of the Wilds as Erys's Bane. There are beetles that live in the canopy, which once a month glow in response to the full moons. They are found in Dan Tynell as well. Arynilas told me that a few are collected each full moon and placed in special glass spheres to celebrate and honour Erys's sisters."

Rowan watched in wonder as more and more lights began to glow in the trees. Her thoughts turned to a black fox moving through the dark shadows of the forest around them.

The Command Tent

King Cerebus slumped into the camp chair and tossed his gloves on the table before him. They landed on the corner of a large map of Pellar, which lay unfurled and weighted down at the corners by various objects: stones, books, a goblet. He wiped his hand across his face wearily and scanned the grim faces of the men seated around the table. Cerebus had slept little in the last three days and he was having trouble thinking clearly.

General Preven reported the details of the strategic withdrawal Cerebus had ordered last night. Yesterday had seen the worst fighting yet. They had lost almost a third of the army to the Raken. Many more would not make it past sunset today. Morale was low and it was becoming more and more difficult to lift the spirits of the men.

Cerebus found it hard to fathom how the prosperous and powerful kingdom of Pellar could be in such dire straights. They had been fighting desperately for weeks against the Raken invasion, and they had been defeated in nine out of the twelve encounters. Cerebus had initially been successful at riding out and eliminating the small groups of the beasts attacking towns and farmsteads. Then the scouting parties had come fleeing back to the outposts with reports of an overwhelming force heading northwest towards the capital city of Pellaris. The coalition forces Cerebus had managed to gather to meet the invasion had been gradually and unrelentingly pushed back towards the capital. Almost three thousand men had answered his summons from the surrounding realms of Tabor and Klyssen. Even mercenaries from as far away as Lor Danith had recently arrived but it had not been enough. The Raken were too strong and too many and they fought with a frightening ferocity.

"The Klyssen cavalry has had the most success against the Raken so far. They can keep the casualties down during our retreat," said Kreagan. "The Raken do not seem inclined to rest on their victory but are pressing their advantage." The horse marshal of the Klyssen Cavalry sat across from Cerebus, his horsehair-plumed helmet and worn leather gauntlets on the table before him.

He was a stern man but very good at what he did. Cerebus had included his own cavalry units under Kreagan's command.

The Klyssen were superb horsemen. They fought from horseback like most soldiers fought from the ground; their well-bred horses trained to maneuver to complex leg commands so the cavalry had their hands free to use their long swords and shields to devastating effect.

Tight formation and precision allowed the cavalry units to cut like a knife into enemy ranks, disrupting their dense lines and creating chaos. The fifteen hundred mounted warriors that Kreagan had brought with him from Klyssen had kept the coalition army from being completely overwhelmed by the Raken.

General Preven, to Kreagan's left, nodded his head in agreement. "It will take time to move so many back to a defensive position within the city; not to mention the supplies. We must protect the supplies or there will not be enough provisions for a drawn out siege. The wells within the city will supply fresh water indefinitely but food will be scarce."

Cerebus sighed. "So it comes down to a siege." Not since Cerebus's grandfather Lendar sat the throne had the city of Pellaris been besieged. Then it had been an army of Taborians, consisting more of foreign mercenaries than men from Tabor, led by Roth the Mighty — the self-styled ruler of what was then lower Tabor — into the rash and foolish attempt to take Pellar's capital city. A city with a reputation for having never been sacked. It had been taken under previous names of course, but history was always written by the victors. It was considered bad luck to keep the old name of a vanquished city. As Pellaris, a city built on the ruins of others, it had never had its walls breached.

Walls, which to their credit, were almost twenty paces deep, surrounded by a moat to the south and guarded in the north by the highest cliffs on the northern coastline. The city was indeed formidable, but Cerebus had never been so arrogant as to believe that it could never fall.

Cerebus's father had been a boy, much the same age as Cerebus's young heir, Daelyn, when Roth the Mighty assaulted Pellaris. The stories about his father and grandfather fighting together along the walls to repel the attack had become legend. They had succeeded. Pellar had remained unvanquished and his father, Doren, son of Lendar, had begun that day to write his own story within the pages of Pellar's history.

Cerebus was raised as his father had been raised, and his grandfather before him. He had learned war and statecraft well, but he always believed strength and pride could be as much a liability for a king as an asset. Cerebus envisioned a different future than his father and grandfather, one where war and the protection of sovereign lands weren't the only endeavours for a king. He believed in a wider world where neighbouring kingdoms could be trusted to hold to oaths and treaties made. Where people under a stable reign could flourish and achieve greatness.

Cerebus wasn't foolish enough to think that such a world could be accomplished without bloodshed. There would always be bullies — nations or men who would take advantage of weakness — but he hoped that one day Eryos could become the peaceful realm of his dreams.

That was part of the reason he had sent Daelyn to Tabor; it was important for a future king to know his neighbours. This war, this invasion, was like no other seen in Pellar. He knew in his heart that darker days lay ahead. His nephew and heir was safe in Tabor, a blessing Cerebus had clung to in the frustration and heartache of the past few days.

Frowning, Cerebus reined his thoughts in and focused on the matter at hand.

"The city is well fortified. It will hold, my lord," said Preven. The general was an unshakable optimist. His belief in the eventual victory of the coalition had been only slightly eroded over the past weeks.

Chancellor Galen, who had been consulting a large leather book in his lap, cleared his throat. "The stores of Pellaris are abundant, my lord. The harvest was successfully brought into the city and many of the refugees have had time to gather and bring their own provisions. There will be enough for a month, maybe a little more." Galen had been chancellor when Cerebus's father sat the throne. His neatly trimmed white beard and hair lent him the air of a distinguished grandfather, but today his long years weighed heavily upon him. Cerebus made a mental note to send Galen ahead to the city where he could rest.

The walls of the small tent billowed in a gust of wind, and the light from the morning sky peeped through the door as the tent flaps blew inward. Cerebus rose and poured himself a cup of strong Drenic from a steaming jug left at a side table. It was one of the only luxuries he afforded himself during this war. There was now a limited supply of the Taborian leaves and it would not be replenished any time soon. He took a sip and savoured the spiced taste.

The tent flaps moved again as a young messenger entered and bowed to Cerebus. The young man looked exhausted, and Cerebus bade him take a seat and handed him his own steaming cup.

The young messenger took the cup gratefully and Cerebus waited for him to drink. “The Raken horde advances on the outpost positions my lord. They are moving fast. Field Marshall Tern sent me to tell you he has the defensive line set and ready to engage the foe.”

Cerebus looked to Horse Marshall Kreagan, who stood briskly and donned his helmet and gloves. “The cavalry will give the infantry time to disengage and retreat.”

“Good. Don’t engage them full on; hit and run tactics,” said Cerebus.

Kreagan nodded.

Cerebus turned to General Preven. “Sound the retreat, General. I’ll not lose any more men to these monsters today.”

The general saluted and the two officers left the tent. Cerebus turned to the young messenger. “Have my horse readied, lad. I will ride with the cavalry today.”

“Yes, my lord.” The young man took a last swig from his cup and quickly followed the others from the tent.

Cerebus made to leave as well but Galen stopped him. “Are you sure it is wise to put yourself in harm’s way, my king? They will do well enough without you.”

Cerebus looked into the eyes of his chancellor. “Not today, Galen. Today the troops will see their king defending them.”

Galen sighed in resignation, nodding his head and moving aside. “Erys go with you, my Lord.”

Cerebus walked out of the tent to his waiting horse.

Of Raken

Six days had passed since the companions had met Rowan and they had neither seen nor heard Raken since the bloody battle at the cleft. Torrin reined in his young black horse to a walk. The game trail they followed was too narrow and twisting for much more. The horse shook his long dark mane and snorted in frustration.

The horse was fairly new to Torrin and he still hadn't thought of a name for him. He had settled on simply calling him Black. His previous horse had been killed by highway bandits; arrow shot from under him. He had been furious about the loss and had made certain personally that the thieves never attacked anyone else. Flyer had been a great horse and was extremely well trained. Torrin had raised him from a spindly foal into a proud battle mount. He'd even made some coin on stud fee over the years from the impressive dun stallion.

Torrin had hopes that this young horse could be as great but it would take time for them to get to know and trust one another. He reached out and laid his palm against Black's neck. The glossy hide was smooth and warm under his hand. Black twitched an ear back toward Torrin and his prancing steps lulled to a slower walk.

The path ahead opened into a small clearing and Torrin could now see more than just Nathel's back directly in front of him. Hathunor, who had been stalking at the point of the group ahead of Arynilas, stopped suddenly and scanned the trees ahead. The others pulled their mounts to a halt and Torrin reined Black in. The young horse laid his ears flat and glared back at Borlin's mare, who had shoved her nose forward to nip at his rump. Torrin doubted Black would kick, but heeled the stallion over to make certain he couldn't.

Hathunor stepped out to the side of the trail and lifted his muzzle to the air, his huge head cocked to the side. He turned suddenly back toward the companions and Torrin could see the red glint of his eyes. The Raken paced smoothly to Rowan and rumbled something, then turned and loped off into the trees, his black body disappearing instantly.

Rowan beckoned to Torrin. The late afternoon sun glinted on her hair and sword pommel as she twisted in the saddle to scan the path ahead.

Torrin touched his heels to Black and the horse surged forward.

"Raken. Hathunor has gone to see how many," She said as he drew close.

"How close are they?" Torrin asked, a prickle running down his spine.

"I'm not sure; Hathunor knows only that they are almost close enough to hear us."

Torrin looked at her sharply. "How much can they hear?"

"We should be safe providing we keep our voices low and the horses are quiet. Hathunor has heard them before they will hear us."

Borlin growled and looked quickly around, pulling his short sword from its scabbard.

Rowan made a calming gesture with her hand. "Raken hearing is far superior to ours. They will be distant yet."

They waited in silence for a short while until Hathunor emerged from the surrounding trees. He walked to Rowan and Torrin and gestured back the way he had come. "Half trieton come fast. We go around." Hathunor pointed to the right. The ground was rocky and the trees crowded together but it was better than walking straight into a large group of Raken. Hathunor looked from Rowan to Torrin and back, his expression worried.

It had taken Torrin a few days to identify his surprising range of expressions. "Lead the way, Hathunor."

The Raken glanced at Rowan again and turned away, stalking towards the dense trees.

They moved as quickly as they dared through the forest while keeping a sharp watch for Erys's Bane in the thick undergrowth.

Torrin looked over at Rowan, who was squeezing her big horse between his own mount and a tree, pulling her foot up out of the way of the trunk. "How is it that Hathunor is able to sense other Raken but they don't seem to notice him?"

Rowan shrugged, eyes scanning the vegetation in front of her horse's path. "From what I understand Hathunor is a different kind of Raken. Perhaps his senses are superior to the others. He could be different from them in many ways."

Torrin hoped so. They would be hard pressed to defend themselves from half a Trieton in this wooded terrain.

They had threaded their way through the trees for perhaps twenty minutes when Hathunor turned north again. They kept their pace quick and were as silent as possible.

Finally, Hathunor slowed and turned to look at Rowan. He nodded, then trotted ahead and disappeared into the trees again, scouting ahead.

Torrin wondered again at the Raken's apparent immunity to the Erys's Bane vine. He had seen Hathunor walk straight through the plant and suffer no ill effects. The rest of them had to be careful not to touch the huge Raken, for fear the poison might transfer to them. Torrin had noticed that whenever they crossed a stream, Hathunor would carefully wash himself down to avoid just such an inadvertent contamination.

They traveled north for the remainder of the day, putting as much distance between themselves and the Raken as possible. The sun was setting when they came to a small clearing with a shallow pond. They set up their camp at the edge of the water and decided not to light a fire in case it was seen from a distance. Hathunor emerged from the trees to join them as they began to share a cold dinner.

Borlin, who was seated next to Rowan, leaned over to her. "Your friend 'as a surprising ability to know exactly when dinner is be'n served. If I didn' know better, I'd be say'n he 'ad Stoneman blood."

Nathel grinned and Rowan's laughter rang softly. "You would want to know where the food was too, if you were that big," she said.

"Aye, that's the goddess's plain truth," Borlin chuckled.

Hathunor sat on the other side of Rowan and looked curiously at the Stoneman, before beginning to devour his meal.

Torrin leaned back against his saddle with his food in hand across from the trio. He readjusted his position to avoid a sharp stone that bit into his hip. Nathel, Dalemar and Arynilas settled beside him.

"It is odd though," said Dalemar, his bite of flat bread stopping short of his mouth. "He doesn't seem to eat nearly enough for his great size. Why over the last few days, I've seen him eat barely as much as Torrin or Nathel and he must have three times their bulk, if not more."

The others looked curiously at their immense companion as he popped the remainder of his meal through his large teeth. He noticed their scrutiny and looked back with puzzlement.

Rowan shrugged. "I had assumed he was catching things to eat when he was scouting." She looked up at him. "Hathunor, do you eat more than this?" she gestured to the food still in her hand.

The big Raken tilted his head to the side, then shook it.

"You don't eat any other food?" asked Dalemar in shock.

Again the huge head shook and then Hathunor pointed upwards. The companions glanced up following his finger. "If sun Hathunor no need food."

They looked at one another, frowning in perplexed confusion.

Then Dalemar gasped.

Rowan watched his friendly expression change from puzzlement into amazement as his mobile eyebrows rose as high as they would go, crinkling his smooth forehead. His bread and cheese was still held up in one hand, completely forgotten. "My goodness! You use the light!"

Hathunor nodded, a sharp-toothed smile on his face.

"What do you mean? Use the light?" Nathel glanced from Dalemar to Hathunor and back.

Dalemar turned excitedly from the Raken. "There is energy in the sun's light! We feel it as heat. Hathunor must somehow be able to harness and use that energy for sustenance."

"He eats sunlight?" Nathel shook his head in disbelief.

"In a sense you could say that, but I doubt it is the same process. Perhaps that is the reason that Hathunor's skin is so black — to absorb more heat — and he is somehow able to use that heat like food."

"Well if he can use light to sustain himself, why does he need to eat food?" asked Nathel.

"The sun does not always shine," said Arynilas.

"Does it 'ave t' be sunlight? What 'bout firelight?" inquired Borlin.

Hathunor shook his head. "Only sun."

Dalemar turned back to the big Raken. “Hathunor, if you had to, how long could you last without the sun before you would need to eat food?”

Hathunor translated the question carefully. “Two days before hungry. Can go long time no food if sun, but Hathunor like food,” he said grinning.

“How fascinating,” exclaimed Dalemar.

Torrin frown in concern. He was no longer listening to the conversation. His mind was racing ahead, to Pellar and an invading army that didn’t need to eat; that didn’t need traditional supply lines; that could set a siege and simply wait out the defenders as they slowly starved to death. The rules of engagement would be completely different. How do you fight an enemy that could survive without food? The implications ran through his mind in cold, frightening clarity. The Raken made for a perfect invading army.

Torrin looked at the huge Raken. “Hathunor, why are you so much bigger than the Raken we fought?” Hathunor stood a good head and shoulders taller than his kin, and he towered over Torrin. An image of having to fight a Raken army of Hathunor’s size flashed through his mind with alarming intensity.

The big Raken pointed to his chest and rumbled, “Saa.” He then gestured back toward where they had circled the half trieton earlier and said, “Drae.” Hathunor pointed to Torrin. Repeating, “Saa.” And then pointed to Arynilas and said, “Drae.”

Torrin nodded his understanding. “You are a different race.”

Hathunor smiled, his frightening expression improving only slightly.

“You do not call yourselves Raken?” Torrin asked.

Rowan shook her head. “His word for his people is unpronounceable to us. Raken kind of suits them though.” She looked up at Hathunor.

He made a strange clicking sound that blended to a grunt. The sound began deep in his chest and ended in his mouth.

Torrin shook his head. He couldn’t repeat the word if he’d tried a hundred times.

“How many races of Raken are there?” Torrin asked.

Hathunor lifted his massive hand and held up four fingers. As he spoke the names of each, he curled a finger down. "Saa, Drae, Cren, Grol."

"Are all Saa Raken as big as you are, Hathunor?" asked Nathel.

The Raken nodded. "Some bigger. Saa – warriors. Big for protecting little brothers."

"Are ye saying the Raken we've bin fightin', these Drae Raken are no warriors?" asked Borlin incredulously.

Nathel drew in a breath and gave a low whistle. "Erys protect us. I wouldn't want to fight a trieton of Saa Raken. The Draes are bad enough."

Hathunor put his head back suddenly and sent up a staccato rumble from deep in his throat. His red eyes were squeezed shut.

Torrin took in the bewildered expressions of his friends and then noticed that Rowan was smiling – Hathunor was laughing.

Hathunor shook his giant head. "Little brothers work hard. Make for high ladies. Make for brothers."

"Who are the high ladies?" asked Dalemar.

"High ladies, mothers to all," rumbled Hathunor.

Dalemar stroked a finger across his blond eyebrow. "Are you saying that Raken have more than one mother?" he asked.

Hathunor squinted as he thought about the question; then he brightened and spread out the clawed fingers of one hand. "Mother not know. All brothers born together. High ladies mother to all."

Dalemar nodded. "So the Raken are born in clutches, in eggs?" he asked.

Hathunor frowned and rumbled, "What egg?"

Rowan held up her hands in the shape of an egg. "You grow inside and then hatch." She mimicked the two halves of the egg splitting apart.

Hathunor smiled his toothy smile and nodded his head vigorously.

"So are there only a very few females among your people?" Torrin asked.

Hathunor's huge head swivelled to look at Torrin. "When sister born, great happiness. Sister high honour."

Arynilas asked the Raken a question then. "Are there other Saa Raken in Eryos?"

Hathunor shook his head sadly. "Hathunor only Saa Raken in this land."

Torrin glanced between Hathunor and Rowan. "Rowan mentioned that your people come from a distant land. Where is your homeland, Hathunor?"

Hathunor's eyes gleamed dully and his thick eyebrow ridges sagged downward, even the perpetual fierceness of his face dissolved into sorrow and grief. "Homeland far. Hathunor no feel. Too far."

"You can feel your homeland?" asked Dalemar in awe.

The Raken sat up straighter. He brought a great hand to his chest. "Feel here."

Arynilas leaned forward, his sapphire eyes glittering in the fading light. "I can feel Dan Tynell. It is like a pull on my soul. Even blinded, I would be able to find the way home."

"How did ye get te Eryos, then?" asked Borlin.

Hathunor stretched out a great muscular arm and pointed to the west, toward the last failing light of the sun. "Hathunor travel far; battle hard. Lose many Saa brothers before great mountains." His face twisted suddenly in a ferocious snarl and a low-pitched growl emanated from his chest. "Blood debt," he hissed.

The companions looked at the Raken in puzzlement so Rowan elaborated for her big friend. "Hathunor and his other Saa brothers were hunted and killed by people from the west. It seems that there are some who find hunting Raken great sport. Hathunor was the only survivor of his small group and traveled on his own, crossing the Great Timor Mountains to get here. Much like me, he was alone in his quest."

"His quest?" echoed Nathel.

"He crossed the Great Timors?" questioned Torrin at almost the same time.

Rowan looked from one brother to the other. "Hathunor was sent by his people to rescue his kin, to find a way to free them. He traveled over the mountains to get here."

"Hathunor search long time. Found few little brothers. They attacked Hathunor, not listen. No soul in eyes. They fight wrong," rumbled the big Raken, pointing towards Torrin's big broadsword. “Little brothers’ metal teeth bad. They no like fight; they like make.”

Torrin raised his eyebrows; he had a hard time imaging a soulful looking Raken. But then looking at Hathunor, as he recounted his tale, Torrin began to have an idea of how painful it had been for the big Raken to kill his own brothers during the battle with the trieton. He also now understood why Hathunor could wreak such havoc among his kin. They were not warriors, despite their speed and strength. The Drae Raken’s nature was inherently peaceful.

The big Raken shook his head and continued in a voice full of despair. “Hathunor killed many but could not kill all. Their death hurt Hathunor. They capture Hathunor. They wait long time, then come kill Hathunor. Rowan save Hathunor. Rowan good friend.” The huge Raken turned to look down at the woman beside him.

Rowan reached out to touch the Raken but caught herself before covering his hand with her own – she couldn’t risk Erys’s Bane transfer from him. Torrin watched her hand hover over Hathunor’s – tiny by comparison. “It is strange,” she said, “Hathunor seems to be the only one immune to the power that controls the rest of the Raken.”

“How is it you have avoided being controlled like your kin?” Torrin asked.

The big Raken heaved a sigh and shrugged his enormous spike-covered shoulders in bewilderment. “Message sent. Hathunor come. Save little brothers.”

Dalemar stirred, removed his freshly lit pipe from his teeth and blew out a puff of smoke. “You received a message from your kin? How?”

Hathunor lifted a finger and tapped his forehead. “Cren lore-keeper hear message. Dream. Tell Hathunor go. Little brothers trouble. Not safe.”

“Hathunor doesn’t know how or why there are Raken here in Eryos, only that they need help. His people believe that there must have been be a Saa or Cren somewhere in Eryos that could send the message,” Rowan explained.

“But Hathunor said he was the only Saa here,” said Torrin.

Rowan nodded. "There are none now. If there were still Saa Raken, Hathunor said he would be able to speak to them or receive a message."

"You can mind speak?" asked Dalemar.

Hathunor nodded. "Saa and Cren speak long distance."

"Hathunor, have you seen any Cren or Grol Raken in Eryos?" asked Dalemar.

Hathunor nodded, "Grol Raken. Smaller than Draes. Sometimes together with Draes, sometimes alone."

"No Crens?" Arynilas leaned forward, his onyx hair falling around his shoulders.

Hathunor shook his great head.

"What do Cren Raken look like?" asked Torrin.

"Crens big. Bigger than Hathunor."

"Lovely," said Nathel sarcastically. "Well I guess we can thank Erys we haven't seen any of them yet." He took a swig from a waterskin and passed it to Dalemar, who ignored it completely.

The Rith's gaze was fixed upon Hathunor. "You mentioned a Cren lore-keeper, Hathunor, what is that?"

The Saa Raken's red eyes glowed in the dimness. "Crens few. Lore-keepers, makers of good. Crens guide brothers, dream for brothers and sisters."

"What a fascinating society you have. The different types of Raken not only perform different tasks but seem to be suited to those tasks physically as well," Dalemar mused.

Hathunor rumbled with humour. "Rith do what man not," he tuned to look at Arynilas and Nathel beside him. "Archer do what Rith not. Fascinating." The Raken's rumble turned into a grating thunder as he began to laugh harder.

Dalemar looked sheepishly up at the huge creature and a grin began to spread across his face. "I guess when you put it that way it's not so unexpected after all."

The last of the Rith's words were drowned out by Borlin and Nathel's laughter as well.

As the quiet once more returned, the Saa Raken stood and stretched his great bulk and then padded softly to the pond where he washed and drank.

Torrin watched him thoughtfully and Dalemar spoke into the evening's silence. "There must be a reason that Saa and Cren Raken are not among the Raken here in Eryos." The Rith turned to look at Rowan. “And why try to kill him instead of using him? Surely whatever or whoever controls the Draes would have no difficulty with adding one more Raken. Indeed, he would be a valued catch, being so much bigger with superior battle skill.”

Rowan turned from watching Hathunor to look at the Rith. “That is a question I have asked myself as well.”

“Perhaps there is something about the Saa Raken and Cren Raken that prevents them from being controlled by whatever it is that rules the others,” said Arynilas quietly.

The first night crickets began to emit their humming-buzz, alternately close and then far distant. They sat listening to the tones as darkness descended and Torrin could no longer make out the faces of his friends. He sat up and stretched muscles that had stiffened in the evening chill and pulled his sleeping roll from the gear behind him.

As the rest of the companions bedded down less the two that were taking first watch, Torrin thoughts returned to Hathunor’s story. The Saa Raken’s journey from the west across the Great Timor Mountains at least answered his earlier question – the Timors were crossable and if the Raken had found a way through, than perhaps others could as well.

For good or ill it possibly represented a profound change for Eryos, and change was never easy.

The Retreat

Cerebus surveyed the advancing Raken as his charger danced restlessly under him. A brisk, chill wind caught the edge of his cloak, billowing it around him before continuing down the slope over the retreating coalition army. It had been a hard morning and Cerebus had lost one of his horses to a Raken spear.

Thorn, a great red stallion he had truly loved, had crumpled under him without warning with a deadly spear buried deep in his stout-hearted chest. Cerebus had been pitched headlong into a line of Raken. Only the surprise of the fall had kept him alive, given him enough time to disengage from the few Raken that had attacked before his own cavalry unit had surrounded him and he'd climbed up behind another horseman.

Now he looked out on the mixed Klyssen and Pellarian cavalry as it harassed the foe. Wedge shaped units kept up a revolving charge, cutting into the Raken ranks and then wheeling to disengage before they were surrounded. So far the tactic had worked well. They had lost few men and the enemy was never given the chance to gain enough speed to swarm the retreating army. They were still many miles from Pellaris though, and much could go wrong.

Cerebus turned to the officer mounted beside him. "Ready the men for another attack." The man saluted and wheeled his horse to gallop back along the line of waiting horsemen. It was time to relieve the Klyssen cavalry.

Word was carried quickly through the ranks and the column began to trot down hill towards the enemy. Cerebus raised a gloved fist and the column split into five smaller units. He nodded to the officer riding beside him and the man raised a horn to his lips. A short blast knelled out and the units began the charge.

Cerebus's horse surged forward, well-trained to the sound of a charge. He adjusted his round shield and drew his sword. When he clapped the visor of his helmet down, his vision was reduced to a narrow horizontal slit. The units sped towards the enemy horde, spreading out in a five-pronged attack.

Cerebus saw the Raken brace for the new onslaught; spear butts ground into the earth and weapons raised. He tightened his grip on his sword. The horses slammed into the Raken. Equine armour deflected most of the spears but a horse to the right screamed in pain. Wood splinters flew up, clattering against his chest. Raken crumpled under the charge as the horses crashed through their lines. The huge beasts were more than a match for men on foot but they could not stand against barrelling horses. They went down under the flying hooves. The small wedge of cavalry cut deep into the Raken and Cerebus sliced down at beasts that got too close.

The din of battle was distant — roars and clashing weapons, Raken screams and men's shouts. His own breath under his helmet was louder. The horse under him reared and clubbed an attacking Raken, hooves flailing. He gripped hard with his knees to keep his seat. Cerebus looked back to see the end of the cavalry hit the line. The widest part of the wedge ensured enough space for the retreat

He spurred his horse, guiding the animal with his legs alone. A Raken club glanced off his side, denting the heavy armour. Cerebus turned to engage the beast but another horseman had assumed the task. A horn sounded — three short blasts that rang over the battlefield. The withdrawal. Around him men were turning their mounts and the column wheeled as one. They thundered back through the opening created by the charge.

Cerebus lifted his visor, wiping at the sweat that seeped into his eyes. He scanned the battlefield. The other units were withdrawing leaving swaths of dead and injured Raken. A horse ran at the end of Cerebus's unit without a rider and several horsemen sported fresh blood.

As the last of the mounted allies cleared the horde, archers at the rear of the retreating coalition infantry sent up a volley of arrows. They fell like rain down among the Raken, killing more of the great beasts.

Cerebus raised his fist and his officer raised the horn to signal another charge.

It would be a hard flight to Pellaris.

Ambush

Rowan pulled her cloak tighter around herself as they rode through the early morning mist. The wet fog muffled the sound from the horses' hooves and a few leaves fell silently to the ground around them. As trees loomed out of the mist ahead and disappeared from view behind, it felt to Rowan as if they were traveling in place, never making any progress. She shivered, imagining the Raken hunting her looming up suddenly like black trees.

Closing her tired eyes, Rowan rested for a few paces. She had not slept well the night before. It had been much colder than the previous nights and her mind had not let her rest. The discussion with Hathunor had expounded upon things that she already knew of her giant friend but she also learned new things about him and his people. The questions of how he escaped being controlled like the Drae Raken, and why his kin were here were the hardest to let go of. Was there any significance to his freedom or was it simply by chance that he had avoided the fate of his little brothers?

Hathunor was very intelligent. She had seen the way he could reason things out and his interaction with the rest of the group spoke volumes about his ability to read and understand people. He was sensitive enough to know when he made others uncomfortable. Rowan had been amazed and gratified to see how easily the big Saa Raken had disarmed the wariness of their new friends, putting them all at ease in his presence.

But although he was friendly and loyal, Hathunor's way of interacting with Rowan and the other companions was distinctly different. He happily answered questions when he was asked and if he needed to tell her something important he would, but he seemed to intuitively understand all of them and therefore had no need to talk to anyone.

Rowan, accustomed to spending time alone, found it soothing not to fill space or time with idle talk or to relate stories of one's past, or hopes for the future. She enjoyed her interaction with the companions and the familiar contact of people again but it was good to have the big Saa Raken's steady quiet friendship in counterbalance.

Hathunor lived entirely in the present. His past experiences were merely what had shaped him and aside from his quest to save his kin, the future was irrelevant. He struggled with the concept of future or years from now. He used the words today and tomorrow interchangeably. His present became the future as he lived it.

Most people were tied down to their past and they carried it around with them like a big stone, dwelling continually on how heavy it was. She supposed it must be a part of why Hathunor was so calm, exuding a sense of peace despite his ferocious appearance. He never worried about what tomorrow might bring.

Rowan gave a wry chuckle as she realized with amusement that she had not slept well the night before precisely because she had been dwelling on what was to come. She closed her eyes again and relaxed into the soothing motion of Roanus's walk, letting go of questions and worries.

After a while Rowan began to feel centered and calm and she silently thanked Hathunor for his wisdom.

"How are you this morning?" Rowan opened her eyes and turned to find Dalemar riding beside her.

"I am well, thank you. A little tired perhaps," she replied.

Dalemar nodded sagely, smooth eyebrows arching. "Thinking of Hathunor?"

Rowan turned to him in surprise. "How did you know?"

The Rith grinned. "I was doing the same thing myself. Didn't catch a wink all night."

They rode in silence for a time until Dalemar pulled a small leather bound book from his belt pouch and flipped through its worn pages. "Rowan, when you told us of your mission after we fought the trieton, you mentioned an omen that was supposed to give a clue to how the summoning of the Wyoraith might be stopped, but you never actually spoke it." Dalemar looked at her keenly. His gray eyes were almost the same colour as the pale mist around them. "What is the message the Seers gave you?"

Rowan saw again the cliff-side fortress of Danum, its black stone walls cut from the volcanic rock. The narrow winding path was barely wide enough for a horse and cart. It snaked precariously up the side of the cliff from the rocky beach below.

The cacophony of circling sea birds that nested in the crevasses beneath the solitary fortress filled the air and their white wings glinted in the first rays of the sun. Rowan had climbed that path alone at first light as she had been instructed. *One and only one of the company is to come to us at dawn. You will know who it is to be.* When she had rapped on the iron door that led through the rising black rock with the hilt of her dagger, the door had been unlocked and opened immediately. The man who opened the door smiled softly and bowed to her. "*Rowan Mor Lanyar, you are expected.*"

Rowan blinked, realized Dalemar was still watching her. The message — it had not been spoken aloud since she had repeated it to her companions as they set sail. She had bid them all to memorize it so each would be able to carry it onward should they become separated or worse. Worse – perhaps the Seers had known all along that she would be the only one to survive the journey into Eryos.

Rowan took a breath to dispel the shiver she felt. It surprised her how much she trusted these people. She made her decision. Nothing could be taken for granted and her journey north would be a dangerous one. Turning to look at the space between Roanus's ears she uttered the words that had first been spoken to her within the black walls of Danum Fortress.

"Look not only to strength or all will be lost for the foe is too great. The gateway must not be opened for ill intent. Bind the Stone with evil. Free the Stone with purity of heart. The path to salvation lies in the hands of the Slayer."

The mist swirled cold around them and the words seemed to fall dead into the wet greyness. Dalemar beside her was silent and when Rowan looked up and ahead, she found Torrin turned in his saddle, looking back at her. The fog obscured him but there was no mistaking the intensity of his gaze.

Dalemar, his brow furrowed in concentration, stroked a fingertip along the leather spine of the book he held. "What Stone does the message refer to?"

Rowan shook her head. "I do not know. I asked the very same question of the Seers the morning I received the message and was told that in time I would come to know what I was meant to know." She allowed some of the frustration she felt colour her words – so many unanswered questions.

"Well, we can certainly search for reference to it in Pellaris's library archives when we get there. I can think of many stones or gems that hold power or are used as receptacles and conduits to access power. Half of the Riths that I know use a stone of some kind."

Dalemar finished scribing the few lines Rowen had spoken, then tucked his book away. He sighed. "If I had thought to unravel some of our mystery, I was mistaken. There is barely enough in those few phases to give any sort of information. The only line that doesn't have more than one possible meaning is the reference to the 'Slayer' and even then — salvation lies in the hands of the Slayer — is it a reference to something the Slayer holds or a responsibility that he will assume? The right answer might be in the literal understanding of the words, or it could have some deeper, hidden meaning. Are your Seers always so cryptic?"

Rowan smiled. "In my experience, almost always. It must have something to do with the nature of the visions they see. Perhaps they cannot be more specific."

"Perhaps they choose not to be."

Rowan glanced over at the Rith. His smooth brow was furrowed in concentration. "Do you know to which 'foe' they are referring?"

Rowan tightened her cloak again. "Until I had reached Eryos, I had always assumed that the foe was the Wyoraith. But it could be the Raken, the Wyoraith or the one who is trying to summon it."

Dalemar nodded and rode beside her in silence until he finally exhaled in exasperation and shook his head, his long blond hair flipping against his dark green coat. "There just isn't enough information. I need a library." He glanced regretfully at his saddlebags, bulging with the books he carried with him. "The few books I have are of absolutely no help with this problem. Words are often misinterpreted or their meanings change over time into something that is very different from what the word meant in an original root language. The dialect of Myris Dar has evolved separately from Eryos's common tongue, and though it appears to be very similar in many ways there could well be words with meanings that have been lost here. Do the Seers of Danum have a reference library?"

"I did see many books and scrolls while I was there and the capital on Myris Dar has a large library as well," replied Rowan.

"Is it possible that they consult artefacts or written references to this Slayer, or do you think the message they sent with you comes entirely from the visions?" asked Dalemar.

Rowan thought for a moment, remembering the ancient stone room she had waited in and the cases of books and scrolls against the walls. There had been a very old sword hanging on one wall and Rowan had looked more closely at it than the books. "It is very possible that they used both to compose the message. I am sorry that I can't be more helpful. It was not a question I thought to ask at the time."

Dalemar sighed, "Knowing would tell us how literally to interpret the message. But no matter, I am sure we will understand it in time."

"What about Arynilas?"

"Hmm? What about him?"

"Perhaps he knows about the Slayer and the Wyoraith. He is older than the rest of us, isn't he?"

"Yes quite. It is possible, but Tynithians do not concern themselves with human affairs and they have a different sense of time than the rest of us."

"How so?" Rowan looked ahead through the mist and glimpsed the black-haired Tynithian riding between the trees.

"A hundred years can pass for a Tynithian, and he or she will have spent it doing one thing only, perfecting that activity. Years blend together for them. There is no reason to mark them because they will go on for over a thousand years."

Rowan frowned, she hadn't though of it that way before. If you were that long-lived then time would not have the same weight, the same importance.

"How old is he?" she asked.

"Over four hundred, I believe."

Raising her eyebrows, Rowan tried to imagine what it would be like to live for four hundred years. The world around you would change but you would remain the same. Humans would be born, walk the face of Eryos and die as you endured. Kingdoms would rise and fall, wars would come and go, and the struggles of people would pass into history. She imagined that were she to live that long it would be easy to lose interest in those transient happenings and turn inward to your own kind. Either that or the pain of continually losing human friends would cause you to withdraw.

The morning sun broke through the mist and the company was bathed in warm light. Rowan focused on the huge dark form of Hathunor as he paced at the head of their column.

She was interrupted from her musing as a piercing howl erupted from the trees to their left. Hathunor became a dark blur as he turned and charged into the bush, toward the sound. He disappeared in an instant, leaving the rest of them in startled suspension.

Rowan reached up to draw her sword from its harness, aware that the others were doing the same. The ringing sound of drawn blades faded quickly in the damp mist as the companions pulled into a tight ring, facing outward to the surrounding trees.

Another howl sounded from within the trees. Rowan recognized Hathunor's voice. It was his signal to run.

"Was that Hathunor?" Arynilas asked from Rowan's right.

"Yes," she turned to Torrin on her other side. "He asks us to flee."

"It's an ambush," growled Borlin.

"We move. Now!" barked Torrin as he pulled his excited horse around. He slapped Roanus on the rump for emphasis, and Rowan's big horse surged under her.

The trees flew by to either side as the six mounted companions fled. Rowan heard Torrin curse and call to Nathel. Then he was beside her, his sword held low along his horse's neck. Nathel spurred to the other side and Rowan was flanked. They passed through a small gully and had to spread out in single file.

A Drae Raken appeared at the exit to the gully, black against the green. Arynilas loosed an arrow to clear the path. The Raken dropped to the ground but another took its place. Rowan glanced back and saw more Raken closing in behind. She pulled Roanus in from his headlong flight, hauling on the reins as her excited horse resisted. They would have to stand and fight.

At that moment blackness flew at Rowan from the right. She had time only to register the huge Raken before it struck. Torrin shouted her name. The beast slammed into her, punching the air from her lungs. She felt her sword spin away. Warm breath blasted in her face and an animal snarl was all she heard as the force of the impact knocked her off Roanus to the stony ground below.

The Raken landed on top of her, obliterating any sense she had left. Her vision swam and she was only dimly aware of the beast as it rolled off and began to drag her into the trees.

Rowan's sight came back gradually. What she saw was a fierce skirmish between the Raken and her friends. Torrin was battling ferociously, his sword flashing. Nathel was down, lying motionless on the ground. Borlin stood guard over him, slaying the Raken that got too near. Arynilas's bow hummed and Dalemar was sending fire from his fingertips.

Rowan fought to stay conscious. She could barely hear the fighting – sound was lost to the pounding in her ears. She reached up, prying at the huge scaled hand that grasped her collar and hair, but her attempts were feeble. She was being dragged away from her companions.

She fumbled desperately for her dagger. It finally came out to her insistent pulling and she raised it with the last of her strength.

The Raken snarled as the blade sliced. Rowan was dropped abruptly. She looked up to see the beast aim a studded club at her. It descended so fast. Rolling aside as quickly as her groggy, weak limbs would allow, she felt the impact of the club as it landed with a thud on the ground beside her.

Sound came crashing back — the clash and ring of steel, the shouts and roars and screams of the battle. There was no time to register how her friends were faring.

The Raken tried to hit her once more. She rolled again, narrowly escaping another blow. Earth flew up as the club landed. She stumbled to her feet. Her knees buckled and she almost went down again.

One of Arynilas's arrows buried itself suddenly in the Raken's chest — a bloom of gold on black. It stumbled back with a grunt. Red eyes refocused on her and it raised the club high again, but Rowan didn't wait for it to take aim. She plunged her dagger into its throat. The Raken toppled backwards to the ground, muscular black limbs sprawling.

She bent trembling to retrieve her blade. Head swimming, she turned to see the battle ending with most of her friends still standing. She took a step towards them and went down again, landing with a groan in the autumn leaves. She sat up and shook her head, trying to clear away the dizziness.

A branch cracked behind her. She pulled in a quick breath as dread rose in her chest; another Raken rushed at her. She tried to scramble back but her muscles wouldn't work properly. She cursed her weakness – there was no way to fight it.

A bright flash sped through the air above her. The Raken was driven back off its feet to land with a thud, a two-handed broadsword buried up to the hilt in its chest.

Then Torrin was there, heaving his sword out of the body with a foot placed on the Raken for leverage. As Rowan climbed slowly to her feet again Torrin scooped her up. He carried her back to the others, placing her upon Roanus. "Can you ride Rowan?" His voice was strained and his breathing ragged. Worry etched his face.

Rowan nodded. "I saw Nathel down," she managed to get out through the pain in her chest.

"A blow to the head. He will be fine, I think. We must be away from here now. Are you well enough to ride?"

"I will be fine soon. I was knocked a little senseless." Rowan noticed blood trickling down Torrin's arm. It dripped from his fingertips. "Are you well?"

Torrin followed her gaze to the wound on his shoulder; the worry was replaced by grim menace. "I gave much better than I received."

He turned from her. "Come, Arynilas, Borlin, Dalemar — we must move.

Dalemar looked up from Nathel's prone form. "But your brother," he protested.

"Lay him across the front of my horse. We will see to him when it is safe to stop."

Dalemar and Borlin lifted the unconscious man. Arynilas trotted back after retrieving as many arrows as he could find.

Torrin reached down and picked something up from the ground. It was Rowan's sword. He presented it to her hilt first. "It is a shame you never got the chance to use your humming blade, Messenger. The battle would have been over much sooner for it."

Rowan took the sword and sheathed it over her shoulder. She held his gaze for a moment. “Thank you.”

Torrin nodded, the intensity she had seen in his face was masked now. He turned away to help with his brother.

Rowan scanned the trees around them, thinking of Hathunor. Unease settled around her. There had been something cunning in this attack. Hathunor had been lured away intentionally. And there was something else, something that chilled her to the bone. They had tried to take her alive.

Into Klyssen

They rode as fast as they dared through the trees. Arynilas was scouting ahead for them until Hathunor returned – if he returned. Torrin scanned the surrounding forest. He hoped the big Saa Raken was safe and would rejoin them soon.

The sun was high over head when the trees began to thin. Stands of dark evergreens and leather birch were replaced with fenic, their distinctive white bark turning the surrounding view into white pole fences. The space between the giant broadleaf trees was wider and Torrin was now able to see glimpses of Arynilas through the trunks.

There had been no sign of pursuit. Perhaps it had been just a small group of Raken but Torrin wouldn't bet on it. It was important to find out how many others there were and how close. He ground his teeth in frustration, feeling blind.

Torrin briefly entertained the idea that the big Saa Raken had led them into the trap willingly. If Hathunor could hear his kin, then perhaps he could communicate with them as well. Torrin shook his head. It sounded logical but felt wrong. Rowan was right. There was no deceit in Hathunor. The Saa Raken had probably led the attackers away from them somehow.

Torrin looked ahead to where Rowan rode on her big gray horse. He frowned as another thought asserted itself — the Raken had tried to take her alive. Why? After so long trying to kill her, why would they want to capture her?

Taking a steadying breath, he let it out slowly as the memory of it flashed through his mind. He saw the Raken crashing into her, dragging her helpless form away. He saw the huge black form trying to smash her with a club as she desperately tried to avoid it. And Torrin, helpless to reach her in time to stop the blows. He gripped his reins until his knuckles turned white.

He had been infuriated to the blinding point, and his own response had shocked him. Losing his reason and mental control in a battle was something he had not done in a very long time. Not since Emma and the girls were taken from him. Torrin closed his eyes and harshly repressed the thought. He didn't think he could bear that much pain again. *Erys help me*, he thought. Not again. Never again.

Rowan seemed to have recovered from the blow she had taken. She was moving more carefully though, more slowly. Torrin would have to make sure Nathel looked at her, providing that Nathel himself was fine. Torrin looked down at his brother, draped across his lap. Worry haunted his thoughts but Nathel was strong. He had sustained worse before, far worse.

Nathel groaned then, as if in response to his brother's attention, and tried to lift his head. "What am I? A sac of potatoes?" The words were groggy, but lucid.

Torrin exhaled in relief and reined his mount in. The others stopped and Borlin hopped down to help. Torrin dismounted and grasped his brother by the shoulders to ease him off the horse. Nathel stumbled slightly but he seemed to suffer no other ill effects. A large red lump had formed over his left eyebrow and he tested its tenderness with his fingertips, wincing. Borlin led Nathel's horse forward and Dalemar handed him a waterskin.

"Are you well enough to ride, Nathel?" Torrin gripped his brother by the shoulder.

Nathel chuckled, "It's just a wee lump, Tor. I'll survive." He glanced quickly around then and relaxed visibly when he found Rowan unharmed. Torrin realized the last thing his brother must have seen was Rowan being dragged away. "Arynilas, Hathunor?" Nathel asked.

Torrin pointed ahead with his chin. "Arynilas scouts, and we've not seen Hathunor since he engaged the Draes at the outset of the ambush."

Nathel nodded and climbed up onto his horse. "He'll be fine, a Raken *that* huge doesn't get into trouble. He brings it to those who decide to bother *him*." His words were meant for Rowan, and Torrin said a silent thanks to his brother. The worry on her face was clear.

"You can tell me all about the battle and how I valiantly passed out as we ride," said Nathel as he turned his horse around. He re-corked the waterskin and tossed it over to Torrin.

Torrin caught the skin in one hand and threw it straight back at Nathel. "You need it more than I do right now, oh valiant one." He swung his leg up over Black and settled once more in the saddle.

Nathel snorted and grinned, taking another swig of water.

They traveled through the thinning trees of the northern edge of the Wilds for the rest of the day. The sun was setting when the trees finally gave way to the open, rolling grassland of Klyssen. From the edge of the Wilds, the vast plains spread out before them — a sea of grasses rippling with wind. It blew through the stems and nodding heads of the ripened stalks in waves that rolled endlessly into the shore of the forest.

The small company plunged into the dry sea, setting out towards a distant outcrop of rock which perched on the plain like a small fortress. It loomed close as the last of the red sun sank below the horizon. The top of the hill contained a shallow bowl and Torrin was pleased to see that it was defensible and offered sheltered from the blowing wind.

Worry and Wait

Torrin sat with his armour and shirt off and his hands loosely clasped around his knees. Nathel was stitching the gash in his shoulder and Torrin, clenching his teeth, was trying to concentrate on anything but the sharp needle poking him. "You're getting better at this Nathel. It only feels a little worse than getting it cut open in the first place." His brother replied with a sharp prick of the needle.

Torrin watched Rowan in the gathering darkness. She was seated on the rim of the outcrop facing back toward the forest, waiting for Hathunor. She had been very quiet since the attack.

During a fight things happen very quickly, with little time to react. Knowing that, though, did not make him feel any less responsible.

Nathel finished the dressing on Torrin's shoulder and handed him his shirt.

"Thanks, Nathel."

"Never a pleasure to see to a wound, brother," said Nathel as he began to pack away his precious medics. He had seen to Rowan first at Torrin's insistence. She was bruised and sore but no bones were broken.

Torrin strode to where Rowan sat, pulling his shirt carefully over his head as he walked. The evening was chilly now that the sun had set. Torrin stopped just behind her. "Hathunor will be fine," he said.

Rowan looked up at him, nodded and turned back to face the distant forest.

Torrin squatted down beside her, his fingertips grasping at long blades of grass.

"How is your shoulder?" asked Rowan.

"It is fine, thank you. Nathel could have been a tailor had he wanted to."

She smiled softly in amusement but when she spoke again her voice was very sober. "I thought I was going to die today. The sight of that last Raken coming at me was terrifying. I had nothing left. No way to fight it."

"I noticed your dagger was put to good use. You never stopped fighting, even though you were hurt," Torrin replied.

A cool breeze stirred around the top of the hill. Once the sun had set the wind had died considerably. The last of the blue twilight was almost gone and the clear sky was sparkling with stars. The expanse of sky was a little unsettling after the cover of the forest.

"The Raken were trying to take me alive today, weren't they?" Rowan hunched her shoulders and crossed her arms. "This attack was different from all the others."

Torrin studied her shadowy form. "It appeared that way," he said quietly. "It was all calculated to get Hathunor away from us and make it possible for them to take you."

The silence stretched and Torrin scanned the distant tree line. They had set a cold camp; a fire would be seen for leagues in the open plains. The others were talking in the hollow, their voices low and muted. They were all worried about Hathunor. Torrin was surprised at his own feelings about their giant companion. He had not realized how fond he had become of Hathunor.

Then Rowan spoke so softly that Torrin had to strain to hear. "I'm so tired of running."

Torrin felt a powerful urge to gather her into his arms. It alarmed him and he held himself rigid as the memory of her being dragged away by the Raken flashed through his mind again. He struggled to control the rush of emotions it summoned. Instead he offered the only comfort he could. "I made you a promise and I intend to keep it. I will get you safely to Pellaris."

Hathunor's Gift

Rowan woke with a start. She had fallen asleep on the edge of the hill. A blanket had been draped over her and it slipped down from her shoulders as she sat up. She stifled a groan as a sharp pain lanced through her side. A dark form was close by, leaning against a boulder. “How long have I slept?” she asked.

Torrin’s voice came from the darkness. “Not long. A few candle marks.”

She hugged herself, feeling again the hot rush of shame and anger that had burned in her all afternoon. The man sitting near her had saved her life today. She had been unequal to the task herself. She had desperately needed the help and she berated herself for letting the Raken surprise her. She should have seen it coming; been able to avoid it before it smashed into her. All her skills and training had become useless after she had taken such a blow. With the titanic force of the impact, Rowan was amazed that she hadn’t passed out completely or had her ribs shattered and her back broken. The Raken must not have hit her squarely.

Rowan pulled the blanket around her shoulders and the pain in her side spread up into her back and shoulder blade. She had not come away from the encounter totally unscathed. She gazed at the glittering expanse above. The skies of Myris Dar were much the same. She turned quickly away from the thought of home – it only served to hinder her here. Rowan sighed. Once again her new companions had been placed in danger because of her mission.

Arynilas appeared beside them. “Someone comes,” he said quietly, pointing down the slope into the darkness.

It took Rowan a while to make out the huge black shadow that moved slowly toward the base of the hill. As it drew closer, she caught a glimpse of a spiky crest. “Hathunor,” she breathed.

The figure stumbled and fell near the base of the hill where it lay unmoving. Rowan was on her feet in an instant, the pain in her ribs forgotten as she ran down the hill toward the prone figure with Torrin and Arynilas close behind. When they reached the huge Saa Raken he did not respond to their voices.

Torrin pulled his shirt off and wrapped it around his hands and forearms before reaching down to grip Hathunor under the arms. Rowan thanked him silently for his presence of mind – in her concern for her friend she had forgotten Erys's bane.

Torrin heaved and the muscles of his back and shoulders stood out in the starlight. Hathunor barely lifted from the grass. Arynilas strapped his bow over his shoulder and bent to help. But even two of them couldn't move the giant far. The job was made that much more difficult because the great Saa Raken was slicked with something wet and their grasp on him kept sliding. Rowan dashed back up to wake the others for help.

They rolled the Saa Raken onto a blanket and dragged him up to the center of the shallow bowl of the hilltop. Nathel was already searching through his healer's satchel for remedies. Borlin lit a small lantern and unhooded it. They gasped at what they saw.

Hathunor was covered in gashes and cuts. Every inch of his dark scaled skin was smeared with blood.

"Sweet Erys!" Nathel breathed. It was the first time Rowan had seen him at a loss. He turned helplessly to Dalemar. "I don't know anything about Raken. He has scales instead of skin. How do you stitch scales? And that is only the outside – what if he has damage inside? He looks to have lost a great deal of blood." Nathel sat back on his heels and stared at the mess before him. He looked at Dalemar again. "I need your help, my friend."

Dalemar rose and stepped around to kneel at Hathunor's head. He placed his hands on either side of the Raken's face and closed his eyes. His palms began to glow with a soft blue light. It seemed as though nothing was happening. Then suddenly the great black body before them arched up violently, every muscle tensing. Dalemar's eyes flew open in shock and he gasped in a great breath. Despite the cool night, beads of sweat began to form on his forehead.

Rowan reached out to Dalemar but Torrin stopped her hand. When she turned to look at him, he shook his head.

Long moments went by. Everyone was frozen, watching in amazement as Dalemar worked his craft. Finally, Hathunor slumped to the ground. Dalemar released his grasp slowly on the Raken and crumpled sideways onto the ground in utter exhaustion.

Nathel helped him to sit up and held a waterskin to his lips. The Rith took a long drink and then sagged back against Nathel. His hands were shaking and he gasped for breath.

The Saa Raken lay utterly still before them. Rowan reached out with a cloth and wiped some of the blood from Hathunor's chest. She gasped in amazement. The scaled skin underneath gleamed smoothly in the lantern light. The wounds were gone.

She looked at Dalemar. "You've healed him!" She wiped more of the blood away, finding more undamaged skin.

Dalemar blinked in astonishment at Hathunor. "That was a most interesting experience – dangerous and a bit frightening, but fascinating."

"You've never healed anyone completely before," Torrin said. "Well done, Dalemar."

The Rith shook his head. "It wasn't me, Torrin, I had nothing to do with it."

"If you had nothing to do with it Rith, then how is he healed?" Arynilas asked with humour in his tilted eyes.

"I don't know. It was like being seized by an immense hand. My power was drawn without my control. I watched the work being done without directing it and was quite powerless to stop it. I learned a great deal actually."

"If you couldn't stop it, how did you break the connection?" Torrin asked.

Dalemar shrugged, his gaze fixed on Hathunor. "It simply let go when the work was done."

"Do you suppose it was Hathunor himself controlling the magic?" asked Rowan.

"It is the only explanation that I can think of," Dalemar said.

"Shouldn't e be wak'n up now at e's healed?" asked Borlin.

Dalemar shook his head. "It may be a while before he regains consciousness. I am always exhausted after working magic. I can't imagine he would be any different."

"More threads unravel in this mystery and our Raken friend seems to be at its heart," Arynilas said quietly.

"Indeed," replied Dalemar, still staring in wonder at the blood-covered body before him. "And I have so many more questions." Arynilas moved to help Dalemar to his sleeping roll.

Rowan began to clean the blood from her giant friend. She felt tears of relief sliding down her cheeks as she found him completely whole. Nathel reached out and began to help as well, then Torrin and Borlin. Together they gently removed all the blood from the great Raken by the light of the lantern.

Of Raken and Magic

Rowan opened her eyes to a lead gray sky. A chill wind whistled around the top of the hill. She was cold and a terrible stiffness had settled into her body during the night. Her right side throbbed painfully as she moved to sit up. A groan escaped her as she slowly unbuckled her leather breastplate, pulled up her shirt and looked at her ribs with morbid curiosity. They were black and blue, with the subtle shades of yellow filling in between the darker bruising. It hadn't hurt this much yesterday. She groaned again, this time in anticipation of the long, painful ride ahead.

She re-buckled the leather straps of her armour and looked around to find Hathunor seated on the ground in animated conversation with Dalemar. Joy flooded through her, bringing warmth for a moment.

Taking up her waterskin, she rinsed her mouth and stood up carefully. Borlin arrived with a cold breakfast of dried meat and cheese, "How's th' pain this morn, lass?"

Rowan smiled ruefully at him as she gratefully accepted the food. She took a bite and watched him walk back to where Torrin and Nathel were saddling the horses. Arynilas was standing watch at the rim of the hill, casting back towards the forest for any sign of Raken.

Shivering, she drew her cloak tighter and cast the hood up as she walked slowly over to the Rith and the huge Saa Raken.

He smiled at Rowan, a flash of jagged teeth.

"I'm glad to see you are well, my friend," she said, grinning at him.

Hathunor's smile widened until she could see every sharp tooth in his mouth.

"The other Raken?" she asked.

His expression fell. "Little brothers dead," he rumbled flatly.

Dalemar leapt to his feet. "Hathunor doesn't remember what happened last night, but he says that all of the Saa Raken have the ability to absorb and use magic!" Hathunor nodded his great head, shaggy crest waving in the wind.

"Truly?" Rowan frowned. Careful not to flex the muscles around her bruised ribs, she sat down to listen to their conversation and eat her breakfast. "But what of the Draes? Its magic that controls them, isn't it? If they had this ability, they should be able to resist or stop it somehow."

Hathunor shook his head. "No Draes capture magic."

The rest of the companions gathered around. Rowan noticed Nathel's forehead looked much like her ribs. She glanced at Torrin and saw that he had found time to mend the slice in his leathers where the Raken blade had cut through to his shoulder.

Dalemar resumed his seat next to Hathunor. "The Draes' ability to harness and use magic must be latent." The Rith tapped his chin with a fingertip.

Hathunor grunted an affirmative and Rowan looked up at him. "Hathunor, how did your people develop this ability?" she asked.

The Raken shrugged his huge shoulders. "It always so."

"Are there people in your land, Hathunor, who can conjure magic?" asked Dalemar.

Hathunor shook his head. "No one make magic like Dalemar."

The Rith frowned in puzzlement. "Then what would it be for? An ability such as this seldom develops without a reason."

Hathunor smiled, ivory fangs flashing. "Good reason."

"Hey? What do you mean, Hathunor?" asked the Rith.

"Hathunor's home magic in land." The Raken cast his arms wide. Borlin had to jump backward to avoid getting whacked in the chest. "In stones, water, sky."

Dalemar eyes widened. "Your people channel magic from the land itself?"

Hathunor nodded.

"But your ability is passive. It can only be used when magic flows into you. That would mean magic must flow freely in your land without anyone directing it!" Dalemar's face was positively alight with this new revelation.

"Only some places magic strong enough use. Flow like great river. Many Raken live near, use magic."

"What do you do with the magic, Hathunor?" asked Nathel.

Hathunor tilted his enormous head. "Shape."

Nathel looked at Dalemar, then back at Hathunor, frowning. "Shape what?"

"All," rumbled Hathunor.

"Do you mean to say that magic is used for everything?" asked Dalemar.

"All," repeated Hathunor, nodding.

"But you said that magic only flows strongly enough in some places. How can you use it for everything?" asked Dalemar.

Hathunor frowned in concentration, then his expression brightened, teeth flashing. "Send magic."

Rowan looked at Dalemar for better understanding. Judging from the looks on the faces of the rest of the companions, the Rith was the only one who completely understood this conversation.

Comprehension dawned on his face. "Sweet Erys!" he breathed. "You channel it over distance?"

Hathunor nodded, shaggy crest waving. "Send magic where need."

"How many Raken can use the magic channelled over distance?" asked Dalemar intently.

"As many as need," replied Hathunor.

"Doesn't the magic dwindle with so many drawing on it?"

Hathunor frowned. "Magic stay strong."

Dalemar leaned toward the Raken. "You don't lose even a little bit?"

"No lose magic. Lathic send far; use magic; give to others; send on next Lathic."

"Lathic?" Rowan peered up at him.

Hathunor turned to look down at her and nodded solemnly. "Lathic strongest Cren lore-keeper."

"So there are certain Raken able to control and wield more magic than others?" Dalemar shook his head in wonder. "Never have I heard of magic being used this way. Riths can channel magic together but it is very difficult and only a few can sustain the link once it is formed. Some of the magic always has to be used for maintaining the link. I've never heard of Riths being able to link and channel over a great expanse. They have to see each other to form the link. If I understand Hathunor correctly, his people can channel magic between themselves in great numbers and over great distance. It's remarkable."

"Then the Cren Raken can use magic as well," said Torrin.

Hathunor nodded. "Cren great shapers, lore-Keepers. Saa use magic heal, defend, send message, small. Not like Cren. Cren great magic shapers."

Rowan tried to picture this complex relationship between the various Raken, their land, and the magic. "Hathunor, if Saa and Cren Raken can channel and use magic so easily and for so many things, why are the Drae and Grol Raken unable to use magic? How is it possible for them to live if magic is used for everything?"

Hathunor's red gaze turned to her. "Drae and Grol need Saa and Cren. Saa and Cren need Drae and Grol."

"Need each other for what?" Torrin asked.

"Drae and Grol need Saa and Cren to use magic, shape for little brothers. Saa and Cren need Drae and Grol get magic. Make."

Torrin frowned, shaking his head. "But you said Drae and Grol Raken couldn't use magic."

"Little brothers no use magic. Make magic." Hathunor concentrated, searching for the right word. "Find magic, change for Saa and Cren."

Arynilas turned from scanning the distant forest, his sapphire eyes intent on Hathunor. "Drae and Grol Raken somehow harvest magic for Saa and Cren Raken to use?"

Hathunor nodded. "Change. Give Saa and Cren. Saa and Cren use for little brothers."

"So Saa and Cren Raken can't use magic without Drae and Grol Raken to help?" asked Torrin, a frown drawing his dark brows downward.

Hathunor nodded again.

Dalemar shook his head in wonder. "It is a completely symbiotic relationship. Drae and Grol cannot survive without Saa and Cren Raken nor Saa and Cren without Drae and Grol."

Hathunor flashed a smile.

"Couldn' a be a tad bit precarious if one side o' the partnership is lost?" asked Borlin.

Hathunor sat up straighter and curled a hand into a fist, placing it on his chest. "Saa protect little brothers. Defend. Keep safe. Cren wise, lead. Drae and Grol sustain all."

"It's like a superior fighting force," said Torrin thoughtfully. "There are generals and captains to make decisions; elite forces, like cavalry to protect the main army; and the infantry, without which it wouldn't be an army."

"Bees," murmured Arynilas. The companions turned to look at the Tynithian as the wind swirled around the hilltop. "Have you ever watched a bee hive make honey? There is a queen, who is looked after by workers who are in turn protected by soldiers that keep the hive safe."

Rowan raised her eyebrows and shook her head in respect for her large companion as the complexity of Raken society sunk in

"Hathunor, can you still feel the magic from your own land?" asked Dalemar.

Hathunor shook his head and his expression fell into sadness. "No feel magic. Too far."

"Is there magic in this land for you to use?" asked Nathel.

Hathunor held up a hand, thumb and fingers close as if holding a pebble. "Little magic here, some places stronger. But no little brothers help Hathunor use."

"But you can use my magic." concluded Dalemar.

Hathunor's toothy smile appeared. "Rith Dalemar strong. Big magic."

"But I cannot access my magic consistently and because it comes from me, I will eventually get tired out," replied Dalemar.

"One day learn get magic from land. Come through, not from, Rith Dalemar."

Dalemar gazed at the giant Saa Raken as though the very contemplation of such a thing took his breath away.

Torrin cleared his throat and Rowan looked up to find a grim expression on his face. "If it isn't possible for the Draes to use magic, how in Erys' name are they to be freed?"

Hathunor growled, a deep, resonant sound from his chest. No one had an answer.

Across the Plains

Rowan exhaled in to the cold air and stilled her mind. She turned inward and concentrated on the feel of the ground beneath her feet and the tension of the muscles in her legs. Pivoting on her right foot, she kicked her left through the air at chest height. She slashed a straight-fingered hand upward toward an imaginary opponent, then swiftly redirected with an elbow to where the opponent's temple would be.

The arrow wound pulled and she felt a small ache but it was almost healed.

Nathel walked toward her with his morning tea in hand and stopped to watch for a moment. "You've forgotten your sword," he teased her.

"Not so," she replied, wiping the sweat from her forehead. "There is much that can be done without a weapon in your hands. The hands themselves become the weapon."

Interest piqued, the rest of the companions gathered around.

"Would you care to demonstrate?" asked Nathel with a grin.

"Would you care to volunteer?" Rowan raised an eyebrow, motioning for him to come closer.

Nathel raised his hand before him. "I'm not walking into that one!" He looked at the others. "You try, Tor. You might learn to use that weapon of yours as a sword instead of as a bread knife."

Rowan supressed laugh as Torrin reacted to the jest with a rare show of levity, rolling his eyes skyward.

She turned to face him. "Try to reach me with your sword."

Torrin sobered and shook his head. "I don't want to hurt you."

"You will not hurt me," replied Rowan confidently.

Again Torrin shook his head.

Rowan sighed. She would not get anywhere like this. "Then come with your bare hands, try to strike me." He hesitated again and she hissed in frustration, "I am not made of glass! Come!"

Torrin raised his fist and aimed a punch – only to find that she was no longer where he was aiming. She dodged forward at an angle so that his extended arm was directly beside her and grabbed his wrist. Using the momentum of his swing against him, she hauled him off balance. When he stepped forward to keep his feet, she stopped pulling and pushed instead, using her leg to trip him. He landed in the dewy grass with a grunt.

Nathel's laughter rang out and Rowan turned, pointing at him. "Your turn."

Nathel started to refuse but Borlin shoved him forward, making Nathel spill his remaining tea. "Ye've got te learn to take yer medicine, lad," chuckled the Stoneman.

Torrin watched closely as his brother was flung to the ground. She reached down to help Nathel up as he grumbled about getting tossed around by someone half his size. Borlin snickered in the background.

When she turned, Torrin was standing before her, waiting to try again. She nodded to him and he stepped forward, hands up. He refused to over-extend himself this time. His first try had been desultory – he was incredibly skilled with a sword and by extension his instincts for hand-to-hand fighting were honed as well. His ability was more than just learned skill. Torrin moved in a way that made him one with his weapon. If he had trained on Myris Dar, she was certain that he could have achieved the highest ranks. With his sword, he would be considered a master.

When it came, his attempt to hit her was quick and tight with little wasted effort. As his punch came toward her face, Rowan brought her elbow up and to the inside of his line. Her movement effortlessly redirected his force to glance harmlessly past her shoulder. As soon as Torrin felt his punch going off the mark, he launched his left hand in an attempt to catch her from the other side. Rowan ducked low under his arm and went for his belly, striking with the heel of her hand in the hollow just below his chest. She then darted up and aimed for the side of his head with her open palm. He pulled back out of the way and brought up his hands to protect his face. The moment he did, she landed her knee into his ribs.

He stepped back, shaking his head ruefully and rubbing his side.

Rowan pointed at her feet, shins, knees, elbows, knuckles, fingertips, the heel of her hand and the crown of her head. "These are my weapons."

"Aye, so ye fight dirty eh, lass?" chided Borlin.

Rowan shook her head. "Would you trust an opponent to be fair? If you drop your sword in a battle, will the man you're fighting stop to let you pick it up again?"

There were nods of agreement.

"I have seen you all do this in battle," she said. "Whether you are conscious of it or not, you use your entire body to fight, not just your swords. Borlin, I have seen you use your targe like a weapon to compliment your short sword; and Nathel, your shield is also used for more than shielding. Torrin, I have seen you use your long legs to advantage, kicking an opponent when your sword was busy elsewhere. When you get hit once or twice the lesson is learned and you adapt your skills accordingly. We each have traits that are unique to us. Just because you have a sword in your hand, does not mean that you can't or shouldn't use your fist as well."

"Would you be as confident when your opponent swings his sword at your head and you have nothing to meet his attack but your bare hands?" asked Nathel, without his usual smirk.

"I would quite possibly have the advantage, providing that I can get close enough. My opponent would underestimate the danger that I represent. He would be over-confident and not on guard for the kind of damage that I could inflict. My place of comfort in weaponless fighting is in tight. Your opponent cannot swing a sword in close quarters. The same rules apply. The sword is the extension of the fist – you avoid the fist and move in close under the guard. You use your strengths to your advantage whenever possible. I cannot hope to match Torrin force for force." She stepped forward and grasped him by the wrist to pull him off balance. It was like trying to move a horse. "But if he is already moving towards me, it is not hard to redirect his own energy and use it against him."

"Thus the grass breakfast," grinned Nathel.

Borlin snorted loudly, "Maybe I should start cook'n ye grass in the morn, lad. Perhaps it'll improve yer fight'n skills."

Nathel refused to take the bait. He looked over at Borlin in mock surprise. "I had no idea grass was an ingredient in your recipe book?" He winked blithely at Rowan.

The Stoneman smirked maliciously. "Seein ye tossed on yer head was mighty satisfying. Just shake yer head over the pot an ye will ha all the grass ye need fer yer meal."

Torrin's attention shifted toward the sun in the eastern sky. "We're wasting daylight," he said flatly, eyeing his brother and the Stoneman.

The exchange of colourful insults continued as the companions began to drift away to saddle their horses and load the gear. Rowan turned from picking up her sword in its baldric to find Arynilas still there.

His tilted eyes twinkled in the morning sun. "I would like to offer you my service in your practice as a drilling partner. Your fighting style is similar to that of my people. Perhaps we can learn something from one another."

It would be an honour, Arynilas." Rowan settled her blade over her shoulder. "I think I will be doing most of the learning, though."

His smooth face was unreadable as they went to join the others in preparation of another day's travel.

The rolling plains of Klyssen unfolded endless as they traveled northward. Rowan looked up at the position of the sun. It felt like they had been traveling for hours but the morning was still young. She closed her eyes and listened to the swishing of the knee-high grass as the horses walked. The golden horizon line was still there –branded into her vision. They were making good speed but she felt as though they were standing still. Each day passing blended into the next as the landscape they moved through remained utterly the same.

Rowan's cloak whipped open and she struggled to wrap it closely around her to keep out the tormenting wind.

Nathel chuckled darkly next to her. "That's thirteen by my count."

Rowan frowned. "You are keeping track? I am wishing for a coat like Dalemar's at this point!" She was used to the wind on Myris Dar, but the moisture-laden breezes of her homeland were born in the warm currents of the Southern Eryos Ocean. The wind on the Klyssen plain was fierce and violent. It blasted them in wailing gusts and swirled constantly, cold and unrelenting, snatching words away, scattering thoughts and pulling at hair and clothing.

"You are experiencing the worst of it now as the autumn rains move over the plains," explained Nathel, "but it usually blows to some degree all year round."

"I am longing for the dense woods of the Wilds," said Rowan, throwing and dark look at the scudding clouds overhead. A few days had dawned with relative calm, offering a blessed relief, but inevitably as the sun rose into the vast sky, the wind would once more begin to blow.

Rowan stretched in the saddle and felt only slight twinges now along her ribs and shoulder. Her injured pride from the near miss with the Raken was taking far longer to ease. The morning drills at least were giving her a way to sharpen her skills. It was a practice she had not followed since leaving the decks of the trading ship that brought her to Eryos and its solid, grounding constancy was a relief.

The harrowing journey through Lor Danith had kept her moving and running almost every waking moment with no time for anything else. Now, trekking across Klyssen with her companions, the desperation of the last weeks was finally receding.

Borlin trotted his mare up on her other side. "Say lass, I've got another good one fer ye!"

Nathel groaned. "Give over, Borlin. Didn't you tell her enough stories last night to get us all the way to Pellar?"

"Don't worry yer thick skull Nathel," replied Borlin. "This is the Tale o' the Wall!"

"Oh well then, onward, but don't let Tor know you told it again, or he's like to split your head for you, little man." Nathel leaned across toward Rowan and whispered, "It changes every time he tells it."

Rowan hid her grin as the Stoneman launched into the setup for the exciting story of yet another battle fought in during the Ren Wars. "An Nathel was in dire straights! Enemy closin' from all sides an 'im wounded in the shoulder so as e' couldn'a swing 'is sword full. Well I tell ye lass, it looked like 'e was finished. Then and there, we was set to mourn fer the rascal. And suddenly a mighty bellow sounded from atop o' the wall! 'Twas so loud that the battle stopped completely as ever'one turned to look up. And there 'e was, standin' like the Lord o' Battle hisself, Torrin. 'E launched hisself down at the melee with that great sword a' spinnin and I swear te ye that time stood still! Thirty feet high it were, if it was an inch to the top o' that wall, and Torrin jumped off te save 'is brother."

Nathel slapped his thigh and laughed out loud. "Borlin, I swear you missed your calling. With your flare for the dramatic, you could have had led the King's Players in Pellaris."

Borlin winked at Rowan. "Poor lad 's soft in the head. 'E canna remember anything clearly any more. Ye know that truth makes fer the best tales."

The rest of the day passed quickly for Rowan as the Stoneman's story telling transported her into the world of Eryos and her companions. "The Warlord's Conclave" told of how Torrin had been able to get the Ren Warlords to agree to tentative peace terms when they wouldn't step into the same room with each other. "Dark Treachery" was Borlin's story of how Torrin lead the companions to uncover a plot that would have trapped them in an ambush. Nathan's quips added to the flavor, and Rowan was so content; even the wind ceased to bother her.

Borlin also spoke of his homeland in the Black Hills and his adventures in mountaineering. His description of stone sculpting and masonry – something he missed a great deal – was passionate and informative. When she asked him about the famous blue glaze the stonemen use on their pottery, Borlin shook a finger at her and tisked with a grin. "Stoneman's secret."

That night they set a fireless camp in a shallow depression. Rowan sat and worked an oiled rag over her sword, watching the last of the setting sun glint from its edge.

Absorbed in her task, she started when Torrin spoke beside her. He sat with his back against his saddle, a cup in hand. "So how high was the wall this time?"

Rowan smiled and tucked her cloth away, sliding her blade back into its scabbard. "Near thirty feet high by Borlin's telling of it."

"That's not too bad. If I recall correctly, he had me fighting a dragon once as well."

The next frosty morning, Borlin lit a small, almost smokeless fire made from a tightly woven grass log he'd fashioned with deft fingers. Then he cooked them a warm breakfast with hot tea to dispel the night's chill.

The stout Stoneman was a surprisingly good cook. "Borlin, this is amazing!" Rowan complemented him between mouthfuls of cereal. "What is in it?"

"Why the grass seed is ripe an' perfect. Harvested me a bag full last night and cooked em up with a little bit o' herbs and such." He chuckled at the look on her face. "When ye enjoy food as much as Stonemen do, ye learn how te cook it properly." Borlin waved at the rest of his friends. "As fer this lot, they couldna boil an egg to save their lives!" A hunk of biscuit, thrown by Nathel, came sailing towards his head; the Stoneman caught it nimbly and popped it into his mouth.

"You're a mystery, Borlin," teased Nathel. "Maybe you should be wearing a dress instead of armour. Make sure no one sees you cooking in Pellaris or you might get whisked off to the local women's guild."

Rowan frowned. "Why should he wear a dress?"

Dalemar closed his book and looked at her with interest. "Women are the ones who cook in Eryos, Rowan, with a few," he looked pointedly at Borlin, "a very few exceptions."

"Ach! Tabor 'as male cooks." Borlin waved a hand at the world. "I canna help it if the rest o' the world is backward."

"Are you saying that men are not allowed to cook?" asked Rowan.

"It is not that they are not allowed, but it is just not socially acceptable for men to cook," answered Dalemar. "It is backward, I know, but it is the way of things here. Men and women have traditional roles that they adhere to. As you have already discovered there are no women in the armies and men fulfill all the leadership roles. Women's duties fall more toward the domestic, like raising children and keeping the home."

Rowan was no longer hungry. Setting aside her food, she got to her feet and took a deep breath, her chest tight; she had a strong sensation of being smothered. She had gleaned much through her travels in Lor Danith but hadn't known that the same views were so widely spread throughout the rest of Eryos. Rowan looked around at the faces of her companions. "On Myris Dar, you choose to do with your life what you want, regardless of whether you are a man or a woman. How can you take away a person's right to make their own choices of who and what they want to be?"

Torrin stood up, his expression gentle. "It is the way it has always been and change comes very slowly to Eryos, Rowan. This continent has been covered in darkness for centuries and still is in many places. You must be prepared for the affect you will have on the people you meet. There will be disapproval and, in some places, outright animosity."

Rowan wrapped her arms around herself as the wind began to pick up. "I cannot change who I am, just to fit in, just to make others more comfortable. I will not."

"No one is asking you to, Rowan. We just want you to be prepared," explained Dalemar.

"There is more you should know," said Torrin quietly. "Ren women are considered the property of their fathers and then their husbands."

Rowan shuddered. "Then young girls must hope to marry a man who is fair and kind."

Nathel snorted. "Scarce traits in the men of Ren."

"What about the other realms of Eryos. Are there no laws?"

Torrin shrugged. "Some, but they are seldom upheld."

"But none of you are like the people I have met," said Rowan. "You have accepted me and what I do. Why are you all so different from the rest of Eryos?" she asked.

Nathel chuckled, "Well look at us, Rowan. Even if there had been a women in our company before you came along, do you think Borlin would have let her cook?"

"The last few weeks have not been without adjustments, as I am sure you have noticed." Dalemar smiled as he cast a look at the others.

"We are an unusual company, Rowan," said Torrin, "Our renown comes as much from that as it does from our fighting record."

Rowan sank down to finish her breakfast as the others prepared for another day of travel.

Arynilas crouched in front of her, his sapphire eyes gleaming. "You are like a pebble dropped in a pond, Messenger.

The ripples of your being here will open minds and eyes that have long been closed."

Torrin stood at the edge of camp in the cold morning air and watched critically as Rowan sparred with Arynilas. The Tynithian's use of his twin blades was very similar to how Rowan used her sword and dagger. They had been training together in the mornings for several days now. The lithe Tynithian was closer to Rowan's size and made an excellent sparring partner. But while Rowan emphasized her sword over her dagger, Arynilas was completely ambidextrous. The Tynithian was also a master at misdirection – a technique he termed the "Vanishing Sword."

Torrin had trained with Arynilas himself and he knew how artful and deadly the Tynithian was. Arynilas' hands were so fast that before you even realized your mistake, his knife was already thrusting from a completely unexpected direction. It was very unnerving.

Torrin dropped his gaze to Rowan's feet and noted with approval that she never over extended herself. Her stance shifted and flowed but was always shoulder width apart, and she balanced on the balls of her feet. When pressure came towards her she would glide with it and allow it to pass her, like a dancer with a deadly partner.

They had all taken the time to practice with Rowan in various campsites, eager to learn more about the use of redirection in her fighting style. And considering that their current adversaries were much larger and heavier than any of them, anything that could give them an advantage was important.

Torrin watched closely now, as Arynilas tested her with redirection and surprise. She was barely a beat behind the Tynithian. Arynilas was not holding back, yet Rowan was managing to get her weapons up in time to protect herself.

Sweet Erys she was good. Torrin had never seen anyone even remotely keep up with Arynilas, including himself, and already she was beginning to anticipate his thrusts. Their breath puffing white in the brisk air, the pair twisted and spun with a complexity that was hard to follow.

Her athletic grace was fascinating – distracting. He frowned, intent on trying to understand her technique. If he could keep his head from getting in the way, he knew there was no one in the world that had more to teach Eryos than this woman.

With a last look, Torrin turned away to help with the horses. As he picked up his saddle and walked toward the picket, a loud pop sounded behind him. He spun, dropping his gear and reaching for his sword.

Dalemar stood with his hand touching Hathunor, while the Raken directed a stream of magic at the ground. After a moment a bubble of water began to seep from the soil. It spread out and soon there was a shallow pool filling the small depression.

"Ha! Wonderful, Hathunor," cheered Dalemar. "Nathel! Come and water the horses."

Torrin shook his head in wonder and turned to retrieve his saddle. It was quite remarkable to see the effortless feats Hathunor could perform with only a trickle of power. Dalemar was learning his own craft at an exponential rate – the Rith could see what Hathunor did with the magic and then make attempts of his own.

Unfortunately, Hathunor controlled the flow of magic through sheer instinct. As a result, Dalemar's lessons became a form of "trial and terror," as Nathel had taken to calling them, with the small party either howling with laughter or bolting for their lives as a spell went awry. Dalemar's rapid progress was remarkable, his skill growing daily along with his confidence.

Hathunor seemed to have recovered immediately from his battle with the Drae Raken. He had submitted to Dalemar's experiments in directing magic with good nature. In fact, he seemed to delight in wielding magic and had begun to play harmless pranks on everyone, blaming them on the Rith. Torrin wondered now how he could have ever mistrusted their giant companion.

*

Sweat pouring down her face, breath coming in gasps, Rowan got her sword in place barely in time to defend before Arynilas moved to the next attack. She danced to the side, deflecting another blow; no time for counter attack. She thought she had his pattern figured out but he changed tactics again, leaving her struggling to catch up.

Rowan spun to keep the rising sun from blinding her, making Arynilas follow her. She slashed at his flank but found his blade there, turning hers aside even as his other one cut towards her middle. She leaped back just in time.

They broke apart and Rowan bent over to catch her breath, feeling like an inexperienced child.

"You are very quick for a human," Arynilas said quietly. "Do not forget that I have had a much longer time to perfect my skill than you have."

Rowan nodded and wiped at the sweat on her brow. "It is true, time helps but it is not necessarily hours spent practicing that makes a master what he or she is. I have studied under the Myrian staff-master Ronithu. Students of different ages come from all over Myris Dar to study under him. I myself spent almost a year under his tutelage when I was twenty. At the time Master Ronithu was fifteen years of age."

Arynilas' dark eyebrows lifted in surprise. "Truly?"

Rowan nodded. "At the age of seven he was one with the staff, better than people three times his years who had practiced with it every day of their lives."

"A virtuoso." Arynilas smiled. "There are those among my people who have extraordinary talents innate within them from birth. As time passes, the gap between those who are born with talent and those who have practiced an activity to perfection narrows. It is said that within each of my people, there is a master of all crafts and only time is required to uncover them."

Rowan laughed. "If only I had a thousand years to practice the sword!"

"You do well enough as it is, Messenger."

Rowan sheathed her sword and dagger and rubbed at her burning shoulders as she and Arynilas made their way back to camp. This time spent with engaging people she trusted, learning their various fighting skills and teaching them some of her own, eased her longing for her homeland.

Their friendship helped bear the weight of the message she carried and her role as emissary from Myris Dar – the first of her people to visit Eryos for hundreds of years. She'd felt honoured when Nathel, in one of his more solemn moments, told her they were proud to accompany her — especially in view of the role women filled here in Eryos.

Her chest tightened. She was not very good at diplomacy and politics. Her cousin Dell had been picked for their mission because he was a diplomat. He would have known exactly what to say and how to behave among strangers. As a man, he would have had an easier time as well.

She prayed to Erys that it would not be too late to deliver the information the Seers had entrusted to her, that it could be understood in time to stop the coming of the Wyoraith. And that she would be able to navigate the uncharted waters of foreign ideologies and beliefs without alienating everyone she met. The hope of Eryos as well as her own beloved Myris Dar depended on it.

Balor

Foul weather set in and the companions were wet as often as they were dry. Early one afternoon, a brief flare of sunlight had slipped out behind the clouds to illuminate the world and Rowan watched the feathered heads of the curved grass stalks glowing around her. She glanced to the horizon, revelling in the sunlit gold of the plain against the bruised purple and grey of the gathering storm. Closing her eyes, she lifted her face to the warmth of the sun, knowing that it would be a short interlude.

"Ye 'ave told us very little of yer home, Rowan," Borlin said, plucking her from her reverie. He nudged his mare closer. "Perhaps I've bin telling too many of me own stories of late," he winked at her. "'Twould be good to hear somethin' new."

Rowan thought for a moment before replying, "Myris Dar is about the size of…"

"No," Borlin interrupted. "Tell us of yer home. Where ye grew up an what yer parents were like. What did ye do as a child, besides play wi wooden swords?"

Rowan heard Nathel snicker from behind them and turned in her saddle to direct a mock scowl at him, but he presented her an entirely innocent countenance. She glanced at Torrin who rode next to his brother. He met her gaze briefly before resuming his constant scan of the horizon. Borlin was still waiting patiently for an answer to his question.

Home.

Rowan's thoughts flew over the blue-green waters of the Eryos Ocean toward the mountainous isle, passed the terraced fields, winding roads and villages, to the steep footpath that led up to the stone house with its wide, concave sloped roof, the carved wooden apex beam and the beautiful finials her father had made. This was the house where she was born. This was where her mother and brother still lived. "I grew up on the slopes of Mount Kori, a few miles from the village of Heria. My home, my mother's house, is perched on an outcrop of volcanic rock and looks out over the Eryos Ocean. My parents raised two children: my brother and myself. We could…"

"What is his name, your brother?" Torrin broke in.

Rowan turned in her saddle. "Andin. He is younger than I and a great mischief-maker." She glanced meaningfully at Nathel, who grinned back without remorse.

"Are yer parents still liv'n?" asked Borlin.

"My mother yet lives. My father died when I was fourteen during a pirate raid on Heria." Rowan took a steadying breath as the familiar mix of guilt and pain washed over her.

"Pirates? I thought ye Myrians were legendary for yer fight'n skills. Why would yer island be target fer pirates?"

Rowan had only been fourteen but she had fought beside her father and mother, a child's drilling sword in her hand. "It is not unlike a master swordsman being challenged by those who want his title. Myris Dar is a lush island and there is great wealth in its land and people. For that reason alone, many a fool has been incited to make an attempt at conquest. It is partly why Myrians have shunned the outside world and fallen out of memory.

"There was a time though, in the distant past, when my people were like sheep at slaughter. Myris Dar was ripe for picking – anyone with strength could land on the island and take what was there. The ancient Myrians would not raise a finger to defend their property or themselves."

"Are you sure we are talking about the same place you come from?" asked Nathel sceptically. "You don't strike me as someone who will stand down when threatened, what with all the throwing people around and such."

Borlin threw Nathel a glare. "Hold yer tongue lad, an' let the lass finish."

"We have always been a proud people," continued Rowan, "but pride can lead to stubbornness, stubbornness to blind and thoughtless adherence to ideas that serve only to shackle us to our own demise. The beliefs of the ancient Myrians decreed that none should harm another. My ancestors were pacifists. Their faith held that harming another, even in self-defence, was a terrible wrong. They held strictly to that belief for centuries but as a result, they condemned themselves and worse, their children, to becoming victims of slavery and abuse.

"They endured one conqueror after another. It is a wonder that we ever survived as a people. Then one day, long ago, a Myrian decided to fight back. A young woman, named Yinnis, no longer able to bear the rape and pillage of our land, decided to take the fate of my people into her own hands.

"Yinnis's mother was not Myrian by birth but came from the mainland to the west. No one knows for sure what her name was or her exact origins. It is known only that she had sailed to Myris Dar on one of the few friendly trading ships and eventually married a Myrian and had two daughters. This woman, Yinnis's mother, is noted in Myrian history because she was a warrior and carried a beautiful but deadly sword.

"She was secretive and kept much to herself but when her daughters were old enough, she began to teach them her skills as a warrior. Her husband, Yinnis's father, was a smith, a kind and generous man. He loved his foreign wife and her fierce warrior spirit. He knew her to be true and generous of heart and mind, but he could not reconcile her willingness to use deadly force when necessary. And so he had to make a choice because to live thus divided was breaking his heart. He chose his wife and family over his long held Myrian beliefs.

"He took to his smithy and forged swords for himself and his daughters. The family's Myrian friends and neighbours disapproved and they were shunned by the folk of the Island. Despite that disapproval, Yinnis lived happily with her family for a time. She learned fighting skills and the ways of her mother's people – to respect others and expect like in return but to protect one's self and the innocent from those that mean to harm.

"Then one day the port where they lived was attacked by raiders – cruel men who came by ship, intent on conquest. The local people offered no resistance and were contemptuously herded into slave lines. Those who were too old or young were summarily executed.

"Yinnis and her family were the only ones to fight back. At first they commanded the element of surprise and were able to free the captives and kill many of the raiders. But they were only four against many and they were quickly overwhelmed. Standing together back to back they fought valiantly until one by one they were killed. All save Yinnis, who took her mother's sword from her dying hands and somehow carved her way to freedom. Her skill with a sword was such that she beat all odds and fled to the hills with her life. She carried with her the weight and grief of her lost family.

"Little is known of Yinnis during the time that followed, but it is told that she moved inland ahead of the raiders, gathering with her those who would stand and fight for their freedom and convincing those who would not to flee. She left behind traps for the greedy men to fall into as they plundered and she used the island's rugged terrain to her advantage.

"After centuries of belief in a way of life that could only be fully realized in a peaceful environment, Myrians began to listen to what Yinnis had to say. She urged Myrians to create and defend their own peace so that the way of life they so value would no longer be threatened. With her mother's sword in hand, she set out to lead my people and to take our land back from our enemies. The history of Myris Dar was changed as she and others vowed never to let their peace go undefended again.

"The defence of Myris Dar and all Myrians has become the cornerstone of our culture, but the legacy of the ancient Myrians still flourishes within the hearts of my people. Despite our martial skills and focus, the culture of Myris Dar is rich in all things beautiful and fair. Respect for life and individuality is paramount."

Rowan glanced over at Borlin and to her surprise unshed tears were standing in the Stoneman's eyes.

"That be a worthy tale. If all people held those values, Eryos would indeed be a beautiful place," he said softly.

"My father's father speaks of Myris Dar as one of the fairest places in all of Eryos," Arynilas said. "He believes the Myrian arts, crafts, their love of the individual and all things living make them brothers and sisters to Tynithians."

"What is the island itself like?" asked Nathel, moving alongside her. "It must be warm that far south."

"The summers are hot and dry and the winters are mild with soft rains and gentle winds. The island is home to many sleeping giants."

"Giants?" said Borlin in disbelief.

Rowan grinned. "We think of them as such. Volcanoes – there are many but the four largest ones are known to Myrians as giants. They rumble in their sleep, shaking the slopes of their shoulders and the people who live on them. They belch out steam and heat once every hundred years or so and once in a long while they will leak forth red-hot tears. The coastline of the island is rugged and irregular and the northeast side, which doesn't face the hottest gaze of the sun, is lush with dense forests and vegetation."

"It sounds like a beautiful place," said Dalemar, riding on Rowan's other side. "I would love to visit the island one day."

"You would all be welcome in my home," said Rowan sincerely.

"And what of Yinnis? What ever happened to her?" asked Torrin from behind. Rowan turned but his eyes were on the horizon.

"Yinnis lived through the revolt and was a key figure helping to lead my people through many other battles for Myrian freedom. Eventually she founded the first High Council to see that what she had fought for was strengthened within the foundations of Myrian culture. She married and had children. When she was finished using her sword – her mother's sword – she passed it into the hands of her eldest daughter, who in turn carried it in defence of Myris Dar."

The dark clouds looming on the horizon finally shut out the light, leaving the vast plain in greyness. When the rain began to fall, it blasted into them in wind-whipped torrents and everyone was soaked to the skin within minutes.

Nathan spoke. "We are nearing the village of Balor."

Pushing her sopping hood back, Rowan watched Torrin rein in alongside his brother. He shook the water from his head, rubbed a hand across his eyes, and stared at his brother. Steam rose from the horses, who waited patiently, heads down in the driving rain. "The weather will clear soon," he said.

Nathel nodded. "There is another village four days beyond. Our supplies will hold till then, right?" He turned to Borlin.

The Stoneman spoke briskly from Rowan's right. "Aye, we can manage."

Torrin turned his horse away from them but his gaze met Rowan's for an instant. She saw naked torment in his eyes.

Torrin put his heels to his mount and the horse surged forward through the sopping grass.

Rowan looked over at Hathunor. The big Saa Raken's stiff crest was laid flat by the water and his red eyes darted warily between Torrin and the others. Peering into the gusting rain, Rowan studied the faces of her companions. She found them all closed, guarded.

Pulling her soaked hood back up, she set Roanus after the others.

Torrin turned in his saddle, looking away from the endless plain ahead and back at his companions. Rowan had pulled her horse up and was dismounting. The others stopped with her as she bent over to examine Roanus's left front hoof.

Torrin turned Black and trotted back. "What is it?" he asked.

Rowan released the hoof and straightened, pushing wet strands of hair out of her eyes. "He has thrown a shoe. I don't know how long ago." She looked back the way they had come through the drenched landscape.

Torrin turned to Borlin, hoping. "Do you have any iron left?"

Borlin eyed the big grey stallion's large hooves and shook his head. "Nay, nothin' as to fit 'is great feet."

Torrin turned a scowl toward the east. He couldn't see it but he could feel it like a pull on his soul: Balor. There were no farmsteads on this side of the town; the land was reserved for grazing livestock. Torrin had led the companions this way for just that reason. As a result though, there wouldn't be any farmers willing to re-shoe the horse. He cursed under his breath. For an instant he was tempted to push on, but knew it was foolhardy to risk laming the horse. Torrin's own horse needed new shoes badly as well. The iron had worn down to wafer thin strips.

His companions were watching him expectantly. Rowan's expression was puzzled. Nathel was masking his concern well, but Torrin could see the tension in his face.

"We head for Balor then," Torrin said grimly.

Rowan gave her grey horse a pat on the neck before remounting.

Torrin reined Black around and spurred towards the east. The cold grey clouds were a perfect reflection of his mood. It seemed he could not avoid Balor's ghosts after all.

Hathunor was still striding along beside them and Torrin cursed again, angry with himself for the oversight. The huge Raken couldn't come into town with them. He'd scare the wits out of the townsfolk and likely get the rest of them run out of the place.

Torrin reined Black in and turned to Hathunor. "I am sorry, Hathunor, but you cannot come with us into town. You must circle around and wait until we leave tomorrow morning. You can meet us on the other side of the town. If you come with us, you will frighten the people and it will go badly for all of us."

Hathunor nodded sadly. "Hathunor understand."

Rowan reached out and patted the Saa Raken on the arm in farewell and they continued onward, leaving their giant friend to head north.

Small herding sheds dotted the plain. As the town came into view on the horizon, Torrin was surprised to see a large wall surrounding the huddle of buildings that was Balor. Smoke rose from the mud brick chimneys, darker smudges against the grey sky.

Torrin studied the wall as they approached the gate at the southern edge of town. It was well constructed and thick, made from the same brick as the houses and buildings within. It only lacked the customary white wash that brightened the rest of Balor.

The rain stopped as they reached the gate. It was well guarded by a small barrack of Klyssen soldiers. Another surprise. The man in the gatehouse stepped out in front of them and Torrin counted four more soldiers along the wall with bows raised and arrows nocked.

"State your business in Balor." The guard's missing front teeth gave his speech an odd lisp.

"We are just passing through, friend. Looking for a warm bed, a hot meal and a farrier for the horses," replied Torrin.

The guard's pale grey eyes passed slowly over the companions. He looked suspiciously at Arynilas, and the Tynithian nodded politely in return. Torrin watched as the guard eyed Rowan. Amusement crept onto his unshaven face when he saw the pommel of her sword. He noticed Torrin watching and his expression soured. He spat into the mud. "Swords are not to be drawn within the walls. Any trouble and you'll find yourselves hung from the gates."

"Understood," Torrin replied.

The guard grunted, stepping aside, and the companions proceeded under the gate.

Rowan looked around curiously as the companions passed into Balor. The main street had been churned to muck by horses. Rowan studied the Klyssen guards standing on the platforms to either side of the gate. They had set down their bows and were already turning to survey the surrounding plain. Their red plumed helmets and silver breastplates glinted even in the dull overcast light. Each had a large round shield slung over his back with a stylized head of a horse emblazoned in the center.

The town was small, little more than a village with a single inn, a large stable and a few small shops along a single main road. Ten or twelve houses clustered haphazardly around the main street. Some of the brick buildings looked close to collapse, tilting ominously over the street. Despite its ailing bones, the town had been painted a creamy white that lent it an air of freshness and pride.

When they arrived at the stable, they found the main corral filled with large, well-bred horses.

"A contingent of Klyssen cavalry came through 'is afternoon," stated the stableman as he ushered them towards empty stalls at the back of the barn. "You'll have to put 'em two to a stall." They thanked the man and passed him some coins for the care of their horses and the storage of their goods.

"Is there a blacksmith available?" asked Torrin.

The stableman nodded and pushed his straggly hair out of his eyes. "Aye, smith is workin' on the cavalry mounts. Oi, Reagon!" he shouted towards a side door.

Into the barn walked a large man with enormous arms and shoulders, silver hair and a short-cropped beard. He looked over their horses, whistling softly when he saw the state of their shoes. "Put a few leagues on these, have you?" Inspection finished, he smiled, his meaty hands brushing the dust from his leather apron. "I should be able to have them done for you by morning. You're staying at the inn?"

Torrin nodded. "If there is any room."

The blacksmith glanced at Torrin's sword. "Might you need a whetting on that blade, as well?"

Rowan unbuckled the cinch strap of Roanus's saddle and let it drop under his belly. She looked over her horse's back and saw Torrin glance around at the rest of his companions, who were busy unsaddling the horses. "My thanks, smith," he said quietly, "but the weapons are sharp enough."

The man nodded pleasantly and left to go back to his work. The stableman lingered though, pretending to be busy while he cast intent looks at Torrin.

Before they left to cross the muddy road to the inn, the stableman finally spoke to Torrin. "Excuse me, Sir, but have I seen ye before? Yer face looks very familiar."

Beside her, Torrin went stone still. With an utterly blank expression he replied to the stableman. "I believe you must be mistaken."

Rowan studied the stableman briefly before turning to follow the others out of the barn. He had the look of a man who knew he had just been lied to and didn't understand why.

Torrin collected coins from them all and dropped them into a pouch which he tucked through his belt. Borlin, delighted to discover they had arrived in Balor on a market day, scribbled instructions for supplies on a scrap of parchment for Torrin, Nathel and Rowan. Then he went off in search of news, ostensibly in the inn's common room, with Dalemar and Arynilas in tow. Torrin shook his head – the last he saw of him, Borlin was already reaching into his vest pocket for his pipe weed.

People from the sparse surrounding settlements had arrived early to sell their wares. The small square in the center of town was bustling with modest activity. Many sellers were still there, though it was late afternoon.

Torrin, Nathel and Rowan threaded their way through the market stalls, avoiding the largest puddles. Water dripped from the covered awnings and the hawker's voices, hoarse from yelling all day, called to them eagerly. The saddlebags over Nathel's shoulder began to bulge with purchases. They were slowly working their way through Borlin's list: salt, thread, dried meat and beans, flour and other dry goods as well as leather for repairing gear.

Torrin and his brother stopped at the words of a seller, espousing the delights of his confectionery wares. Torrin had been listening to Nathel's growling stomach for a while and purchased three. When he looked up Rowan was no longer with them. He spotted her twenty paces ahead.

A man stood blocking her path, a wide smirk on his face as he spoke to her. She ignored him, turning her head to follow a second man, who stepped behind her. A third man got up from his seat on a barrel. All three were laughing at her.

Torrin's world contracted to that small muddy section of street. Anger and dread rose in his chest so quickly that it stopped his breath. Before he knew what he was doing, his sword was ringing free of its scabbard. A hoarse shout choked his throat. His vision wavered and the world spun around him. A keening scream seared through his memory.

"Tor!"

Torrin pushed away the grip on his shoulder, twisting away from the restraint. He had to get there before they could hurt her.

"Torrin!" the voice punched through his sickly spinning world. An arm wrapped around his chest to halt his forward momentum. Torrin snarled with rage and spun to confront the men holding him down.

"Tor, it's me, Nathel! For Erys sake, brother, calm yourself."

Torrin blinked in confusion. He was standing facing Nathel with his sword raised. Nathel's face was stark white and he reached up to grasp Torrin by the shoulders. "Seven years, Tor," he whispered, looking Torrin hard in the eyes. "It was seven years ago."

Torrin's sword felt too heavy in his hand. He let the tip drop to the mud. He brought a shaking hand to his forehead and squeezed his eyes shut. If Nathel hadn't been there, Torrin would have killed those men. He knew it for certain.

Torrin turned quickly to look back at Rowan. She stood very still as the three men around her continued to laugh and make jokes. Torrin turned and began to stride toward her. Nathel tried to grab his arm again but Torrin shrugged him off roughly.

"I'm fine, Nathel." Torrin slammed his sword back down into its scabbard.

As he drew closer to Rowan and the three men, he caught a glimpse of her face in profile. He was surprised to see disappointed resignation rather than fear.

As the man from the barrel reached out to snatch at Rowan's arm, the man behind her reached for her sword pommel, full of swagger, intent on taking it from her.

Neither man was able to touch her. Her hands and feet moved so quickly that Torrin wasn't sure what he had seen. The brothers stopped in amazement.

The two men who had tried to touch Rowan were suddenly down on the muddy ground before the smile had left the first man's face. He looked down at his companions in dismay — one hunched over, hands covering his mouth, trying vainly to stem the flow of blood from his nose; the other on his side, groaning. The remaining man cursed loudly and pulled a carving knife from his belt. He lunged at Rowan, his face contorted in anger.

She stepped smoothly out of the blade's range and caught the man's wrist as the weapon swept past her. She wrenched his thumb and wrist backward and he dropped suddenly to his knees to keep the bones of his arm from breaking. His cry of pain stilled the surrounding buyers and sellers who turned to gawk.

Rowan stripped the knife from his nerveless fingers and knocked him in the side of the head with the butt. He crumpled to the mud next to his friends. Rowan threw the knife down between her attackers, where it buried to the hilt in the mud.

A snicker escaped Nathel as he walked up and bent over to look at the three injured men in exaggerated sympathy. “Come, come Sweetling,” he said to Rowan, “Let’s not make any widows today. You know how sad you left those poor women in the last town. Surely these fine gentlemen don’t deserve such harsh punishment for a little lack of manners?”

Rowan turned and walked away. The people nearby who had witnessed the incident watched her with wide eyes but Torrin stood rooted to the spot where he had watched it all unfold. Ignoring Nathel’s banter, he focused on slowing his breathing. He clenched his fists by his side to quell the shaking of his hands. It was the second time he’d lost control and this time he hadn’t even been fighting for his life in battle. There was no excuse – she had not even been in need of help.

Nathel followed Rowan but only after he had nudged the bleeding man with the tip of his toe. “You should really get that looked at, friend. Perhaps next time you will show a little more respect. A lady is still a lady, even if she can knock your lights out.”

Rowan glanced back at Nathel’s antics to see Torrin turn his back suddenly and stalk away from them. She took a step to follow but Nathel reached her and looped his arm through hers.

“Let’s get that list of Borlin’s finished so we can go enjoy a cup. Can’t let that scoundrel have all the fun while we are out here slaving away for the greater good.”

“Where is Torrin going?” asked Rowan.

Nathel forced a grin. “I think your little demonstration reminded him to see to the weapons. Are you going to put on that show in every village we pass through? Because I will sell tickets for the next one.”

Rowan smiled at his joke but she felt uneasy. Something was very strange here.

The Inn

The rain poured down from beyond the stable doors. Rowan patted Roanus on the nose and threw her damp saddlebags over her shoulder. The others were waiting in the lantern light beside the doors. All except Torrin.

Rowan swung the stall door closed behind her and deposited her bags on the pile of their gear, which now bulged with new supplies. She was looking forward to being dry for a change, and a warm bed and a hot meal would be most welcome.

The short run across the puddle-filled street saw them almost soaked through again. The inn's bright interior spilled out onto the dark street and the noise from inside increased as they approached. It had been a long time since Rowan had been in such a place, surrounded by people and sound. There was music and cheer, as though the dire events of the world could not find this place.

Klyssen soldiers, like the ones at the gate, occupied most of the tables. Local villagers were also there catching up on any news the soldiers had brought.

A plump little man with a sparkling white apron came bustling over to them. He was sweating freely and wiping his hands. The little host ushered them over to a table in the corner, beside a roaring fireplace.

"We have a little of the venison stew left and my wife has made some lovely mincemeat pies." He rolled his eyes at the busy room, ringing pudgy hands. "It never gets this busy so we don't stock enough for so many."

Dalemar made a soothing gesture. "We'll have whatever you are offering, master innkeeper."

"Of course, of course. I will bring some ale. Would you perhaps care for something a little sweeter, my lady?" His round eyes were on the pommel of Rowan's sword.

"Ale will be fine, thank you," replied Rowan. The little man turned on his heel to trot away.

Once Rowan was settled comfortably, she looked over the folk at the other tables. Her gaze stopped on a man seated alone in the darkest corner. His back was to them and she could barely see him. She realized with a start that she was looking at Torrin. She began to get up to let him know they were there, but felt a restraining hand on her arm and looked down to find Nathel holding on to her.

He shook his head, his expression serious. "He knows we're here. He'll come when he's ready."

Rowan slid back down in her chair and looked again at Torrin.

The rain poured down outside, lightening flashed and thunder shook the walls. It was the most intense storm Rowan had yet seen in the lands of Eryos. She was thankful to be sitting with her companions in the warm common room of the inn. Nathel recounted the afternoon's incident to the others, much to Borlin's delight.

The Stoneman pounded a wide fist on the wooden table, rattling the cups, "Good fer ye, Lass! Give the bastards hell." He looked like a proud father, amber eyes twinkling and his wide mouth stretched in a grin.

Rowan laughed warmly at Borlin and resisted the urge to reach across the table to give his short beard a tug.

"You're my hero," Nathel teased her.

Rowan snorted in disgust, kicking him under the table.

"Ow! What?" Nathel reached down to rub his shin.

A shadow covered the table. Rowan looked up to see Torrin pulling out a chair to sit down with them. She watched his face as he set his tankard down on the table. He and Nathel exchanged a cryptic glance but the conversation continued as though Torrin had been sitting among them all evening.

"We are being watched," Arynilas said. He had not missed a single detail of the noisy room.

Torrin nodded. "Klyssen officers. I've been watching them watch you for a while."

"How soon do you reckon it will take them to come over and satisfy their curiosity?" Nathel asked.

"I give them about five more minutes, especially now that I've sat down," Torrin said.

Borlin shook his head, his beard bristling as a grin crossed his face. "A silver piece says ten minutes."

"Three," said Dalemar, "and only the young one will come, *and* he will speak to Rowan first."

Rowan laughed quietly as Nathel winked at her.

It took the younger of the two exactly three minutes to get up and saunter over to their table.

"Lieutenant Lorn," he introduced himself to Rowan.

"Nice to meet you, my name is Rowan," she suppressed a grin as coins were passed covertly to Dalemar.

Lieutenant Lorn wore an oiled moustache and had close-cropped hair. He was well polished and trim. Rowan suspected he had only worn his officer's uniform for a short while.

"And where might you be from?" he asked, pulling up a chair next to her.

"Myris Dar." Ignoring his blank look at the mention of her distant island home, she introduced him to her friends.

"My Lady," he intoned with drama, "surely a creature such as yourself should be traveling with an honour guard." His eyes flickered to her sword pommel, but he continued blithely as though there was nothing out of the ordinary. "It is no longer as safe as it once was, you know. Perhaps I can arrange for you a contingent of the Klyssen cavalry to accompany you to where you are traveling? Just let me know your destination and I will look after everything else." He kept her gaze, refusing to look at her companions.

"My thanks to you for your concern. I do not require an escort, though I am sure you would be of great service," said Rowan.

The officer smiled. "My name is widely known in these parts. I have been through many battles and I am somewhat of folk hero. I would be most happy to tell you of some of the more exciting tales of my military exploits."

The innkeeper arrived with their meals and many apologies for the tardiness of the service, and Torrin took advantage of the interruption to ask the young officer what news there was of King Cerebus and the war in Pellar.

Lorn leaned back and waved a hand in dismissal. "Oh they should be making out well enough by now I would imagine, what with the Klyssen cavalry we sent as reinforcements."

Torrin leaned forward, his expression intense. "How many?"

"Fifteen hundred, the most ever sent out to a foreign war."

Torrin shared a look with Nathel and the others and he shook his head imperceptibly. There was no way to know if the fifteen hundred would make a difference in the fight against the Raken.

"Where are you headed, Lieutenant?" asked Nathel.

"We are heading out on border patrol, making sure none of these Raken things are coming across from Pellar."

"Oh aye? Have ye met with any of 'em yet?" asked Borlin.

"Not as yet, but if we do, it will be a sad day for them," the lieutenant said flatly.

"You would be wise not to underestimate them," Torrin said quietly.

Lieutenant Lorn snorted in amusement. "Not even a marauding Raken hoard can diminish the might of Klyssen cavalry. The King of Klyssen sent the cavalry, mounted I might add on Horse Clan stock, to Pellar as a friendly favour to a neighbour in need. We are vigilant and will not be caught unaware by some foreign invader."

"Your border patrols, have they increased?" asked Dalemar.

"Yes, but it is only a precaution."

"Have you ever seen the Raken your comrades have gone to fight?" Rowan regretted the question as soon as she uttered it.

It launched the young lieutenant on a diatribe of the virtues of Klyssen cavalry. "There is nothing to match the awe and fear created by mounted horsemen thundering down on an opponent," he stated dryly.

She winced and shrugged in apology to her companions for having prolonged the pain. Nathel grinned wickedly at her and she buried herself in her plate of food. It was a while before she realized that Lieutenant Lorn had ceased speaking and was looking at them all expectantly; like her, the rest had tuned out his droning voice and were blinking at him as if he had only just appeared.

"I asked why four humans, one of them a Stoneman, and two Tynithians, travel together?" He had mistaken Dalemar for a Tynithian and the Rith stared in astonishment at such an apparent error.

Nathel leaned back in his chair and waved a hand dismissively. "Oh, we travel together because there is nothing that can match the awe and fear created by a thundering Stoneman and his friends."

Borlin's great guffaws resounded suddenly in the noisy room and he nearly fell off his chair. Heads turned to see what the ruckus was. Dalemar chuckled when Borlin pounded Nathel on the back so hard he spilled his ale. Even Arynilas and Torrin wore grins.

Rowan almost felt sorry for the lieutenant, but then she noticed the tiniest smile on his face. It disappeared as quickly as it came. "You must forgive my companions," she said smoothly. "They have been on the road for longer than is wise for one's sanity. Perhaps it would be best to withdraw before our thundering Stoneman decides that he needs to make a demonstration."

Borlin's renewed cackles emphasized her suggestion. Lieutenant Lorn nodded sagely and withdrew from the table, casting a nervous glance back at the Stoneman. Rowan turned back to see tears streaming down Borlin's face into his red beard. She met Torrin's gaze, and shook her head.

"It sounds as though Klyssen is mobilizing," said Nathel as the laughter died away.

Borlin nodded, casting a sober glance across the room to where the lieutenant had resumed his own seat next to the other officer. "I pity the poor fool. 'E as no idea what 'ees up against."

"The Raken don't seem to be coming out of Pellar in large numbers yet then," said Dalemar. "That's something at least. Perhaps the ones we saw before we met Rowan were advanced scouting parties of some kind."

"Scouting parties do not murder entire towns," said Arynilas grimly.

Nathel nodded. "More likely they were intent on spreading fear. Invading a country is not hard when the people are terrified of you."

Dalemar frowned. "Perhaps they were all sent to look for Rowan. We assumed until now that whoever controls the Raken knew where Rowan's company was landing. What if they didn't know for sure and had to send enough Raken out to all the likely places the Myrians would arrive. The Raken might then have had the dual purpose of spreading fear while they searched for Rowan."

They all turned to look at her and Rowan frowned, feeling a rising dread at the cunning behind the Raken tracking her. Would there have been Raken waiting for her and her Myrian company if they had come ashore somewhere else? And what of the Seers of Danum and their insistence that Rowan and her party sail to Dendor and travel overland? Rowan shook her head. There were too many questions, too many unknowns and few answers.

Nathel took a sip of ale. "Whoever is controlling the Raken will not be content with Pellar alone. Why conquer only one kingdom, when you can have them all?"

Torrin nodded. "One at a time. Secure your position then move on without having to worry about your back. It's how I would do it. Take the kingdom that is the biggest threat first. Once Pellar has fallen, it will be easy to head south. With the Erys Ocean at their back, it will be almost impossible to stem the tide," he said grimly.

The silence stretched around the table until the rotund little innkeeper came over to clear their plates. Torrin asked him if there were rooms available.

"Oh forgive me sir but all have been rented by the soldiers." He looked as though he might cry at the thought of an unhappy customer.

"How about the hay loft above the barn?" Torrin asked.

The innkeeper brightened at the proposed solution. "Indeed, you would be comfortable there, and no charge. Breakfast is served at sunrise."

As Torrin paid for their meal, he asked the innkeeper what news he had heard of the war in Pellar.

The little man drew in his breath and rocked back and forth from one foot to the other. "Not good sir, not good. The City of Pellaris is under siege and King Cerebus and his advisors are trapped within."

Rowan closed her eyes briefly, her heart sinking. How was she to get her message through into a city under siege?

"When did the siege begin?" Torrin asked in a tight voice as his gaze traveled around the table and stopped at Rowan.

"Oh I can't rightly say, I've been hearing bits and pieces of rumour for several days now."

"Have you seen any Raken around here? Any attacks?"

The innkeeper looked positively scandalized. "Goodness no, Thank Erys. I've never even seen a Raken, and frankly," his voice sank to a whisper, "I think their description is much exaggerated."

Torrin thanked the man and he trundled off to see to other customers.

"At least Pellaris is well suited to a siege," said Nathel.

Torrin nodded. "Nathel is right, they could hold out for over a month, longer if the food stores are good." He noticed Rowan's puzzled look and explained. "The city is perched on a promontory over-looking the sea. An army can only attack from two sides. It is nigh impenetrable provided that it is well defended."

Rowan shook her head. "That's not the point. If Pellaris is under siege it means that we have no way to get into the city. No way of delivering the message."

Borlin looked at Dalemar. "Perhaps there is a way to get through the Raken with out being detected."

The Rith nodded. "I can think of several things that might work, but it would be risky."

"There is another possibility," offered Torrin quietly. "But this is not the place to speak of it." He glanced meaningfully at Nathel whose pale blue eyes reflected an immediate understanding. Both Torrin and Nathel turned together to look at Rowan. "Rest assured," said Torrin, "the message will be delivered."

The five companions all nodded. Rowan felt a deep affection wash over her. She sighed in relief and curled her fingers around the warm cup of mulled wine, which the innkeeper had brought her along with her ale. Rowan was happy he brought her a more ladylike beverage, for she was greatly enjoying its warm, heady sweetness.

Trying not to think of the uncertainty ahead, she focused instead on the good things at hand. The room was cheerful, with people talking and laughing as they ate and drank. She had received the usual stares and disapproving glances, but they had not affected her this time. The entire group she sat with was odd; what was one warrior woman compared with a Rith, a Tynithian, two huge northern men and a Stoneman?

She smiled to herself and took a sip of wine. As she lowered the cup, she noticed an old woman sitting on a rickety chair next to the big ale barrels. Tiny and bird-like with bright blue eyes, she watched Torrin intently. Rowan glanced across the table at Torrin. He was in conversation with the others and had not noticed the scrutiny.

Rowan looked back at the old woman, who had risen to her feet and was making her way slowly through the tables with the aid of a wooden walking stick. She was thin, dressed in homespun wool. Her long grey hair was pulled back from her face and tied in a bun. Her eyes never left Torrin as she moved toward them.

Rowan looked quickly back at Torrin. He had seen the old woman now and was watching her approach with the wariness of a trapped animal. A flash of pain washed over his features.

Rowan looked up as the old woman moved past her. She placed a thin, speckled hand on Rowan's shoulder for support as she walked around the table to Torrin. He rose from his chair as she neared him. The old woman reached out with shaking fingers and took hold of Torrin's hand. Her pale, papery skin stood out against his sun-dark complexion. She tilted her small head back to speak to him and Torrin leaned down to listen.

Despite the noisy room, Rowan heard her words distinctly from across the table.

"Erys bless you," she said in a high voice. "I have prayed to the Sweet Goddess all these years for the chance to see you again, just once, so that I may thank you. She has seen fit to grant me that wish before I die." A smile crinkled the woman's lined face and tears leaked from her eyes. "My granddaughter lives. She has grown into a lovely young woman and has married a good man. She will have a child in the spring. She has not forgotten, but she has survived." The old woman released her grip on her walking stick and reached out to touch Torrin's chest. "The loss you suffered that day was balanced in part by the lives of those you saved. We have not forgotten you in our prayers. May the Goddess bless you and bring happiness to your life." She reached up to touch Torrin's face before turning to leave.

Torrin stood for a moment, his hand still extended to where the old woman had grasped it. He stepped forward and gently took her arm to help her from the inn.

Rowan's eyebrows lifted in wonder as Torrin led the tiny woman protectively from the noisy common room. When she turned back, tears were standing in Nathel's pale blue eyes and her questions stilled on her tongue. The rest of her friends were silent and grave.

Torrin returned with his calm restored. He met Rowan's gaze briefly but offered no explanation.

The next visitor to their table was the senior officer who had been watching them earlier with Lorn. Although similarly polished, his demeanour was confident rather than cocky.

"You must forgive my young lieutenant; he is rather inexperienced yet but he has the makings of a good officer. His rash enthusiasm is something I hope time will temper." He spoke in a deep voice and though he looked at all the companions, his words were for Torrin.

Torrin nodded to an empty chair, asking the man to join them. As the officer took a seat, Rowan leaned forward and said, "Do not underestimate your man, sir. He is not as inexperienced as he appears."

The officer looked at her in surprise and then a slow smile crept across his face. "My name is Ganor Welan." His eyes took in all their various weapons, lingering the longest on Rowan's sword. "Forgive me but your party is hard to miss among the simple folk of Klyssen."

"It is good to meet you Captain Welan," said Torrin. Rowan glanced at the horizontal stripes on the shoulders of Welan's uniform and made a mental note. "My name is Torrin, my companions and I are just passing through."

Welan nodded thoughtfully, his gaze traveling around the table. "On your way to Pellar? To answer a summons?"

"We will do what we can," Torrin said.

The captain turned to look pointedly at Rowan. "We? Surely not all of you? My lady, Pellar is not the best place to travel at the moment, even with an armed escort."

Rowan returned his gaze steadily. "I thank you for your concern, Captain, but believe me when I say, Pellar is our destination."

He glanced down to her hands, clasped loosely in front of her on the table – noted the sword calluses. He looked back up at her face, his grey eyes studying her with an eyebrow lifted. He nodded and turned to look back at Torrin. "Mercenaries are not often welcome in Klyssen, especially in this little town. Let us just say it has an unfortunate history when it comes to the subject."

Torrin scowled suddenly and Rowan was shocked to see the anger in his face after the calm indifference. Nathel's glance darted between Welan and his brother.

When Torrin spoke his voice was very low. "We are people of honour, Captain. Your implication is an insult to us all."

Their eyes locked across the table and the seconds passed. The Captain broke eye contact and leaned back in his chair. He pulled out a pipe, filled it and lit the bowl with the small oil lamp on the table. He took a puff and looked around at the companions. "The Raken beasts are beginning to come across the border from Pellar. Be on your guard as you head north. We have had a few reports from the scattered outposts, but the numbers are not solid."

Rowan scanned the common room of the inn. They might have had to fight these men, had Welan decided they were not welcome in his country.

"What do you hear of Pellaris and King Cerebus? Is the city truly under siege?" she asked.

Welan turned to look at her. "It is, my Lady. I have only just heard myself but I do know that the host of Raken before its gate is vast. If you go to offer aid to Cerebus, you will not likely get into the city."

Torrin leaned forward, "If the King of Klyssen were to send more cavalry to aid Pellar, how many could he spare?"

Welan shook his head. "Another fifteen hundred perhaps, but that is for King Daesis to decide should a call for aid be issued. I only go where I am sent, do what I must."

Torrin nodded. "Have you engaged any of the Raken yet?"

"No, though we have heard rumours. Most of my men tend not to believe such wild tales."

"And you?" asked Nathel.

"I do not discount anything I have not seen with my own eyes."

"If you have a choice, don't engage any more than your own number; even then it will be a hard fight," said Torrin quietly.

Welan's gaze sharpened. "You have fought them, then." He looked again around the table at the others. They nodded.

"More than we would have liked," said Nathel.

"They are fast and extremely large," warned Torrin. "Do not let them breach your guard. Cavalry units will fair better than infantry."

"They can hear over great distance," added Dalemar.

"And we suspect they can outrun horses over long distance," said Rowan.

Welan sat and carefully absorbed all the companions had to tell him about the nature of Raken. His pipe forgotten, his gray eyes watched each speaker intently and he asked a few pointed questions.

When they had finished, Welan placed his cold pipe in his coat pocket and rose from his chair. "It is late. We likely all have an early start in the morning. My men and I will be heading northwest to the border. I'd offer to escort your group but I imagine you'll be taking the most direct route to Pellar. I thank you for the information; you've given me much to think about. I will be sending a runner back to King Daesis with this new information. I think this Raken invasion is more serious than most people believe. I wish you luck and speed on your journey." He bowed courteously to Rowan and nodded to the rest of them before turning from their table and leaving them in thoughtful silence.

Hauntings from the Past

The sun beat down on the bone-dry street of the small town. A hot, dry wind swirled the dust. Torrin could hardly see through the tears in his eyes. He strained to look at Emma as she screamed incoherently; bent down in the dust over two small bodies – their daughters. The man standing above her was looking down at the fruit of his labour, methodically cleaning a bloody dagger.

Torrin wrenched and heaved against the rough ropes tying his wrists behind his back. Warm blood slid over his hands. A knee was planted heavily between his shoulders. More weight was on his legs. All his straining and fighting was in vain – he could barely move.

He looked at his little girls; their small, sweet faces were peacefully asleep. He could almost convince himself of it except for the red stains spreading through their dresses where the dagger had plunged into their small chests. The man above them continued to clean that dagger, watching with satisfaction as Torrin struggled.

"Erys no! Please, not my little ones." Torrin choked on the dust.

The man who had killed them tucked his dagger into his belt, listening coldly to Torrin's sobs. He walked slowly around Torrin's keening wife and crouched down in front of a broadsword. Torrin's sword.

"Hold his head up." The man rasped to his four companions holding Torrin down. "I want him to see this." A slow snarl spread on the man's dirty face, he was missing one of his front teeth. He reached forward and grasped the hilt of Torrin's sword, dragging it toward him through the dirt, his gaze fixed on Torrin. When the blade was closer he hefted it, pretending an interest in the weapon's weight and balance. Encouragement and laughter drifted from the surrounding audience. Murderers and thieves they were to the last.

Torrin struggled, a terrible rage engulfed him and his vision bled red with it. The remaining bandits were spread out in the empty street, watching their leader exact his revenge for the seven men Torrin had killed. Torrin envisioned these monsters dead, just like their murdering companions he'd already killed. As surely as they stood over him and his family now, they would be dead, all of them by his hands. He would see to it. He clung to that knowledge and it fed him.

A hand grabbed his hair, wrenching his head back. Torrin strained with all his might, felt the sudden burning of a vein bursting in his left eye. The leader was behind Emma now. She was oblivious to the danger. Her long auburn hair was undone, hanging like a curtain around her face. Nothing existed for her but her daughters.

"Please!" Torrin begged, his voice hoarse from the sharp angle of his head. "Please don't do this! Take my life! I give it to you freely! Please don't kill her. Emma!"

The man raised Torrin's sword, a snarl on his face. "You killed my brother, you bastard, and I will take your family for it!"

The blade flashed in the bright sun. Emma's keening was ended abruptly, and Torrin began to scream.

He woke suddenly in the dark, sweat-drenched and breathing in ragged gasps, his heart pounded in his chest. He reached with shaking fingers, fumbled in the dark for his water skin and took a long drink. It did nothing to quench the dryness in his throat.

It had been a long time since he'd had the dream and it left his chest tight and his body spent. He glanced around the dark loft where they were sleeping. The forms of his friends were nestled comfortably in the hay. Borlin, as always, was snoring softly. Torrin's screams must have been only in his dream. Water plunked softly into the hay as it dripped from cracks in the barn roof but it was nothing to the sound of rain hammering on the roof boards above.

"Are you well, Tor?" asked his brother's voice behind him.

Torrin turned and saw Nathel sitting on a bale of hay near the opening of the loft, wet blackness beyond. It was still some time until dawn. Nathel was standing second to last watch.

Torrin got up slowly and moved quietly to where his brother was sitting. He found an old bucket, set it upside down and took a seat. "Just a dream."

Nathel looked at him closely. "Ghosts?"

Torrin sighed. “I had hoped these people wouldn’t recognize me. It’s been seven years.” The last vestige of the dream finally and thankfully began to fade.

“That day was not something anyone could soon forget, Tor. You underestimate the impact you had on these people. It was a terrible thing but they would have lost everything if it weren’t for you. People place the hope of the future in their children. Those young village girls you saved kept a nightmare from becoming an utter tragedy.” Nathel scratched his face and looked tentatively at Torrin. “You also killed the men who committed the crimes. You exacted justice for the people of Balor, and for Emma and your daughters.”

Torrin sighed again and leaned back against the corner of the opening, his head turned to look down on the dark street below. The old woman at the inn had wished him happiness but Torrin had long since accepted the joylessness of his life. In a way he welcomed it – it was recompense for his guilt.

Returning to Balor was harder than he thought possible. Torrin took another deep breath to steady his swirling emotions, surprised at finding himself willing to talk about it. “It didn’t ease the pain.”

“I don’t think it was meant to, brother.”

Torrin glanced at Nathel’s face in the dimness. His brother was the only one who understood the devastation that day caused.

Torrin could still see the surprise on the faces of the men who had killed his family. It had taken him five long days to track them down once he had recovered enough from the savage beating they had given him; leaving him for dead in the dusty street.

Those terrible days had passed in a haze of grief and pain. He had attacked the bandits in their camp while they slept, with the spoils of their raid on Balor strewn about them. His sword wreaking vengeance, Torrin had completely surrendered to his wrath. The faces of Emma and his daughters Deana and Arial had driven him like a lash.

The bandits had kidnapped six young women and girls from the village for their amusement. In the bloody aftermath Torrin had heard their sobs and followed the sound to find them huddled together in a filthy tent. It had taken him half an hour to coax the terrified victims out and convince them he would not harm them.

He barely remembered getting the girls back to their homes and worried families in Balor. After that, Torrin had wandered in a fog of madness, unable and unwilling to deal with the pain and guilt of his family's deaths. When Nathel had finally found him months later, living almost like a wild animal, Torrin had hardly recognized his brother. Nathel had brought him back from his self-imposed exile, healing his body and mind enough for Torrin to function again.

Torrin had flatly refused to return with Nathel to Pellaris though, and his brother, unwilling to let Torrin disappear again, had stayed with him.

Torrin looked down the dark street through the rain to the bulk of the inn, unchanged from that day long ago. "I never thanked you for telling Emma's parents for me."

Nathel shrugged, "You would have done it if you'd been able."

The silence stretched between them for a while as they scanned the night outside. At length Torrin broke the silence. "Time for my watch. You should get some sleep."

Nathel nodded and rose from his seat. Before he left to find his blankets he placed a hand on Torrin's shoulder, squeezing. "It will not haunt you forever, Tor. One day you will move past it."

Torrin glanced up at his brother. He wished he had Nathel's faith. He turned away to watch the street outside with the company of ghosts to occupy him.

An Unexpected Friend

The morning dawned clear. The sun shone brightly across the saturated landscape, but the ever-present wind blew cold from the north. Torrin was pleased to discover the blacksmith true to his word and their horses all soundly re-shod. They paid the man for his work and made ready to leave.

As they saddled their mounts, the smith walked over to Rowan, who was tying her saddlebags onto her saddle. Roanus stood quietly while she worked, resting a rear leg and swishing his tail. Rowan turned as the blacksmith tentatively caught her attention.

Torrin pulled up on his cinch strap and watched over his horse's back.

"Excuse me, Miss," said the smith. "I couldn't help noticing that the sword you carry looks to be of the finest craftsmanship. I was wondering if I might be permitted to see it?"

Rowan's guarded expression softened and she smiled at the silver haired man. She reached up behind her shoulder, grasped the pommel of her humming sword and pulled it free of the scabbard, holding it out, hilt first.

The smith's face lit up in delight as he held the slim sword. He gently traced the length of the blade with his fingers, and he peered closely at the scrolling words inscribed into the metal. He rested the sword horizontally, just under the guard, nodding to himself at its perfect balance. Tipping the hilt up, he looked carefully down the length of the sword, watching the light play across the blade's folded surface.

The blacksmith sighed with pleasure and nodded respectfully to Rowan as he handed it back. "I thank you, Miss. That is truly a worthy blade. I've never seen a Myrian sword but it is everything I imagined it to be."

Torrin blinked, not sure if he had heard the man correctly. He looked at Rowan for her reaction. Her eyes widened and an expression of delight spread across her beautiful face.

"It brings gladness to my heart to see a Myrian walk the land of Klyssen again," said the blacksmith. "I wasn't sure when I saw you yesterday but now I know for certain."

Rowan reached out and caught his sleeve as he turned away. "Please, can you tell me how you know of my people?"

The man smiled widely and bid them to follow. He led them to the back of the barn where a large wooden door opened into a clean private residence. The smell of herbs and beeswax welcomed them as they stepped into his simple home. The smith strode to an old iron chest set against the far wall of the main room. Its hinges creaked as he lifted the lid. From under a blanket he withdrew a round, cloth-wrapped object. As the soft covering was removed Torrin caught the glint of metal. It was a beautiful light shield, decorated with designs similar to Rowan's armour.

Rowan gasped and reached out to touch it. The outer edge of the shield was etched with interweaving designs and from the center, curved lines arched out, spiralling to the outer band. Her voice was full of awe. "This shield bears the name of Mor Lanyar."

"What?" Torrin looked at Rowan in shock. She turned to look up at him, her eyes wide, then back at the shield. Nathel and Borlin let out surprised exclamations and moved in closer for a better look. Dalemar's eyebrows rose in amazement and even Arynilas looked astonished.

The smith looked around at them all in puzzlement. "You know what the designs mean?"

Rowan nodded. "It is ancient Myrian script and it spells the dame name of a Myrian house." Her fingers traced the engraved center of the shield. It was identical to the curling script that ran down the blade of her sword. "*My* name is Mor Lanyar."

The blacksmith's eyes grew round. "Truly?" he breathed.

"Yes." Rowan gaze was fixed on the shield. "Where did you get this? It is very old."

The smith scratched his silver beard. "It has been in my family for generations. My great, great grandfather received it from his father and so on. I have no idea how long ago, but it was given to one of my forefathers by a Myrian woman who was traveling through Eryos. She had needed aid and received it from a blacksmith, my ancestor. In return for his help the Myrian gave him this shield. When I was a child, my father would tell me the stories told to his ancestor by the Myrian woman – stories about Myris Dar and its people. When I saw your leatherwork and sword, Miss, I was certain you were from the fabled isle. If your name is what is inscribed on the shield, then unbelievable as it may seem, it was your ancestor the shield belonged to. I should be honoured to have you accept it as a gift. It rightfully belongs to you."

Rowan shook her head. "I thank you, sir, but I could never take that which was bestowed in gratitude. It belongs to you. I ask only that you remember Myris Dar and that the name Mor Lanyar means friend to you." She offered her hand to the blacksmith. "My name is Rowan Mor Lanyar and it is an honour to meet you."

The man clasped her hand, enthralled. "Reagon Smith. The honour is mine, my lady Rowan."

Reagon had just met the Emissary of Myris Dar.

Torrin reached out next to shake the man's hand. Reagon tore his eyes away from Rowan to greet Torrin. The rest of the companions properly introduced themselves as well.

"Please," said Reagon, "let me offer you a cup of tea. I am a widower and my home lacks a woman's touch but I can at least serve you some little comfort before you leave."

Torrin sat down with the others and looked across at Rowan who was listening to Reagon as he placed out cups and teapot. "I have kept the shield tucked away because Bess didn't care for it. She said it was not a thing for inside a home, clashing with the flowers and such." The smith smiled wistfully.

Torrin realized he had no idea if Rowan liked flowers or lace or if she desired the pretty things that most women enjoyed. She wore no jewelry except a simple necklace that featured a smooth but asymmetrical green stone, which was inscribed with the same emblem that decorated her sword. If he were to give her something it would more than likely be a weapon, or a piece of armour. He almost laughed; then noticed Rowan was returning his gaze. Her green eyes were curious and Torrin took a swallow of tea to dispel his strange turn of mind.

"You and your family have taken great care of the shield. It is in remarkable condition," said Rowan. "I'd say it is in good hands."

Reagon beamed as they finished the last of the tea and rose from the table.

As they were stepping back into the barn from Reagon's quarters, the smith handed Torrin the coins he had charged them for his farrier services. Torrin tried to hand them back. "You did good work, Reagon, you should be paid for it."

The smith shook his head emphatically. "If Rowan will not take her family shield, I cannot take your silver. It is the way of friendship."

Torrin nodded and tucked away the silver. "I won't likely return to Balor, but if I do, I will look you up."

Reagon looked searchingly at Torrin. "I wasn't here seven years ago when bandits massacred many of the people of Balor and kidnapped the village girls," he said quietly, "but I understand from the stable man that it was you who righted the wrong and gave justice to Balor along with the return of its children."

Torrin took a deep breath and let the pain wash over him. The urge to push past the man was powerful, but he looked the smith in the eye. "Understand Reagon, what I did was for my wife and daughters. I had no notion of justice for the town. I was fuelled only by wrath and vengeance."

"Yes, but you did what the people of Balor could not and it granted them peace, even if you could not find it for yourself. I wish you good fortune, Torrin."

Peace.

The word reverberated through Torrin like a taunt. He closed his eyes for a moment. He nodded to Reagon, then strode into the barn and took up Black's reins, leading the horse outside to where his companions were mounting up.

The bright morning sun was in stark contrast to the blackness he had been sunk in for the last few days. He climbed into the saddle and guided Black around a large puddle in the muddy street. Torrin focused on the gate at the end of the street and let the buildings of the little town pass unmarked. There was no need to remember Balor – its single street and cluster of houses would forever be seared into his memory.

Northward

As the sun rose over the plains of Klyssen, the companions rode northward at a brisk pace, their breath white in the crisp autumn air. Torrin glanced back. Balor had faded into the distance and he began to relax. Then he caught himself watching Rowan. Facing forward, he gritted his teeth, focusing on the horizon.

The company of women was fleeting for soldiers and mercenaries and that suited Torrin fine. Emma and their daughters were a fragile dream from a lifetime lost and gone; since then, the rare occasions when he'd shared his bed always ended in a brief and unemotional farewell as dawn paled the sky. He never looked for more. Resigned to his loss, he was as content as he would ever be.

He frowned. Until Rowan – she pulled his gaze to her; her voice drew him; his pulse quickened at her touch. She was a danger best avoided. Were it not for his duty to get her and her message to Cerebus…

A dark shape rose up on his right and he reined up, reaching for his sword. Hathunor loped toward them, his fierce smile stretched wide to show sharp teeth. Torrin sheathed his sword as the great beast wrapped his arms around Rowan. She grinned up at him, dishevelled from his embrace. "Hathunor!"

The companions rode at an easy pace through the flattened grass, the sodden ground squelching under their horses's hooves. Rowan closed her eyes and lifted her face to the clear sky, relishing the sun's warmth, happy to be dry for a change.

She was still stunned at the idea that one of her relatives could have been here before her. Although she had never heard of a distant aunt or grandmother traveling to Eryos, she supposed it could have happened.

The shield was in remarkably good shape for its age. It had been well tended and protected from the air over time. It was quite possibly as old as her spell sword.

Rowan shifted in the saddle and felt the familiar, reassuring weight of her sword against her back. Her spell sword was different from regular weapons. The spell bound to it protected the sword from damage, making it difficult to know how old it actually was. There was no one left now on Myris Dar who knew how the blade was made and Rowan had yet to come across other examples of Myrian spell swords. It might be that her sword was the only one left to her people.

The name Mor Lanyar itself was centuries old. Rowan glanced down at the leather vembraces her brother Andin had made for her, following the flowing Myrian script etched into them. Names in Myris Dar did not die out easily. Women kept their own names when they married. Each new generation of daughters secured the survival of the names of their mothers, in the same way the names of sons perpetuated the names of their fathers. It was one of the hallmarks of equitable society that Myrians took great pride in.

The name on the shield was scribed in ancient Myrian, which dated it at over a thousand years old. Though the name itself was no guarantee that a Mor Lanyar was ever here with it. The shield could very well have been stolen or passed outside the family as a gift or payment for services. There was no way to know for sure, but she liked Reagon and his shy way. It made her happy to know that someone here knew of her home and that she might be walking in the footsteps of a distant ancestor.

The wind was beginning to blow again and Rowan sighed with resignation and reached back to untie her cloak from behind her saddle. Torrin rode ahead of her, his broad back relaxed, one hand resting on his thigh. His dark hair ruffled in the wind and she knew his blue eyes would be constantly scanning the distant horizon for Raken, ever vigilant.

Once she had buckled the clasp of her cloak, Rowan glanced across at Nathel. She touched her leg to Roanus, urging the big grey horse to move sideways until she was right beside Nathel and his mount.

Nathel looked over at her and smirked. He twitched his reins, moving his horse around a large rodent hole in the ground.

Rowan launched right in. "I need you to tell me what happened to Torrin. Why he was so uncomfortable in Balor and why he keeps himself so closed."

Nathel's head snapped up and he glanced around. "That is Torrin's story to tell," he replied bluntly.

Rowan sighed sardonically. "You know he won't tell me."

Nathel cast Rowan an accusing look and shook his head firmly. Rowan gave no ground and Nathel finally heaved a sigh and glanced ahead to his brother. He turned to look at her. "I tell you this only because it might help him move beyond his past, but he will not be happy about it."

Nathel quietly recounted the reason Torrin had left Pellar and become a mercenary. Listening in dismay, her gaze fastened on Torrin's back as she heard the last of the terrible story, Rowan finally and dreadfully understood.

Torrin rode near the front of the group of companions. The melody of an old song threaded sporadically through his thoughts and he concentrated on silencing it.

To his far right, Hathunor stopped mid-stride and looked up at the sky. Torrin stopped his horse and followed the Raken's gaze. Thin wisps of cloud were scudding by. There was nothing to see except a pair of hawks wheeling far above. Hathunor turned to look expectantly at Dalemar, who was also gazing skyward.

Dalemar shuddered suddenly. "I can feel it also."

"What is it?" Torrin heeled his horse closer to the Rith.

"A spell of some kind." Dalemar tilted his head this way and that.

Torrin strained his ears and heard nothing but the wind.

"It is a very powerful spell for me to be able to feel it." Dalemar drew in his breath and stiffened in his saddle. "I think it's a tracking spell! And it is moving very quickly!"

"Can you tell what its target is?" Torrin asked.

Dalemar shook his head. “Not from this distance, but it would be wise to take precautions.” He glanced around at the surrounding land and pointed at a shallow depression in the ground twenty yards to the left. “Take cover in that hollow. Quickly!”

Dalemar spurred his horse towards the dip and the others followed close on his heels. He bade them all dismount and then he turned to Hathunor. “I may need your help my friend. I have not attempted this on such a large scale before.”

Hathunor nodded and strode to the Rith’s side.

“Is there anything we can do to help, Dalemar?” asked Rowan anxiously.

“No, you must stay within the circle once I have erected the shield. And do not touch it.” Dalemar closed his eyes and raised his arms above his head. For a moment only the wind disturbed the silence. Then a crackling blue light erupted from his out-stretched fingertips. It spread upwards and began to cascade to the ground. Torrin watched as the blue shield filled itself out around them. He remembered the last time Dalemar had preformed this spell, creating a magic umbrella to protect them when they had been caught out in the open during a raging hail storm. The fist-sized balls of ice had shattered upon contact with the shield, keeping them and their horses safe from the storm. The shield’s creation had been through sheer luck then.

Now they stood within a circular dome of transparent blue. The wind was cut off abruptly, and in the silence the breathing of the horses was loud.

Dalemar opened his eyes and lowered his hands, happily inspecting his work. “I certainly couldn’t have done that a few months ago!”

Hathunor was staring in wonder at the blue shield around them, and Dalemar was pleased to have come up with something new for him to see

“Won’t the tracking spell be able to detect the magic of the shield?” asked Rowan.

“It would, except I believe I have inverted the spell so that it can only be detected from within. I saw Hathunor do something similar once. The only concern I have is that the tracking spell might have already detected us before I could erect the shield. If I could feel it, there is a good chance it could also feel us and has already sent its findings back to its creator."

"Ye canna tell who the maker be?" asked Borlin.

"No," said Dalemar. "I know there are several Riths that sit on the high council that are capable of creating such a spell, but if there is a way of detecting the spell caster's identity, I do not know of it. The magic felt stretched, if that makes any sense, as though it had come from very far away. I also cannot be certain that the spell was sent to find *us*." He sighed in frustration. "If only I had more experience, I'd know for sure."

Torrin looked around at the faces of his companions. "We must presume that this tracking spell was intended to find the Messenger. We should also assume that it has found her. If whoever sent it also controls the Raken, then the beasts will be looking for us here." He turned to Rowan. "There are five days of travel left between here and the bog lands, and I would not like to be caught out in the open. Speed might be our only chance."

"Agreed," said Rowan.

"A race it is," growled Borlin as he loosened the cinch of his saddle for his mare. Arynilas pulled a bag of grain out of his saddlebags to feed the horses.

Torrin also began to loosen his own cinch so his young horse could rest without restriction. He glanced up over his saddle to find Rowan looking at him. She lowered her eyes quickly but not before he read something odd in her gaze. He glanced at Nathel; he, too, lowered his head and turned away.

Torrin frowned and studied his brother. Then he understood – Nathel had told Rowan about Emma. Torrin shook his head in disgust.

They stood in the quiet of the protective dome as the minutes crept past. Torrin threw his arm over his saddle to lean some of his weight on Black. The young horse eyed him and shook his mane, then dropped his head to crop at the long grass, his soft muzzle seeking the youngest and sweetest shoots.

Arynilas, Nathel and Borlin sat down to relax and Rowan busied herself with finding some food in her saddlebags. Hathunor crouched down on his haunches and watched the blue flickering of the dome. Dalemar stood in concentration to keep his spell from disintegrating. The temperature inside the dome gradually increased as the sun beat down without the cold wind to steal away the heat. The companions began to remove their outer cloaks and coats.

After half an hour, Dalemar deemed it safe to remove the shield. It shimmered, fading slowly, and the wind began to scour them again.

As the others remounted, Torrin led his horse to where Rowan was tightening the cinch of her saddle. He stopped and leaned down towards her. She turned to look up at him and he locked gazes with her. "I do not want your pity, Rowan," he said very quietly. "Save it for those who need it."

Her eyes widened and she glanced quickly toward Nathel. Her cheeks flushed, but when she looked back at him her gaze was steady. She nodded and turned to put her foot in her stirrup.

Nathel watched their exchange from horseback, his expression a mix of guilt and defiance. Torrin cast him a withering glance and turned to mount his horse. He spurred the animal into motion, striking north once again.

Spell Casting

Miroth stood looking to the west. From this height, in the uppermost room of the great east tower of Lok Myrr, it was possible to see for miles. The surrounding peaks of the great Krang Mountains never lost their ice fields even in summer and the white snow glinted diamond-like in the late sun. The clear mountain air was cold and held the scent of coming snow. A ragged line of mongrel mountain people trudged away from the fortress on the westward road towards their distant hovels, pleased no doubt with their trifling acquisitions from the market held graciously once a month for their benefit in the bailey of the keep.

Cold wind swirled through the open window, banging the wooden shutters against the ancient stone of the tower. Neither the stunning view nor the wretched people of Krang held any interest for Miroth. He was eager to close the window and return to the work waiting in the large room behind him. There was much that he was immune to. The slow march of years had given him time to perfect control over many things but cold he still could not ignore.

Miroth hissed with impatience. There was a man in the room behind him that was almost ready for the final stage of the spell Miroth was working. If he did not return to him soon, the labor of the previous hours would be wasted.

The young ones who fought made the best conduits, the life force in them being strong, and the results always more powerful. Young women, he had discovered long ago, gave the best release. But he had to take what he could find in this sparsely populated land. Rumour had leaked out and now the superstitious mountain peasants kept their daughters away from the fortress.

A groan sounded softly from the darkness behind him. Miroth's chest contracted with anticipation but he resisted the urge to turn away from the window. His tracking spell would be coming any moment and traveling such distance would need his guidance to hold together. With any luck it will have found what he was searching for.

Miroth scanned the horizon again, searching. The Raken runners were swift but time was growing short. The beasts' limitations were infuriating after the long years it had taken him to bring enough of them here, to breed them and bend them to his will. He refocused his thoughts on the distant horizon and leaned on the window ledge.

Miroth heard Sol adding a log to the fire. He felt a sudden surge of irritation at the thought of his assistant – if one could even call him that. The little fool bungled the simplest tasks but Miroth didn't have the time to find someone to replace him. Miroth glanced sideways as the boy returned to his place to cower. Sol would not even offer much in death, thought Miroth sourly – the boy's weak will would taint any spell.

Miroth's late assistant, Darion, had assured him that the boy would one day make a fine assistant, but Darion was only a human. He had served for almost seventy years and then died at a most inconvenient time. Darion's skills were sorely needed now and Miroth had to take precious time from his work to do tasks that had been securely left to his old assistant. True, the man had been ancient by human standards, but a tiny part of Miroth was disappointed that Darion would never see the great heights achieved by his Master.

Miroth turned his mind to the King of Pellar as he awaited his returning spell. The Myrian girl was bringing a message to Cerebus but Miroth would make certain he was not free to act upon it. Once the Wyoraith was free, Miroth would no longer be subject to the restrictions of his flesh. Pellaris would fall and the south and west would follow. And then the Rith city in the Timor Mountains. He allowed himself the tiniest feeling of triumph at that last thought.

Yet doubt flickered – a ribbon of unease thrashing whip-like through his mind. He had already miscalculated where the Myrian was concerned. It was a mistake that could have cost him everything.

He needed her in hand. Miroth felt the truth of it throughout his entire being, the knowledge vibrated in his chest like his own power. She was the right one.

An eddy of cold wind blasted into his face. Miroth narrowed his eyes as he watched the last of the sun slip below the ring of mountains. He focused on the future and a slow smile stretched across his pale face, pulling tight across yellow teeth.

A hint of something teased his mind and brought him back to the present. He cast his thoughts out to find his returning spell skimming over the mountains from the west. It was barely cohesive. When he had sifted through the information it brought, his smile widened.

"I see you, Myrian," he whispered.

With the last of his strength he cast his mind again out over the mountains, seeking the one he wanted. The Raken he had bonded with was not far from where he had expected to find him. He implanted his instructions in the beast's mind and then withdrew.

The mind link was a useful tool but the Raken had proven harder to bond with than he had expected. He was still searching for a way to bond with more than one creature at a time without the two beasts sharing each other's thoughts as well. They became too difficult to control when they were linked together. It worried him, but it could be regulated, and soon it would no longer matter.

The regrettable part of the bond was the effect it had on him when the Raken he was linked with died while he was present in its mind. It had taken Miroth four days to recover.

Rage flashed through him. It settled in the pit of his stomach, a hot coil that eased the cold in his limbs. The Myrian had much to atone for. Physical pain was of no consequence; it was the lost time that angered him.

He turned his back on the cold dusk and motioned impatiently for the boy to close the shutters. Sol scurried forward, his brown eyes turned fearfully to the man bound to the table in the center of the room. This was the first time Miroth had allowed Sol up into the tower; the first time the boy had witnessed the complex spell casting that gave Miroth his strength and long life.

Miroth approached the table, glad to be once again within the warmth of the room. Weariness threaded through his body and he leaned heavily on the edge of the table, oblivious to the blood that soaked into his red robes. The death Miroth was spell casting with was approaching.

He looked down at the dying man bound before him. Fear and anger clearly shone out through the haze of pain in the man's eyes. Miroth was pleased and a little surprised to find the anger still there. It would color the spell with a distinct flavour and add to its power. The important task now was to insure that a subject embraced death willingly and with gratitude, thus irrevocably attaching the spell's release to the spell caster.

Miroth studied the many complex weaves of his spell, calculating. He must extract as much as possible from this one. The man's breath came in shallow gasps; he was unable to draw full breath with his lungs exposed to the air. It really was quite remarkable what the human body could endure before death finally came.

Shaman of the Horse Clans

Torrin poured the last of his tea into the dead fire. The rising sun was a small span above the flat horizon and about to disappear into the low cloud cover. It was likely all they would see of it for the day. He bent over his gear, stowed the cup and tied the straps of his saddlebags. A loud crack accompanied by Dalemar's excited exclamation sounded to the left and Torrin looked up.

The Rith was watching carefully as Hathunor directed his magic in a rope thin blast of Rith fire. It lanced into the distance where stones had been set up, blasting into them with an explosion of rock shards and dust. Torrin straightened and watched as Dalemar refined his attempt after Hathunor. It was a perfect copy of Hathunor's blast and the great Raken grinned in encouragement as Dalemar struck the remaining rocks. Torrin had never seen Dalemar direct Rith fire with that kind of accuracy. The trial and terror seemed to have passed, thought Torrin with relief as he reached down to heave up his gear. Dalemar had figured out how to copy Hathunor's examples perfectly.

As Torrin walked toward the horses he watched Hathunor direct Dalemar's own magic back at him while the Rith blocked it.

"Would you like me to move that for you, Torrin?" asked Dalemar, his voice sounding as though he spoke from right beside him.

Dalemar now worked his magic to move his own saddle and bags to where the horses were being loaded. Dalemar grinned at him with enthusiasm.

Torrin shook his head and pointed with his chin. "Help Borlin."

The Stoneman crossed his thick arms and scowled at Torrin. "Do ye see me needin any help?"

Nathel snickered. "Strength doesn't count for much, Borlin, when you can't reach the top of your horse's back."

Torrin ignored the ensuing insults and lifted his own saddle up onto his horse's back. The more time that passed without sign of their pursuers the more Torrin's unease increased. He tightened the cinch and Black turned to look back at him. Torrin gave him a pat on the nose and then heaved once more on the strap. There was little point worrying – it was a soldier's pragmatic view. An endless litany of "what ifs" was always a commander's burden. When you started fretting too much about what might happen, about what could go wrong, you opened the door to doubt and that's when you lost your nerve. A little doubt was a good thing; it kept you sharp and humble. But too much was paralyzing.

He picked up his saddlebags and settled them in place and glanced across at Rowan. She was saddling her own horse with her head down, concentrating on the task.

Torrin frowned and looked back at his own work. He couldn't seem to follow his own rules. Thoughts of harm befalling Rowan tormented him. He became quick to react to the slightest danger and his loss of control in Balor's market caused him to rein himself in even tighter. Last night he had woken suddenly with his dead wife's scream in his head, only to realize with dread that it had been Rowan's voice he'd heard, not Emma's.

His need to get her safely to Pellaris drove him through his waking hours. Though he cursed himself for a fool for thinking a besieged city offered any more protection.

Somewhere deep down, where he seldom looked, he feared he would never be able to keep her safe.

Rowan pulled the loose hair that had been teased out of her braid away from her eyes. Her fingertips were rough and dry. Dirt had ground into the crevasses of her skin, creating a fine spidery web over her fingerprints. The oil that she used to clean her weapons was the only thing that kept the skin of her hands from becoming painfully cracked.

Torrin's saddle creaked beside her and she glanced over as he leaned back to reach into his saddlebags.

"Riders." said Arynilas suddenly from ahead, "On the horizon to the northeast."

Whatever Torrin had been searching for was forgotten as he swivelled around to look in the direction the Tynithian indicated. "The Horse Clans," Torrin murmured to no one in particular.

Rowan studied the four small dark dots in the distance: men on horseback. She could make out nothing more.

"Dalemar." Torrin turned to look behind them at the Rith. "Do you or Borlin have any pipe tobacco to spare?"

"Aye," said Borlin from Rowan's other side as he guided his mare closer to them, "I've a spare pouch at'll do." The stoneman patted the chest pocket of his under-vest.

Rowan looked over at Torrin, raising an eyebrow. "Pipe tobacco?"

Torrin's glance flicked away from the riders on the horizon for a moment to look at her. "Tribute. In return for crossing Horse Clan lands. If they do not receive tribute from travelers, they will likely exact a more expensive payment in the form of horseflesh."

"They'll steal the horses?" Rowan asked.

Torrin smiled grimly. "They will try. The young men will. Horses are about the only thing of value to them."

"But they will take a small pouch of tobacco instead of a valuable horse?"

Torrin shook his head. "The tribute is only a token, a sign of respect; it has nothing to do with worth. It is an acknowledgement of their right to these lands. It must be something small and useful, easily carried. A Horse Clansman would be greatly insulted by a tribute that most other men consider valuable – they have no interest in trinkets or coin. Horses and the training, tending and breeding of them is the only thing important to them. A man's worth is measured in horseflesh, not gold. They honour mounted skill in battle with bow and spear and a man is awarded the same status as his horse. The lives of the Horse Clans are moulded completely around their steeds. They look for omens in foaling cycles and mare's milk, and the death of a horse is considered great misfortune, especially if it dies because of a man's folly."

Hathunor looked up at Rowan from the crouch he had assumed when Arynilas had spotted the horsemen. His red eyes were bright. "Hathunor wait and follow at distance. Will come if you need Hathunor." He cast a baleful glare at the distant men, then staying low on all fours, he moved back toward the rim of a shallow depression keeping the group between him and the distant riders. Rowan watched his swift progress and was surprised to see him disappear completely in only a few moments.

The companions spurred their horses forward once more, angling their course to meet the waiting horsemen. The wind increased as they closed the distance, lifting cloaks and whipping the horses' manes.

The four mounted men resolved into fierce looking warriors with spears braced in their stirrups. Their armour was made of thick leather, tanned red and ornamented with small copper disks. Their clothes were made of a softer leather. All four had long sandy-coloured hair which they wore tied behind their heads like tails. Horsehair tassels, lifted sideways in the wind, were tied to the tips of their spears. Each man had a re-curved bow strapped to his back and a short sword at his hip.

Torrin, riding ahead of the rest of the companions, pulled his horse in when they were twenty paces from the warriors. Rowan, Dalemar and Borlin drew up beside him on the right and Nathel and Arynilas stopped on his left. The two parties regarded each other in silence.

Finally, the man in the middle of the group moved his horse forward a few steps and nodded his head formally. "You ride Horse Clan lands."

"We offer tribute to ride across Clan Lands," replied Torrin calmly.

"The Mora' Taith of Clan Shorna is waiting for you. He sent us south to watch for your coming."

Rowan blinked and glanced sideways in surprise at Torrin. He sat very still, a frown on his face. "You have been waiting for us specifically?" he asked.

The guard grinned insolently. His eyes caught and wandered with interest over Rowan's big grey stallion. "The Mora' Taith of Shorna is the most powerful shaman among the Horse Clans. You are either blessed or extremely unlucky for him to mark you so." The horsemen behind him laughed.

A cold tickle ran up Rowan's back and across her shoulders. She kept her face still. Torrin and Nathel were tense, their expressions guarded and wary.

"Has the Mora' Taith been waiting for us for a long time?" asked Torrin.

The man shrugged, his eyes still fixed on Roanus, appraising his chest and girth, his hooves and legs. "Who can tell what lives in the heart of a shaman? We were sent to watch for you three days ago." The warrior sighed and tore his gaze from the horse. "My name is Jari and these are my brothers."

"How far are we from your Clanhold?" asked Torrin.

"A full day and a half's ride, your horses look as if they are swift enough to keep up. We will make good time." Jari's tone was just shy of contempt.

"What say ye, lad? I've never met me a Mora' Taith," said Borlin boldly.

Nathel chuckled, but his eyes on the mounted warriors in front of them were still measuring.

Torrin looked at Dalemar and Arynilas; he received silent nods from both. When his gaze met Rowan's, she said quietly, "Better to know than to wonder."

Torrin turned back to Jari. "Lead the way then, my friend. We should not keep your Mora' Taith waiting."

Jari barked out an unintelligible command and the three horsemen behind him launched forward, two circled around behind the companions and the third fell in with Jari as he wheeled his sorrel horse around and led the way through the long grass.

Rowan turned as Torrin heeled his horse close to her and spoke softly. "Be wary of what you say. The Horse Clans are proud and fiercely independent; they hold allegiance to no one. We cannot be certain if their Shaman wishes us good or ill."

"Or neither," Rowan replied.

Torrin said nothing but he eased his sword in its scabbard.

The pace set by the Horse Clan warriors was fast but no faster than Rowan and her friends had driven themselves over the previous weeks. Jari and his brothers spoke little as they journeyed and Borlin's attempts to draw them into conversation largely failed. It left the Stoneman's usually jovial manner with a surly edge.

Although Rowan was pointedly ignored, her horse sparked much interest. They talked loudly amongst themselves, gesturing with much shaking of their heads. The language they spoke was coloured with a bit of the common tongue of Eryos and Rowan understood a few words but nothing else.

Finally, after hours of riding, Jari guided his sorrel horse toward Rowan, giving Arynilas and Dalemar a wide berth and a furtive glance. He nodded respectfully to her but instead of addressing her, he directed his question at Torrin in the common tongue. "We have a small wager that affects the stud services of my brother Kylor's horse. It concerns the lineage of this stallion." He indicated Roanus.

Torrin looked at Jari for a moment, his eyes weighed the man. "If you have a question about her horse, you should ask Rowan; she is not wed."

Rowan watched then in amazement as the warrior's bearing toward her changed instantly. He turned to look her directly in the eye for the first time and a wide smile lit up his face. "I wonder please if you could settle a debate my brothers and I are having about the lineage of your beautiful stallion?"

"Roanus traces his sires back for almost three hundred years in the Myrian studbooks." Rowan watched Jari's expression change from surprise to awe.

Then it was her turn to be surprised when Jari nodded sagely. "We have not seen a Myrian horse before but they are listed in our record scrolls. The description of them is quite accurate, based on what I see in your horse. I thank you. I believe I have just won the wager. What is his full name, please?"

"Roanus D' Enyain. Enyain D' Emius is his sire's name," replied Rowan.

Jari repeated the name as he gazed at her horse. "A most noble title." He spurred his horse over to his brothers where he told them with excited animation.

Rowan looked at Torrin and he answered her question before she could ask it. "It is considered extremely offensive to look at and speak with a married woman. Most Horse Clansmen will assume a woman is married rather than risk insulting a husband. I'm surprised that these Clansmen are observing the custom with foreigners. They don't care enough one way or another about folks who are not Clan to worry about insulting them." Torrin glanced down at Roanus. "Perhaps he's the reason they are treating you with such respect."

When the sun set, the wind dropped with the temperature and they were given respite from its driving force. By unspoken agreement the four Clansmen stopped in a shallow depression and began to set up a simple camp. They cared for their horses before any human comfort was sought, watering them with their own waterskins and checking hooves and legs thoroughly.

Dalemar slowly walked through the swale, with his head cocked. The clansmen watched him surreptitiously as he stopped and crouched down to touch the ground at his feet. He closed his eyes for a moment and Rowan could see the faint blue glow around his hand in the fading twilight.

Then Roanus whickered in interest and the other horses began to nose forward toward the Rith. Rowan walked her big gray over to where he could drink from the runnel of spring water that Dalemar had called to the surface. The four Clansmen edged closer to see, their mouths falling open in wonder as the rest of the companions brought their mounts forward to drink.

Dalemar winked at them. “Bring your horses before I release the water.” The Clansmen traded wary glances. “It is spring water from deep in the ground. It is clean and pure and quite safe,” said Dalemar. They tentatively led their horses forward, but tasted the water themselves, before allowing their animals to drink.

Afterward, they shared some of their food with him and nodded to him whenever he was near. But they still could not be engaged in conversation.

Rowan was woken in the darkness by a hand on her shoulder. She could barely make out Torrin above her. “Time to go,” he said quietly.

Rowan would have liked to stay curled under her warm blankets, but the camp around her was stirring to life. She sat up and began to pack her gear.

The companions and their escort were in the saddle and traveling again toward the Clanhold before the sun rose. Rowan watched the last of the stars fade as the morning sun crested the horizon. She ate in the saddle with the others. By late morning Arynilas spotted smoke in the distance – a smudge against the low cloud. They soon began to see small and large herds of horses grazing on the surrounding plain. Without exception, mounted and armed Clansmen guarded the herds.

Rowan looked closely at the horses they passed. Like the mounts of the Clansmen escorting them, the animals were all of the highest quality – swift and strong.

They reached the encampment and followed their escorts into a circle of round tents with peaked roofs. It was like a small town with streets winding between the distinctive tents. The smell of mead and roasting meat wafted toward them on smoke from cooking fires, and Rowan watched the people busy with various tasks. The clank of a hammer on anvil sounded nearby and large, lanky dogs with flopping ears charged around the tents chased by screeching long-haired children.

Many of the people they passed looked curiously at them but soon resumed whatever they had been doing before the arrival of the strangers. This Mora' Taith, shaman of the Horse Clans had seen fit to inform his people of the imminent arrival of Rowan and her friends. He was obviously certain that they would accept his invitation, or perhaps he simply knew they had and were on their way.

Rowan swallowed, seized with a cold dread as she looked around. What if the nameless thing that hunted her was at work here? Sometimes she felt as though she could sense it, hovering just behind her, reaching for her with malice.

A few children stopped their rough game of tag to point and dance about before trailing after the arriving party. They cast wary glances at the Clan Warriors guiding the companions as though expecting to be chased away at any moment. Rowan blinked, and shook away the sense of doom. There was no comparing these people to the thing that hunted her. This place did not hold that dread.

The four men escorting them stopped and dismounted in the center of an open field between the tents. Another knot of warriors strode forward and briefly exchanged words with the escort. Rowan could not hear what was said.

She swung down out of her saddle and stretched, then stepped forward with the rest of her friends to greet the men waiting for them.

The new group of warriors was similar to those they had met out on the plain, except for the tallest man in the center who strode forward and looked them over sternly. In addition to his copper-disked armour, he wore a cloak made from an enormous bear skin and his long sandy hair was not tied back but fell loosely over the dark fur of his mantle.

The man planted his large fists on his hips. "I am Brynar, Clan Chief of Shorna. You are?" His voice was gruff and low and his small grey eyes severe.

Torrin tossed a small leather pouch out to the chief who caught it in his thick fingers and proceeded to untie it.

"My name is Torrin, my friends and I seek passage across Horse Clan lands."

Brynar squinted at the contents of the pouch and brought it briefly to his nose to smell it. He nodded his approval.

"We were told that Shorna's Mora' Taith wished to see us," Torrin said.

Brynar raised a hand. "Not you, Northman." He jabbed a finger at Rowan. "The Mora' Taith has been waiting for her." He signalled to his men with a flick of his wrist and several of them stepped forward; one actually reached out to grab Rowan's arm.

Rowan stepped back, striking the man's hand away. A metallic ringing filled the air as Torrin instantly drew his sword. The surrounding Clansmen stilled. Brynar's face changed, the arrogance replaced by the look of a wary hunter.

Bows were drawn, arrows nocked and aimed at Torrin's chest. Nathel reached for his own weapon with the rest of the companions. Arynilas' gold-fletched arrow sought the chief's heart, on the verge of release.

Torrin stepped close to Rowan and scowled at the man who had tried to touch her. The clansman rubbed at his forearm.

"Is this how the Horse Clans honour a tribute?" Torrin's voice was low and menacing.

Brynar looked around through the circle of bristling weapons at his men. He took in the companions and the golden arrow held unwaveringly on his chest. Then he threw back his head and laughed loudly, with true humour. The Clansmen around him blinked in confusion for an instant and then lowered their weapons. "Indeed, Northman," Brynar's laughter coloured his words. "We seldom have well-intentioned visitors these days and we take the word of the Mora' Taith very seriously." He spread his arms and bowed his head slightly but kept his small eyes fastened on Torrin's. "May we offer an *escort* for you and your friends to the tent of the Mora' Taith?"

Torrin sheathed his sword slowly. Rowan relaxed her grip on the pommel of her dagger and the others stowed weapons.

"Lead the way, Chief Brynar," she said evenly and stepped forward.

They were led through the camp to a large circular tent with a horsehide flap hanging over the arched door. Brynar and two warriors went through the door first and Torrin followed them more slowly. As Rowan passed the entrance into the darkness beyond, she was hit with the sudden warmth of the interior. Instead of walking forward, Rowan stepped to the side; clear of the door but with her back to the wall. Torrin had done the same and his familiar bulk was a reassurance.

Rowan began to make out the interior of the tent. Low benches strewn with soft animal hides sat around a sunken fire pit that smoked up into the ceiling and out through a flap that let in the only light. A tiny man sat on a raised platform on the far side of the fire, covered in a furred mantle. His eyes were completely covered in a pale grey film and his head was turned to look right at Rowan. Gooseflesh rose along her arms – she felt as though he was looking into the heart of her. The warm air of the tent became oppressive.

A slender young woman who was sitting on the ground next to the old man stood and bade them to sit on the benches that circled the pit. She picked up a large jar warming by the fire and poured out bowls of mead, passing them out to Brynar, his men and the companions. She regarded each of them with silent interest.

As she passed the drink to Rowan their fingers touched briefly and the girl smiled softly before returning to sit beside the old man.

When the Mora' Taith finally spoke, his rasping voice seemed to encompass far more strength and power than his frail body could contain. "So you have finally come to my fire, swordswoman. I see you clearly now." A toothless smile spread across his crinkled face and he nodded to himself with a jerky movement.

Rowan glanced to the young woman.

The slender woman stirred and looked up at the old man. "I am my grandfather's practical eyes, but he sees very well in other ways."

The old man leaned forward near the edge of his fur-covered platform, his opaque eyes fixed unerringly on Rowan. She swore she could hear the creaking of his bones. "You have been in my dreams often of late. I have watched you journey far and endure much hardship. You will face much more in time, but you will also find here what you could not find in your own homeland."

Rowan frowned; more cryptic riddles. The old man's blind gaze was unnervingly like that of the Lady Therial; his prediction similar to the one the ancient crone had delivered.

"I did not come here expecting it to be easy, Shaman, and I look only to fulfill my mission," Rowan replied. Brynar stared at her from the other side of the tent.

"Nevertheless, swordswoman, what you search for will be found here."

"Do you refer to the Slayer of the Wyoraith that we seek in Pellaris?" asked Rowan bluntly.

The little man's smile deepened for a moment. "Your quest here is but a beginning. It is meant to prepare you."

"Prepare me for what?"

"I do not see the end of your path, swordswoman, only its beginning. What you search for is not what you think it is."

Before Rowan could ask him to clarify he turned to gaze sightlessly around the tent, when his eyes passed over Arynilas he nodded in greeting. "Be welcome, Shape Shifter. We have not seen your kind for many generations." His grey eyes passed on to Dalemar and he paused for a long moment before continuing to Borlin and Nathel. Torrin's scowl deepened as the old man's scrutiny fell on him, challenging.

The filmed eyes turned once more to Rowan. "There is one among you missing. Tell me, where is your large black friend?"

Rowan felt as if she had been struck and Nathel, sitting on Torrin's other side, pulled in a breath in surprise.

Torrin leaned forward abruptly. "What is your reason for summoning us, old man? Speak plainly and leave off with the hints and shocking revelations," he growled.

Brynar glared at Torrin and began to rise to his feet but before he could speak in reprimand the old man began to cackle in delight.

Torrin drew back and looked piercingly at Rowan.

The old man's laughter drew to a coughing close. "Well said, Northman. You speak the truth, but leave an old man a few of his pleasures." His next words held no trace of humour. "I have *summoned* you here to give you warning. The one you seek searches for you also. And I fear he is close."

Rowan's skin went cold and she struggled to breathe, crushed under the terrible weight of the old Shaman's eyes. "You—" she gasped as the dying screams of her kin sounded in her head. Blinded by a vision of ambushing, howling Raken, she reeled from the memory and reached out desperately for something, anything to cling to. A strong, warm hand gripped hers and brought her slowly back from the terror.

Rowan opened her eyes to find Torrin staring at her with concern. She reluctantly pulled her hand from his and looked over at the Mora' Taith. His blind eyes were fixed on her, as she knew they would be. He had something to do with the intensity of the memory.

"You've seen what hunts me?" she asked in a hushed voice.

The Mora' Taith raised his hand to point northeast. The furs fell away from his skinny, twig-like arm. "He sits in shadow there, where the land lies always frozen. I do not see him clearly but he is strong, very strong. He has wintered a thousand years and he has spent much of that time waiting for the day when he will unleash darkness across the land. This I know for certain: that day will be upon us soon."

The summoner of the Wyoraith. Rowan's chest hurt and she realized she was holding her breath.

Dalemar spoke into the charged silence. "You are certain that he has lived for a thousand years?"

The shaman turned to the Rith. "I am certain, Magic user."

"Is there anything specific that you can tell us about him?" asked Dalemar insistently.

"You should know better than anyone, Rith, how the sight works," rasped the Mora' Taith. "I give to you only what I have been shown, the rest is for you to discover." He turned his gaze on

Rowan once more. "He will dog your steps and he will not give up. Like the wildcat on the scent of a newly dropped foal, he will not stop until you are his."

"Why does he hunt me?" Rowan was surprised to find her voice steady.

"He hunts you because you will help him."

Rowan shook her head vehemently. "Never –"

The Mora' Taith held up his hand to stop her. "What I see is only *his* intent." He reached down and picked up something small, which he passed to the young woman. She nodded her head and gracefully stood and walked to Rowan. The object she handed to Rowan was warm and smooth. It was a carved stone with a hole drilled through its center. Threaded through the hole was an intricate braid of knotted horsehair, tied with a string of stone beads. It was small enough to fit in the palm of her hand but Rowan found its weight too heavy for its size. She looked up at the shaman.

"It is a protection stone, Swordswoman," explained the Mora' Taith. "I made it a year ago and when I first dreamt of you. Keep it always with you and the strength of the Horse Clans will become your own."

Rowan closed her fist around the stone. She sensed that this gift was not given lightly. "I thank you. For your warning and your gift," she said gravely. "What did you mean, this quest is only the beginning?"

The Mora' Taith was silent for a while. "What I see of your fate, Swordswoman, is shadowed by the one who hunts you. All I know is that this is only the beginning. In the dark days to come may your horse be strong and your aim true."

That signalled the end to the audience. Brynar and his two warriors rose and began to usher the companions out of the tent.

Torrin stood. "Why have you told us this, to what purpose do the Horse Clans help outsiders?"

The Mora' Taith's voice sounded for the first time like a very old man's. "Because the darkness ahead will cover us all."

The Flight

Hathunor's black bulk crouched near the campfire close to Rowan; the others cast smaller shadows against the hollow. The faint sound of water from the brook at the bottom of the shallow vale echoed around them.

Dalemar finished filling his pipe, then passed the leather pouch to Borlin, who pressed weed into the bowl of his own pipe with thick fingers.

The Rith leaned forward to light Borlin's pipe, then his own, the white light of his power briefly illuminating their faces. "A thousand years," he said to no one in particular.

Standing on the other side of the fire, Torrin pulled his cloak closer around his shoulders. "Only Tynithians can live that long," he said quietly.

Rowan shivered and glanced at Arynilas. His steady silence led her to believe that even among his kind there were those who broke laws and custom. Still, she had trouble seeing a Tynithian at the root of what hunted her. She turned to Dalemar. "Is it possible that the one hunting me is using Riths to do his work? The tracking spell, the control of the Raken—those aren't things a Tynithian would be able to do."

Dalemar's pipe glowed in the darkness as he drew through it. He removed it from between his teeth and shook his head. "It is not a Tynithian, at least I don't believe it to be. I'm afraid it is far worse. I'm afraid there is a Rith at the heart of this."

"But Riths only live for a few hundred years; three hundred and fifty is extremely long in the tooth for a Rith," said Nathel. "You told us that yourself, Dalemar,"

"Yes, yes, I did. You are correct, Nathel. A Rith has not lived beyond the age of three hundred and seventy in centuries. But a very long time ago, when Riths still lived and worked among the other races of Eryos, there were some who developed a way of extending life. In secret, a small group began to work certain spells, terrible spells. For almost eight hundred years they went undetected." Dalemar closed his eyes for a moment. "For eight hundred years, countless victims fed the glutinous appetites of these monsters. When others of Rithkind discovered the spell-working, they strove to put a stop to it, believing the gain of immortality was not worth the moral depravity that Rithkind would sink to. It sparked a civil war.

"When the first blow of the war was struck, it was done with magic and the ensuing battles raged for almost fifty years. A third of Rithkind was lost to the struggle. There was great destruction and many Riths cared little for the innocent bystanders that got in the way. Eventually those who wanted to end the spell-working were victorious and formed the new Rith high council. They declared the use of such knowledge anathema to all Rithkind. Any scrolls and books that pertained to the use of the spells were destroyed and laws were passed to forbid the practice of them. Anyone caught dabbling with the life-extending knowledge was sentenced to death.

"Rithkind withdrew into the mountains in self-imposed isolation. The high council believed that keeping themselves separated from humans would keep such dreadful tragedies from recurring." Dalemar put his pipe back into his mouth and stared into the flames.

Rowan looked at her silent companions. "People have forgotten the Rith war and its cause haven't they?"

Torrin added another grass log to the fire and the light flared. "That the fifty years of battle between the Riths had in fact been largely for humanity's sake? Yes, very few now know."

Arynilas sat forward. "Their deeds are not your own, Dalemar. We are, each of us, linked to the past in our own way, but it is a way that we must make for ourselves. To bear another's shame for them only makes it more difficult for them to bear it themselves, even in memory. To remember a deed and stand witness to the immorality of it so that we may learn from it does not mean that we must also feel guilt for the acts of our fathers."

Arynilas held Dalemar's gaze until the Rith nodded in acceptance.

Rowan held out her hands to the new warmth of the fire. "Dalemar, the spells to extend life – what was so terrible about them?"

Dalemar looked at her and sighed. "The spells used humans, people who were killed in horrible, agonizing ways in order to give Riths that which was needed to extend life –

another's life essence." Dread crawled across his face. "I fear that a Rith has resurrected this ancient knowledge and is using it now."

"Or perhaps never stopped using it," added Torrin ominously.

Gooseflesh prickled Rowan's arms and back. In the silence even the sound of the nearby stream seemed muted. She looked up at Torrin and took a shaking breath. "Do you think that is the reason why whoever controls the Raken tried to take me alive in the wilds, instead of killing me?"

Torrin balled his hands into fists.

Arynilas nudged the grass log further into the fire. "Are you certain that this summoner of the Wyoraith, if he is indeed the one controlling the Raken, was trying to kill you before? When we fought the Trieton in the Wilds, I saw only blunt weapons aimed at you, Messenger."

"With the exception of my battle to free Hathunor, I remember mostly clubs and cudgels but when we were ambushed near Dendor, my company was assailed with swords." Rowan sighed and rubbed her temple. "There doesn't seem to be any pattern."

"We've noted that the Draes are clumsy with weapons and Hathunor has told us they are not warriors. Perhaps they slipped up," suggested Nathel.

"Aye and when they shot ye Lass, they might ha' bin aimin for yer horse," said Borlin.

The silence stretched. Torrin spoke finally, his voice quiet. "It does tell us one helpful thing about our enemy." He looked around at them all. "That he is fallible. That he makes mistakes and perhaps does not control the Raken as completely as we thought. If the captive Raken were able to send a message to Hathunor's homeland, then maybe this Summoner has weaknesses we can exploit."

*

Rowan shivered, her face was cold and her white breath whipped away as soon as she exhaled. She rode with her cloak pulled tightly around her, one hand clutching the hood to keep it from blowing back, the other molded around the reins of her horse. She frequently exchanged hands to let warmth flow back into the one that had been exposed. The wind seemed to drive right through her doeskin gloves and her heavy cloak. Torrin and Nathel ranged beside her, similarly muffled. The rest of the companions spread out behind them.

They had been riding for two and a half days across Horse Clan lands. Sometime during the freezing morning a dark smudge had grown visible on the distant horizon. They had reached the edge of the great marshland and its low bulk spread past seeing.

The brothers were quiet beside her and she glanced over at their faces. Torrin had been angry with Nathel for telling Rowan about his past, but she sensed no anger between them now. He treated her no differently than he had before and she deemed it wise to do him the same courtesy. She had a hard time envisioning the stern warrior with a family.

Rowan pulled her hood back up yet again. She was thankful now for the heavy garment. Torrin and Nathel both wore heavy winter cloaks as well with leather gloves. Dalemar was wrapped in a fur-trimmed mantle that sat over the shoulders of his long green coat and Borlin almost disappeared under a sheepskin-lined vest that made his barrel chest look even deeper. Arynilas wore a long grey cloak that blended so well with the surrounding landscape that Rowan wouldn't have been able to spot him from a distance without the dark bulk of his sorrel horse.

The only one of the companions who seemed unaffected by the cold weather was Hathunor. He strode along beside the horses, his gleaming, black scaled skin exposed to the icy wind, his spiky crest of stiff fur waving in the gusts.

Rowan was wondering how he could possibly stand it when he stopped mid-stride and turned his ferocious visage to look behind them. She pulled Roanus in, glancing to Torrin who was also turned to follow the direction of Hathunor's gaze.

A low growl emitted from deep inside the Saa Raken's chest. "Draes." The wind blew his crest flat against his skull.

"How do you know?" Rowan asked.

Hathunor tilted his head. "Hathunor hear them."

The companions looked at one another in alarm. Borlin worked his sword free in its scabbard and Arynilas reached up and pulled an arrow from his quiver.

"How close are they?" Torrin spun his charger around and squinted into the distance, looking for any sign of the approaching foe.

"Hathunor not know. Wind carries the sound to Hathunor."

"Arynilas?" Torrin glanced to the Tynithian, but after a moment of scanning the horizon behind them Arynilas shook his head.

Torrin turned to look back at the distant marshes, judging the distance. "If we make it to the bogs we will have a better chance to defend ourselves, but we must not exhaust the horses, or we won't have a chance to escape." He looked back to Hathunor. "Can you tell how many Raken approach?"

Hathunor cocked his head. "More than thirty," he said at last.

"Then we will have to outrun them," said Nathel grimly. "How fast can Draes run, Hathunor?"

Hathunor reached out a huge, clawed hand and gently patted Roanus on the rump. "Fast as four legs." Then he puffed out his chest. "Saa Raken faster."

"Wonderful," groaned Nathel.

Torrin turned to Dalemar. "Any chance you can slow them down?"

Dalemar shook his head. "Not at this distance, with nothing to aim at."

"Then we ride!" Torrin launched his big horse towards the marshes, his dark cloak swirling. Roanus jumped forward as Rowan touched his sides and the rest of the group charged after them through the wind-whipped grass. The horses were excited, catching the collective mood of their riders, and they had to be reined in from a crazed gallop.

Torrin set a fast pace but a sustainable one and the six horses settled into their stride, hooves pounding hollowly. Rowan fixed her gaze on their distant goal, and its scant offer of salvation. Her eyes watered in the cold wind and the dark blur on the horizon disappeared. Dread settled over her; they could not win against so large a group of Raken out in the open, nor would they be much safer within the cover the mashes offered.

The long grass sped by under the horses and clods of earth flew up from churning hooves. As they came closer to the bogs, Rowan began to make out the distinct shapes of stunted, gnarled trees.

"Aie!" shouted Arynilas. Rowan turned in her saddle to search the grassland behind, but couldn't see any thing. "They come on quickly!" cried the Tynithian. "We will not out run them at this pace."

"Dalemar!" shouted Torrin.

"As soon as I can see them, I can send back a nasty surprise," the Rith called back.

Torrin urged his mount onward. The big black warhorse responded with a surge and they began a headlong flight toward the marshes.

Rowan concentrated on the ground ahead, steering Roanus wide of any potential obstacles. She snatched a look behind and gasped. There were at least three Trietons – a dark, boiling mass. Dalemar was muttering under his breath as he turned in his saddle and stretch forth a hand, fingers extended.

Nothing happened. Rowan was beginning to think perhaps his spell had failed when a great concussion sounded behind them. She looked back to see a large cloud of dust expanding outward from where the Raken had been.

Nathel whooped, and Torrin slowed his horse, pulling him to a plunging stop with the others. "Arynilas, what do you see?" asked Torrin.

The dust was beginning to drift away and even Rowan saw movement as the Raken ran forward through it.

"There are some Raken down, but not enough," said the Tynithian.

Dalemar raised his hand again and concentrated on the distant creatures. Rowan watched in suspense. Moments later a great spray of earth and dust exploded upwards from the Raken, followed by the loud crack of the explosion.

The horses stood blowing, heads down and nostrils wide. Rowan leaned forward to stroke Roanus' sweat-slicked neck, watching the distant dust, waiting for it to clear.

Dalemar suddenly swayed in his saddle and Nathel reached out to steady him.

"Tor!" Nathel called.

Dalemar held out a hand. “I am fine, but I will not be able to manage another one of those.”

“They stir!” Arynilas said.

“Can you count them?” Torrin asked.

“At least two Trietons.”

Sixty. Rowan felt her hopes fall; they stood no chance against so many.

Borlin pulled his sword from his belt and prepared to kick his tired horse toward the distant foe.

“Hold Borlin,” called Torrin.

“I’ll not end me life flee’n, Torrin.”

Torrin shook his head. “You will get your chance my friend, but Rowan must get to Pellaris, we will have a better chance in the boglands.” Torrin cast a sidelong glance at Hathunor, who stood looking as fresh as ever. “We certainly won’t outrun them.”

They wheeled around and asked their weary horses for a last effort to take them into the marshes ahead. As they fled, Rowan began to hear the distant calls of the Raken behind them. She leaned low over Roanus’ neck, urging him onward. The big horse was nearing the end of his endurance. The horses were sweat-soaked and covered in flecks of foam from rubbing tack.

The Raken grew louder and she glanced back, shocked at how close they were. As she turned forward again the first of the stunted trees flashed by. Their pace slowed as the horses began to weave around the new obstructions.

Roanus stumbled suddenly. His head went down, his front legs folding under him. As Rowan pitched forward over his head she tucked herself into a tight ball, somersaulting, and landed with a jarring thud, skidding on the grass. Above her, she saw her horse’s back legs, hooves pointed to the sky, flailing down towards her. Scrambling out of the way, Rowan turned to see Roanus on his back, belly exposed. She gasped, watching in fear as he began to struggle to his feet.

Torrin and Arynilas, who had been racing behind, hauled on their horses, changing direction to intercept her. Before Rowan had a chance to see if Roanus was injured, Torrin’s big charger was upon her. Torrin leaned down out of his saddle, arm extended. She reached up, grasped his outstretched hand and he hauled up behind him.

Raken howls intensified from close behind as they spotted the downed horse. Rowan turned back to see her grey stallion struggle to his feet and launch himself after the rest of the fleeing companions. Ears pinned back, he pelted after them, stirrups flying loose.

Rowan wrapped her left arm tightly around Torrin and reached up to draw her sword. Behind them, Arynilas rode with his bow out, an arrow clutched in one hand. She felt Torrin change direction and craned over his shoulder to see where they were headed.

"To me!" he shouted. Now Rowan saw what Torrin was heading for. It was a small knoll with a stand of larger trees gathered around its crown, but what caught Rowan's attention was the shallow pond that curled around the back of the hill, protecting it.

They galloped up the rise to the top and Rowan threw herself to the ground before Torrin had completely stopped his mount. He jumped down after her and slapped the big black horse on the rump, sending it towards the trees near the lake. He inspected the top of the hill. The others dismounted and drew weapons, gathering. Rowan looked at the Raken – now only a few hundred paces away.

"Erys save us! Look at the monsters!" Nathel stared in dismay at the enemy horde. He glanced wildly around then back at the Raken.

Torrin strode to Dalemar. "Are you well?"

The Rith nodded, his face drawn. "I've got enough left for a trick or two." He turned to Hathunor. "They can't find what they can't see."

The huge Raken bent down to listen to Dalemar's instructions.

Torrin looked at them all grimly. "Fan out. Protect the Messenger. Erys shelter us."

Torrin and Nathel flanked Rowan and the rest of the companions placed themselves on ether side: Dalemar and Hathunor to one side, Arynilas and Borlin to the other.

Arynilas began to loose arrows up into the air. They flew in a great arc to land among the on-coming Raken. Rowan drew her long dagger and brought her sword up to her forehead, whispering the spell words. The sword began to hum and the cold in her limbs receded, replaced by the sword's energy.

"One day you will have to show me how that sword works." Torrin eyed her weapon.

"If we survive this, you have my word," she promised.

A seething mass of black bodies rushed toward them. They would be swarmed, overwhelmed. It would be over quickly. At least she would die with her sword in her hand, fighting next to people she cared about.

The Raken were closer now. Rowan could see their red glinting eyes, the jagged ivory of bared teeth, black scaled skin.

Rowan glanced at the grim, determined faces of her friends. They would not give in so easily. *But they would still die.* Out in the wild where no one would know.

As the Raken approached, they spread out, cutting off escape. One hundred paces, seventy, thirty.

Then the Raken slowed, trotting to a halt. The Draes began to cast about in confusion. Rowan blinked in baffled amazement.

She looked over to Torrin and gasped. Her companions were gone. She was alone on the hilltop. Panic rose in her chest as she spun to look behind her.

"What?" It was Nathel's voice. It came from right beside her but there was no one there.

"Dalemar!" Torrin on her other side.

She turned quickly to look at the empty air.

Dalemar's voice came out of nothing. "Can you tie it off Hathunor? So it stays without one of us holding it?"

"What have you done, Rith?" There was true surprise in Arynilas' voice.

"They can no longer see us, hear us or smell us. It is as though we have disappeared," said Dalemar.

"We 'ave disappeared, or at least ye 'ave! I can see meself." Borlin's gruff voice sounded somewhere to the right.

"You said hear and smell as well? If we cannot see each other, then why can we still hear each other?" Arynilas had moved back behind.

"That is an interesting question," said Dalemar.

"Hathunor needs to hear friends," rumbled the Saa Raken.

The Raken were advancing cautiously towards the hilltop. One Raken in the center of the line cast his arm out, speaking in a guttural voice. The rest began to fan out, huge heads swivelling from side to side.

"We need to get out of the way. Unless your spell made us formless as well." Torrin's voice came from behind Rowan now.

"Hathunor has done a good job!" exclaimed Dalemar, "Each of us is wrapped in a blanket of magic. I'm not quite sure what he has done but I think it has something to do with bending the senses. You are right though, they will eventually stumble into us."

"They will be easier to kill," growled Borlin.

"It would still be risky with that many Raken," said Torrin from behind Rowan. "Eventually they would close in on us, regardless of whether we are invisible." She felt a light touch on her back – Torrin had been trying to locate her. His fingertips skimmed leftward to her arm and then down her sleeve until he grasped her hand in his. Rowan sheathed her dagger and properly gripped his hand in return. It felt good to have more contact than an eerily disembodied voice.

"The spell only extends to the edge of the hill to hide us and the horses," said Dalemar. "We cannot leave it or the Raken will see us."

"We need a diversion," said Rowan. "Something to lead them away."

"Hathunor, do you think you can out run them?" asked Torrin.

The Saa Raken's gravelly laughter rumbled from their left. "Hathunor will lead them far away."

"We will make due north," said Torrin. "Once you have lost them, head back that way. Our progress will be slow."

The searching Drae Raken approached the foot of the knoll. There was silence on the hill top except for the whistling wind. Were it not for Torrin's warm hand holding hers, she would have believed she stood utterly alone. Rowan tightened her grip on his hand and received a strong squeeze in return. She felt the roughness of the back of his hand with her fingertips and the steady rhythm of his pulse. For a moment the beat of her own heart matched his and she could feel the energy of his presence next to her.

Suddenly there was a splash to the far left, down by the vegetation along the water's edge. Rowan turned to look for Hathunor, but the trees screened the water from view.

The searching Raken whipped their heads around to look for their quarry. Most of the Draes launched themselves as one toward the water, howling, in pursuit of Hathunor. The few that remained began to scour the area from which the companions had vanished

Torrin pulled on Rowan's hand. "We need to back up. Let's hope they don't run into any of the horses before their mates are out of hearing."

Stepping carefully backward, Rowan watched the Raken slowly advance on the hilltop. They snuffled the air, red eyes darting around. Two Raken were getting close to them. Torrin's grip tugged her insistently back. They were going to run out of room soon.

A horse nickered from the left. Rowan turned towards the sound. A Raken bumped into the invisible animal and slashed at it with long claws. A squeal of pain sounded. The horse must have kicked out with its hind legs because the aggressor was sent flying backward to tumble heavily to the bottom of the hill. The remaining Raken watched confounded as their brother rolled past them down the slope.

"That's it!" Torrin said beside her. He released her hand and she felt him brush past.

Arynilas's bow hummed from thin air to the right. Arrows thudded into black bodies. The Raken scattered, diving for cover. When they rushed to the place the arrows had come from, they found nothing.

Confused and questing around the hilltop, the Raken died swiftly. The companions called continually to one another to ensure they didn't hurt each other by accident.

"Is anyone hurt?" asked Torrin.

As the others called out around her, Rowan noted their positions. "I'm well."

"Why didn't the Raken disappear when they got to the top of the hill?" Torrin had moved back toward the trees.

"I'm not sure. Perhaps because they were not on the hill when Hathunor cast the spell," said Dalemar from the right.

Whatever the reason, Rowan was relieved the Draes had remained visible. She envisioned a frightening picture of stumbling into Raken she could not see. Hopefully Hathunor was able to lead the main group of Draes far away. "Do you think the Draes chasing Hathunor heard the battle?"

"I doubt they could hear much above the racket they were making themselves," replied Nathel from somewhere behind Rowan.

Rowan's sword was still humming in her hand and she stilled it with the spell words. The battle left her feeling weak, but no longer cold. She could hardly believe they were still alive.

"We need to get off this hill so we can see each other," she called.

"That would be wise; I do not know how long the spell will last." Dalemar's tired voice was right beside her but it came from low down. Rowan reached out, groping through the air. Her hand touched the soft leather of his coat.

"Are you alright, Dalemar?"

He sighed. "I am very weak is all."

Rowan reached up to re-sheathed her sword, then bent to find the Rith again. "Come rest your weight on me." She felt for his hand and helped him to his feet.

"Dalemar?" Nathel was beside them. Rowan reached out and found the healer's outstretched hands and guided him to Dalemar's other side. Nathel shouldered much of the Rith's weight as they moved down the hill toward the edge of the spell. When they finally passed its boundary, Nathel and Dalemar winked into existence beside her and Rowan breathed a sigh of relief.

Dalemar was grey with exhaustion. They carried him away from the spell's edge and gently lowered him to the ground.

As Rowan turned to look back at the hill, Arynilas appeared carrying her cloak. Had she pulled it off before the attack? "Thank you," she said as he handed it to her.

Torrin appeared next, pulling a cluster of reins that fanned out behind him to suddenly become four horses. Borlin appeared shortly afterwards with the remaining two.

Rowan looked closely at Roanus. Her horse seemed uninjured from his fall. Borlin's poor mare had four long claw marks on her left flank, though, and the Stoneman patted the bay horse consolingly as he inspected the wounds.

Nathel retrieved a waterskin and some food from his saddlebags and knelt down, offering them to Dalemar.

"We should move as far from here as we can, in case they return." Torrin squatted in front of the exhausted Rith. "That was quite something, Dalemar. You saved our lives." He reached out and grasped him by the shoulder.

"Nonsense, I didn't do it, Hathunor did."

"Hathunor could not have done it without your idea and magic, Rith Dalemar," said Arynilas.

As Torrin rose his eyes met Rowan's. There was unrestrained relief on his face. Even after the battles in the Wilds, she had not seen that expression on his face.

She looked around at the rest of her companions. The sickening realization that they had all been willing to die to protect her hit like a fist in the gut.

She turned away and went to see to her horse.

Dalemar soon recovered enough to mount, allowing them to move deeper into the great marsh. The ground softened and the wind died down within the expanse of twisting trees and shallow ponds.

Rowan noticed none of this. She rode in silence, her eyes locked ahead but not seeing. They were all safe for the time being, but she couldn't seem to feel the relief of her companions. More Raken would come; they would try to reach her some other way. The deaths of her friends would be her fault, just as it had been her fault when her father had died.

She sighed. It was one thing to tell yourself there was nothing you could have done, to hear it said to you over and over, but it was quite another to truly believe it in your heart.

The day her father died flashed through her memory and this time she did not fight it, did not push it away. It settled around her like a dream. She had been afraid. Not yet tested in real battle.

She knew she was not ready. Her mother knew it and so did her father. Still there had been little choice that searing hot day when the sparkling blue of the Eryos Ocean seemed to expand into the very air itself.

The marauding ships had somehow breached the ring defences of the Myrian fleet, enabling them to land in the small harbour of Heria. Rowan remembered how amazed she was that so many men could come from so few ships.

Her parents had kept her between them. Already she was beyond most with her sword; even then it had been a calling her family had taken seriously. Her brother, Andin, had done chores for her so she would have more time to practice. Her mother and father saved to send her to study under a master swordsman, until she could earn the honour that allowed her to train for her homeland.

The moment the pirate's sword struck her father down in front of her, sending his blood spraying like rubies, she had known. As her mother screamed in rage, Rowan had known it was her fault. It had been meant for her, the sword that killed her father. He had stepped in front of it, given his life to spare hers.

It was his sacrifice that had driven her to train so relentlessly over the years, bringing her skill with the sword up to the highest levels, always seeking to improve and learn new things.

No one would ever need to step in front of a blade for her again.

The shadows around them deepened as the sun set. Rowan gradually pulled free of the dark power of that memory – a sinkhole of grief and guilt.

The companions began to search for a safe haven for the night. The idea of heading deeper into the marsh and placing more distance between themselves and the Raken was very tempting, but they needed rest more than reassurance.

Arynilas found a campsite within a dense thicket. They pushed their way through the scrubby trees, collecting burrs and dead leaves. A tiny clearing opened up showing the first glittering stars in the evening sky. There was enough room for a small camp and space to tether the horses.

The animals were exhausted. They stood together in the gathering dark, heads down, muzzles near the ground, eyes closing. Rowan went to see to them, still needing to be away from the others. Her fingers fumbled with the leather cinch on her saddle, and she bit down on her bottom lip. The knot finally loosened and she tugged at the strap.

She should have insisted on traveling alone through the wilds and Klyssen. The voice in her head named her for a fool; brave or not, she had condemned her companions. Now she was torn between wanting to protect them from her enemies and needing their help to get to King Cerebus.

She sensed movement and turned to find Torrin watching her.

"Something is wrong." he said quietly.

Rowan pulled her saddle down to place it on the leaf-strewn ground. "I am fine."

"Not good enough. I know something is bothering you."

Rowan was surprised when the tears came. It had been a long time since she last cried. She tore open her saddlebag, her vision blurring.

Torrin strode forward and grasped her arm, turning her toward him, his expression concerned.

"I am fine," said Rowan rubbing at her cheeks with the back of her hand. "It is just the strain of battle."

He shook his head, amusement flashing over his face. "I have seen you in battle. Most war-hardened men would be blubbering on their knees before you would crack. No, this is something different."

Rowan sighed and tugged her arm free. "Stubborn man," she whispered under her breath resuming her search for a brush. "I cannot bear the thought of any of you getting killed because of me. Like my fa – " she could not say it.

"Like what?"

Rowan shook her head. "Because of this Erys-forsaken mission, you were *all* almost killed, and not just today. I don't think I could live with myself if any of you died because of me. I should have continued on my own like I had wanted to when I first met you."

"You would have died," Torrin said flatly.

"Perhaps, but at least I wouldn't have led you all into such danger."

Torrin crossed his arms, scowling. "If you think you are responsible for the decision we made to see you to Pellaris, then you are greatly mistaken. The summons we were answering from King Cerebus was to come to his aid. *You* are his aid! Even if your mission was not so akin to our own, we would never have let you carry on alone with a Trieton of Raken on your heels."

"At least you would have made it to Pellaris safely, without your lives at stake every step of the way."

"And you think I'm stubborn!"

Rowan exhaled in exasperation.

"You feel guilt over the straits we find ourselves in," he continued, "but that guilt is not for you to take. You have no right to hold yourself responsible for the decisions of grown men. We knew the risks, and I know that each of us would make the same choice again. Not to mention the fact that each of us cares for you and would never want to see you hurt." He lowered his voice, adding menacingly, "And if you think to slip away and journey without our protection, know this: I will hunt you down and personally drag you back kicking and screaming."

Rowan's eyebrows rose at the undignified image.

She scowled back at him. "Wishful thinking."

"We shall see."

Torrin turned his back and walked over to his big black horse.

Rowan watched him, realizing abruptly that much of her guilt had been replaced with anger. His touch was gentle and he spoke softly to the animal as he removed the saddle and began rubbing his sweat-encrusted coat.

Rowan turned back to Roanus and began to brush him. Much of what Torrin had said was true but it would not change the responsibility she would feel if any of them got hurt.

Her mother's voice sounded in her head. *You must not take so much on your shoulders, Cheria. There are always others to help carry the burden. It was* his *choice. Your father would not have wanted you to feel this way.*

Guilt sat on her shoulders, but its weight was lessened. You couldn't make people's decisions for them, even to keep them safe.

When they had seen to the horses, Rowan finally gave in to her weariness. The air was cold and crisp and there was blessedly little wind. Borlin had built a merry fire and she craved its warmth. The surrounding thicket leaned in like crowding tree creatures protecting them with outstretched twig limbs and spindly fingers.

The Bog Lands

Torrin opened his eyes to a thick blanket of mist, muffling sound and concealing the world. The air was moist and thick and as he sat up his blanket fell heavily into his lap. His friends were indistinct humps around the dead fire and the horses had disappeared. All he could discern of the thicket surrounding them was the odd thrusting branch.

Arynilas appeared and strode to the fire. Torrin would have started had he not been so used to the Tynithian's stealth.

"When did the mist rise?" he asked.

Arynilas squatted and began to relight the fire. "Before dawn."

The rest of the companions were stirring now and Borlin's exclamation came as if from far away. "How long till it burns off?"

"Not until the sun is high," Arynilas answered. "It will be like this every morning now that the temperatures have dropped."

Torrin rose and stretched his limbs, working the tightness out. Arynilas had the fire going quickly and Borlin began to make tea. Torrin packed his gear and went to see to the horses.

Rowan was with her big stallion, brushing him as he ate his grain ration. Torrin felt a powerful relief; he had half expected her to make good on her threat to leave them and try to travel alone. He knew what guilt could do to a person.

After a quick breakfast the company was in the saddle and wending their way through the mist, deeper into the twisting swamp.

A fly bit Torrin's neck and he swatted at it. Black shook his head furiously, trying to dislodge the insects crawling into his ears, stamping a hoof in frustration. Torrin sincerely hoped the ear covers Borlin was working on for the horses would be finished soon. The poor animals were being driven mad by clouds of biting flies.

Arynilas turned back towards them and shook his head. Torrin frowned and waved the flies away from his face. He pulled on his reins and gave Black a leg to turn him around on the tight game trail.

"Another back track?" asked Rowan.

"Looks like it," said Torrin.

Nathel groaned.

The horses began to pick a path carefully back through the squelching mud and hummocky moss. Another trail that looked deceptively clear had become impassable, narrowing into walls of tangled reeds and dark water. Although Arynilas knew the direction they needed to travel, finding clear paths was proving a challenge.

Thick reeds clustered along the trail, and small birds and animals skittered away as they passed. Torrin steered Black around a shallow pool of stagnant water, keeping him way from the edge. They had discovered that what looked like open, solid ground surrounding the pools were in fact mats of moss and grasses floating over viscous mud. Borlin's mare still sported the mud from a plunge up to her belly earlier today.

Torrin pulled his scarf up to cover his nose and mouth and urged his horse after the others. The sun was beginning to set now and they would need to find a campsite soon. The darkness would bring a relief from the bugs, but the maze of bogs transformed as the light faded into a haunted wasteland. Spooky stories about the bog lands were traded like currency among the children in Pellaris. Giant beasts as tall as houses were said to roam through the swamps and snakelike monsters lived in the dark water. One toe dipped in the fetid muck could doom an unwary traveler. As he looked over the endless expanse of twisted trees with their gnarled branches tricking the eye into seeing things that were not really there, Torrin could well understand where the stories came from.

Swatting at more flies and steering Black through the reeds, Torrin recalled the chilling tales told by the guards in the bailey of Pellaris keep about wraiths that would rise out of the swamp water at dusk and travel the marsh by night, killing all those they touched. A brave soul could be deceived into believing there was nothing to fear during the daylight, but when the sun sank below the horizon, the mist rose to link the living with the dead. Torrin rolled his shoulders and grimaced as he dug out another biter crawling beneath his collar. The truth was almost worse.

A flock of birds with bright plumage flushed up into the air to the right. Black startled in response and Torrin put a hand on the young horse's neck to calm him. The birds wheeled about with a cacophony, before settling again in the twisting trees. Already they had seen an amazing number of birds: huge wading herons with knife-like bills for spearing fish; eagles and hawks and tiny jewel-like kingfishers. Bright blue-and-yellow ducks floated on some of the larger ponds and shiny black darters rested in the trees with their wings outstretched to dry in the sun. Torrin watched the birds as they chattered and flew. Stories about the marshes never mentioned the beauty of the wildlife.

Arynilas turned off the trail they were following to head into a thicket. The companions leaned low over their mounts as they pushed through the dense vegetation. Torrin caught a glimpse of Rowan's tense expression in the dusk light. He had noticed her frequently casting back for a possible glimpse of Hathunor's return. Of the Raken, they had seen nothing but he hoped that Hathunor had led his pursuers far away.

Torrin's turn came to push through into the thicket. When he emerged from the clinging, scratching branches, he saw a clearing much like the previous night's camp. He experienced a moment of disorientation, wondering if they were just blundering in circles.

The creeping pace of their progress was a source of frustration. After the open grassland of Klyssen Torrin felt as though they were standing still, with the world continuing on without them. They were all getting to rest though, and for that at least Torrin was thankful.

"What say you, Tor? Four or five more days to the border of Pellar?" Nathel came to where Torrin was sitting, oiling his broadsword in the light of their small fire. Each of them had to take extra care of their gear here. In the moist air, metal began to rust very quickly. Rowan and Borlin were sitting across the fire from Torrin performing the same task.

Torrin stretched his shoulder muscles. "Sounds right, providing we don't have to retrace our steps too often." Torrin accepted a mug of hot tea from Nathel before his brother settled next to him.

"How long do you reckon it would have taken us to go around the bogs?"

"Three weeks at least," replied Torrin.

Nathel sighed. "Perhaps the Raken are hoping to set up ambush on the other side."

The rest of the companions looked up from their various tasks of repairing gear and cleaning weapons, their hands stilled. Rowan frowned, Arynilas lifted one smooth eyebrow and Borlin removed his pipe from between his teeth, puffing out a curse with the smoke as he dropped the last pair of ear guards for the horses to the ground in disgust.

Dalemar cleared his throat. "If Hathunor has led the Raken on the merry chase I think he has, it will take them a good while to make it out of the bogs and get to the other side to meet us. Unless there are more that we do not know of waiting to intercept us, we should be well ahead of the group tracking us.

"So we best be on our guard at the edge o' the bogs," said Borlin darkly.

"There are also the Raken besieging the city of Pellaris itself," said Nathel.

Torrin shook his head. "Their focus will not be on us though."

Rowan began to clean her sword once more. "In Balor, you said that there was a way into Pellaris around the siege?"

"Tunnels," answered Nathel.

"Tunnels?"

Torrin nodded. "They run beneath the walls of the city and extend quite far into the surrounding forest. Depending on what the Raken movements are, we should be able to enter the city undetected."

"How do you know of them?" Rowan asked.

"Tor and I discovered them when we were kids," said Nathel with a grin. "Our father was a king's man fairly high in King Cerebus's favour and we had the run of the fortress when we were young. We discovered the tunnels one day down in the old quarter playing Dragons and Demons with some kids." He chuckled. "We got ourselves into a lot of trouble in those days."

Torrin glanced sideways at his brother. "You mean *you* got us into trouble. I was always trying to make sure you didn't break your neck or crack open your fool's head!"

Borlin's guffaw sent the birds roosting in the surrounding trees scrambling for cover.

Torrin frowned, he hadn't thought of his father in a long time. Ralor had been a career soldier in the Pellarian army – a man of great renown for his battle and leadership skills. He had risen through the ranks swiftly until he reached the king's side, serving as captain of the King's Guard. Ralor and Cerebus had become friends – a rare thing in palace hierarchy where a common born soldier and a king only crossed paths fleetingly. But they had recognized something in each other and relied upon one another like brothers.

Torrin's father served Cerebus as captain and friend until he died in a border skirmish with a renegade Taborian warlord. Ralor had taken an arrow that had been meant for Cerebus. Torrin and Nathel were teenage boys when their father died. Their mother had passed on years earlier and the boys had no other relatives to look after them, so Cerebus had taken responsibility for Ralor's sons. Torrin was old enough to look out for himself and Nathel but Cerebus had insisted that they stay at the keep in their father's quarters as long as they wanted to.

Torrin had grown up groomed to take Ralor's place at the king's side and when Ralor died, Cerebus had turned to Torrin, hoping to find in him a man like his father had been. Torrin was young but he had proven himself capable and in time he surpassed even his father's skills. When Torrin was only twenty, King Cerebus placed him in command of the elite King's Guard, a position that Torrin kept until he married the lovely daughter of a prominent member of the healers' guild. King Cerebus blessed the union and promoted Torrin to commander at arms for the Pelarian army.

But after the terrible events of that day in Balor, going back to Pellaris and carrying on with the life he had led was unthinkable. He could never have faced the people he knew – the people who had known and loved Emma and his daughters. It was far easier to face the unknown life of a mercenary, surrounded by men who didn't know him or his past. He was just another sword arm, another soldier for hire.

Gradually he and his brother garnered a reputation among the men they fought with, a reputation based not on Torrin's past but on his skill as a warrior and his ability to lead men in battle. Few soldiers and mercenaries fighting in the Ren wars hadn't heard of the big northern brothers who brought death to the enemy. And when they met Arynilas and Borlin that reputation grew even further.

Torrin studied his brother who was stretched out staring into the fire. He marvelled that Nathel had left his life in Pellaris, following Torrin into his own private hell. Nathel was everything that Torrin was not. Before Torrin had lost his wife and daughters, there had been many similarities between them, but the pain of the last seven years had scoured away the light-hearted man Torrin had been, leaving only a hardened, battle-scarred shell full of grief and bitterness – his guilt refused to let him heal.

And so Nathel, a rogue at heart, had developed more of the traits that Torrin had lost, living fully for both of them. He laughed and joked when his brother could not, was quick to smile when Torrin had forgotten what a smile felt like on his face. There was nothing Torrin wouldn't do for his brother. He knew he could never repay Nathel for his loyalty so when Cerebus's summons had reached them in the south, Torrin had decided to return to Pellar for his brother.

Torrin sheathed his sword and took up his cooling tea. Nathel was looking forward to returning to the northern city. But seven years was a long time. People changed; places changed. He hoped his brother wouldn't be disappointed.

Torrin rubbed a hand down his face. He was dreading the return.

Movement across from him caught his eye. Rowan put away her gear and stood, bending over the fire to pour herself a last cup of tea. Her long braid swung forward over her shoulder, its golden strands glinting in the firelight. She was absorbed in her own thoughts and the pensive expression on her face made her look even more beautiful in the light of the fire.

They finished the last of their tea and began to roll themselves into their blankets around the dying fire. Torrin closed his eyes; felt the stillness of the bog lands like a weighted heaviness – the calm before the storm. Out beyond the glowing fire and the sleeping forms of his friends, battles were being fought for the kingdom of his birth and although he no longer considered Pellar his home, he couldn't help but feel old loyalties stir.

Arorans and Tynithians

Rowan woke the next morning to the cold grey of the perpetual morning mist. She rolled out of her blankets to find Borlin already stooped over a small fire, preparing breakfast. After packing her gear away into her saddlebags, she made her way to the fire. A cluster of pots sat above the fire on a grate. She lifted the corner of one lid to peek at the contents and a billow of steam escaped.

Borlin growled at her. "Ye'll let all the steam out, an breakfast 'l be ruined. I'll tell ye lass, never interrupt a Stoneman and 'is cookin."

Rowan laughed and raised her hands in submission. "As you say Borlin, but it's hard to resist when it smells so good."

The Stoneman puffed up his chest and handed her a steaming cup of tea.

"Thank you." Rowan wrapped her hands around the hot cup, enjoying the warmth that spread through her cold fingers.

"You're welcome, Lass. I'd not like to see you starve."

Rowan grinned into her cup. Borlin believed he was the only one among them who claimed any skill in cooking. Rowan was disinclined to alter that opinion. The culinary arts of Myris Dar were taught to most children, but the lure of the practice yard made her time spent in the kitchen grudging at best.

Borlin seemed to have an inexhaustible store of ingredients hidden away in his voluminous saddlebags. Indeed, they had eaten remarkably well for travelers. Borlin collected herbs and spices from every place they traveled. A special box containing packets of the different flavours was one of his prized possessions.

Rowan almost jumped when Torrin and Nathel materialized from the direction of the horses, and she greeted her companions as they gathered around the fire.

After breakfast they broke camp and saddled up. Borlin went around instructing them on how to attach the ear socks he had made for the horses. Roanus shook his head in irritation as Rowan tied the last cord to his bridle cheek strap. He settled quickly though, seeming to understand that the alternative was far worse.

Rowan mounted up and the companions pushed their way through the thicket, back out onto the game trail. If it weren't for Arynilas and his unerring sense of direction, Rowan wouldn't have known which way to go in the eerie white. The ghostly calls of birds sounded around them as they began to wend through the reeds. The horses' hoof beats resounded with dull thuds and even the jingle of tack was hard to hear. Rowan turned in her saddle to look behind at Borlin – already indistinct directly behind her. Another five days Nathel and Torrin had said. She was not looking forward to more Raken on the other side, but she would be happy to see the end of this expanse of marsh and its biting insects. The bird life was the only thing she would miss. She sighed and turned forward again – it reminded her so strongly of home.

The morning passed as they threaded their way through the twisting trees and tall marsh grass. Rowan's thoughts turned to Hathunor. Her giant friend was out there alone somewhere in this vast morass. The more time that passed without Hathunor's return the more worried Rowan became. She envisioned his scaled skin covered in wounds and blood. She saw him lying dead in the waters of the bogs, having somehow been caught and overwhelmed by the Drae Raken that pursued him. She strove to dispel such dark images from her thoughts by reciting the message she carried. It ran through her mind again and again. The words lost their meaning, becoming a string of sounds in her head.

It wasn't until Nathel's horse stopped in front of her and she had to rein in, that she realized how lost in thought she had been. Arynilas spoke quietly from the mist ahead, but his voice carried to her. "Something comes. It is large!"

The companions gathered into a defensive circle, and Rowan reached up and drew her sword. The ring of weapons leaving scabbards was muted by the mist.

After a few moments Rowan heard the sound of movement ahead through the screen of trees. But it was the vibrations in the ground that told her something huge was approaching.

Roanus tossed his head, ears flicking uncertainly. Rowan placed a hand on his neck to calm him. The sounds became louder – the blowing of a great breath was clearly audible.

The mist ahead of them darkened as a huge shape loomed over the trees. Rowan gasped and Nathel whistled in wonder. A gigantic beast materialized out of the swirling fog. Seeing the companions, it stopped. The beast looked at them carefully, its small eyes passing over each one. Rowan held her breath, staring in wonder.

It looked as though Erys had taken different animals and combined them to create this behemoth. Its short tan hide was covered with dark vertical stripes; the huge head held on its short, massive neck sported an elongated snout, which was busy chewing the marsh grass that dangled from its mouth. The creature's legs were long and its three-toed feet wide. Its tail, which ended in a horsehair-like tuft, swung continuously from side to side, brushing away the annoyance of insects.

The beast snorted and the horses spooked at the percussive sound. Then the enormous creature turned away and continued into the fog, fading back into the grey of myth as though it had never existed.

"What in the name of Erys was that?" asked Nathel in the silence.

Dalemar opened his mouth, but it was Arynilas who spoke. "It was an Aroran, a creature that used to roam across Eryos. They have dwindled to a few pockets of inaccessible land where they cannot be hunted. Most people have forgotten them – much like you, Messenger, and your homeland of Myris Dar."

"An Aroran." Borlin shook his head, dismounting and opening his saddlebag. The mist was dissipating, and a relatively dry hummock nearby provided an opportunity for a respite and a midday meal.

Rowan saw to Roanus, then sought the Tynithian. "Have you seen Arorans before?"

"Many hundreds of years ago they were found all across Eryos. When I was a child I once saw them move in a great herd over the land, but even then there were not as many as there had been."

"How long ago was that?" Rowan asked.

"Four hundred and sixty human years I believe."

"And how long was your childhood?" Rowan wondered if she was being impolite, but Arynilas's tilted eyes twinkled.

"A Tynithian is no longer considered a child once he or she has passed their hundredth human year."

Rowan's eyes widened. "Are you are still considered young for a Tynithian?"

"Fairly. I am still before my middle century. I would be considered about 30 in human terms."

Rowan looked down at the wedge of cheese and dried meat still uneaten in her hand as she tried to imagine having a childhood that lasted a century. Her own scant years seemed less than a blink in comparison.

As if Arynilas had heard this thought, he said, "To have a thousand years to live a life is also to give up that which shorter lived people hold dear – time. Each precious moment of life is no longer noted and savoured. I believe we lose as much as we gain."

"Humans lose reverence for life far more easily than you think, Arynilas," Torrin said quietly. He lay stretched out and propped on one elbow, listening to their conversation as he carved off bits of dried apple. Arynilas looked over at Torrin, his gemlike eyes holding a knowing look.

He looked back at Rowan and then pointed to the marshes around them. "Do you not feel it here, in this place?"

"Feel what," asked Rowan.

"A suspension of time," answered Torrin for the Tynithian.

"I thought you might be able to feel it," said Arynilas.

Rowan glanced between them. "It does feel different here, heavier, as if we are standing still."

Arynilas nodded. "It is how I feel when I take the shape of the fox. This place forces us to be in a moment suspended. To be in a place of stillness."

"Like Hathunor," said Rowan. "I have noticed that he does not dwell on the future or the past."

"He is like a Rith Piryon, a master at time travel." Dalemar came to sit beside them. "The Piryons are a small closed sect of Rith society that believes the passage of time is only a concept in our minds, a way to link seemingly separate events. Piryons claim to be able to travel through time because they see all of history as one point that can be accessed in a suspended moment which is continuously *this* moment." Dalemar shook his head. "Most Riths do not completely understand the Piryons and their abilities, but I do see some of their philosophy embodied in Hathunor."

Rowan thought again of the black fox, remembering its dark shadow during a full moon night. She wondered what it must feel like to take such a shape. "When do Tynithians learn to shape shift?"

Arynilas looked squarely back at Rowan. "My people search for their animal form during the first few hundred years of their lives. I was very young when my other self found me; only one hundred and fifty. Some Tynithians search for three hundred years."

"The fox found you?" Rowan asked.

Arynilas nodded, black hair swinging forward, and Rowan saw in her mind the waving tail of the fox. "We are all searching for our true selves. Sometimes when we meet another person we find a part of that self in them. Tynithians also search for that self in animals. It is why we live in Dan Tynell, the Great Green Hall – to surround ourselves with the creatures of Erys so that we might meet the one we are looking for. So that it might find us."

"Are you saying that the fox and you are actually separate beings that are somehow joined?" asked Rowan.

"No. We are the same. The search for our animal self is a spiritual one. A journey within that takes us far further than any physical path that we might travel."

Rowan frowned. "Is it true that some Tynithians choose to live only in their animal form?"

"It is rare but it does happen. When we become our other selves, we access a different world from this one. We are still a part of this one, but our perceptions are altered such that we see things we cannot normally see. When I take my other form, the fox changes me. My traits are still there but they become superseded by the fox and what he sees. The same is true of this form – the fox is still in me but my Tynithian traits are stronger. Those of my people who choose to exist completely in animal form are lost to those of us who do not. They forget the Tynithian in them and can no longer return to that form."

Rowan nodded. Arynilas's superior senses, his tracking ability and physical agility were from his fox, then. "What do you see, when you become the fox?"

Arynilas studied her with his dark sapphire eyes, his expression grave. "I see that which these eyes cannot. The magic plane." Arynilas turned to Dalemar. "The place where Rith kind access their power. It is all around us but we do not see it. Dalemar will one day be able to see it completely."

Dalemar, listening as he smoked his pipe, nodded his head. "Now I see only glimpses of it, and only when I spell-cast."

Rowan looked back at Arynilas, "Why then do you not take the shape of the fox more often if it is possible to see such wondrous things?"

"Because it is dangerous to do so. The fox, though part of my true self, is more powerful than I. He lives by instinct and primal need. To exist too long in that form is to risk loosing myself to him."

Rowan nodded. "You are closely connected to Erys."

Arynilas tilted his head. "Yes."

"We have so much to learn from you," Rowan said quietly.

"The opposite is also true." A faint smile pulled at the corners of Arynilas's mouth and Rowan realized that was precisely why Arynilas chose to travel with Torrin and his companions.

"Most Tynithians believe there is little to learn from the other races of Eryos," Arynilas said. "I have decided otherwise."

Torrin gave a short, cynical bark of laughter. "So that is your reason for following a madman and his foolish friends across Eryos?"

"Friendship is also the reason, and a life debt."

Torrin sobered. "You've repaid that debt a thousand fold, Arynilas. I would gladly follow you, my friend."

Arynilas shook his head. "Some are *meant* to lead."

Returning through Mist

Rowan rode behind Dalemar through the swirling white mist, his form already indistinct in the short distance between them. Ahead of the Rith, Torrin was little more than a dark mass. The fog this morning was the thickest they had yet encountered. The only link between the companions was the rider in front and behind.

They periodically moved through pockets of clearer air and took the opportunity to check and make sure everyone was together. Twice now they had needed to stop and call out to each other.

Rowan was soaked. The air was so laden with moisture that it settled into her clothing and hair. She was cold and hoped they would stop soon. The birdcalls around them were muffled and Rowan had no idea how far the morning had progressed.

Then a whistle came from behind – a bird not of the marshes. Rowan turned quickly to look back. Borlin, riding behind her was pulling his short sword from its scabbard, craning around to peer into the thick whiteness behind.

Nathel had rear guard. Hooves pounded dully from behind and the dark bulk of man and horse appeared. Nathel had his sword drawn.

Torrin, Dalemar and Arynilas loomed to Rowan's right, having turned their horses around and moved back down the trail.

"What is it?" Torrin's voice was quiet.

"We are being followed," replied Nathel.

"Did you see who?"

Nathel shook his head. "Whoever it is, they are close."

Metal rang through the air as as Torrin drew his broadsword. Rowan reached up over her shoulder, fingers grasping the cold hilt of her blade. They gathered in a tight semi-circle facing back the way they had come.

Roanus perked his ears forward, listening. His head came up. Rowan strained to hear and see through the fog. Twice she thought she saw something moving only to realize that the mist was to blame, uncovering trees and shrubs creating darker shadows through the white.

Her companions were leaning forward in their saddles, tense with anticipation. Arynilas raised his bow and aimed.

Rowan heard something, a foot squelching in mud perhaps. The Tynithian held his bow steady, waiting.

Then, out of the fog a big dark form materialized, pitch black against the white. A staccato rumble carried to them.

Rowan jumped down from her horse with an exclamation, and ran through the mist. Hathunor became clear as she approached him, his fangs exposed in a wide grin. Rowan laughed in delight as as he scooped her up into his huge arms. She wrapped her own arms around his thick neck, careful to avoid his spikes. By the time Hathunor set her on the ground, the rest of the companions were patting him on the back and shoulders as they exchanged greetings. The big Saa Raken grinned happily down at them all, his spiked crest heavy with moisture.

Rowan closed her eyes in relief as the tight band of worry that had been around her chest faded.

"What happened?" asked Nathel in excitement.

Hathunor cast an arm back the way he had come, encompassing the mist behind, and rumbled, "Hathunor lead little brothers very far. They not see Hathunor. They followed for long time."

Torrin nodded from horseback, a rare smile on his face. "Thank you, Hathunor. I'm glad you are back with us."

Hathunor clapped a large clawed fist to his chest and nodded his head.

"You must have led them away for a long time, Hathunor. It has been almost three days since we entered the marshes," said Rowan.

Hathunor nodded, pleased. "Little brothers followed Hathunor two days. Then Hathunor make little brothers lost."

Nathel snickered. "Well done. Let's hope they spend a while bumbling around in this Erys-forsaken mist."

"Little brothers find way soon but not too soon," rumbled Hathunor.

"Won't they be able to follow your trail to us?" asked Dalemar.

Hathunor shook his head, water droplets flying from his crest. "Hathunor travel here in wet."

"You waded through the ponds?" Torrin looked surprised as Hathunor nodded, fangs flashing.

Rowan looked closely at the Saa Raken and shook her head in wonder; he looked as fresh as always.

"Do you think we can make it to the edge of the marshes before the Raken pick up our original trail?" Rowan asked.

Torrin nodded. "We have to be getting close to the edge." He turned to look a question at Arynilas.

The Tynithian pointed at the ground. "The way underfoot has been gradually getting harder. It will not be long before we see the end of the bog lands."

As the companions neared the edge of the bog lands, Rowan felt as though they were stepping from an enchanted realm of stillness into a perilous world of turmoil. Like Arynilas said, time had seemed to move differently in the bog lands, as if the world beyond had simply ceased to exist.

Hathunor and the Tynithian ranged ahead, scouting. The giant Saa Raken took particular delight in resuming his scouting duties. His long-limbed body was loose and relaxed as he moved, disappearing into the vegetation. Rowan steered her horse around a clump of bushes and looked back at the expanse of twisting trees. She thought about the giant Aroran they had seen and almost wondered if it had been a dream, a hallucination brought on by the monotony of the bogs.

The soggy, hummocky ground was finally hardening and the sucking mud gave way to long stretches of grass-covered earth. They encountered water less frequently; the trees grew much taller and straighter, and as clumps of dense vegetation thinned they could see further into the distance.

Now that they no longer had to move in single file, Rowan found herself riding beside Torrin. "How far is it to Pellaris?" she asked.

"About seven days, six if we hurry."

"What will you and the others do once we have reached King Cerebus?"

Torrin glanced over at her and a frown creased his brow. It was a while before he answered. "We will do whatever Cerebus requires of us. Though I don't know what use five extra swords will be against a Raken horde."

"You do not give yourselves enough credit," Rowan said quietly.

"What of you? What will your course be after you deliver your message to the king? Will you return to Myris Dar?"

Now it was Rowan's turn to frown. She had not thought beyond her goal of getting to Pellaris.

Before she could answer, Torrin spoke again, his tone regretful. "There is no need for you to go to Pellaris itself. Dalemar and the rest of us know the message. We can deliver it to the King."

Rowan shook her head. "No. I am honour bound. Truthfully, the message is only half of my mission. Dell's role of emissary and ambassador for my people fell to me when he died. Reaching King Cerebus and delivering the message is the priority, but once that is accomplished, the responsibility of representing my people will begin. Though to be honest, I'm not certain I know how to fulfill that role."

"You will do fine." There was amusement in Torrin's voice and Rowan glanced over at him curiously.

Torrin returned her gaze and one of his eyebrows rose. "You truly do not know?"

"Know what?"

"There is no role of emissary for you to fulfill. You simply *are* the emissary of Myris Dar. It is in everything you do and say, how you speak to people and the bearing with which you conduct yourself. We have been traveling with you for a long time, Rowan, and I have seen the emissary many times."

Rowan's eyebrows rose in surprise. "Well I suppose my people are known for their martial skills. Perhaps I can represent Myrians through my sword. I could help defend the city."

Torrin's expression darkened and he turned to look ahead. His posture remained relaxed but his jaw tensed.

The silence stretched. Rowan reined her horse to the right to avoid a broken stump and she switched the rein to her other hand. "There is of course still the Slayer to be found. Who knows, maybe I can help find him."

Torrin nodded. "Dalemar hopes to find information pertaining to the Slayer in the Library of Pellaris. It seems like a small chance."

Rowan had often thought of the man that they must find. It was unlikely that King Cerebus would know who the Slayer was. With nothing to go on, they would have to search through dusty old books, not likely to be a promising venture.

"We will miss you when you decide to go home," Torrin said quietly. "I will miss you. It has been an honour to travel with you and fight by your side." His voice was gruff.

Rowan caught her breath as a pang of sorrow rose in her chest at the thought of being apart from this stern warrior whose quiet strength had slowly and gently surrounded her – a shield between her and the world.

Rowan frowned, shaken. "I shall miss you all as well."

Part II

Pellar

Torrin kicked Black into a lope across an open expanse of rolling parkland, toward a large stand of trees. Although Arynilas had scanned the surrounding woodland before they headed out into the open, Torrin checked again to the sides of the wide opening. The transition here was gradual, unlike the border along the Klyssen Plains, where the bog lands sat like a fence along the horizon.

He slowed Black as they reached the trees, turning to scan behind as the rest of the company made it into the forest. All was quiet. The calm of the bog lands, it seemed, extended into Pellar's parklands as well. They had not run into Raken and Torrin dared to hope they wouldn't catch them before they reached King Cerebus.

He urged his horse further into the trees, wending around the large trunks. Pellaris was only a few days away. The fortress city and capital of Pellar was the center of civilized Eryos and it glowed like a beacon in his mind's eye.

He could see the city perched high on its promontory. It commanded unobstructed views of everything around it. To the west, the parkland continued until it reached the cold moors of Tabor. To the east, Krang in its mountain vastness sat huddled like a gray wall upon the horizon. And to the north, the Eryos Ocean surged against the foot of a sheer cliff upon which the citadel was built.

Torrin sighed. Despite himself, he longed to see the city again; though it would bring back more than he wanted to remember. Years had past since he had last walked its narrow, teeming streets. Emma had walked beside him, her hand in his as they searched for a birthday present for their older daughter, Arial. They had left soon after on their fated trip to Klyssen. Torrin pushed the memory aside.

Rowan moved abreast of him, her big grey stallion walking easily on a loose rein through the red and gold leaves covering the ground. Torrin frowned. Rowan had withdrawn from them a little as the goal of her mission drew nearer. He would gladly shoulder the weight she carried, but she would never let others bear the responsibility for the Message. Erys willing, they would not be too late.

They came to another clearing. The temperature was dropping and the last of the evening sun just touched the uppermost branches of the surrounding trees; dead leaves drifted softly down, carried on a light breeze. Torrin reined in his horse. "This looks like a good place to camp for the night." He stepped down from Black.

Torrin stopped Borlin as he was reaching down to pick up a branch for firewood. "No more fires now, Borlin. We are getting too close."

"Aye, tis true." Looking crestfallen, Borlin opened his saddlebags for some trail rations.

With the horses seen to, the companions gathered together while they ate. The trees had already become ghostly poles against the surrounding darkness.

Torrin leaned back against his saddle and brought his knees up. Rowan passed along a cloth bag of nuts, and he murmured his thanks.

She turned to the Rith. "Have you been to the great library?"

Dalemar shook his head. "No, I have never been to Pellaris, but I've heard the city's library has the largest and most extensive collection in all of Eryos, with the exception perhaps of the Rith city of Tirynus."

Rowan turned back to Torrin. "Are you and Nathel are the only ones who have been to Pellaris?"

"Yes, though we have not been back for over seven years."

Rowan's green eyes clouded in sympathy, then steadied. "Tell me about Pellaris. What is the city like?"

How to describe the most magnificent, most terrible place in all of Eryos? Nathel saved him the trouble. There was pride in his brother's voice as he spoke. "It is the largest city in the north. Dendor in the south matches it in size but I do not believe Pellaris is matched in splendour by any other city in Eryos. The city is built on a large promontory that juts out. Cliffs – three hundred paces high protect it from invasion from the sea to the north, and a great wall, seven men high and twelve paces deep, protects the city's southern flanks. Pellaris's keep is perched on the very edge of the cliff. Part of it was carved from the stone itself centuries ago and the view of the water and the great harbour below is spectacular from its upper levels."

"If there are such high cliffs, how do you reach the harbour?" asked Rowan.

"A great stair carved through the stone allows access. Most of Tabor's trade comes through Pellaris harbour and it can be a busy place through the shipping season. The tides on the north coast are exceedingly high, especially when the moons are full. A unique floating wharf system, devised during the reign of Cerebus's grandfather, allows the ships moored there to rise and fall with the water level. A pair of gigantic bronze rings slide up and down poles set into the stone of the cliff."

Rowan nodded. "And the library?"

Nathel shrugged. He was never much for books.

Torrin tossed the bag of nuts to Borlin. "The library is located across from the great Temple. It is the third largest building in Pellaris after Temple of Erys and it houses an enormous collection of books and scrolls."

"If the Priesthood had had their way, they would have made their temple larger than the keep itself," said Nathel sarcastically.

"The Priesthood?" echoed Rowan.

"The Priesthood of Erys." Torrin shook his head in disgust. "They have become very powerful in Pellar and Tabor over the last hundred years. Their wealth comes from taking food and money from the poor in the guise of spiritual redemption and guidance. Their power comes from political maneuvering and manipulation of the king's generosity."

"This priesthood – they are like monks, but you don't approve of them?" Rowan asked.

"No," said Torrin flatly, "I do not. King Cerebus, unlike his father before him, is a generous man. He believes a king's responsibility, aside from protecting the kingdom, should be to guide his people with tolerance for individual rights. Cerebus, though he is a decorated warrior, will try peaceful means to end conflicts before reaching for the sword. The priesthood uses every chance it gets to take advantage of that generosity and plot against him. They know just how hard to push before backing down to avoid pitting themselves directly against the king. Power is what motivates the Priesthood and little else. Their spiritual goals are a crutch and a pretext to keep them above reproof."

Torrin felt Rowan studying him and he turned to meet her gaze.

"They can't all be corrupt," she said. "Surely a little of what likely began as a noble faith yet remains?"

Torrin shook his head.

Rowan broke eye contact and was turning away when Torrin reached out and stopped her with a hand on her arm. He held her gaze for a moment. "You will need to be very careful around them."

"That's putting it lightly!" said Nathel.

Rowan looked from one brother to the other. "Why?"

"The Priesthood would like women to do little more than bear children," said Nathel. "It has made the repression of women its philosophy in the name of Erys. Even thoughtless men such as us can see it."

Rowan frowned. "I don't understand. Erys is the Goddess. How could a group proclaiming to worship her get away with repressing women?"

"It is all about power," explained Torrin. "Originally the Priesthood's views on women were moderate, but when Cerebus was newly crowned he wanted women to have the same rights as men. And they do now in the eyes of the law, thanks to the king, but the Priesthood was sorely threatened. After all, Erys is female; who better to represent her than women? But there have not been priestesses in many generations and the priests, do no want to see women rise again in their ranks. They proclaimed that to truly honour the goddess, women should follow the ways of Erys and be the creators of man. To do this, the Priesthood decided that activities other than child bearing and rearing would distract women from the holiness of Erys' calling. Women who defied the teaching began to disappear or were excommunicated along with their families."

"And women stand for this?" Rowan hissed with disgust. "What hope is there for young women, if their prospects for life are already chosen for them? It is unjust. Some of the finest architects, physicians, metal-smiths and soldiers in Myris Dar are women. Women hold many of the highest seats in the great council. Women and men are not the same; it is true. We have different solutions and approaches to all that life offers. A man's way is not any better than a woman's way. Our strengths are different but we are each just as capable. People should choose to make of their lives what they will regardless of what is between their legs."

Torrin raised his eyebrows and studied her.

"It is true, much in Eryos is unjust but it has been that way for hundreds of years," shrugged Nathel. "Within Pellar, Tabor and Klyssen at least there are laws to protect women from abuse and mistreatment."

"What good does it do to protect the body when the mind is not free?" Rowan's voice was quieter, but no less vehement.

Torrin frowned. With a degree of shame, he had to admit that until he had met Rowan, he had never truly seen women as equals in many respects. He suspected most women themselves would be scandalized at the thought of joining the army or knocking on the door of Pellaris's esteemed physician's guild and asking to be admitted to study.

Torrin expelled a breath and rubbed at the stubble on his chin. Rowan's role as emissary of Myris Dar was far more complicated and dangerous than he had thought.

The Besieged City

Torrin shifted his position, careful to avoid lifting his head above the crest of the hill. His view from this high vantage extended over the large plain that spread between the ridge top where they hid and the city of Pellaris.

The late afternoon sun gleamed upon the copper roofs and spires of the city. It looked as large as Torrin remembered, streets crowded with houses and shops marching up the hill towards the citadel – the crown of the city. Flags and pennants snapped atop the towers and battlements in the cold breeze. His gaze slid to the right of the citadel to the pale stone buildings of the great temple square. The grand complex rose above the rest of the city, on the same level with Pellaris keep.

Pellaris looked deceptively peaceful but it was what covered the plain before the city's gates that held his attention. An enormous army spread across the fields between the city and their hiding spot. Torrin exhaled, his hackles rising as his gaze wandered over the hoard. A vast, black sea of towering bodies stood shoulder to shoulder facing the city. The innumerable host of Raken stood ominously in eerie stillness, as though frozen in time.

Nathel, who lay on his stomach next to Torrin, emitted a long, low whistle and swore softly. The brothers and Arynilas had crawled to the top of the rise to get their first look at the Raken army besieging the city.

Torrin rubbed his gritty eyes with his fingertips. Constant vigilance had been required over the last day and a half to avoid the small groups of the Raken that came and went from this huge army.

Yesterday afternoon their course had merged with the wake of the invasion and the grizzly aftermath of the running battle. Abandoned farms and villages, with household goods strewn about in haste as people fled to the safety of the city, dotted the landscape. They had kept a parallel line, moving from cover to cover.

Looking down at the army before them, Torrin's heart sank – any reinforcements Cerebus had received would not be enough. No army held within the city could hope to match the sea of black creatures standing before its gates.

Torrin inspected the walls. As far as could tell, the Raken had not succeeded in breaching them. There was evidence of failed attacks – rubble and bodies littered the ground before the city gates. From this distance it was impossible to tell how many of Pellaris's dead lay among the grim harvest.

Nathel poked Torrin and pointed off to the left of the city where the surrounding trees were the nearest. Torrin nodded, remembering the entrance to the city they had discovered long ago. The trees were dense and Torrin was relieved to see there were few Raken in the area. He scanned the possible routes, hoping the tunnel entrance was still open.

King Cerebus was truly trapped. Even if the secret tunnel remained secure, there was no way to smuggle a sizable army through a cramped space meant for small parties or single messengers at best. They could never hope to bring enough soldiers through fast enough to oppose the vast number of Raken surrounding the city. Any gathering force would be detected before it could properly stage.

He thought of Rowan down at the bottom of the hill with the others, holding the horses to keep them quiet. Her message had to get through; somehow it had to get through.

The main army of Raken was still and focused on the city, but as they watched, small squads of Raken moved along the edges of the immense host. The companions would have to circle wide and approach the tunnel with the utmost stealth to avoid the Raken patrols. Any attempt to reach it would have to wait until dark.

Torrin, Nathel and Arynilas slid carefully back from the ridge until they were out of sight and scrambled back down the steep slope to where the rest of the companions waited. The group retreated silently back into the trees.

They stripped the horses of all gear that jingled, and smeared mud over anything pale or metallic, then settled in to wait. They would try for the tunnel before the twin moons rose. Torrin's biggest worry was cave-ins. The tunnels were barely big enough to lead a horse through, and he had a vision of trying to back their steeds all the way back to the entrance.

Darkness fell slowly. The wind died and the companions waited. Borlin dozed intermittently; Arynilas sat with his legs crossed, bow across his lap. Rowan rested with her back to a sapling, her green eyes occasionally opening, contrasting starkly with the mud she'd smeared over her features. Dalemar sat reading, squinting in the near darkness. Hathunor was next to him on his haunches, only his glowing red eyes moving. And Nathel reclined next to Torrin.

The distant boom of the surf was almost more like a pressure than a sound. Torrin closed his eyes and envisioned the crashing waves, letting their ceaseless assault upon the vertical stone of the cliff wash away his tension. He could smell the salt tang in the air; felt the hardness of the tree trunk at his back; the currents of air moving over his exposed skin. His senses stretched as they always did before a possible battle.

The shadow deepened. Soon Torrin could no longer make out the forms of his friends, their mud covered faces blending with dark.

A Raken patrol moved past their hiding spot. Nathel and Borlin carefully took hold of the horses to keep them quiet and everyone soundlessly drew weapons. But the small patrol did not detect them and the black Raken disappeared into the dark.

Torrin could sense Rowan's growing restlessness, though she didn't move from where she was. Once the darkness was complete, and it was finally time to leave the trees, she was the first one ready.

Torrin gathered the reins of his horse and led him after Arynilas. He moved carefully, testing his footsteps. They wove through the tree trunks and foliage leading the horses like a line of silent wraths. Hathunor moved parallel between the company and his kin, listening.

Shadows and Stealth

Rowan watched in awe as Arynilas began to shimmer before her. His form, what she could see of it in the darkness, shrank from the slim framed Tynithian into the form of a large fox. The shimmering dissipated and the fox settled into focus. He wagged his long fluffy tail and turned to trot into the surrounding trees.

Torrin stooped to retrieve Arynilas's clothes and weapons and stepped after him as though nothing out of the ordinary had happened.

Rowan shook herself and stepped after Torrin, Roanus following in her wake, the horse's breath warm on her neck.

Torrin's black horse all but disappeared in front of her and she had to be careful not to walk into him. They stopped frequently as Arynilas trotted silently ahead to scout the way; they waiting quietly until his black shadow materialized again. The night wore on and the companions gradually closed in on their goal. Rowan was tense, her neck and shoulder muscles pulled tight, her senses straining in the darkness.

A faint rumble sounded beside her. She turned and saw Hathunor looking back the way they had come. Everyone froze. Then the shadow that was Arynilas trotted to Torrin and placed a paw upon his knee. Torrin looked down and nodded then returned his attention to the right.

The sound of many feet was heard now, coming from behind. A large group of Raken moved through the clearing to the right of where they hid. The Raken drew level with them and continued onward. She could only see the glint of starlight on their scaled skin. Her chest began to hurt and she realized she was holding her breath. Soundlessly she released the air from her lungs.

Movement to her left – Torrin's horse tossed its head, its eyes rolling in fear at the Raken so near. Rowan divided her attention between the Raken and Torrin's horse. She reached up and placed a steadying hand on Roanus's smooth neck, hoping he wouldn't pick up young horse's anxiety.

Black was quieting. Torrin's hand gently stroked his horse's head, and he was whispering softly into Black's ear. What was he saying that had such an affect on the young horse? Black had grown completely still, one ear cocked to his master's voice.

Rowan's skin prickled. This was a part of Torrin she had not seen before – the part she suspected was there but was kept locked away in the cage of his grief. Rowan found herself leaning toward him, straining to hear, her heart pounding in her chest. She realized with a start that she'd forgotten the Raken, and she closed her eyes, forcing her thoughts away from Torrin, willing her heart to calm.

She was not prepared for this.

Into the Tunnel

Torrin handed his reins to Borlin as he and Nathel moved silently away from the group. He judged it had taken about three hours to reach the thicket where the tunnel was located. "Do know the exact location?" he whispered. "I just remember the boulders and that it was at the base of them." The fact they had actually found the outcrop in the dark was a wonder.

Nathel pulled on his arm. "This way."

They found the iron doors set into the ground at the base of the rocks. An ingenious spring and beam system held a clump of dead bracken over the doors. Nathel held the beam and Torrin reached down to pull on the handle. Nothing. He heaved and it moved a little with a loud screech. Torrin swore and released the handle.

Borlin found some cleaning oil in his saddlebags and passed forward. Torrin unstopped it and drizzled some over the rusted hinges. He reached for the handle again and this time with Nathel and Borlin assisting, managed to pry first one, then the other up. The hinges squealed in protest but not as loudly as they had.

A black hole gapped before them. Although disturbed at being forced into such a tiny space, the horses moved quietly forward as the companions led them down into the tunnel. Hathunor was the last to enter. Torrin stood in the pitch dark looking back toward the opening with the others. The huge Raken stood silently, listening for a moment before he stooped down into the blackness of the tunnel. Torrin and Nathel closed the heavy doors and heard the scratching of the bracken hide as it slid back over the iron.

The clicking of Borlin's firestones filled the enclosed space. Then light bloomed from his small lantern. The companions blinked at the sudden flare. There was barely enough room for two people to walk abreast, and the horses certainly wouldn't be able to turn around. As Torrin squeezed past the horses to the front, he once more fervently hoped the tunnel had not collapsed anywhere.

Arynilas stepped out of the blackness as Torrin reached the front of the line. He was once more in his Tynithian form, his skin gleaming palely in the light. Torrin pulled Arynilas's clothes and weapons from his saddlebags and handed them over.

Nathel had another lantern out and was lighting it from Borlin's. The twin lights pushed back the oppressive blackness as they set off through the passage. Torrin looked back along the line of his friends to see Hathunor hunched over. The tops of the horse's ears brushed the ceiling where tree roots dangled down and the damp smell of earth was strong.

Torrin set a pace that matched the horse's strides. He slowed a little as the tunnel floor began to rise gently. There was a quiet weight to the air in the tunnel and his friends spoke in subdued tones. The lantern he carried showed nothing beyond the gradual twisting and turning ahead. It was hard to gauge how long they had been walking.

Torrin slowed as his lantern light fell on something different. A giant tree root grew horizontally through the tunnel at hip height. Torrin stopped at the root and reached out to touch the wood, considering.

Nathel and Borlin squeezed forward, their shoulders scraping along the dusty wall and pulling loose pebbles and debris from it to land in piles on the uneven floor.

"I could cut it away wi' me ax." Borlin's voice sounded loud after the long silence.

Torrin looked at the huge root. He judged the height of the obstruction against the level of the horses' bellies. The steeds might be able to scramble over it with some pushing and pulling. In the open the horses could all have easily jumped it, but not here. He sighed. "We will have to cut it out of the way. The wood is dry and hard. If it takes too long, then perhaps Dalemar can help somehow."

Borlin went back for his axe but before could return, Hathunor shouldered forward between the wall and horses. He stooped over the root, wrapping his enormous arms around it. His spiked back strained as he heaved upwards. A dry cracking echoed through the tunnel as the thick root began to split. Again the big Raken heaved and with a loud ripping the root splintered into two. Hathunor pushed the shorter end down, removing the sharp spikes of wood that might hurt the horses. Then he lifted the longer section and pinned it against the other wall. The Saa Raken held it there and motioned them to lead their animals through the gap.

As Torrin led his horse forward past the root he looked closely at it. Its girth measured almost as wide as his torso. He shook his head and eyed Hathunor.

They trudged onward unimpeded for quite some time before the lantern cast up against an iron grill. Torrin reached out to test it and found the metal rusted. He looked back down the line. "Nathel, was this here when we were exploring?"

"I think so," said his brother. "But it was open."

Torrin turned back to the grill. Well, it was locked now which means someone had been in the tunnel after Nathel and him all those years ago. "Anything you can do, Dalemar?" Torrin asked over his shoulder.

The Rith came forward and laid a hand on the lock. A pale blue nimbus surrounded his palm. With a squealing shudder, the door swung away from his hand. Dirt sifted down onto their heads.

On the other side of the grill the tunnel became rough-hewn stone. The passage was wider now and water seeped from the stones, dripping in the darkness. They were passing under the city itself. Torrin's lantern revealed another path entering the tunnel ahead. As he approached, he found a crumbling stone stairway leading downward into darkness. He stopped and looked back at Nathel for confirmation. He saw Rowan looking forward over the backs of the horses. Her expression was grave and intense.

"There were no stairs after we came down from the first cellar," said his brother.

Torrin nodded, turning away from the stairs, and they moved onward. Twice more they came to intersections and he paused to consult his brother. Both he and Nathel had a fairly clear memory of what they had seen the last time they had traveled this tunnel. Some of the openings off the main corridor were completely caved in, but the passage that led where they wanted to go was clear but for a few fallen stones.

The next intersection presented a cluster of different corridors. Torrin cast the glow of his light into all the openings, which radiated outward in different directions – one passage was level, one plunged into darkness and one climbed steeply upward.

"Time to start climbing," said Torrin, as he and Nathel looked around at all the various options. His brother nodded but then stopped as he was about to return to his horse. Nathel indicated a descending spiral stair. "Do you remember going down there, Tor?" he asked.

Torrin looked down into the blackness and a chill settled over him. He remembered it well. Two full days he and Nathel had been lost down there searching for a way out. When they had finally found the marks they had been making on the stone walls to keep from losing their way, they were down to a single guttering torch. The pair of them had vowed never to come down here again – a pact which lasted for as long as the punishment they received for being away from the keep with no explanation for so long.

Torrin led Black up into the sloping tunnel. The company followed with the sound of hooves on stone. It soon levelled off and finally they came to another door. Its rust-pitted surface gleamed dully in the lantern light and, unlike the first grate, this door was solid and heavily reinforced.

Torrin waited for the others to slide past the horses and gather around the door.

"Where are we?" Rowan asked, her voice echoing.

"We are outside the cellar of a guard outpost. Likely it is used now as a garrison, so there will be soldiers. They will think us the enemy at first." Torrin cast a glance at Hathunor. The Saa Raken was bent over double, his huge fists against his knees.

"Perhaps we should just knock then," suggested Dalemar.

Torrin shook his head. "I doubt we'd be heard."

Dalemar nodded and moved to place his hand upon the door.

"Wait!" Torrin gestured at the faces of his companions. "We should remove the mud first."

Nathel grinned, white teeth in a dark face. Borlin pulled out rags and Arynilas doused them with water. They wiped the worst of the now-dried mud from their faces.

Dalemar replaced his hand on the door and closed his eyes. With a hollow boom and a metallic squeal, the lock gave way. The iron shuddered.

Torrin and Nathel placed their shoulders against the door and pushed. It moved only slightly. Hathunor waded forward and his huge clawed hands wrapped around the edge. The bottom of the iron door grated against the stone floor as he shoved it inward. Loud clatters and metallic clinks echoed in the room beyond, drowning out the sound of the squealing metal. A table piled with supplies and weapons had been placed directly in front of the door and it tipped, tumbling armour and swords onto the floor.

Nathel dusted off his hands. "Well they certainly haven't used this in a while, I'd say."

Hathunor helped them move the table out of the way. Then he reared up to his full height and Torrin felt dwarfed again. Looking at his mud-smeared friends, he wondered how in Erys' name they could avoid being taken for spies and enemies.

Shouts echoed above. Booted feet sounded loudly on the stone steps that led up out of the cellar room. Torrin moved to stand next to Rowan. She looked up at him and he nodded once in encouragement. She took a deep breath and turned expectantly to the stairs.

Borlin began to pull out his sword but Torrin held out a hand. "Be easy, we are among friends."

The Pellarian soldiers reached the bottom of the stairs, swords drawn and shields donned, shiny helms on their heads. There was a moment of stillness as they registered the odd collection of invaders. Then they raised their eyes to Hathunor.

Battle oaths reverberated off the stone walls and the soldiers launched themselves into an attack.

Torrin leaped to stand in front of them, his arms outstretched, palms empty. "We answer summons from King Cerebus and escort the Messenger from Myris Dar. We are not your enemies! Please put up your swords."

The soldiers arrested their attack and warily looked at one another, but did not lower their weapons.

"My name is Torrin, son of Ralor. King Cerebus will know that name. We are here to answer his summons and to bring him a message."

Rowan stepped forward then, tossing her long braid over her shoulder. "I am Rowan Mor Lanyar of Myris Dar. I have an urgent message for King Cerebus." The soldiers blinked at her. Hathunor loomed behind her, ready to snatch her back out of harm's way.

The captain in front scowled at them. "You say you are friend to King Cerebus, yet you bring a Raken spy with you. Explain yourselves or you will understand what it means to be an *enemy* of King Cerebus."

Rowan reached back and grasped one of Hathunor's huge hands. "This is Hathunor, a Saa Raken, and unlike his brethren before the city, he is free."

"Hathunor friend to Cerebus," said the Saa Raken and he brought his other hand up to his black chest in salute. The soldiers gaped in surprise.

"Send a runner to the king, Captain," said Torrin. "We will wait here under guard until you hear word."

The captain appraised them speculatively for a few more moments before sending one of his men running back up the stairs.

Pellaris

Rowan wiped her brow. She was hot despite the cool air in the cellar and the smell of the horses was strong in the small space. She curbed the urge to pace, focusing her attention instead on the armour and weapons collected in the room. They were of competent craftsmanship, simple in line and function.

The silence had grown awkward. Borlin and Nathel had tried unsuccessfully to engage the remaining Pellarian soldiers in conversation, finally subsiding to seat themselves against the wall with Arynilas and Dalemar. Borlin lit his pipe and smoked.

Hathunor crouched on his haunches close to Rowan, his red eyes wary, and Torrin remained standing near her, arms crossed over his chest, exchanging guarded stares with the captain. The rest of the soldiers were too intent on Hathunor to spare much attention for much else.

Leaning against the wooden table, Rowan glanced back to Torrin, then closed her eyes. Black tunnels and the moonless night filled with Raken enemies played across her mind's eye; through it all Torrin's whispering voice threaded like a song. She opened her eyes and took a deep breath, working to clear her wits for the meeting ahead. The message would be delivered tonight; she must focus on the end of her goal.

Footsteps echoed down the stone stairs and Rowan looked up; her friends rose from their seats as the soldier came pelting down into the cellar, gasping for breath.

"The king would like to have his guests brought to the citadel," he gasped, "with honour guard for the Messenger, and her friend." He glanced up at Hathunor. An honour guard. Rowan smiled grimly. Of course they would never be allowed to walk freely through the city with a Saa Raken.

The captain nodded. "Get the escort ready then, Corporal." He turned to Torrin again as the soldier dashed back up the stairs. "It would seem you are known to the king and welcome, but the Raken," he paused to look up at Hathunor, "will be watched. If he tries anything, he will be killed."

"As you say, Captain," replied Torrin smoothly.

The captain measured Torrin for another moment before nodding. "Follow me please. I will take you to the king."

Rowan led her horse up amid the clattering of hooves. Roanus suddenly went down on one knee as his iron shoes slid with teeth-grinding screeches on the flags. Rowan gave him the rein as he struggled to get his legs under him. He righted himself and she patted his neck, looking back to see that two men had been left to guard the old iron door. No more unexpected guests.

Rowan emerged from the tight stairwell with the others into a brightly lit hall. From here there was a direct route out onto the cobbled street, where she took a deep breath of fresh air and looked around. An escort of Pellarian cavalry was standing ready with torches guttering in the darkness.

Torrin was there then, tightening the cinch of her saddle for her. "Whatever you need, Rowan," he said quietly, looking her in the eye, "we are here for you." Rowan swallowed and nodded her thanks. He stood back and held the reins formally as she mounted. Then he turned to mount as well and the cavalry formed up tightly to escort them through the city.

People appeared at their windows and in doorways, no doubt drawn by the sound of so many horses. Some gasped and pointed at Hathunor, but most stared silently. The darkness concealed the toll the Raken siege had taking on the city, but it showed plainly in these haunted faces.

Rowan studied the men around her – their armour and bearing. She looked for a resemblance to Torrin and Nathel and found it in their size, colouring and the strength of their prominent features. They were tired; their serious faces wearing the pragmatic expressions of soldiers.

Torrin rode beside her, torchlight playing over the angles of his face. His inscrutable expression masked anything he might be feeling at this homecoming. Was he glad to be back? She suspected not, although she truly hoped he would one day come to terms with his past, she may never know.

Rowan took a breath to steady herself as she approached the crossroads of her path. A rush of affection flooded her chest as she glanced at her companions. She didn't think she could ever repay them for their help and friendship. And now it was almost done – she would stand face to face with King Cerebus, unburden herself. How strange, to no longer be traveling toward Pellaris. The words of the Mora' Taith came back to her "*Your quest here is but a beginning. It is meant to prepare you.*" Rowan shivered.

The cobblestone street widened onto a huge square, lined with shops and houses. The buildings were larger with grander entrances and surrounding gardens. The huge keep of Pellaris loomed above, its lit windows bright in the dark city. The big main doors stood open with torch light flooding the stone steps leading up to them.

The escort stopped; Rowan and her friends dismounted as sleepy stable boys came forward to take their horses. She took her saddlebags down from Roanus, and gave the horse a pat. "A well deserved rest my friend," she whispered to him. His ears twitched and he nuzzled her palm in response.

They were led up the steps and through the grand archway of the entrance. Pellarian castle guards pulled the massive doors closed with a boom. Rowan blinked at the blazing candelabras and sconces which lit the soaring foyer. Their escort led them through the spacious entrance hall, hung with rich tapestries, to the end of the foyer where a broad stair swept up to a high corridor.

A tall, dignified elderly man stood waiting for them at the bottom of the staircase. He wore a black scull cap atop his white hair, and his trim white beard framed his face. He was dressed in long elegant blue robes, and despite his apparent age, stood straight, watching them with silent composure.

Nathel exclaimed in surprise. "Galen!"

The old man nodded his head as his eyes passed over them, pausing on Rowan and Hathunor. "Indeed, Captain Nathel, it is I."

Nathel looked as though he would like to pick Galen up in a hug, but deemed it wise not to ruffle the old man's dignity.

Galen turned to face Torrin. "It has been a long time, Commander. Welcome back to Pellaris. Your presence will lift the king's spirits greatly."

Torrin nodded in return. "Galen, it is good to see you." He turned to indicate Rowan. "This is Rowan Mor Lanyar, a messenger from Myris Dar and emissary of her people. She has traveled a long way through much hardship to reach Pellaris and deliver her message to King Cerebus. Rowan, may I present Chancellor Galen."

Galen bowed formally to Rowan. "It is a great pleasure, my Lady."

Torrin turned to the huge Raken at Rowan's side. "This is Hathunor, also a messenger of sorts."

Galen's eyes narrowed as he looked at the Saa Raken. He inclined his head but said nothing.

Torrin introduced Dalemar, Arynilas and Borlin, and Galen nodded to each politely in turn. "The king is waiting for you all, if you will follow me please." He turned and proceeded up the wide stairs.

Rowan climbed the stairs with the others, trying to take it all in; noting their escort of soldiers was still with them. Galen led them down a broad corridor, lined with more tapestries, huge mirrors and marble tables set with lanterns and sculptures. High windows at the end of the corridor were dark now but Rowan guessed they looked out over the ocean. Its salty smell made her think of home; she was looking forward to seeing the great water again.

Galen turned before the high windows to follow a smaller corridor. They walked through a set of carved double doors, depicting cavalry bearing standards and entered a large audience chamber. More high windows looked out over the north and hearths, crackling with fires, stood at either end of the room. The carpet from the corridor proceeded up the middle and ended at the foot of a small dais upon which two carved and elegantly upholstered chairs stood. A man occupied one of the thrones – the King of Pellar. He was surrounded by a group of men dressed in armour.

"Please wait here." Galen walked up the aisle toward the dais.

Rowan took the opportunity to study the king. She could see only a little of him as the men around him shifted and moved. He sat looking down at something on the floor; a man on his left squatted down to point at what he looked at. The king spoke a few words and the men around him bowed and turned to leave. The crouching man picked up a large map, which he rolled swiftly in his hands as he bowed to the king and followed the others.

Two men remained standing before with the king. An older, thick set, blond warrior wearing bronze battle armour; the other by contrast, was slim and dark and robed in black.

When the officers had filed out through a door near the back of the room, the king sagged back into his chair and covered his face with a hand. Rowan felt a tug of sympathy – it was a gesture of utter exhaustion.

Galen approached the throne and the two men standing in front of it turned toward him as he spoke. The king looked up from his hands and his eyes traveled to the doors where Rowan and her friends stood waiting. His demeanour changed and he drew himself up as if finding a reserve of strength.

Galen returned and beckoned them to follow. "The king will see you now."

Rowan stepped forward. The king was a handsome man; the heavy mantle of worry and exhaustion had transformed his face but there was strength in the set of his shoulders. His eyes met hers and any doubts she might have had about him fled. The care and weariness that marked his features had touched his eyes too, but had been absorbed into the far stronger intensity of who he was. They were the kindest eyes she had ever seen. Rowan was reminded forcefully of her father – she did not want to disappoint this man.

Galen stopped and bowed. "My King, may I present Commander Torrin Ralor; Captain Nathel Ralor; Lady Rowan Mor Lanyar, the Messenger of Myris Dar; Hathunor; Dalemar the Rith; Arynilas of Dan Tynell; and Borlin of the Black Hills."

Galen turned to the companions. "I present King Cerebus of Pellar."

Rowan bowed with her friends.

The king sat silently looking over his visitors, then he stepped down. "By sweet Erys, I never thought to lay eyes on the pair of you again!" Rowan raised her eyebrows as Cerebus clasped hands with Torrin and Nathel. His voice was deep and affectionate and his warm smile eased the exhaustion on his face.

Nathel wore a wide grin as he pumped the king's hand.

"It is good to see you again, King Cerebus," said Torrin. His tone was courteous but his face tight.

Cerebus looked closely at the big swordsman, searching. "It has been a long time. It is good to have you back among us, both of you. The sons of Ralor have been missed in Pellaris." The king turned to the two men in front of the dais who watched Hathunor warily. "Gentlemen! I give you two of the best swordsmen in Pellar!"

The man in bronze armour stepped towards them. He was hawk-nosed with a grizzled beard above a barrel chest. "I need no introduction to these two." He clasped hands with the brothers. "It's about time you boys decided to come home."

Nathel chuckled. "General Preven. We figured you could have gotten on well enough without us. Are you trying to prove me wrong?"

The general barked a laugh. "Same old rascal!"

"General." Torrin nodded. Again he received an appraising look.

The man standing next to General Preven stepped forward and Galen introduced him. "Tihir N'Avarin, Priest of Erys."

Rowan shifted, disturbed by the fevered gleam of disapproval in his dark brown eyes as he looked at her. Her attention was snagged by the heavy gold medallion, embossed with the image of the Goddess, that hung centered on his thin chest. His long black robes hung from sharp shoulders and his face, entirely devoid of softness, wore an ascetic expression that pinched his features.

Torrin spoke and Rowan was relieved to have the priest shift his gaze away from her. "We came as soon as we received your summons, but we were far in the south and it has taken us a while to make the journey."

Cerebus sighed. "Many have come to offer aid. It is welcome. I thank you for answering my call." He turned to Rowan and bowed. "My Lady Rowan, it is an honour to meet you. The fabled land of Myris Dar is mostly forgotten here in Eryos, and I am proud to be the first king in centuries to welcome a Myrian to Pellaris."

Rowan smiled, surprised to find Cerebus familiar with her homeland. "I thank you, King Cerebus. I am relieved to finally be here." The king looked at her curiously, noting her clothing and sword, but said no more. He moved on to the other companions, greeting each one in turn.

"Rith Dalemar, your presence is most welcome. It is heartening to know that the world of men is still of some importance to Rithkind."

Dalemar smiled sadly. "Alas, your majesty, I cannot speak for Rithkind. I have not been home for many years and I doubt those of Rithkind would listen to my council."

King Cerebus nodded in acceptance and stepped in front of Arynilas. “Arynilas of the Great Greenhall; you honour us with your visit.”

“Your Highness,” replied the Tynithian with a graceful bow of his head.

“Many Pellarians believe your people exist only in myth. Is that not so, N’Avarin?” Cerebus turned away from Arynilas to look at the priest.

N’Avarin watched Arynilas and the king uncomfortably, dark eyes glittering. “It is true, your highness. Perhaps when those who do not believe see your guest, they will change their minds.”

Cerebus turned his back on the priest and moved to stand in front of Borlin. “Borlin, be welcome; your coming is like the addition of ten men.”

The Stoneman bowed his head and coughed self-consciously. He smoothed his beard, his brown eyes sparkling with pride.

When the king reached Hathunor, who towered over him, Rowan saw their armed escort inch closer, hands upon weapons. “Hathunor is it? I will be interested to hear what you have to say regarding your friends outside.” The warmth was gone from Cerebus’s voice.

Hathunor bowed his head and drew a clawed fist to his chest. “Hathunor does not like what has happened to little brothers. Hathunor will help if possible. But Hathunor’s first duty to Rowan.”

Cerebus turned to look at Rowan with wide eyes. “You have the loyalty of a Raken?” He walked over to stand in front of her, regarding her anew. “Galen said you were a messenger, Lady Rowan. Tell me, what message do you bring to us in this desperate hour?”

Rowan met the king’s gaze. Torrin and the others shifted, subtly gathering at her back. Cerebus noticed and his grey eyes traveled over them. His bearing stilled.

Rowan took a deep breath. “I was sent by the Seers of Danum with a message for you, King Cerebus of Pellar. I have traveled far to reach you and would not have made it but for these friends.” Cerebus’s glance flicked to Torrin. “I was sent to find you in Pellar,” Rowan continued, “because the Seers believe

Pellar is where hope of victory against a grave threat to the world is to be found."

Cerebus's eyes narrowed. "You speak of the Raken invasion?"

Rowan shook her head. "Unfortunately, your highness, the Raken outside the city are only a small part of this threat."

"Small part?" protested Tihir N'Avarin. "Dear girl, have you *seen* the host beyond the walls?"

Cerebus's gaze never left Rowan's face, his eyes held a look of resignation. "Tell me."

At that moment an alarm bell began to toll stridently in the distance. It was echoed almost immediately within the walls of the keep.

Preven turned to stride away, barking orders to the companion's escort, sending men running.

King Cerebus closed his eyes briefly. "Forgive me, my lady Rowan, but we must continue this meeting later. The Raken attack and I must look to the defence of the city." The king turned to the chancellor. "Galen, will you please see to the comforts of our guests."

Torrin stepped forward. "Your highness, we came here to answer a summons for aid." He glanced at the rest of his friends and his blue eyes stopped at Rowan with a regretful look. "I speak for all of us when I say we would not sit within the keep while the city fights for survival."

Cerebus sighed wearily and nodded. "I thank you all. Preven will see to where you will be most helpful. I must prepare for battle." Cerebus turned away as a young squire came running through a door behind the dais with the king's armour.

Rowan's heart pounded as she and her companions followed General Preven from the audience chamber. She cast a glance back at the king – she would not be delivering her message this night after all.

*

Rowan was breathing heavily when they reached the walls. A booming resonated from the assault on the solid iron doors of the main gates. She could not make out a single call amid the deafening noise from atop the walls. Torches burned at close intervals, casting movement on the battlements in an eerie glow.

The escort of Pellarian soldiers was with them but the men were now as preoccupied with the battle atop the walls as they were with keeping and eye on Hathunor. The weariness Rowan had felt earlier was gone now, swept away in the tension and turmoil.

Rowan felt a hand on her shoulder. It was Torrin looking at her with concern. He said something but his words were drowned out. He leaned down with his face close to her ear, his warm breath on her cheek. “You still have not delivered your message. It would be better for you to stay away from the fighting.”

Rowan shook her head. “I’ll watch your back if you watch mine.”

He frowned, leaning down once more. “Stay close then. No heroics. Agreed?”

“Agreed.”

They mounted the stairs to the top and Rowan, choking at the stench of blood and burning pitch, took in the wide space above the gate. Soldiers at the edge of the wall fired arrows down at the enemy. Several scaling ladders had not been repelled and Raken were scrambling over. Men drew swords and archers tried to fire at close range. Raken tumbled backwards from the wall. Screams and shouts filled the night punctuated by the clash of steel and roars and snarls of the attacking Raken.

A creaking moan sounded beside them accompanied by a great whoosh. Rowan ducked as a massive sling send forth a barrel of burning pitch. It whistled streaking through the darkness to land among the Raken army with a deadly splash of fire. The soldiers manning the huge weapon turned the cranks fiercely, drawing the sling back to be reloaded. Rowan looked down the wall and saw the massive slings set at even intervals, launching in alternating succession.

A scaling ladder hit the wall in front of the companions. A soldier fell unconscious to the stones as the weight of it struck him. The defenders hurried to place long poles against the top rungs and strained to push it away. One pole splintered suddenly and the ladder twisted violently to the side. The remaining pole slipped from its place and the heavy ladder cracked back down onto the wall.

Raken scrambled over and leaped down, cudgels and swords swinging. The men nearest were sent flying like dolls. The soldiers trying to hold the breach fell back quickly.

Torrin leaped forward into the fray. Rowan charged after him with her friends around her. The bright flash of golden-fletched arrows whipped past Rowan and she saw a streak of thin blue Rith fire arc overhead to hit the top of the ladder where it exploded the wood. Raken still leapt over the wall, but at slower intervals. Rowan's sword hummed in her hand and she pulled her dagger from her waist. Hathunor bounded past, crashing into the smaller Drae Raken – a boulder rolling into pebbles.

A soldier near them aimed an arrow at her friend, mistaking him for an enemy. She rushed forward and grabbed the man's arm, pulling it downward just as he reached full draw. "The big Raken is an ally! Do not harm him or you will die by my sword!" she yelled over the din. "Pass it on."

The man gaped at her in disbelief.

"Pass the word along!" she shouted again. Rowan waited only long enough to see the man nod before she turned to help her friends. They were in the thick of the fighting where the line had been breached.

A Raken dove from the fiercely burning ladder and rolled past Hathunor. The beast stood up with its skin smouldering and turned to attack the nearest man, a Pellarian soldier with his back turned as he fought desperately with another Raken.

The man turned just in time to see the huge beast bearing down on him, but could not raise his sword in time to parry the giant's blow. Rowan's sword hummed as it sank into the beast's side. The Raken flinched and twisted toward Rowan, its red glowing eyes focusing on her. It lunged and Rowan jumped to the side to avoid its rush, her dagger slicing up into the throat. The beast recoiled and Rowan drove her sword through its chest.

Another beast roared and charged. Rowan raised weapons to meet it. But a soldier pushed her out of the way. "Get out of here woman, before you get killed!" The shouted words were filled with disbelief and contempt.

Rowan growled in irritation. The soldier met the Drae Raken, but wasn't strong enough to trade blows with the beast. His sword was ripped from his grasp; the Raken's free hand whipped out to rake down the soldier's breastplate, knocking him backward. The beast bellowed and sent its mace flying at the man's head.

Rowan jumped forward and deflected the weapon with her sword. Sparks glittered as the metals met. She sliced down with her dagger, severing tendons. The Raken lost its grip and snarled in pain-filled rage. Its warm breath blasted her in the face as she killed it.

She turned to find the soldier staring at her in shock. Rowan picked up his sword and tossed it to him. She pointed with her blade to the breach where her friends still battled. The man watched her with wide eyes as she moved past him but he followed her into the melee.

Rowan reached Torrin's side and helped him drive a Drae Raken back towards the smoking remains of the scaling ladder. Torrin spun his great broadsword around him as if it weighed nothing. The Raken he fought roared as his blade cut into it. The beast made a last charge before it died with both their swords in its chest. They shoved it from the wall and Torrin turned to face her. He was blood-splattered and his eyes were fierce. "I told you to stay close!"

"I *was* close. Close enough to watch your back."

Torrin scowled.

Borlin heard and barked out a laugh. "Well said, lass."

Nathel, Hathunor and Dalemar gathered beside them to look down at the broiling mass of Raken below the wall. Arynilas rained arrows down with precision, picking off Raken that climbed too high up the nearest ladders.

In the brief respite, Rowan looked at the soldiers around them – all eyes were staring at Hathunor.

A horn rang to their right. Rowan turned to see a frenzied skirmish further along the wall as more Raken made it to the top and rampaged through the defenders.

The beasts were being killed but several men were down in the stillness of death. A bronze-clad warrior among the silver of the Pellarian soldiers caught her eye like a beacon.

"Isn't that General Preven?" she asked.

"And the king," said Torrin from beside her.

Rowan looked past the general to a knot of defenders led by a warrior in exquisitely wrought armour.

"Come on! We're not done yet," said Torrin.

They ran to reach the beleaguered defenders. The soldier Rowan had saved ran beside her. He watched them as though afraid to miss something important. Rowan was reminded of her younger brother following her to the practice yard. She shook her head and raised her sword.

And then they were in the midst of the fighting. Hathunor once more charged to the ladder where he ripped into the Raken as they tried to gain the wall. This time the companions kept together, following in the huge Saa Raken's wake. Rowan watched to make sure nobody mistook him for an attacker again.

The flow of Raken coming over the wall ceased with Hathunor hurling them back. Rowan fought with her sword and dagger in the close press. Men's shouts sounded behind her and she turned to find General Preven down on the paved stone of the wall with King Cerebus standing over him, keeping the Raken at bay. The general was struggling to gain his feet but the Raken kept him pinned. King Cerebus took a blow to the shoulder, but it glanced off his armour and he kept his balance.

Rithfire streaked through the press and blasted into the Raken trying to kill the king. Four more Raken materialized and closed on the king and general; they came simultaneously from different directions. Rowan ran forward to intercept one of the beasts.

"To the king!" Torrin bellowed from beside her as his sword slashed a Drae Raken in the chest.

Nathel took a cudgel on his shield and thrust it aside, his blade swept across the Raken's flank. Rowan's attack on the Raken nearest Preven gave the general time to struggle to his feet. She deflected an over-head blow from a mace, stepped to the right of the Raken and its weapon whipped past. She sliced in quick succession and the Raken went down. The humming of Rowan's sword had increased – its cutting edge razor-sharp.

Preven stepped up beside her as the next Raken came at them. Working together Rowan and the General stepped away from each other as the beast blasted toward them. It had to choose a target. As it veered to assault the general, she dispatched it.

Rowan glanced around in the moment of stillness. She took in Torrin and Nathel battling next to King Cerebus, Dalemar was next to the ladder, sending Rithfire down over the wall. Borlin fought with hew and hack next to Arynilas who danced through the remaining Raken with his blades. Hathunor moved like a black wraith, torchlight flickering on his scaled skin. The smaller Draes were no match for him and soon there were none left to fight.

As the last of the beasts were felled above, the horde at the base of the wall turned away suddenly and retreated out of arrow and sling range. Preven shouted orders and the massive trebuchets were stilled to conserve ammunition.

Amid the carnage Rowan stood as her breathing slowed. What had been dull to her perception during the heat of battle now seemed appallingly vivid. She stilled her sword and sheathed her dagger, her palms sticky with drying blood.

Torrin stood, his back to her as he scanned the battlements, turning until he found her. Their eyes met and relief passed over his face.

A man groaned at her feet and she look down to find a soldier with a deep gash in his left side and the helm on his head staved in. Rowan knelt to gently remove the helmet and he looked up at her through pain-hazed eyes. She could hardly see his features through all the blood on his face. His breath came in shallow pants.

"Are you the blessed Goddess?" He whispered. "Are you come to take me into the next life?"

Rowan wiped some of the blood from his forehead. "Nay soldier, I do not think your time has come yet." She looked up, searching. "Dalemar, Nathel! There is a man here who could use your skills."

Rowan made to stand but the soldier grabbed her hand. Nathel arrived to look at the man's injuries and Rowan pried herself free. "Rest now soldier. You have defended your king and city well."

Hathunor was gently lifting his brethren and carrying them to the edge of the wall where he dropped them over. When he turned from his last grizzly task, she reached up and placed a hand on his arm. "I am so sorry for your loss, my friend."

Hathunor rumbled in response and his sad red eyes looked out at the distant army of his kin, illuminated by fires yet burning out on the plain.

Torrin, Borlin and Arynilas gathered next to them. Torrin passed a cloth to her so she could clean the blood from her weapon. She wondered strangely where he had found it.

"It would seem that we have a friend wearing the enemy's face," said a deep voice behind them. They turned to find King Cerebus watching them. He was blood-spattered, his face was grey with exhaustion in contrast to his resplendent armour. "My thanks, Hathunor, for your courageous deeds."

The big Saa Raken sighed and rumbled, "Hathunor must help, for brothers lost."

"My thanks to all of you," Cerebus continued, his eyes lingering on Rowan's sword as she wiped it clean. "You have brought honour to yourselves."

Rowan shook her head. "No your highness, it is you and your soldiers who have acted with great courage and honour – to repeatedly repel attacks such as this one. No doubt they have all been as heated and chaotic. The greatest warriors of my homeland would be impressed by your perseverance."

Cerebus inclined his head and turned to Preven who arrived with news. The general listed out a brief casualty report and an assessment of the damage wrought by the siege attempt.

Cerebus turned back to the companions. "There is work I must attend to. Please take your ease at the keep, if that is possible in these present circumstances. I will be convening a meeting in the great council chambers tomorrow morning to receive to your message, my lady Rowan, as well as hear the news you and your companions bring from afar." The king eyed Hathunor. "The General will arrange an escort for you back to the keep. It would not do to have our guest mistaken for a hostile." He turned away, torchlight glinted on his armour as he moved through the soldiers offering praise for their well-fought defence.

Rowan strode wearily through the splendid, high-ceilinged corridors of Pellaris Keep with her companions. She was completely exhausted and covered in grime, sweat and blood. A memory rose to mind – Rowan and her brother Andin as youngsters, covered in dirt from playing outside and her grandfather, chuckling as he lifted them onto his lap, wrinkling his nose and proclaiming that he had found a pair of *mudlings in a silver cup*. Rowan almost giggled as she looked around at the fine interior.

Chancellor Galen paced ahead of them with his blue robe swishing around his legs. He led the companions higher into the upper stories of the citadel. The broad corridors shrank, becoming intimate and quiet. Rowan noticed that despite the smaller size, these halls were lovely and elegant with a calm, soothing air.

Galen stopped before a broad wooden door and lifted the heavy latch. The door swung smoothly inward and revealed a beautifully appointed sitting room with a crackling fire burning in a large hearth.

The sitting room gave way to a small vestibule with another carved wooden door. Opposite was a hall with several smaller doorways. "My lady Rowan, your room is ready for you. I have taken the liberty of arranging for you to have the largest of the suite's rooms. The bath should be drawn and ready for you. Please feel free to ask the servants for anything that you require." Galen gestured toward the hall across the sitting room. He cast a dry glance over Torrin and the others. "I trust that your companions will not mind sleeping two to a room? A lady should have her own space, I think."

Torrin's blue eyes flicked from Galen to Rowan.

Nathel reached out and took her hand, bowing over it. "M' Lady," he said with a wicked grin.

Borlin's face reddened as he stammered out, "g'night."

Dalemar smiled and patted Rowan fatherly on the shoulder. "Enjoy your rest, my dear."

Arynilas gave her a formal bow before turning to follow the others across to the other bedrooms.

Rowan sighed heavily, watching them disappear down the hall, feeling as though she'd been stripped of something precious. She turned and pushed open the large door to her room.

Once in the room, Rowan pressed a hand to her forehead. The message was to have been delivered by now. She frowned and began to pull off her armour. She supposed one more night would make little difference.

Breakfast and Danyl the Great

Rowan woke to the sound of bird song and bright sun streaming through the glass door of the balcony. Raising her head, she glanced blearily around the large guestroom and fell back against the pillows, burrowing back into the cozy warmth of the feather bedding, willing herself back to sleep.

It was no good. Peering out, she focused on one of the four carved wooden pillars of the bed, tied with brocade drapes. It was the largest bed she had ever slept in. Rowan twisted and propped herself comfortably and gazed about the elegant room. In the daylight she inspected the monstrous dark wardrobe and the round table with comfortable padded chairs. The hearth was cold now and it occurred to her that she could likely fit herself into the fireplace with room to spare. She laughed softly and turned over. Despite a wonderfully restful night – the first in a long while where she had not had to stand watch – she still felt like she could sleep for a week.

Events of the previous day crowded in and her pleasant drowse vanished. Groaning, she sat up, swung her legs over the side and stepped down onto the stone floor. She shivered as the cold seeped up through her feet and splashed water from the bedside basin over her face.

Her clothes were neatly folded on the table by the window; clearly she had slept through the return of the servant. Rowan eyed the sumptuous bed, frowning. Fatigue and the safety of the location were no excuse for carelessness. Dressing swiftly to cover her goose bumps, she inhaled the fresh scent of laundry soap. The stains and dirt of the past weeks had been scoured away.

Rowan stood contemplating her freshly cleaned and oiled armour, silver buckles gleaming. There was no practical reason for wearing them in the keep yet she reached for them anyway. She had a role to fill here as ambassador to her people. Although she wasn't a diplomat, she was a warrior and that was as much a statement about her people as anything.

Once she was dressed, she reached for her saddlebags and opened an inner pocket. She paused and took a breath, then withdrew a small cloth-wrapped bundle she had not touched since the day her cousin Dell had died. With trembling fingers, she removed a leather strip that unrolled into a v-shaped shoulder mantle. It was a simple thing, yet the gold and pale green designs were exquisitely wrought. In the center of its six-inch width, where the two sides met, was a crest with flowing script of ancient Myrian – the title of emissary.

Rowan carefully inspected the length of the mantle. Her fingers traced the tooled lines that evoked the essence and beauty of her home. She sighed and let the memory of sun on waves wash over her. The light from the window sparkled on the gold and green dye and she saw the rich green hills of Myris Dar and smelled the moist air. Lifting it carefully, she settled it over her head and onto her shoulders. The weight of the leather was slight but she felt the heavy burden it represented. Finally, she picked up her cleaned and oiled sword and slid it into its scabbard over her shoulder.

A knock sounded on the door as she finished braiding her hair, and she flipped the plait over her shoulder as she went to open it.

Nathel stood on the other side, clean and well rested. "Breakfast," he said with relish, rubbing his large hands together. His ever-present grin was especially bright.

Rowan laughed. "What? You're tired of travel rations?"

Nathel leaned forward and whispered conspiratorially, "Even Borlin can't work miracles with only beans and dried meat. I swear my teeth have been worn down to nubs over the last few weeks." He offered his arm with a courtly bow. "Shall we dine, my lady?"

Rowan rolled her eyes and slugged him affectionately in the shoulder. "You honestly think there is going to be much better food to be had in a city under siege?"

Nathel moved along beside her. "Ah, but you haven't yet met Danyl the Great."

Borlin, Dalemar and Arynilas lounged in the well-stuffed chairs of the common room, and Hathunor was curled near the huge fireplace, basking in the heat. Borlin eyed her green mantel, stood and inclined his head. "Well met, Lass."

Rowan grinned at the Stoneman and shot a mischievous glance at Nathel. "Nathel was just telling me how much he was looking forward to some real food."

Borlin's brows drew down and he glowered at Nathel. "Ye shouldna bite the hand that feeds ye, Lad or ye'll be findin' rocks in yer stew."

Casting a dismayed glance at Rowan, Nathel backed away a pace from the offended Stoneman, his hands up. "Even a great artist can do little with only a single color!"

Mollified, Borlin moved to the door with the others and Hathunor rose from his spot, giving Rowan a toothy smile.

"Do you know where Torrin is?" Rowan asked as they walked through the corridor.

"No," said Nathel. "I know he slept at least some of the night, because I heard him leave some time before dawn, but I have no idea where he went." He glanced down at her. "He just needs a little time."

As Nathel led them through the citadel and down to the kitchens, which were located on main level near the large bailey, they began to see servants, household staff and soldiers hurried past.

Rowan looked around as they entered an enormous hall full of long tables and benches where soldiers and other people bent over their food. The sound of chatter and the clank of dishes reverberated through the space, but a ripple of stillness followed Rowan and her friends as people stopped to watch their progress through the hall. The huge black bulk of Hathunor held their attention. He strode, loose armed and feral in their midst, his red eyes curious.

A pair of doors at the end of the dinning hall opened into the steamy, fragrant chaos of the keep's kitchen, and Rowan side stepped as a young boy went hurtling by with an overloaded wooden tray held above his head, shouting a "Pardon, please," over his shoulder. Rowan turned at the sound of a low whistle of appreciation from Borlin. The Stoneman's eyes were wide and a great grin split his bearded face.

The light from the morning sun streamed into the hot interior of the kitchen through huge wooden doors that were swung opened at the far end of the room; beyond them, in the large inner bailey of the keep, a wagon was backed up so that supplies and firewood could be delivered directly into the heart of the scullery. Between Rowan and those doors was spread a wonder of culinary delights: sideboards strewn with flour and fresh bread as it was pulled from the rows of brick ovens; vegetables tumbling out of baskets and bowls full of ingredients spread out across tables; giant caldrons simmering with savoury mysteries in the giant hearths.

She stood, blinking and trying to make sense of the directed confusion that was Pellaris Keep's kitchen when she noticed, presiding over it all – the center of a spinning top, the most enormous man she had ever seen. His eyes were fixed on Nathel.

"By the sweet Goddess, you scoundrel," he cried. "Come to pilfer my honey cakes and steal the hearts of the kitchen maids?" The great man waded through the activity until he was standing before them, looking down at Nathel. His girth was so impressive, Rowan doubted she could reach halfway around his great bulk.

Nathel turned with a flourish. "May I present Danyl the Great, head cook of Pellaris Keep."

The giant cook captured Rowan's hand and delicately kissed the back of it. "We seldom enjoy such important and lovely company down here in the kitchens!" His eyes darted in the direction of Nathel and he whispered conspiratorially to Rowan, "It's usually only the ruffians that come down here looking to wheedle the tastiest morsels out of us."

Nathel frowned at the insult. "I always brought you good conversation in return!"

The other cooks and scullery maids laughed and Danyl the Great rewarded them with a mock scowl. "See to your pots, then!"

Rowan's jaw dropped to see the enormous man launch into action. He moved almost as effortlessly as Arynilas. Feeling like she was caught in whirlwind, Rowan was suddenly seated at a table with steaming food heaped before her. She closed her mouth and inhaled the aroma.

Borlin had not sat down with them and she glanced around to find him leaning over a simmering pot, dipping a large spoon into the contents. The giant cook noticed him as well and caught him just as he lifted the spoon to his lips to sample it.

"Here now! What do you think you're doing? You'll ruin my sauce! Get off with you." Danyl trundled around the large counter towards the Stoneman.

Borlin, ignoring the huge cook completely, tasted the sauce, raised his eyebrows and smiled in appreciative delight. "Tell me, 'ave ye used Tiepan or Savoury Fernisen in this?"

The huge cook stopped in mid-stride and appraised the Stoneman with renewed interest. "Tiepan. Savoury Fernisen is very hard to come by this far north, especially now that all trade has been suspended."

Borlin nodded thoughtfully. "This would 'ave a subtle difference with Fernisen. Me store o' the spice is still full. It would be interesting to try it, no?"

Danyl's face lit up. "You have some Fernisen?"

Borlin smiled, "Oh, aye. I 'ave quite a few lovely spices picked up from me travels, some I 'ave not even tested in a dish as yet."

The giant cook nearly quivered with delight and the two fell into an excited conversation about the possibilities.

Rowan turned to the others and asked quietly, "I thought you told me that women do most of the cooking in Eryos?"

Nathel smiled. "Cerebus found Danyl in Tabor. It is one of the few kingdoms where men cook. Danyl was head chef to the king of Tabor and Cerebus managed to entice him away from Tyrn. He has been here a very long time now."

The food was delicious but Rowan found she could not get much down. Her stomach tightened as she thought ahead to the coming meeting with the king.

Nathel leaned over and said quietly, "It will be fine. Cerebus is a good man, and he will listen and act upon your message. You will make a fine impression. Just be yourself."

Rowan looked at him with surprise and he winked at her. She nodded and swallowed. That was it, she thought. She was acutely aware that her message wasn't the only thing required of her. As the Messenger of such strange information they would look to her to understand it and as a woman she would have little credibility in the eyes of the men she needed to convince.

A wave of hot frustration washed over her. Nothing had been easy since she had left her native soil. She looked at Nathel again, at all her friends. That wasn't necessarily the truth.

Memories

The streets of Pellaris looked clean and clear. A dawn storm had quickly passed and now the early morning sun shone as the clouds broke apart. Wet surfaces glittered, making the old buildings look new.

Underfoot, the cobblestones changed to the rough, rounded style of the oldest part of Pellaris and Torrin was pulled from his cluttered, crowded mind. He was in the old quarter, and had been wandering for more than three hours.

After an almost sleepless night, with the suffocating memories of time spent with his wife and daughters in the citadel threatening to overwhelm him, Torrin had left the keep. Wandering through the sleeping streets had unfortunately done little to alleviate this feeling and he let go the futility of holding the memories at bay, letting them wash over him.

He had shunned the great market square, where Emma had loved to go – had passed it by three streets and still felt its pull. Instead he turned to walk through the merchant quarter with its elegant homes and expensive shops. His path took him further back into memories not touched by pain. Eventually he arrived here where his carefree youth had brought only pleasure.

The narrow streets were crowded like crooked teeth with two story houses and shops that leaned precariously into the street. The ancient buildings were slumped, their mortar nearer in composition to sand than stone. This was a place of history. It spoke of the simple folk of Pellar who, generation upon generation lived and worked in these streets under whatever ruling king was in power.

As a boy, *this* had been Torrin's favourite place.

He and Nathel had played hide and seek in the twisting alleys, oblivious to the dangers such a place could present to a pair of young boys. Looking at the streets now, he wondered that their father had let them come unescorted. Perhaps they had only assumed themselves clever enough to elude the castle guards and escape to the old quarter, he thought reflectively. There were always plenty of other children to play with, some half-wild and orphaned, but the promise of adventure was all they needed.

Passing a dark alley where the morning sun had yet to penetrate, he peered down its gloomy length, remembering he and Nathel, torches in hand with a cloth wrapped lunch for the exploration ahead. They had felt like treasure hunters, exploring the dangerous underground labyrinth of catacombs and tunnels under the city. In the course of their frequent visits and mapping they had discovered the decaying bones of the ancient city that lay beneath Pellaris.

A man wearing seaman's clothes with a sack tossed over his shoulder nodded to Torrin as he passed, heading to the harbour.

Now there was a place to fuel a boy's imagination. The great sea wall on the north side of the city looked out over the harbour at a forest of ship's masts swaying with the swells. The stone of the cliff created a natural sweeping hollow, protecting the bay from the prevailing winds. Torrin and Nathel had prided themselves on being able to name every kind of ship that came into the harbour. Sloops and cutters bobbed among the larger galleons; occasionally a tall ship arrived from the mysterious west, filled with exotic spices, foods and fabrics. All were moored at the same quayside amid the bustle and hum of sailors and shipwrights.

On the few occasions the boys were allowed to descend the tunnel stair to see those ships up-close, they had glimpsed a few of the pale-skinned westerners, slaves who manned the great ships, climbing to and fro in the rigging to repair sails and mend ropes with an agile grace that Torrin had admired. Slaves already mixed into crews were allowed, but the slave ships themselves were not permitted in Pellarian waters. They had to sail further northeast to Krang or make the long dangerous journey around that mountainous realm to sail south and east all the way to Ren. It was a journey only the most experienced – or the most reckless – captains made through the deadly, roiling gambit between the ice flows and northern Krang.

Torrin frowned. Thoughts of Krang brought him full circle to the Raken and their origin. He took a deep breath and released it slowly. The council would be held soon and Rowan would finally deliver her message. All his will had been bent towards getting her here to King Cerebus, a man Torrin trusted. A part of him was relieved, but another part – a greater part – was wary.

Everything they had learned pointed to a sinister intelligence and plot behind the Raken.

The sun was higher now and the folks of the old quarter were stirring and opening windows and shop fronts. Torrin turned right up a narrow, twisting street, shrugging his shoulders uncomfortably as he passed beneath the precarious lean of the jutting second floors overhead. He struck out with a purposeful stride, his long legs carrying him quickly over the uneven cobblestones. The street zigzagged but it headed in the direction that he wanted to go. The memories surrounding him fell away to be left in the doorways, alleys and corners – more history to add to the oldest part of Pellaris.

The Council

Rowan followed Chancellor Galen down a long, elegant corridor, rubbing her palms against her thighs and needlessly adjusting the vembraces on her forearms. She registered the enormous tapestries and the gilded stand lamps, but was more focused on calming her racing heart.

Here in the public wing, people sat on benches along the corridor or stood in small clusters. Rowan tried to ignore the reaction Hathunor's enormous figure drew as people shrank back against the walls, looking wildly around for more enemies, and focused instead on Galen's thin, straight back, trusting the escort of Pellarian guards that strode with them to soothe the people. Nathel and Dalemar walked to either side of her and the others followed. Rowan sighed, missing Nathel's snickers and jests that had kept her mind from worry during breakfast.

Nathel assured her that Torrin wouldn't miss the audience; still, Rowan found herself seeking his tall figure among the people in the corridor.

The hall opened into a high circular lobby, its stone walls reverberating with footsteps and voices. Rowan crossed an inlaid marble insignia in the floor – gold stars arranged in the constellation of the Great Northern Huntsman on a red field. At the opposite end of the foyer a pair of arched copper doors stood open; through them was an enormous circular chamber lined with tiers of benches. There, a tall, broad figure detached itself from the milling crowd and Rowan felt a flutter of relief as Torrin walked toward them, his intense blue eyes fastened on her. He looked tired but his clothes and armour were clean, and the broad eagle wings and crest stood out boldly on the center of his polished leather and bronze breastplate. He fell in beside her and together they walked through the doors into the council chamber.

Galen stopped. "My lady Rowan, if you please, there is a place for you and your company on the floor to the left." The chancellor indicated a row of seats behind a polished wooden table. "Make yourselves comfortable. Refreshments will be brought to you in a moment. Forgive me, but I must see to the king."

The lean old man bowed, then walked across the council chamber to stairs leading up to a pair of ornate chairs, set between two carved wooden doors. He disappeared through one of the doors.

Rowan followed Torrin as he strode across the floor to the row of seats Galen had indicated. She ignored the low babble of voices from the people already sitting in the tiers of benches and looked up at the high arched ceiling. Morning light streamed through four large windows set high in the walls of the chamber, lighting the stone interior with a warm glow. The soaring construction of the room was clean and though ornamentation was minimal, Rowan noted the craftsmanship was exquisite.

At the table, she sank uneasily into a padded chair between Torrin and Dalemar. Her stomach flip-flopped. She had not expected to give her message to an entire audience.

The top tier of seating was packed with soldiers dressed in their battle gear, prepared for a call to arms on a moments notice. Women in fine gowns and men in equally fine tunics ranged in the first two tiers above the chamber floor. Behind them the next two tiers were quickly filling with people dressed in less expensive garb. They had the look of trades people and guild members. In spite of the siege, it seemed that folk were still concerned with the machinations of governance.

Rowan cast a wry glance at her huge black friend. The big Saa Raken was crouched easily on his haunches, just past the end of the table, clawed hands relaxed and dangling from his bent knees. Hathunor was as much the reason for the crowd as being privy to the decisions of King and council.

A group of older men wearing long robes similar to that of Chancellor Galen began to file into the chamber. Rowan counted fifteen in total. They dispersed to the lowest seating, padded chairs and glossy tables like the one Rowan and her companions occupied.

Most of these latest arrivals resumed their conversations once seated, casting speculative glances at Rowan and her companions. A few, though, sat back and surveyed the chamber with dignified or haughty expressions.

Servants clad in gold and red Pellarian livery entered the chamber with trays carrying goblets and flasks of water, which they placed on the tables. Hathunor reached out a clawed hand circumspectly to ask for some as a serving man passed, making the poor fellow jump and squeak like a child. With his face drained white, the man cast wide eyes at the rest of the companions before tremulously holding out the pitcher he had been carrying. Hathunor received the vessel and exposed long ivory fangs in a grin. The man paled even further and scuttled away as Hathunor swallowed the contents of the pitcher in one gulp. The huge Saa Raken's red eyes shone with amusement and he emitted a low rumble as he placed the jug on the table.

Nathel chuckled and Borlin snickered into his goblet. Arynilas, eyes twinkling, surveyed the chamber through his ever-calm sapphire eyes. Dalemar cleared his throat in suppressed laughter and even Torrin to her other side lost the edge from his stern demeanour. Rowan breathed out a shaky breath. She would have laughed too if her stomach had not been in knots.

General Preven walked across the floor flanked by two soldiers. He still wore his breastplate and the long red and gold cloak of the Pellarian army. The two men following him looked to be officers as well. The tall man on the right wore the armour of the Klyssen cavalry, his horsehair-plumed helmet tucked under an arm and his stern hawk-nosed face looking straight ahead. The man to the left was shorter and darker in appearance and wore armour consisting of many overlapping plates. It looked to be both flexible and light.

Torrin leaned over and said quietly, "He looks to be a commander in the Taborian army. I saw Taborian infantry last night as we fought on the wall."

Rowan nodded without taking her eye from the warriors; they both looked to be experienced fighting men. "And the Klyssen officer is a captain?"

"Yes, same as our friend, Captain Whelan."

The men made their way to the last table on the floor directly below the thrones. One final person strode purposefully into the hall. The ascetic figure of Tihir N'Avarin reached the centre of the council floor and paused. As if on cue, the giant chamber doors closed with a hollow boom. His dark, glittering gaze swept the chamber contemptuously, lingering on the well-dressed nobles. He turned toward his seat, black robes swishing about his ankles. Rowan watched him and saw something else in his dark eyes. It was there for only a moment before disappearing – hunger. She shuddered as he swept by.

The noise in the vaulted room ceased as all eyes turned in expectation toward the dais. A staff struck the marble floor twice and echoed through the silence. A man and a woman emerged through one of the doors. They came to the thrones and surveyed the council chambers.

Chancellor Galen stood to the left of the thrones. "Ladies and lords of Pellar, I present to you King Cerebus and Lady Queen Elana." The chancellor's voice reverberated through the stone room with a strength that belied such a slender old man.

Rowan hastened to her feet as the people in the council chambers stood and hailed the royals. King Cerebus looked much as he had the night before. His armour breastplate and shoulder guards were polished to a gleam and he wore a fur-trimmed cloak. His sword was sheathed at his hip and one large hand rested comfortably on its hilt.

Rowan studied the woman beside him. Queen Elana was beautiful, with pale hair twisted about her head in intricate braids and her proud form clothed in a creamy gown trimmed with gold stitching. She was a match to the king in every way. Though she was slight and fine-boned, she radiated the same strength and conviction that Rowan had seen in the king. The chamber fell away as Rowan gazed at the queen. Not since leaving her homeland had she encountered a woman this powerful. It was innate in her every fibre; if had Elana been a scrubbing woman in the keep's kitchens, she would still exude that same strength.

King Cerebus raised a hand and his voice rang out over the chamber. "Please be seated." He waited until the rustle of clothes and the scuffing of feet died away. "I have called this council for one reason alone. Our attentions are limited to the defence of this city and time is short so I would ask that the ceremony be dispensed with so that we might proceed with all swiftness to the matter at hand." His gaze turned to Rowan and her companions. "We have with us today those who have travelled far to reach our beleaguered city to offer what aid they may and who bring with them a message from afar. I myself have heard but some of the message and felt that it warranted our fullest attention."

Cerebus seated himself beside Queen Elana and nodded to Chancellor Galen. The old chancellor stepped forward and spoke in his sonorous voice. "The lady Rowan Mor Lanyar, Messenger and emissary from Myris Dar."

There were murmurs and sounds of exclamation around the chamber. The name of Rowan's homeland had likely not been uttered here for a very long time.

Rowan took a deep breath, rubbing her hands on her knees under the table. Before she could stand, she felt the sudden warmth of Torrin's large hand closing over hers. She turned to look at him and found his blue eyes steady on her, an expression of encouragement on his face as he squeezed her hand.

Rising, Rowan adjusted her sword in its scabbard and strode out to the centre of the council chamber floor. There, she stood, feet slightly apart, shoulders back. The comforting weight of her armour grounded her. Thankful for heft of her sword on her back, the tooled leather armour of her homeland that covered and protected her like a second skin, she steeled herself against the collective weight of every gaze in the chamber.

She had no idea how she would present her people to this council or if she was even a fit representative for Myris Dar. A sword and armour did her no good in circumstances such as these, but it was all she knew.

Rowan looked up at King Cerebus and smoothly knelt down on one knee. Her long golden braid slipped over her shoulder as she knelt and its end touched the floor beside her fist as she bowed her head. This was a man's pose and she heard whispers among the watchers. Then, without waiting for leave she rose to her feet and waited.

Cerebus inclined his head. "It is indeed long since one from the fabled isle has visited this land. I thank you for the honour you do us, and bid you welcome to Pellaris, though the circumstances are dire. I hope we can one day repay that honour."

Rowan smiled, remembering the look in King Cerebus's eyes upon their first meeting. That same gaze shone through the formal tone of this public audience and her stomach unclenched a little. "The honour of fighting by your side in the defence of your home and your lives is repayment enough for any Myrian, your highness."

Cerebus blinked and the queen sat forward with an intrigued expression. Rowan nodded to her, then turned to look at the entire assembly before returning her gaze to the king. "I bring with me the good will of all my people. Those who fight for freedom and justice are ever high in our esteem and though I am but one warrior, I would lend my sword to that for which you fight. But first I must deliver the message I have been charged with bringing to the city of Pellaris and the king who rules here.

"I was sent by the Seers of Danum, an ancient sect of mystics in my land who are bound to the protection of all Erys's creatures. For centuries they have guarded against a darkness that will bring chaos and destruction to the world. In their visions, the Seers foresaw the peril hanging over Pellar and sent me in the hope that this doom will be somehow thwarted."

Rowan paused and felt the expectant silence in the chamber. She pulled in a breath, feeling like a lodestone, absorbing the charged energy of the space.

"The message is this: *Look not only to strength or all will be lost for the foe is too great. The gateway must not be opened for ill intent. Bind the Stone with evil. Free the Stone with purity of heart. The path to salvation lies in the hands of the Slayer.*"

Rowan closed her eyes, acutely aware of how cryptic her message was. She silently railed against the Seers for not giving her more. When she opened them again, the faces she saw were blank and perplexed. "When the little moon is hidden by her sister, the darkness of which I speak will be unleashed. Unless it is stopped, this city will fall."

A councillor wearing red robes, a long dark beard fanning out on his chest stood with an amused and patient expression on his broad face. He spoke as though to a child. "My dear lady, you came across the ocean and journeyed through Eryos to bring us news of the Raken hoard that stands beyond our gates?"

Uncomfortable chuckles rolled through the crowd.

Rowan turned to look the man in the eye. Her voice cut through the murmurs of people and echoed around the room. "I do not speak of the army besieging this city," she said darkly. "I speak of the coming of the Wyoraith."

The councillor snorted with indignation. "The Wyoraith! Bah, children's tales. My fellow councillors we have a real enough threat arrayed before the gates of this city without being distracted by nonsense. We should be seeing to the defence of our city!"

There were grumbles of agreement around the vaulted chamber and a few hands were slapped upon the wooden tabletops of the council seating.

Rowan spoke over the noise and all eyes turned to her once more. "Here in this land the Wyoraith has slipped into legend, just as my homeland of Myris Dar is no longer remembered as truth; but as I stand before you real, made of flesh and blood, so too does the Wyoraith exist. The Seers of Danum have guarded against its coming for centuries and they believe here is where the wisdom and strength to battle that enemy will be found.

"There is one who can meet this threat, one known as the *Slayer of the Wyoraith*. Just as the Seers foresaw the coming of the Wyoraith, so too do they tell of the one who will battle it. They do not know who he is or where in Pellar he is to be sought, only that he will be found here. The Seers must have hoped that someone here would understand the message and know what to do about it."

As Rowan finished, utter silence descended on the council chambers for a few heartbeats, then it erupted into cacophony. Councillors strove to speak over one another and the citizens in the upper tiers chattered loudly to each other.

Rowan looked helplessly at her companions. Hathunor's great head swung from side to side and he looked ready to leap to his feet if anything more than shouting occurred. But then she met Torrin's steady gaze and felt some of his strength flow into her.

A stout red-faced councillor bellowed through the din, "Are these Seers of Danum well known? How are we to verify the truth of their warning?"

"Oh please, Marik," scoffed another councillor. "Shall we convene a committee to look into it and wait until next spring for an answer?"

"Or perhaps we could send a delegation to the island of Myris Dar to ask them to please elaborate upon this information that they have sent," mocked another.

Rowan frowned and scanned the council chambers, looking from face to face as the fifteen council members argued among themselves.

Then she looked into the dark gaze of Tihir N'Avarin. His expression was hard, cold and disapproving. He sat quietly and the circular seal of Erys on his chest glowed like an eye against the black of his robes.

"Enough!" roared the king.

Silence fell over the chambers but councillors continued to eye one.

"We have precious little time as it is without wasting it arguing over irrelevant points," said Cerebus. "When we have the luxury of time, I will be happy to open the floor to debate as to how Pellar shall respond formally to Myris Dar. For now I will myself vouch for the honour of the messenger, for I have seen her risk her life in the defence of Pellaris."

"Hear, hear," called General Preven, the scowl on his bluff face softened by the wink he gave Rowan.

The soldiers sitting near the top of the rows of public benches began to stamp their feet in unison.

Cerebus raised his hand once more for silence. He sighed and rubbed his brow. "My Lady Rowan, the news you bring is perplexing to say the least. Is there anything else that your Seers would have you say?"

"Only that the Wyoraith is but a tool, it can only be used by the one who summons it. If the one trying to call it forth can be found and stopped, the Wyoraith's coming will be thwarted. The Seers also believe that the Raken invading this land are connected to the one that is trying to summon the Wyoraith."

Cerebus sat forward, his grey gaze intense. "So by stopping the one trying to summon the Wyoraith, the Raken will also be stopped? Are you certain?"

Rowan nodded. "I have the word of the Seers, but for myself I do not need it. From the time I first set foot in Eryos, I have been hunted by Raken. That they should pursue me so relentlessly, tells me that my message and the Raken are connected."

"Do the Seers know who it is?" Cerebus's voice was intent.

Rowan shook her head sadly. "The one trying to summon the Wyoraith is hidden from the Seers."

"What of the Stone in your message?" asked the queen. "*Bind the Stone with evil. Free the Stone with purity of heart.* What does that mean?"

Rowan shook her head once more. “Forgive me, your Highness but I do not know. The Seers answered few of my questions. Either they couldn’t or they wouldn’t answer them for reasons of their own. I had hoped that the answers would lie here in ancient Kathorn – in Pellar.”

Queen Elana nodded and Cerebus frowned in concentration. He turned to Hathunor. “Your Raken friend, why is he so different from the army outside?”

Rowan beckoned for Hathunor to join her. She registered a collective gasp as the huge Saa Raken rose smoothly to his feet and padded across to her, the clicking of his claws on the floor audible and his red eyes sweeping the chamber. He stopped next to her and Rowan reached out to touch his arm.

“Hathunor’s kin beyond the gates are under a spell. They are enslaved and have no choice in what they do.”

A murmur of exclamation spun through the council chamber.

“Hathunor owe Rowan rrrrffethhtickh.” The last word began as a rumble and ended in an odd clicking. The giant Raken looked curiously at the shocked faces around the chamber, then tilted his head and said, “Life debt.”

“You saved *his* life?” General Preven asked incredulously.

Rowan nodded. “Even the largest and strongest among us need help sometimes.”

Tihir N’Avarin rose to his feet and cleared his throat, turning to address King Cerebus. “Your Majesty, I beg you to consider the full ramifications of what has been placed before us. The Lady Rowan –” Tihir cast a dark glance at her – “has proven herself valorous in the defence of our beloved city but I must stress the consequences of placing such trust in one who has strayed so far from Erys’s appointed path. The Goddess in her wisdom created men and women to fulfill specific roles. To deviate from that path flies in the face of Her righteous judgment. We must beware the follies of what our visitor brings with her. Although her intentions might be pure, she lacks the benefits of proper schooling and as such represents a danger to our way of life. We must beware what her message brings, tainted as it is with the intentions of the unfaithful.”

As the priest spoke Rowan clenched her hands into fists, anger blooming in her chest. She understood now why Torrin felt as he did about the Priesthood.

Cerebus sighed and shook his head. "N'Avarin, Rowan Mor Lanyar is a foreigner and stands outside of the jurisdiction and judgment of the Priesthood. Her message, though cryptic, must be considered with the fullest respect and seriousness."

"Are these Seers always right? Does what they see always come to pass?" asked N'Avarin, his dark gaze boring into Rowan.

"The Seers are not all-seeing," replied Rowan. "They catch only glimpses of what has passed and what is to come. The fullest understanding of what they see only comes after years of contemplation and study."

"Then how are we to know what these Seers say is even true?" N'Avarin turned to address the assembly. His voice was slowly rising and its power held the listeners enthralled. "It could be gibberish. Flights of fancy in which we are told we must place our trust. Why now after so long does Myris Dar wish to make contact with us? They send into our midst a single woman with a wild tale and expect us to accept without question what they say? My king and fellow councillors, am I alone in seeing the true danger here? Why should we bow to the whims of heresy from a foreign land? Are we to now take our orders from blasphemous Myrian fanatics?"

Heat flushed Rowan's face as all that she had faced and overcome to get to this city with her message was spun by the priest into an act of dubious and hostile plotting. The man not only impugned Rowan, but maligned her people as well. Wide eyed she looked at the priest; her worst fears coming to pass. She tore her gaze away from N'Avarin to look to the king and queen. They had their heads together, and Elana speaking quietly to Cerebus. They seemed not to be swayed by the priest's words. It was a mercy Rowan clung to.

As Tihir N'Avarin finished, there were echoes of agreement from the robed councillors and many nodded heads in the rest of the crowd.

Rowan stood up straighter and stepped forward, taking a deep breath to defend herself and her people. Before she could speak, a large figure appeared beside her. She turned to place a calming hand on Hathunor but found Torrin instead. By the look on his face, Rowan thought he might draw his sword. His dark expression took in the entire assembly and then settled with weight on Tihir N'Avarin.

His voice held something dangerous. "You would speak of heresy? Of blasphemy and fanaticism? Be careful priest, for you are treading dangerously close to hypocrisy."

Tihir N'Avarin's eyes went wide and he drew himself up. But Torrin didn't let him reply. "When we met this woman," he turned to look at Rowan, "she was traveling through the Wilds with a Raken trieton chasing her." Torrin glared back at N'Avarin and lowered his voice. "Have you risked *your* life in the face of a Raken hoard?" His eyes traveled around the faces in the council chamber, then back to N'Avarin. "When Raken killed her party in Dendor, she set out for Pellaris *alone* to bring you this message. Raken pursued her the entire way. Tell me, why would they have been interested in one woman if she was but a single seed planted by another nation with designs on Pellar? One lone woman would present little threat to a Raken invasion of Pellar unless she had something they wanted, threatened them in some way. Whoever controls the Raken beasts knew what she was bringing to you and very nearly stopped her." Torrin raked his eyes over the listeners. He pointed back to the walls of the chamber as though he could see through them and out over the city. "That army waiting out there, is that the way a normal army acts? Standing like statues under the sun and rain as though waiting constantly for a signal. Then they attack without warning – no commands given; no sound; only the sudden unexplained attacks. Look at this Raken we call friend," Torrin indicated Hathunor, standing behind Rowan. "Does he act like the Raken outside the gate?"

Torrin looked back at N'Avarin and his voice dropped with menace. "Do not forget the facts that stand before you when you try to spin a tale for your own purposes, priest."

Rowan felt tears just below the surface. None of this mattered – what people decided to think of her and her homeland was irrelevant. She knew who she was, and her friends knew it also. The last of her distress and anger slipped away and she turned to look at Cerebus.

The king was watching Torrin with interest. "What can you tell us of the Raken? If they are being controlled by someone, how is it being done?"

Dalemar answered, striding from the table to stand with them on the floor of the council chamber. "We are not certain, King Cerebus, but as they are being controlled, we believe there must be a way they can be freed of that control. There is something about Hathunor that saved him from the same fate as the Drae Raken beyond your gates."

"Drae Raken?" asked Cerebus.

Dalemar nodded. "Hathunor has told us that there are four races of Raken and that two of them are being used here in Pellar. As far as we know, Hathunor is the only Saa Raken in Eryos. He is from the warrior class of his people. His enslaved kin are like our common people. The reason that he has not been enslaved we believe lies in the ability of all Saa Raken to capture and use magic."

Cerebus blinked. The people in the chamber looked at Hathunor with renewed interest.

"He can wield magic?" asked Queen Elana.

Dalemar nodded.

"Then he is like a Rith," said General Preven.

Dalemar shook his head. "His ability is passive; he can only use magic that flows into him. The land that he comes from has magic that flows through it naturally and undirected. The Raken have developed the ability to use it."

Astonished conversation filled the chamber as Cerebus considered the full weight of what the Rith claimed. "Then you believe the Raken are being controlled through the use of magic, and have been brought here from some other land? To what end?"

"I can see no other way for so many to be controlled. It must be magic, and it is not a thing lightly done. Whoever is behind it, is *very* powerful. We have no reason to question Hathunor's word that the Raken have been somehow brought here from his homeland. But to what end," Dalemar exchanged looks with Rowan and Torrin, "we do not fully know."

"A Rith then is behind this invasion?" asked one of the councillors.

Dalemar sighed. "There are more questions than answers, but yes a Rith or someone with an ability to control Rithkind as well and bend them to his will."

Queen Elana stirred, her skirts rustling. "Where are they from? You mentioned their homeland. Why have we never seen their kind before now?"

"Hathunor's people are from a land far to the south and west beyond the great Timor Mountains," replied Dalemar. "We have no idea how his kin were brought here, but when Rowan found Hathunor, he was about to be killed by Drae Raken under the spell. She saved his life."

The chamber hummed.

"These Drae Raken at the gates do seem to have magical abilities," said Preven. "We have not been able to discover how they are supplied. As you said Torrin, they stand as though waiting. We have not seen them eat or drink. They do not act as a normal army would; far from it."

Torrin nodded grimly. "They are not like a normal army, General; though I do not believe it is magical. They do not need to be supplied. They can and will eat but they can go great periods with no food because they are able to gain sustenance from the sun's light."

Tihir N'Avarin's scoff was quiet. "Nothing in the Goddess's creation has such abilities."

"Do not forget," said Dalemar, "these creatures are not from Eryos. The rules of Eryos do not apply to them, nor does our knowledge of the world extend much beyond the borders of our land."

"How?" asked Cerebus in a low voice, "How could they possibly use the sun to survive?"

"It is not very different from a snake or lizard that needs the sun to warm its flesh before it can hunt or move quickly," answered Dalemar. "The heat in the environment affects their ability to move. The Raken must be governed by a similar process."

At this, Hathunor's gravely voice rumbled forth, "Raken eat sun."

Rowan sighed at the confused faces. Many of the people in the room were simple soldiers.

Torrin cleared his throat. "Suffice it to say, this army of Raken can survive without the conventional supplies an army normally needs. They can and will outlast the city's stores provided the sun continues to shine."

The grim silence that greeted this statement was absolute

The general cleared his throat loudly. "We will have to await the reinforcements from Klyssen and Tabor, we cannot hope to confront the army outside the gates without more men."

Torrin frowned and shifted his stance, looking at all the faces staring back at him. This should have been a private audience. Rumours would spread throughout the city like wildfire. The power of suggestion was potent in warfare – a hint of fear could swell and grow into a tide of terror transforming a disciplined army into chaos.

He glanced sideways at Rowan. She stood proudly, but her straight back and tense stance belied her otherwise calm appearance. The audience stared at her with disapproval and, he sensed, a certain amount of wonder. Perhaps this was what Cerebus was counting on.

"You've sent messengers out to call for more aid?" he asked.

Preven nodded. "Four separate parties."

"Are you certain they got through the lines?" asked Nathel from the table.

Preven wiped a hand across his face. "We've had no word, but then I didn't expect there to be any. If the reinforcements from Klyssen and Tabor come we will at least be able to launch a combined attack. The Raken will be caught between the armies and we will have a chance." He glanced uneasily at Hathunor.

"How many are you expecting?" Torrin asked him.

"Couriers were sent to Klyssen to request a thousand armed mounts," replied the Klyssen captain.

"We are hoping for the same amount from Tabor," added Preven.

The Taborian commander's overlapping armour creaked as he leaned forward. "Rest assured, General, Tabor will send troops." He scowled at the Klyssen Officer.

Torrin sighed, even under these dire circumstances the two countries could not get along. “How often are they attacking?”

General Preven shook his head. “There is no set pattern. It is very unnerving. The Raken do not need to muster because they are already standing ready. We’ve had to post more lookouts because there is so little time to prepare for an attack.”

“We have seen them exchange places with each other,” said the Klyssen officer with the hawk nose and slanting eyebrows, “but we do not know where the relieved Raken go once they leave the field. Until now we assumed their supplies were hidden from our view beyond the plain.”

“When we approached the city,” said Torrin, “there were smaller patrols we had to avoid, but we had no hint as to what they were doing.”

Arynilas stirred. “Despite the strange power over the Raken, whoever controls them cannot push them past their endurance or they would be of no use to him. Even Hathunor needs to rest, though his stamina far outstrips our own.”

“If they wanted t’, they could swarm the walls an’ breach yer defences,” observed Borlin. “It looks as if ye barely ’ave enough t’ man the walls.”

Preven scratched his jaw. “We have no explanation. The attacks are brief. You are right, Master Borlin, if they wanted to they could over-run the walls during a sustained attack. But they break off their assaults before we are tested to that point.”

Torrin tapped a finger on the pommel of his sword, his frown deepening. How was it the vast army before the gates had not yet taken the city? It made no sense. A commander wouldn’t prolong a siege, using up precious resources without good reason. But then the Raken army had no need of supplies. It cost whoever was controlling the Raken nothing to keep them occupied with Pellaris, conventionally speaking anyway. He glanced at Dalemar – given how exhausting it was for his friend to use skills, Torrin couldn’t imagine the power it must take to control the Raken army. Perhaps –

Rowan spoke his next thought even as it formed. “Maybe he is waiting for the right time to launch a final attack. Perhaps there is something else he needs to do and is simply keeping Pellaris contained for the time being.”

“The Wyoraith,” Cerebus said.

Rowan nodded.

"It could be that the one behind the Raken invasion is extended to his limit," said Dalemar. "The summoning of the Wyoraith might be of more importance at the moment than the capture of Pellaris, or perhaps he hasn't enough strength to achieve both goals at once. I imagine the Raken are fighting his control. It could be that he hasn't the strength to force them into a prolonged attack. Keeping the Raken from breaking free of his control is one thing but forcing them to actually act against their collective will would take a great deal more power."

Cerebus nodded in agreement. "Then it would seem our task is to determine who is controlling the Raken and find a way to break his control over them."

"Indeed," said Dalemar.

"What would the Raken do if they were no longer controlled?" asked Elana.

"Raken brothers not attack if no reason," rumbled Hathunor. "They never attack and fight unless in defence. They like quiet place. Brothers miss homeland." He lifted one of his clawed hands and tapped himself on the chest. "Hathunor miss homeland." There was a deep well of sadness in the huge Raken's voice, and the audience fell silent.

Rowan spoke. "If the summoner is dead, his control of them will be ended."

Torrin turned at the finality in her voice and saw in her face the shadings of things to come – they scoured through him like a cold, hollow wind. He clenched his fists, his heart contract in his chest. He took a breath to calm his racing heart. "What of the city's storehouses? How long can Pellaris last against this siege?" He was surprised to find his voice steady.

A questioning murmur spread throughout the chamber.

"There is perhaps a month's worth of provisions, maybe more," said Preven. "The chancellor will know the full extent."

"There have been many questions from citizens," said a green robed councillor, rising to his feet. "Are there enough stores to last until the reinforcements?"

"We have not had an update from the chancellor's office for days," stated another councillor. "What is the rationing schedule?"

Elana leaned forward, ignoring the councillors, her penetrating gaze levelled at Rowan. The queen's voice cut through the chatter. "Is there anything more you can tell us about this *slayer*?"

Rowan shifted and drew in a breath. "The Wyoraith was last summoned a thousand years ago. There was a man, believed to be born in this land, a man who grew up to become the *Slayer of the Wyoraith*. It is not known how he was able to kill it or what part of Pellar he came from, only that he was found here in this very city. The Seers sent me to give the message to the king of Pellar in hopes that he would understand. In hopes that you might know who the *Slayer* is."

Cerebus released a long breath and his eyes held regret. "I fear we do not."

Torrin's slight hopes plummeted like a stone dropped to the bottom of a pond.

"What of this gateway?" asked the king.

Dalemar replied and Cerebus looked at him. "The *gateway* could be the portal through which the Wyoraith will enter this world."

Cerebus leaned back in his chair and steepled his fingers. "It would seem we have many more questions."

"Your library is rumoured to be one of the largest in all of Eryos," said Dalemar. "Perhaps the answer to these mysteries can be found there. A thousand years ago Pellar did not exist but there may yet be an echo of the realm that covered these lands. If records were kept, they would be older than Pellar's history."

Cerebus turned to Galen. "Advise the head archivist to begin searching for any reference to the *Wyoraith* and a *Slayer*. Any Kathornin scrolls and texts would be a good place to start. I seem to recall a fairly large Kathornin collection. Also advise Craius to accommodate any requests from the Lady Rowan and her party. He is to give them full access to the entire collection." Cerebus looked directly at Rowan. "Your message, it seems, begets another quest. I do not know whether the answers to the questions you have brought before us can be found, but we will try. Tell me, Lady Rowan, what would your Seers suggest be done if we are unable to find this *slayer* in time?"

"The Seers of Danum sent no advice, King Cerebus." Rowan's voice was solemn. "For myself, I would send a force, however small or large as can be spared, to find and kill the summoner."

Torrin nodded in approval. In her voice he heard the sound of a commander giving no quarter. He saw Preven and the other officers were in agreement.

Tihir N'Avarin's cold voice, laced with sarcasm, echoed around the chamber. "And I suppose *you* are the one, sent to our aid by the grace of your Myrian Seers, to stop this summoner?"

"If I must. If no other way were found; if there is no *slayer* to send; then yes, I would go. I would try." There was only quiet sincerity in her voice.

The room was silent, all eyes fixed on Rowan.

Torrin drew a deep breath, fierce pride radiating through his body.

Cerebus also took in a long breath and let it out. "Let us hope that will not be necessary."

"It would seem that our gratitude must be given to this brave woman," said Elana, her gaze fixed on Rowan.

Cerebus nodded. "Indeed, regardless of the nature of the message, she deserves our gratitude for the risks she took to deliver it." He looked at all of the companions. "You all deserve our deepest thanks."

The king of Pellar stood and his deep resonant voice echoed through the circular room. "To those of you who fight bravely for our freedom and our lives, whether you are a soldier, smith, healer or servant, I offer you now that which I see in front of me – hope. It comes in the form of good will and courage from a woman not of our land and her companions who have traveled through great hardship to bring us a message.

"That message, thought it is not fully understood stands now between Pellar and despair. It offers light beyond the grinding pain and exhaustion of our days and nights; hope that we may yet prevail against the enemy outside our walls. Now we have a solution to look for and a course to chart through these treacherous waters. I ask that each of us remain steadfast in our duty to Pellar; to our freedom; to our lives until the day when this doom is lifted and the Goddess's sweet light is no longer dimmed by the suffering of our people."

A great collective shout erupted from the listeners as Cerebus finished. The soldiers on the top tier were on their feet;

their shouts the loudest of all. "Hail King Cerebus! For Pellar!" reverberated around the chamber.

Torrin smiled with admiration amid the noise. *This* is why it had been a public meeting. Although more questions were raised and the path was obscure, it *was* possible to end the siege. Hope had been given to a city in need of it.

The Balcony

The sun had set over the distant horizon and the city of Pellaris was cast in hues of pale pink and mauve. Lanterns had been lit in the large square before the keep and lights had begun to appear in windows, twinkling in the dusk. From up here, on the wide balcony near the guest quarters, it was difficult for Rowan to see the damage wrought by the month-long siege of the city.

The top of the city wall was just visible between the houses with the black sea of the Raken army beyond. Rowan frowned and leaned against the balustrade for a better look. If the power over them was broken, what would happen?

An image formed instantly in her mind – the huge beasts looking around in confusion as though waking from a dream. They discard their unlikely weapons and cast red-eyed glances back at the walled city as they disappear into the forest, melting like dark smoke into the shadows of the night with feral grace. Rowan blinked and came back to the balcony overlooking the city, goose flesh rising on her arms. Was that a glimpse of the future? She pushed the thought away and continued her inspection of Pellaris.

The rolling swells sounded hollowly from the bottom of the harbour. Rowan turned and looked out across the expanse of the ocean. It felt good to be close to the sea again. The breeze carried up the faint sounds of shouts and creaking rigging; at the docks, crews readied the Pellarian fleet in case a final retreat became necessary. Five ships had already departed for Tabor, loaded with women and children, the sick and elderly. The season for storms on the northern ocean had begun and there was ever increasing risk to any who set sail. A large number of folk though, had refused to leave their homes and businesses, their city.

The council today had been long. Rowan folded her arms and began to pace. Although her message had finally been delivered in full, she felt a growing unease. She had proclaimed she would go in search of the summoner if the Slayer of the Wyoraith could not be found. When she said it today in the vaulted chambers, her own shock had matched everyone else's but it was an intent truly declared. Where would she even look for the one trying to summon the Wyoraith? Her gaze was drawn eastward toward the distant line of the Krang Mountains – a dark jagged strip against the dusk sky. The first stars were beginning to appear above it. They were treacherous, Dalemar had told her, but from this distance they looked beautiful to Rowan. It was hard to believe that mountains could be so tall and steep; the mountains of her homeland seemed soft and round by comparison. Dalemar had spoken also of the Great Timor Mountains to the west beyond Tabor – mountains from which explorers often never returned. They were twice the height of the Krang range. Like a great wall, they spanned the length of Eryos cutting it off from the lands to the west. Rowan shook her head; it was a thing beyond her experience.

An image of Clan Shorna's Mora'Taith came to her, his spindly arm stretched out toward the northeast. *The one who hunts you sits there*. Rowan swallowed. If the summoner and her unknown enemy were one and the same, then perhaps she would know which direction to head.

She tore her gaze from the horizon. Shivering, she hugged herself; the fabric of her sleeves silky under her fingers. This lovely dress was a gift from Queen Elena, and while Rowan was thankful to have something appropriate to wear to tonight's banquet, the full skirts and tight bodice were uncomfortable. It felt so strange to wear a dress after months of travel clothes, and she wished briefly that she had thought to pack some Myrian garb formal enough to for the occasion. Silly, she thought, twirling to watch the skirts flare out.

Last night after their arrival, after the battle on the city walls, a glorious bath had awaited her. Her room had smelled of roses and the petals had been left floating on the water. Rowan, bone weary and utterly filthy, caked still with the mud they had used to cover themselves and splattered with blood, had left her soiled clothes in a ragged line on the floor, set her sword within easy reach of the bathtub, and slid into the hot water in absolute bliss. Her smile deepened as she looked forward with relish to another hot soak tonight.

But first, the banquet arranged in her honour, a generous effort while the city was under siege. Given the present rationing she doubted it could be much of a feast. Glancing once more over the city, she smoothed down the skirts of her dress.

A soft noise sounded behind her and she turned to find Torrin standing beside the fountain watching her. Rowan's eyes widened. His armour and sword were gone, and he looked handsome in a dark blue tunic, trimmed with red at cuffs and collar; his hair, which had grown over the past weeks to curl over his ears and the back of his neck, was cropped shorter.

Rowan's face flush with heat as his eyes traveled over the dress she wore. It was silly, the gown concealed more then her usual leggings, but she felt more exposed in it. Her hair was loose, lifting in the breeze, and she brushed a few strands from her face.

"You look beautiful," Torrin said, walking towards her.

"Thank you."

Leaning over the balustrade, he surveyed the city. "I went to your room but you had already left."

"It is difficult to get used to the indoors after so long spent out upon the land."

"I know what you mean." A slight smile curved the edges of his mouth. He looked toward the distant Krang Mountains. "Your task is finished. You have fulfilled the duty placed on you. You can rest now, if you choose to." His voice held a note of appeal.

"I wish I could feel happy about it. I thought I would be relieved, but I fear the task is not finished."

Torrin was silent, his gaze returning to the city below.

Rowan turned to face him squarely. She took a deep breath. "You were right, Torrin. I would never have made it to Pellaris and King Cerebus to deliver my message without you and the others. In a strange land where I found few welcoming faces and even less comfort, you and the rest of your company aided me, saved my life more than once and gave me the irreplaceable gift of your friendship. I owe you all a debt I can never repay." Rowan reached out, placing her palm on Torrin's chest in the Myrian fashion of paying tribute to a comrade in arms – an acknowledgement of a bond between warriors. "It has been an honour to fight at your side, Torrin, son of Ralor, and I thank you." Rowan placed her other hand over her own heart and curled her fingers into a fist in salute.

Torrin's eyes were intense. "Rowan Mor Lanyar," he replied with equal formality. "You have returned all and more than you have received from us. You have brightened all our lives over the last weeks." His voice shook and he reached out to gently touch her face, his fingers, warm and rough but light as a whisper, tracing the line of her cheek.

Then he bent down and kissed her. His arm slipped around her waist and the fingers of his other hand twined through her hair. Breathless, Rowan found herself enveloped by his warm strength, swept through his wall into richness and love; her heart ached as she witnessed the depth of him.

Falling into Torrin, she surrendered, wrapping her arms around his neck and returning his kiss with everything of herself, matching his depth with her own. His arms tightened around her in response and heat spread through her, tingled on her skin where he touched her, on her mouth as his lips pressed on hers.

Releasing her suddenly, Torrin stepped back and Rowan gasped as his walls slammed down, shutting her out. The balcony spun as she struggled to calm her racing heart. The splashing of the fountain was too loud and the lights of the city, once warm, were now cold and bleak. She drew in a shaking breath, concentrating on keeping her feet.

Torrin reached out to steady her. "Forgive me," he said quietly. "I should not have done that."

Rowan shuddered at the finality of those few words, at the denial in them. There was unconcealed anguish in his face; his gaze was dark with pain. She reached out to him, but he closed his eyes, turning away to lean on the stone railing, shoulders tense, breathing heavy.

"I'm sorry, Rowan. I can't." His voice was strained.

"It wasn't your fault, Torrin. You do them a disservice by continuing to blame yourself."

He turned on her suddenly. Rowan took an involuntary step back. His brows knitted together and the lines of his face were set in bitterness and despair. "You don't understand," he said hoarsely. "I have lived with the pain of their deaths for seven years. They died because *I* couldn't protect them. I go on living because I must, because any other choice would be a coward's way, but I died the day they were killed. The man I was and the life I had was lost; and it's only a fraction of the price I should have paid!" Torrin spoke the last words through clenched teeth.

Rowan wiped at the tears on her cheeks. "No," she said quietly. "But I understand guilt, Torrin. My father died to save my life. I may not have lost as much and I was only a child, but I do know it was my fault he was killed. He died because I failed to protect myself."

Torrin watched her silently. The wounded look in his eyes was replaced by reserved distance.

"The dead always haunt the living," Rowan whispered. "My mother told me the hard part is learning to embrace their spirit without losing ourselves. I never really understood this until now. Behind the walls of your grief, the man that you claim is dead *still* lives. I have seen him, waiting to be released from his prison."

More tears spilled down her cheeks as she turned and left the balcony.

Torrin's brother found him still standing at the stone balustrade, looking out unseeing into the dusk. They stood in silence for a while.

"Emma would want you to find love again Tor," said Nathel finally. "She would have liked Rowan."

Torrin sighed. "It's not Emma. I know she would have wanted my happiness." He closed his eyes, but the vision of their deaths was still there. "She's willing to go to death's door, Nathel. How can you keep a woman like that safe?"

"She is not like other women. She is a warrior and doesn't need you to keep her safe. In fact, I know it for truth she would poleaxe any of us who stepped in when she did not need our help."

Torrin knew the truth of that, but still couldn't reconcile it with his fear for her safety.

"Do you love her, Tor?"

The question was weighted. Torrin turned to look at Nathel's earnest face.

"Sweet Erys help me, I've loved her from the moment I first laid eyes on her. But I can't do it again."

"Would it hurt any less if you were to lose her now, without ever telling her how you feel? With the love between you denied?"

Yes. Yes, it would, surely it would…

"No."

Nathel clasped him on the shoulder, smiling. "Then what truly do you have to lose, brother?"

Veiled Threats

The wide wooden table was loaded with glasses and goblets glinting in the candlelight. Empty plates and crumbs littered the boards. The food eaten had been wonderful, though the portions sparse. Rowan popped the last of a savory into her mouth. If Danyl the Great could spin such magic in his kitchen today, what would a banquet be like during a time of plenty?

A few diners lingered at the tables – one man snored softly, his head down, fingers clutching an empty goblet. Most of the people had cleared the tables and benches out of the way and were gathered at the far end of the great hall, dancing.

Her eyebrows rising, Rowan watched with amusement as Nathel tried to teach Hathunor to dance, as Borlin and Dalemar offered encouragement. When Hathunor rose to try, he had to gently removed the clinging cargo of children one at a time. They followed him with their little arms reaching up.

The queen, sitting beside her, leaned over with a smile and pointed at the big Raken. "He has proved a great attraction for the few little ones left in the keep, you know."

Rowan grinned, watching the children clamber over Hathunor's huge form, like explorers upon a spiked mountain. The Saa Raken patiently endured the attention, occasionally lifting one of the children up before his face to look more closely, amusement shining in his red eyes.

Rowan shook her head as Hathunor tried to follow Nathel's instructions with little people hanging from his arms. "I don't think he has ever danced before."

"Do you think these are the first human children that he had seen?"

Rowan looked at the parents that hovered near by, unsure of the Raken with their children but beginning to relax. "It is quite possible, yes."

The queen was silent for a while and Rowan turned to find herself being studied closely. "Do you always wear men's clothing?"

"In Myris Dar, dresses are worn for formal occasions, but for everyday wear it is a matter of personal preference. Women wear what they wish. For practical reasons, most usually wear breeches, though the styles are different from men's."

Elana drew back, eyes wide, a delighted smile creeping over her beautiful face. "I would one day like to visit your home."

"You would be most welcome, your Highness. I would very much enjoy your company."

"You must tell me all about it, Rowan. We will get together soon, just the two of us." Elana turned as Chancellor Galen bent down to speak quietly to her. She nodded and sighed. "I am sorry Rowan, there are duties I must attend to. I do hope you will enjoy the festivities." The queen nodded towards dancing.

Rowan stood with the queen and inclined her head as Elana and Galen stepped away from the tables to disappear through the door behind the dais. The king had left a while ago, surrounded by his officers, and Torrin had left as soon as proper etiquette allowed, bowing formally to Cerebus and Elana. Rowan sighed, feeling fresh tears near the surface. It felt like there was even more distance between them now and she was angry with herself for thinking, hoping that Torrin would be able to overcome his past so easily.

Nathel approached and offered her an arm. "The party is just getting started! Come and dance."

"Have you got some Pellarian steps to teach me that are all the rage?" Rowan asked, relieved at the distraction.

"But of course."

Taking his arm, she looked at the revellers as they made their way toward the dancers. "Has Arynilas left too?"

Nathel nodded. "I sense he is feeling somewhat trapped within the stone walls, surrounded by so many people."

"I know how he feels."

The musicians had just begun a lively reel and Nathel pulled her into the thick of the crowd, spinning her around. Rowan caught her breath as people and bright colours flew by. He exuberantly taught her the footwork for the dance, cracking jokes and making her laugh. Borlin cut in, grinning as he elbowed Nathel aside and swept her around the dance floor with a twinkle in his eyes. They ended up face to face with Dalemar who took a stately turn with her.

The song ended and Rowan stood panting for breath, a grin plastered on her face as she clapped for the musicians. They began a more subdued song and she turned to find the soldier she had saved on the wall before her. “Will you take a dance w – with me, my lady?”

“With pleasure, sergeant, is it?”

He dipped his head and held out his hand. Rowan was acutely aware of her role as ambassador this evening, of representing her island home. “How goes it on the wall?”

“We are maintaining.” His voice steadied and he spoke now with assurance. “The slings are having better effect now that Commander Torrin has adjusted them.”

Rowan’s eyebrows rose. Torrin had been advising on the wall.

The sergeant cleared his throat. “May, may I ask how you learned to wield a sword, my lady?”

“Please, call me Rowan. I have trained my whole life. All Myrians train to a certain extent. I would be happy to work with you and your men if you would like.”

The sergeant blushed and stammered out a thanks as the song ended. He bowed and left to return to his friends at the edge of the hall who crowded around him. Rowan sat down at a table to watch the next dance. Leaning back into the chair, she contemplated a hot bath and her bed with longing.

A figure loomed to her left and Tihir N’Avarin sat down next to her. Even sitting, the stern priest held himself pole-straight.

“Could I have a moment, my Lady?”

He was not asking permission. She kept her expression neutral.

“I must apologize for my scepticism this morning,” he began in a silken voice. “It was not personal, you understand. As a priest of Erys and one of the king’s councillors, I must make certain that I see the world clearly and to that end, I question everything. I do hope that you were not hurt or offended by my remarks. I had no wish to cause harm to so rare a visitor to our Kingdom.”

Was that an apology? “No offence taken, Master N’Avarin, I would gladly take a rousing theological argument over a battle with a Raken Trieton.”

N'Avarin blinked, eyes glittering, lips pressed into a thin line. "Well yes, I am sure."

Rowan almost regretted her dig – this man could make a powerful enemy.

"It must be difficult, my Lady Rowan," the word *Lady* rang with disdain, "to miss out on the honoured role women have in Eryos."

Rowan smoothed her brow before turning to look at him. "What role is that?"

"Why, Erys made women in her own image, to bring life into this world. That is a woman's primary role. Like Erys, she is the bringer of life. Men are rightly left to manage the more mundane and onerous tasks."

Such as doing what they please and following their own desires.

"So you believe women should do nothing but bear children?"

"It is as Erys has shown us," he said piously.

The Priests of Erys had found a way to imprison women with the very thing they celebrate in their Goddess. If Erys were here now, what would the Goddess say? In N'Avarin eyes, Rowan represented everything he would take from women to keep them under his control. But there was more to his hatred than religious doctrine – this man was a tyrant who couldn't rule absolutely so he took a perverse pleasure in stripping away the dignity and rights of others.

Rowan looked him in the eye. "I must apologize then."

"Oh?" He raised his eyebrows.

"I have not yet had any children and have no interest in assuming a woman's *primary role* anytime soon. I do quite enjoy managing the more mundane – was it? – and onerous tasks in this world. Indeed, I am quite good at some of them."

Tihir N'Avarin worked to keep his expression calm. "Of course, you are new to these lands and have not been properly educated in our ways," he said with condescension. "You may find them simple but I assure you the people of Pellar find comfort and peace in them. We take a certain pride in that."

"Pride? Master N'Avarin, for certain the people of Pellar are great and noble in the purest sense, but do you truly believe the Goddess would take pride in such restrictions of freedom?"

N'Avarin's eyes narrowed. She was going too far, but didn't care. "A very wise man I once knew on Myris Dar told me that if the people chose for themselves how they wanted to be educated, they would take further into their hearts what they learned."

"Your land sounds very intriguing; perhaps one day the Priesthood will have the good fortune to visit." The words were spoken with polite precision but the threat was clear.

"The Island is warded," she said flatly. "Free thought and speech being one of the primary tenants of my homeland, I'm afraid your Priesthood would be unwelcome in Myris Dar."

"The unenlightened often fear the ways of the righteous," he said quietly.

Rowan bit back a scathing reply as N'Avarin continued with a practiced patience. "You must have faith in the Goddess. Only she can bring you into the light of her wisdom."

Rowan sighed. Her anger left her as quickly as it had come. What he said was true but it was not something he understood beyond his narrow doctrine. "I have faith in myself, Priest," she said with conviction. "The light of the Goddess is for each of us to understand in our own way. I hope the Priesthood will one day understand that, for the sake of Pellar."

N'Avarin's pious expression flickered for an instant into intense hatred, quickly replaced by something she did not expect – envy.

He looked up past her shoulder, and his features underwent another rapid transformation, this time into a bland mask of civility. As he got to his feet, Rowan turned to see Nathel, his blue eyes hard.

"Master Nathel," said N'Avarin smoothly, "I was just apologizing to Lady Rowan for the tactless ways of a sceptic. She has assured me that she took no offence. It has eased my mind."

"The Lady Rowan has a forgiving nature, not the least of her many talents. We are indeed fortunate to have her with us." His pleasant tone contrasted with the deadly look on his face.

N'Avarin backed away, but his dark eyes flicked back to her. "It has been a pleasure, Lady Rowan. I look forward to speaking with you further about your charming homeland. Master Nathel." He spun on his heel and stalked away.

Nathel scowled at the man's back.

"My thanks, I was not enjoying his company," said Rowan.

A smirk pulled at the corners of his mouth. "I feared for his health."

Rowan frowned. "I think I have just made an enemy."

Nathel shook his head and the smirk slipped away. "You are a likely target for him regardless of your actions, but you must take care. The Priesthood of Erys is very powerful here and has say in the king's court."

Rowan nodded. "So I have discovered. Cerebus doesn't strike me as a man who would endure someone like N'Avarin."

"I don't think he has a choice." Nathel's grin slid back onto his face. "Shall we dance?"

Rowan held up her hands. "I am finished. I will be dancing back to a bath and bed!"

"Oh, you crush me. We were having so much fun and I think Hathunor has got it now."

Rowan laughed. "Goodnight, Nathel!"

She walked slowly back to her room through the empty halls and corridors – a relief after the noise of the banquet. Her thoughts were chaotic and scattered from the wine. In her room she carefully removed the gown she wore, hung it in the huge wardrobe and sank gratefully into the soft bed, sparing only a thought for her missed bath before sleep came to claim her.

Intruders

Rowan woke in the darkness of her quiet room. The twin moons cast a pale light through the open balcony door. Her mind was instantly awake, her muscles tensing. She lay still, listening.

The balcony door had been closed.

Carefully, Rowan slid her hand up under the pillows. The cool weight of her dagger was a reassurance. Her bed was in shadow and she climbed silently out to stand with it between her and the windows. Anyone standing in front of them would be in silhouette. She waited, straining to catch a sound.

The faintest whisper came from the shadows by the balcony doors. Rowan concentrated on the spot. It seemed there was a deeper blackness there. The curtains stirred in the light breeze, shimmering in silvery moonlight. There. The sound again, closer this time, along the wall near the bed.

A soft scuff came from behind her.

There were two of them!

She was grabbed roughly from behind. Rowan twisted violently, slicing with her dagger. A gasp of ragged breath sounded loudly in her ear. She smelled stale wine and tobacco mingled with the stench of body odour. For an instant the grip relaxed and then she was lifted and thrown on the bed. Landing heavily on her back, she immediately rolled, not away from her attacker but towards him. Her fist connected with flesh – something soft. There was a grunt of pain and a thump as knees hit the stone floor.

Rowan scrambled off the bed, groping along the floor for her sword. It wasn't where she had left it!

"Bitch, I'm gonna kill you for that!" The words were husky with pain.

"We are to take her alive, you fool!" The second voice spoke from the shadow by the balcony.

"She has a knife!" hissed the voice by the bed.

Rowan backed towards the door of her room. Light bloomed suddenly in the dark as a lantern was un-hooded to revealing two burly men, raggedly dressed and unshaven. One was crouched by the bed, holding his bleeding forearm. The other moved towards her. "We're not going to hurt you, lovely, but you have an engagement elsewhere that you are expected to attend." The man was eyeing her up and down, smiling – she wore only her small clothes.

Rowan sprang for the door but he was closer and cut off her escape. The other one, on his feet now, was warily stalking her. Sidestepping to keep from getting between them, she scanned the room for her sword. It was under the bed; the man she'd hit must have kicked it there.

There was a moment of stillness, of weighing the possibilities. The man between her and the door had a scar over his left eyebrow; the smell of their unwashed bodies mingled with the burning oil from the lantern; the light cast the room in an eerie glow from below.

They attacked together. Rowan launched herself at the nearest man – the one she'd cut. He overshot his grip and she struck upwards with her knee. Air whooshed out of his lungs. Her palm connected with his chin and his teeth cracked together as his head snapped back.

She spun as he fell to the floor and threw her dagger at the second man. He ducked and it shot just over his head, burying itself in the wooden door with a loud thud.

Rowan glanced at her sword but it was out of reach. The man had drawn a knife now; was watching her carefully. His companion was unconscious on the floor.

He came swiftly, knife raised. Rowan sidestepped, blocking his thrusting forearm with her elbow. Grabbing his wrist and thumb, she twisted sharply. He cried out and the knife went clattering away. She punched him in the face and he staggered back, blood streaming from his nose. A kick planted in his chest sent him sprawling.

He was quick to get up but Rowan was diving for her sword. Her fingers closed on the hilt and she stripped the leather scabbard, facing her attacker, still on her knees. The man launched himself at her again, a look of desperation on his face.

Then the door crashed open, slamming against the wall with a boom. Torrin bulled into the man shoulder first, carrying him up off his feet to land on the hard floor. He hit him hard with his fist and the man sprawled in unconsciousness.

Torrin took in the room, ready for another fight but the other man was already down. "Are you hurt?"

Rowan climbed to her feet, slowing her breathing. "I'm fine, how did you know?"

"What?" Torrin looked at her and she was aware again of how little she wore.

"How did you know they were here?" Rowan reached for her clothes draped over a chair by the bed and began to dress.

"Oh." Torrin looked away quickly. He bent down and searched the unconscious man's pockets. "I heard the sounds of the fight."

Rowan glanced at the door, which now stood lopsidedly against the wall, one of its hinges completely torn away. Her dagger blade had gone right through the wood. "You heard the fight from your room?"

"I wasn't in my room." He was searching the second man now. Rowan realized he was fully dressed; he hadn't been sleeping.

To avoid thinking about the implications of that, Rowan bent down also to study one of her attackers. The man was unremarkable but filthy. Her adrenaline spent, Rowan straightened and sheathed her sword. "They smell like they haven't washed in a year."

Torrin looked up at her from his search, his eyes traveling over her carefully. "Are you sure you're alright?"

Rowan nodded. This was the last place she would have expected an attack – safe in her room in a guarded keep.

Footsteps sounded behind them. The rest of their companions appeared at the door. Nathel's face was worried. "Are you alright?"

"Yes I'm fine, Torrin helped." She waved at the damaged door.

Borlin's eyebrows rose, he turned to look at Torrin. "Ye did that?" he asked, rapping his knuckles on the thick wood as they filed into the room.

Torrin didn't answer; his attention was on the men before them.

A young castle guard arrived at the door next, followed by two more of his comrades. They peered in at the scene.

"Summon the captain of the castle guards." Torrin said to the man.

The guard hesitated. "The captain of the guard is on the city wall, Sir."

Torrin took an intimidating step towards the man, his voice angry. "I don't care if he's on his death bed. A guest of the king has just been assaulted in her room. Get him!"

The guard swallowed and left.

"Bring some rope," Torrin told the two remaining guards.

They disappeared from the doorway, hastening to follow his order. Nathel picked up the lantern and set it on the table near the balcony. Torrin tossed the contents from the men's pockets down on the table. Coins glittered in the light, a roll of rough string, a wine cork and a key. Torrin picked the key up and weighed it in the palm of his hand.

He looked at Rowan and passed the key to her. It was quite heavy and large, with a long shank and an ornate end. It was not the sort of item one would expect to find in the pocket of a grubby street tough.

"So these men 'ad help gettin into t'keep," growled Borlin.

Torrin nodded, his eyes still on the key in Rowan's hand. The guards returned and bound the unconscious intruders, then the captain of the castle guard came through the door, disheveled and breathless.

"How goes it on the wall?" asked Nathel.

"No siege attempts so far tonight," he answered. "I was just arriving back at the keep when Jensen found me. What has happened here?"

Rowan stepped forward and handed him the key. "Do you recognize this? Any idea what it unlocks?"

The captain took the key and examined it, leaning over the lantern for better light. "It looks like one of the bailey keys. There is an iron gate in the side of the wall from the square. It is usually guarded but with so few to defend the city walls, men were pulled from that duty to fill in elsewhere."

The captain pulled a large ring of keys from his pocket and searched through them, when he found the one he was looking for, he held it up to the key Torrin had found. They were identical.

"How many people have keys like that?" Rowan asked with a chill.

The captain looked over the keys at her. “Only a few people, my Lady. You were not hurt, I trust?” He eyed the sheathed sword still in her hand.

“No she wasn’t.” There was still anger in Torrin’s voice. “But she could have been. I want to know who that key belongs to.” He eyed the two unconscious men now being dragged from the room. “They got it from someone.”

The captain nodded. “I will look into it immediately, Commander Torrin. The intruders will be interrogated when they wake up. If you will excuse me, I must inform the king.”

The rest of the companions gathered around as he left. “Any guesses as to who sent them?” asked Nathel darkly.

Before anyone could answer, Arynilas called to them from the small balcony. When they looked over the railing they found a rope tied to the bottom of one of the stone pillars. It hung down to the balcony below.

“Been tied from above, that ’as,” said Borlin, squatting down for a better look.

“Someone went to a lot of trouble to set this up,” said Nathel.

“From now on I want one of us with Rowan all the time,” said Torrin quietly. “If there are enemies in the keep with access to these rooms, they could very well try again.”

“Hathunor not leave Rowan,” growled the Raken, hunkering down in a corner of the room.

Torrin nodded. “Good.”

“Did they say anything to you, Rowan?” Dalemar asked.

Rowan shook her head. “Only that they were to take me alive.”

“What were their exact words?” he asked intently.

Rowan thought for a moment, then she remembered. “One said I had an engagement elsewhere that I couldn’t miss.”

“An engagement?”

“Yes.”

“The Summoner,” whispered Torrin, looking at Rowan with concern.

Rowan touched Dalemar’s sleeve; she needed to think about something else. “Have you had any luck in the library?”

The Rith shook his head. “Not yet, but Craius the archivist has quite a collection of ancient scrolls. They are kept locked away because of their delicate condition. I am hoping that there will be a reference to the *Slayer* and the *Wyoraith*. But I will need time to search."

"I'll come and help you tomorrow – the more eyes the better." She wanted something to do, anything; she would not sit quietly and wait for them to come for her again.

The Interrogation

Torrin followed Captain Rienns of the castle guard down through the many levels of the citadel. Rowan walked behind him with the others. Their expressions were grave – little had been said since the attack. The temperature cooled and the air became heavy with moisture below ground level. The corridors narrowed and the ceilings lowered

They made their way through several locked grates with Captain Rienns's keys rattling and clanging against the iron. Torrin glanced at Rowan as they waited at the final grate into a guardroom. She looked calm and collected. Nothing to betray the violence of the night before, save the intense look on her face.

Two young guards stood up quickly from their game of dice as the captain entered. A corridor set with locked heavy iron doors stretched into the darkness. The cells beyond were silent.

Rienns opened the door to a small interrogation room. The captain motioned Torrin and Rowan into the room with him – it not large enough for everyone. When Hathunor made to follow Rowan, Torrin put a hand on the giant's forearm. "Wait a few moments before you come in, my friend."

Torrin entered behind Rowan. He took a deep breath, his chest and throat tight with anger.

These two men had tried to take her.

He held no illusions about Rowan's ability to handle them on her own but the implications of an abduction attempted inside Pellaris keep had a cold knot of apprehension growing in his belly to counter the heat of his rage.

Rienns carried a torch into the small room and placed it in a bracket by the door. The two men who had attacked Rowan were revealed in the guttering light. They sat tied to their chairs, hoods covering their faces. Torrin gritted his teeth and took another breath – they needed answers not retribution. The latter would come when they found out who had given them the key.

Torrin strode forward and pulled the hood from one of the captives. It was the man Torrin had slammed into. Blinking in the sudden light, the prisoner looked around warily, his gaze lingering on Rowan.

Captain Rienns pulled the hood from the other man. Both men had bruised faces, split lips; dried blood smeared their skin. Rienns had not been gentle with his interrogation.

Torrin leaned over the first prisoner. He let his wrath suffuse his expression and held the key out before the man's face, inches from his nose. "Where did you get this?"

Fear crawled across his face and the man opened his mouth to speak, but then shut it again, his teeth clicking together.

"Someone gave this to you so you could get into the keep, I want to know who." Torrin put menace into his voice.

The man looked at the key, but said nothing. Torrin glanced at Rienns.

The Captain shrugged. "We could get nothing out of them. They have refused to even give their names."

Torrin turned back to the door, raised his voice. "Hathunor!"

The iron door swung inward, squealing, and the huge Raken's form filled it. He had to duck to get through and when he stood up inside the room his spiked crest brushed the stone ceiling.

Hathunor growled a low rumble and bared his sharp fangs, his red eyes burning. Torrin looked back down at the man in the chair and watched his eyes grow round as marbles; watched the blood drain from his face.

"Do you know who this is?" Torrin asked quietly.

The man's eyes rolled back to Torrin. His breathing was laboured, coming in short gasps.

"This is a very good friend of the woman you tried to abduct last night. The last man who tried to harm her had his arms ripped from their sockets. Very unpleasant sight." Torrin smiled grimly, certain it *could* happen.

The prisoner glanced at Rowan again. She stood with arms folded across her chest, a frown on her face. Hathunor loomed behind her like a mountain.

Torrin tossed the key up and caught it. "Rowan can control him; keep him from tearing your spine out through your belly, if you tell us who gave this to you."

Gaze flicking toward the giant Raken, the man shook his head, more a convulsion. "There is nothing you can do that will be w-worse than him."

Torrin leaned forward, his leathers creaking. "Who?"

The prisoner licked split lips. "He will kill me."

Torrin frowned and pointed up at Hathunor. *"He* will kill you *now* if you do not answer my question. Now or later, it's up to you. Choose."

Suddenly the prisoner convulsed against the ropes, retching. The air rattled in his throat.

Torrin stood back. Something was wrong with him – a seizure perhaps.

Dalemar was there, squeezing past Torrin, packing the already tight space. He bent down, examining the man closely. Captain Rienns leaned around to watch what was happening.

Dalemar laid a hand on the man's chest, pulled it back sharply. "There is a compulsion spell on this man, a very powerful one!"

He placed his hand on the prisoner's chest again where it began to glow softly blue. The prisoner jerked more violently, his head thrashing back and forth. Spittle flew from his mouth. Captain Rienns moved to hold him still but Dalemar shook his head. "Please do not touch him."

The Rith removed his hand after a moment. "It is too complex, I have very little experience with this kind of spell and I cannot see all of it."

Slowly, the man's thrashing subsided until finally he was still, sitting limp in the chair, his head hanging.

"Even if he wanted to tell us, he could not. It would kill him for trying." Dalemar crossed his arms over his chest and frowned down at the captive, one finger tapping his chin.

Captain Rienns watched the Rith with interest. Dalemar turned and looked up at Hathunor.

"Would you care to try something, my friend? It shouldn't take a lot of strength, but a considerably lighter and more sophisticated touch than I posses as yet."

Hathunor nodded his massive head and stepped around Rowan.

"It looks much like an intricate net covering him. I could not see all of it but it is simply a matter of loosening a few strands here and there to allow him to speak."

Hathunor and Dalemar moved to flank the prisoner and the Rith reached up to touch the Saa Raken on the arm. Hathunor stood for a moment in concentration, then brought a massive clawed hand gently down on the man's drooping head. The captive gasped in a ragged breath and threw his head back. With Hathunor's enormous hand covering his face, all Torrin could see was his open mouth and pink tongue. After a moment the Raken removed his hand and the man blinked at them in a daze.

Torrin waited for the prisoner's eyes to focus once more and then stepped forward again. "Who sent you here? Who has bound you to his will?"

The man swallowed and looked up at Hathunor again. "He comes into my dreams. He gives me orders." His voice dropped to a whisper. "He does terrible things and I wake up feeling like I'm dying."

"Who," asked Torrin insistently. "Who does these things?"

The man opened his mouth to speak but nothing came out. He worked his jaw and his lips moved, peeling back over yellow-stained teeth. Veins popped out along his forehead and his face slowly turned purple and then blue.

Hathunor suddenly reached out a massive arm and grabbed Torrin, pulling him back away from the thrashing man. The other prisoner began to wail horribly, a high pitched keen filled with animal fear and pain. Torrin wanted to clap his hands over his ears.

Hathunor placed himself in front of the man, blocking Torrin's view. Rowan, just behind the Raken, was cringing at the inhuman sound with her eyes squeezed shut.

A blinding light flashed outward. The huge Saa Raken was silhouetted against the brilliance.

The force of the blast threw Rowan against Torrin. He had time only to wrap his arms around her before they were hurled against the wall. The back of Torrin's head struck stone. His vision burst into a multitude of tiny white pinpoints. Rowan's weight forced the air from his lungs and he barely registered Dalemar and Rienns as they too were flung back into the walls. Hathunor was the only one unmoved. Torrin slid slowly down the wall, landing heavily. Rowan, still clutched in his arms, was unconscious, her head on his shoulder.

With the last of his strength, Torrin rolled them both over and placed Rowan between himself and the wall. Then all faded into blackness.

Something moved in his arms, pushing. “Torrin!” Rowan’s voice? He cracked opened his eyes and groaned as pain blossomed at the back of his skull. He was still curled around Rowan and she was struggling to shift his arms and extricate herself.

Hathunor appeared above them, his fierce face concerned. Torrin released Rowan and rolled over. Had he been burnt? He touched the skin of his face; it was undamaged. Hathunor hauled them both to their feet. The pounding in Torrin’s head increased blindingly. He bent over, placing his hands on his knees. Slowly the pain eased and Torrin stood up to inspect the small room. Scorch marks along the walls and ceiling attested to the heat. Dalemar was stirring and getting to his feet with Hathunor’s help but Captain Rienns lay sprawled against the door, unmoving. The two prisoners were still in their chairs, heads back, blood seeping from ears and noses.

A shuddering breath wrenched the captive they had been interrogating. Torrin took a quick step toward the man. Grasping the captive’s head, he lifted it so his airway was less restricted. The man gazed up at him in search of redemption. His lips moved but no sound came out. Torrin brought his ear down close and heard the faintest whisper on the prisoner’s last breath. “Lok Myrr.”

Pounding came from the other side of the door. The captain’s body blocked it, keeping it from opening. Rienns was dead, his ears and nose seeping blood like the captives. Without Hathunor to shield him, the spell had hit him full force. Hathunor moved the captain out of the way and Nathel and Borlin peered into the tiny room, with Arynilas and the two other guards looking in from behind.

Torrin released the man’s head and straightened. Rowan was staring at the prisoners, her green eyes dark in the torchlight. She stood utterly still. Torrin grasped her by the shoulders and tilted her face up away from the grizzly sight. “Come away from this place.”

She nodded mutely and turned towards the door with the others. Torrin took a step to follow but he trod on something. He bent down and picked up the ornate key from where he had dropped it. Glancing once more at the dead prisoners, he gripped the key until it bit into his palm.

Rowan felt she was suffocating, a giant weight on her chest. The constricted space deep under so much stone made her feel trapped. Tears began to well in her eyes, spilling down her face. She turned away from the others and began to walk up the passage. All the time she had spent in Eryos, through all the hardships, sorrows and dangers with so few tears shed, and now here she had cried twice in two days. She shook her head.

It was a release of tension, but it was also a deep terror of a power that was strong enough to track her across Eryos; to enslave Raken and besiege a city. A power that was strong enough to send two men, against their will, to take her to Erys knew where, for reasons she did not even want to speculate about.

A sudden searing anger rose in her chest and burned there helplessly. She quickened her strides. They were directionless and floundering in a doomed city – simply hoping for some clue to lead them forward.

A soft touch on her shoulder stopped her. She turned to find Arynilas behind her. Even here, in this dark place, he was a peaceful presence.

Rowan began to wipe away the tears on her cheeks but he reached out a slim hand and gently brushed her face. When he lifted his hand before her, a single shining tear rested on his fingertip.

"Do you know that my people believe tears to be gifts from loved ones and ancestors beyond this life? We believe they are sent as messages to teach us about ourselves. Each single one is a valuable lesson, if we are only willing to listen."

Rowan swallowed but the lump in her throat would not move and her voice trembled. "Arynilas, I have never before felt fear like this. A nameless dread has come upon me and I do not know how to fight it."

The Tynithian studied her for a moment. "Perhaps it is not meant to be fought but simply to be endured and accepted; learned from, to gain strength. My grandsire once said of the Myrians: 'They are unlike any other; their resilience is greater than any race I have encountered in this world.' He spent many seasons among your people and grew to love them. Just as I have grown to love you, my Myrian friend. Know this, whatever darkness lies ahead; you will not face it alone but with friends at your side. With those who love you."

Rowan released a long breath. With it went some of the paralyzing dread, and her pounding heartbeats slowed in her aching chest.

"Thank you my friend," she whispered.

A Traitor to be Found

Rowan took in the king's study as they were ushered in. Cerebus turned from the maps and scrolls spread out on the table before him. General Preven looked up from the other side of the table, a cluster of plans in his burly hand.

"My Lady Rowan, I am glad to see that you are all right." There was concern and disquiet on Cerebus's face. "I was told of the attack in your room last night. Forgive me, I would have attended to you sooner but there was a great deal of movement during the night and we feared an attack."

"Please do not worry yourself," Rowan said. "There were only two intruders and I had the help of my friends.

The king's gaze was sharp as he took in the companions, lingering on Torrin. Leaning back against the table, Cerebus across his arms. "What has happened? I am told that Captain Rienns was killed this morning."

"Someone went to a great deal of trouble to control those men," said Dalemar, "to make sure that they completed their task. It kept them from revealing the truth about their mission." The Rith touched Hathunor's dark, scaled arm. "Thanks to Hathunor, we all might have been killed. Unfortunately, Captain Rienns took the full force of the spell."

Torrin stepped passed Rowan and handed the king the key. "They used this to get into the bailey last night and we believe someone else, someone who had full access to the keep, went into Rowan's room and secured a rope from the balcony. It was tied from above and the men climbed up in the night. She was attacked while she slept."

"So you believe someone within the keep has betrayed us? Sweet Erys." Cerebus wiped a hand over his face and stepped forward to clasp Rowan's hands in his. They were warm and strong but his eyes were tired, regretful. "Lady Rowan, please accept my deepest apologies for this assault, I assure you the one who gave them this key will be found." The king handed the key to Preven. "I want every person with a key to the bailey accounted for. Get it done quickly please, general."

"Yes, my lord," replied Preven. "Be assured, my Lady, the traitor will be found." He bowed and strode out of the study.

"Were you able to get any information from the prisoners?" asked Cerebus.

Borlin shook his head. "T'was for naught for no information came o' it." His voice was bitter.

"Not completely," said Torrin. "Does *Lok Myrr* mean anything to anyone?"

Cerebus went still. "Are you certain that is what he said?"

"Yes. Do you know who that is?"

Cerebus frowned. "Not *who* but *where*."

Rowan held her breath and looked up at Torrin. He returned her glance with raised eyebrows.

Cerebus closed his eyes and shook his head. "It seems now as if I should have expected this. Lok Myrr is an isolated fortress in Krang. It is the seat of power in that land; at least it's the only one that we have been able to discern. I have sent two envoys to Lok Myrr in the last year. The first was turned away and they returned without even being allowed to treat with the lord there. The second should have returned some time ago. There has been no word and I fear the worst; we should have received a message before the city was sealed.

"My father never believed Krang to be of any threat or interest beyond the barrier of the Krang Mountains, but over the last years, word has trickled out of a new power growing there."

Cerebus turned to a map of Eryos unfurled across the table. He reached down and placed a finger on the vellum. Rowan stepped forward to see. Her friends gathered around the table. The wide swath of the jagged Krang Mountains formed an arc across the map, separating Pellar from the eastern realm of Krang. The dark ink on the page delineated a border and the major villages and towns in Pellar, but beyond, little was marked other than the massive range of peaks. Cerebus's finger rested at the end of a long wide valley surrounded by more mountains.

"Lok Myrr," he said.

Torrin leaned over the desk to get a better look. "Who controls the fortress?"

Cerebus shook his head. "We have been able to discover very little about the so-called Lord of Lok Myrr, which is how most of the local people refer to him. He is greatly feared by the sparse population between the border and the fortress valley. The people of Krang are mostly goat herders and subsistence farmers. They have a superstitious fear of strangers and it has been very difficult to gather information. We have heard the him referred to as Master Miro, Master Mithro and Master Miroth."

Dalemar gasped. "Miroth!" He shook his head. "No, it's impossible; he would have died hundreds of years ago. He must have, there has not been a whisper of his whereabouts."

"Who?" The hairs on the back of Rowan's neck stood up. "Who would have died?"

"Do you remember when I told you about the Rith Wars and the trials of the vanquished – the Riths using human deaths to gain power? There was one among them who never went to trial. He disappeared, taking with him some of the most ancient and powerful scrolls from the Tirynus archives; many of them contained the arcane knowledge the war was fought over. Riths were sent after him and for a time they were able to follow his trail but it went cold. He was never found and held to account. Miroth was one of the most powerful Riths of that time."

"Do you think it is him?" asked Torrin.

Dalemar frowned. "Riths live for about three-hundred and fifty years on average. The oldest known Rith was Warick the Great and he lived to an exceedingly old age of four-hundred and seventy-two. If Miroth were alive today, he would be almost fifteen-hundred years old."

"That means he would have been alive during the time of the last summoning," said Nathel with a measure of awe.

"If it is him, then he has been extending his life through the use of treacherous magic," said Dalemar. "Sweet Erys, no wonder the people of Krang fear him."

"Do ye remember what t' Mora T'aith said 'bout sittin in the Nor'east where the land lies frozen?" asked Borlin. He leaned with fists planted on the table looking darkly at the map.

"He also said the one we sought had wintered a thousand years," said Arynilas quietly.

Rowan shivered and looked down at the worn map – at a star inked in black. "The Summoner." she declared softly. "Now all we need to do is find the *Slayer*."

The Concerns of the People

Elana was finding it hard to concentrate. After the astonishing events of last night, the security she had always relied on was in question. Someone Cerebus trusted had let two men into the bailey and the intruders had attacked the Myrian woman.

She sighed and lifted a sheet of parchment from the pile at her elbow and scanned it without seeing. At least Rowan had not been hurt and had subdued her attackers largely by herself. What must it be like to enjoy such physical self-sufficiency? When Elana left the keep, a guard always accompanied her. There had never been any need to learn self-defence; those within would never lay a hand on their queen. She was still fit for her age, her figure slender. She imagined herself learning swordplay – laughed at the uproar it would cause.

A certain confidence was inherent in the ability to protect one's self and Rowan did carry herself like the warriors she traveled with, moving like a graceful cat. She behaved like a noblewoman but lacked the arrogance and superiority. It was refreshing. Were all Myrians like that? Elana smiled and dropped the page. She could see why Torrin was so smitten. He hid his feelings well but she and Cerebus new the sons of Ralor.

Torrin.

Dear Erys, but she remembered such a different man from the one who had returned. It was true Torrin had always been more serious then Nathel, but he had been as quick to laugh as anyone. There had been a quality about him that set him apart from others, a confidence of spirit that drew people to him. He certainly stood out now, but for his hardness, his distance. The pain he must have endured to loose Emma and those sweet little girls in such a way. Elana shook her head as she remembered the stricken look on Nathel's face when the terrible news reached them. He had left immediately to go in search of Torrin. Ralor's boys had been like sons to Cerebus and it had hit him hard when the brothers never returned home.

Cerebus loved his nephew Daelyn. The young man would one day make a good king, but she knew her husband had seen in

Torrin what he had truly hoped for in a son. The son he and Elana had never been able to have –

She quickly closed herself off from that line of thought; she had no time for that now. Daelyn had become their son in all but name and she loved him deeply. She whispered thanks to Erys that he was safe in Tabor where Cerebus had sent him. The young man had been furious at being sent away, but Cerebus had been adamant. Pellar's heir could not be lost along with its king and capital.

A light tap on the door pulled her from her thoughts and she looked up. Tihir N'Avarin opened the door walked into her study. He folded his hands piously before him. "My Lady, if you have a moment there is something of importance that I must discuss with you."

Elana suppressed a surge of irritation and sat back in her chair. "I am sorry Tihir N'Avarin, but now is not the best time, I am very busy. Perhaps you could come back later when I can devote my entire attention to your matter." She plucked up the parchment that she had been unsuccessfully reading before his intrusion.

He cleared his throat and stepped further into the room. "My Queen, I understand that you are very busy, but it is the very safety of Pellaris that I must speak to you about."

Oh very good. She would appear unsympathetic to her city if she were to refuse him now. "Very well, what is it you would like to say?"

Without permission, N'Avarin strode forward to take a seat in front of her desk. "My Lady, I hate to burden you with this, but as the king is so busy with the defence of our fair city, I can see no other alternative."

Her sworn duty was to see to the administration of the city during a time of war. N'Avarin had been *there* when Cerebus publicly passed the Seal of Pellaris to her before leaving to meet the advancing Raken. "Speak, N'Avarin and then leave me to my work."

He looked curiously over the pile of documents strewn across her desk. "As a member of the High Commission of the Priesthood, it is my pleasure to inform you and the king that the Priesthood has agreed to take further action to ensure the safety of the city from the Raken invaders."

Elana raised her eyebrows. “Oh, how so?”

“The Priests wish to have a more visible presence within the city…to take on essential tasks beyond our simple role as spiritual leaders. We would like to lend a hand and shoulder some of the weight that is being bourn by so few.”

“I must say the Priesthood’s intentions are most noble, Tihir N’Avarin, and I gratefully accept,” Elana said. “There are barely enough men to keep the walls covered as it is.”

N’Avarin frowned. “My Lady misunderstands.”

“You had something else in mind?” She knew only too well.

“We wish to take on a more progressive role in helping with the administration and coordination of the city’s welfare. The king and his advisors are clearly stretched to their limits and there are many tasks being neglected as a result. The Priesthood is offering to assume responsibility for those tasks. We are here to serve the people of Pellar after all.”

Elana worked to keep her face smooth. The Priesthood was ever steady in their quest for power, but to seek it in the midst of a siege? N’Avarin request was not even concealed in religious doctrine. She supposed she should not be surprised, they had been maneuvering for years now, seeking to gain a greater foothold in Pellar’s circles of influence. It was alarming to see how they were succeeding. More and more of the powerful families in Pellar and Tabor had fallen under the sway of the Priesthood over the past few years.

What Elana didn’t understand was why, when their own safety was at stake, would they keep pushing to gain greater control? Perhaps the questing for power was too deeply ingrained.

“Tihir N’Avarin,” Elana replied evenly. “What Pellaris needs most are reinforcements. We need hands to wield swords to protect our city from the Raken outside its gates. I myself would pick up a sword to help, if I could.”

N’Avarin narrowed his eyes. “Of course, my Lady, but surely there are other…more suitable roles we could fill for the benefit of our citizens, until these dark days have passed?”

Elana sighed, feeling tired. “I will consider the Priesthood’s offer, and consult with the king at his earliest convenience. In the meantime, I request that the Priesthood ask its ranks for volunteers willing to stand in defence or to administer to the wounded." Tihir opened his mouth to respond but Elana gave him no opportunity. "The priests should at *least* be able to serve as runners and medics. There must be something they can do besides performing the last rights of Erys for the dead and dying."

N'Avarin stood and bowed, his expression stony. "As my Queen requests." He turned and stalked out.

She stood and turned to the window, looking out over the city below. The truth was they needed all the help they could get when it came to the proper administration of the kingdom. With the army at the gates, Cerebus had little time for statecraft. But they could not surrender more power to the Priesthood.

The Earl of Lochom had detested the Priesthood and been a strong voice in support of Cerebus among the other noble families. But he was killed in the first battle with the Raken and his sons were still squabbling over the estates. The balance of power shifted and the Priesthood wasted no time in swaying more of the weaker families to their side. Cerebus had neither time nor energy to deal with the increasing threat now.

Pellar's strong central government kept it largely free of the constant maneuvering for power that afflicted other lands. Compared with a realm like Ren, Pellar was a paradise; but the subtle currents of power struggles still ebbed and flowed.

The Priesthood was not a rival lord whose claims could be dealt with quickly and openly. They had the support of the people, however erroneously, and their quest for power was buried under layers of subterfuge. Many of its more powerful supporters, blinded by religious zeal, were unaware of the ulterior motives. Others would align with the Priesthood simply because they perceived its star rising.

Elana had fond childhood memories of the Priesthood. She remembered kind, soft-spoken men in multi-hued robes that represented the diversity of all life as the Goddess's creation. They helped to ease suffering, working and living with the common folk and bringing the light of Erys into people's lives in simple ways. Now that joyous faith was buried beneath dogma and restrictive rules. Elana could not have said when politics became more important to the Priesthood than the care and tending of Pellar's spiritual health. It happened too gradually to pin point any one incidence or give people who disagreed a rallying point.

She feared if something weren't done to halt the Priesthood, Pellar would slide into the darkness of a religious dictatorship.

Another knock sounded on the door. She turned; half expecting N'Avarin to be standing there but the door remained closed.

"Come." She moved back towards her smothered desk.

The door opened to reveal Chancellor Galen. "Forgive the intrusion, my Queen. I can return later if you are busy."

"Chancellor! Please, come in. Sit." She ushered him to a chair and returned to sit behind her desk. "I have not seen Cerebus this morning yet. What news is there of the two men who attacked Lady Rowan last night? Have they confessed? Do we know who let them into the keep?"

Galen sighed and shook his head. "I have just seen General Preven. The men who breached the keep last night are dead."

Elana drew in a sharp breath. "How?"

"It would seem they were under a powerful spell of some kind and when the Rith Dalemar tried to counter it, the spell was released, killing the two men in the process. Unfortunately, Captain Rienns was also killed."

Elana brought a hand to her mouth, her eyes stinging. The loss of Captain Rienns would be a huge blow to the morale of the guard. The Captain had been a fine man, devoted to his duties and his king. Magic. So the men who had attacked Rowan were not acting of their own will. "Who put them under the spell?" she breathed.

Galen frowned. "It is as yet a mystery, my Lady."

"And the traitor?"

"The General is only now verifying that all the bailey keys are accounted for," said Galen. "I myself have just given him my key and I believe N'Avarin was on his way to see Preven as well."

Elana frowned, thinking of the priest. "N'Avarin was just here to see me."

"Oh?" Galen's white eyebrows rose.

Elana nodded. "The priesthood would like to assume control of the city's bureaucracy to aid us during the siege."

Galen smiled thinly. "Always pushing for any advantage. Do not worry too much, my Lady. It will take some time of course, but once the siege is over the king will begin to block any inroads that they have made."

"My worry is that the siege *won't* end and the political struggle with the Priesthood will cease to matter," Elana said blackly.

The chancellor's white eyebrows drew together. "My Lady, you must not give up hope. The reinforcements will come from Klyssen and Tabor and the Lady Rowan's arrival has brought new hope as well."

"Yes, but now we have a traitor within our Keep." Elana began rubbing her temples; she was getting a headache.

Galen rose from his seat and went to the counter beside the window where he poured a goblet of wine. He placed it gently in her hands.

"Thank you, Galen. You are a good friend." She took a sip of the wine without tasting it.

Galen placed a pair of rolled parchments on top of everything else on her desk. "These are the reports that you requested, my Lady." He paused, a frown on his lined face. "You should let me take care of this work, Queen Elana."

Elana shook her head. "Nonsense, Galen, you have more than enough to do as it is. Leave the day to day worries to me. You just take care of Cerebus, he's barely sleeping."

The Chancellor nodded seriously. "I will make sure he has everything he needs, my Lady. Between Preven, myself and the other officers we will look after him."

Elana nodded. "I thank you, Galen."

The old man bowed and left her to the work piled before her.

The King's Study

Torrin sat stiffly in the large chair next to the fire. He had only been in Cerebus's study a few times and he looked around at the book-lined walls. The room was simple and comfortable, made for work and reflection. A large window with a stunning view of the Eryos Ocean let in plenty of light and the high ceiling with its redwood timbers gave the room a spacious feel. There were a few chairs placed about the room and of course the large polished wooden desk, much of which was covered in maps and scrolls. Cerebus sat behind the desk in a high-backed chair. He sipped his Drenic silently, eyes unfocused on the desk before him.

Torrin had not tasted his Drenic yet and he brought the steaming cup to his lips. It had been a long time since he'd had the brewed leaf and he enjoyed the strong aroma and flavour. He looked up at the large map of Pellar hanging on the wall above the fireplace. Krang and the dark mark of Lok Myrr drew his gaze.

"Do you believe the answer to defeating the Wyoraith lies with sending a force into Krang after Miroth?" asked Cerebus.

Torrin looked away from the map to find the king watching him intently. "He will not be defeated here," was all he said.

Cerebus leaned back into his chair, fingers steepled before him. "During the council the Lady Rowan offered to go after the summoner of the Wyoraith herself. If that means going into Krang after the lord Miroth, do you truly think she would?"

"Erys herself might have a hard time stopping her."

Cerebus's eyebrows twitched. "And you would not let her go alone."

Torrin looked down at his cup. "I would keep her safe if I could," he replied guardedly.

"Even if this siege is broken," said Cerebus. "Miroth will still have to be dealt with regardless of whether or not he is the summoner. He must answer for the abduction of the Pellarian envoy."

"If we can find this slayer, perhaps we might have a chance," Torrin said.

"And if no slayer is found?"

Torrin shrugged his shoulders. "Miroth is ancient and powerful, but like all Riths he can still die."

"Indeed." Cerebus frowned, his grey eyes fixed on the cup before him. "Let us hope that Dalemar is able to find something helpful in the library." Cerebus looked up at Torrin. "You and you brother have come back to us with very interesting friends. Tell me, how did you meet them?"

Here then were the questions Torrin dreaded.

He told the king succinctly of the Ren Wars and how they met Dalemar, Arynilas and Borlin. To his surprise the king asked nothing about his family and their loss. Torrin found himself beginning to relax and enjoy Cerebus's company. "I have not seen Daelyn. Is he here, he must be almost a grown man now?"

Cerebus sighed. "Daelyn is not here. I sent him to Tyrn, to safety. He was not happy with me."

Torrin nodded. He knew Daelyn, or at least he remembered the ten-year-old boy who had trailed after him and Nathel.

Cerebus shook his head sadly. "I could not take the risk of Pellar loosing its capital and king as well as its heir. I do not believe he will ever forgive me for sending him away from the battle."

Torrin sighed, acutely aware of his own need to keep loved ones safe. To keep Rowan safe.

"Nathel has not changed a bit," said Cerebus, changing the subject.

Torrin frowned and ignored the inference. There was nothing to say and nothing could change the past. He placed his empty cup on the table beside his chair and rose. "I should get down to the walls and see to the rest of those recommendations you asked for, Sire. Thank you for the Drenic." His chest was tight with the need to escape.

Cerebus stopped him as he was pulling the door open. "Torrin, I understand how difficult this must be for you. I do not presume to know what you went through, but I want you to know that I am glad you have returned. There is a place for you here. Your father's place, if you want it."

Torrin released the latch and clenched his hand into a fist; he closed his eyes for a moment then he forced himself to turn around and face the king. He offered a short bow, carefully controlling his voice. “I thank you, King Cerebus, but my return to Pellaris was for Nathel and duty to you as my king, not for myself. The man you seek died seven years ago and what is left of him cannot find peace here.”

“And is there peace to be found wandering from one war to the next without a home or a country, away from those who love you?”

Torrin took a deep breath, released it. “There is contentment of a sort, an ease to the restlessness.”

Cerebus sighed. “You are a natural leader, an experienced master swordsman as well as a talented strategist. I’ve seen the Pellarian soldiers look to you for guidance, even in the short time that you have been back with us. If you cannot find peace here, perhaps at least you can find fulfillment and a worthwhile use for your skills.” The king stood and turned to face the window. “Give it some thought, Torrin. That is all I ask.”

Torrin turned away and the king remained at the window looking out at the roiling sea.

Atop the Battlement

Torrin leaned on the stone battlements looking down across the vast Raken army. The black skin of the Raken seemed to absorb the light of the midday sun, sucking it from the air. They stood like statues, just out of arrow range.

Soldiers arrayed along the city's wall, kept watch continuously on the enemy below, but the bulk of Cerebus's army rested just behind the walls in provisional dormitories. The buildings closest had been commandeered for the purpose and the army bedded down in whatever room could be found: warehouses, shops and stables; and the lucky ones in the few houses found close to the battlement steps built at intervals along the wall. When the Raken attacks came, it was a short hustle to get up and into position.

Arynilas and Hathunor had seen Rowan up to her room, while Nathel, Borlin and Torrin after his meeting with the king, had come down to the battlements to make their assessments of the defences. *The more experienced eyes and minds we have behind us the better*, the king had said.

Torrin scanned the line of trebuchets, arrow and pole stores. Aside from minor changes to the placement of the burning pitch and arrows for easier access and deployment, there was little left to change. The slings had already been shifted for better effect after he advised the captains to move them the other night.

Arynilas materialized beside him.

"How is Rowan?"

"She is well," said the Tynithian. "Hathunor will not leave her side."

"Good."

"She is afraid," said Arynilas, "But her fear does not control her."

Torrin nodded grimly. "I just wish I knew what this Miroth wants with her. If he is in fact the *Summoner* we are looking for." Anxiety fluttered in his chest at the thought of Rowan in the hands of a black Rith.

"Dalemar worked at healing as many of the wounded as he was able in the keep's infirmary before he went to the library again to search. My knowledge of Miroth is limited. We hear of the rest of Eryos as faint whispers from within Dan Tynell, and this Rith disappeared before I was born."

Torrin glanced at the waiting army below. "I hope he finds something soon. This city is a trap. Rowan is right; the fight must be taken to the Summoner himself and time is running out. But without more information, without knowing who this *Slayer* is or where to find him…" Torrin ground his teeth in frustration, his fingers drumming on the stone.

The meeting with the king had been unsettling, but he had learned one thing: Cerebus was thinking about sending a force into Krang.

"They stir!" Torrin looked to where the Tynithian pointed. There were ripples of movement within the press of black bodies.

Torrin shouted to the nearest soldier. "Raise the alarm! The Raken move." The young man hurtled down the steps and bells further along the wall began to ring.

There was a surge of activity – weapons drawn, men running up the steps from below. Soldiers rolled the huge vats of boiling pitch over to the edge of the wall and made ready. Archers knocked arrows and the giant slings crews released the safety latches so they were ready to fire.

Torrin looked back down at the Raken, they were moving in a solid line now towards the wall. Torrin heard the first distant howls as the wind carried the sound up to the ramparts. Arynilas waited, a golden-fletched arrow in his slim hand. The Tynithian still leaned on the wall, ignoring the activity around him, tilted eyes upon the foe.

Torrin caught sight of Nathel and Borlin jogging along the wall towards them. The Pellarian soldiers had lined up now behind the crenelation, arrows aimed down into the enemy ranks. All stood poised, awaiting the signal.

A horn blasted into the air. Bowstrings thrummed as arrows were loosed. The men who had shot stepped aside quickly, already reaching for new arrows. Another line of archers took their place, aimed and fired. Torrin saw many of the beasts go down but it was like drops of water lost to the sea.

Beside him Arynilas drew and fired in one fluid motion. Before his arrow found its mark, and Torrin knew it would, the Tynithian already had another missile set.

The Raken came on. Scaling ladders and grappling hooks appeared. Torrin and Arynilas stood on the widest part of the wall over the huge iron gates of the city. It was the only place without water in front of it. Raken all along the front lines leapt into the fetid moat, scrambling over rotting bodies and debris. Torrin coughed at the stench as decomposing gases were released to waft up.

A grappling hook clanged against stone beside him. Torrin ducked as stone chips flew outward. Leaning over, he looked down the length of rope to the Raken climbing quickly up; he sliced his sword through the rope. Nathel and Borlin reached them and shoved a scaling ladder out from the wall with long poles. The soldiers atop the gates began to pour the burning pitch down upon the Raken and screams rose up from below.

The first Raken made it up over the wall. It was killed quickly, surrounded by Pellar's defenders. Torrin's world contracted to a span of battlement and the sword in his hand. A beast jumped at him over the ladder and died. Nathel and Borlin were beside him. Arynilas whirled through the press, dealing death. They rallied the soldiers when the Raken broke through the lines; kept the battlements clear of enemy. Time disappeared and there was only battle.

When the Raken finally withdrew, Torrin and his friends stood weary and sweat drenched. Then the glint of a familiar golden braid caught his attention and he swore. What was Rowan doing here? He had thought her safe in the castle. Sheathing his sword, he stalked over to where she stood, surrounded by Pellarian soldiers.

"What are you doing here?" Torrin noted the blood she was cleaning from her weapon. He realized he was searching her for wounds and stopped himself.

Rowan lifted an eyebrow. "I heard the alarm raised and came to lend my sword."

"One more sword wouldn't have made a difference. You should have stayed where it is safe."

Rowan's expression hardened, green eyes glinting. "I would rather be down here doing *something* to help, then sitting up in the keep safely doing nothing."

At least Hathunor had been with her. Torrin glanced around, looking for the huge Saa Raken. Rowan gestured behind him. Hathunor stood up from a crouch and the men around him fell back to give him space. The soldiers were looking at Rowan, their expressions rapt.

Rowan reached up and slid her sword into its baldric. "Shall we go find some food? I haven't eaten since last night." She turned on her heel and walked off along the battlements, her golden braid swinging down her back.

Torrin heard Nathel snicker and turned to glare at his brother, who lifted his hands in submission and backed away. "I'm going to see if I can help with the wounded, I'll see you at the keep later, Tor."

Nathel halted as he was turning away to stare at something over Torrin's shoulder. With a last glance at Rowan's retreating figure, Torrin turned to see what had captured his brother's attention.

His eyebrows rose as a group of black-clad figures wound toward them through the soldiers in the aftermath of the attack. Small golden disks glittered on their chests and they all wore bright red strips of fabric around their upper right arms. The Priests were handing out food and water to the weary defenders and stopping to administer aid to the wounded.

"Huh, I haven't seen the Priesthood up on the battlements before," said Nathel. He shook his head in amused wonder and shared a glance with Torrin as he pulled his healer's satchel from beneath his armour and moved away.

Everything Torrin knew of the Priesthood was contradicted by the quiet, humble behaviour of this group. A short priest with sandy hair and a boyish face came over to him. "Erys's blessing upon you, warrior. Your defence of the city is honoured and appreciated." His brown eyes looking directly up into Torrin's.

Torrin nodded warily.

"My name is Thaius, is there anything you require of us, food perhaps or water?"

Torrin accepted the proffered cup and drank deeply; the water was cold and refreshing. "My thanks. I had not expected to see the Priesthood upon the front lines," he said flatly.

Thaius cast him a knowing look. "It is truly a pity that Pellar does not have more faith in the Priesthood of Erys, but I am ashamed to admit that the lack of trust is not unwarranted."

Torrin looked more closely at the young priest. "You do not espouse what the Priesthood stands for?"

"Oh on the contrary, I am deeply committed to the teachings of Erys, but to the first and true teachings," said Thaius with a twinkle in his eye.

Torrin frowned and folded his arms.

Thaius set his bag down. "The wisdom of Erys, as passed from the first of her priests, teaches us to honour women and men alike as the blessed creations of the Goddess. Women were imbued with her wisdom and ability to bring forth life and men with her strength and loyalty to that life. Sadly, what passes today for the teachings of Erys is but a shadow of her true wisdom."

"Forgive my scepticism, but how could these ideas be part of the repressive, heavy-handed ways of the Priesthood?"

Thaius sighed. "There are some of us within the Priesthood who have been working quietly to restore the Goddess's true teachings. The Priesthood has been corrupted by the quest for political power, twisting Erys teachings into a dogma used to control people. The path to Erys is one that each of us make on our own. It cannot be imposed upon us or Her true wisdom is lost. We have been blocked repeatedly and threatened with heresy, but when the request came from the king and queen for aid from the Priesthood in a more tangible form, many of us volunteered in order to begin the Restoration."

"The Restoration?"

"It is what we call the reform we seek from within the ranks of the faithful. I and my fellow priests have been waiting a long time for the opportunity to engage with the people of Pellar directly without the interference of members of the Priesthood who would see us cast out for our views."

"Word will reach those members and you will face punishment, is that not so?"

"Indeed, I do not deny that there will be a price to be paid, but with the city under siege and the royal decree for priests to minister to the army, we will have the best opportunity to achieve our goal. It is in the people of Pellar that the true power rests and my fellow priests who do not see that will one realize how lost they are in their own greed."

Torrin looked back at the black-clad figures moving along the city wall. "How many of you are there?"

Thaius smiled secretly. "You would be surprise at how strong the true teachings of Erys have once again become." The young priest then reached out and touched Torrin briefly on the shoulder. "Do not abandon the Goddess because her followers have lost their way. She encompasses so much more than our hearts and minds can comprehend."

Torrin bent down to retrieve the priest's bundle of food for him. "You take a great risk, my friend but I wish you luck. As for the Goddess, she abandoned me long ago."

A Sending

She ran through darkness – an endless corridor of weeping stone. It was cold but she was sweat covered. Something terrible pursued her. A vile yellow-green light emanating from behind her revealed what little she saw. Fear beat around her, driving her relentlessly. It was the light that hunted her and yet it was something else also. Her mind was useless – a fluttering bird in a cage. She reached for her sword but it was not there.

A wall loomed out of the darkness as the corridor came to a dead end. There was no where to run. She reached the wall, hands scrabbling across its surface for some way to escape – nothing. Panic descended in a cloud. She turned around to face the sickly green light as it expanded toward her, flowing like a wind.

A wave of nausea washed over her, bringing bile into her mouth. Unable to move from its path, she stood frozen; she heard screaming and realized it was her own voice.

The light hit her in the chest, blasting her against the hard wall. Pain seared through her and she was suddenly suspended in nothing. Plummeting. The darkness engulfed her and a nameless dread rose up to meet her.

Rowan awoke with a gasp, bolting upright in the bed. Sweat beaded on her forehead and her heart pounded like a drum. Her chest hurt badly and she fumbled to open her shirt with shaking fingers, expecting to find a raw wound. Her skin was smooth and undamaged though. She wrapped her arms around herself and rocked back and forth until the searing pain began to fade. Slowly the rhythm of her heart returned to normal. She lowered her head onto her knees, taking deep steadying breaths. Her room, with the late afternoon light filtering in through the windows, was in sharp contrast to the horror she had just woken from. It hadn't felt like an ordinary dream, though she had no idea what it meant. She had never been so afraid.

A knock sounded lightly on the door. Hathunor had stationed himself outside the door, so whoever it was had his approval. Rowan rubbed the sleep from her eyes and padded to the door, trying to shake off the last vestiges of the terrifying dream. She glanced at the balcony; the doors were still locked. Smoothing her hair and flipping her braid over her shoulder, she reached for the handle.

Elana was there holding a small tray. She smiled brightly. "May I come in?"

"Of course, Queen Elana, you are welcome." Rowan stood aside. Hathunor, standing by the door gave her a sharp-toothed smile. Rowan grinned back at him.

"Please, just Elana, I get so tired of the formality." The queen stood studying the door with its hastily mended hinges and splintered frame. "My, someone wanted to get in here quite badly, didn't they?"

Heat rose in Rowan's cheeks and she stepped forward to take the tray from the queen.

Elana sat in one of the comfortable chairs, arranging her simple gown around her. The late afternoon light showed the fine lines that radiated out from the her eyes. Her sandy hair was pulled back into a selection of braids, and the many angles of the layers shone in the sun. Rowan sat opposite as the queen reached for the tall, steaming decanter on the tray and poured the dark liquid into two silver cups. She passed Rowan a cup and looked at her seriously. "How are you doing, my dear? It has been a trying couple of days."

Rowan accepted the warm cup. "No more trying than the last two months." She looked curiously at the contents of her cup and took a sip. "Is this tea?"

"It is called Drenic, it comes from a leaf like tea, but it is far stronger. It is often taken with a bit of honey." She motioned to the small silver pot and spoon on the tray.

Rowan nodded, reaching for the sweetener.

Rowan's sheathed weapons were laid out on the trunk at the foot of the bed and Elana eyed them as she sipped from her cup. "Do all women in Myris Dar fight with the men?"

"Yes, the martial schools accept all applicants regardless of gender, but not everyone is admitted. Both men and women participate in the defense of our land."

"Word has spread quickly of your skills. I doubt there are any in Pellar that have not heard of your valor defending the city's walls. Preven says the men are passing stories of your deeds among themselves like currency. You have become something of a legend."

Rowan frowned. "I do not understand it. I am no different from anyone else with battle skills. I started out with little knowledge of combat just as they did."

"This is not Myris Dar, traditions are different here. Most people believe that women are not even capable of what you do."

"And it is largely the Priesthood of Erys that perpetuates and enforces those traditions, am I right?"

Elana sighed. "The leadership of the Priesthood is interested very much in power it is true." She made a vexed sound. "They have succeeded in putting women under their thumb while at the same time espousing their virtues. Since before Cerebus's reign the Priesthood has been firmly entrenched in Pellar. If he stood against them, he would make enemies he can ill afford."

Rowan nodded and sipped her Drenic. "I had the pleasure of speaking to Tihir N'Avarin last night."

Elana sat forward. "He is very powerful. I do not know what he is capable of but I do know that he will not hesitate to bring you down if he can."

Rowan frowned into her cup. "Where is the Temple of Erys, where the Priesthood congregates?"

Elana turned to look out the window. She pointed over the rooftops of the city below. "Do you see that spire, the tallest one?" Rowan nodded, studying the copper roof of the building in the distance. It stood surrounded by a space of its own, a square perhaps. "That is the Temple of Erys and the seat of the Priesthood's power in Pellar."

"Have they helped in any way with the siege?" Rowan asked.

Elana frowned and tuned back to face Rowan. She looked very tired and Rowan perceived a little of the immense burden this woman carried to keep her people sheltered from the civic chaos that could so easily rein in times like these. "They have done nothing that can be criticized but they have helped little. Cerebus works tirelessly to keep the Raken from taking the city and the Priesthood takes every advantage they can while his guard is down."

"Why have they not evacuated with the other citizens of Pellaris?" asked Rowan. "Perhaps they know something we do not."

Elana gave her a calculating look turned again to look out across the city toward the Temple.

Rowan brought her cup to her lips and discovered it already empty. Reaching for the steaming decanter, she offered the queen another cup and then served herself.

Elana placed her cup on the table and smoothed the skirts on her lap. "Would you truly venture into Krang to try stopping this *Summoner* of the *Wyoraith*, or were your words merely meant to shame Cerebus into sending a force of his own?"

Rowan stopped mid-sip. So the queen knew of the evidence pointing to the Lord of Lok Myrr. She swallowed, placing her cup down. "This battle against the *Summoner* concerns us all. I would welcome anyone who decided to make an attempt to kill him to prevent the coming of the *Wyoraith*. If it comes to it, I would carry the fight into Krang. Though to be honest I had no clear thought on how the attempt could be made. I still don't."

Elana shook her head in wonder. "You would likely die."

"If the Wyoraith is released, we might all die."

"You sound like Chancellor Galen. A pragmatist he has been all his long years."

Rowan frowned, her own deep commitment to finding and stopping the summoning was something she had not fully explored or understood. She gladly accepted the change of topic. "How long has he been Chancellor?"

"Galen was Chancellor to Cerebus's father Doren, but his roll was very different then."

"How so?"

"Doren's reign was not concerned with educating the people of Pellar, or collecting knowledge. The civil court system we have is only here because Cerebus created it. Doren wasn't a bad ruler, but he was far from the man Cerebus became. Under Doren, the nobles and wealthy families of Pellar held sway, gathered around the King's court to curry favor. The rest of the populous was there to grow the food and make the goods for the kingdom." Elana shook her head. "Pellar was powerful, but not great.

"Galen, as king's chancellor had more power than anyone save the king himself, but when Cerebus rose to power after Doren's death, he set about changing a great many things. People became accountable for their actions. They could no longer expect favor simply because of familial associations. His advisors he hand-picked and set on an equal footing, those of his father's time that he trusted and respected stayed, those he did not were sent away well compensated.

"The common people were given greater rights and freedoms. It made many people very angry. Cerebus made enemies but he also made many friends who believed in what he was doing.

"The formation of the council of fifteen was his greatest service to Pellar. Each councilor speaks for the people of a certain region so that everyone has a voice before the king. Decisions made take into account all the varied visions of the kingdom. The power to override any decision the council makes rests with Cerebus but he rarely uses it. The decision making process slows down but I believe the fair representation of the people out-weighs the added bureaucracy."

"That must have been quite a change for Galen," Rowan mused.

Elana frowned. "I suppose it was but he never seemed to resent it. He has always been loyal to both Doren and Cerebus. The rise of the Priesthood however, and their ensuing quest for power is unfortunately in part due to the climate of tolerance that Cerebus has fostered. But as they grow more powerful and the freedoms that Pellarians enjoy become threatened by the Priesthood's dogma, he will have to take action for that is unacceptable"

The late afternoon sun was almost gone and Rowan's room had grown slowly darker as they spoke.

"Listen to me go on, I have intruded upon you enough for one day," apologized Elana. "I shall take my leave of you, and thank you for a lovely visit."

Rowan stood with the queen, shaking her head. "It has been a pleasure to receive your company. Your insights have helped give me a greater understanding of your Kingdom."

Elana gave Rowan a shrewd look. "You are an inspiration yourself, my dear."

An Emissary

Sol was worried. He had been waiting in the icy wind for almost two hours. The Master would be very angry if Sol did not bring the visitor soon. He squinted for the hundredth time through the heavy iron grill of the massive portcullis. As he leaned past the protective stone, the wind blasted into him, making his eyes water. The road leading to the fortress ran into the lonely distance of the wide valley. It was completely empty. Sol knew better than return to his master empty-handed. He'd rather spend the entire night out here in the freezing bailey waiting than tempt Miroth's wrath.

But there was no one coming. No visitor. What if the Master was mistaken, and no one was going to come? Sol couldn't imagine his Master being wrong about anything, ever.

He blew into his numb hands; the fingernails were blue like the pretty dyed cloth tapestries from the Master's study. Tucking his fists under his armpits, he hoped for a little warmth. The Raken guards at the gate and on the walls above seemed utterly oblivious to the cold, their black skin exposed to the biting mountain air. Sol fumbled with the wool scarf Zerif had made for him, wrapping it more tightly around his neck. Of the entire fortress's staff, old Zerif was the only one that took care of Sol, not like his mother used to, but Zerif was kind in her way.

Sol longed to see his family, his sisters, but he knew Master Miroth would never permit him to leave. The Master kept his people close and once someone entered his service, whether willingly or otherwise, they never left it alive.

Most of the servants and staff of the huge fortress were slaves brought into Krang from the Bay of Tyros. The slave ships from exotic shores far beyond Tabor in the west were banned from Taborian and Pellarian waters but received welcome in Krang.

Little was known of the west. It lay like a vast dark mystery in Sol's mind, full of riches and strange people. Despite the impenetrable barrier of the great Timor Mountains separating Eryos from the west, Sol fantasized about someday seeking his fortune in that unknown land. The fortress servants, the pale skinned ones who had come to Krang on the slave ships, told Sol stories of the west while he stared in fascination at their white hair and pale grey eyes.

He risked another peek through the portcullis and almost withdrew again before his eye snagged on something in the distance. A black dot was moving along the road near the far entrance to the valley – a man on a horse.

Sol pulled back out of the wind once more. How had the Master known? There was no way he could have seen the approaching rider behind the mountains even from the top of the tower. Gagging at the thought of the tower room, Sol swallowed hard to stop the bile that rose into his throat. The nightmares woke him every night. Sol hadn't known Pernic well, only what he'd heard from other servants, but the man's face was burned into his mind.

Shame and guilt washed over Sol in a hot wave. The Master had been amused, looking at Sol to see how he might react to Pernic's screams for help. Sol had stood shaking, rooted to the floor in a corner of the hateful room, trying not to watch, trying desperately not to hear. He squeezed his eyes shut and tears froze on his cheeks. He didn't think he would survive the next time Miroth requested assistance for his dreadful work in the tower.

Shivering and tucking his arms tighter about himself, Sol checked on the progress of the rider. The horse was moving quickly; they had covered almost half the distance to the gate. Only a bit of the spiky backs and crests of the Raken guards on the wall above him were visible. He stepped away from the protective wall and called up for the grate to be raised in the name of the Master.

One of the Raken turned to look impassively down at him with red eyes. Then the thick iron spikes at the bottom of the portcullis ground in their stone resting pits and began to move upwards. Sol stared avidly as the huge cogs and chains wound at the top of the gate. The massive gate wasn't opened very often, but he always made sure he was there to watch it if he could. The grill rose slowly and clanged to a jerky stop half way up.

Sol stepped clear of the wall. The horse galloped along the dirt road a few hundred paces away now, dust drifting up as it came. It was big, high stepping and proud and black as the cloak that covered its rider.

Trying to control the shaking of his frozen limbs, Sol stood and waited for the visitor. His stomach growled – he probably wouldn't get a chance to find some bread for his dinner.

The horse pounded toward the gates, hoof beats audible now. The rider had the hood of his cloak up, clutched with one black-gloved hand. Flecks of foam flew from the horse's churning legs as the rider galloped through the gate and plunged to a stop. Sol cringed back as the horse towered over him, its sides heaving and its nostrils blowing. Very little of the rider's face could be seen inside the dark hood as he swung down and passed the reins of his horse to the young stable boy that appeared.

"I wish to see Rith Miroth." The tall visitor had a flat commanding voice. He did not lower his hood.

"Master Miroth is waiting for you," said Sol.

The rider made no reply and so Sol turned toward the main doors of the fortress to lead the way. Sol's hands and face began to burn in the warmth of the fortress after the freezing bailey. As they walked down the main corridor towards the east tower, Sol cast furtive glances up at the visitor pacing beside him. The man ignored the Raken guards trailing behind them, escorting them from the gates. Sol was impressed. Used to the giant creatures as he was, he still had difficulty not trembling in their presence.

They finally arrived at the great wooden door of the Master's tower. The two Raken to either side of the door glared at Sol and the stranger.

"A visitor to see the Master." Sol was proud of how steady his voice sounded.

He pushed on the great door and led the man into the warm rooms beyond. He noted how the visitor looked around at the luxurious surroundings. They reached the inner door of the study and Sol jumped as it opened of its own accord. Had the visitor noticed his fear?

The study was dimly lit as usual and Sol stepped carefully forward, bowing low when he reached the huge desk. The stranger followed on his heels.

Miroth sat in shadow behind the desk. He lifted a hand and waved with irritation. "Leave us, Sol, but wait out in the corridor. Our guest will not be staying long."

The words were softly spoken but they crackled around the room.

Bowing and backing out of the study, Sol closed the door softly before hurrying to the outer door and the cold corridor. Just before the inner door had shut though, Sol caught a glimpse of the visitor lowering his hood. He was fair skinned and blond – a Pellarian.

Sol stood quietly in the passage, staring at the Raken. They were so huge and different and beautiful in their fierceness. The Raken, both the ones guarding the Master and the two that had followed them from the gates ignored him, standing like statues in the corridor.

The day the biggest Raken had turned on the Master, Sol had been down in the breeding cells where the young Raken and the breeding pair were kept. Old Darius was assisting the Master and required Sol to carry his instruments and tools. Carrying Darius's tool kit was always hard – the wooden box was heavy and awkward. It was always cold down beneath the fortress too and Sol was afraid of the screams and snarls of the Raken in their cages.

Darius and the Master were working on the big Raken and Sol hated to see what they did to the beasts to gain control of them. The big Raken was something to see though and despite his fear, Sol was excited to see the giant creature again.

He didn't understand why the Master and Darius were so puzzled by the big Raken. At first it seemed like all the others but as it grew it began to develop other traits that the smaller Raken didn't have. It grew much taller and broader and it had longer claws and stronger limbs, but what Sol remembered most about it was its eyes. The other Raken had frightening eyes, but the big Raken had a gaze that seemed to look right through you into your heart. And when the Master worked on it, the big Raken's gaze never shone with fear like the smaller beasts.

Darius told him that the Master was going to try once more to control the big Raken and Sol must be very quiet so as not to disturb Master Miroth at his important work because if this attempt failed, they would have to destroy the beast.

Sol would never forget his surprise at the look of fear on the *Master's* face that day as he used his powers on the beast. Master Miroth had sunk to his knees; his gaunt face twisted into a grimace as he wildly motioned for Darius to kill the giant beast chained to the wall. Sol didn't understand completely what had happened, but he knew that for a few moments the big Raken had taken control of the Master.

Old Darius had stumbled over the weight of the great axe as he swung it again and again, burying it in the big Raken's chest. In the moment the beast died, its red eyes held a look triumph as it stared at the Master. Only when it was dead could Master Miroth climb to his feet with help. What had the big Raken had done to bring the Master to his knees? And why had its dying expression been one of victory?

Time passed as he stood in the corridor outside Miroth's tower. Sol's empty stomach began to growl loudly. His feet were getting sore and he could only stare at the Raken guards for so long as he waited for the stranger to reappear. He twiddled the knotted ends of his scarf, unwinding threads for a while; then frowned and pursed his lips as he looked at it. Zerif would refuse to make him another if he ruined this one.

The door to the tower swung inward and the visitor stepped out into the corridor. Sol pushed away from the wall and struggled to keep up as the man walked down the passage at a clipped pace. The two Raken from the fortress gate detached themselves from the shadows and stalked after.

The man was silent as he strode with the dark hood back up to cover his face. Sol doubted he'd even taken off his gloves.

As the man was mounting his large black horse in the fortress bailey, Sol caught a glimpse of gold that peeked out like a tiny sun amid the black folds of the cloak. He blinked in surprise – a medallion of Erys.

He knew that gold disk well from the priests that occasionally traveled through the mountains; they were among the few visitors that had ever come to the isolated farmstead his family kept. Sol held the precious scrap of information to himself, felt it warm him. He was not important enough to know of the wider world and how it affected the Master but he was smart enough to know that the Master's deeds were far reaching. He smiled, pleased to have found out something that his Master didn't necessarily want him to know – a secret little pleasure in the cold fortress of Lok Myrr.

The man whirled the horse and launched out the gate as soon as the heavy portcullis was raised. Sol watched him gallop away down the road for a moment. He wondered where the man was going to stay tonight. The sun was just setting over the mountains at the end of the long valley and it was going to be a cold night.

Sol thought longingly of dinner, and then sighed. The Master would likely want him to work tonight. He turned back to the wide steps of the main entrance and began the walk back to his Master's tower.

Sol sighed and pushed aside his fancies – they would never come true anyway. He averted his eyes as a pair of Raken guards marched past. He had to move aside to avoid being trampled by the huge beasts; Their red eyes pierced him briefly as they swept by.

He passed few people, except for the Raken guards. Lok Myrr was a very lonely place; the master kept only enough people to run the keep. Most of the servants lived in fear of being taken to the east tower for the Master's work. Sol shuddered as Pernic's face swam into his vision. He plucked at any thought other than the horror of that day. The fortress was haunted. Yes, haunted – he knew for certain. There were places down in the dungeons where the root of the mountain groaned under its own weight and moans whistled up from the black depths. Sibilant whispers called to him, making the hair on the back of his neck rise. Sol had almost understood them which made his heart pound even more. As much as he feared the Master, Sol all but clung to Miroth's robes when they went down to those forbidding places.

Sol shook his head and squeezed his eyes shut for a moment – that memory was almost as bad. He cast his thoughts to the recently departed Priest. What had the Master wanted from the Priest? The Priesthood of Erys was very powerful in Pellar and their power was growing into neighboring kingdoms. He remembered what his father, who was a smart man, told him about the rest of Eryos. Father was one of the few men from the village his family lived near who had ever traveled beyond the Krang Mountains. His father had relished the visits from the occasional priests. Father always bade them stay, and mother – who father was proud to tell had given birth to no less than eight children – cooked a meal far greater than any they normally ate.

Sol would sneak down the stairs from the bedroom he shared with his brothers to listen to his father and the Priest as they spoke of the rest of the world. He'd learned that Tabor now boasted a Temple of Erys almost as large as the one in Pellaris and the Priesthood would one day be more powerful than the kings themselves.

Sol still wasn't sure where Tabor and Pellar were, except that they lay somewhere beyond the Krangs. But that hadn't stopped him from imagining. He had been excited the day Master Miroth's men had passed their remote house to demanded payment in the form of servants for the lord of Lok Myrr. Finally, he would get to see the rest of Eryos. Sol hadn't understood his parent's tears the day he was led away on the back of a rail-thin mule, with his meager belongings clutched in his hands. He understood now.

Master Miroth was wise to form an alliance with the Priesthood. The master must be very pleased to have had such an important visitor. When he reached his Master's rooms though, he could tell Miroth was angry. Sol's belly contracted with fear as the Master looked up from the faded yellow scroll he was reading. Sol bowed and kept his eyes averted, focusing instead on the object-strewn table.

Miroth sat forward and his head gleamed in the firelight. Sol braced himself. A long, bony finger crooked at him and Sol stepped forward. Miroth slid a small piece of parchment across the gleaming wood of the table. Sol reached out tentatively to take the scrap. It was a list with ingredients scrawled in a spidery script.

"Get this prepared for tonight, leave it here when you have finished." The cold gaze that Sol feared so much barely glanced over him before returning to the scroll on the table.

"As you wish, Master." Sol bowed again as he backed away and hurried from the room, thanking Erys that he had gotten off so lightly. Walking back down the long corridor away from the east tower, he looked more closely at the list in his hand. It was a short list, only four ingredients, but he recognized it immediately. It was a potion his Master asked him to make when he was about to undertake difficult magic. It was a tonic to rebuild his strength quickly. It was one of the few tasks of magical importance the Master trusted Sol with. Not that the potion itself was magical, it was merely a brew of different herbs and such, but Sol took it very seriously.

He hurried through the fortress to old Darion's workroom. If the Master needed this tonight, it meant he was going to do something big. Sol shivered, trying not to think of what that might be.

The Great Library of Pellaris

Rowan stood in the cool morning shadow of the mammoth Temple of Erys. She and Hathunor gazed up at the eight-story high walls that curved away from them in either direction, creating the circle of smooth stone. It held aloft a massive copper-covered dome. Rowan could just see the top of the tall spire that rose up to meet the blue sky like a spear. There were lush gardens and fruit trees spread in a swath at the base of the curved walls and a row of circular clearstory windows, inset around the structure.

Bells began to clang suddenly in the stillness, startling doves from the dome's spire. Hathunor growled and shook his head.

Rowan looked up at him. "What is it my friend?"

"Hathunor's ears hurt."

Rowan motioned for him to follow and they moved away from the temple and into the square. A trickle of people came and went up the wide stone steps of the temple and through the huge arched doors, which stood propped open for visitors. With the majority of the population evacuated, those who had chosen to remain behind were looking to Erys for solace. Priests dotted the square, robed in red and black, large gold medallions suspended on their chests.

As they walked, Rowan turned her attention to the smaller building across the square. The great library of Pellaris was a perfect example of Pellarian architecture – a beauty with clean, simple lines and a minimum of decoration, which only enhanced its size and weight. It was rectangular, with four great columns in front rising to its domed copper roof. There was something very refreshing about it. Rowan admired Pellaris, its people and architecture. It was completely different from Myris Dar's soaring arches, open filigree and ornate, patterned surfaces.

The people stared at Hathunor as they passed, pointing and whispering. Word had spread of the friendly Raken within the city but Rowan kept a watchful eye just in case.

They reached the wide stone steps and went up to the double doors. It was cool inside and brighter than expected – light flooded through windows below the dome into the space. Rowan looked up and gasped, smiling with delight. The dome's ceiling was painted to look like a beautiful cloud-swirled sky.

"My I help you, my Lady?" said a soft voice beside her.

Rowan turned to see a slight young man wearing a brown tunic. "We are looking for Rith Dalemar."

The young man motioned for them to follow, eyeing Hathunor warily as he turned and strode across the marble inlaid floor. Was he more concerned for himself or the books?

They proceeded across the main hall, their footsteps echoing. The stone floor was inlayed with intertwining red circles, sprinkled with the stars of Pellaris. Large bookshelves soared up to the high ceilings and ladders on rails provided access to the topmost books. Rowan saw only two other people working in the quiet. One elderly man looked up at them from repairing a large tome and another other man was carefully packing away scrolls and books into crates.

The young man led them to the end of the grand hall, where a staircase spiralled down into darkness, took a lantern from a peg and began to descend. They emerged on the lower level, where a hallway stretched back again the length of the building. This one was not so grand, with lower ceilings and plain stone construction. Their guide led them to the end of the corridor where a door stood open; yellow lantern-light from within cast a long, bright slash across the stone floor. He nodded. "There, my Lady."

"Thank you." As Rowan pulled the door open, Dalemar looked up from his reading and a smile lit his face. He was covered in dust, with smudges across his face. Rowan almost laughed; the Rith was certainly in his element – seated at a table with scrolls and dusty pages spread open before him. The room was filled to bursting with shelves crammed full of ancient leather-bound books and faded rolls of parchment. Some of the volumes looked as though they might disintegrate at the first touch.

Dalemar rose and cleared a space on the nearest chair, scooping up scrolls and dumping them unceremoniously on the table. He began to clear a second chair and then paused, looking Hathunor up and down with a bemused expression. He shook his head and left the chair as it was. Hathunor positioned himself by the vault-like room's only door and, with a low rumble, crouched down and regarded them with glowing red eyes.

Rowan sat, and the musty smell of old parchment and cracked leather greeted her. “Have you found anything interesting, Dalemar?”

The Rith nodded. “A few things, yes.” He picked up a roll of parchment from a pile at the corner of the table and passed it to Rowan. “Take a look at this, in the second to last paragraph there is reference made to the Wyoraith. It is rather vague, but gives us a little more than we had.”

Rowan scanned the parchment. The script was elaborate and very faded, the ink disappearing in places. She found the passage Dalemar had mentioned and read through it. The script was in the common tongue but the phrasing was archaic and it took a moment for her to decipher it. One line near the bottom made reference to the Wyoraith and the Gatekeeper. She looked up, the hair on her arms tingling. “The ‘Gateway’ in the message – it must refer to the Wyoraith then.”

Dalemar nodded and sat down. “Whoever wrote this believed the Wyoraith would come into this world through a literal Gateway – I have found a few other such references. It would seem that anyone who summoned and controlled the Gatekeeper would have access to the Wyoraith.”

“So the Summoner is not the Gatekeeper?” asked Rowan.

“Based on the references I have read, they are two different people, although the Gatekeeper hasn’t been confirmed as a person,” replied Dalemar. “It might well be an object of power that the Summoner must use.”

Rowan glanced over the passage again. “I wonder… If the Wyoraith is a tool, as the Seers believe, is it possible to summon it for positive intent?”

Dalemar’s eyebrows shot up. “Indeed.” He stared at Rowan for a moment with wide eyes. “That reminds me of the reference to the ‘Stone’ in your message. I have been looking but I’ve yet to find any reference to a stone.” Dalemar sat back in his chair and frowned at the book-crammed room.

“Is it possible that the Stone from the message is another reference to the Wyoraith itself? Asked Rowan. “Or maybe the Stone *is* the Gatekeeper, an object of power that the Summoner must use.”

Dalemar's frown deepened. "It is an interesting thought. The two must be linked somehow, otherwise there would be no mention of a Stone in a warning about the Wyoraith."

He sat forward and heaved a large, worn, leather book towards her. Rowan peered at a page but found the text indecipherable. "What language is it?"

"It is an ancient form of Kathornin, which is a similar language to that spoken today in Pellar and the neighbouring kingdoms but it is far older. The realm of Kathorn once covered the Kingdoms of Pellar, Tabor and Klyssen. It was an empire that reigned for over six centuries. I still have much more to translate, but it looks promising. The text deals with the history of Eryos. I'm hoping there will be a reference to the Slayer of the Wyoraith, but it will take some time."

Rowan studied the ancient script; it was flowing and precise. She slid the text back to Dalemar who took it reverently. He indicated a stack of parchment to her right. "I have those yet to go through, if you're interested. Most of them are written in the common tongue; it is somewhat antiquated but you should be able to read them."

The parchment crackled in Rowan's hands and she carefully traced her fingertips across the brittle pages. The language in Myris Dar stemmed from the same language as Eryos's common tongue; despite the long isolation from one another, the languages had remained remarkably similar.

On the voyage across the ocean to the port of Dendor, Rowan and her party had taken time to accustom themselves with the common language. Even though many words were different, they could be understood because the root hadn't changed, only its pronunciation or spelling.

It was dark when the three of them finally emerged from the library's basement to make their way through Pellaris, back to the citadel. Rowan rubbed her tired eyes and tried to blink away the gritty sensation. She had a mild headache from squinting at small, faded text in the torchlight and her back was stiff from the hunched position she had maintained all day.

The warm, torch-lit foyer of the keep was welcoming, and they made their way to the huge dining hall. They found Torrin and the others sitting by the huge hearth, sipping ale.

"There ye are!" Borlin's head was wreathed in pipe smoke. He passed his fragrant tobacco to Dalemar who sat down with a sigh.

Rowan sat as well and Hathunor crouched in front of the fire. A warm bowl of soup found its way into her hands and she realized how hungry she was. She ate quickly as Dalemar told of his findings in the library.

A pleasant drowse came over her and, gazing into the fire as she listened to her friend's voices, Rowan remembered the eerie light from her dream the previous day.

"Dreams," she said quietly, remembering the prisoner who had attacked her. "He said: *He comes into my dreams*."

Dalemar looked across at her, blowing smoke from his mouth. "What did you say?"

The others had stopped talking and were looking at her, waiting.

"Can Riths enter your dreams?" she asked.

Dalemar frowned. "It is a forbidden practice, but yes, the knowledge exists."

"Why?" asked Torrin.

"I was just curious. I had a strange and frightening dream yesterday afternoon." Rowan shook her head and frowned, it was a little silly complaining about a nightmare.

"Tell me what the dream was about, Rowan," Dalemar said quietly. His pleasant expression had sharpened into intense scrutiny. It made the hairs on the back of her neck rise. "It is very important that you tell me exactly what happens in the dream."

Rowan glanced around at the suddenly concerned faces of her friends. The dream and the pain in her chest were still vivid. "It is a nightmare. That in itself is not so strange, but the dream was odd, more real than a dream usually is." She described it and the terrible dread and fear she had felt in that dark, cold place came back full force. Rowan shivered as she finished and noticed that she had wrapped her arms around herself protectively. She forced her hands down into her lap. "When I woke, the pain in my chest was real. I expected to find a terrible burn when I checked."

"How long have you been having the dream? How many times have you had it?" Dalemar's face was worried.

"Just yesterday, during the afternoon."

"You think it was caused by magic?" The alarm in Torrin's voice caused Rowan's unease to grow. He leaned forward in his chair, intent and frowning. "What does it mean, Dalemar? Could someone somehow have access to her dreams?"

Dalemar sighed. "I am sorry, Torrin, I have no answers. I know some Riths have the ability to project their thoughts into another's mind. It is most likely a form of this ability that lets the Summoner reach the Raken he is controlling. It's one thing to reach another's mind to communicate something, but quite another to compel that person to act against his will. Whether he is using this ability or something different is impossible to say. Dreams are mysterious ground. It could be that your dream is a form of warning, something that your mind has created from the various things that you have learned and done." Glancing around, Dalemar smiled at their puzzled expressions. "Haven't you ever wondered where your dreams come from?"

"I just thought they were based on our memories," said Nathel, "or things we wished for. To tell you the truth, I rarely remember my dreams."

Rowan glanced again at Torrin's expressionless face. She knew what haunted his dreams.

"In part, yes that is true," said Dalemar, "but there is more. Some of the Riths I studied under believed that a person had two minds, a waking one and another one that lies beneath. The first is where we think and feel while we are awake. The latter rules our sleep but is not bound to it. Although the wakeful mind cannot feel the second one, it is still there, taking in everything, and when we sleep it forms our dreams to help guide us in our lives. There are sects within Rith society that devote their lives to deciphering dreams."

"Tynithians take dreams very seriously, for they are often our teachers" said Arynilas. "It is how we find our other selves."

Dalemar nodded. "Rowan's dream could be based on an anxiety about the Summoner and his plans. The mind is a powerful thing."

"I don't know about anyone else, but I've never had pain follow me from a dream into the waking world," said Torrin darkly. "Emotional pain, perhaps, but not physical."

"Aye, that sounds a wee bit more serious than a simple dream," said Borlin.

"Yes," agreed Dalemar. "Unfortunately I do not know enough to ward your sleep if someone is sending you this dream." He sighed again. "I'm sorry that I can't be of more help. You must tell me though, if you have another one."

Rowan nodded, looking down at the bowl in her hands. The last of her soup was cold but she wouldn't have been able to finish it anyway. No one had mentioned Miroth's name, though they were all thinking it. A fifteen-hundred-year-old Rith – he had sent men to abduct her. If he could control them and reach right into her mind while she slept, she wouldn't be safe from him anywhere.

The Note

Elana hissed in exasperation as the scroll she was reaching for rolled off the desk and onto the floor. Her fingers were stained with ink and her eyes ached from reading. Yet another petition for extra food, a dispute between two men over the theft of a horse, and the heads of Pellar's various guilds who had not evacuated — all were requesting audience with the king, and their requests had been added to the pile of parchment spread across Elana's desk. Standing to pick up the errant scroll, she wondered how Galen kept up with it all.

Galen – she needed to consult him on the guild requests. Cerebus had no time to meet with the guild masters, so they would have to settle for the queen's ear, but she needed some more information from the chancellor before she met with them. Now was as good a time as any, and now that she was up out of her chair, she was loath to return to it. She left the scroll where it had fallen.

The corridors were silent this afternoon. She passed only a few servants and a pair of the castle guards, who strode towards the great hall. They stopped to bow but she waved them on. There were more important things these dark days than following etiquette to the letter.

Galen's rooms were near the ground level so he didn't have to contend with the staircases. If Elana didn't find him in his study, he would likely be next door in the city's record room, where he kept Pellaris's civic history perfectly catalogued and filed. He rarely let anyone into the huge room stacked with shelves of scrolls and leather-bound ledger books without supervision. How *did* he find the time to do it all? She shook her head. Turning to enter the corridor leading to his study, she stopped.

At the far end of the corridor Galen and N'Avarin stood close together, speaking quietly. She had never seen the two men give each other more than a cool, grudging respect and here they were, heads bent together, whispering like conspiring boys.

Galen stepped away from N'Avarin suddenly and turned to open the door of his study, but N'Avarin plucked at his sleeve, bowing and offering him a scroll of parchment in a deferential manner. Galen took the scroll briskly before closing the door on the Priest. N'Avarin straightened his robes needlessly and then turned to walk down the corridor away from Elana. Neither man had seen her.

When she reached Galen's door Elana paused; Tihir N'Avarin had already turned the corner and disappeared from sight. Odd, she mused; she had never seen the priest act so submissively.

Rapping briefly on the wooden door, she pulled it open. Galen stood near the fireplace, where he tossed N'Avarin's scroll into the flames. He turned quickly, his face dark with anger, and a look of surprise passed over his lined features when he saw her.

"My Lady!" He glanced quickly down into the fire, and then moved discreetly to stand in front of it. "Whatever brings you here, my Queen? You should have sent someone. I would have attended you in your rooms."

"Never mind, Galen, it is just as easy for me to come to you, besides I needed to get away from my work for a little while." Elana watched the chancellor's face carefully. "Tell me, when did you and Tihir N'Avarin become so close?"

Galen raised his eyebrows. "Oh, you must have seen him speaking to me outside. N'Avarin was attempting to obtain my help in gaining greater access to the King's ear. Naturally, I listened to his requests, and then sent him on his way." He smiled warmly at her. "Come and sit, my Lady. Tell me what has brought you all the way to my study?" He went to a small table near the fire, poured two goblets of wine and brought one to Elana before sitting down in the chair opposite hers.

Elana felt silly; after all, this was Galen. It was ridiculous to suspect him of actually supporting the Priesthood in their quest for power. He had spent the last seventeen years working tirelessly for Cerebus and Pellar, longer before that for King Doren. She took a sip of wine to cover her embarrassment.

"I have need of your advice, Galen. The guild masters have requested an audience and before I meet with them, I would like to review their recent activities."

"Of course. I'll collect the documents right away for you, if you don't mind waiting a moment." Galen put down his cup and rose to his feet.

"Thank you, Galen. One other thing," she said quietly as the old Chancellor pulled open the door. "What was it I saw you burning when I entered?"

The old Chancellor turned, his hand still on the door to his precious city records. His face was expressionless, but his eyes were hard, his jaw set. "Oh, that," he said lightly. "It was a list of concessions the Priesthood of Erys hoped to gain from the king. I should not have burned it, I suppose, but with everything that is happening, it angered me." With a shrug of his narrow shoulders, Galen turned and disappeared into the record room.

Elana rose and paced to the window, a frown on her face, unable shake the dreadful thoughts that spun through her mind. What was the Priesthood trying to gain now? What was the point of going though Galen, when she herself had already refused their latest requests?

Elana found herself pacing. Galen's study was austere, the furniture functional and beautiful but not overly ornate, neat and organized like Galen himself. She cringed inwardly at the thought of her own office, with its mound of scrolls.

The only thing out of place here was a desk drawer partially open. Elana glanced down at its contents as she wandered past. She froze in mid-stride, and an icy cold gripped her chest. Down in the drawer, nestled among scraps of parchment and old inkwells, was the corner of a small, hinged box lying open and filled with clay. The queen's mouth went dry as, hardly breathing, she reached down to shift aside the parchment with a trembling hand, knowing what she would find yet willing it not to be true.

The clay was dry and cracked now, but pressed into it was the detailed impression of an ornate key.

Silenced

Rowan sat on a low stone bench on the large balcony overlooking the city cleaning and oiling her sword. She glanced over to the railing - where Torrin had kissed her.

They had not spoken about it since. Rowan was certain he wanted to talk to her but was holding back. Perhaps he was afraid of what it might lead to. She worried that if she told him of her own feelings for him, it might drive him further away. There was a strain between them now and Rowan longed for a release of it – a return to the easy camaraderie of their journey to Pellar.

The wide fountain splashed soothingly behind her and she shifted her gaze to the view of the city. The late afternoon light glinted from the domes and copper rooftops of Pellaris, and the pennants snapped in the breeze. Beyond, she could see the Krang Mountains. The fortress of Lok Myrr, hidden beyond that range, sat in her mind like a stone.

The day was quiet. The Raken had not attacked the gates and Rowan had spent most of it down in the basement of the Great Library with Dalemar, pouring over dusty tomes. Arynilas and Nathel had joined them in the cramped room and even Nathel's jokes did little to improve the frustrated atmosphere. Despite the addition of several new sets of eyes, they had turned up nothing of use.

Rowan felt caught, trapped and oddly suspended in time. The frightening dream had awoken her again last night with the same terrible pain in her chest. It had been identical to the first. Dalemar and the others looked on with concern when she told him about it this morning, but there was little they could do.

Her need to do something, to find out why she was a target for this Miroth, burned inside her. It was impossible to make plans or decisions until they knew what they were up against. Dalemar was more than halfway through his translation of the Kathornin text, but still no reference to the Slayer.

Rowan sighed. Finding some vague reference to the Slayer in old, dusty books did not necessarily mean they would find the man.

An image of Torrin, fighting through Raken, his double-edged sword glinting in the sunlight, flashed through her mind. Perhaps the Slayer had been here all along, under their very noses. She smiled, it was a nice thought but they had no way of knowing if Torrin — or even Nathel, for that matter — was the Slayer.

Her smile faded abruptly; either way, they were running out of time. If they did not act soon, it would be too late. Her hands stilled on her blade, while her gaze strayed again to the distant line of mountains. She closed her eyes to dispel the odd tugging sensation she felt toward Krang. It must be the stress and the knowledge of who the Summoner was.

She rose from the bench and re-sheathed her sword, then rubbed the excess oil from her hands with a rag before trailing her fingers in the fountain's water. She turned at the doors into the keep to gaze back one last time at the slate-grey mountains huddled on the distant horizon.

Hathunor stirred from where he had been curled in the sun against the wall. Standing to his full height, he stretched like a giant cat. The huge Saa Raken was one of the few sure things in these last days of uncertainty and Rowan was glad of his presence.

Just as they were about to enter the cool, dark interior she heard the alarm bells rising on the wind from below. The Raken were attacking. She spun and looked out across the city to the gate where the sun reflected in glints and flashes from armor as the soldiers broke into frenzied activity atop and along the wall.

Time to fight again.

She wheeled and plunged through the door into the keep with Hathunor following on her heels.

They raced through the citadel, running down empty corridors towards the main entrance; most of the castle guard was already down at the walls. Sprinting down the corridor that led to the grand entry, Rowan slid to a halt. Someone lay in the middle of the smooth floor, unmoving. She trotted closer and recognized the intricate golden braids.

Rushing forward, Rowan fell to her knees beside the queen. Elana lay sprawled on her back, her arms flung wide, a large pool of blood forming under her head.

Rowan touched Elana's chest and waited, barely breathing. There was a heartbeat, but it was faint.

Rowan turned to Hathunor. “Find Dalemar quickly! The library.”

The Saa Raken hesitated, looking down at Rowan with an anxious expression.

“Go! I will be fine, my friend. Dalemar might be the only one to save her.”

Hathunor blinked, then launched himself down the corridor, his long claws striking the stone flags.

Rowan bent to examine the large, profusely bleeding wound on the side of the queen’s head. She had been struck with a sharp object of some sort. There was no way she could have received a cut like this by falling and hitting her head. The blood on the floor had not yet begun to congeal. It must have happened moments before.

The pool of blood on the floor was rapidly spreading. Springing to her feet, Rowan dashed to a low table, pulling the fabric runner from its surface. A vase crashed to the floor behind her as she ran back to Elana and crouched, winding the cloth tightly around the queen’s head.

Satisfied that she had at least slowed the bleeding, she sat back on her heels and brought her hand to her lips, took a deep breath, and whistled as loudly as she could, three short blasts.

She waited only a moment before she heard the sound of running feet. Three members of the castle guard raced down the corridor towards her. They slid to a stop when they recognized their queen. One of them, a sandy-haired man, turned and barked orders to the other two guards. “Artel, find the King! Blain, fetch the royal physician—and bring back a stretcher!”

More people were trotting down the corridor now. Servants and maids, they gasped and some of them began to weep. The guard who had taken charge ordered the nearest servant to relay a message to the captain of the guard.

A stretcher arrived, the royal physician, a rotund and ruddy-faced man, trundling along in its wake. “Here then, give me some room, give me room!” He waved his large hands as he burst through the small crowd.

Rowan stood back and looked at the people surrounding Elana. Ironic that so many should be here now when moments ago the hall had been empty, with no one to see what had happened.

The physician knelt down with surprising alacrity. His face was cast in dismay but he went about a brief and thorough examination, peeking for a moment under the increasingly blood-soaked cloth Rowan had applied to Elana's head. The physician looked up at Rowan. He noted the blood on her hands. His gaze was piercing. "You found her?"

"Yes," Rowan replied.

The physician's attention was already on Elana again before the word had completely left Rowan's mouth. He directed the stretcher to be laid beside them. As Elana was lifted gently onto it, a deep voice called for a way through.

Cerebus.

The King moved forward, his expression fierce. People fell back to give him room. Falion, the new Captain of the castle guard was by his side. Cerebus knelt down with a horrified exclamation.

The physician spoke quietly to the king. "It is a head wound Sire. I must get her moved to her quarters where I can treat her."

Rowan swallowed, tightness gripping her chest at the anguish on Cerebus's face. His hand had seized one of Elana's and he was gripping it hard.

"King Cerebus," she said, "I have sent Hathunor to find Dalemar. He will be able to help."

The two men looked up at her. The physician motioned for the guards to lift the stretcher, and he led them away down the corridor bearing Elana's unconscious form.

Rising, Cerebus turned to the captain, hard anger in his voice. "I want to know what happened! Did someone attack my wife in my own keep? Did anyone see what happened?"

The sandy-haired guard gestured at Rowan. "The Lady Rowan found the queen, Sire."

As Cerebus turned to Rowan, she became painfully aware of Elana's blood on her hands. "Hathunor and I were on our way down to the city walls when we found her lying in the middle of the corridor," she said. "We must have found her only minutes after it happened. There was no sign of anyone, but I believe she was struck by something sharp. I am sorry that I cannot be of more help."

Cerebus turned back to Captain Falion. "I want everyone in the keep questioned. I want to know if anyone saw this attack."

Falion nodded, but cleared his throat. "What of the walls, Sire, the city's defences?"

"The sons of Ralor and General Preven are down on the walls, they will defend our city."

"Yes, Sire." Falion saluted and strode briskly away.

Rowan realized Cerebus was talking about Torrin and Nathel, and her thoughts flew to the defenders on the city walls. A need rose up to find her friends, to help fight at their side. There was little she could do here.

Before she could leave Cerebus turned to her. "Walk with me, Lady Rowan."

Rowan looked down the corridor towards the entry hall. Then she nodded and strode after the king as he followed his wife's stretcher.

"Was she awake when you found her? Did she say anything to you?" asked Cerebus.

Rowan sighed. "I am sorry, King Cerebus. The queen was unconscious when we found her, and looked to have fallen to the floor that way."

"I see," he said softly. Rowan became aware of his carefully controlled breathing. "The keys to the bailey, like the one found on your attacker the other night, have all been accounted for. Whoever it was that gave the two men the key must have had a duplicate made."

"Then anyone who has a key could potentially be the traitor," said Rowan.

Cerebus nodded, a scowl on his face.

They walked in silence toward the royal residence. Rowan had not been in this part of the keep before. The corridors were laid with intricate carpets and the walls hung with tapestries. The doors they passed were skilfully carved and stained glass decorated the wall sconces, scattering candlelight in bright colors across the stonewalls.

They reached a pair of grand double doors, one of which stood ajar. The two castle guards who had served as stretcher-bearers for the queen were just returning to stand guard on either side of the doors.

"I want you to admit the Rith Dalemar when he arrives. Otherwise no one save the physician or anyone that I approve personally is to get within ten feet of the queen, Understand?" Cerebus's voice shook with anger.

The guards saluted the king briskly as Cerebus turned to the door and pushed it open.

Rowan hesitated but Cerebus motioned her forward. The suite beyond was beautiful with large comfortable chairs gathered around an enormous hearth. Artisans' work from all over Eryos decorated the tables and shared the shelves with volumes of leather-bound books, including Stoneman blue glazed urns and vases and what looked like Klyssen copper-work.

"Please make yourself comfortable, my lady. Wait here for Rith Dalemar and send him in as soon as he arrives." Cerebus disappeared through a door.

Rowan stood for a moment. Elana's touch was everywhere, though there were several sets of armour – Cerebus's collection. She recognized a Taborian suit and what looked like formal Klyssen armour, also a suit of simple bronze with a helmet that looked a lot like what she'd seen in Dendor. One she didn't recognize; an ancient suit, it was beautifully etched and riveted.

Turning, Rowan widened her eyes in astonishment. A Myrian suit of armour, complete with sword and shield, stood carefully displayed in one corner.

She moved to stand before the Myrian suit. Unlike the practical, light leather she wore, this was a ceremonial suit, made of silver and bronze, etched with the scrollwork and the spiralling emblems of Myris Dar. Nevertheless, it was completely battle-worthy. Myrian men and women who wore these suits were of the highest quality – the most renowned fighters. This suit was sized for a man.

Rowan reached out and reverently traced a finger across the etched surface of the metal. It was cool but alive somehow too. She exhaled the breath she had been holding as a childhood memory washed over her – the capital city of Mykrian where her parents had taken her and Andin to see the Myrian ceremonial guard. It had been one of the defining moments of her young life. Rowan shivered as she felt once again that sense of destiny – the absolute knowledge that she would one day wear that armour. The shining helms and breastplates had glinted in the sun like fire, the bright red plumes added to the regal effect and the guards, each standing resolute, radiated power and strength.

"I thought that might interest you."

Rowan blinked, pulled back to the present and turned to find the king watching her from the doorway.

She lowered her hand, and took a steadying breath. "How is Elana?"

Cerebus's face was drawn. He shook his head. "The physician is stitching her wound; he says that she lost a lot of blood and the blow to her head is keeping her from waking." The king walked to a chair by the fire and sank into it. He rubbed his hands across his face and gestured to the seat across from him.

"Please have a seat, Lady Rowan. We've not yet had a chance to speak informally. Now is as good a time as any. In fact, it would help keep my mind off Elana."

Rowan walked forward and sat down in the chair facing the king. Cerebus looked away from the fire and focused his attention on her. "Do you recognize the armour?"

Rowan glanced back over to the ceremonial suit and nodded. "Where did you acquire it?"

Cerebus sat back in his chair and propped his chin in his hand. "My great grandfather bought it from a trader when he was a young man. The trader insisted the armour was a gift from the Myrian man who'd once worn it, and that the warrior was an old man by the time he gave the suit to the trader. I've always doubted the tale myself. A ceremonial suit that beautiful would not be simply gifted away."

"Actually, it is considered very honourable for a Myrian to give armour or weapons to another, especially if that gift has been used in the defence of Myris Dar. The very act itself is thought to bestow the light of freedom on those who are in need."

"Truly?" Cerebus's face lit up. "What a noble idea. Your people are somewhat of a contradiction: expert in war and fighting, yet gentle and generous of heart."

Rowan smiled. "We are very simple in many ways."

Cerebus watched her steadily. "The fact that you rescued a huge Raken for no personal gain, and the loyalty of your friends, speak of anything *but* simplicity. Do you know there are tales circulating around the city about you? The soldiers who have fought beside you have taken to wearing a blue strip of cloth tied around their right arm."

"They are fine men, courageous and steadfast in the face of an overwhelming enemy. It has been *my* honour to fight with them." Rowan looked down at her hands searching for her next words. "King Cerebus, I must apologize for my lack of diplomatic skill. My cousin Dell was the ambassador among our group. He would have truly enjoyed your great city." Rowan's voice quavered and her chest ached.

Cerebus shook his head. "You have represented your people admirably. Many emissaries are little more than messengers. You have given us *so* much more than your message – a sense of the nobility and spirit of Myrians and their intention to make contact with Pellar and the rest of Eryos. You have brought Myris Dar back to shine brightly in the minds of Pellar's people from the dim shadow of legend."

There was a light tap on the door and Dalemar popped his head through. His smooth face was marked with worry.

Cerebus stood up quickly. "Come in, Rith Dalemar. Thank you for coming so quickly."

Dalemar bowed. "How is the queen?"

The king gestured for him to follow as he walked to the door of the room Elana occupied. "She has lost much blood and will not awaken. Please, anything you can do for her…" Cerebus trailed off as Hathunor ducked under the doorframe and followed Dalemar into the room. Two guards, with hands on the hilts of their swords and looks of dismay on their faces, followed the great Raken.

"Forgive the intrusion, King Cerebus, but I will likely need Hathunor's help," explained Dalemar.

Cerebus nodded and dismissed the guards, leading them into the room beyond. Rowan watched from the doorway as they gathered around the bed. Elana lay still and pale on the wide pillows as the portly physician bent over her, stitching up the wound. So involved was he in the work that he failed to notice the new occupants. Cerebus lay a hand on his shoulder and he started, glancing up at Hathunor and then rising in alarm. The king gestured for him to step aside.

Dalemar touched Elana's forehead and sighed. "It is a grievous blow. She may not regain consciousness right away, but we will do our best." He nodded to Hathunor and the huge Saa Raken stepped forward.

The physician made a strangled sound and moved to intercede but a soft word from Cerebus froze him in mid-stride.

Dalemar placed one hand against Hathunor's black, scaled arm; his other hand, still on Elana's forehead, began to glow softly. Even from the doorway Rowan could see the wound on Elana's head shrink slowly and disappear, leaving only a smear of blood and the dark thread the physician had been using.

Elana's color became healthier, the blue circles around her eyes faded and her shallow breathing expanded.

Dalemar swayed on his feet. Rowan hurried forward and placed a hand under his elbow. The Rith acknowledged her wearily. "The wound was grievous. She will be fine but I cannot say how soon she will wake. Her body needs to rest now to regain the blood that was lost. I will send Nathel with a dose of Winoth root to speed the rebuilding of her strength." He sagged against Rowan.

The king, who was beside Elana now stroking her head where a terrible wound had been, nodded. "My deepest thanks, Rith Dalemar."

The royal Physician was staring at the Rith with an open mouth, the curved stitching needle still between his bloody fingers.

Rowan and Hathunor helped Dalemar to the door and through the sitting room beyond. She glanced back through the open door at the queen. What, if anything did Elana know about who attacked her — and why?

The Sons of Ralor

Torrin ducked. He couldn't get his sword up in time as a Raken's club descended. It struck his shoulder guard and glanced down the metal rings to a chinking halt. He gasped as the shock splintered along his upper arm. There was nowhere to move in the press of bodies and the Raken had surprised him from behind. Torrin swore. He barely heard his own voice above the staccato snarls and roars, the shouts and screams of men. How had they gotten behind the line?

Pulling his sword arm free, he stepped forward and stabbed the Raken. It flailed its arms, knocking a soldier down in its pain. Torrin yanked his weapon out and re-swung, cleaving the beast between neck and shoulder.

Nathel was a few paces away, his blond-hair stark against the black as he battled against the sudden onslaught of Raken. The beasts had focused their attempt to take the wall in one spot and the Pellarian defenders were being pushed back at an alarming rate. Torrin glanced around, taking stock of his friends among the soldiers. General Preven, wounded earlier, had been forced to retreat from the fray.

Torrin silently thanked Erys that Rowan was not here.

The line of defenders was ragged but they were holding, barely.

Further along, a man slipped and went down. Then another tripped over him and was killed by a Raken. As Torrin watched, a hole opened and the Raken streamed through.

He launched himself along the wall and hit the first Raken before it had a chance to turn on the soldiers from behind. "Hold the line!" he bellowed. "To me! Hold! For Pellar!" The battling men around him solidified. Shouts rang out among them, echoing his call. The breach was slowly closed – inches and feet won in blood.

Torrin swept his sword up to meet a curved blade, then pivoted it into the Raken. He kicked out, hitting it squarely in the gut and sent it plummeting off the back of the wall. He smiled grimly. Rowan would have approved.

Another huge beast leaped for him. Torrin stepped sideways, raising his blade and closing the distance. The Raken was too late reacting. The next was upon him and all he saw was the red glare of its eyes. It spun lightning-quick to avoid his sword thrust. Torrin grunted with the effort of blocking its spear. The wooden shaft splintered, and his next thrust took the Raken in the heart.

Torrin looked quickly around, his chest heaving. There were no more Raken behind the lines. Turning back, he dove into the crush of battling men and Raken, careful of swinging weapons as he pushed through to the front.

The men around him were tiring, faltering. Torrin spotted Nathel as his brother worked his way closer through the melee. They needed to give the soldiers a chance to regroup above the gate. Borlin and Arynilas were closing in on the dense pocket as well.

The four of them came together at the head of the mass of Raken and, battling for Pellar, they cleared ground. Protecting each other's backs, they fought seamlessly – Borlin roaring, smashing his targe and cutting deftly with his short sword; Arynilas, spinning silently, knives flickering; Nathel beside Torrin, his teeth gritted, his sword and shield wet with gore.

Eventually the Raken's advance slowed, finally stopped. The Pellarian soldiers took advantage of the lull and surged forward to push the beasts backward. Scaling ladders tumbled back down to the field below. Raken were shoved from the wall, plummeting down and taking others with them, clawing for purchase.

As the Raken below began to turn in unison away from the city, Torrin shouted, lifting his sword and pointing down into the retreating Raken. "Archers!"

Soldiers scrambled to take aim.

"Fire!"

Bowstrings thrummed and a wave of the foe fell. Torrin called orders to fire again while ruthlessly thrusting down the sympathy that rose in his heart for the Raken.

The beasts swiftly moved beyond arrow range, leaving behind newly fallen and turned once again to stand facing the city walls.

Torrin assessed the battlements, wiping the sweat from his forehead. Their losses were many. The top of the wall was littered with bodies; far too many of them were Pellarian soldiers. Men had already begun the gruesome task of dispatching the Raken still alive. Wounded soldiers struggled to stand.

Arynilas materialized beside Torrin. The slight Tynithian looked to have barely broken a sweat.

"You'll need to fletch more arrows after today, my friend," said Torrin darkly. "We barely held them."

Arynilas cocked his head. "The defence held. It might not have though, if you hadn't closed the gap."

Torrin looked for Nathel and found him already moving among the wounded to apply field dressings with Borlin's help. The black-robed priests of Erys were also there and the young one who had offered Torrin water the day before looked up just as Torrin's glance passed over him. Thaius locked eyes with him for a moment and they nod to each other.

Torrin accepted the strip of cloth Arynilas passed to him. He looked over the Raken army as he wiped the blood from his sword. They were blackness covering the plain. He shook his head and shoved his blade into its scabbard. The Raken could have easily won through this afternoon if they had just kept coming.

"I need to find Preven and give him a report." Torrin turned to find the general himself stalking up the steps to the top of wall, his arm in a sling.

Preven reached them quickly and he scanned the army below the city and the carnage atop the battlement. "My gratitude to you and your companions for a battle well fought. This attack was the strongest yet. I only hope we are given enough time to recover before the next assault."

"Agreed," said Torrin. "How is your arm?"

Preven glanced down and wiggled the fingers peeking out of his bandaged arm. "It'll do. These old bones don't break that easily. I've received word from the King, though. Queen Elana was attacked. She suffers from a grave head wound. The lady Rowan found her."

Torrin's skin went cold, tiny prickles running across the back of his neck. He had been relieved Rowan wasn't in the battle, while up at the Keep she might have been in worse danger. He cleared his throat and swallowed. "Have they sent for Dalemar?"

Preven nodded. "I was told the Rith was on his way to her."

"Do you know who attacked her?"

The general shook his head in frustration. “There were no witnesses, and Queen Elana remains unconscious.”

The general moved off to take command of the wall and Torrin raked a hand through his hair. An attack on the queen in the middle of the afternoon in Pellaris Keep was akin to an act of war. Were the attacks on Rowan and Elana related?

Of course they were.

The certainty of it chilled his heart. Whoever was behind it all was getting bolder, or worse – desperate.

Torrin turned and frowned up at Pellaris Keep, perched at the top of the hill. Desperate men were always far more dangerous than bold ones.

The Temple of Erys

Galen strode across the vast, austere marble floors of the Temple of Erys. It was late; nothing stirred in the vaulted chamber. Starlight and a pale glow from the twin moons bled through the high clerestory windows, illuminating the massive dome with silver. He was used to the sight and did not pause to look upwards with awe as so many did.

At the back of the circular Temple, behind the glittering alter of Erys, was a small door of polished wood. Casting a glance over his shoulder, Galen inserted his key and swiftly passed through, locking it again behind him before climbing the spiral stairs. At their top, another small door provided entry to a large room—as yet unoccupied. Galen sighed in relief. He needed time alone to clear his mind, time to think. He must be calm.

Two lanterns glowed at either end of the chamber. He considered lighting more, but the dimness was an appropriate backdrop for the seriousness of the deliberations held here. Tonight's business would usher in the next era for the priesthood.

Galen took a deep breath and stepped forward, walking slowly past the ring of chairs that formed a circle around the perimeter. Large and throne-like with seats upholstered with red velvet, all were identical save for one – into its gilded back was carved the circle of Erys.

Pausing, Galen laid a hand on its armrest. The wood was worn smooth, the collective presence of all those whose wise counsel had guided the priesthood through the ages. "If only you could have led us through these troubled times yourself, my old friend." He closed his eyes. "Erys took you too soon." Galen owed much to the last patriarch of the priesthood, Palior N'Allrion. During the last days of the eminent leader's life, Galen had promised his dear friend that he would guide the priesthood through the coming turmoil.

Tonight, a new patriarch would sit here.

Galen turned away, the next leader of the priesthood could never be as wise, nor blessed with the same scope of vision, as Palior N'Allrion.

A small, ornately carved wooden table stood at the center of the thick red carpet, a cushion on its glossy surface cradling the scepter of the priesthood. A formal reminder of the gravity of this process, it would remain untouched until this momentous decision had been made. Solid red gold, with the largest ruby ever mined from the Great Timor Mountains set in its top – the preciousness of the material was nothing compared with the power the sceptre represented.

Galen had a great deal of influence over who would wield it next. And in return for that influence, he could expect to strengthen his own position, becoming even more indispensable to the upper echelon within the priesthood. As he once more secured his position as councillor to the patriarch, Galen would ensure that *his* guidance was followed in the future decisions to be made, and that his promise to his old friend was kept.

Palior was entitled to that promise and much, much more. The old patriarch and the priesthood had been an island of refuge for Galen when, shortly after the succession of Cerebus to the throne, Galen found himself on unstable ground while all that he stood for and cared about in his beloved Pellar was systematically jeopardized by the new king, a man that Galen was sworn to serve.

During King Doren's reign, Galen's place had always been assured. The two men had fostered a relationship of mutual respect for their individual talents throughout the years. Galen knew the king's mind and was fulfilled by the role he had played in raising Pellar to the preeminent military and economic power in Eryos. Doren was a proud man and his ambitions as a king were simple: power, strength of arms and absolute rule. Galen's one regret was that had never found a way to better instruct Doren on the finer plays of statecraft.

As chancellor of Pellar, some of Cerebus's education fell to Galen and he was initially pleased to find an intelligent and subtle mind in the young heir. But as time passed, Galen became disturbed by many of the ideas and opinions the young man expressed. He had warned Doren, but the king was satisfied that his son was well-versed in statecraft and well-blooded in battle, and had little interest in pursuing philosophical avenues with Cerebus. When Cerebus ascended to the throne of Pellar, Galen knew he would be a very different king than his father had been.

At first he had hoped that the idealistic young king would outgrow his foolish dreams of a Pellar ruled by its people, but Cerebus's vision and ambition for a much different Pellar grew and took root in his many public works and projects. It was a fine enough fantasy, but in reality it just wasn't possible.

Wealth that should be going towards strengthening the army and filling the crown coffers was being dribbled away on books and learning and convoluted court systems, on alms for the poor and schools for girls. A grubby farmer or a fat baker would never pick up a sword to freely help defend their Kingdom, regardless of how happy they were. They had to be paid for it or forced into it.

Galen watched his own world disintegrate as Cerebus made decision after decision to pull apart all that Doren and he had built together. Cerebus kept Galen on as king's chancellor, but increasingly disregarded his wise council. Then Cerebus married Elana, and to Galen's dismay, the king found an avid cohort and fellow idealist in his queen. The chancellor lost all hope of tempering Cerebus's rule. So he bided his time, covering his resentment and fostering his role as the loving uncle whose days of true service were past; as such, he was beyond suspicion.

Until now.

Turning away from sceptre of Erys, Galen shook his head regretfully and assumed his seat next to the Patriarch's chair. Cerebus could have become a great king, far greater than his father even. If only he had not been blinded by a misplaced sense of responsibility for the social and philosophical health of the people. Such things only bled away the strength of a king. And when strength mattered most in the workings of a kingdom, ideas like Cerebus's led to ruin.

People *needed* to be ruled by a strong and steady hand. As soon as citizens were given the right and responsibility of making decisions, the realm would grind to a crumbling halt. People could never agree with each other about how things should be run. The kingdom would eventually tear itself apart.

One only needed to look to the south, at the quagmire Ren had become without a strong central power, to see that Cerebus's grand plans would never work. The changes Cerebus had made during his reign had transformed Pellar in ways that were of little importance. The people of Pellar were happier, it was true; still, weighed against the weakening and destabilizing of the kingdom, it counted for nothing.

Desperate to save his beloved Pellar, the king's chancellor turned his great expertise to the purpose and cause of the Priesthood of Erys. Palior had been only a priest when they met, content with his station, but Galen's great knowledge of secular politics and governing brought Palior to see the possibilities of what the Priesthood of Erys could become. With Galen as his guide, Palior had risen quickly through the ranks of the priesthood and finally to the office of the patriarch itself.

Through the broad reach of the Priesthood, Galen was able to oppose the king's many plans. The priesthood began to court the more powerful families in Pellar, establishing ties of obligation. And when Cerebus sought support for his various projects, he found his past allies had united with the priesthood. By instilling the priesthood's values in the minds of the public, values that Galen and Palior knew to be counter to the king's policies, they were able to thwart Cerebus through the very means that he valued most – the opinion of the people. Together, Galen and Palior brought the priesthood into Pellar's political arena, applying for a seat on the council so they could work from within the government.

It had been a risky relationship, and his work with Palior had to remain a secret. Galen could not be seen to align with the priesthood or he would lose what little power he had left to temper Cerebus's plans and decisions with his circumspect counsel. It was difficult; the king was an intelligent man, and over the years Galen had to tread very lightly. But the risk had paid off. As the priesthood grew in power, Galen became increasingly certain it offered the strong leadership the Kingdom needed – a great central pinnacle that people could look to for direction. Soon, the priesthood would supplant the crown, with him at the patriarch's side to once again realize his dreams of a strong Pellar.

The latch on the door clicked, and the first commission member filed into the room. Tihir N'Avarin's usually austere features were flushed with expectation.

Galen frowned at the priest. N'Avarin inclined his head. "Chancellor."

"The others?" asked Galen shortly.

"They will be along. I wanted the opportunity to speak with you privately."

"You do not trust I have everything in hand for the vote?"

N'Avarin flushed more deeply. "No, I am sure tonight's proceedings will be smooth. Erys has blessed this succession," he said piously. "I wished to speak of how it is with the king and queen. She is recovering, I am told."

"Yes, the Rith was able to heal her wound." Galen sighed with frustration and regret. "Things are getting out of hand, N'Avarin. The queen should never have been involved. If you hadn't been so impatient to speak with me, she would not have suspected anything." Galen took a deep breath and relaxed. He did not want to inflame the man before the others arrived. They would have to come to accord if they wished to accomplish all that was planned.

"Perhaps if the Myrian woman had been handled more carefully," said N'Avarin in a cold voice, "some of this would have been avoided."

"I am afraid even Miroth underestimated her on that account. He was explicit – only is his own men were to capture her. The fault lies with him." Galen smoothed out his robes, smothering another moment of irritation. Miroth's proposals demanded much and gave little in the way of assurances for the priesthood's future gain beyond vague promises of a place in the new order of Eryos.

"The Lord of Lok Myrr," said N'Avarin with distaste. "He is not to be trusted, I fear."

"I share your concern, N'Avarin. But our agreement allowed us to make necessary arrangements before the Raken army arrived at the city gates. We are as well positioned as possible with such a dubious ally."

"And what if he decides to turn on the priesthood? Perhaps the king –"

Galen shook his head. "Any bridges back to that possibility have now been irrevocably burned. As misguided as Cerebus's ideals are, his commitment to them has proven unshakable. And now with Elana coming to harm, he will be relentless in pursuit of the culprits."

"But Miroth –"

"*We* have what Miroth needs, N'Avarin. Do not forget that. For whatever reason he is bent on acquiring this Messenger. We will use that to our advantage."

N'Avarin stroked his chin, his dark eyes flashing with a new confidence.

"This alliance will leave the priesthood in a position of absolute power once the siege of Pellaris is over," said Galen. "Remember, Miroth made first contact. We have the upper hand. By now Miroth's spies in Pellaris will have sent word of the failure to capture Rowan. He will be looking for another opportunity to take her, and the priesthood will prove indispensable to him. Now, do be seated, N'Avarin; you must be seen to be pious and unconcerned. You are here to serve the priesthood in your leadership, not yourself."

The priest's expression hardened but he said nothing and moved to his own chair. As he sat, the door opened and the rest of the commission began arrive.

Watching them file in, Galen turned his thoughts to the work at hand. He didn't have much time do what needed to be done. Elana's condition was improving and things were moving very fast. The new patriarch had to be in place and Galen safely concealed by the priesthood before the queen regained consciousness. New plans also had to be made to improve the bargain struck with the Lord of Lok Myrr.

He had already removed his most valued possessions from his study and left the keep with little regret.

His true home was here with the priesthood.

Truth Revealed

Cerebus paced impatiently between the large bed and the window, passing a hand across his face, feeling rough whiskers. Late morning light filtered through the laced curtains. He had hardly slept all night, keeping watch over Elana, checking to make sure she continued to breathe easily.

He turned back to face the bed, where she still lay sleeping, marvelling again that there was no sign of the terrible gash that had rent her scalp open yesterday. Elana was strong in so many ways, but sweet Erys it had been terrifying to see her so badly injured. He'd taken the safety of the keep for granted until Rowan was attacked – and now… Cerebus muttered an oath, berating himself for the hundredth time. Elana should have had an armed escort. She had scoffed at the idea, told him every man was needed on the city walls and of course she was right. Still, if only someone had been with her. Cerebus closed his aching eyes.

He heard a soft murmur from the bed. Elana had moved her head; she now faced him and the window. Cerebus bent over her, placing a hand lightly on her forehead.

Her eyes fluttered open. It took her a moment to focus on his face. A small smile curved her lips at the sight of him.

Relief flooded his chest "My love, we have been so worried for you," he said softly. "How do you feel?"

Elana's eyes wandered over the room then back to his face. "Groggy, and rather weak," she replied in a whisper. "Cerebus, how did I come to be here? I have no memory of it."

Cerebus clasped one of her hands in his own. "You were unconscious when they brought you here. You were found on the floor of the main side corridor with your head split open."

Elana frowned in concentration. She reached up to touch the side of her head where the wound had been. "I remember being hit. The pain was terrible."

"Elana, did you see who attacked you?"

Elana shook her head and then closed her eyes. "No. I… I was coming to see you. It was important."

"What was important?"

"I can't remember. I think…" His wife's face blanched suddenly and her eyes widened. She reached out and gripped his arm, her fingernails digging in. "Cerebus, where is Galen?"

Cerebus frowned. "Where he always is, I would assume. I have not seen him since yesterday morning. Why? What is it? Is he in danger?"

Elana closed her eyes and sagged back into the bed. "Cerebus, you must find him. He's the one. He is the traitor."

"What?" Cerebus pulled away. "What are you talking about?"

Elana's eyes were suddenly very clear. "I know it's hard to believe, I didn't believe it either; I tried to justify it; I tried to think of some plausible explanation. Cerebus, I found something in his study."

Cerebus felt as though the air was being pressed out of his lungs. He couldn't take his eyes from Elana's earnest face. "What, what did you find?"

"A small clay-lined box used to make a copy for casting. It held the impression of a key, Cerebus. The bailey key."

Cerebus straightened and gently pulled Elana's fingers from his forearm. "Do you know what you are saying, love? Galen? He's been like a father to me, to us both. How can you be sure that you're not jumping to the wrong conclusion?"

Elana struggled to sit up against the pillows. Her face was pale. "That is not all, Cerebus. Before I got to his study yesterday, I saw him speaking very closely with Tihir N'Avarin. He received a note from the priest. When I walked into his study, I caught him burning it. I asked what it was, and he said it was just a list of the priesthood's latest demands. But why would he burn that?"

Cerebus turned away and walked to the window, a sick feeling growing in the pit of his stomach. He'd known Galen all his life, had relied on him for guidance and support. Galen would lay down his life for Pellar. How could he be involved with giving a key to men who were sent here from Miroth? Impossible! Galen had as much dislike for the priesthood as Cerebus. How could the chancellor be allied with them?

He turned back to his wife. She sat up in the bed watching him gravely, her braided hair dishevelled. Erys help him – one of the two people he trusted most in the world was telling him the other had betrayed them.

Cerebus strode back to the bed. He leaned down and brushed Elana's forehead with his lips, touching her soft cheek with his fingertips. "Rest, my love. I'll send one of your ladies in with some food. Guards are posted outside. I have to go." He began to turn away but Elana stopped him.

"What are you going to do, Cerebus?"

He looked back down at her, unable to bear the thought of anyone hurting her again. He sighed. "I'm going to find out the truth. I need to speak to Galen. I owe him that much at least."

"Please be careful," she whispered. "Do not go alone."

Out beyond the curtained window and the city below, the alarm bells began to sound again.

Fight in the Great Temple Square

It happened in broad daylight, in the great Temple Square, as they made their way to the library to help Dalemar. Nathel had just cracked a joke and Borlin was laughing as they walked. Hathunor paced loosely beside Rowan.

She breathed in the fresh air and sighed, not looking forward to the prospect of another day spent in the cramped, dusty room.

A small troop of castle guards approached them from the opposite end of the square, about twenty or so. Rowan frowned; something was odd about them but she couldn't identify what. Keeping her eye on them, she turned her attention back to the conversation. As they drew nearer to the guards, Rowan noticed a black robe amongst the red and gold of Cerebus's colors. The priest had been walking with the guards but split to move away towards the Temple.

It was too far to see his face clearly but something about the way he walked and the glances he cast at them over his shoulder gave warning.

"Did anyone see that?" Rowan interrupted Borlin.

"I did," said Nathel, reaching down to ease his sword in its scabbard. The move solidified the group – all now had their attention trained on the priest and the castle guards coming toward them.

"That was Tihir N'Avarin, wasn't it?" Rowan asked.

Nathel nodded, casting a quick glance at the Temple before looking back at the guards.

The sun broke free of the clouds and as the huge square was plunged into sunlight, Rowan drew in a breath. "Look at their feet!" Mud-splattered boots of different shapes and colors. They were close enough now to see that the red and gold uniforms were ill fitting.

So it comes to this, she thought, not surprised to find Tihir N'Avarin involved.

Nathel swore. "The library is too far away." They were almost at the center of the square. The guards would intercept them if they made a run for it.

Rowan cast a glance back and her heart jumped into her throat. "They are behind us as well." Another group of ten castle guards, all impostors, blocked the street entrance. They were trapped. The approaching guards to the front were only a hundred paces away.

Nathel nodded to the huge fountain in the middle of the square. "We might be able to defend that."

Without another word they altered course for the circular pool of water. A huge stone statue of a knight on horseback rose up out of the center and cast a long shadow over the space before the fountain. The stone knight gazed sternly down at them without pity.

Rowan, Nathel, Borlin and Hathunor reached the fountain and drew their weapons, backs to the statue. Hathunor let out a menacing growl.

"Erys but I wish we had Torrin and Arynilas with us," said Nathel quietly.

Rowan closed her eyes. Torrin.

The guards reached the fountain and spread out to surround them. They were rough looking men, much like the two who had attacked Rowan in her room.

One guard stepped forward. "There is no need for bloodshed." His eyes flicked to Hathunor. "Rowan of Myris Dar is under arrest for crimes against the crown," he said with a snarl. His eyes traveled over the group until he was looking at Rowan. "If you come quietly, we will spare your friends."

Nathel laugh sharply. "Go back and tell Miroth he will have to try harder than this. Rowan is going nowhere with you." There was dead seriousness in his voice.

The man grinned, showing crooked teeth. "You're a little out numbered, big man, even with the beast." His eyes darted again to Hathunor, then back to Rowan as he folded his arms and cocked his hip arrogantly. "It's your choice, lovely. You come quietly or they die."

Rowan looked up at Nathel. He was scowling, his pale blue eyes wrathful. Her heart wrenched – he looked just like Torrin. "Don't you surrender yourself for us, Rowan. Don't you dare!"

"Aye, Lass," Borlin growled. "The lad speaks truth." He clapped his short sword against his round shield and glared at the enemy. "Come on then, ye toad swill!"

The leader spat on the ground. "Wrong answer." He signalled and the posing guards charged.

Rowan whispered the name of her sword and it jumped to life in her hand. Hathunor became a black streak as he launched himself at their attackers. He bowled into them taking four of them down to the ground. The men around him hacked at his exposed back and flanks. He spun on them and they stumbled back in alarm. Hathunor swiped the weapons from their hands; knocked them senseless or ripped out their throats.

Rowan met a burly man in a uniform too small for him. She parried his sloppy thrust, slicing upward with her sword. He screamed. Blood sprayed across her face.

Two more came. Between the moving bodies, she saw her friends dealing with three or more attackers each.

Her heart pounded in her chest; sweat slicked her palm and she clenched her blade tighter. One man attempted to wrap his arms around her, pin her. She deflected his arm with her sword and smashed the pommel into his face. He stumbled back, his broken nose gushing blood.

The ten from the square entrance arrived then, crowding in. There were too many. She was pushed back, expending all energy on just protecting herself.

She saw Nathel take a short blade in the side. He grunted with pain and sent his own sword slashing through the man's collarbone. Borlin was bloodied as well, struggling to wield his weapons in the press of bodies. There were men behind them now, wading through the shallow water of the fountain. They were swarmed.

Rowan was clouted on the side of the head. Her vision swam black for an instant but she never stopped moving her sword. She felt it slice into something, smelled sour breath as it was exhaled into her face. When her vision cleared, a man was dropping to the ground in front of her. She leaped back as he tried to wrap his arms around her knees.

Her back collided with something solid and she glanced back. It was Nathel, fighting desperately. He bled from a dozen shallow cuts and the deep wound in his side.

Her attackers were trying to disarm her or knock her out. Miroth wanted her alive – her companions were not so lucky.

Nathel grunted again behind her. He grasped her baldric and pulled her back close to him. Borlin was down bleeding on the flagstones but he was too far away to protect. She couldn't see Hathunor anymore. If she left Nathel's side they would lose what little advantage they had left.

It was so hard to swing her sword in the press. A cudgel flew at her head. She dodged, raising her sword to deflect it. It glanced off her shoulder and she ground her teeth against sudden pain. There were at least ten men around her now.

She could no longer feel Nathel at her back.

Panic rose in her chest. She fought it like she fought the men. *On this day when blood is to be shed, let this sword be true, let this arm be strong in the defence of my land, my people and myself. On this day when blood is to be...* The words rose unbidden and she clung to them.

Her sword humming and whirling around her, she fought a losing battle. She was cracked again on the side of the head. Pain sheared along her scalp and the sunlit square dimmed. Her hands lost all strength. Her sword clattered to the paving stones. The dagger was ripped from her grasp.

The alarm bells rang from the wall, but their sound was faint and fading.

Torrin, I'm sorry. She was roughly lifted as the world went black.

The Raken Master

Miroth withdrew from the mind of the Raken, leaving behind the walls of Pellaris as his army withdrew once more. The disorientation, the odd stretching sensation as his mind sped back towards his own body left his head swimming. Bonding to the Raken beasts was always an unsettling experience. He focused on his goals for a moment until the peculiar feral awareness passed. He had almost expended too much energy.

The limits of his mortal body continued to be a source of burning frustration. Even with fifteen hundred years of toiling and knowledge, there were still boundaries he could not cross, things he could not do. The time would come, though, when he would finally cross those boundaries to the realm of perfection – fatigue and weakness never to plague him again.

What would his teachers think of him now? A familiar wrath seeped through his veins, offering strength for his purpose. Images of Tirynus rose unbidden from the far-off depths of memory. The beauty of its tiered streets of carved stone and the breathtaking views from its mountainous heights inspired a mix of longing and vengeance.

The faces of his teachers swam forward over the images of his countless victims. They had screamed for mercy in the end too. Miroth had granted none, just as *he* had been granted none as their pupil. They had sensed in him a strength that would one day outstrip their own and had conspired to break him, grinding him into the stones beneath their feet. The dusty tombs of Tirynus now contained *their* disintegrated bones, while he had gone on to surpass their most envious expectations. And when he escaped the Rith war trials, he took the forbidden knowledge with him.

Soul Taking – the ancient, forgotten art that Miroth alone now possessed. Over the centuries he had perfected his skill, growing in power and refining his techniques. Living longer than any Rith in history, Miroth was immortality itself.

The great Rith city in the Timor Mountains represented all that he hated and all that he would possess. He would raze the Rithspake to the ground when he returned. The place where they had pronounced judgment upon him would be rubble. He would see every last stone of it destroyed and the names of his accusers wiped from the granite monuments. He would sit upon a throne of the sorrows and agonies of his enemies and be free in the knowledge that none would sit higher.

Miroth sighed and reached out to close the shutters, plunging the circular room into restful darkness. The mountain air was cold but at least there was no wind today to scour away his warmth. He turned to face the giant hearth's crackling fire that glowed on the furniture and contents of the study. Miroth stood embracing the heat, stretching his long-fingered hands out towards the flames. He curled them into fists and the sharp fingernails bit into his palms.

Time – he'd had so much of it, had mastered it in ways no other had; yet it seemed now to be bleeding through his hands.

He turned and reached across his desk to pick up the scroll. Unrolling the cracking parchment, he held it up to the firelight, careful not to let it get too close to the flames. The ancient writing was spidery against the translucent surface.

The star charts he had collected over the years gave only hints of the precise timing required for the summoning, until he had found this one scroll. A scroll which contained almost everything he had been searching for – he just needed time to decipher it. But now he was running out of time.

He returned to his desk, pulled an ancient book towards him and gently laid the scroll down beside it. His old bones creaked as he stooped down to scan the text in the dim light. He glanced at the candle next to him; the tip of his staff glowed ominously from where it leaned against the desk as the candle lit up.

Many layers of complex spell casting would have to be accomplished. Each and every layer had to be in its exact time and sequence to allow the summoning to work and to bind the Wyoraith to his purpose. If one thing was missing, or something miscalculated, it would fail.

Time – it was moving too fast. He could feel the ancient power beneath Lok Myrr growing, stirring like a slumbering beast ready to awaken. But it had to be properly chained and fettered before it could be allowed to come to life.

Taken

Torrin didn't listen to the rest of what the young soldier had to say before he was running. Chest pumping, long legs eating up the cobblestone streets, his breath came in short gasps as he raced up the winding road towards the keep.

"They were dressed as castle guardsman – were able to get close enough without raising suspicion – Rowan was taken – his friends seriously injured" The words seared through him as he ran, burning. He pushed himself faster.

Arynilas ran lightly at his side. Torrin had forgotten the Tynithian until he had caught up. He forgot his fatigue from the battle on the walls. He forgot reason. There was only Rowan – *Sweet Erys, no.*

The time it took to run the distance between the city walls and the citadel felt like an eternity. Torrin was covered in sweat and his lungs aching by the time they got there. Preven was waiting for him in the castle foyer. The general held up his hands, making absurd calming gestures.

"What happened, where are they?" Torrin gasped out the words. "Where is Rowan?"

"Every available man is searching the city as we speak," said Preven. "We will find her. As for your brother and friends, they have been taken to the infirmary. Torrin, your brother is in bad shape."

Torrin turned to Arynilas. "Find Dalemar."

The Tynithian nodded and sprang away.

Torrin left the general and began to run again. His mind was numb, only one thought was coherent – I should have been there.

I should have been there.

The keep's infirmary on the lower level did not take long to reach; he gagged at the odour as he entered the room. Cots containing Pellar's wounded lined the large vaulted room. Narrow aisles were left between the rows to allow healers to tend the casualties. Torrin scanned the room, hardly seeing the soldiers with terrible battle wounds. Then he found what he was looking for – his brother and friends laying still, unmoving. Torrin couldn't tell if they were unconscious or asleep. Hathunor had been placed on the floor; no cot was big enough for the Saa Raken. Fresh bandages had been applied to their many wounds. A bloom of blood seeped through the pristine white of the cloth wrapping around Nathel's bare chest.

Cerebus and Elana were both there. The queen looked tired and weak but determined. A part of Torrin noted that if Elana was awake, Cerebus might know whom the traitor was.

With mounting dread, he moved silently forward. It seemed as though he walked through water and couldn't make his limbs move faster. When he reached Nathel, he knelt at his brother's side, grasping the hand that was almost identical to his own, squeezing gently. Nathel opened his eyes slowly. His face was pale, his arms and chest were criss-crossed with shallow wounds. He rolled his head across the pillow to look at Torrin and whispered, "I'm so sorry, Tor. I couldn't protect her – there were too many. Forgive me."

Torrin's throat clenched. He dropped his head to Nathel's shoulder, breathing deeply to steady himself. When he could, he looked back up. There were tears in Nathel's blue eyes.

Torrin squeezed Nathel's hand again. "There is nothing to forgive, brother. I know you would have given your life for her and I will always be grateful to you. I should have been there. It should have been *me*." Torrin began to shake. He gripped Nathel's hand tighter. "I never told her, Nathel. I never told her how much I love her. Erys forgive me, she doesn't know." Anguish closed his throat and the room began to fade in a haze.

Nathel's insistent grip pulled him back. "Tor," he murmured, "she knows. She knows how you feel."

Torrin shut his eyes. He could hope.

A familiar wrath began to burn through the painful band around his chest. But this time it was controlled and calculated, not tainted with madness. He clung to his rising fury and it gave him strength, purpose.

Torrin released Nathel's hand and stood. He turned to Elana, seated on a stool alongside the cot, the king standing behind her, their faces stricken with grief. "How long since they took her?" Torrin's voice was calm, steady. He *would* find her.

"About an hour. Torrin, I'm so sorry…" began Cerebus.

Torrin shook his head. "Miroth wants her alive. They're taking her to him."

Elana brought a slim hand to her mouth, horrified. "What for?"

"We don't know yet. All we know is that he wants her for something. Did anyone see which way they took her?"

Cerebus shook his head. "People fled the square as soon as the fighting started. When the castle guard got to the scene, the battle had ended. Rowan was gone and Nathel and your friends were in bad shape."

Torrin frowned. "Are there any tunnels out of the city from the square? Anything close by they could have used to escape the city?"

Cerebus began to shake his head then narrowed his eyes. "The Temple of Erys. If there was an escape route anywhere, it would be there."

Nathel clutched at Torrin's hand. "Tihir N'Avarin…" He squeezed his eyes shut against sudden pain. "He was there – left the guards before they attacked us."

Torrin's pulse quickened. Tihir N'Avarin – he would kill the man if he could, but not until he'd dragged a full confession from him. He leaned forward and gently kissed his brother's forehead. Nathel was cold. Torrin reached down and gently pulled the blanket up to cover him. He glanced at Borlin and Hathunor; both were still unconscious but didn't look too seriously injured. He released Nathel's hand and looked up at the king.

"I'm going after N'Avarin. If you want it to be official, send Preven with me and some guards; otherwise I'm going to take matters into my own hands." It was no way to speak to his king, but he was beyond caring.

Cerebus lifted a hand. "Torrin, wait, there is more that you should know." He looked down at Elana. "Chancellor Galen is the traitor."

Torrin blinked. Old Galen was the last person Torrin would have suspected. "Are you certain?"

The king nodded. "It appears he was the one who made the copy of the bailey key used by the men who attacked Rowan in her room." Cerebus shook his head and heaved a sigh, looking at the queen again, "And we think he attacked Elana."

Torrin looked down at the queen. "I am sorry, Your Majesty." He took a deep breath and let anger for her abuse add fuel to his wrath.

"He has not been found anywhere within the keep," continued Cerebus. "He is a man of habit, or at least I thought so. He would never stray far without letting me know. If he was not guilty, why would he disappear?" Cerebus sighed in bewilderment. "I just wish I knew."

"What about N'Avarin? He was seen with the men who took Rowan."

Cerebus nodded. "We believe there was a concealed relationship between Galen and N'Avarin."

"Then they must be found and persuaded to share their intentions," said Torrin blackly.

The king looked hard at Torrin, then turned to the nearest guardsman. "Assemble a squad of castle guards. Have them wait for us by the keep entrance." The man saluted and dashed out.

Cerebus turned back to Torrin. "We will solve this together."

Torrin looked at Nathel who nodded. Then he bowed to the queen. "Please, my lady, will you look after them until Dalemar arrives?"

Elana patted Nathel on the shoulder. "Be assured, Torrin, they will receive the best care."

With the king of Pellar at his side, Torrin made for the door. At last his fury was given direction.

The Slayer

Afternoon sun slanted through the open doors of the keep's vaulted entry. Torrin and King Cerebus strode down the steps to where the guardsmen were gathered before the huge doors. Red and gold uniforms filled the hall – it looked as though every member of the castle guard stood assembled. Cerebus stopped to speak to General Preven. They could not all go and leave the keep undefended.

Torrin paced impatiently. He turned back toward the door just as Dalemar came flying through. The Rith's long green coat flapped behind him and his face was painted with excitement. He ran up to Torrin, breathing hard. "I've found it!"

"Found what? Did Arynilas find you?"

Dalemar frowned in puzzlement. "Arynilas? Why no, was he looking for me?" Before Torrin could answer, he rushed on. "I've finally found it, the reference to the *slayer*! Well to be precise, it's the *keeper* not the *slayer* but I know who it is!"

Torrin's eyebrows rose; he had completely forgotten. "The man from Pellar? The Wyoraith Slayer, you know who it is?"

Dalemar shook his head, a crazy grin on his face. "Not from Pellar, it's been right under our noses the whole time! The original *slayer*, all *slayers* for that matter, came from Myris Dar."

Torrin's skin prickled along his neck and down his arms. Something shifted perfectly into place within him and the truth of what Dalemar said resonated like a bell. "The *slayer* was Myrian?"

Dalemar nodded excitedly. "I stumbled across a list of sorts, detailing the history of the *slayers* or *keepers* rather. It seems there was a grammatical error at some point. The text spoke of three *slayers*, all of them Myrian: two men and a woman. And Torrin, it was there!"

"What was?"

"The design that covers Rowan's armour and her sword, the one that looks like a leaf with a dot in the center and lines spanning outward?" Dalemar held up a scrap of parchment and on it was a small drawing of the recurring symbol from Rowan's armour. That same image was also inscribed into the small green stone she wore around her neck. "I found it within the text, drawn in the margin. Torrin, it has been her all along. Everything makes sense now… Miroth, the Mor A'Taith, the Raken trying to take her alive."

"Rowan –"

" – is the *slayer*," Dalemar finished happily for him.

Torrin frowned and shook his head. Dalemar was just now noticing the activity in the entry hall. He glanced quickly back at Torrin. His excitement replaced with worry as he noted Torrin's dark expression, the sweat still drying on his shirt under the leather of his breastplate. "What has happened? Why was Arynilas looking for me?"

"Miroth has taken Rowan with the help of the Priesthood of Erys and Tihir N'Avarin. They have smuggled her out of the city, we think through the Temple of Erys. We are on our way there to find N'Avarin and, if I'm lucky, take the bastard's head."

Dalemar's eyebrows rose and horror crossed his face. "I will come with you."

Torrin shook his head. "No, Dalemar. You are needed here. Nathel, Borlin and Hathunor were all injured in the attack. I do not know if Nathel will make it without your skills."

"Where are they?"

"The keep's infirmary."

Dalemar nodded and began to head for the wide stairs. But he turned back. "Miroth wants her alive, Torrin. She will not be harmed until they get her to Lok Myrr. There is still time for us to catch them." Then he was gone, dashing up the stairs two at a time, long green coat twisting behind.

Torrin watched him go. Yes, he would hunt them – into the very heart of Lok Myrr if need be.

Revenge or Justice

Although the bodies of the false guards were gone, the blood that stained the cobbles in front of the central fountain had not been washed away. Torrin clenched his teeth and balled his fists. Was Rowan's blood there as well? There was far more than could have come from his friends, so they had put up a good fight.

The vast interior of the Temple of Erys was cool and dark after the bright square. As Cerebus's guards fanned out quickly to secure the exits, Torrin scanned the various robed figures and worshippers. The one face he sought was absent

A plump older man in black robes hurried towards them, his gold medallion of Erys swinging wildly back and forth, in an attempt to head them off. "What is the meaning of this? You are in the house of Erys. Show respect!" The priest was puffing, his face flushed red in anger. "Why are all these armed men here?"

"Where is Tihir N'Avarin?" Cerebus asked.

The furious priest turned to the king, his eyes widening. He adjusted his tone. "Your Majesty, forgive me. Patriarch N'Avarin is in his study but he does not wish to be disturbed." The priest trotted along beside them, his arms held wide, vainly trying to contain the column of guards interrupting the afternoon service.

Torrin clamped a hand down on the priest's plump shoulder. "I don't care if he is taking his bath, you will see us to him now." The priest flinched and squeaked as Torrin squeezed.

Darting a glance at the king and his guards, the priest nodded. Torrin kept a firm grip on him as the man led them to a side door beyond which was a set of spiral stairs. Guards started forward to take the lead but Torrin halted them. "We do not want to alert him."

Cerebus nodded curtly and he and Torrin proceeded first up the stairs, their footsteps and the puffing breath of the priest echoing in the space. Torrin frowned down at the sweating man stumbling up the stairs beside him. Rationing hadn't tightened his belt. How many of Erys's senior priests hadn't bothered to sacrifice for the good of Pellaris? Apparently they didn't find it necessary to share with their junior priests, either; young Thaius and most of the novices were gaunt.

The stairs opened onto a wide corridor that curved in a circle around the main space of the temple. Even through his simmering anger, Torrin noticed the smoothly interlocked stonework and the perfect curve of the wall. And what of the probable tunnel lying below the Temple? An image of Rowan being dragged through narrow darkness rose in his mind and he gripped the pommel of his sword.

The plump priest stopped before a large polished wooden door with hinges and latch made of shining bronze. Torrin thrust the man aside into one of the guards and grasped the handle. The door swung silently inward and he stepped into the room beyond.

He stood for a moment, looking for the occupant amongst the opulent furniture and luxury that crowded the room. Seated behind enormous desk, half-hidden behind ornate lanterns and small carved wooden chests was the man he had come for.

Tihir N'Avarin looked up with annoyance at the intrusion, then rose and walked around the desk. His dark eyes flashed over Torrin, taking in the guards in the hallway beyond.

"My King, what brings you to the Temple?" N'Avarin asked smoothly.

Cerebus frowned. "The Lady Rowan was abducted this afternoon. Witnesses place you there."

N'Avarin spread his hands. "Then they are mistaken, Sire. I have not left the temple for the last two days." He lifted his chin and stared haughtily at them. "There is quite a lot to be done as you know and the Priesthood has been trying to relieve some of the pressure on the city."

Torrin stepped forward. "Someone I trust explicitly saw *you* leaving the company of men who captured Rowan of Myris Dar this afternoon."

N'Avarin barked a derisive laugh. "I don't know what you are talking about. I've been here the entire day. Any of the temple priests can vouch for this."

Torrin balled his fists and felt the blood pumping through his veins. He dropped his voice. "They survived, you know, Rowan's companions. They did not die as you expected. The odds were in your favour, weren't they? How could four take on – what was it – twenty, twenty-five?" As Torrin spoke he moved towards

N'Avarin, whose eyes darted past him to Cerebus and the guards. Torrin smiled with satisfaction as the arrogance was slowly replaced by uncertainty and fear. "They wore stolen uniforms which were taken from the barracks. Smart really – it allowed them to get close enough to attack the messenger. And then there is the matter of a certain key. Was it *you* who gave the two men the bailey key? Was it *you* who tied the rope from Rowan's balcony so they could surprise her after nightfall?" Torrin drew his sword. The metallic ring of the blade sliding from the scabbard reverberated in the quiet room.

The priest bristled. "How dare you accuse me of such things. I am the new Patriarch of the Priesthood, sanctified last night by Her holy commission. I would not consort with lowly criminals and bring ill repute on the name of the Priesthood." He frowned over at Cerebus. "The Priesthood will hold *you* accountable for the actions of this man. You must not defile the Temple of Erys!"

"Where did they take her?" Torrin leveled his sword at the priest, barely containing his rage. "How did they get her out of the city?"

N'Avarin shrank back against the desk.

"Torrin!" Cerebus's voice cracked like a whip.

"He is guilty!" Torrin didn't lower his sword.

"I know he is. And he will be dealt with in accordance with Pellarian law. Evidence will be brought against him and he will have his chance to defend himself. For now, it should suffice that he was arrested for treason against the king and Pellar."

N'Avarin sat up and looked at Cerebus in disbelief. "You wouldn't dare," he spat.

Cerebus smiled thinly at him. "There is also the matter of the chancellor's treason. Tell me about Galen, N'Avarin. Did he give you the duplicate key to the bailey or did he give it to the two men who breached our walls *himself*? How long have the two of you been plotting against me?"

N'Avarin's face blanched, but he recovered his composure quickly. It was enough conformation for Torrin though.

"My lord," N'Avarin said with feigned puzzlement. "I only see Chancellor Galen in the keep and in your council chambers. I have no idea what you are speaking about."

"You'll certainly have time to figure it out while sitting in the keep's dungeon," said Cerebus. "Your downfall, N'Avarin, is your arrogance. The Priesthood of Erys is not above the king's justice. If you act openly against me, then you will face the consequences. In your ambition, you failed to keep that in mind." The king flicked his hand and the guards moved past him to arrest the priest. When Cerebus spoke again his voice was low. "And if I find out you were involved in attacking the queen, I'll take your head myself."

Tihir N'Avarin clamped his mouth shut and rolled his wide eyes between Torrin and the king as the guards bundled him unceremoniously from the room.

Torrin ground his sword tip into the plush carpets. He leaned on the hilt, nursing his unfulfilled fury and stared across room at Cerebus.

"You cannot have your revenge, Torrin. Not here, not now."

"You know he will probably get away with it. Politics will get in the way of justice, as it usually does." Torrin hefted his sword and slammed it back into the scabbard.

"I did not create the laws so that you or I could stand above them. You of all people should know that. I would be no better than the tyrants you've been fighting in Ren if I allowed him to be killed now without due process. Revenge is not the same thing as justice."

Torrin scowled. He had little patience for Pellaris's politics. His concern was Rowan. He took a last look around the repulsively extravagant room. "Your hands may be tied, but mine are not. I am going after Rowan. I will free her or die trying. She is the *slayer*, and if the Myrian Seers are right, *she* is our only hope."

Cerebus stood stunned, his dark-circled eyes widening. "Lady Rowan is the *slayer*?" He shook his head in wonder. "Truly?"

"Truly. Dalemar discovered it this morning in your library. I suppose we've all been blinded by our own expectations, but when Dalemar told me, it was as though I'd always known. He discovered that all the *slayers*, also known as *keepers,* were Myrian."

Cerebus nodded slowly, a faraway look in his eyes. Then he refocused on Torrin. “But your companions, your brother. Will you will leave without them?”

Torrin shook his head. “With Dalemar’s help and a bit of luck, they will be ready to travel by now.”

Cerebus’s face had altered and Torrin studied him. The king still looked tired but there was something else – a look in his eyes. What was it?

“Take whatever you need, Torrin – men, food, horses. The hopes of Pellar go with you.”

That was it, thought Torrin.

Hope.

Torrin stepped through the postern door into the keep’s bailey with Cerebus and the guards. He exhaled, relieved to find his brother healthy and waiting with the others. Their horses were ready with bulging saddlebags strapped on. Rowan’s big grey stallion stood patiently while Borlin worked on his tack. Torrin stopped to stroke Roanus’s dappled neck and the big horse whickered softly in response. He twitched his ears and pitched his head as though eager to be off after his mistress.

Torrin clasped forearms with his brother. “Are you fit to travel?”

Nathel looked tired but he smirked. “Thanks to Dalemar and Hathunor, I’m as right as rain. Dalemar healed him first and then together they turned their skills on me.”

“Wee bit o’winoth root, Nathel me lad, and don’t ye forget,” said Borlin lightly.

Nathel closed his eyes and swallowed. “You’d better watch Borlin. He suffered a blow to the head and may have lost his mind.” His brother’s words were light but he was very weak – it had been a close thing.

Arynilas waited close to Dalemar, who stood by his horse, looking worse than his patients. Hathunor loomed behind them.

Torrin strode to the Rith. "Thank you, my friend. I hope you are recovered well enough for the long ride ahead."

Dalemar nodded. "We will ride through the night and beyond, Torrin."

"Find Rowan now," Hathunor rumbled.

Torrin's chest ached at the simple emphatic statement. He sighed gratefully – none his friends had suggested they wait for morning to go after Rowan. The trail would grow no colder.

Torrin tightened the cinch of his saddle and looked up at the walls. The light was almost gone now and the clouds were lit orange with the last rays of the sun. The courtyard was cast in dim shadow as they made their final preparations. Rowan – the *slayer.* He shook his head. It didn't matter, she was who she was and he was going to find her. Torrin closed his eyes. *Sweet Erys, please keep her safe.*

King Cerebus and Queen Elana came down the steps. Torrin stepped around his horse to meet them. Elana held out a long, cloth-wrapped bundle for him. A faint humming came from it. He reached out and drew back the fabric to reveal the hilt of Mor Ranith – Rowan's spell sword.

"It has been like this ever since it was brought back to the keep. The guards were afraid of it." Elana smiled up at him but her eyes held a pleading hope. "You must return it to her. She will need it if she is to defeat Miroth and the Wyoraith."

Torrin grasped the hilt and slid the sword carefully from the cloth. He hefted the light blade and felt its exquisite balance, then whispered the words Rowan had taught him in the marshes. "Dyrn Mithian Irnis Mor Ranith." The sword ceased its humming and he reverently re-wrapped it and secured it to the front of his saddle, looping a strap tightly around the guard. Cerebus stepped forward and handed him Rowan's dagger next, which he slid behind his belt.

"Are you certain you will not need more men with you?" asked the king.

Torrin shook his head. "Thank you, Sire, but we need to move fast, and a small party will be more difficult to detect then a large one. The provisions are welcome though."

Cerebus reached out and clasped Torrin's shoulder. "You will find her, Torrin. She will not be lost to you, my friend." Pulling Torrin forward into an embrace, he repeated with quiet conviction, "*She* will *not* be lost to you." The terrible burden Torrin had carried for so long eased in that moment and strength flowed through his limbs, settling into his chest. Nodding, he returned Cerebus's embrace.

A soldier came pelting down the steps. "We have found the tunnel, Sire," he said, puffing. "It was well hidden but large enough to accommodate horses."

Torrin's pulse quickened – finally. He swung into the saddle and turned Black, his friends falling in behind him as he exited the bailey. But when Torrin passed through the gate, he halted his horse, pulling in a sudden breath.

The entire castle guard and many of the Pellarian infantry and officers stood arrayed across the square in front of the keep – a forest of pikes, glinting in the last sun. As one they lifted the pikes and hammered them into the flagstones with a resounding crack. A horn sounded and a multitude of deep voices rang forth in salute to the lost warrior.

As they rode past, Torrin noticed a group of soldiers, smaller and slighter than the rest.

A swell of pride filled him.

They were women.

The Chase Begun

Torrin ignored the scandal they caused as they clattered through the vast Temple of Erys – shod hooves ringing on the polished marble floor. Priests flapped around them, a flock of angry birds but the guards Cerebus had sent to search for the tunnel waved them on toward the door to the catacombs.

Dismounting, Torrin led Black through the door. The stallion balked only a little before plunging down the steep stairs. The horses slid and clattered down in a chaotic scramble until the bottom opened to a dark corridor with storeroom doors and small cells, presumably for the priest initiates. Torrin walked toward the end where a guard was stationed next to the entrance of a large cold-storage cellar. Torrin nodded to the guard as he led his horse through into the cellar. Barrels and kegs stood stacked and rolled to the side to reveal the tunnel entrance. Its metal door stood open to the yawning darkness beyond. Torrin frowned as he scanned the room. The priests had been keeping much of their hoarded food here. As Dalemar led his horse in, Torrin called to the guard. The man squeezed in past the horses. "Yes Sir?"

"Find Priest Thaius," said Torrin. "And put him in charge of arranging for the redistribution of this food to the soldiers on the wall and the remaining people of Pellaris. Tell him it is for his Restoration."

The soldier grinned. "As good as done, sir."

Torrin turned to his friends. "Ready?"

"Aye, Torrin," said Borlin with his lanterns already lit. The others nodded and Hathunor stooped down to enter the dark passage. Torrin took one of the lanterns from Borlin and followed the Saa Raken.

Like the tunnel through which they had entered the city, it was just large enough for a horse to be led through single file. Torrin steeled himself against the slow pace but as each footstep carried them deeper into the darkness, his frustration increased. The black, twisting way seemed to go on and on with no sign of an end. Finally, Torrin halted and called back to Arynilas. "Can you sense if we are past the city yet?"

"Yes, we passed its walls some time ago. I feel only parkland above," said the Tynithian.

Torrin swore. "It must stretch further into the surrounding hills than the other tunnel." He stepped forward again and pulled on Black's reins. Let this *end* so the hunt can begin, he thought desperately. The darkness was stuffy and dense and Torrin felt as though he was breathing water, drowning in shadows. Rowan was being taken further and further away at a swift pace.

A rumble from Hathunor sounded through the blackness ahead – an end. Torrin jogged forward pulling his horse. His lantern illuminated an entrance like the one they went through in the temple. Hathunor looked down at Torrin; his expression, lit from below, was nightmarish. Together they pushed on the door and felt a sudden breeze of cool, fresh air. Torrin sucked in a deep breath in relief and they pushed harder. The metal squealed and the door opened enough for them to bring the horses out. "Can you check outside, Hathunor?" asked Torrin. "I want to know what we are walking into."

Hathunor rumbled and slipped into the night. A moment later her was back. "Hathunor sense no others."

They filed out and gathered a short distance from the entrance. Torrin looked up at the twin moons and starry sky; it was good to be above ground. Even the horses tossed their heads and snorted in pleasure.

"Well at least the tunnel has taken us far away from Pellaris and the Raken army," said Dalemar. "There should be little worry of being detected this far out."

"Here!" Arynilas, who had stepped further away, came back to the horses and began to shed his clothes.

"Have you found the trail?" Torrin walked to the Tynithian.

"About fifteen men, mounted and moving in single file. Their trail is saturated. It will be easy to follow." Arynilas stuffed his cloths into his saddlebag and began to shift.

"Stay close to Borlin's lantern so we can follow *you*," said Torrin.

The fox yipped and then disappeared – a black shadow against a black night.

Torrin hastily tightened his cinch and swung into the saddle. The trail left by Rowan's captors led due east from the tunnel entrance, straight towards Krang.

Borlin's lantern bobbed through the darkness. It lit the ground in a small circle as he swept it back and forth in slow arcs to keep the black shadow that was Arynilas in sight. Despite Torrin's frustration, they *were* making good time with Arynilas following the scent.

Torrin pulled his eyes away from the lit trail to let his night vision return. He stretched his cramped shoulders and rubbed his gritty eyes. There were maybe two hours now until dawn, and he longed for the light of day when they could follow the trail rapidly. He glanced ahead to the distant horizon beyond the teeth of the Krang Mountains where dawn glowed like a beacon. The sky glittered with stars in the midnight blue and the cold air carried the hint of snow. He hoped Rowan was warm enough.

Torrin had no doubt they would catch up to the men who had taken her. Freeing her was *all* that mattered now, but then what? He had some vague notion of assassinating the Black Rith but until they located him and could see what they faced, there was really no way to plan.

The light had increased imperceptibly, and the surrounding trees and rolling hills of Pellar were now visible as dark shadows. They were at least seven hours behind the men they tracked. It might take a full day to make up the distance.

Torrin willed the dawn to come faster.

Part III

Painful Awakenings

Pain – the world slid between blackness and a swirling, sickening jumble. A wash of sound slipped forward and then receded: a creaking and jingling; a muffled voice; laughter. The blackness was a relief but the pain always returned. It flared suddenly – hard, jagged and razor edged. The surface of the world was close. Sounds became clear: jingling tack, creaking leather, the thud of hooves. A Bird called and the air was cool.

Rowan regained consciousness with a sickening lurch. The sounds were smothered beneath the pounding, searing pain that lanced across the side of her head. Her face felt swollen and hot; blood beat in her temples. Her shoulders and wrists were on fire, the joints pulled into strained angles.

She opened her eyes and the ground rushed by, her long braid hung swaying. Nausea swept over her and she closed her eyes, clamping her jaw shut, fighting as the blackness came for her once more.

Focus. Where am I?

The thought was groggy, slow.

She tried to move and the pain in her arms punched through the pounding in her head. She gasped and felt the blackness move closer.

A horse, I am on a horse.

Re-opening her eyes slowly, Rowan steeled herself against the sweeping nausea. Turning her head caused the pain in her skull to increase, and tears sprang to her eyes. Through them, she saw a line of horsemen spread out ahead of the horse she was tied to. She counted seven before she had to close her eyes and wait for the rolling sickness to subside. To the rear were at least ten more, spread out single file, wending through a forest in cool greyness. Was it dusk or dawn? Rowan thought hard – A bird call. Dawn.

She closed her eyes again, straining to remember. The scenes of the desperate battle in the square flashed through her mind: too many to fight; the touch of Nathel's back against her own suddenly vanishing and her friends down; panic; the final blow to the side of her head. What had happened to Nathel and Borlin and Hathunor?

I am being taken to Krang. A shiver ran up her back. How far from Pellaris had they brought her? How much time had passed while she lay like a sack on the back of a horse? She pulled herself away from why Miroth wanted her. I am not there yet, she thought grimly. I have to get away from these men.

Even if she could get loose, she doubted she was in any condition to run or fight. Testing her bonds sent ripples of pain along her arms, and she couldn't stifle her groan.

"She's awake!" yelled someone from behind in a rough voice.

The column halted. Saddles creaked and spurs jingled as riders dismounted. A man walked into view but all Rowan saw was a pair of thick legs covered in grease-stained leather. A large, dirty hand reached for her braid, grasped it and coiled the hair around thick fingers before yanking upwards.

Rowan gasped as pain lanced through her head and neck. The man's fearsome face swam into her vision. He was completely bald with a long, white scar cutting down across his brow and through his eye, puckering the lid. The eye itself was completely white.

"Get her watered and fed." His breath reeked with of sour wine, and his voice was raspy and low as though his vocal cords were damaged.

He released her, and someone grasped her legs and hauled. Her chest scraped across the saddle and she noted thankfully that she still wore her leather breastplate. As the world tilted back upright, she almost blacked out again.

When her feet touched the ground, her legs collapsed and she went down with a grunt. Laughter came from the surrounding men. Rowan took deep breaths, waited for the pain and nausea to subside. They were tending to horses and finding food – sprawling in the dew-drenched grass to gnaw on hunks of bread and dried meat.

Some of them sported cuts and gashes hastily tended. One man unstopped a waterskin and squatted in front of her, pouring as much of it over her as into her mouth. He was missing his front teeth and had a broken nose with purple bruises spreading to his eyes, and she remembered suddenly – it had been the pommel of her sword that had smashed his face. She smiled grimly through the pounding in her head, regretting it immediately as the man snarled, backhanding her across the jaw. The blow blasted her head sideways, flaring new pain in her head. He reached out and grabbed her roughly by the collar of her leather breastplate, shaking her.

The men around her laughed again. "You show 'er, Gil. Teach the bitch a lesson fer breakn' yer nose."

"Oi, save some fer me!"

The rasping voice ended the men's laughter, and they fell back, suddenly finding something of supreme interest elsewhere. The man holding her was clouted on the back of the head and Rowan fell backward as she was released.

As her blurred vision cleared, she looked up to the scarred face of their leader. "The package is to be delivered undamaged or payment will not be made in full." His raw voice carried clearly in the early morning, and she noted the criss-cross of more scars covering his bare arms. He saw her appraisal and bent down. "Best not be thinking of escape or causing any more trouble, lovely, or you'll lose what privileges you have. I've no problem with keeping you unconscious and slung over the back of a horse all the way to Lok Myrr." A grin split his face and several gold teeth flashed.

"How long have I been unconscious?" Rowan's voice came out a thick whisper. Her jaw hurt and her throat was raw.

Scarface smiled again, his white eye eerie. Ignoring her question, he turned away to spit into the grass. "Mount up!"

The men scrambled to their feet and made ready to leave. Rowan was hauled to her feet and supported her as her legs buckled again. The ropes around her ankles were sliced and the cords at her wrists untied. Blood rushed into her fingers, warming them, and she gritted her teeth in agony as they pulled her hands forward and retied them in front. She was lifted up onto the horse, her tied hands lashed tightly to the high pommel of the saddle.

The column began to move again as the morning sun crested the horizon.

Teeth gritted, Rowan tried in vain to free her hands. She was as weak as a newborn kitten. There is time, she thought. It was a long way to Krang. She would gather her strength and wait for an opportunity.

Rowan opened her aching eyes and looked up at the sun – still only midday. *Sweet Erys it felt like forever*. Her mouth was parched and the nausea came in rolling waves. Her horse stumbled and a new burst of pain exploded through her stupor. *Please, let them stop*. She swayed in the saddle and longed for rest. A cold wind gusted and Rowan shivered – apart from her leather cuirass and various armour pieces, only one layer of cloth protected her. She sucked in a breath of the chilly air. Maybe it would clear her head a little. The column traveled through foothills with copses of deciduous trees clustered against their slopes. Hawks circled above, an occasional cry piercing the silence. Burning circled her wrists and blood had dried from the rope cuts. Rowan tried to flex her fingers but her hands were numb. She winced and closed her eyes.

A whistle sounded and her horse halted with the column. Two men came forward and untied her from the saddle. Rowan held her breath as they pulled her roughly down and dumped her on the ground. They tossed a waterskin next to her and she struggled to sit up so she could reach it. With her hands tied in front of her, at least she would be able to drink on her own. Gasping at the pain in her hands, she attempted to unstop the skin with near-useless fingers. Finally, she got it open and drank as much as she could. A man approached and pulled it from her grasp before she was done. He thrust a piece of hard, dried meat into her hands. Rowan looked at the meat and her stomach heaved. She swallowed hard, fumbling to tuck it away for later into her breastplate. Exhausted, she collapsed back onto the ground and closed her eyes, concentrated on relaxing every muscle while taking deep, steadying breaths. After a moment, the sickening spin of the world stilled and the pain in her head eased.

She awoke with a man holding her in a vice-like grip while he applied a sticky, stinging paste to her head wound. He released her and stood back; behind him, Scarface watched with his glaring white eye. They roused her roughly to her feet, lifting her to be re-tied to the saddle. Rowan steeled herself as the thudding pain and dizzy spiralling returned.

The afternoon waned; the column stopped again and Rowan woke from a doze. The two men walked up on either side of her horse from behind – they were not going to underestimate her. Rowan frowned; it would make escape more difficult. Once again she was untied and pulled from the horse.

Scarface came over and squatted down in front of her. He reached out and grasped her chin, turning her head to look at the wound. Rowan pulled away from him, her head spinning. "My condition has not changed. Rest assured you will likely get your full payment."

He smiled, gold teeth flashing. Reaching out, he laced his fingers through the hair at the back of her head and wrenched her towards him. His lips brushed her cheek. "The terms of payment are for undamaged merchandise," he whispered. "Nothing was said about spoiling the wares in other ways. It's a long way to Lok Myrr, sweetness." His whisper was surprisingly free of the rasping that marred his speaking voice.

Rowan stilled as his grimy fingers trailed down her neck. He licked her ear and she suppressed the urge to strike him. With her hands tied in front, she could still inflict serious injury but it would only get her another beating. *Wait – a chance will present itself.*

Instead she whispered back, "You will come to regret that touch, taken without my permission – and when you die with my sword in your belly, you will remember this moment."

He drew back, surprise flickering over his face. Then he leaned forward and kissed her roughly.

Rowan stiffened against the onslaught – the foul taste of his mouth, his teeth scraping against hers. He broke off with an arrogant grin and thrust her back down into the grass. Standing, he licked his lips and looked around at his mercenaries. "Very nice." There were chuckles and snickers from the men.

Rowan lay still, ignoring them and focusing on calming her pounding heart. She willed herself to relax as frightening possibilities ran unchecked through her mind.

All too soon it was time to move on again. Someone kicked her leg, and before she could sit up by herself they grabbed her, lashing her tightly to the saddle once again. As the column began to move east, Rowan tested her bonds. The rope tying her to the saddle was a little looser than usual – only a little.

The column crested a small rise, and a deep valley spread out below with a huge river flowing through it. The broad expanse of water had carved out a steep canyon to the left as it sped on its way towards the Eryos Ocean. Evergreen trees carpeted the high shoulders of the canyon, their tops just catching the last of the slanting sun. She remembered the map in Cerebus's study with the blue line inked out as it made its twisting way from the great marshland. It was the Pellar River – there was no other large river between Pellaris and Krang.

The line of horsemen began the descent to the river below. The swirling current of water was fast but shallow enough for the horses to cross where the river spread out before the narrows of the canyon. Rowan worked at the ropes holding her to the saddle. Clearer than she had felt all day, she turned again to look at the canyon where the water disappeared. In the evening light, the shadow of the canyon concealed the course of the river and it was hard to say how rough it was. The seed of a plan formed. *I will never outrun them but maybe, just maybe –.*

The first few riders entered the dark, swift waters and began to work their way out into the main current. The horses were shoulder deep by the time they were halfway across. The men in front of Rowan heeled their mounts down the steep bank. Ignoring the searing pain in her wrists, she pulled harder at the ropes binding her. When her horse balked at the water, dancing sideways along the bank, it almost unseated the man holding its lead line.

Two men from behind rode up on either side of her. They cursed at her spooked horse, slapping its rump. The animal suddenly launched itself out into the fast current. Rowan gasped as the ropes tore at her wrists but they gave a little. Cold water splashed up at her and she tested the lashings again.

The two men flanking her kicked their horses into the water to keep their positions. She waited until her horse was halfway across, watching the current sweep by under its belly until it rose to cover her feet and shins. This should be fast enough – it had to be.

Rowan took a deep breath. She wrenched at the ropes, clenching her teeth against the pain and pulled back to stretch the lashing as far as they would go. Then she twisted her hands forward to drag herself free of the saddle pommel. Most of the rope came away but the end was still wrapped and she had to wind her tied hands around and around the pommel to free the rest.

The men riding beside and ahead were focused on the water in front of their horses. But a sharp cry came from behind and they jerked their heads up, turning to look. The man on her right made a grab for her just as the last loop came free. Rowan leaned away from him and then swung her hands with fingers laced into a double fist. She hit him in the jaw and his head snapped back, unbalancing him so he had to scrabble at his saddle to keep from being dumped in the river.

The man on her other side clamped a hand around her upper arm. Rowan swept her arms up and around in a circle, binding his thumb. He cursed and released his grip; then tried for another. She kicked him savagely in the ribs.

Head pounding with the exertion, dulling the shouts and commotion around her, Rowan spun to assess her chances. The men behind were plunging their skittish horses into the river amid plumes of spraying water. Ahead of her, men along the line struggled to get their mounts turned. A horse slipped in the fast current and went down, dousing its rider and getting swept downstream several paces before finding its feet. Scarface had wrenched his horse around and was splashing back towards her, screaming orders and cursing his men.

Kicking her right leg over her horse's neck, she jumped into the river. The shock of the freezing water sucked the air from her lungs and she gasped in a ragged breath; her legs and arms went numb. She passed under the neck of the horse beside her. Its rider reached down but the water swept her from his grasp. Rowan stuck her feet out in front of her, kicking her legs to keep her head above water. Her hands, still tied, floated in front of her and she struggled to free them. She risked a glance back. The river had already taken her far downstream. Scarface was waving his arm and shouting; men were jumping into the water after her but their metal armour and chain-mail sucked them under the surface.

Rowan turned to face the river ahead. The steep walls of the canyon were approaching fast and the river's current was growing rougher. Cold water washed over her face; her boots had filled and she struggled to keep her head above the churning surface. Her right leg glanced off a stone beneath the water, spinning her around. As she kicked frantically to turn herself forward again, another wave splashed over her and she swallowed water, coughing.

Now she was between the high canyon walls. The roar of the water echoed from the cliffs and the sheer walls of the canyon plunged directly into the water. The racing current had smoothed the stone into rippling sheets of rock without a finger-hold to cling to. She focused all her energy on just keeping her head above the surface as the violent river rocked and spun her about. She risked another glance back up stream but couldn't tell how far the waters had taken her.

The river bent sharply and the current sped up, swinging around as the canyon turned. Rowan cried out as she struck a large rock below the surface. She was spun sideways and struggled to pull in a full breath.

I have to get out of this – the thought sluggish. The icy current and the adrenaline had cleared her head but now her limbs were wooden. She hit another rock but felt no pain this time – only the force of the blow.

Her head slipped under and she kicked weakly to regain the air. She broke the surface and filled her lungs before the river sucked her back under. Her legs would not work properly. Opening her eyes, she looked up at the light but couldn't get there. Shadowy forms of boulders and riverweeds sped by as she tumbled through the dimness. Her lungs burned and her heart pounded in her ears. She no longer knew which direction to swim. The cold was gone now and she felt only tired. It was so calm here in the weightless, watery world. Wasn't the world above a harsh place? Wasn't this far better, quiet and safe? Her panic receded and peaceful contentment slid into its place. Why was it so important to reach the surface? She fumbled dimly for the answer, her vision fading.

Her feet struck something. Gravel gritted against the soles of her boots. Her legs relaxed until her knees crunched as well. The need to draw breath was on one hand overwhelming but on the other – why bother? Surely this calm dark place would keep her safe.

Her father's face smiled at her and her heart wrenched. How could he look at her with such pride when she had failed him? Scenes from her life floated through her mind – random images of home; her mother; her little brother and the pranks he played. Her friends were there too, their faces concerned – and Torrin, his expression intense. He was speaking but she couldn't hear. It was important, his gaze insistent, compelling.

Torrin.

The clouded haze of her thoughts burned away. She connected to something so much greater – infinitely larger and unknowable than her own life. With all the strength she had left, Rowan kicked off the river's bottom.

Her head broke the surface and she pulled sweet air into her lungs. In that instant the world glowed with crystal clarity – the beads of water that flew from her head; her own breath resonant and filled with life; every detail and nuance of the high canyon walls revealed in sublime clarity

I am exactly where I am meant to be.

She sucked in a second breath. *My life has always been moving towards this place.* The death of her father was a catalyst for an unbroken chain of events bringing her here. Even Miroth, working his evil deep within Krang, was as he should be – an opposition to be realized and overcome.

Rowan pulled another less portentous breath and the heightened consciousness began to fade, but an encompassing peace remained. Her friends were out there somewhere, searching for her. The knowledge settled around her like a protective cloak.

The water's surface was smooth and calm; she was in an eddy, away from the tumult of the river's current. She kicked feebly with her legs, unsure if her limbs were responding. Her foot hit gravel, then her knees and her still-bound hands. Rowan crawled forward out of the water, sopping clothes dragging at her body. Unable to lift herself free of the water, she rolled and squirmed up the gravel bank. A clump of bare bushes offered scant shelter. Curling into a tight ball, she fell instantly into a heavy, exhausted sleep.

The River Pellar

Torrin watched the flurry of activity along the shoreline below. In the dusk light, the broad expanse of the River Pellar glinted like a silver ribbon. Arynilas and Nathel lay nearby, all of them hidden from view by the long grass at the top of the rise. Torrin rubbed his tired eyes and re-focused below, frowning. He counted eighteen horses but only fifteen men, some of whom were being dragged from the fast flowing water.

There was no sign of Rowan.

Torrin searched again. Five riders whirled their mounts on the far shore and headed downstream at a gallop. Another five splashed back across the river toward the rise. Torrin tensed as they reached the shore, their horses scrambling up the bank amid flying sand and gravel. Instead of riding up the slope to where the three of them lay hidden, the riders turned and headed downstream as well. Two of the remaining riders waited by the opposite shore. While one scavenged the bodies of their drowned companions, the other held the riderless horses, his bald scalp glimmering in the gathering dark. One of the horses – Torrin's breath caught.

"Arynilas, can you see if one of the horses has no bridle?"

The Tynithian searched for a moment. "There is a mount with only a halter and long shank. It is tied to the pommel of the bald man's horse."

Torrin nodded

"They look as though they have lost something, don't they?" said Nathel. Torrin glanced at him. It was the first time his brother had spoken in hours and he almost sounded like his old, irrepressible self. Nathel turned and caught his eye, a faint smile played around his mouth.

Downstream, the riders were disappearing into trees that covered the top of the high canyon. Torrin turned his attention back to the haltered horse. Rowan had been tied to that horse. But where was she now? It would be a good opportunity to escape, provided you were a strong swimmer. The men who had been dragged from the water had either been knocked in or had jumped in after her; but wearing chain-mail and breastplates – they would have sunk like stones. A slow appreciative smile spread across his face, then it vanished. *I just hope she was able to swim the rapids.*

He turned to the others. "We go downstream."

Nathel and Arynilas were moving even as he spoke.

Once mounted, they kept below the rise, circling wide to enter the dense trees without being seen. Arynilas quickly found the trail left by the five searchers and they picked up speed.

We have to find them before they find Rowan.

Torrin caught glimpses of the river down in the canyon and his heart jumped into his throat. He swallowed hard. The Pellar narrowed to a fierce torrent through these tight, sheer walls; black and formidable in the dim light, it tore past huge boulders huddled ominously in the center of the flood, spraying white foam against the darkness.

If she survived the water, they probably wouldn't be able to find her until the morning. Torrin shook his head, frowning. *She is strong.* He focused on the path ahead.

Arynilas held up a hand and they all stopped. Over the blowing of the horses, Torrin caught the faint sound of shouts – men calling back and forth across the canyon. Arynilas turned to look at Torrin, his black hair blending into the surrounding shadow, making his pale face glow.

"They are three hundred paces ahead, maybe less."

Torrin nodded, drawing his sword. The others took up their weapons and they moved forward through the dark trees.

They took the five men utterly unaware. Arynilas's arrows took two before the remaining three even knew of the danger and began to draw their swords. Torrin killed one from the back of his horse and Hathunor, who was swifter than the horses, dispatched the last two in a blur of claws and teeth.

The mercenaries had been well armed and provisioned. Torrin cleaned the blood from his sword and moved to the edge of the canyon to scan the river below. They needed to find a way down to the water so they could begin to search for Rowan.

They mounted up and continued along the top of the canyon, moving carefully through the gathering darkness. Faint shouts carried across to them from the other side of the canyon – hails to comrades that would never be returned.

Hard Won Freedom

Rowan woke shivering and gasped as she tried to move. Everything protested with pain – back aching sharply; arms, wrists and head needled with pain. She tried to bring her hands to her face but they were still tied, the end of the rope snaking underneath her side. She looked groggily around. Dawn brought only a little light into the deep canyon. Huge boulders rose around her like a forest and the canyon wall glimmered, pale, behind her. The river roared past ten paces away, its rolling surface charcoal black.

Her shivering increased as a cold wind stirred the bush she was curled under, waving leafless branches at the lightening sky, where a few stars still sparkled.

She rolled painfully onto her stomach, gritting her teeth as her cold, wet shirt pressed against her chest, then levered up slowly and crawled awkwardly from under the bush. When she sat back on her heels, pain flared in her right thigh. The fabric of her leggings was torn and blood oozed from a gash beneath. Casting a look around her to make sure she was alone, she brought her hands up to her face to better see the rope around her wrists. The knot wasn't complicated but the water had swollen the rope, making it tighter. She worked at prying it free with her teeth, ignoring the ache it caused them and the burn in her wrists as the coarse, sodden fibres rasped against her skin. Eventually she worked it free. Her hands warmed a little as blood pumped into them, and she rubbed them together, blowing into her palms, until the shivering increased and her mind began to fog.

I have to get up and move. Warm up.

Somehow she summoned the energy to push herself to her feet, locking her knees to keep her legs from buckling. A single tremulous step sent pain shooting through her right leg, but it was bearable. Another step. Her feet stung as the blood was forced through them. Another step brought her to the nearest boulder and she reached out to steady herself against the rough stone. She took a deep breath; at least the spinning sensation and nausea had passed, but she weak and shaky.

The canyon was still steep here but the bottom was wider, strewn with large boulders and small trees and shrubs. In the increasing light she could make out the dense trees at the top of the canyon. She would need to walk downstream to find a way to climb out. *How long was the walk back to Pellaris*? She frowned – first she had to survive the elements and her injuries.

Rowan hugged herself, looking up at the high canyon. The men she had escaped last night would surely be searching downriver. There was more tree cover near the canyon wall to the right, where she could hide under the spreading branches. Pushing herself away from the rock, she took a step toward the shelter.

She took another step and saw the rope she had pulled from her hands lying coiled on the pebbles. Making her way to it, she picked it up – she might very well need it and she couldn't take the chance that the men searching for her would find it.

As Rowan neared the trees she was heartened to find her limbs slowly becoming more responsive, but with the improving blood flow the pain in her leg grew more intense, overshadowing the throbbing aches from all her other wounds combined.

Progress would be slow and painful.

River Search

In the pale light of dawn, Torrin peered through the mist that hung thick in the bottom of the canyon, obscuring everything. Nearby, he could barely see Hathunor's tall, black form, huge head swinging as he walked; somewhere across the canyon were the rest of his companions, searching through the fog. He couldn't tell rock from shrub without getting almost close enough to touch them. If Rowan was unconscious, they could walk right past her and never know it.

Arynilas, in his fox form appeared ahead, trotting with his nose to the ground in search of Rowan's scent – nothing so far. At least that meant she was still upstream, or so they hoped. Dalemar emerged too and as the mist began to clear, he could see Nathel and Borlin as well across the fast-flowing current.

The call of a bird sounded over the rush of water. He cocked his head to listen for a reply. It was not a bird of Pellar – they had used the whistling sound as a contact call for years. Even when there was no danger of unfriendly ears hearing voices, they used it. Rowan would recognize it.

If she heard it.

Torrin sighed and rubbed his eyes. *She would be fine; she had to be!* He cast his gaze out over the misty riverbed again, his vision snagging on anything that looked like a figure. Dalemar, his blond hair blending with the mist, headed toward the canyon wall on the right to search a stand of trees. Arynilas waited panting, as Torrin caught up. The footing was treacherous next to the water's edge with dew-slicked rocks that could easily turn an ankle. The fox navigated them effortlessly, while Torrin had to place each foot carefully.

Bringing his fingers to his mouth, he blew a sharp whistle that drew to a warbling close. The taste of salt lingered as he waited for a return call, hoping.

With the exception of Arynilas in his fox form, they had decided to wait for the moons to rise before starting the search – too much risk of passing by Rowan in the darkness. The wait had been unbearable for Torrin. They had tried to rest during the few hours it took for the pale half moons to rise high enough. But visions of Rowan injured and needing help had flashed through his mind, each worse than the last. Before the moons had risen completely, he had bolted to his feet, chased by the image of her caught among the boulders like spring storm debris. Stumbling to the river's edge, he had peered into the black shadows and forced his eyes to look for shapes in the dark.

An echo of the whistle cut through his thoughts. Torrin froze. Arynilas stilled and perked his ears. Torrin glanced quickly across the river. Nathel and the others were behind them. It couldn't have come from them.

Torrin repeated his whistle, waited – breath held.

A faint echo of it filtered back to him from the thinning mist. He scrambled forward, slipping on slick stones. He whistled again. The call returned, stronger now. Unmistakable.

Torrin searched the mist ahead – trees, boulders, river, his eyes swept over them all looking for what he wanted to see, needed to see.

And then she was there, her slim figure gaining mass and deepening in color, emerging out of the paleness. She was moving slowly and Torrin closed the distance. When he could finally make out her face, her grin was all he saw and his own face stretched to mirror it. Smiling foolishly, his weariness falling away, Torrin swept Rowan up in his arms, spinning around and crushing her to his chest.

"What took you so long?" she breathed.

Torrin barked a laugh and placed her back on her feet but the smile slipped from his face when her knees buckled. He caught her he and looked at her carefully.

Her brave grin couldn't cover the pain and exhaustion in her face. Dark circles rested under her eyes; a purple bruise spread across her jaw and a long gash on the side of her head, just past her hairline, was inflamed and covered with dried blood. Torrin took her cold hands in his. Her sleeves only partially covered the angry red burns and raised welts where ropes had been tied. A large slash in her leggings revealed dark blood crusted over a wound on her right thigh.

And that was only the damage he could see.

Rowan shook her head. "Mostly scrapes and bruises. I will be fine."

Torrin nodded and reached up to push the loose hair back from her face. His fingers lingered on her cheek. "I thought I'd lost you."

Rowan closed her eyes and a tear slipped down her face. "Me too."

He swallowed and gently pulled her into a hug – there was so much he wanted to say but just to have her standing safe before him was enough for now.

Arynilas was there suddenly, black bushy tail wagging and then Dalemar. Nathel and Borlin waved madly at her from the opposite shore. Rowan caught sight of them and laughed. "Thank Erys Nathel is recovered," she said. "The last time I saw him he was gravely wounded."

Hathunor splashed across the river as though it was a creek and flew past Torrin to pick Rowan up in his huge black arms. When he set her down she turned to hug Dalemar as well. Arynilas yipped and she scratched his head, a smile on her cracked lips.

Torrin pulled his water skin out and unstopped it, placing it in her hands. Her fingers shook so he cupped his own around them to help her raise it to her lips. Dalemar stripped off his long coat, placing it around her shoulders. She nodded in thanks.

"There are at least fifteen men looking for me, I don't know if the river claimed any of them." She scanned the top of the canyon.

Torrin nodded grimly. "There were twelve when we caught up with them at the crossing. It must have been just after you escaped. Ten were sent downstream, five on each side. We have not yet come across the ones on the east side, but on this side they will not return to their comrades."

Rowan looked closely at him and nodded.

Torrin turned and waved across the river at Nathel and Borlin. They would have to walk back downstream to the place they crossed earlier. He took a quick scan of the canyon. The mist was almost gone; it was time they started back to the horses and looked for a concealed campsite where Rowan could get warm and have her wounds seen to.

As they took their first steps back down stream though, Rowan stumbled. Her shivering had increased. Torrin scooped her up into his arms. She felt so light it made his heart ache.

"It's alright, I can walk," she protested.
Torrin ignored her. It was an excuse to hold her close.

Safe Harbour

Rowan rested her head against Torrin's neck. His skin was warm and rough with whiskers. She breathed in his comforting scent of leather, oil and horses. Despite her protests, she would collapse the moment she was placed on her feet. For the first time in a very long while, she allowed herself be taken care of. Her eyelids dragged downward; her shivering slowly subsided.

Torrin murmured to her under his breath and she was reminded of the night they traveled through the tunnel into Pellaris. She listened with a small smile on her face as she descended into sleep, warmed as much by his quiet voice as by the heat of his body.

She awoke as Torrin placed her gently on the ground. Bereft of the warmth from his body, she began to shiver again but didn't have the strength to open her eyes. She heard Dalemar's soft voice and felt his warm hand touch her forehead. A hot tingling sensation spread through her, flowing out to her fingertips and down to her toes. The pain in her body disappeared.

She fell back asleep.

A rocking motion woke her a second time. She found herself wrapped in a blanket and nestled in Torrin's arms once again as he rode. Dense trees passed by on both sides and mid-morning light filtered down through the canopy. Nathel rode in front of them and she caught a glimpse of Hathunor's dark form further ahead.

Torrin looked down. "How are you feeling?"

She smiled sleepily. "Better, thank you."

"Dalemar was able to heal most of your wounds."

She nodded. "And you? How are you?"

"We are all tired and in need of sleep."

"That is not what I meant."

The muscles in his jaw jumped, and he swallowed. His blue eyes were very dark. "There is so much I should have said to you in Pellaris. When I thought I might not ever be able to tell you how I felt, I realized how wrong I've been."

Rowan's heart quickened but she kept silent.

"I've been trying so hard to keep from reliving the pain of seven years ago when Emma and the girls were taken from me that I lost sight of the truth. To lose you without saying what I needed to say, without letting you know how I feel would have been unbearable." Torrin searched Rowan's eyes and took in a deep breath. "I have loved you from the moment I first looked into those challenging green eyes of yours, standing alone and barely keeping yourself upright with five strangers surrounding you. I spent the time since trying to deny it, fighting the way I feel – telling myself it was the message you carried, the mission that was important, but that was my fear speaking. I love you."

Rowan closed her eyes, tears close to the surface – something deep within shifted, as though a part, missing all the years of her life was set into its rightful place. *Torrin.*

"And I love you," she whispered. "I realized it fully the night we entered Pellaris. Like you, I think maybe I have always known but the message was too important. There was no room for my feelings. I knew you were wrestling with your past and it did not seem there was a chance for more."

He traced a fingertip down her cheek. The tension left him and his eyes sparkled as a smile transformed his face. "Can you ever forgive a fool for fearing to look beyond the ghosts of his past?"

Rowan grinned. "You may be many things, Torrin, son of Ralor, but you are no fool. Stubborn perhaps would be a better description…"

He chuckled and reached back down to his reins, guiding his big black horse around a fallen tree.

Rowan sighed drifted off again, content, caught between blissful dreams and semi-awareness of the movement of the horse and Torrin's presence next to her.

No doubt the future held more terrible struggles, but for the moment all was right upon Erys's wide world.

Traitor's Chance

Galen looked out the window toward the city's walls, but saw neither the late afternoon light on the rooftops nor the birds that circled the dome. He rarely spent time this high up in the Temple and the tiny room he was occupying felt like a cell. Though Galen could hardly compare it to the black hole in which the patriarch must be locked, deep in Pellaris Keep. The dungeon, under Cerebus rule, was rarely used for the kind of dreadful things that occurred there in the past – but the waste of it was intolerable. The patriarch was needed here. Galen hissed as a wave of frustration and anger washed through his chest.

He turned from the small window to the desk that had been brought up for him. The high commission members would come here to him until it was safe for him to leave the confines of this room. Cerebus had posted castle guardsman throughout the temple after they had conducted an extensive search for him. But the Temple of Erys offered much in the way of protection for its priests. The secret passageways between the walls had been more than adequate to hide Galen. The priests had led him back through areas that the guards had already searched to hide him again.

Eventually the guards would be recalled to help defend the city and if not, then they would be taken care of once the coming plans were put into play. The discovery of the tunnel beneath the Temple by Cerebus and Torrin was not a surprise. Galen had expected a thorough search to uncover the passage. Fortunately, the second tunnel leading from the city beneath the great Temple, was known only to Galen. Palior had confided the location to him – a secret kept by the patriarchs of Erys. And its value was soon to be tested.

The hard part was going to be getting Tihir N'Avarin out of Pellaris keep's dungeon. Galen was working on a plan but he was having difficulty with the high commission. There was great outrage within the ranks of the Pricsthood over the treatment of the new patriarch, but little will to act.

Galen sighed, if he couldn't have N'Avarin here now, at least the man's ambition would be tempered in a cell for a while.

Once he rescued the priest, his influence over N'Avarin would be secure as well. But members of the commission were pushing hard for an interim patriarch to be elected to lead the Priesthood until N'Avarin was released.

Galen picked up the list of candidates that had been given to him by the commission secretary and scanned the names once again. None of the men on the list were ones he would support. For now, Galen was directing the commission and the Priesthood – a situation that needed to be maintained until his plans were accomplished. To install someone unfamiliar in the office of Patriarch now, someone Galen couldn't control, would be disastrous. Much depended on timing and quick decisions; he needed to give orders and have them followed without question.

Cerebus had acted faster than he had expected. After Elana regained consciousness and imparted what she had learned, Galen thought the king would take more time to search for him before moving so openly against the Priesthood. Now with N'Avarin locked away awaiting a trial that might never happen, Galen had to consolidate his position before the high commission became too restless.

He dropped the sheet of parchment back onto the small desk.

None of Galen and Palior's plans and communications with the Rith Miroth were known within the high commission; there were some who would openly oppose those plans. He was regarded with approval for his tireless work on behalf of the Priesthood and many would not question him, but he needed a way to be sure of the commission's support.

He picked up the large leather-bound volume of the Priesthood of Erys's Theocratic Laws and Edicts. The book was already opened to a page that gave him his best chance at seeing a positive outcome for the Priesthood and Pellar. Tracing his index finger down the page to the paragraph at the bottom, he reread the text, carefully weighing all the implications. By invoking the *Precept of Wartime*, Galen could legitimately ask for and receive fealty from the members of the Priesthood. The hard part was going to be convincing them that he had the right to invoke what only the patriarch could. If N'Avarin passed temporary authority to Galen, then he could legitimize his role as leader of the Priesthood.

Galen placed the heavy tome on the desk and lowered himself into the chair. He reached for a fresh piece of parchment and dipped his quill into the ornate inkwell he loved so well. It was one of the few things he had brought with him from Pellaris keep. Now ink from that well was going to be taken back inside the walls of the fortress. The message had to be cryptic in case it was intercepted. Galen thought for a moment; something only Tihir would understand … carefully he placed his pen to the page and began to write. The pen scratched across the smooth surface of the parchment as his precise hand grew sure and swift, committing to this new strategy.

The Keeper

Rowan woke in the early evening, in an already-set campsite within the dense thicket. Yawning and stretching, she felt only a little soreness in her leg and arms.

"Welcome back." Torrin sat beside her with his back to a tree trunk, mending a torn buckle on her breastplate. Rowan smiled up at him and cuddled deeper into the blanket. Her friends were busy about her, mending gear and cleaning weapons.

She inhaled the smell of something wonderful Borlin was cooking and her stomach rumbled loudly. She hadn't eaten in almost two days.

Nathel eyed her from across the fire. "Borlin, you'd better get some food into Rowan before she gives away our position."

Dalemar chuckled, exhaling pipe smoke.

Rowan's arms and hands shook as she accepted a large wooden bowl full of savoury stew from the Stoneman. She leaned back and relaxed for a moment before trying to wield the spoon. Food had never tasted so good. Borlin's little pouches of spice had worked magic on the simple meal.

Before she knew it, Borlin was bending over her, his brown eyes twinkling. "Perhaps I'll just put a wee bit more in yer bowl. The wood doesn'a taste as good as the stew, ye know."

Rowan smiled sheepishly as he took the bowl she had been scraping clean and refilled it with another helping. She leaned back against the tree with Torrin and concentrated on actually chewing her food as she ate. "How was it in Pellar when you left? How is Queen Elana?"

"She is better," said Torrin, "though it will take awhile for her to rebuild the blood she lost. It was Chancellor Galen or Tihir N'Avarin who assaulted her."

"Galen? I would never have though him capable of something like that."

"Galen is missing; it was he who copied the bailey key that allowed the men who attacked you to gain access to your room. That is what the queen discovered in his study before you found her unconscious. Cerebus had N'Avarin arrested for conspiracy and treason. We found the tunnel they took you through under the Temple of Erys."

Rowan nodded, watching his strong fingers deftly thread a line of sinew through her tooled leather armour. "We saw N'Avarin leading the impostor soldiers." Rowan glanced across at Nathel. "Your brother and Borlin fought ferociously. It was a close thing wasn't it? The wound I saw him take –"

Torrin's hands paused as he looked at Nathel. "Yes, it was close. I don't know if he would have made it if Dalemar and Hathunor had not been able to help him."

Rowan swallowed and closed her eyes as she remembered losing touch with Nathel's back under the swarm of enemy.

Torrin placed her mended breastplate beside her. "Rest for a while. There are things we need to discuss after we eat." He reached to pick up something else from beside the tree.

It was her sword.

She sighed. "Oh, Torrin, I had not dared to hope you might have recovered it. Thank you."

He held it out hilt-first with the flat of the curved blade resting on his forearm vembrace. He had replaced the soft leather wrappings on the hilt for her. The metal gleamed in the setting sun as she reached out to take it. Its weight felt good in her hand – complete.

"I'm the *slayer*?" Rowan rose to her feet and looked around in disbelief at the calm faces of her companions.

Dalemar nodded, a smile on his face. "Don't you see, Rowan? The *slayers* – all of the ones that I found reference to – were from Myris Dar, and some were women. The *slayers* the seers refer to were indeed found in Pellar but none of them were Pellarian. I wouldn't be surprised if they too were sent by the Seers of Danum as messengers to warn of the Wyoraith's return."

"But wouldn't the Seers have known the identity of the *slayers*? Even if the Seers didn't know the *slayers* were Myrian at first, surely they would have made the connection by now." Rowan frowned. *How could this be possible*?

"Perhaps they couldn't tell you for fear of altering the course of events. If you had known from the start you were the *slayer*, would you have acted the same way you did, made the same decisions?" Dalemar asked.

Rowan sighed and shook her head. "No, I suppose not. I likely would have gone in search of the *summoner* instead of traveling to Pellar."

"Perhaps the time you spent traveling through Eryos to Pellaris was important for something," said Dalemar, "to find something or to gain strength and knowledge before you went after the *summoner*."

Dalemar's last words rang through her head. She looked at Torrin and sank slowly back down onto the log she was sitting on. He returned her gaze steadily. Perhaps he was what she needed to find. She looked at all her friends, each of them watching her. Perhaps she had needed to find them all. She rubbed her temples – it was crazy! "Even if the past *slayers* were Myrian, that doesn't mean the one we're looking for is *me*. You are basing all this on a single reference in an ancient book. What if the *slayer* was one of the Myrians I came here with? My cousin Dell was a renowned warrior – it could have been *he* who was meant to slay the Wyoraith, or Lesiana." She turned to look at Torrin and Nathel. "It could be either of you. I was sent to find the *slayer* in Pellar, a *man* – the Seers could not have been this wrong."

"We did find the *slayer* in Pellar – you," Torrin said calmly.

"You truly believe this?"

Torrin nodded. "When Dalemar told me, it was like learning something I had always known but had never fully realized. It also explains why you are so drawn to Krang." He nodded as her eyebrows rose. "I've seen you gazing east, looking for the distant Krangs even when they could not be seen. During the council, your mention of taking the fight to the *summoner* resonated with the deepest truth whether you knew it or not. It is written in your words and deeds, Rowan. You are the *slayer*."

"But that was conjecture. When I said I would go after the *summoner* during the council, I – I meant as a last resort. Only if the *slayer* wasn't found."

Torrin snorted, his dark brows lowered and his eyes glinted in challenge. "Now you're reaching, Rowan. You and I both know how seriously you took the proposition. I heard it in your voice that day. Search your heart; you will find the truth there."

Rowan stared at him.

"How long has that symbol been in your family?" asked Dalemar, pointing towards the repeating motif that covered her armour and sword.

Rowan glanced down at the vembraces her brother Andin had made for her. The symbol was something she had always taken for granted. "It is the Mor Lanyar family crest. I have no idea how long it has been in my family."

"Rowan, I found that symbol inscribed into a book describing the last few thousand years of Kathornin history. It was labelled as the insignia of *slayers*," said Dalemar, frowning. "There cannot be any doubt that you are linked to the *keepers*."

"You've referred to the *slayers* as *keepers* a few times now — why?" asked Rowan.

"It has to do with an error in translation. I think whoever translated the text I found mistook the word Chelvir, which means keeper in an obscure dialect of Kathornin for Chavor – slayer. All subsequent referrals to and translations featured the word *slayer* rather than *keeper*," explained Dalemar. "I have no idea, though, what a *keeper* of the Wyoraith is supposed to do to stop its coming."

"How did you figure out that this obscure word meant keeper?" asked Rowan.

"It was in another scroll that was correctly translated into Kathornin. I came across the same language – 'Mo ranithea a chelvir'. It was translated into 'Guard the Wyoraith and its keeper.' It made sense," said Dalemar. "Why would the Wyoraith need protecting if a slayer was meant to kill it? And then I remembered your sword's name."

Rowan barely heard Dalemar's last words. The phrase he had spoken in that ancient language resonated through her with strange familiarity like a forgotten memory or a childhood song. Her whole body went still as she listened for something she could not identify. "My sword –" She looked at Torrin as the implications sank in.

"Mor Ranith," he said quietly.

"The name of your sword is almost the same as the word meaning Wyoraith in that language," said Nathel in surprise.

"It is possible that one is a derivative of the other," said Arynilas.

Dalemar was looking at Rowan with expectation. "I believe 'Mo' might be the root of 'Mor'. Perhaps your name, your sword's name, Mor Ranith, means literally to guard or guardian of the Wyoraith."

Rowan reached up and pulled her sword from its leather scabbard and ran her fingertips along its surface. "I had always assumed that Mor Lanyar was ancient Myrian, a dame name no one remembered the meaning of. But if it isn't Myrian at all … " Rowan trailed off as she gazed at her weapon. "I have no idea how old this sword actually is."

"Maybe ye had an ancestor way back who was not from yer homeland," suggested Borlin.

Rowan nodded absently, studying the etched script that led down the blade's length. She had an impression of this same sword in the hands of all the *keepers*, marching back through time. Gooseflesh rose along her arms and back and she shivered.

"It makes a poetic sort' o sense, lass." Borlin stood and bent over the fire to pour a cup of tea. "I can feel it in me bones that ye had a greater role te play in this." He passed the cup to her, his amber eyes gleaming with affection and respect.

Nathel accepted a second cup from Borlin, looking at her over the steaming brim. "If anyone can be the *slayer* or this *keeper*, its you."

Rowan frowned; she wasn't in the mood for his joking but his expression was as serious as the afternoon in the square where they fought for their lives.

Arynilas regarded her seriously. "Some things are not meant to be questioned, Messenger. Sometimes the reasons behind the way things are do not matter. It is only the truth that is important. From the start, your quest had the weight of great events hinging upon it." He shrugged. "What will be; will be. It is the way of all things."

Hathunor, seated next to Nathel, smiled a broad, toothy smile. He believed in her regardless of whom or what she was. She couldn't help but smile back.

Her chest ached as she looked around at her friends. They had helped her get to Pellaris to deliver her message. They believed that she was the keeper they were looking for – accepted it as though someone had told them the sky was blue.

I don't want to let them down.

If she was the *keeper*, it would at least help to explain the strange dream.

Torrin's voice cut through her musings. "What is it?"

Rowan stirred. "Maybe it is why I am having the dream. It is more than just a nightmare. The paralyzing fear of it and the pain I feel afterward is too real."

Torrin's face darkened, a deep frown shadowed his blue eyes. "Miroth thinks you are on your way to Lok Myrr tied up as a neat package for him to do with as he wants. You'll get there, but on my life it will not be as he expects."

Rowan shivered in spite of the warmth from the fire. *Keeper* or not, they were going after Miroth and all that entailed. *But what do I do once we are there?* "I don't even know what the Wyoraith is; let alone how to stop it."

"You will know what to do when the time comes." Torrin said softly. "We will all be with you. You will not go into Lok Myrr alone."

"Perhaps that is why the Seers never told me, if indeed they even knew," said Rowan. "Maybe more than the *keeper* is needed to stop the Wyoraith."

In the silence that followed this statement, Borlin barked a laugh. He ran a thick finger down the blade of his short sword. "Ye might have someth'n there, lass. I've been spoil'n for a good fight for some time now."

Nathel grinned and slapped his thigh. "Well said, Borlin!"

Rowan shook her head – the crazy fools.

Torrin watched her as Nathel and Borlin traded boasts over expected glory. His expression held a hint of the worry he must be feeling. It would be hard for him to see her in any danger. He nodded – they would be fighting together for all of Eryos.

Dalemar trickled a little power into his pipe to relight it. "At least we have one possible answer to why Miroth wants Rowan enough to send men into Pellaris for her."

"I assumed it was because he knew she was the *slayer* or *keeper* and could stop him," said Nathel.

"Perhaps, but I have a suspicion there is more to it than that," said Dalemar.

Torrin frowned, leaning forward; his glance took in Dalemar and then Rowan. "If he knew she was the *keeper*, why would he want to bring her closer, alive, to Lok Myrr? Why not try to kill her?"

"The Summoner would not be interested in doing such a thing unless there was good reason for it," said Arynilas. "We have seen little purposeless action from him." He was tending his bow and his slim hands moved deftly over the weapon.

"I'd stake my life on it having something to do with the summoning of the Wyoraith," said Torrin.

Dalemar nodded. "As the *slayer*, it is true there would be no logical explanation to risk bringing her to Lok Myrr. But as the *keeper*, it makes a lot more sense. Think about it. The word *keeper* connotes someone who has control or power over something." Dalemar blew out a mouthful of smoke. "Or someone who is charged with protecting something. It could be that Miroth cannot summon the Wyoraith on his own, that he needs her to help him somehow."

"Bah! I've known Stonemen who've gone to as much trouble o'er revenge. Who's to say the Black Rith is interested in anyth'n more than that?"

Torrin turned to look at Borlin. "It is true; we cannot discount that his reasons might be purely personal."

Rowan shivered again. If that were the case, she couldn't imagine what she had done to warrant such action. She frowned – it was no help to worry about the unknowable. "What of Lok Myrr? What do we know of it?"

"None of us have been to Krang –" began Dalemar.

"I have been there," said Arynilas.

They all turned to look at the Tynithian in surprise.

"I guess if you live for hundreds of years, you have time to explore the world," chuckled Nathel.

"What do you remember, Arynilas?" asked Torrin.

"I was there during the summer months, on a ship that plied the waters off the rugged coast. It was many seasons ago and I visited a few of the accessible harbours. Krang is far from a hospitable place. The people I came across were downtrodden; frightened of strangers and even more frightened of the lawless brigands that travel the inland roads. The entire realm was covered in steep mountains and the settlements were very isolated. Of Lok Myrr itself, I have no knowledge."

Dalemar reached into his saddlebags, rummaging around until he pulled out a folded parchment. As he opened it, Rowan recognized the map from the king's study. Dalemar held it out before him and frowned down at it. "Krang is indeed completely covered in mountains. They are rugged and high. There is but one pass through them from Pellar into the interior. It is located about five days' hard ride south and east. The pass is high but we should still have time to get through before it is packed with snow. The late warm weather this autumn has ensured that it will be open."

Torrin sipped his tea. "We have a little information on Lok Myrr itself from Cerebus's first envoy. They made it to its gates, but were turned away without entry. They described the fortress as impenetrable, with walls fifty span high and great towers rising from the corners. It is situated northeast of the pass in a narrow, barren valley."

"We have to assume that the approach through that valley can be seen from the fortress itself," said Nathel.

Borlin dropped another log onto the dying fire, sending up sparks. "And the road that leads te it is likely watched."

Torrin swirled the remaining dregs in his cup. "Cerebus said the men in that first envoy were not experienced officers. There was a diplomat from the council and city guilds, a messenger from the king himself, and several mid-ranking castle guardsmen to serve as escort. It is more than likely they overlooked something, and saw with inexperienced eyes only the size of the walls in front of them. We will have to wait until we reach the approach to Lok Myrr before deciding how to proceed. Stealth and surprise are going to be our strengths but we must assume that the way into Krang is watched and that Miroth might know we are coming." He looked at Rowan. "We will somehow have to get you inside the fortress so you can do what you need to do."

Rowan laughed without humour. "What ever that may be."

Darkness had gathered in the dense trees around them and the trunks creaked as they swayed gently in the wind. Torrin stood. "Let's get some sleep; we have a long ride ahead of us and the remaining mercenaries are out there somewhere, still looking for Rowan. We should keep double watch."

Rowan wrapped her cloak around herself and made her way to where the horses were tethered. She hadn't seen Roanus since Pellaris. Her big horse nickered as she approached, dipping his head. His muzzle was soft as she cupped her palm under it, feeling his warm breath. His whiskers tickled her hand and she stroked his forehead. "Hello my big fellow. It's good to see you." He shifted his weight, rested one hind hoof and shook his long silvery mane.

Rowan turned as Torrin came towards her. "I have something else for you," he said, walking to the gear where he pulled a cloth-wrapped object from his saddlebags. As the fabric was pulled away, Rowan drew in her breath. They had found her dagger as well.

She took it in her hand, tracing the Mor Lanyar insignia with her fingertip in the darkness. "Thank you," she whispered. "I had hoped it was not lost."

"Use it well, Rowan of Myris Dar," he murmured. "Use it well." Then he gathered her into his arms and kissed her. The stars overhead began to glitter and for a while the world and its troubles receded.

An Account Settled

Torrin woke to a muffled shout and an explosion of movement beside him. He bolted upright, prepared to engage attackers, but all was still.

A soft sob of despair sounded beside him and he turned to see Rowan sitting up and clutching her chest, tears glistening on her cheeks in the silvery moonlight. Arynilas, who had been keeping watch, was on his feet beside her, a look of concern on his face.

Torrin shifted closer to Rowan and took her face in his hands, wiping her tears away with his thumbs. He whispered gently to her – trying to call her back from the horror. Slowly, her eyes focused on him, and she blinked.

"Torrin?"

"I'm here. You are safe; it was just a dream. Everything is fine."

Rowan shuddered and collapsed toward him, hugging him fiercely. He pulled the blankets up over them and held her as she wept silently against his chest.

How could you save someone from the demons that haunt from within? The question struck him with intense irony as his own ghosts rose to mind. The answer was simple. You couldn't – they had to save themselves.

Torrin stayed awake until the sky began to lighten, listening to the slow rhythm of Rowan's breathing long after she had fallen back to sleep. He hardly dared to believe that she was safe and curled in his arms. The pale morning light slowly revealed her smooth cheek and the arch of her brow. He longed to see those green eyes but didn't want to wake her. Their camp stirred and Torrin got his wish as Rowan woke and gazed at him. He traced a finger down her cheek and she smiled, but her tired eyes told a different story.

The sun was touching the treetops as Torrin swung into his saddle. Black tossed his head and danced sideways, kicking the remains of the breakfast fire, which steamed into the cold morning air. Torrin guided the eager horse out of the ashes and glanced around at his companions as they mounted.

Rowan adjusted her saddlebags and pulled her cloak closed against the chilly air. She was recovered from her injuries, thanks to Dalemar's talents, and her strength was rapidly returning. Her green eyes were calm as she glanced up – no evidence now of the terrifying way she had woken in the night.

Torrin's breath steamed in the sun as he exhaled. There was little warmth this morning and he had been glad last night for the sheepskins that Cerebus had sent with them. The horses looked woolly with their winter coats growing in. There would be snow any day now.

They guided their horses through the tangle of trees and bare shrubs, which sheltered the camp. Torrin pulled Black in at the edge, and scanned the rolling foothills spread out before them. Since crossing the Pellar River yesterday morning they had seen no sign of the mercenaries, but they were still out there somewhere, hunting Rowan. A cold rain had obliterated any trail the seven remaining men might have left.

They traveled eastward at an easy pace toward the distant wall of the Krang Mountains. Torrin led them through the winding valley bottoms of the foothills, keeping any silhouettes they might create against the slate coloured sky to a minimum. Gradually, more dark evergreens clustered among the bare branches of the deciduous woods as the parkland was replaced by denser forest. The land rose steadily towards the shoulders of the mountains. They saw deer moving through the landscape and a reddish fox, but only the winter birds were left in the north.

The companions stopped by a swift creek as the sun rose high, and passed around a cold meal. Ice still coated the reeds at the waterline, but the horses were glad of the cold water and stood, fetlock deep, slaking their thirst.

Torrin sat next to Rowan on a fallen log, and handed her a piece of flat bread and dried meat. She had been very quiet all morning and didn't speak now as she accepted the food and began to eat slowly. He had seen it many times – battle stillness.

The afternoon wore on as they continued to ride eastward, slowly approaching the ominous barrier of grey stone on the horizon.

Torrin shaded his eyes against the sun's glare. Arynilas and Hathunor were moving back down the slope of the hill ahead. Torrin reined in his horse to wait with the others as the two scouts reached the bottom and closed the short distance. The Tynithian's face was calm, but he moved with a purposeful intent – they had found something.

Arynilas stopped beside his dun coloured mare. "Men are at the end of the next valley, set up for an ambush."

"Our friends?" Torrin asked.

Arynilas nodded and Torrin looked over at Rowan. Her green eyes were very bright as she returned his gaze

"We'll circle around; surprise them from the rear," he said, glancing at Arynilas again. "Unless they've posted a rear watch?"

"No."

Torrin smiled grimly. "Even odds… They shouldn't pose much of a problem." He turned to Rowan. "Will you save any for us?"

"There is only one I want," she replied quietly.

His friends wore dark expressions.

"Split up; circle wide; signal when you are in position." Torrin turned Black around and set his heels to the horse. The companions split – Hathunor guiding Borlin, Nathel and Dalemar south and Arynilas with Torrin and Rowan turning north.

Torrin dismounted and crept forward with Rowan and Arynilas at his side. They crawled silently forward on elbows until they could peer through the dense shrub at the scene below. He shook his head in disgust. The mercenaries stood exposed, hiding behind a thicket of trees – all eyes watching the approaching valley and the ambush they believed they were setting. They had two archers but they would not match Arynilas and Dalemar – nor Hathunor for that matter.

Torrin heard the bird-whistle signal off through the trees to his left. He glanced back down through the screen of foliage to the men below. They had not stirred at the call. He put his fingers in his mouth and returned the birdcall quietly, then counted to ten while he silently drew his sword.

Rowan reached up and placed a hand on his shoulder. "Scarface is for me." She looked fiercer than he'd ever seen her, even more beautiful for it.

Torrin wanted to argue but he wouldn't get far – it was her privilege. He glanced down at the mercenaries again, found the leader and took stock of him. He was big, muscle-bound and carried command easily.

Arynilas set an arrow to his bowstring. Torrin whistled once more with higher pitch, and the three of them rose and moved through the cover. Breaking into a run they charged down the slope. There was a blur of motion to the left – Borlin and Nathel stormed from their concealment with Hathunor, a huge black streak outstripping them all, hurtling towards the men below.

Three men spun around with shouts. The rest turned, cursing and fumbling with weapons, trying to free them in time. One of the enemy archers took aim at Hathunor, but Arynilas let fly his own arrow. It punched into the man, dropping him like a stone. The second archer shot his arrow but a fine ribbon of blue Rith fire incinerated the missile before it hit the Raken.

Hathunor bowled into the remaining archer and another man, smashing them to the ground, his long claws rending and tearing. Their screams cut off abruptly, throats ripped out.

Torrin reached the enemy with his sword held high as Rowan pelted past, further into the fray. The mercenary he met swung low at his stomach. He parried the swing and drove his sword through the man's chest. Planting a foot on the body and wrenching his blade free, he turned swiftly to meet the next opponent. Disappointment welled up when the man he turned to face was neither bald nor scarred.

He yelled and charged, his sword sweeping down at Torrin. Ducking low, Torrin sliced the man's chest, stepping past as his assailant crumpled forward with a screech of pain.

The battle was finished, almost. Nathel killed one man and Hathunor two others, Torrin took two and Arynilas one. That left only one. Torrin turned and found Rowan circling with the mercenary. Scarface.

The man was even bigger than he had looked from above, about Torrin's height but more heavily set. His broadsword swung with the formidable force of his bull-like shoulders. A network of white scars criss-crossed his face and he was blind in one eye.

Keeping his sword out, Torrin stood tensely as the two faced off. Scarface was furious, using his weight and strength against Rowan with little success. The mercenary swung, aiming at Rowan's side with enough force to fell a small tree. Rowan refused to meet his blow head on and he paid for his mistake with blood.

Realizing he was not going to win this fight, the mercenary swore at her in a rasping ruin of a voice. "Cowardly bitch. Stand and fight! Or do you need your useless friends to finish the job? They couldn't save you before, could they? Have you decided to fight for yourself this time? Little girls shouldn't play with swords if they are afraid to put them to their proper use."

Torrin clenched his fists, gripping his sword, but stayed where he was. He would enjoy killing this man, but death at the hands of a woman half his size would bring the brute far more pain than any Torrin could inflict.

Nathel stepped forward, broadsword in hand. Torrin grasped his brother's arm, shaking his head.

A small, calm smile appeared on Rowan's face. Now fully enraged, Scarface screamed and charged at her. Rowan met his heavy over-handed blow full on and the clang of metal shivered through the trees. Torrin gasped in a breath, trying to follow the flicker of her curved blade as she redirected it.

The mercenary looked down at his chest in surprise, dropping his sword as his arm went limp.

Rowan had slid her sword perfectly between his shoulder guard and breastplate. Blood seeped from beneath the plates. She leaned forward, still gripping her imbedded sword, and whispered something. Scarface looked down at Rowan, his face blanching to match his eye as he sank to his knees. She pulled her sword free as he toppled backwards.

The man who would have delivered her to Lok Myrr was dead before he hit the ground.

She turned from the body and Torrin met her gaze.

He saw Miroth's death in those green eyes.

The Pass

Torrin studied the rock above, taking in the wide scree falls built up from centuries of tumbling stones spilling down into the tree line. Grey granite dominated but bright seams of red iron ran in striations across the surface. The setting sunlight was slowly receding up the mammoth stone walls, bathing the sheer cliffs in gold and leaving the companions in cool shadow on their horses below. Four days' hard riding had brought them here – to the foot of the steep Krang Mountains. Now, they gazed upward in awe.

A glacial creek fell down from the heights and rushed past them. Black thrust his nose toward the water and Torrin released the reins so the horse could drink. He turned to look south along the slopes marching into the distance. They were still half a day's ride from the pass.

Torrin sighed – it would be slow going from now on. The foothills had become increasingly rugged, forcing them to take longer than he had hoped to get here. Still, it was gorgeous country.

A hare flushed from beneath the shrubs along the creek, and Black jumped. Torrin gripped the stallion with his legs to keep his seat; the horse snorted loudly and turned to look at the offending rabbit.

Rowan laughed softly as the hare and horse squared off, before the former darted away.

"Well Tor, it has been a nice interlude," said Nathel, guiding his horse into the water beside them. "But it looks like things are about to get tough."

"Aye, we'll be seein' a bit'o snow soon I reck'n." Borlin stepped down from his saddle to loosen his mare's girth.

Torrin patted Black's neck as the horse resumed his drink. He cast a look back at the landscape they had traveled through.

"You enjoyed the journey here, didn't you?" Rowan had moved her horse closer.

Torrin glanced at her, smiling. "I'd like to come back here some day to explore it further."

"It was good to forget for a while," she said, looking west with him.

Torrin studied her face. *If only we could just stay right here*. He frowned, clearing his throat. "We'd best look for a suitable campsite. The temperature drops fast this high up."

As he turned Black to the gravel bank, Torrin looked and could almost make out the valley they would head for tomorrow – a path to lead them up into the rock and timber fastness of the Krang Mountains.

A path to Miroth.

"There's a likely spot just o'er the creek." Torrin followed Borlin's outstretched arm to a dense copse of trees located up-slope and commanding a good view.

"As good as anywhere," he replied, and they splashed out of the creek and up the slope.

The last of the sun finally slipped below the horizon as they entered the thick stand of trees to set up camp. Within minutes Borlin had a merry fire going and water boiling for tea. Thanks to the mercenaries, they had acquired another packhorse and more supplies, though Borlin had shaken his head in disgust at all but a few of the dry goods.

Torrin pulled his saddle down from his horse and placed it on the ground with the rest of the gear. He untied the warm fleece mantle Cerebus had supplied and tossed it over his shoulder as he walked toward the fire with his saddlebags and bedroll. Rowan, already wrapped in a fleece, was seated on a log they had pulled closer to the heat. Torrin silently thanked the king for his foresight – extra blankets had been the last thing on his mind as they left Pellaris.

He stowed his gear next to Rowan and stole a kiss before going back to look after the horses. Borlin's gruff voice carried across the quiet evening as he spun a tale of the mountain creatures found in the Black Hills.

"Large as hillsides, they are, and covered in white shaggy fur. Not a Stoneman among us was taller 'n its waist. Its skin was thicker 'n boiled leather — and claws! Ye should a seen its claws! Talons they were, wickedly curved, an' I swear by me mother, I saw serrated edges."

Nathel laughed. "You've got to be exaggerating just a little, Borlin."

The Stoneman shook his head, short red beard bristling. "Nay lad, 'tis no tale, I saw it with me own eyes. Me sword bounced right off its damnable hide!"

Horses seen to, Torrin made his way back to the fire. As he settled himself, Rowan passed him a steaming cup of tea. She leaned forward to toss more wood on the blaze and her fleece slipped down. Torrin pulled it up for her, his hand lingering on her back.

"Are there any such creatures in the Krang Mountains?" asked Rowan.

Borlin nodded sagely. "Most assuredly, lass."

"You've never even been into the Krangs, man!" scoffed Nathel.

Borlin puffed out his barrel chest and placed his hands on his hips. "I've been a far sight more places than ye 'ave, pup!"

Nathel just laughed harder, holding his hands up in submission.

Rowan laughed with him – a ringing sound that filled the night with pleasure. Torrin closed his eyes, savouring this rare occurrence.

The dream was coming to her every night, sometimes twice a night. Torrin slept close beside her in the cold darkness, ready to pull her tightly in his arms when she gasped awake in terror and pain. Holding her until her heart stopped pounding and her breathing slowed, his lips close to her ear, as he whispered calm reassurances that concealed how helplessness he felt.

They did not speak of it anymore; nothing could be done and Dalemar had exhausted what little knowledge he had, trying vainly to find a remedy. Refusing to give in, Rowan would drill with her sword each cold morning to warm her body and ease her mind, moving through the long days with a quiet resolve.

Torrin relaxed back against the log, drinking his tea. His companions were bedding down around the fire, transforming into fleecy humps – Borlin's snores already emitted from one. Rowan leaned back into his chest and he wrapped his arms around her. *If only we could just stay right here.*

*

Whiteness greeted Torrin when he woke the next morning. A thick blanket of snow covered everything – saddles, gear, rocks, shrubs and sleepers. He lifted the extra weight of the snow on the fleece up and Rowan yelped beside him as snow sprinkled down onto her neck. He peeled the fleece back and stood to shake it out, looking around at his stirring friends. "Best to just get going and eat breakfast in the saddle."

"Or we could just sit in a pile of snow and shiver," said Nathel with a frown as big wet flakes began to fall anew.

Borlin pulled out oiled canvas to cover the packhorses. "Come on lad, help me wi' the beasties. Sooner we get it all packed the sooner we can 'ave a bite o' breakfast."

The ride toward the pass was slow and treacherous as they picked their way through the fresh snow. When they finally reached the wide valley that cut up into the wall of mountains, it was almost noon. The snow was still falling, and higher up the peaks were concealed in thick cloud.

Nathel shook the snow out of his eyes. "Perhaps we should wait and attempt the pass at dawn so we have a full day to travel it."

"We cannot risk waiting any longer," said Dalemar, "or higher up it may become impassable." His horse bent down to rub frost-covered eyelashes against its front leg, then snorted, expelling white plums of breath upward.

"It will mean traveling down the other side in darkness," said Nathel. "We will have to move slowly or seek shelter somewhere."

"Aye, there may be caves we can find," said Borlin.

Arynilas studied the shrouded peaks as though already seeking a trail. "I cannot see though cloud and mist, but there are other ways to detect dangers. We will eventually have to lead the horses on foot when the snow gets too deep, and possibly rope together so we don't loose each other."

The heavy snow deadened the sound around them, muffling the horses and muting their voices. Torrin followed the Tynithian's gaze up the winding path that cut through the surrounding slopes. The forbidding peaks seemed to close over them like a warning. He looked at his friends – all of them were poised to walk through a doorway into uncertainty and possible death. It was a sensation they were very familiar with, but never before had so much been at stake. Torrin drew in a deep breath as he stared upward.

Arynilas and Hathunor stepped forward to lead the way. As they began to plod up the steep path, Torrin realized it was more like a narrow road. Parts of it were cut out of the stone, others built up with masonry to allow a horse and cart passage. He hoped the entire route through the pass was like this, giving them a chance at getting through in the dark.

Rowan, riding in front of him, turned in her saddle and looked back. The fleece mantle around her shoulders framed her face and there was snow in her hair. Torrin's chest clenched, stunned once again by her beauty. He felt like he was seeing the world through someone else's eyes – what grey darkness had covered his life before this.

They stared at each other for a moment. She said nothing but there was determination in her eyes – she was unsure about being the *keeper,* and none of them knew what they would face in Krang, but she would not turn back.

Torrin kissed his gloved fist, touched his forehead to salute her.

A memory surfaced then – a conversation between Rowan and Nathel as they traveled over the endless Klyssen plain. While she and his brother had practiced, Nathel asked if she was considered a master swordswoman in Myris Dar.

Rowan had paused and lowered her sword. "A true Master always wins his or her battles without fighting."

This was one battle she would not need her sword for. She was strong – possibly the strongest person he'd ever known – but her strength was slowly being sapped and it frightened him to see it.

If Miroth knew Rowan was the *keeper*, perhaps he was sending her the nightmare to wear her down before she was finally brought to him. Despite his strength, power and long years, perhaps the Rith feared her. Was he still vulnerable to the *keeper*, even when he thought she was captured and under control?

The idea brought Torrin fragile hope and he prayed Rowan could resist the *summoner's* power.

The thick cloud ceiling grew closer as they climbed higher into the pass. When they finally entered the swirling mists, all sense of time disappeared. The world shrank to the pale ribbon of the narrow, winding road – a slight path through a dull white landscape. Snow began to fall heavily and gusts of wind swirled the flakes around them, into eyes and mouths and down exposed necks.

Torrin pulled Black up as Rowan's horse stopped ahead. She stepped down and Torrin followed suit. The snow was almost knee deep. He motioned for Dalemar and Nathel behind him to dismount and could just make out Borlin bringing up the rear. Torrin patted his exhausted horse and moved to walk in the furrow created by those ahead. He pulled his scarf up over his nose and rubbed at the ice on his lashes. Soon he was gasping for breath, his chest aching. Even with frequent stops to rest, Arynilas couldn't keep up the pace indefinitely – Hathunor maybe but not the rest of them. *It's the altitude.*

Torrin struggled through the snow past the horses which stood with heaving sides, to where the Tynithian squatted, resting. "How are you, my friend?" The light was fading and the temperature had dropped wickedly.

Arynilas looked up, his black hair dark against the whiteness around them, "Well enough."

"Will you be able to lead us in the dark?"

The Tynithian nodded. "Yes but it will be slower yet and I will need to use the Fox's wiles."

Torrin handed Arynilas his water skin to drink his fill. "Keep those sharp eyes out for some shelter. Even if you and Hathunor can go on, the rest of us and the horses can't."

Torrin and Arynilas stood as Hathunor's black form appeared out of the swirling white ahead. He seemed unaffected by the cold and snow but without the sun he would eventually run out of energy to break through the deep snow for them. Torrin looked back to see if the others were ready to continue.

Rowan's face was pale behind the scarf she had pulled up.

He took a step toward her. "Are you alright?"

She nodded and looked past him. He turned to find the black fox standing before him. Arynilas wagged his fluffy tail before setting off with Hathunor, his nose to the Raken's snow-churned path. Torrin retrieved Arynilas's clothes and weapons and stowed them in the Tynithian's saddlebags. Then he gathered the reins of Arynilas' dun mare and coaxed her into the deep snow beside the path so Rowan could walk ahead. He picked up his own mount to follow; the two black pathfinders had almost disappeared ahead.

The temperature plummeted as the last light faded. Torrin pulled his hood down and rewound his scarf, leaving only a slit for his eyes. He scanned back frequently to make sure Nathel and the others were still there. Wind whistled and moaned loudly, driving the snow like daggers.

We must be close to the top of the pass.

If Arynilas didn't find shelter soon, they would have to rely on Dalemar to conjure a shield to protect them from the elements. But to create and maintain a shield large enough for an extended period, the Rith would be taxed to his mortal limits – not to mention the message it might send to Miroth.

Rowan suddenly stopped in front of Torrin and he pulled up just before he walked into her horse's hindquarters. She moved foreword again but to the left toward the steep rock looming out of the dark. He searched for his companions but could only barely make out Nathel.

"This way," he called. He waited for Nathel to signal before turning to follow Rowan again.

They moved passed the rock face and the ground became uneven and sloped. Another cliff appeared and Torrin gasped in disbelief as Rowan vanished into its dark stone surface. When Torrin reached the wall he discovered that it was not as flat as it looked. A long cleft ran into the stone, narrowing to a split that burrowed deeper into the granite. The opening was just large enough to fit a horse through. He pulled on the reins and stepped into the cleft.

The darkness within was complete. Torrin reached out and found Roanus. "Rowan?"

"I'm here."

Torrin moved along the side of her horse. Rowan gripped his hand but he could barely feel the pressure with his numb fingers. "We need to move the horses further in to make room for the others." They pressed into the darkness, Torrin keeping hold of her hand.

Borlin finally entered, swearing as he fumbled around for his lanterns. Warm yellow light bloomed in the blackness as he lit them and they looked around in surprise at the very large cavern they stood in. The howling wind outside was muted to a whine and the drip of water came from somewhere in the shadowed recesses.

The horses tossed their heads and snorted in fear. Torrin pulled off the snow-matted cloth that he'd wrapped around his face and a powerful stench assailed him – a ripe animal smell of wet fur and dung. He scanned the cave, trying to pierce the dark corners.

Arynilas, bare skin gleaming in the lantern light, reached swiftly for his bow, nocked an arrow and aimed into the shadows at the far end of the cave.

There, against the wall of the cave, a huge form stirred, then padded forward into the light, blinking. It was the largest cave bear Torrin had ever seen. Baring yellow fangs at them, it roared with deafening sound in the confines of the cavern.

Arynilas pulled his bow taut, taking careful aim. "I tracked his scent to the cave opening, it was very faint but once I got close enough to the entrance, it was like a horn call. He has resided here for many years." There was regret and respect in the Tynithian's voice.

Hathunor reached out, placing a huge hand on Arynilas's shoulder. Arynilas relaxed the string as the Saa Raken stepped in front of him. Hathunor beckoned Dalemar to come and the surprised Rith stepped forward to touch Hathunor's back. Pale blue light glowed around his hand as he sent his power into the Raken.

Hathunor stood motionless and stared at the bear. The animal swayed back and forth, head and muzzle pointed upwards, its small brown eyes fixed on Hathunor. The bear finally shook its great, shaggy head and turned its back on them, padding silently away, its back feet turned inward. Short tail bobbing, it disappeared into another cleft that Torrin hadn't noticed, leaving only its strong smell behind.

Torrin sighed in relief and looked at Hathunor.

"Well, if you don't mind the smell, it looks as if he's willing to have house guests," laughed Nathel into the stunned silence.

"Goodness," murmured Dalemar as he withdrew his hand from the Raken's back.

"Did you see how he did it?" Rowan asked Dalemar.

The Rith nodded excitedly. “Yes, but I don’t know if I can duplicate it. Honestly, I had never thought to use magic to communicate with animals!” He looked up at Hathunor. “Could you talk to the horses, calm them down?”

Hathunor grinned and Dalemar again placed his hand on the Raken. This time the Rith peered into the space between Hathunor and the horses. The animals relaxed, lowering their heads. Their wide eyes calmed and their tails swished as they shook the wet snow out of their manes.

Dalemar smiled widely. “It’s more of a sending of reassurance than actually communicating with them. That might come in handy some day.”

Despite the strong smell, the cave gave them welcome respite to tend the horses, warm up and dry out.

Exhausted, they bedded down alongside the fire. Torrin lay with Rowan relaxed against his chest. She was soon asleep with her long golden braid draped across his torso. Torrin was fairly certain the bear wouldn’t return during the night; Hathunor’s intervention had been surprising, but persuasive. None the less, Dalemar was taking first watch, speaking quietly with Hathunor.

Torrin frowned. Did the Black Rith know this much about the Raken he controlled? Somehow he doubted it.

Fear is Not My Master

Rowan ran – heart pounding, breath tearing in her throat. It was close, seeking, driving her onward into the winding corridors ahead. She knew she could not last much longer. Her chest seized, burning with pain, lungs pushed to their limit. If she stopped, it would catch her.

A wall loomed out of the blackness, lit from behind her by the eerie greenish light. Rowan knew what was coming. She stumbled to a halt against the wall, gasping, sweat drenched.

She turned her head to the right, nothing but rough-hewn rock. Her fingers clutched at the stone before her, panic rising.

Something was different. To the left the wall continued into the darkness, the corridor hadn't ended. The passage had turned.

Rowan willed her exhausted body to move. She ran on. The light hunted her. Suddenly the walls were gone and she pitched headlong into complete blackness. The floor was all that she could feel.

Dread beat at her. It was in front of her now as well as behind. She stumbled wildly ahead, tripping and landing heavily on the cold stone. She sobbed, struggling to her feet, and ran blindly forward, arms outstretched.

She ran into stone, elbows cracking against the surface and she barely kept from striking her forehead. She reached outward feeling for an edge. There was nothing.

Rowan turned around. The light bled through an arched opening behind her – a doorway she had run through. Fear clouded her mind. Her legs went weak and the light pulsed toward her.

No.

Rowan ground her teeth, forcing herself to stand. She reached up for her sword –knew she would not find it.

Death expanded out from the light, rushing for her. She couldn't move as it came. Rowan closed her eyes. *Fear is not my master. I control my fear. It will no longer govern me. Like a stone thrown in still water, the ripples will wash over me and leave only calm. Fear is not my master.*

She willed herself to move, diving sideways as the light came for her.

It hit the wall where she had stood, splashing outward, sizzling across the surface. The space was illuminated for a blazing instant and she saw an enormous cavern. Rowan rolled, stumbling to her feet but her legs gave way and she sprawled across the floor. Blackness fell once more but the light was coming again.

Despair rose in her throat. It was too hard. She climbed wearily to her knees. The light expanded. She finally gained her feet and stood tremulously just as she was hit in the chest. The light tore into her, shuddering through her entire body and burning the flesh from her bones. She screamed and began to fall into endlessness.

Rowan struggled awake, trying to draw breath around the pain in her chest, blind to everything but the fear. She clenched her teeth, tasted blood in her mouth – she had bitten her tongue.

Something touched her face and a deep voice softly spoke her name – Torrin. His concerned face swam into focus, along with the dimly lit cave and sleeping figures of her friends.

Rowan took a deep breath, closing her eyes in relief as Torrin gathered her into his arms – waiting as the searing pain in her chest eased and invoking the meditations Dalemar had taught her. She and the Rith had spoken at length about being conscious while dreaming – knowing you were dreaming while it was happening. Even if Miroth was controlling the dream, it was still a dream and Dalemar reasoned that she should be able to control at least some aspects of it.

Why? Why was Miroth sending the dream?

This time the nightmare was different. I chanted the fear litany in the dream!

She twisted in Torrin's arms so she could look at him. "I fought back this time. I tried to at least. I haven't been able to do that before." She touched his face, wanting to reassure the worry in his eyes but her fingers shook.

Torrin held her hand and kissed her fingertips. "You are stronger than anyone I have ever known, Rowan. He will not overcome you."

Rowan rested her head on his chest. “It was still terrifying and real, but I think I knew it was a dream this time. I finally felt like I had a little control.”

Rowan realized she had something hard clutched in her other hand. Opening her fist, she found the circular talisman that Clan Shorna’s Mor’A Taith had given her. The polished stone was hot, as though it had been set beside the fire.

It is a protection stone, swordswoman. Keep it always with you and the strength of the Horse Clans will become your own.

Into Krang

Rowan took a deep breath as she stepped out of the cave. The early morning air was clear and crisp – a relief from the foul-smelling cavern. They had not seen or heard from their reluctant host during the night, but were ready to travel with first light.

The snow had ceased falling in the hours before dawn and lay deep outside the cave entrance. A pale orange glow from the sun beyond the rim of mountains to the east washed into the dark blue of the sky. They waded through the snow to where they had left the road and stood looking down into the steep valley below.

"All down hill from here – well, almost," said Nathel lightly.

Torrin stepped up beside her, smiling with reassurance and pointing. "There is the summit." It stood like a beacon with the barest hint of the winding path to show the way.

Hathunor strode through the deep snow with ease and they followed in his hip-deep wake. The snow was heavy and wet, sticking to the horses' shod feet in large clumps. They stopped frequently to pick away the balls of snow before it compacted into ice and caused the animals to slip or strain tendons in their legs. As the sun rose and the temperature warmed, their stops became less frequent. Making good progress, they reached the summit by mid-morning.

Rowan rubbed her tired eyes and scanned the view toward the interior of Krang. Clouds still nestled in the valley below, but here the sun glittered on the snow around them with glaring intensity. The crystalline peaks of the vast mountain range spread out before them. There was a calm stillness to the landscape under its blanket of white; snow sat like huge mushroom caps on all the treetops, sifting silently down and falling like silken veils in the light breeze. Shifting her attention back to the valley, she sought a route through the sharp outcroppings of rock and snow-filled crevasses below.

Nathel whistled beside her. "No wonder Miroth has been undetected here for so long. Who in their right mind would venture into that maze?"

"Well we all know ye don't 'ave a right mind," chuckled Borlin, "So I guess ye would. We're just along to save yer flea bit'n hide."

"How about some food Borlin?" said Torrin darkly from behind them. Pre-empting more banter.

Borlin cast a concerned look at Rowan. "Aye. T'would do us good."

Rowan sighed and closed her eyes against the glaring light, leaning against Roanus's neck. She had been visited by the dream twice during the night and had awoken exhausted.

Torrin gripped her by the shoulders and turned her to face him. The look of concern on his face made her wince. "I am just tired, Torrin. Please do not worry."

"Come and sit down."

Her nose and cheeks were cold but her body was warm under the heavy fleece. Her breath misted white before her, its moisture crystallizing on her face as she followed him.

Rowan sat down on the fleece he had laid out. "You know, despite how exhausted I feel, I am also hopeful."

Torrin stood looking down at her. "The dreams last night? You said they were different."

"Yes, though I still don't understand it, I feel as though I have made some small progress." It was like a glimmer of light in the darkness spreading before her. "I think the dream is a sending, a message of sorts." Rowan shook her head, frowning. "I can't explain it. I just know the closer we get to Lok Myrr, the more it will haunt me."

"So you think it will get worse?" He crouched before her, his eyes intense.

"Yes, but I can fight it now. I know I can and that sense of hope, however small, has been with me all morning."

Torrin reached out, caressing her cheek with warm fingers. "Then you fight him, Rowan, fight him like I know you can – and we will guard your back. You must tell Dalemar of your progress. He may be able to help further now."

Rowan swallowed and nodded. Torrin bent forward and kissed her forehead before standing to help with the horses. She leaned back against the packs and closed her eyes again. Whether the dream sent by Miroth was a warning or simply a strategy to weaken her before she got to him made no difference. She felt almost as though it represented a hidden part of her – something she had never touched before. In her relentless drive to be one with the sword, she had never realized that the need to fight her own battles, without exception, was an unattainable aim. The world was not that simple.

There is no shame in needing help.

Rowan took in a shuddering breath – tears close to the surface.

I understand now.

Her father had offered his help – his life, not out of obligation or disappointment in her, but rather, because he loved her.

The land of Eryos had tested her to her limits and many times she had needed help to survive. That help had been given freely by these friends around her and by those she met in Pellaris. Rowan opened her eyes to watch her companions, here at the top of the bright snow-covered pass, and shook her head in wonder. Blinded by her pride and disappointment in herself for having needed that help, she had missed the full gift of it.

For certain I will need their help again.

Sweet Erys, please keep them all safe.

The air warmed further as they descended, and melting water dripped into the snow, forming tiny, blue holes in the flawless surface. A few animal tracks criss-crossed the white expanse – a testament to the life hidden beneath winter's cover.

From these heights they could see two valleys running off at angles from the bottom of the pass. One went southeast toward the distant coast of Krang; the other followed a long line of mountains that marched northeast into the mysterious center of the realm – leading them to Lok Myrr and Miroth.

Rowan drew in a deep breath and let it out. Based on Cerebus' map, it would take them three or four days to reach Lok Myrr from the pass. There were no other details on the simple chart, other than the location of the fortress they sought. Nothing was known with certainty, Rowan thought grimly. *It hasn't been since I accepted this mission and left my homeland.*

What would the Seers of Danum say now? For the sake of her friends she hoped they had chosen wisely in sending her to Eryos.

The winding road narrowed and Rowan peered down at the sheer drop that fell dizzyingly away to the right. She gripped her legs tighter around her horse and gave silent thanks they had found shelter last night and not continued in the dark.

Back toward the summit, glinting in the afternoon sun, a vast glacier was now visible on the mountain across from the pass. It supplied water to the river in the valley below and as they traveled lower, Rowan could see its milky flashes through the crowding trees as it rushed past.

The path finally widened and Torrin rode forward and reined in beside her. He looked at her critically then twisted in the saddle to call back to the others. "Let's rest here for a while." He pulled out his water skin and passed it over to her.

Rowan accepted it and pulled the stopper to drink. The water was sweet and cool – snow melt from earlier that day. She surveyed the endless march of jagged peaks. The cloud cover from earlier had lifted and she could see far down the valley.

"The mountains seemed so much smaller from above," she said.

Torrin stepped down from his horse, glancing up the valley as he untied the flap on his saddle bag. "Only the Great Timor Mountains are higher."

Rowan swung down and loosened her saddle cinch for Roanus. She looked back up the pass and leaned against her big horse. Torrin ducked under Black's neck and came to stand beside her. He handed her some dried bread and a hunk of cheese. While she took a bite, he opened a small leather pouch full of nuts and spilled some out into her palm. The others gathered and Torrin passed what food he had out among them.

"Are there are people living here, in the mountains?" asked Rowan.

"Yes," said Arynilas, "although they are few and far between. Small pockets of people live along the valley bottoms where they raise goats or hunt and trap."

"'Tis a mean life in this rugged country, an' no mistake," said Borlin with a shake of his head. "Sun sets early an' summer months are brief. 'Tis a realm where news is slow te travel an' movement nigh impossible durin' the winter."

"A perfect place for the Black Rith to entrench himself," said Nathel darkly.

Arynilas dusted crumbs from his slender hands. "Warlords ruled Krang until a few hundred years ago. They warred against each other over the vast territories, and exacted tribute from the scattered people."

Dalemar nodded in agreement. "Miroth must have wrested power from them when he took Lok Myrr. It is likely that the people of Krang were relieved by the relative stability brought by the succession, and quietly accepted Miroth's rule."

Nathel snorted. "The Black Rith would be a ruthless ruler, taking whatever he wants and brutally suppressing opposition."

"If he stays isolated in his fortress, like a spider in a web, chances are many of the folk have rarely had to deal with the terror he instils," said Torrin grimly as he stowed away the food in his saddlebags.

Rowan frowned. "Surely there are stories, rumors of his evil." She sighed then. *I am experiencing first-hand just how the Black Rith uses terror.*

Torrin re-cinched her saddle and gave her a leg up. He squeezed her knee and gazed up at her. Rowan caught her breath as, for an instant the terrible fear for her safety and his helpless rage against an unseen enemy flashed through his eyes. He masked it quickly before turning away.

He has his own nightmares.

The Interior Within and Without

Rowan started awake, sweat-drenched, shivering with cold. She curled herself into a tight ball around the burning pain in her chest. Wind tugged on her loose hair and she burrowed deeper into the fleece and blankets piled on top of her until only the crown of her head was exposed to the cold gusts.

Torrin had not woken. His warm back lay pressed against hers. She must have awoken from the dream without a violent outburst. The pain that followed her from sleep did not seem quite so acute either, but perhaps she was only becoming desensitized to it.

Once again, the dream had been different. Her sword had been there this time – its cool metallic touch like an oasis in a desert. The ring of the blade as it slid free of the scabbard had sounded so real. She frowned. Her scabbard was made of leather. What would make me hear a ringing when I drew my sword? The unlikely event that the slim sword could defend her against the horrible light did nothing to dispel the feeling of power and strength she received from the presence of the weapon.

Dreams were often symbolic, Dalemar had told her. The sword in her hand was an emblem of protection – she took solace from it.

The fear litany was still spinning through her mind like wisps of smoke from a doused fire. *Fear is not my master*; *I will control my fear.* The pain eased, and her fear faded with the last of the calming words as she drifted once more to sleep.

For the remainder of the night, her slumber was untroubled, touched by nothing more than the need to keep warm in the cold.

They drew steadily closer to Lok Myrr over the next cold, clear days. The ill-kept road they traveled guided them through shaded gullies and rock-strewn ridges. Krang's interior was considerably drier than the mountain pass they had struggled through, cold and parched with the frigid breath of a land that never truly thawed.

About two days out they began to see scattered settlements of low, round stone buildings covered with sod roofs. Wood smoke curled up from jutting chimneys and mixed livestock, in rough wooden enclosures, bawled in the cold air. The dense forest of the lower slopes of the pass had thinned and the valleys they rode through now were barren and craggy. Meagre plots of fallow ground – a testament to hopeful farmers – dotted the land around the huddled dwellings.

They encountered only a few people, careworn and weathered beyond their years, who offered brief nods with eyes averted from the well-armed warriors riding along the path to Lok Myrr. The questions they had tried to ask of the small, wiry men had been met with fear and suspicion. The folk hurried on, shaking their heads, hands up in submission. The few women and children they saw fled at the sight of the companions.

The road slowly lifted in elevation and the temperature chilled further. Herds of wild sheep, with huge curling horns that swept back almost as far as their rumps, traversed narrow trails high on the bald slopes. There was little gazing for the horses, and they were forced to use their stores of grain.

Rowan sat cross-legged on her fleece with her eyes closed, focusing on the cold wind and taking deep breaths. She conjured the image of the passages of her nightmare and the dreadful light that pursued her. She imagined reaching up to find her sword and holding an ancient Myrian shield for protection – felt the concussion of the light as it struck the shield and scattered outward harmlessly. Rowan sighed and opened her eyes. Now the dream was coming almost every time she fell asleep, and despite the fear it still induced, she had finally been able to take greater control of her actions within it. The last few times the dream had come she had been able to awaken herself before she was hit with the searing fire and sent into nothingness.

These changes she believed were possible because she was slowly learning to control her fear: where it had paralyzed her before, now she could master it enough to take action. Indeed, when she was not so afraid, the nightmare seemed to lose its power over her and she could wake from it.

Could Miroth sense her coming? Was he increasing the sending because she was getting close, or because she was no longer as afraid?

Rowan pulled her cloak tighter around her and watched her companions setting up camp. Torrin looked at her and she waved in reassurance. She smiled wearily – their caring concern and help was welcome now.

The closer they drew to Lok Myrr the more oppressed the atmosphere grew. Snow lay thinly over the ground and the few straggling clumps of heavily grazed grasses were bent in the slicing wind. Vegetation grew close to the ground among sharp stones.

Movement caught Rowan's attention far upslope and she shaded her eyes to see what it was. A small herd of scrawny goats was moving higher up, herded by a small child in bulky sheepskins, skinny bare legs exposed to the cold air. The child was urging the goats onward with a stick, glancing fearfully down at them.

A shadow fell over Rowan and she turned to see Torrin, laden with sleeping rolls and blankets. "You should try to get some sleep while you can, Rowan."

"How close are we to the fortress?"

"Arynilas and Hathunor should be back soon with news from their scouting of the fortress's vale. They will be able to tell us of the distances and how best to approach without being seen. We won't ride out until just before sunset." Torrin knelt down beside her and bundled a blanket behind her for a pillow. He gently pushed her back to rest. "I know it is hard to rest, but you look like you could fall asleep in the midst of a battle."

Rowan groaned and curled up on her side, closing her eyes as Torrin covered her with another fleece. She reached into her belt pouch and retrieved the smooth hard weight of the Mor'A Taith's gift. "Tell Dalemar the visualization is getting easier and more clear. Tell him it is helping – I sometimes find the things I visualize in the dream."

Rowan surrendered to the heavy pull of sleep as a last thought trickled through her mind.

It is now only a matter of time. For good or ill, the dream will end when we reached Lok Myrr.

Lok Myrr

Rowan squinted into the dusk as a cold breeze lifted loose strands of her hair. She shifted on the hard, frozen ground and lifted her head higher to see over the ridge. Grey and brown rock greeted her. Snow dotted the valley and the higher slopes, and gigantic boulders sat immovable throughout the landscape. Lok Myrr fortress was set within a ring of peaks at the end of the long valley. It jutted upward, like a stiff-fingered hand perched on the flank of one of the mountains, each high tower aligned with the four directions. Cut directly from the granite rock of the mountain, the lower half of the enormous structure hulked with squat proportions and a depressive air. Its top half was crudely built of huge rough-hewn blocks, quarried from the same stone as the lower section but probably added later. It was cold and sullen, like a giant's toy that had been put together clumsily. The fortress boasted a long drawbridge that spanned a steep chasm between the front gate and the surrounding rock. Buttresses soared upwards to thick crenellated battlements which commanded a clear view of the narrow road cut through the barren valley leading up to the fortress. The massive arched gate with its heavy iron portcullis stood closed and unassailable.

Rowan closed her eyes and rested her forehead down on her hands. The fortress didn't seem to have any weakness.

Torrin, lying on his belly next to her, cursed quietly under his breath.

"The attempt will have to be made in the dark," said Nathel from Rowan's other side.

Torrin grunted in agreement. "Can you see anything, Arynilas? Any weakness?"

The Tynithian shook his head. "Not as yet."

"We're going t' need ropes an' grappling hooks," said Borlin, the most experienced climber among them.

Rowan lifted her head. "Is it possible Miroth could have magical wards set around the perimeter?"

They turned to look at her, disquiet in their eyes.

"Isn't that a lovely thought," said Nathel sourly.

"It is something I would do if I could," said Dalemar.

Torrin looked back at the distant fortress, chewing on his lower lip. “Will you be able to detect any wards we come across?”

Dalemar nodded. “Detect them, yes. Get us through them without alerting Miroth… that is another thing entirely.”

Rowan switched her attention to the mountain behind Lok Myrr. The slope was steep but looked to be navigable. “Couldn’t we circle around and climb down the mountain face behind the fortress? Maybe the defences won’t be as strong at the back. It is the least likely place to be attacked.”

Nathel nodded. “The moat doesn’t look to circle the entire fortress. It might be our best chance. What do you think, Arynilas?”

“You are right; the chasm does not completely circle the fortress. The mountain slope is steep but we should be able to climb down it. Also the battlements are not as high at the back because of the mountain’s rise.” The Tynithian looked over at Torrin. “It would seem to be the best course.”

“Then we must make for those slopes, circling around behind,” said Torrin. “When we get close enough to see what kind of force is manning the walls, we can make further plans.” He looked at his friends and received nods from everyone.

As the others began to crawl back away from the ridge top, Torrin reached out and caught Rowan’s hand. His grip was warm despite the cold. “Are you sure you want to go through with this? There might be another way to stop Miroth, something else we can do. Even if we make it inside, we have no idea what we will face. There could very well be an entire Raken army in there.”

Rowan swallowed, her mouth very dry. “Are you trying to scare me into turning back?”

Torrin chuckled sardonically. “If I thought that was possible, I would have attempted it a long time ago.” His gaze turned intense. “No, I just know that its going to get much worse before it gets better. Miroth wants you for something and that frightens me more than you will ever know. I won’t insult you by asking you to stay behind. You are the Keeper and this mission will likely fail without you, but I want to make sure this is truly what you want.”

Rowan squeezed his hand. “I don’t believe we have a choice. Even if there *is* another way, we can’t afford the time to look for it. Pellaris cannot stand for much longer – we are their only hope, Torrin, the only ones in a position to stop him. We have to try, even if it means failing." Rowan took a deep breath. "As for what Miroth wants with me… we will find that out soon enough."

He sighed, bringing her cold fingers to his lips, his eyes never leaving hers. "You mean more to me than life, Rowan Mor Lanyar. I will give my own to protect you."

Rowan closed her eyes and felt tears roll down her cheeks. She shook her head, trembling. Torrin tightened his grip on her hand. She exhaled the breath she had been holding. "I can't bear the thought of it."

"It's the truth, my love."

She nodded, her chest tight. "We will keep each other safe."

They both turned to look one last time at Lok Myrr fortress, its walls fading in the Twilight.

Shadows in the Night

The black bulk of Lok Myrr fortress loomed out of the darkness below. Rowan scanned the battlements and towers in the dim bluish glow from Bashelar, just rising above the rim of surrounding mountains. Fortunately, clouds were massing and would obscure most of the light soon – it was a gift. Of Raelys, there was no sign yet.

Rowan tucked her sore hands under her arms against the cold wind and tried to imagine what the eclipse of the two moons would look like. Dalemar had shown her the detailed star charts he had been given by the head archivist at the great library, but they had been just lines and points on a parchment to her. Dalemar had poured over them, finally concluding that the eclipse foretold in Rowan's message would happen tomorrow night. Rowan focused on the wide battlements below and tried to will her tense muscles to relax. If they breached the fortress below, they would have no way to confirm Dalemar's prediction of the twin moons' fated positions.

If we gain entry to Lok Myrr, it won't matter if there is an eclipse tomorrow night. There will be no turning back.

Rowan turned as Arynilas appeared beside her on the ledge they had climbed down to. He checked her ropes and began to take up the slack for the next leg. The rope was little more than a precaution for the Tynithian, who scaled the rocks effortlessly, but Rowan relied on it heavily. She craned to look back up at the ridge from which they had started the descent over an hour ago, but she could see nothing beyond the face they had just come down. Borlin, leading the way with Dalemar, had carefully selected the route down to the scree slope below. Torrin, Nathel and Hathunor were still above, lost in darkness.

Rowan turned to look back down. Borlin and Dalemar were small shadows clinging to the rock near the bottom. She had been amazed to see the wealth of climbing gear Borlin had produced from the packs strapped to one of the packhorses. Ropes and harnesses, buckles and circular loops and strange little devices used to jam into rock crevices so lines could be attached. The

Stoneman handled the gear with expertise and she noted the rest of her friends were not strangers to it either.

Myris Dar had many volcanoes, new and old, but the climbing she had done at home had been free-hand where there were easy foot and handholds.

Thick clouds passed in front of Bashelar, obscuring what little visibility they had for long moments. When the moon light shone once again Arynilas stepped lightly forward, positioned himself facing outward, and touched her on the shoulder to signal that he was ready for her to descend once again.

Rowan turned her back on the fortress below and, crouching, placed her hands carefully on the rough rock. She had already abraded the skin on her knuckles from placing her hands too quickly. She felt for her holds, then repeated the process for her feet. She leaned briefly against the rope and pushed herself away from the rock face, confident that the Tynithian would hold her, to survey the route down. Straining to see the possible foot and hand holds in the darkness, she began to move down. Climbing down was harder than climbing up, Borlin had told her. She had learned quickly why as she sought to place her feet blindly. The first few times she had panicked and wanted to move back up, but now she was able to calmly trust the tactile assurances of her toes.

The dark form of Hathunor appeared to her right as she placed her feet into a small crevice. The Saa Raken had refused the rope when offered, not that any of the companions could have held him had he fallen, but they soon discovered he was almost as at home on the vertical cliff as he was on the ground. He moved past her across the rock face – a shadow slipping before the moon.

Rowan returned her attention to the next foothold and began to climb down. It was a slow, laborious process and she could see almost nothing of her companions above and below. When she finally reached the broad scree slope at the base of the cliff, her arms and fingers were weak and aching.

I hope I will be able to grip my sword properly.

Borlin, busy coiling ropes and stashing gear behind a large boulder flashed a broad grin at her. Hathunor was crouched not far away, looking down at the fortress. Rowan looked up at the sound of rope scuffing against stone. Arynilas landed softly beside her a moment later. She began to unbuckle her harness, cursing her useless fingers, then moved to help collect the remaining rope as it came down below Torrin and Nathel. The brothers reached the bottom and Torrin whispered, “Borlin, pass out some food and water. We need to catch our breath and regain some strength before moving on.” They sat among the boulders to watch the battlements below.

Rowan sat next to Torrin and accepted the cheese and dried meat Borlin handed her. She took a bite and studied the huge fortress. Up close, the four towers were very tall and wide. The tapered tops rose far above even though they looked down on the battlements from the base of the cliff.

After a few moments, Arynilas hissed and pointed. Just coming around the north tower were two Raken guards. They walked slowly across the battlement until they disappeared around the east tower.

Nathel counted quietly as they waited. After a long while two more guards appeared around the north tower, following the same route. For good measure they waited once more for the next guards to appear. The timing wasn’t exact, but it was close.

“We’ve got two hundred-count or so between guards,” whispered Nathel.

Torrin stirred beside Rowan and looked away from the fortress to Dalemar. “Anything?” he asked quietly.

Dalemar shook his head. “I can’t sense anything.”

Hathunor stiffened and emitted a low growl from his throat. He gestured toward the fortress below with a large black arm, his head cocked to the side, listening intently.

“What is it?” whispered Torrin.

Hathunor turned to look at him. “Hathunor can sense Draes in there,” he rumbled.

Torrin looked back at the fortress below and then at the Saa Raken again. “You can sense the Raken? Why now?”

Hathunor shook his head. “Saa Raken can sense little ones to protect better.”

“Little ones? Do you mean children, Hathunor?” asked Dalemar quietly.

Hathunor growled fiercely.

“The bastard’s breeding them,” hissed Borlin.

“How long do you suppose it took Miroth to amass his army?” mused Dalemar.

"It matters not," said Arynilas softly, "but it does mean that some of the Raken may not be fully mature."

"Erys bless us." Nathel chuckled quietly. "We'll have one advantage in there if Hathunor can sense some of them. It should even the odds a little. At least we will know in advance when an overwhelming force is coming to kill us."

Torrin shook his head. "Why would Hathunor suddenly, after all this time be able to sense his own kin?"

"Perhaps Miroth has been cloaking them somehow and doesn't feel the need for that secrecy here," said Rowan.

Dalemar's pale head turned towards them. "If as Hathunor said, he is able to sense the younger ones, then perhaps the army within is made up mostly of children or sub-adult Raken."

Torrin turned to the blacker shadow that was Hathunor. "We will need you to guide us through the fortress to avoid your kin, Hathunor. Whether you hear them or can somehow sense them some other way, it will help us navigate."

The Saa Raken's pale, sharp-toothed grin was all they could see of his expression in the darkness.

"Are we all ready?" asked Torrin quietly.

They waited in silence until the moonlight was dimmed by the clouds. Then Torrin, Borlin and Nathel stood and hoisted the three scaling ropes with grappling hooks that Borlin had attached while they waited. Rowan stood with the others and they began to move down slope as quietly as possible, clambering carefully over the loose, unstable footing. The night had become more overcast and they used its darkness well, pausing to scout ahead each time the moon shone down and moving on once the scudding clouds brought shadows.

As they neared the bottom of the rocky slope, the huge wall reared upward in front of them. The darkness was deeper at the base of the wall and Rowan felt a shiver run through her as she looked up toward the top of the battlements of Lok Myrr.

Miroth is beyond these stones.

The wall was not as tall here as elsewhere, but it still soared as high as the ramparts of Pellaris. Hundreds of years of falling rock from the peaks above had built up a slope at the rear base of the fortress.

Torrin stepped back to gain room and began to swing a rope and hook. A very strong toss would reach the top of the battlements.

Nathel, keeping count, nodded when the guards had passed again. Torrin released and the rope whirred softly up into darkness, then the shaft of the cloth-wrapped hook glinted in moonlight as it flew beyond the shadow. A dull clink sounded above and Torrin quickly took up the slack until the hooks bit into the stone lip of the battlements.

Arynilas, his bow strapped across his chest along with the other ropes and hooks moved quickly forward. The fastest climber by far, he fluidly began to ascend. Rowan adjusted her footing and strained in the darkness to see up the wall. Once at the top, Arynilas would secure the other two lines, making certain the grappling hooks were hidden. His arrows would silence any Raken that might discover them.

The rope ceased to move – Arynilas had made it over the top. The other two ropes dropped down to land with a slithering hiss at the foot of the wall. Once the hooks and lines were attached, Arynilas would disappear into the shadows of the battlements.

I hope he finds somewhere to hide.

Nathel, still counting quietly under his breath, tapped Torrin on the back when it was clear above again.

Torrin, Borlin and Hathunor stepped forward and began their climb. They stopped to wait near the top, hanging silently on the ropes as another patrol passed on their perpetual rounds.

The ropes stilled as Torrin and the others gained the battlements. Rowan stepped to the wall to make ready. Nathel, still counting, touched her on the shoulder and she reached up to grasp the rough rope. Finally allowed to take action, she exhaled deeply and heaved herself upward with Dalemar and Nathel climbing beside her. Her hands were numb from the cold and it was difficult to feel the rope. They had left their warm fleece hidden beyond the ridge with the horses. The bulky garments would only serve to hinder them in a fight but Rowan missed the warm mantle now as the frigid wind blew through her clothes.

Breath coming in short gasps, she glanced up – halfway there. She gripped the rope hard and pulled herself up, placing her feet on the wall in front of her.

Nathel hissed suddenly from her right and she froze with the others, straining to listen – faint footfalls above approached and receded again.

They climbed once more.

Rowan was sweating, the cold forgotten when she finally reached the top. Torrin was there, his hand extended to help her up through the crenel.

They gathered the ropes and piled them in the darkest shadows along the wall of the fortress, where Arynilas and the others had hidden from the passing guards.

Torrin drew his sword slowly, silently. "We move with the Raken guards to the east tower. Keep close to the wall."

Lok Myrr was built for war. The wide battlements were a barren no-man's land between the fortress and the wall – nowhere to defend from Raken. They would not get away with hiding in shadows much longer. Rowan drew her sword and followed Torrin. Narrow murder holes set in the walls of the fortress above stared out into the night, vertical black voids from which archers could wait to send deadly arrows down. Rowan hunched her shoulders, feeling the potential threat of eyes watching from the sinister openings.

No doorways into the fortress yet. The portal, when they found it, would be small, easily defended by only a few.

The huge east tower loomed above them as they warily moved toward it. Dalemar stopped and spread his arms. "Hold!" he whispered. He stepped forward carefully and leaned toward something unseen. They waited tensely; Arynilas, his bow loosely drawn, watched behind them.

Slowly Dalemar backed away from whatever he had been examining. He shook his head, whispering, "It's a warding spell... a very powerful one. It encircles the entire east tower. This is where Miroth spends most of his time. I am certain of it. I cannot break through it and if I tried, he would know immediately. We will have to turn back and find entry into the north tower instead. Miroth will likely be able to sense me using magic this close, so I must avoid giving us away too soon. We will have to rely on our other skills for now."

Torrin cursed quietly. Rowan rolled her shoulders and took a deep breath, willing herself to relax. She cast a look up at the soaring stones of Miroth's tower. The faintest hint of light emanated from one of the high openings, and in her mind's eye she saw Miroth, up in his lair with his black thoughts and blacker heart, plotting his foul deeds.

Her grip on her sword tightened. She took an involuntary step toward the tower.

A hand on her arm stopped her and Rowan turned to see Torrin, his face obscured by darkness. He shook his head. "Save it for the right battle, Keeper," he whispered intensely.

Rowan looked back up at the east tower.

I will meet you, Black Rith. And when I do it will be on my terms.

Resolve settled over her like another suit of armour. She turned her back on the tower and Miroth, moving swiftly back the way they had come.

The Walls of Pellaris

Cerebus looked up as the young soldier came pelting into the room, sweat-soaked and panting. "The Raken, my lord! They attack the city walls."

Cerebus nodded and rose wearily from his desk. "Call for my squire quickly."

The soldier gave a short bow and then spun around, running from the room.

Cerebus strode after him, pulling his determination around him. *Sweet Erys but I'm tired...* he had not slept more than a few hours in the last days. The frequency of the Raken attacks had increased and Pellaris's resources were stretched to the breaking point. It was becoming harder and harder to push back the assaults.

As he left the room, he saw his squire come running down the corridor toward him, silver armour rattling over the lad's shoulder and glinting in the candle light. Cerebus no longer removed his under padding. He continued walking as his squire helped him settle the breastplate and shoulder pieces in place, the young man dancing along beside him. Gorget, brassards, vembraces—by the time he reached the bailey, he was almost fully dressed in armour. A castle guard had his horse ready to take him down to the walls.

One of General Preven's lieutenants waited with a small escort, torches held to light the night. Cerebus nodded to the man and mounted up. Glancing up to the wide walkway above the bailey, he saluted Elana; her pale hand returned the gesture. He spun his horse and clattered out the gate, his escort following after.

His wife had been tireless in keeping the city running during the siege. He owed her more than he could ever repay. His time had been taken up entirely by tactics, supplies, arms and soldiery. While he had been so consumed, Elana had seen to the day-to-day responsibilities. Disputes still needed to be settled and criminals tried, food stores to be distributed to the remaining population of the city, wounded to be treated. Grief-stricken wives, parents and children of lost soldiers needed solace. The queen had worked as hard as he had, and slept as little over the last weeks.

As they drew closer to the walls, Cerebus heard the ring and clash of steel, the roar of battle. The Raken had made it to the top of the wall again. He spurred his horse faster. Pulling up short of the wide steps that led up to the battlements above the gate, Cerebus jumped down and looked for Preven. He found him in a knot of desperate fighting above the gates, the General's bronze plated armour flashing among the red and gold and black of soldiers and Raken.

As Cerebus started up the stairs, a deep pounding shook the battlements. He looked quickly to the gate; the great wood and iron doors still held. Even if the Raken made it through the gates, they would still have to come through the tunnel and the huge iron portcullis. Above the tunnel, murder holes riddled the ceiling; soldiers stood ready to rain arrows and hot oil down on their trapped foe

Reaching the top of the stairs he surveyed the scene. The Raken were mounting the battlements on ladders all along the wall. Most were killed or sent back over to fall among their kin but there was no end to them. They came on and on, a swarm of giant black ants from an agitated nest. The cold wind whipped at the tripod torches along the wall, sending sparks skyward into the night and casting eerie light over struggling men and beasts.

A trebuchet whumphed to the left but Cerebus spared only a glance at the burning missile as it launched out over the Raken. He moved forward, sword drawn, and shouted over the noise to Preven.

The General extricated himself from the fighting to join the king. He was blood spattered and heaving, sweat plastered his dark hair to his forehead. "They are advancing much stronger than before, my lord," he rasped. "If this assault does not abate, our forces will crumble."

"It is as we feared, then. Miroth must be close to his goal." Cerebus moved to the edge of the wall and peered down through a crenel. A sea of black boiled before the city, blending into the darkness. "How long can we hold before we need to withdraw to the keep?"

Preven leaned close to Cerebus's ear. "At this intensity the men will tire quickly... no more than a few hours, my king."

Cerebus nodded. "Order the evacuation of the city. Have the last of the supplies taken up to the keep."

Cerebus strode into the nearest battle. Shouting salutes and flashing smiles, his soldiers redoubled their efforts, beating the Raken back, sending the ladders tumbling from the wall. Cerebus moved on to the next fight, his sword covered in dark Raken blood.

Into the Demon's Lair

Torrin ran with his friends through the dark band of shadow under the huge north tower. He slowed as they rounded the curved base of the tower, searching for a doorway into the fortress. All was dark above them. Only the faint glowing candlelight bleeding from a window halfway up the east tower provided evidence of the life within – Miroth's lair. He cast a glance back at Rowan but couldn't see her expression in the dark.

The bulk of Lok Myrr was becoming visible against the lightening sky.

Please let us find a way in to this Erys-forsaken place.

Hathunor, moving silently through the shadows beside Torrin, growled softly and halted. Torrin looked up at him – his huge head swung from side to side. There was nowhere to hide here; the battlements were narrow with the tower swelling outwards from the walls of the fortress. Hathunor stilled and turned to face the way ahead. Torrin stepped back behind his huge form, shielding himself along with his companions, who stood braced against the wall of the tower with their weapons drawn. He tightened his grip on his sword – maybe if all they saw was another Raken…

Around the curved wall came not two but five Raken guards, walking in a tight cluster. They continued onward, and Torrin held his breath.

The lead Raken stopped and threw out his arms. He cocked his head and stared at Hathunor. A moment passed, then he barked a guttural command to the others, reaching for the horn slung across his broad chest.

The thrum of a bowstring sounded almost at Torrin's ear, and he twitched his head to the side reflexively. With a quiet thump, the arrow struck its mark in the heart of the Raken trying to give warning. The creature toppled backwards amid the confused guards. Growls and roars erupted and they rushed forward.

Hathunor launched himself at them, whirling among the smaller Drae Raken. Torrin ran forward with his sword high, wincing at the sudden sound of metal clanging against metal.

Raken hearing was good. It would only be a matter of time before more guards were upon them.

The fight was fierce and short. Arynilas stood clear and sent arrow after arrow into the Raken. Torrin met one Raken, ducking sideways to avoid a heavy club. He swung his sword and cut deep, letting his momentum carry him past. Howling, the Raken shied from the sword but shot out a clawed hand. Talons raked across Torrin's leather shoulder guard, grabbed hold and heaved, throwing Torrin backward. He slammed into the wall of the tower with force, barely keeping his head from bouncing off the stone. Twisting violently, he broke the Raken's grip and sliced upward with his sword, catching the Raken in the heart. The creature collapsed at his feet.

He swiveled. Rowan leapt to one side as the remaining Raken brought its massive club down, crunching it against the battlements where she'd stood. She stabbed up ward through its heart and it toppled slowly off the battlements. They heard the sickening thud of the body landing on the stones below.

Rowan's sword hummed; Torrin scanned the battlements, listening...

Arynilas retrieved his golden fletched arrows, sliding them back into his quiver, and the others heaved the bodies of the Raken to where the first had fallen below.

The clouds parted and bright moon light shone on the battlement. Torrin

looked up, frowning in confusion. Bashelar and Raelys were almost side by side in the sky, a pair of glowing eyes. Cold dread tingled up his back. By this time tomorrow night, Raelys would be tucked behind the blue surface of Bashelar. *The eclipse.*

Rowan gasped. "When the little moon is hidden behind the larger…"

His friends stood gazing up as the clouds once more began to cover the moons.

Torrin shook himself. "Let's move!" he hissed.

They rounded the last curve of the tower, and there was the dim outline of a door concealed in the shadow of the joining angle. Torrin reached out to test the handle doubtfully. It was locked. Hathunor stepped forward and leaned his considerable weight against the iron-clad door; it groaned and shuddered, but would not open.

Torrin clenched his teeth in frustration. *We should have been deep inside the fortress by now.*

The door's smooth, riveted surface fit tightly into the stone wall, offering not so much as a keyhole.

Dalemar laid a hand on Torrin's shoulder and spoke softly into his ear. "We will have to hope that a little trickle of magic will not be detected by Miroth."

Torrin nodded; more Raken would come at any moment, drawn to the sound of the fighting. *Miroth will know we are here soon if he doesn't already.* He tried to shake the sinking feeling that their mission was failing before it had truly begun.

Dalemar moved forward and pressed the palm of his hand against the handle. Blue light flared faintly around his hand. After a faint click, the door squealed as it swung outward, revealing pitch blackness within.

"Erys! That is unpleasant," said Nathel, inhaling the stale odour from within. "A lantern would be good now, Borlin."

"Light it inside." Torrin hefted his sword, trying to watch both directions at once.

One by one, the companions crossed into the dreaded darkness. Rowan hung back as though stopped by an unseen force. Her expression made his heart clench – it was exactly how she looked when she woke from the nightmare.

He placed a hand on her shoulder. "Are you ready, Keeper?"

She turned back to face the door. "I am," she said and stepped forward.

With a last look up and down the battlements, Torrin plunged into the unknown labyrinth of Lok Myrr fortress after Rowan.

Intruders

Miroth raised his head suddenly from his work, looking across the room at the rich tapestry without seeing it. Magic had just been used within the fortress. It had been a bare trickle, but he had felt it just the same. He frowned; he had not noted the Raken pass through his ward for quite some time.

He hissed in irritation. The work before him had consumed him, leaving little room for anything else. He had barely noted the presence of the boy standing motionless in the corner of the room, head down, eyes on the carpet.

"Bring me the Raken guards from the door!" snapped Miroth. "Move!"

Sol jumped and fled the room.

Who would have the impudence to try entering Lok Myrr? A glimmer of worry tainted Miroth's thoughts. He stood, back muscles aching in protest. With his long robes swirling, he began to pace.

Miroth hadn't been in contact with other Riths for almost five hundred years, and he was certain none would be bold enough to come without invitation in the middle of the night. Perhaps Cerebus had found a way to send an attacking force. Miroth shook his head. No army could approach the walls of Lok Myrr without being seen.

Where are my beasts? Miroth's irritation grew deeper. He had no time for this! His attention was already divided enough. As he strode past his desk, he cast a longing eye at his work, then noticed the cup of tonic that Sol had brought – he still hadn't touched it. Miroth's hand shook as he picked up the goblet. He bumped an ancient scroll and it rolled off the edge to land amid the books stacked around the carved legs of the table. He left it where it fell.

Inhaling the sharp tang of herbs, he brought the cup to his lips. He hated the brew but it did work – rebuilding his strength quickly. He went to stand in front of the roaring fire, basking in the heat. After taking another mouthful of the bitter infusion, he placed the goblet on the stone mantle. He gripped the fire-warmed stones to steady himself and cast his mind out briefly to the bonded beast he had in Pellar. He held the contact only long enough to see his army of Raken swarming over the walls of Pellaris. Yes, good.

He returned quickly, sagging against the mantle, and reached for the goblet. The shaking was worse. No matter – there was a man above in the uppermost room of the tower waiting to give his life for his master's cause.

Miroth stared fixedly into the flames and felt a pull of yearning, an itch to feel the power that would come from the slow ebbing of life. Very soon now, the essence that he took from each death would not bleed away like the life that had given it. Soon he would have the strength to keep pushing the Raken onward. They would not stop their assault on Pellaris this time.

The ancient Soul-takers were mere apprentices compared to the heights he had reached with the magic. Through his own ingenuity and talents, he had discovered the complex and subtle variations of the art.

Certain emotions, when fostered at the moment of death, added different flavours to a casting – different traits that when combined in specific ways could give the soul-taker what he needed to achieve his goals. The emotion of anger gave power but little stamina; happiness created quickness of thought; sadness gave the ability to see with clarity; and fear, fear gave the longest lasting effects of strength.

Some emotions were very difficult to achieve during the final moments of life and the nuanced blending that came from a mix of different emotions could be extremely fulfilling. Miroth had worked for centuries meticulously cataloguing and testing the effects of the different combinations. Fear and anger was by far the most successful and useful combination he had found. The two emotions, when experienced at the moment of death in the exact mixture of almost equal amounts, allowed a soul-taker to gain long lasting strength and power. Power that augmented his own to a great degree, enabling him to perform feats that far outstripped what he would otherwise be capable of.

But that particular blending offered little in the way of exhilaration or pleasure. Once, many years ago, Miroth had been able to achieve the emotion of love at the moment of release. Not just love for life or family; his victim had experienced a profound love for him as she died. It had left him weeping on the floor in ecstasy.

Miroth sighed So much more was possible. There were always more layers to be peeled back, deeper depths to be sounded through skin and blood, muscle and bone at the moment when life, in all its variations, crossed over the threshold to death.

Miroth's mastery of the lost skill of soul-taking had made the task of deciphering the Summoning spell far easier. Although the spell needed to summon the Wyoraith was incredibly complex, there were similarities between *its* structure and the spells at which Miroth was adept. As the Soul-taking spells were constructed and the power was woven to build upon itself until it vibrated with its own life, so too did the Summoning spell build and mount to its climax. The weaving needed to summon the Wyoraith was like a vast lake compared with the ponds in which Miroth worked to soul-take, but a lake only required more time to fill.

Miroth forced himself to sip from the goblet again. He glared at the door. Where was Sol and the Raken?

Like his soul-taking work, emotion would be very important during the summoning, not just the victim's but his own as well. He had discovered that the Wyoraith would resonate with the intention of the Summoner. If he was not fully committed to the task at hand and clear in his purpose, the Wyoraith would be less potent – or, worse, a useless tool.

Miroth pulled in a harsh breath. His ancient heart shuddered erratically as cold panic bled through his chest. *I cannot fail.*

The Myrian woman was close; he had felt her drawing nearer over the last days. The gift he had been sending her, paired with the conditions of her journey, would be doing its work well by now. Miroth had been explicit in his instructions to the Priesthood of Erys. The men selected for the task of escorting the Messenger were to be brutal in their treatment of her, but were never to cross the line. The expectation of real violence needed to be an ever-present companion for her.

Fear – it was the key to the potency of the summoning. She had to be terrified.

Miroth had taken the utmost care in constructing his sending for the girl, making sure it was not too strong to overcome her completely. Most of the subjects that he had worked this form of mind projection on eventually went insane as the dream took over their waking lives. She would be stronger than most, and able to keep madness at bay until the very end.

He bared yellow teeth and clenched his jaw as saliva pooled in his mouth in anticipation. Several loose teeth shifted. Very shortly *he* would become the caretaker of her suffering. Let her be worthy of her fate.

He cast his mind downward toward the cavern deep below the fortress. Slowly, almost imperceptibly, the force within it swelled upward in anticipation of release. He sighed and came back to himself.

Miroth had recognized the presence that dwelled beneath Lok Myrr long ago, when he had wrested possession of the fortress from the Krang Warlords. It was the place he had searched for so relentlessly. Finally, he could begin his true work in earnest. In their own crude way, even the Warlords had understood that great power slept beneath the fortress – attested to by the pointless but appropriate victims they had hurled into the chasm to appease it.

Miroth had looked down into that pit of darkness with his heart racing, knowing that with the dormant inhabitant at his command, he would be able to reach the great heights for which he was destined. Since then all his energy had been channelled toward this end. Uncounted years had bled away like the lives he had taken to gain the power he needed to finally release what slept below – an eternal entity waiting for resurrection and release by a hand that could control and direct its vast power.

Miroth hissed and drank down that last of his bitter tonic. Focus! There were still so many urgent tasks yet to be done, each as important as the next and demanding his undivided attention. He resumed his pacing.

Two Raken stepped into the room. Sol slunk in after them, trying to hide behind their bulk. Miroth spoke to them, the harsh sound of their speech odd in his mouth as always. The beasts nodded once and turned without uttering a sound, almost trampling his stupid assistant in the process.

Anger rose like bile to Miroth's tongue. "I have been kept waiting, my attention taken from vital work."

Sol began to back away, stammering out an apology. "My Lord, th-the Raken w-were n-not at their post. I had to run down the –"

Miroth motioned impatiently, cutting Sol off with a thread of power squeezed around the boy's throat.

"I do not have time for your excuses, idiot," he spat. "Go with them! I want to know who trespasses in my fortress. Bring whoever it is to me alive."

Miroth released his hold and stalked towards his work, barely registering the boy scuttling from the room. The scroll on his desk was ancient, disintegrating even as he read it. It would be destroyed once he had memorized what was needed from it. Only a single phrase was left, but it had to be recited exactly or all the work for the Summoning would be in vain.

There is no room for error.

Dark Passage

The shadowy corridors of Lok Myrr were cold, ominously still. Despite the chill, Torrin reached up to wipe sweat from his brow. Borlin's small lantern cast a dim illumination in the blackness.

A light bled out of the dark ahead – a torch smoking in the damp air. They were near the center of the huge fortress now. As they moved into the light Torrin looked back at his friends. Their expressions were set, wary. Rowan returned his gaze steadily.

The plan was to find their way as quickly as possible to the east tower where Miroth would be behind his ward. What they would do when they found him… Torrin frowned; they had a few surprises for the Black Rith. Hathunor for one – Miroth might not know about the Saa Raken's abilities to control magic. Surprise itself was also a weapon to be used. Rowan freed, and here of her own will was another.

They came to a junction of corridors. Without slowing, Arynilas turned east and headed down the dim hallway to the left. A wavering torch was set far down its length.

Hathunor growled. Torrin and the others stopped, listening. Ahead of them, they began to hear the faint tramp of many running feet.

"What are the chances they are *not* looking for us?" asked Nathel.

"Slim to none." Torrin ground his teeth, looking at Rowan. "We will have to find another way to the east tower."

She nodded and turned back the way they had come, spell sword grasped in her right hand. Quickening their pace, they took the left passage at the junction – the next best route into the darkness. They had to move as far into Lok Myrr as possible; couldn't waste precious time and energy engaging enemy Raken.

They jogged through a corridor with doorways that yawned open darkly. Only a few were closed and one or two had light seeping from under the threshold. The bare rooms were depressing – servants' quarters.

Torrin skidded to a halt with his friends as an old man stepped out of a room directly ahead of them, his swinging lantern casting a swooping light across the stone walls. He froze as he saw them. Standing ghostlike, with his long white hair draggling over bony shoulders and parchment-pale skin illuminated from below, he stared with round, milky eyes. Torrin wondered if he was blind. Then it dawned on him – this was a man from the west, like the ones that laboured on the ships he and Nathel had watched in Pellaris's harbour as children. He had never seen a Westman this close.

Arynilas drew his bow, aiming to silence the pallid man before he could shout warning. But the Westman quailed back from them and cast himself upon the stone floor, covering his head. His lantern sputtered to darkness as it rolled to a stop near Torrin's feet.

"Wait!" Torrin bent swiftly over the frightened man, grasping his skinny shoulders. "How do we find Miroth's tower?"

The man began to sob, squeezing his eyes shut.

Torrin modified his tone. "We will not harm you. All we want to know is how to get to the Lord of Lok Myrr."

The man's toothless mouth opened, but no sound came out.

"Will you show us the way?" asked Rowan urgently beside Torrin. The Westman's pale eyes opened, rolled over to Rowan, and he nodded weakly.

Torrin lifted him from the floor and set him back on his feet, motioning forward. "Lead."

The old Westman stumbled a few steps in the direction they had been going, but it was quickly apparent that he was too old to travel at their pace. After getting a few stammered instructions out of him, they bundled him into an empty room and continued onward.

Soon another hallway branched off toward the left, heading east. It led to a set of spiral stairs; they began to climb. Hathunor stopped and Torrin pulled up sharply to avoid running into him. The Saa Raken pointed up the stairway. "Hathunor sense Draes."

"How many?" Torrin asked.

Hathunor tilted his head. "Hathunor cannot tell. Little Brothers feel faint."

Torrin looked down the stairs at his companions.

"Me thinks we'll no make it further wi'out a fight," Borlin said quietly, hefting his short sword.

Nathel looked down a step at Dalemar. "Any element of surprise we had is gone. Miroth knows we are here now. Why not hide us with magic like you and Hathunor did in the Boglands?"

Dalemar shook his head. "Miroth would be able to locate us through the magic we would be wrapped in."

"Yes but the goal is to reach Miroth with as little fighting as possible. If we can evade the Raken to get close enough to take out the Black Rith, then we should try it," said Nathel.

"Don't forget how difficult that spell was on Dalemar," said Rowan. "We will need Dalemar at full strength when we confront Miroth."

Torrin ground his sword tip on the stair. "I agree. Dalemar, you must conserve your strength for when it matters most. Use magic only when necessary; the less information we give Miroth the better."

Hathunor motioned to the others.

Torrin took the steps two at a time until he reached the curve near the opening at the top, then flattened himself against the wall as the rest of the companions followed. Arynilas darted out of the opening and instantly blended into the shadows on the other side. Borlin shuttered his lantern, leaving Hathunor's glowing eyes as the only light.

They could hear the sound of the approaching Raken now – a large group. Torrin risked a peek through the stairwell entry, and cursed silently under his breath. Twelve Raken were striding through the passageway towards them with several torches. They looked different somehow. It took Torrin a moment to realize they had no crests and their shoulder spines were blunt. They were also very small – Torrin and Nathel's size, in contrast to the bigger Drae escorting them.

Hathunor spoke in a low rumble. "No kill these Little Brothers. They are cubs. They should not be here. This terrible fate for little ones."

Torrin stared up at Hathunor. In the oncoming torchlight, every fang glinted in a snarl the likes of which Torrin had never seen.

He looked quickly back out the door. These Raken were children!

"What should we do, Hathunor?" Rowan asked in a whisper.

The giant Raken swung his huge head to look at the companions, and then he focused on Dalemar. "Power, give Hathunor a little magic."

The young Drae Raken were almost upon them. Dalemar did not hesitate, reaching out for Hathunor. Blue light flared in the darkness and Hathunor stepped through the doorway, stretching out his hand.

The little Drae Raken stopped, staring up at their giant kinsman, but stood for only a moment before collapsing to the stone floor. The full-grown Drae stood unaffected and Arynilas released his arrow. A clean kill – the big Drae collapsed dead among the smaller Raken.

One of the young Draes closest to the doorway reached out. Hathunor swiftly crouched over him and they spoke in the strange gravel-slide Raken tongue. The small Raken closed his eyes and Hathunor gently laid his great hand upon the little one's chest.

Hathunor stood, clenching his clawed hands, and threw back his great head, venting forth a ferocious snarl. The sound of it echoed down the corridors and into the shadows beyond.

Dalemar stepped forward, studying the forms of the young Raken. "What is it, Hathunor? What angers you so?"

Hathunor's voice was filled with sorrow. "Miroth enslaves Sisters."

Torrin stepped through the door with Rowan and the rest of the companions to stand next to the Rith and the Saa Raken. He looked down at the still forms of the young Raken – they did look like children.

"Did ye put them t' sleep?" asked Borlin.

Hathunor nodded. "Young ones not strong enough to withstand sleep spell."

"How does Miroth force such young Raken to do his bidding?" asked Rowan. Borlin lifted the shutter on his lantern, augmenting the sputtering torches, and they saw the dreadful answer. The young Raken were covered in fresh wounds, long thin cuts and welts criss-crossed their bodies like stitching on a quilt – whip marks.

Hathunor stood looking down rumbling softly in despair. Nathel reached up and grasped the Saa Raken's arm. "We will find them, Hathunor, your Sisters. We will find them and free them." His voice hardened. "We will free them *all* somehow.

Weary Dawn

Cerebus's sword was heavy in his hand. The burning in his shoulder and arm was excruciating and sweat ran into his eyes, stinging. His fingers slipped on the hilt of his sword; he readjusted his grip. His leg was numb where blood leaked from a long claw gash.

Another ladder clattered against the stone wall, then another. Black Raken swarmed over the wall into the recently cleared space. He moved forward to help force them back. The men were exhausted – Raken were being repelled more and more slowly and the extra time allowed the enemy to cause greater damage. Bodies littered the battlements and blood made the footing treacherous.

A woman appeared beside him. Her short sword cut at a Raken flank. The beast screamed and spun to attack. The woman retreated, sword awkwardly raised before her. There was fear in her eyes but also determination. Cerebus was shocked when he realized how young she was – perhaps only sixteen.

Dear Erys!

Intercepting the Raken, he took the blow meant for her on his shield. His left arm shuddered and he gritted his teeth as he thrust the shield upward and spun, slamming his sword through the beast's chest.

The young woman was there again, thrusting her sword into the black, scaled skin as the beast fell. She wrenched her sword free and turned to face the wall as the next Raken scrambled over it. She cast a quick look at Cerebus; he nodded to her. Her beautiful young face lit up as she realized who he was.

Cerebus killed the next Raken as it landed on the battlements, and the young woman picked up the pole to push the ladder back. It hardly moved; he grabbed the pole behind her and heaved, grunting with the effort. The ladder slowly moved away from the wall, then fell backward quickly as gravity took over.

Cerebus stood, gasping, looking along the wall for more Raken. It was clear for the moment. In the pale dawn light, he saw more and more women among the men. They wore miss-matched light armour. Many held bows, firing down at the the swarm of Raken on the ladders. Others fought with short swords and small shields like the girl beside him.

Cerebus saw Preven along the wall and hailed him. The General wore a blood-soaked bandage around his head under his helm. Cerebus moved to meet him, taking the brief reprieve to shake out his sword arm.

"I thought I told you to keep the women away from the front line," he said.

"No choice, Sire. We would have been overrun without them." Preven wiped sweat from his eyes. "As it is, I turned them away twice, but more and more came; some with kitchen knives and hatchets. I have been trying to arm them with the light armour but…" He shrugged.

Cerebus sighed. "Yes, you are right. They might not have skill in battle but their determination is making up for lack of experience."

Rowan of Myris Dar had inspired much in the people of Pellar.

It was just as well, thought Cerebus wearily; they needed as much help as they could get. "Any word on the cavalry and reinforcements promised from Klyssen and Tabor?"

"No, Sire. it looks as though they will get here too late, if at all."

Cerebus looked along the battlements. The Raken had been assaulting the walls now for five hours. The early morning light painted the sky above in pale pink – an echo of the blood washing the stones.

The army of Pellar was taking heavy casualties; the city was now evacuated to the keep. Those on the walls were dying as they tired. But there was nothing to be done for it, no one to relieve them.

New scaling ladders cracked against the wall where they had cleared them.

Cerebus closed his eyes – all they could do was keep fighting. Try to hold the walls as long as possible before retreating to make a final stand at the keep.

He hefted his sword and shield and stepped forward to face the next wave. Preven and the young woman stepped with him.

Escape

Galen waited impatiently in the dark tunnel entrance. He he hated being this deep underground. He could picture the flurry of activity in the marbled halls of the Temple, but the silence down this deep was complete. Galen could well imagine how that stillness had been broken when the tunnel had been used earlier by the party going in search of the Myrian woman. At the time he had been moving through the Temple's secret corridors with the remaining High Commission members and a few priests for escort, carrying torches and provisions.

He looked back through the small opening into the dim basement vault. Several priests were praying silently to the Goddess for her protection. Galen's prayers were not to Erys, but to the execution of well-laid plans.

The sound of footsteps echoed through the quiet and Galen stepped out of the tunnel in time to see two priests dressed as castle guardsmen enter the basement vault, followed by a third figure.

"Thank the sweet Goddess, Patriarch N'Avarin! We have been so worried," said one of the priests as the High Commission members moved forward to surround the three arrivals.

The guardsmen-priests turned to close the door and bar it, revealing the thin, scarecrow figure they had been escorting. Tihir N'Avarin's usual austere appearance was marred by a dirty face and scraggly hair. The borrowed layman's clothes he wore were crumpled and soiled. His dark eyes were sunk deep into his skull and they burned with a feverish intensity.

Galen stepped forward to greet the Patriarch. "I am so sorry for your ordeal, Patriarch. It must have been dreadful for you."

N'Avarin's expression in the torchlight flashed briefly with anger before he covered it. "It is good to see you, Chancellor Galen. I understand that I have you to thank as the architect of my emancipation from Cerebus's dungeon. It was not a pleasant experience, but with Erys' help, I have endured it. You have my lasting gratitude for your tireless work on behalf of the Priesthood."

"It was my duty, Patriarch, one I did happily. I am just glad that you are safely delivered to us," said Galen blandly, motioned for the priests to gather the torches and gear. "It is time that we leave, Patriarch, provided that you are up for the journey. Horses will be waiting at the other end to take us safely away until such time as we can return to our beloved city."

"If there is even going to be a city to return to," said Commission member Pothiern darkly. He fussed with the Scepter of Erys where it was hidden under his black robes. Galen frowned. He was regretting entrusting him with its safety.

One of the priests disguised as a guard came to his side and reported quietly. "The King and all the army are upon the walls. They will not last much longer."

Galen nodded, imagining the chaos along the battlements. There would be no hope now for Cerebus. He turned to Pothiern. "Do not worry yourself over the fate of Pellaris, brother. The city has seen far worse in its history and its stone walls have endured. When we return, there will be a new beginning for Pellar under the guidance of the Priesthood of Erys. Now let us move; we have a long way to travel."

An Unexpected Turn

Sol ran as fast as he could down the long corridor. The sound of his breath and the slap of his feet on the stone echoed loudly. His lungs were burning.

She was here! He knew the Master was expecting her but not this way. Sol had been trailing along behind the Raken when he found Zeben in the servant's quarters. The old man was shaking, tears leaking from his pale eyes, as he told Sol in a cracked whisper about the strange people he had seen.

The Master was going to be very angry. Sol's heart lurched in his chest. He passed the Raken guarding the huge wooden door to Miroth's tower and pushed the thick portal open wide. He moved through the first room with all its lovely furnishings and tried unsuccessfully to slow his breathing.

Miroth looked up when he entered and Sol bowed.

"Well?" the Master's voice was angry, impatient.

"Master Miroth, she is here, the Myrian is here!"

Miroth rose to his feet, a sudden smile stretching his papery skin; Sol glanced away from the yellow teeth, the cold eyes.

"Good..." The word was drawn out in an audible whisper.

Sol shook his head, desperate to be clear. Fear made his tongue dry as the smile left Miroth's face and his terrible stare bored into Sol. "No Master, she is not here as you expected. She is with men and… and an enormous tame Raken. They are fighting in the corridors below!"

"What of the mercenaries bringing her here?" the words crackled through the air. Sol quailed in dread; he had no answer to give.

Miroth seized his long wooden staff and swept around his desk, robes billowing. The air on Sol's face from the Rith's passage made him shudder; he hunched away but followed as quickly as he dared on his master's heels. He would be punished for not being within easy reach.

When Miroth reached the Raken guards outside the door, he spoke in their harsh guttural language. The two Raken turned and loped away down the corridor, their clawed feet clicking over the stones.

Miroth spun on Sol. The tip of his staff flared suddenly, sickly green. Sol was blasted back against the wall and held there. His head cracked on stone and his vision dimmed. When he could see again, Miroth was standing directly in front of him, his burning eyes only inches from Sol's face. Sol tried to turn his head away but couldn't move. His feet were a pace above the floor. Panic rose in his chest to suffocate him.

"You will begin to make the final preparations for me. See that there are no mistakes." The cold sinister voice burst through his skull and excruciating pain followed it.

Miroth turned away, and Sol was released to fall in a heap. In a haze of painful dizziness, face pressed against the stone floor, he watched the swishing black hem of his Master's red robes recede down the corridor after the Raken guards.

Inside the Belly of the Beast

The sound of Raken howls erupted from close behind. Rowan looked over her shoulder at the doorway they had just come through, expecting to see their black forms spill from it. The large vaulted chamber they raced through intensified the sound, echoing it from all directions. Howls sounded distantly ahead of them now as well.

The Raken were closing in on them.

They ran, weaving through tables and benches – a mess hall. Rowan had an incongruous vision of people sitting eating, talking in hushed voices. Even under Miroth's heavy hand, life went on.

At the head of the group, Hathunor altered direction and sprinted to the right. They followed wordlessly. It had been perhaps twenty minutes since they had encountered the child-Raken and Hathunor had been leading them through the dim corridors, keeping them just ahead of his kin.

Rowan pulled in a big breath, side stepping an over-turned chair. Frustration beat in her chest along with her heart. They were no closer to the Summoner – getting pushed further away from the east tower. Arynilas could sense the moons pointing them unerringly eastward. But more often than not, they were not free to choose that direction.

We are running in circles.

Lok Myrr was vast and multileveled. Corridors ran in every direction as though different architects had not consulted one other. There was little regard for design or symmetry; the passageways were graceless. A mad tangle of string – and they were scrambling through the hollow threads.

The sun must be rising outside.

She glanced up at Torrin running beside her, blood-spattered, his dark hair wet with sweat and his expression grave.

Hathunor loped forward ahead of them with determination, his crested head down. An arched door loomed ahead and Hathunor led them through it. The sounds of pursuit diminished.

Rowan's mouth was dry. She reached up and wiped the sweat from her forehead; her sword still hummed in her right hand.

The mission was failing. Miroth was still an unattainable ghost – like his presence in her dream, a barely glimpsed foe that she would never get close enough to fight.

Rowan shook her head. *Don't think, just move.*

Hathunor barked a warning as they came to a meeting of corridors. Raken pursuit was loud again; Rowan and the others slowed. Hathunor headed right and they followed – away from the east tower. Away from Miroth.

"They close!" called Arynilas.

Rowan turn – there were about twenty Raken running down the same corridor on the other side of the junction.

"Stop," called Torrin. "We cannot outrun them."

As one they formed up to face the enemy. The hallway was narrow – a few could defend it, providing no Raken came from behind.

"Come, Hathunor, let us see if we can even the odds," said Dalemar, stepping toward the charging Raken. He raised his arms, pointing down the corridor at them. Hathunor stepped with him.

Rowan felt sudden heat as something whooshed past from the other direction, ruffling her hair. She frowned, trying to understand what was happening – Dalemar hadn't released magic yet. He was struck violently from behind by an unseen force; snapping his head back and sending him sprawling on the stone floor. He lay crumpled and unmoving.

Rowan turned in horror – the corridor that had been empty only a moment ago, now held the object of their hunt. A wan yellow-green light illuminated a figure clothed in long robes, striding toward them.

Miroth.

Rowan gasped and took an involuntary step backward, squeezing her eyes shut. She bumped into something solid – Torrin. He gazed down at her, his blue eyes resolute. It gave her strength. She looked back at the Black Rith coming toward them. More Raken followed Miroth – many more. They blackened the space behind him, a boiling mass of spikes and stiff crests jutting toward the low ceiling.

Miroth wanted her for something; he wanted her alive and uninjured. If she could make it to him before the Raken closed in….

Rowan lifted her humming blade up before her. "On this day when blood is to be shed, let this sword be true, let this arm be strong in the defence of my land, my people and myself." The litany rolled off her tongue, calming her.

Torrin hefted his sword. "We are with you."

She looked up at him and back at the others. "May your blades be true, my friends."

"And yours, Messenger," said Arynilas, drawing his bow and firing.

"Aye, let it be done!" Borlin rapped his short sword against his small shield.

Rowan drew her dagger from her hip and spun it into her hand. She launched herself down the corridor.

This was the reason she was here, the reason she had left her homeland and traveled so far into an unknown land.

It was time to end it.

She ran and Torrin and Nathel ran with her, flanking her, barely a step behind. Borlin and Hathunor brought up the rear; the big Saa Raken had Dalemar's limp form clutched under his arm. Arynilas trailed behind, sending the last of his arrows into the chasing Raken.

The features of Miroth's face became clearer; his eyes were set deep within shadowed sockets, bald head reflecting the light as he stalked towards them. Crimson robes swished about his feet. Even from this distance she could feel his gaze burning into her. He carried a long staff, its tip glowing the ugly colour of her nightmares.

Miroth stopped and, without taking his eyes off Rowan, issued a command over his shoulder to the Raken. His minions leapt forward and streamed around him, water past a stone.

No, I have to reach him!

The distance closed quickly between them and Miroth's Raken. They came together, crashing waves of steel and flesh. Rowan heard shouting – realized it was her own voice. Torrin and Nathel slammed into the Raken, their broadswords cleaving and hacking in the tight space. Hathunor launched past them, scything into the Draes.

Rowan looked desperately for Miroth – a wall of huge, black bodies filled her vision. The Raken tried to grab her, disarm her. She kept her sword whirling before her. It caught arms, hands, fingers. Beside her Torrin and Nathel fought desperately.

Borlin and Arynilas faced back, meeting the Raken from behind; they were caught in a black, scaled vice. She ducked under Nathel's backswing, felt her elbow jab into Borlin's back.

The sound was deafening – Rowan knew the sword in her hand was still humming by the vibrations. Stinging sweat seeped into her eyes; she gasped in breaths.

A Raken clawed Torrin's chest, long gouges down his breastplate. She was knocked forward – Borlin had been shoved backwards and collided with her. As he regained his footing he had the presence of mind to latch onto her and yank her back upright.

The Raken had weapons, but they were careful not to use them on her. Her friends were not so lucky.

Hathunor's growls and roars sounded from somewhere in the press of black bodies. A club slammed into Nathel's side; he grunted, stumbling to one knee. Rowan sliced at the Raken, defending Nathel while he regained his feet. Rowan's throat was raw, her lungs burning. Her sword arm was tiring; blood and sweat hampered her grip. The floor was slick now with splattered gore.

Something struck her leg. A Raken had lunged low while her attention was on Nathel. Rowan kicked out hard, catching the Raken in the face. She brought up her sword, swivelling the grip, and plunged it down between the spiky, black shoulders.

Her sword stuck in bone. It wouldn't come free as more Raken came for her. Torrin was there, defending her with his great sword. Rowan wrenched as hard as she could, finally freeing the blade as Borlin and Arynilas pressed harder into them from behind. She almost tripped on Dalemar, lying unconscious against the wall between them.

Miroth was nowhere in sight – their small chance was passed. It would only be a matter of time before they were overcome. Then a blow made it past her guard; pain bloomed in her side and she stumbled, slipping in the blood. Torrin snatched her back up before she could fall.

No! We cannot fail! Rowan railed against the despair rising in her heart. She fought harder, ignoring her fatigue. Sword humming, dagger slicing, she wove pain and death through the Raken before her.

A dark shape loomed above them suddenly – a Drae Raken scrambling over the shoulders of its kin, spiked crest brushing the ceiling. It leapt at them, a black streak.

They raised their swords, impaling the creature as it fell on them, but its weight and momentum was enough to carry them to the floor with it. Rowan was pinned, her blade buried deep in the creature's side and the hilt jabbing painfully into her ribs – she could not free it. Grunting, thrashing; muffled sound. She heaved but couldn't budge the Raken atop her; she could hardly breathe.

"Rowan!" Torrin's voice was strained.

"I'm here," she called. More weight landed on her, forcing the remaining air from her lungs. Her vision began to dim. All she could perceive was a thin strip along the floor. Clawed Raken feet filled the space. She could see nothing of Torrin or the rest of her friends.

The weight crushing her was nothing compared with the pain in her heart.

They had failed.

As she was losing consciousness, the weight on her was lifted. Rough hands grabbed her arms, pinning them behind her. Then she was hoisted up over a Raken's shoulder and spikes bit into her waist. She struggled, straining to see the others – caught sight of Torrin and Nathel briefly between the black bodies. They were on their feet at least. The Raken clamped down hard. She stilled. Time to save her strength, take stock.

They were marched through the endless corridors of Lok Myrr. The Raken took them down stairways and descending passageways – always downward. Rowan's head began to pound with the blood rushing to it. The memory of being tied over a horse outside Pellaris flashed through her mind. She glimpsed her sword, and those of her friends, in Raken hands behind her.

"Dyrn Mithian Irnis Mor Lanyar," she whispered. The Raken carrying her sword lifted it and looked curiously at it when the hum ceased.

Finally, they stopped before a rough iron-bound door in a cramped corridor. They were so deep within the fortress now that

Rowan swore she could feel the groaning of tons of rock pressing down on them. The Raken carrying their confiscated weapons had gone, disappearing ahead down the narrow corridor.

Of Miroth, there was no sign.

The door squealed as it was opened and its thick bottom ground against the stone floor. She was lifted from the Raken carrying her and thrown into blackness. Pain flared through her shoulder when she hit the floor. Someone else landed behind her with a soft grunt – Arynilas.

Rowan twisted around to look at the doorway. Torchlight bled over the stone floor at its opening. She saw Nathel shoved forward by the Raken into the darkness and then Torrin, blood dripping down his face.

Ignoring the pain in her shoulder, Rowan scrambled up. Dalemar was tossed in next and Torrin and Nathel barely caught him before he hit the hard floor. Borlin finally stumbled through, cursing eloquently.

The door slammed shut, plunging them all into blackness.

Hathunor was missing.

Betrayal

The sun had reached its zenith in the clear blue sky when Cerebus ordered the retreat to Pellaris Keep. The lines of the Pellarian army were no longer holding the Raken at bay.

Cerebus fought next to General Preven, refusing to leave with the first wave of soldiers heading back up into the city.

The young woman also fought by their side, favouring a broken arm where she had been hit with a Raken club. It was not her sword arm, she had explained, when Cerebus bade her to retreat behind the line. She was untrained but had courage and knew instinctively to get in close, make a strike and get out again as fast as possible.

Cerebus bled from a long gash on his arm and his thigh oozed from a stab wound. He had to continuously wipe at another cut over his left eye to keep his vision clear. Sweat slid into the wounds, stinging. Cerebus welcomed it – it kept him sharp.

The soldier beside him went down, whether from a slip on the gory stones or a wound, Cerebus didn't know. Another man stepped forward to take his place, but only here, where their king fought.

Cerebus looked along the battlements. Now when men fell, no one took up their place. The Raken were getting through in ever-increasing numbers. They had broken through the outer gate and the beasts were now working at the heavy portcullis. The murder holes in the ceiling of the tunnel had been put to good use, but there were no longer enough soldiers to man both walls and gate.

"My Lord! My Lord!" Cerebus turned to see a young soldier run up the steps from the gate below.

"What is it?"

"The Raken are within the city, Sire. They are coming towards the walls in great numbers." The young man's voice wavered in panic.

Cerebus looked again along the walls. "Where? Where are they getting in?"

"They are coming out of the Temple of Erys, my Lord, scores of them."

Cerebus's blood ran cold. The Priesthood.

He looked back up toward the Keep. A black tide of Raken was washing down the main avenue toward the gate.

His heart sank. *The city can never hope to stand now.* The army was cut off. It would be over soon.

Preven cursed, his grey eyes filled with disbelief.

A short blast from a Klyssen horn sounded down behind the wall, and hooves clattered over stone. Cerebus tore his gaze from the Raken in the city, looking toward the sound. It was Captain Kreagan – the Klyssen cavalry rushed into view between the battlements and the buildings. They wheeled tightly and launched a charge up the main avenue at the Raken from the Temple.

Cerebus was jostled from behind and turned his attention back to the knot of battling men surrounding him. He would have to leave the Raken coming from the traitorous Priesthood's Temple in Kreagan's hands

"Sound the second stage retreat, General." Cerebus lifted his sword again, his arm like lead.

Elana. He would never see her again, never touch her or hear her joyful laugher.

In the bright noonday sun, Cerebus saw something flash – in the distance, across the trampled field before the city, at the edge of the trees. Slowly his tired mind grasped what he was seeing – armoured men on horseback. He blinked, wiped the sweat and blood from his eyes and looked harder. They were still there, forming up for a charge at the Raken army's rear.

Preven was lifting the horn to his mouth to give the retreat order.

Cerebus grabbed his arm. "Wait, Preven look!" He pointed to the distant army, all his fear and weariness lifting. The ally reinforcements – they had made it.

There were thousands of them. He recognized the green and white of Klyssen and the yellow of Tabor. The long awaited aid had finally arrived and the clear call of a horn drifted to his ears on the wind as he watched his allies charge into the Raken army from behind.

Shouts and cheers went up around him. Men renewed their fighting – the Pellarian army found new strength as flagging spirits rose.

Cerebus stepped forward to defend Pellaris's walls. The girl and General Preven were with him.

The Summoner

Miroth meticulously tested the edge of the dagger. Satisfied, he placed it reverently in its velvet-lined case, closed the lid on the carved wooden box and threaded the small ornate bolt through the closure holes. He motioned for Sol to pack it in the chest.

It was the last of the items Miroth needed for the summoning. He looked around the interior of his study; the hours he had spent here melted away into the dim past. Once the Wyoraith was free and under his control, he would set forth from here to finally claim his true place.

He reached for his staff and caressed its smooth surface, fingers stroking wood almost as old as he was. The sapling had been green the day that he had cut it down to carve into his focus. Over the years, the wood had slowly turned black as he drew his power through it. It had become an extension of his own body and, despite its brittle age, he was still attached to it. The ravages of time had done far worse to his flesh, but he had kept himself alive for this day.

Miroth swept from the room. Reaching the cold corridor, he spoke a command to his Raken, then strode down the passageway without checking to see if they, or Sol, straining under the weight of the chest, followed.

Footsteps matching the beating of his heart, the Black Rith moved with a singular purpose fused now with the energy pulsing in the cavern below the fortress. His entire body vibrated with excitement. The power from the Soul-taking spell he had worked up in the tower coursed through him. It had been regrettably rushed and when the man died, Miroth had been unable to receive the full force of the death release. He had enough to complete the task ahead, though, and that was all that mattered.

His thoughts turned to the woman in the dungeon. The Myrian was perfect. That short time before his Raken had overwhelmed her and the warriors was enough to tell him all he needed to know. That final verification of who she was before the Summoning would not be necessary. He was looking forward to meeting her up close, looking into her eyes, and feeling the gateway to the Wyoraith through her.

Miroth turned down a short corridor leading to the main stair into the dungeons. He flared his staff to illuminated the way more clearly and began to descend.

Terrible Purpose Revealed

Torrin traced the edges of the door for the fifth time – looking for any cracks, any weakness. It was no use. The darkness was so complete the companions had to grope along the walls to explore their prison. They searched every inch of it, running hands over the tightly fitted stone walls. Even the ceiling was scoured, with Rowan boosted up onto Torrin's shoulders.

He sighed and dropped his hands, turning back to face the room he could not see. "Anything Nathel?" His bother had been examining Dalemar as best he could in the dark.

"No, he is still out, but I can find no blood or wounds, so that is something."

"Anyone know how long we have been in here?" Torrin had the impression that many hours had slid by in the darkness. He caught himself reaching for his sword; felt naked without it.

"I believe two hours have passed," said Arynilas.

Torrin rubbed his face. Miroth would come for them soon. Unless Dalemar woke, they would be defenceless.

Torrin felt a light touch on his arm. He turned towards it as it slid down his arm; a hand nestled into his – Rowan. He reached out to gather her to his chest. She embraced him strongly in return and they stood together in the darkness.

"Hisst!" Arynilas whispered. "They come."

The tramp of many feet sounded faintly, growing louder until it stopped outside the door. A jingle of keys clanked against the lock and the metal squealed.

Torrin backed away from the door, pulling Rowan with him. It ground open slowly, flooding the stone cell with torchlight. The companions squinted in the brightness and Torrin scanned the room to find everyone but Dalemar standing tensely.

Five Drae Raken entered, bristling with weapons. More crowded in the corridor outside. Torrin's heart sank.

Rowan squeezed his hand and he looked down at her. She nodded grimly – whatever they faced, they would face it together. His heart pounded faster in his chest. Erys he loved her!

He turned to see the Black Rith step into the room, ebony staff clutched in a bony hand, deep-set eyes searing each of them in turn with cruel intent, scowling as his gaze lingered on Dalemar's unconscious form. Miroth saved Rowan for last. A slow, sinister smile stretched his withered lips as he looked her over as a slaver would his property. Torrin clenched his fists and stepped in front of her; Nathel was with him.

Miroth refocused on the two men blocking his view and Torrin felt a physical impact from the dark gaze.

"Fools," hissed the Black Rith. "You think you can protect her from me?" He raised his staff and levelled it at the brothers. Its tip began to glow a florid yellow-green and Torrin tensed.

Before Miroth loosed his magic, Rowan pushed between him and Nathel to stand in front of them with her head held high. "Stop. It is me you want."

Miroth lowered his staff. "True." His black eyes scanned them once more. "You will all be kept for useful purpose later." The Black Rith took a step toward Rowan, finishing his appraisal of her. He took his time – dark eyes wandering over her, studying her clothes and armour, her face and hair.

Rowan stood firm. "What have you done with Hathunor?"

"Is that what you call it? Your pet Raken?" Miroth narrowed his eyes. "I assure you it is quite safe. I am grateful for the opportunity to study it further. I will take more time with it later. The few that I have had the pleasure of working with have died quite early in the experimentation process." He watched Rowan intently for a reaction, his vindictive expression hardening into hatred. "You have cost me much in resources." He glanced toward the nearest Raken. "All that energy spent trying to bring you here and you show up entirely on your own." His rasping chuckle was mirthless, and when he spoke next, his voice rustled around the stone cell like a spectral wind. "Time is running short now, Keeper. We have much work to do, you and I."

Torrin closed his eyes. *Sweet Erys, he knows she is the Keeper.* He silently cursed himself for a fool; he had brought her straight to the enemy.

Miroth laughed once more. "You seem surprised, yes? I sent them to wait for you in Dendor and in other ports. I had agents and Raken waiting for months before your arrival." Miroth leaned toward Rowan and dropped his voice so that Torrin had to strain to hear. "It is a shame that your countrymen – the two who survived the journey here from where you were ambushed, had to die so slowly in order for me to learn that neither of them were the one that I sought."

Rowan flinched as through she had been struck, but she kept her head up.

"I discovered, much to my delight, that Myrians have considerably more endurance for pain than the people of Eryos. But what I was looking for was not to be found with them, or the bodies of the rest of your brave company."

The Black Rith watched Rowan with satisfaction as she stared at him in mute horror. Then he noticed something at her throat and reached out with his desiccated hand. Rowan turned her head away as he traced traced a finger down her neck like a lover. Shaking with suppressed rage, Torrin took a deep, steadying breath and willed himself to stay calm. Miroth's fingers hooked the leather cord near her collar, and he drew the green amulet from beneath her breastplate, rolling the stone between his fingertips before releasing it. He tapped the leaf-like insignia that decorated her shoulder guard. "I knew the Keeper was a Myrian coming to Eryos, I just needed to find the right one."

The Black Rith turned away. Rowan sagged against Torrin and he slipped a supporting hand under her arm. The Raken closed in.

Rowan's long braid suddenly slid up and around her neck of its own accord, twisting tightly. She reached up reflexively but couldn't get her fingers under it. Torrin took hold of the end of the braid, trying to pry it from her throat; it would not budge. She could still breathe – but barely. The black Rith was ensuring that she was under control.

Miroth looked back at her. "You have eluded me for a long time. But perhaps this is as it should be. The Keeper should come willingly to release her charge, yes?"

He approached Dalemar and looked down upon his fellow Rith with contempt. The tip of his staff flared as he lowered it over Dalemar's chest.

"He is no threat to you." Rowan said quickly. "He lost his staff in the fighting. Your Raken did not think to bring an old piece of willow with them when they took our weapons. He is young and helpless without it."

Miroth regarded her for a moment. "Perhaps it will be a small gift to you in return for what you will give me. You see the Wyoraith needs a soul to guide its way into this world, but not just any soul – the Keeper herself must relinquish her control to the Summoner. You will make a perfect sacrifice."

"Erys take you!" Torrin snarled, launching himself at the Black Rith.

Rowan whirled, planted her palms on his chest before he could be impaled by the Raken.

"No, Torrin." He pulled his glare away from Miroth to look down at her. Tears stood in her green eyes. "Please," she begged. "He will kill you without a thought, and I cannot face what is to come if you die now."

"We will all die anyway." The tears spilled down her cheeks and Torrin wiped them away.

"Please wait," she spoke very quietly. "There may still be a chance." She glanced meaningfully to Dalemar. Torrin closed his eyes, sighing.

Miroth spoke to the Raken, and the Draes grabbed Rowan.

"I love you," she whispered as they pulled her from his grasp. She stretched out a hand towards him; Torrin reached for it. Their fingertips brushed, then she was gone, swallowed by the towering, black scaled bodies.

I love you….

Not this. *Please* – a familiar curtain of madness descended over him. Torrin sobbed, lunging after her. Nathel shouted his name, grabbed at his arm but he shook it off. The Raken turned to meet him with a flurry of blows, knocking him down. Somehow he avoided the spears and regained his feet to assault the slamming door. He was only dimly aware of the others beside him trying to keep the door from closing. The light snuffed out and Torrin was left hammering at the thick iron.

"Rowan!" he screamed, hoping she could hear him. "Hold on Rowan! I will find you!"

He slammed himself into the door, pounded on it and kicked it as hard as he could. It stood unmoved – a testament to his powerlessness.

When Emma and his girls were murdered, he had been lost along with them. Not again. Never again. The blinding rage slowly lifted and Torrin subsided, panting with his forehead pressed against the cold door.

Sweet Erys protect her. Please give me the strength to save her before that demon can hurt her!

His breathing slowed; the rage and frustration overcome to reveal an unwavering purpose. He turned away from the door to grope in the dark for Dalemar.

The Offering

Rowan was swept along the dark corridor, her feet lifted clear of the floor. Tears streamed down her face as the last of Torrin's shouts receded. Miroth paced ahead, his scarlet and black robes flickering in and out of her vision between the black bodies.

Despair yawned, a pit before her. Only the hope that Dalemar could be roused to free Torrin and the others kept her from that endless fall. She couldn't see the path they were taking. There were doorways, locked iron grills. They paused for a moment, Rowan dimly registered the grinding of stone and then they were moving again.

The corridor began to slant downward; the walls were less finished. Water seeped down the rough stone and cool air flowed up from the way ahead. The sickly green light from Miroth's staff lit the way and torches held by the Raken guttered. The choking smoke curled up toward the low stone ceiling.

Blackness ahead, blackness behind.

Her arms hurt where the Raken gripped her tightly. Her pounding heart shook her entire frame and her chest began to burn as if Miroth's terrible light was already searing into her. The terror of the dream reached out for her – she was trapped, running from the dreadful fire. She began to lose herself to spiralling fear. It beat down on her, stealing reason, stealing thought. Her frantic mind could find no escape.

They had failed, failed utterly. They could not stop Miroth, and they had given him the very thing he needed to complete the summoning of the Wyoraith. *Her*. That was why he had hunted her so relentlessly; he needed her to help him bring about the downfall of Eryos, of *everything*. She had come here hoping to slay Miroth; instead she would be hastening his dominion over the land.

She sobbed, tried to fill her lungs against the crushing weight. *How could we have been so foolish?* How could the Seers not have foreseen this?

The corridor walls vanished, replaced by blackness. The glow of Miroth's staff flared. A huge round room was revealed, its circular walls dimly lit and the ceiling vaulting upward into shadows.

Rowan's breath stilled in her constricted chest – horrible recognition bloomed.

This was the end.

In her dream she was never able to escape beyond this point. Dread settled over her. She had died here over and over in bitter pain and paralyzing fear. Rowan clamped her teeth shut, fighting the impulse to scream. Panic rose like bile in her throat.

Soft laughter echoed around the vast space. Miroth turned to look curiously at her, his eyes burning her almost as much as the Rithfire in her nightmares. He said nothing, simply nodding his head.

Miroth had sent her the dream and there was something that he wanted from her in return. She didn't know what it was but she vowed never to give it to him. She could not give in to the terror. For the sake of her friends who had risked everything for her, she could not fail in this. It was such a small thing compared with what was about to happen to her but it was the *only* thing she could give them now.

Rowan closed her eyes; shut out Miroth, the Raken and the vast chamber around her. *Fear is not my master. I control my fear. It will no longer govern me. Like a stone thrown in still water, the ripples will wash over me and leave only calm. Fear is not my master. I control my fear. It will no longer govern me. Like a stone thrown in still water...*

Rowan's breathing began to slow and the pain in her chest eased a little. With the calming words running through her mind, she opened her eyes.

This is not the dream.

The Raken brought her forward and without the haze of panic, she noticed the chamber was actually quite different from the one in her nightmares. It was much larger and there were three openings into the vast space. The cavern in her dreams had a great pit in the center of it but what she saw in the middle here was a rising pinnacle with a flat top that thrust up from the darkness of a chasm that surrounded it like a moat. Each of the three entries into the cavern led to a bridge that was suspended across. Miroth strode over the nearest bridge to the center pinnacle, where a young man stood waiting for him.

As the Raken holding her followed Miroth across, Rowan focused on the chasm. The depth was unfathomable as it descended into purest black. Even the light from Miroth's staff illuminated only a short distance down the sides of the abyss. She felt a presence emanating from its depths, palpable in the cool, damp air. There were no words to describe the power and force in that presence. It raised the hair on the back of her neck, closed her throat, and yet it had a familiarity that was calming even in the depth of her fear.

A great, raised stone slab stood in the center island, with four large iron rings set in the corners. Its surface was worn and stained and Rowan knew why.

Miroth, standing at the edge of the chasm, raised his arm, indicating the slab. She shook her head; panic thumped her heart. She struggled madly, twisting and heaving against the Raken. It was useless – she was a blade of grass caught between stones.

The Raken lifted Rowan, placed her upon the stone, twisted the rope around her wrists and ankles and pulled it through the iron rings. Metal clanked loudly as the rope was cinched tight, straining her muscles and tendons. She couldn't move.

Her breath coming in shallow gasps, Rowan sought calm again; found it slowly. As she rolled her head from side to side, trying to see, she became aware of a deep pulsing in her body that came from deep in the chasm. It throbbed with the rhythm of her heartbeat.

Miroth was there then, standing over her, gaunt features lit by his staff. "I have waited a long time for this, Keeper." He beckoned to someone behind her and Rowan tilted her head back. The young man – a boy really – stepped forward with stark fear molding his features. He avoided her gaze, holding an ornate dagger out to Miroth with shaking fingers.

The Black Rith took the weapon and dismissed the boy impatiently. He held the knife above her, then slid it under the straps of her leather breastplate and began to slice. She was jostled with the force of the blade until it cut through the hard leather. When he had cut all the straps, Miroth tossed the protective garment aside.

His eyes traveled her prone length. Then he sliced open her shirt with the dagger, exposing her belly and small clothes. Rowan strained against the rope, felt it cut into her wrists. Miroth traced a line down her bare stomach with his cold finger. Rowan squeezed her eyes shut, shuddering. He cackled softly. "Patience, my love. You make it much harder on yourself by struggling, yes? You were destined for this day."

Drawing in a deep breath, Rowan focused inward, seeking calm in the fear mantra and the pulsing coming from the earth below. If she was truly the Keeper of the Wyoraith, then its power was also hers. She reached for it, opened herself and let its pulsing fill her.

The knife touched her stomach. Cold metal on hot flesh – then Miroth cut.

She clenched her teeth against the sudden pain. It was a shallow wound, but she could feel warm blood sliding down her side. Miroth put down the knife and held his hand out over her, palm down. His staff flared. Blood from Rowan's belly began to drip upwards, bead after bead until it became a stream of viscous red, where it collected just below his hand, swirling in a tight liquid ball.

The young man stepped forward with two golden bowls. He held first one and then the other under the blood. It splattered as it dripped into the vessels.

Miroth took the first bowl and walked to the edge of the chasm. He began to chant with the bowl held out before him. The words were strange, guttural, almost like the Raken tongue but deeper and more earthbound. The pitch of his voice was low and Rowan could feel the power beneath them responding to it.

She lifted her head, scanning the room – there was almost a full Trieton of Raken positioned by the entrance they had come in through. They stood impassively, awaiting their master's command.

Miroth's voice echoed around the circular chamber, bouncing off the hard stone walls, louder and louder until the words were shouted. His staff flared brilliantly. Rowan squinted in the sudden light; could see the arched dome of the ceiling high above. Holding her breath, she rolled her head over to watch the Black Rith. The bowl had lifted above his hands and begun to rotate. His voice reached a crescendo and abruptly ceased, leaving echoes in the silence.

The bowl, and its offering, hurtled downward into darkness.

Sacrifice

Cerebus stumbled in exhaustion. The knot of tired men around him tightened as he regained his balance. The young woman at his side darted forward to slice at an exposed, scaled leg. She held her broken arm protectively against her chest. Cerebus couldn't believe she was still on her feet. She was young and quick. It was what had saved her thus far.

He could no longer see how the battle fared outside the walls. He was fighting in the square before the shattered gates, amongst the tattered remnants of the Pellarian army. The Raken out side the walls had turned back to face the attacking Klyssen and Taborian reinforcements, causing the assault on the battlements to slow and then cease.

But the Raken streaming into the city from the Temple of Erys were more than a match for the beleaguered defenders. Cerebus had not seen Preven for over an hour. He had no idea where the General was or if he was even alive. Kreagan and his cavalry had cleared many of the streets but the Raken were everywhere within the city now. Insects burrowing into rotten wood, they roamed in groups through the streets and alleys, attacking suddenly from unexpected places.

The low evening sun highlighted the upper levels of the citadel, glinting on windowpanes and the copper domes.

Erys please protect the Keep.

He dodged sideways to avoid a descending club, his mind snapping back to the battle. The weapon missed him but the man beside him didn't see the strike. It hit him squarely in the side of the head, sending his helmet flying. Cerebus heard the crunch of breaking bones; could do little but watch as the doomed soldier slumped to the ground.

Both Cerebus and the young woman attacked the Raken as its club-stroke carried it off balance. The beast screamed as two swords plunged into its chest.

Cerebus wrenched his sword free of the falling body barely in time to defend himself from another Raken. He almost lost the grip on his sword as he parried the downward stroke of its scimitar. Cerebus sliced diagonally across the beast's chest. Another broadsword was driven into the Raken from behind, splattering blood over him. He couldn't see who had wielded the weapon.

Cerebus turned and saw the young woman struggling to draw her short sword from the chest of the Raken they had killed together. He stepped forward and took hold of the hilt to help her remove it.

He was looking into her eyes as the blade slid free. Her sudden change of expression warned him, and Cerebus spun to see a long spear blade jabbing towards his chest; he couldn't get his sword up in time. In a blur of ivory fangs and red eyes, the Raken thrust.

He twisted, turning his torso – presenting a narrower target. He lost his footing and felt the spear glance off his breastplate as he fell to the cobblestones. The Raken snarled in frustration and yanked the spear back to thrust again.

Cerebus was on his back; couldn't get to his feet in time. His sword was somehow pinned under his own leg. He tried to pull it free.

Movement flashed above – long blond hair flying loose. Then the Raken screamed in pain, even as its spear thrust found its mark. The beast slowly toppled backward with a short sword buried in its throat.

The young woman stumbled and then fell backward into Cerebus as he was struggling to his feet. The spear, meant for him, was sunk deep in her chest.

Cerebus caught her and wrapped his arms around her, one hand clutching the shaft of the spear to keep it from causing further damage.

Her head rolled back and she looked up into his face, a small but proud smile on her lips. She weakly reached out and clutched at his hand. Cerebus released his grip on the spear and took her hand. He squeezed it gently and his tears fell on her forehead.

She died quickly.

Cerebus almost didn't get up again.

The men fighting around him needed him, needed his leadership, but he needed the young woman before him – needed her to live, to grow old with a family, with children and grandchildren; needed her not to have sacrificed herself for him. He had never in his life felt so unworthy.

Placing her gently on the ground, he drew the spear blade from her body. She looked so young with her eyes closed, that smile still on her beautiful face – a face that would burn in his memory to his dying day.

He didn't even know her name.

Hope

Torrin paced in the blackness – exactly ten steps from the iron door to opposite wall. He counted, focusing on his steps; anything but what Miroth was doing to Rowan. The images came flashing into the darkness.

It felt like they had been trapped in here for hours. It had been only minutes but every second was an eternity. He reached the door again and turned, one, two, three...

His companions had been silent, waiting. Only Nathel could be heard trying to rouse Dalemar. Rowan's quick words had saved his life and given them the only hope they had of escaping to rescue her.

A groan sounded in the dark. Torrin turned quickly towards it.

"What – where?" A light bloomed and Dalemar's face was illuminated in the glow from a small ball of flame, hovering in his palm. Torrin rushed to gather with his friends around the light.

"How do you feel?" asked Nathel.

"I have a blinding headache, but I think I am fine."

"Can you get us out of this room? Miroth has taken Rowan." Torrin's impatience coloured his words.

"Dear Erys!" Dalemar grimaced and scrambled to his feet with Nathel's help. "Get me to the door please."

Torrin took one arm, Nathel his other. Dalemar's face was set and angry as he laid a hand against the door. It shuddered, then exploded outward; twisted shards of iron flew into the corridor beyond. The four Raken guarding the door scattered in surprise. They turned to attack and Dalemar sent a blast of blue fire at them. It struck with a loud crackling, splashing the stone walls and ceiling with sizzling blue. The Raken collapsed in smoking heaps.

Torrin cleared the door and sprinted down the corridor, following the direction he had heard Miroth take Rowan.

They came to another iron door. Torrin pressed his face to the small grate set in the top. Torches lit the room beyond and he felt another surge of hope; their weapons were laid out on a long table.

He stepped back as Dalemar reached him. The iron door was no trouble for the Rith, and they jumped over its twisted metal remains to get into the room.

Torrin found his sword and tossed Borlin his short sword and targe. The others quickly gathered up their weapons and belongings. Torrin cast around for Rowan's blade. It wasn't there. There were a few other swords though and he looked around for one that was small and lightweight for her to wield. Then a thought occurred….

"Dyrn Mithian Irnis Mor Lanyar."

Nathel turned to look as a muted humming sounded behind them. Torrin followed the sound. It was coming from a long, tooled wooden box, sitting on a shelf. He reached up and pulled it down. The box was locked. Miroth had noted the value of the weapon.

Torrin set it on the table and smashed open the lock with the hilt of his sword.

As he flipped the wooden lid back, the humming sounded clearly in the room. He took up the sword, spoke the words to quiet it and slipped it under his sword belt.

There was only one other exit from the room – an unlocked door leading to a dark, downward-sloping corridor. Torrin set a hard pace as they followed the passageway. The next iron door stood open, and they ran through it into a large square room. As Dalemar's light illuminated the contents of the room they stopped in horror and stood staring.

Three walls of the room were set with iron shackles, and several heavy wooden tables stood festooned with chains and thick riveted iron manacles. Black dried blood covered everything. On the fourth wall, like a collection of grizzly trophies, hung tools of torture.

"Sweet Blessed Erys!" whispered Nathel. "These chains are far too heavy for humans."

Torrin looked more closely at the manacles.

"This is how 'e controls 'em, through torture?" asked Borlin.

"It likely only one of many forms of control that Miroth employs," replied Dalemar with disgust.

"Dead end," said Arynilas quietly.

Torrin cursed. “They didn’t come this way.” He clenched his fists – could not abide the thought of having to search through the maze of Lok Myrr’s dungeons, giving Miroth all the time he needed to have his way with Rowan.

He turned his back on the horrible sight of Raken torment and made quickly for the door, his hope fading. But Dalemar halted him.

“What is it?” Torrin turned back.

The Rith was moving towards the wall hung with torture implements, hands held out in front of him. “There is a space behind this wall.”

“You can feel a spell on the wall?”

“No, I can feel a draft, there is cool air moving through it.”

They each moved to the wall, examining it closely, shifting aside whips and pincers and dreadful-looking things they had never seen and didn’t want to see again.

“If it’s a door, I canna see no latch te work it,” said Borlin with disappointment.

Torrin hissed in frustration. “This is taking too long! Can’t you blast it, Dalemar?”

“I could but need to conserve what strength I’ve regained. We do not know what we will face beyond.”

“Aye and Miroth would feel it as well, if ’e hasn’t already felt the two doors. ’E’ll send ’is Raken afore we can get close enough te help the lass.”

“At least it would distract him from Rowan,” replied Nathel quietly.

Torrin frowned and looked at Nathel. His brother’s expression was painfully grave.

“Aie!” Arynilas leaned closer to the wall and reached behind a long branding iron to push a small incongruous stone. It slid deeper into the surrounding stones and they heard a series of sharp clicks within.

Torrin placed his palms on the wall and put his weight into it. With a grinding sound, the wall pivoted a few inches to the right, close to where Arynilas had found the trigger. The rest of them pushed and the wall pivoted further inward to reveal a dark tunnel beyond.

“This is it.” Torrin drew his sword; it rang as it cleared the scabbard and he launched himself into the darkness. Dalemar lit the way for them with a suspended ball of flame above his hand.

Enemy at the Door

Elana ran down the corridor towards the main entry of the keep. The castle staff had not lit torches as night fell. Loud booming sounded from the tall, carved wooden doors. Shouting filled the vaulted chamber ahead and when she reached the wide steps, she saw the castle guard frantically trying to shore up the main entrance with anything they could find.

Evacuees from the city were milling around in distress. Crying children clung to the skirts of frightened mothers, who tried in vain to calm them. Near the bottom of the staircase sat the elderly, with bundles of their quickly gathered belongings heaped in their laps. There were even a few animals including dogs and a goat.

Elana swept down the steps to the nearest guardsman. He was very young.

"Guard."

He turned, and his face blanched in recognition. "My Lady, you must go to the upper levels! Somewhere safe."

Elana ignored him. "Where is the Captain of the Guard?"

The young man shook his head. "He went down to the battlements to help with the evacuation hours ago."

"Then who is in charge?"

The guard turned and pointed across the entry to another young man who was trying to help several others lift a long table to add to the barricade.

The great entry doors shuddered violently with another boom. The ornate iron grill that had been lowered just inside the doors would not hold for long after the Raken broke through the outer wooden portals.

Elana shook her head. This chaos was going to kill them. The guard was looking at the doors, panic on his face. She took hold of his arm and pulled him around to face her.

"Tell me who the oldest guard is left in the castle," she said.

The young man blinked at her for a moment and Elana resisted the urge to shake him.

"Uh, Nate. Nate is the oldest but Blain has seniority." He turned to look back at the doors as another boom sounded hollowly throughout the camber.

"Where is he, where is Nate?" Elana asked insistently.

The guard pointed off to the right, where a group of guards were bringing benches through a doorway from another room. An older man with silvering hair was directing them: Nate. Yes, Elana recognized him.

She turned back to the young guard. "What is your name?"

"Brec, my Lady."

"Brec, I want you to get together a few guards and get these people out of here and up to the mess. Then I need you to recruit assistants to bring the wounded from the infirmary there as well. They will need help carrying the stretches."

The guard hesitated for a moment and Elana's voice cracked like a whip. "Now, Guardsman!"

The man bobbed a quick bow and then raced off.

Elana strode to Nate, calling his name, and she registered the same worry for her safety in his eyes. Before he could voice it, she spoke.

"Nate, you must take charge of the castle guards. There are no experienced officers left in the castle. Can you organize a defence if the Raken break through the doors?"

Nate surveyed the men trying to brace the huge doors. He ran a hand down his exhausted face and then nodded. "Yes, my Lady. I believe I know what needs to be done."

"Good, see to it then. If the Raken win through, they must not get further than this entrance. Use archers. Position them at the top of the stairs to contain any that get past you."

Nate looked at the staircase, nodding. He clapped a fist to his chest briskly. "It shall be done, my Lady. I must request that you remove yourself to the higher levels. The King, may Erys protect him, would never forgive us if anything –"

Elana held up a hand to cut him off. "Erys be with you, Nate."

"And you, Queen Elana."

But Elana was already turning to see to the people who were being led up the steps by Brec and his fellow guards.

Rebellion

Sol crouched on the ground, hunching his shoulders as his master's voice echoed around the vast room. The weird chanting made the hair stand up on the back of his neck. Sol gripped the keys in his hand – keys to the cells where the huge Raken and the Messenger's friends were held. The Master had tossed the ring at Sol when they were no longer needed. The Master wanted no unnecessary hindrance for his special work.

Sol looked over to where the woman was tied down to the stone altar. She was very beautiful and Sol felt sorry for the pain Miroth was causing her. It was wrong. Whatever his master was doing was wrong. Sol knew it, but he was afraid. He would be killed or worse if he tried to stop his master. He felt tears sliding down his cheeks.

Miroth's chanting ended abruptly. There was a heavy silence broken only by the woman's ragged breathing. Then the room shifted sickeningly. Sol fell forward and grazed his elbows on the hard rock of the island. He looked over to the chasm, dread rising in his chest. Miroth stood on the edge with his arms outstretched, his staff lit an eerie green.

A silent concussion rippled through Sol's body. The room grew darker, as though the light and air had been sucked down into the blackness. Then there was wild laughter – Miroth's laughter.

The wrongness of what his Master was doing made Sol's skin crawl and itch. He wished for nothing but to be away from this horrible place, from whatever evil Miroth was working.

All around them, a grey, murky mist rose up from the abyss. It lifted high over the pinnacle and like a wave, curled inward, and poured down toward the altar at the center of the island.

Sol whimpered in fear. The fog began to murmur and as it gained momentum it whined and then wailed. When it hit the woman, her back arched up from the stone in distress. Sol watched in horror as the mist entered her. It seemed to absorb through her neck and chest and Sol thought he saw a faint green glow from where it penetrated. It was not the dreadful green of the Master's staff, but a soft green like spring grass after rain. More and more the mist poured into her and Sol could not understand where it went. She was not big enough to contain it all.

Tears blurred his vision and he shook his head. Pernic's face swam into his mind, along with the terrible things the Master had done to him. Sol knew Miroth would do the same to the lovely woman tied to the stone.

Sol heaved in a great breath and clenched his fists. His chest ached. Something long forgotten in his fear-tainted existence swelled in him, bringing heat to his face. It rose into his throat, choking him. He began to tremble, but his shaking was no longer from terror. Sol felt a strength that amazed him. His tears dried on his cheeks and his teeth clamped together in sudden resolve.

No more. He hadn't had the courage to help Pernic, but maybe it was not too late to help this woman.

He reached down to where he had dropped the keys and curled his fingers around the cold iron ring. Sol looked back at his Master, consumed by the magic he was working. He looked at the woman writhing on the altar.

Sol darted towards one of the bridges. It was left of the one they had crossed to get to the island pinnacle. He glanced back only when he was halfway across the span. The fog had completely disappeared into the woman now and the Master was standing over her with his back to Sol, oblivious to all else but his terrible work. Sol felt something wet in his hand and looked down to find blood seeping from his fist. He was gripping the keys so hard they had cut into his palm.

A Lesson for the Teacher

The moment Rowan felt the dense fog enter her body, she knew it – it was a part of who she was, had always been a part of who she was. It pulsed through her like her own blood. Her muscles hardened and flexed, arching her back as the power was pulled ever faster into her. There was heat at her throat and burning fire coursed through her. She gasped in air, could not feel the sensation of her own body. There was no longer any separation between her and the vast power of the Wyoraith whistling violently through her.

Rowan understood then what it meant to be the Keeper of this earthbound power. She understood how important it was to keep it from being used for evil purpose.

As the last of the Wyoraith was absorbed into her, Miroth loom over her. His face was painted with excited triumph. He reached down and picked up the second blood-filled bowl and brought it to his lips. His black eyes never left hers as he swallowed. Rowan shuddered in understanding – the Wyoraith would be drawn to her blood as he consumed it.

He pulled the bowl away from his mouth. Blood dribbled down his chin and ran into the creases and folds of loose flesh under his jaw. His eyes closed for a moment in pleasure as he savoured the taste. Then he drank once more, but didn't swallow. Instead he arched backward and spat up into the air above them – a fine spray of red. His staff glowed as the mist of blood reached its apex. It hung there, a scarlet cloud – above where Rowan was tied.

Once again Miroth spoke words of magic to summon the Wyoraith and the roiling, seething power within her began to rush outwards once more. Rowan gritted her teeth as it scoured through her and up to the suspended blood. Her body shook and as the last vestige of it spilled forth, she lay bereft.

Miroth filled his lungs and dropped his chin until it almost touched his chest. His eyes slid closed and for a third time he began to chant. This time, his speech was laced with all the blackness of his heart.

Rowan cringed with revulsion as his voice mounted. The greyness of the Wyoraith contracted and she watched in despair as its color began to change.

Deeper and heavier came Miroth's voice, soaked with a terrible malevolence. The Wyoraith began to revolve as it darkened. Rowan was helpless to stop the energy above her from transforming. It began to absorb and reflect all the evil that was Miroth.

Waves of nausea washed over her. The Wyoraith was swirling faster and faster, becoming a roiling blackness that sucked heat and life from the cavern. She could feel it all. The Wyoraith was linked to Miroth's emotions – a thousand years of hatred that had festered in darkness, growing and twisting into madness and an insatiable lust for vengeance was now swirling like a hurricane through the Wyoraith, tainting its essence. She felt the Black Rith's unbridled scorn for all life and his terrible need to control it. Miroth's own personality, his true nature – the Rith he had been when he was young – was but a faint glimmer of sanity lost in a sea of anger, pain and an overwhelming desire to inflict suffering and agony on others.

Rowan's fear of Miroth the Rith paled when compared with the dread she held for his creation. With the enormous power of the Wyoraith under his control, the Black Rith would reign supreme.

The presence now swirling above was beyond evil, it was the antithesis of life, hammering at her. Rowan groaned in loathing as the taint now within the Wyoraith oozed through her own body. It fed on her fear, taking from her all that she held dear. She desperately wanted to look away, but couldn't.

*Fear is not my master…*Rowan clung to the mantra.

And then she felt it – an island of calm in the storm. There was a small aspect of the Wyoraith that hadn't been completely consumed by Miroth. Rowan folded her will around it; protected that tiny spark of rightness within the morass of corruption. She willed it to strengthen, to stand against the wickedness of the Black Rith. She fed it, pouring her love for Torrin, her friends and homeland into it; felt it respond and grow. She gave it her own courage, her own will to fight for what was right. Her father's face came to her and her mother and brother. She fed the Wyoraith her love for them.

She was its Keeper and she *would* keep it safe and uncorrupted.

The Wyoraith was almost touching Miroth now. The spinning vortex at its center had extended down over his head. Miroth lifted his face to it and reached out his hand to caress his creation. He drew back suddenly from the contact.

"There is something wrong," he said in shock. "It is not as it should be! It is not complete – not nearly powerful enough. Not fully mine."

Rowan clenched her teeth and focused harder on the Wyoraith.

Miroth looked at her, his dark eyes filled with wrath. "What have you done, Myrian?"

Rowan gasped – a flash of comprehension. The dream Miroth sent her was meant to instil fear. As the Keeper, she could influence the summoning. Her fear was intended to make Miroth's conquering of her and the Wyoraith absolute. For the summoning to work properly, she had to be terrified. But she was afraid – only not as afraid as she would have been without the dream to teach her to control that fear.

Satisfaction settled over her, calming her further. She fed that calm to the Wyoraith; it lightened a shade. Miroth had prepared her well but not for the task he expected.

Rage etched across his skeletal face. He was breathing heavily, a wild, mad look in his eyes. "You have ruined the spell, marred the summoning."

Rowan looked up at him with defiance. "It is you who taught me to master my fear, Rith. You should be proud of me. I have learned your lesson well."

Miroth hissed at her with clenched teeth. He grabbed the dagger, his hand shaking with fury. "We will see how afraid you can be, Myrian. There is still time to correct some of the damage before the rest of the sacrifice is needed. You will see that pain can be a teacher as well." Spit flew from his mouth, landing on her bare skin, burning her.

He reached down, bony fingers sliding across her stomach; long nails scratching. The blade of the knife touched her and she gasped – it was like ice. Slowly he drew a line down her middle with the flat of the blade. Then he pivoted it up until the tip bit into her lower abdomen.

“Now you will suffer.” The tip of the knife pressed harder and Rowan braced herself against the coming pain.

A loud blast shook the room. Miroth whirled to see what was happening, the knife still in his hand. Dust sifted down from above. Rowan lifted her head, straining to see. Another blast jolted the chamber, sending a tumble of rock from the cavern ceiling to land on the Raken standing guard at the entrance.

A crackle of blue fire; the flash of an arrow; the sound of clashing steel in the passage beyond the entrance.

Torrin.

Miroth shrieked in rage and levelled his staff at the door. A bolt of liquid green fire blasted from the tip. It exploded into the Raken guards indiscriminately.

Rowan saw Torrin then, fighting furiously to get through the Raken; his great sword flashing blue in the Rithfire. Hope surged through her.

Miroth aimed his staff again, directly at Torrin. Rowan screamed out a warning; the green Rithfire flashed. Torrin saw it too late, even as he began to move, to duck – he couldn’t avoid it.

Time slowed, a moment, an instant suspended. Rowan watched helplessly with perfect clarity as Nathel stepped in front of his brother, shielding him. Miroth’s bolt hit Nathel squarely in the chest. He was blasted backward to slam into the stone wall, collapsing to the floor.

Battle in the Great Cavern

"No!" screamed Torrin. He lunged under the Raken blades to where Nathel lay against the wall; lifted his head into his lap.

"Nathel! Oh sweet Erys, no. Nathel!"

His brother slowly opened his eyes. His chest was burned and blackened, his chainmail and armour destroyed and hanging in tatters with bits of metal and leather fused into the terrible wound. Nathel's shallow breath was laboured and he shuddered in pain.

"Nathel?" Torrin registered his companions form in a defensive ring around them; saw Dalemar as he turned to confront the Black Rith, sending blue fire streaming outward from his hands towards the hated figure. Saw Rowan, lashed to the stone beside Miroth. He registered all this in an instant, as though there were two of him – one watching his friends, wanting desperately to get to the woman he loved and to kill the enemy who had done this to them. The other, holding his brother, the only family he had in this world, whose life was slipping away.

Torrin looked at Dalemar, hoping beyond hope that the Rith would be able to heal his brother; save him before it was too late, but knew when he saw Dalemar battling with Miroth that the young Rith would die the moment he tried to disengage himself.

"Tor," breathed Nathel. Torrin bent close to hear. "I couldn't let it happen again," Nathel coughed weakly, trying to get air into his ruined lungs. "Couldn't live with the thought… of you losing her like Emma." He closed his eyes.

"Nathel!" Torrin no longer heard the tumult surrounding them; was straining only to catch his brother's words.

Nathel opened his eyes and gazed up at Torrin. "Go to her. Save her, Tor. She needs you – I love you, brother…" Nathel's eyes closed and did not open again.

Torrin hugged his brother's body to him, his chest aching and grief rising like a tide. *Go to her. Save her, Tor…*

Tears blurring his vision, he let Nathel gently down and took up his sword. He clenched his teeth and stood to face Miroth and his beasts.

Dalemar was locked in desperate struggle with the Black Rith. Blue fire from his outstretched fingers connected to Miroth's eerie green, creating a pulsing column. It crackled and snapped, splintering away in threads of light. The green fire was pushing back Dalemar's blue. The young Rith stood shaking, teeth bared in effort and hands flowing with fire.

Arynilas was out of arrows, his flashing knives cutting into the Raken around them. Torrin helped Borlin in pushing a Raken over the edge.

A blur of movement to the left caught Torrin's eye. Hathunor came barrelling through the arch at the next entrance into the great chamber. The huge Saa Raken slid to a stop, his great head swivelling to take in the scene. Then he launched himself across the bridge and even at a distance Torrin could see the the snarl on his face.

A small figure stumbled into the chamber after the Saa Raken – a lanky boy with a ring of keys in his fist.

Hathunor reached the center pinnacle; then he stepped into the Rithfire.

When the giant Raken stepped into the stream of magic it winked out behind him and Dalemar sagged to the floor. Miroth's eyes widened in surprise and then fear.

Hathunor faced Miroth, capturing the Black Rith's magic, and absorbing it into his great black body. He turned his head and looked back toward the desperate battle at the cavern entrance and cast out a long arm. Green light flared from his clawed hand – a pure green, cleaned of Miroth's vile taint. It shot towards the Drae Raken, piercing them like lightning.

Torrin arrested the swing of his sword, watching warily as Miroth's Raken were transfixed, backs arched and arms thrown wide. The sound of magic hummed throughout the cavern and the light it cast bleached the shadows.

The flow from Hathunor ceased and the light flickered and faded around the Drae Raken. The beasts staggered as they were released. Torrin backed away but kept his sword up as they looked around in confusion – waking from a terrible dream.

As one, they dropped their weapons with a clatter and turned to watch Hathunor as he fought their oppressor.

Torrin launched himself forward, jumping over fallen bodies, dodging past the Drae Raken. He sprinted over the bridge, past Hathunor and Miroth. He reached Rowan, staked out on the slab; saw blood glistening on her bare stomach; relief in her eyes.

Slashing his sword down at each corner, Torrin severed the ropes binding her. He pulled her up into his arms and lifted her clear of the hard stone. She was shaking.

Miroth screamed then. He reached up toward the swirling black vortex above him. The Rithfire that connected him to Hathunor arced upward into the Wyoraith, where a section of the streaming magic touched it. Hathunor roared in pain. Then he was thrown backward, landing heavily and unmoving near the edge of the abyss.

The Black Rith, looking shaken, turned towards them. His expression of fatigue resolved into burning hatred.

A Warrior's Sword

Rowan watched as Miroth aimed the tip of his staff directly at Torrin. She shoved Torrin as hard as she could; he went with the force, diving behind the stone slab just as rancid green fire lanced through the space he had been.

Rowan glanced up at the dark mass of the Wyoraith swirling over Miroth. An icy cold radiating from it now. Large coils of it snaked down through the air, circling the Black Rith, twirling around and through him, drawing his attention.

Rowan inched closer – the dagger he had used on her was only a few paces away. She gathered herself to dive for it, hoping to get to Miroth before he could react. But he looked back at her and she froze.

His eyes were strange – the power of the Wyoraith clouded them. "It is time, Keeper." His staff glowed brightly. "We must complete the summoning."

"Rowan!" Torrin threw something towards her. It glittered in the green light – a long flash of metal. Her sword. Rowan lunged forward, caught the hilt, then spun.

"Dyrn Mythian Irnis Mor Ranith!" she shouted. The sword leapt in her hands, humming. Miroth shot deadly Rithfire at her; she dodged, barely avoiding it. Pain lanced across her skin with the searing heat of it.

Then her sword connected, but it wasn't Miroth it hit. A yellow-tinted shield of magic had sprung up between the Black Rith and her sword. Rowan's arm shuddered with the impact. The humming of her sword increased when it connected with the shielding, becoming a high-pitched whine.

Miroth glared at her from behind the safety of his magic.

Rowan drew her blade across the transparent surface of the shield. The humming increased in pitch again; a piercing whistle overlaid the thrumming now.

The shield gave a little.

Miroth glanced down at her sword in apprehension.

Rowan gritted her teeth and pressed harder. The sword's song increased again, hurting her ears and the shield gave a little more. Amid the screaming din of the battling magic, Rowan felt her sword finally slip through the barrier. She shifted her weight and lunged forward with all her strength, pivoting the blade so it would stab through the small opening.

The Black Rith crumpled forward as the razor-sharp spell sword took him in the chest. The shield flickered and died. Miroth dropped his staff with a clatter and the poisonous green light snuffed out.

The black tendrils around Miroth recoiled, pulling away from him. They snaked back up to the swirling Wyoraith above.

"No!" Miroth screamed as the Wyoraith withdrew.

He staggered forward and latched onto Rowan. His skeletal hands were surprisingly strong. They stumbled toward the edge of the pinnacle. She wrenched at her blade, still trapped in Miroth's flesh, but he clung tighter to her, carrying them to the edge.

Rowan heard Torrin shout her name. It was too late, she felt herself slip, pulled down to the ground and over the edge into the blackness below.

To Catch a Falling Hero

"Rowan!" Torrin shouted in horror as she was pulled over the edge into the chasm by the Black Rith.

He launched himself forward, diving. Threw his arms out; his sword spun away. He landed on his stomach and skidded across the ground. His head and shoulders crested the rim of the abyss and were suspended over the edge; his arm stretching, straining, fingers reaching.

An eternity passed in that moment, then he caught Rowan by the wrist.

The sudden weight wrenched at his shoulder, threatening to pull him over the edge as well. The fingers of his other hand and toes griped the ridges and cracks of the ground, barely holding. Rowan swung down and slammed against the wall of the pinnacle with a groan. Miroth still clung to her.

Torrin couldn't pull them both up with one arm. Rowan looked up at him – she knew it as well. He was slowly sliding over the edge.

He felt weight then on his legs. His friends were gripping his feet. The inexorable sliding ceased.

Rowan let go of her sword, still buried in Miroth's torso. She struck the Rith with her free fist, then her elbow, but he clung frantically to her.

Torrin turned his head and closed his eyes, willing his straining muscles to hold on. When he opened his eyes, he saw a golden dagger lying on the floor next to his free hand – Miroth's dagger. He glanced back to Borlin and Arynilas, holding his feet, then chanced it. He let go of his tenuous hold and grabbed the knife. He called out to Rowan and tossed it over the edge.

She caught the spinning hilt and, in one quick movement, sliced the blade across the Black Rith's throat. She dropped the dagger, took the hilt of her sword again and heaved on it.

Miroth's nerveless fingers finally released their grip. He slid from her sword and fell into the blackness of the abyss.

Torrin heaved Rowan up, the muscles of his arm burning. When she could reach, she shoved her sword up onto the island's top and slipped her free hand around his neck. Her feet scuffed at the sheer side of the pinnacle, and then she was finally up and over the edge.

The black, rotating mass hovering above them had slowed its spin. It began to lighten, the darkness and evil infused into the Wyoraith by the Black Rith could no longer adhere and it returned to a muted grey. Miroth's evil released was condensing into a black ball, shrinking in upon itself, smaller and smaller. A silent concussion reverberated throughout the great cavern.

Then it exploded.

Torrin threw himself down and over Rowan. The air around them swirled, gusts pulling at their clothing and hair like a gale. A groaning shook the foundation of the rock.

When it was over, Torrin pushed up to look at Rowan under him. Her fingers shook as she touched his face then she clasped her arms around him, pulling him back down. He crushed her to him with relief.

Battle's End

Cerebus was fighting somewhere in the streets of Pellaris. The renewed hope created by the arrival of reinforcements from Klyssen and Tabor had faded. The broken Pellarian army, scattered throughout the city, battled in tight groups, sheltering against buildings or retreating into the houses to make valiant stands at doorways.

Cerebus growled under his breath. He should have let Torrin kill the Patriarch in the temple. Galen, if he was ever found, would hang for treason.

Cerebus's exhausted mind wandered from the dark street – wondered what had happened to the brothers and their companions. He had hardly thought of them in the days after Torrin had left in search of the Myrian woman, the Messenger, the Slayer, or was it the Keeper? He shook his fogged head. Rowan had made quite an impression in Pellaris. Cerebus could see why Torrin loved her.

He had not expected to see the sons of Ralor again. Seven years was a long time, and after the horrible news of Torrin's family, Cerebus had given up any hope of welcoming him home again. He remembered their father with great love and respect. Torrin was just like him – Cerebus had been surprised by just how much.

He hoped they were safe now… *It was a fool's errand* – setting off into the icy land of Krang, but Cerebus believed in his heart what they were going to attempt was the only way Pellar would survive. A part of him had longed to go with them – to take the battle to Miroth himself, but a King's place was with his people.

A knot of Raken came streaming through the gap between the two buildings ahead; black shadows against the night. Only the gleaming on their black scales from the torches lying on the cobbles revealed them.

Cerebus shook his head. *Focus.*

He brought his sword up in front of his face but his arm, black with blood, didn't look like his own. His hand was stuck to the hilt with dried gore. His armour was gone; he had no memory of discarding it.

Cerebus refocused his attention as a soldier went down in front of him. Slicing at the Raken, he hauled the man out of reach of the sharp claws.

Red eyes burning, the Raken launched itself at him. Cerebus raised his sword, wishing he still had his shield. He stepped to the side, barely avoiding steel. The Raken spun; Cerebus stumbled backward, almost went down.

The beast lunged. Cerebus braced himself. He no longer had the strength to fight, to move beyond its reach.

But the Raken didn't strike. Instead it fell to its knees, its great black body arching backward.

Cerebus stepped forward to press the unexpected advantage.

The creature opened its mouth and an ear-splitting roar erupted forth, stopping Cerebus in his tracks. All the Raken were down, their heads thrown back, bodies stiff. He wanted to cover his ears but couldn't raise his arms. The howling ended but continued to reverberate through the street.

Looking around in confusion, the Raken climbed to its feet. The creature's red eyes, which a moment before had glared with a mindless ferocity, blinked in surprise – looking remarkably like Hathunor.

The men in the street stood stunned, too exhausted to do more than watch in astonishment. The beasts looked down at the weapons in their hands and dropped them, clanking and clattering on the cobblestones.

The Raken before Cerebus looked appraisingly at him for a moment, then turned to its nearest kin. It spoke. Cerebus was surprised to hear a precise and measured speech filled with clicks and burrs and guttural sounds.

Then the Raken turned in unison and melted away into the darkness.

Cerebus swayed. He looked around at the battle devastation and body-strewn street.

They are leaving. He was supposed to feel relief – or something.

The man down on the ground beside him groaned. Cerebus dropped the tip of his sword to the ground, grating it on the cobbles and leaned down to see to the soldier.

"Sire?" An uncertain voice sounded behind him.

Cerebus turned. "Send men to the keep, I want to know what damage there is and if the queen is safe."

The soldier saluted. "What of the Raken, sire?"

Cerebus wiped a hand wearily down his face; it came away covered in blood. "It is over. For now, it is over. Find the General; there is much to be done."

As the soldier limped away, the only thing that kept Cerebus from curling up on the street in the guttering torchlight was the wounded man in front of him and worry for his wife.

A Brother's Lament

The wind died from the explosion of Miroth's taint. Rowan wept at the relief on Torrin's face as he lifted himself off her. She reached up and pulled him back down, kissing his lips, his cheeks, his brow. He held her tightly, his warm breath on her neck a salve.

When he drew back she asked softly, dreading the answer. "Nathel?"

Unshed tears stood in his eyes; he shook his head. He got slowly to his feet, pulling her up with him and they stood looking around the dim cavern. The Wyoraith was still suspended above them. Miroth's legacy – the foulness he had poured into the summoning, fell like black ash, drifting down on them and slowly into the chasm after the dead Rith.

Borlin and Arynilas, crouching over the gigantic form of Hathunor, looked up as they approached.

"He is alive and I can find no wounds." said Arynilas. "He is simply unconscious."

Torrin nodded mutely.

Rowan began to shiver as they started across the bridge. Torrin wrapped his arm protectively around her and she leaned into him with relief.

They crossed the chasm to where Dalemar sat next to Nathel. The Rith was shaking his head, rocking back and forth over the dead warrior. He looked up, tears streaming down his face, his hands clasped at Nathel's temples. "Forgive me, Torrin, I was too late. There was nothing I could do. He was already gone – "

A tremor passed through Torrin and Rowan tightened her arm around his waist.

"I know," Torrin said in a constricted voice. "Hathunor still needs your help, my friend."

Dalemar nodded, but didn't move.

Arynilas and Borlin came to stand behind him, the Stoneman weeping silently. Rowan reached down and squeezed Dalemar's shoulder, her own tears wet on her face. She pulled in a ragged breath as profound sorrow for Nathel's sacrifice and

Dalemar's struggle to save the fallen warrior flooded through her. It moved from deep in her core and welled outward beyond the boundaries of her body.

The Wyoraith flowed through her once more, but it was smooth and calm. It passed out through her hand and into Dalemar. The Rith stiffened as it moved through him. Brilliant white filled her vision and peace swelled with it – so unlike the hatred and cruelty of Miroth.

"What?" Borlin exclaimed in surprise.

The Wyoraith settled into Nathel through Dalemar's hands, still clasped to the sides of his head, but there was nothing for it to connect with. It simply emptied into the dead warrior.

The whiteness faded as the last of the power left her and Rowan's strength went with it. Her knees buckled and her vision swam.

Torrin was there, lowering her to the ground. "Borlin, your water-skin."

Rowan took a swallow of cool water and, when she could see clearly again, she looked at the others. Their expressions were wondering and hopeful.

"What happened?" Torrin's voice was laced with expectation.

Dalemar was staring at Rowan. "That was the Wyoraith, wasn't it?"

Rowan nodded and looked up, knowing that the formless grey mist was gone. "What did you see?"

"We couldn'a see, lass, for the brilliance of the light," said Borlin.

Arynilas was watching the still form of Nathel. "It surrounded all three of you – the purest white."

Dalemar and Torrin leaned over Nathel, checking for signs of life. They waited, hoping; praying to Erys for a miracle.

After a while the Rith leaned back on his heals and sadly shook his head. "Whatever happened has had no effect on him."

"Come, Dalemar," said Arynilas softly. "Let us see to Hathunor."

Dalemar, bone weary from his battle with Miroth, accepted the Tynithian's help and he, Arynilas, and Borlin returned to the pinnacle to revive the great Raken.

Torrin wiped at the tears on his face but they wouldn't stop. His hand shook as he reached out to touch his brother's forehead. He took Nathel's sword-callused hand – the healer's hand – and brought it to his lips. His brother's face was peaceful and Torrin kept imagining him waking up, but the dreadful wound in his chest forbade any hope. Torrin wanted to cover it but wouldn't dishonour Nathel's bravery and sacrifice.

Rowan reached up and undid the leather cord of the small amulet she wore. The green stone was luminescent as she placed it in Nathel's other hand, wrapping the leather around his palm and closing it in his fist. She placed his hand over his heart and left her own clasped over it. "For your bravery and unwavering strength in the fight for freedom, I honour you, Nathel son of Ralor. Your valour will not be forgotten. Irinis vaen Mor Lanyar – the house of Mor Lanyar honours you."

Torrin stared at his brother's face. He felt strangely calm. Grief welled in his chest but instead of fighting it, turning away and ignoring it, he embraced it. He had not fully faced the death of his family until he was forced to choose between the pain and guilt consuming him or Rowan. His brother's death, his sacrifice, completed something. It brought Torrin full circle to redemption. He sighed, closing his eyes. Nathel was a part of him, he could feel his brother's presence – grinning at him. *Don't you see Tor, what else could I have done but give you this?*

The great cavern was very still. Miroth's Raken were gone, but their weapons littered the floor. Torrin heard footsteps behind and turned to see his friends stepping off the suspended bridge. He was relieved to see Hathunor looming behind the others. Rowan went to embrace the great Saa Raken and he rumbled softly as she disappeared within his trunk-like arms. The young boy – the one with the keys who had freed Hathunor – was still there. He was timid, but it took bravery to defy Miroth.

Nathel had made a promise to Hathunor. Torrin beckoned to the boy. "What is your name, lad?"

"S-Sol, sir. My name is Sol." The boy's wide eyes strayed to Hathunor and Rowan before returning to Torrin.

"This is my brother, Sol. He gave his life so that we could slay Miroth. Without your help in releasing Hathunor, we might not have succeeded. You have our thanks."

Sol flushed and looked at his feet.

"My brother made a promise to free the captive Raken here. Are there female Raken kept here, Sol?"

The boy nodded wretchedly. "Yes, down in the breeding cells. I can take you there." Sol looked up at Hathunor. "I am very s-sorry for what Master Miroth did."

Hathunor reached out a huge hand and gently patted Sol's skinny shoulder.

Torrin turned from the others and crouched beside Nathel. He lifted him gently to a sitting position and slid his other arm under his brother's legs.

Borlin and Arynilas stepped forward to help.

"No." Torrin shook his head. "I will carry him."

Borlin nodded and picked up Nathel's sword and shield. Arynilas handed Rowan her armour breastplate, collected from the pinnacle where Miroth had discarded it.

Tears wet his face as Torrin carried Nathel up the sloping corridor with his companions following. Rowan paced beside him, her hand on the small of his back. Relief and pain washed over him in waves.

One saved, one lost.

Sol led them past the dreadful torture chamber and through the guardroom. Hathunor lifted the remains of the twisted iron door out of the way. They went past the cell where Miroth had locked them and down a series of dark tunnels until they reached a row of cages set with iron bars. Torrin gagged on the stench of the Raken imprisonment and Rowan covered her mouth. He stood against the wall in appalled silence, cradling Nathel in his arms, as Hathunor and the others opened the cages. Five female Raken had been held there; for how long, Torrin couldn't guess. They were in poor shape – the conditions of their confinement would have killed humans. Their emaciated forms were covered in sores, red eyes sunk deep under their spiny brow ridges. Hathunor treated them like a reverent son, his voice pitched low as he spoke to them in the Raken tongue.

When they reached the bailey, the night was cold and clear with stars twinkling overhead. A bedraggled line of people stood waiting, many of them white-haired and pale-eyed like the man they had seen in the servants' quarters. Almost all had their meagre belongings strapped to their backs.

Torrin glanced at Sol. "They are leaving?"

The boy nodded. "They were the Master's slaves."

"They must have known Miroth was dead when the Raken deserted," said Rowan quietly.

Borlin shook his head. "Like spirits the Raken are, te jus' melt away."

As the companions passed slowly down the line of people, they received nods from each of them. A pale young man led a horse out of the stable with a stretcher tied to the stirrups of the saddle.

Torrin, shaking with fatigue, stepped forward and laid Nathel upon it. Rowan was there, helping to fold Nathel's arms across his chest, and Borlin and Arynilas laid his weapons down with him.

They turned when they reached the windswept gates and looked up at the hulking darkness of Lok Myrr. Much of the sinister, repulsive quality of the fortress was gone, leaving it merely ugly and unsavoury.

Sol, who had opened the gate with help from the other slaves, wrapped a ragged knit scarf tighter around his skinny neck and bowed. "Thank you for freeing us from the Master." Tears shone in his brown eyes. "I have sisters, but I didn't think I would get to see them again."

Rowan stepped forward and kissed him gently on each cheek. "Thank you for your help, Sol. I hope you find your way back to your family."

Torrin closed his tired eyes, remembering a similar token of thanks on a balcony in Pellaris.

Pulling on the reins of the horse, Torrin stepped out onto the pale ribbon of road stretching into the dark valley. Rowan, walking alongside him, slipped her hand into his. They had a way to travel to reach the place where they left their horses and gear.

Erys he was tired, but the thought of walking – just walking, without having to fight; without the bleak prospect of an impossible mission looming over them was such a gift.

He looked at Rowan. She would no longer be tracked and hunted; no longer be tormented by Miroth's nightmare. He squeezed her hand and pulled her closer. She looked up at him and nestled in as he wrapped his arm around her shoulders. It was over.

Sweet Erys, it is over.

Rowan stepped back as Torrin placed the last stone on the Nathel's grave. She pulled her cloak tighter against the cold night. The jagged Krang Mountains were black shadows around them in the stony vale, and the great Northern Hunter slanting across the heavens was gradually disappearing in the coming dawn. Torrin stood and bowed his head.

Borlin came from the packs with a blue glazed bottle. "'Tis not much, but I've bin sav'in it." He passed it to Torrin and patted his shoulder.

Torrin accepted the bottle and uncorked it. He hesitated, then took a sip. "To Nathel." He cleared his throat. "Thank you, brother." Stepping forward he poured a little on the stones of the grave.

Rowan accepted the bottle from him and took a sip. It was sweet and burned a little as it slid down her throat. "To Nathel. Thank you my friend." She poured a little out for him and passed the bottle to Dalemar.

The companions took turns saluting a fallen comrade. Rowan took a deep breath as fresh tears slid down her cheeks. It was done, but they had paid a dear price. She looked at Torrin – pain was written across his face as he listened to the farewells. In another time and place she would have believed Nathel's death and Torrin's grief her fault. Guilt would have kept her from the people she loved.

Nathel rested now with his sword, shield, and his healer's satchel. There was a gift from each of them – a piece of blue ribbon drawn from a secret pocket next to Torrin's heart, the last and only remnant of a lost life; a carved Stoneman dagger; a golden-fletched arrow; a small leather-bound notebook; a lock of coarse, reddish Raken hair; and a small green stone amulet carved with a leaf-like emblem.

Light from the rising sun touched the top of the mountains, bringing a new day. It was a strange feeling to see the sunrise with the prospect of no Miroth.

They stood as the sun rose, saying farewell to a comrade, a friend and a brother.

Aftermath

Elana ran down the steps of the keep, ignoring the calls of the soldiers following doggedly at her heels. They were determined not to let her go unescorted into the city. She navigated the steps to the square, weaving around the bodies. The fighting had been desperate here; the castle guard had just barely kept the Raken at bay. It was over but the toll was dreadful.

The Raken had been about to breach the doors when they had mysteriously stopped. She had watched from the balcony above the square, leaning over the edge as it ended.

Elana walked through the dark streets, searching, marking each dead soldier's face. The guards lowered their torches so she could see – so many valiant men. She saw women among the dead too, swords still griped in their slim hands.

Rowan. Had Rowan and Torrin succeeded?

There was no sign of the Raken, only the huge bodies of the slain ones. A soldier limped toward them, looking dreadful, covered in blood and grime. He stopped before her and bowed slowly, barely keeping from falling over.

Elana coaxed him upright. "Now is not the time for such formality. What news of my husband? Is the king alive?"

"Yes, your majesty, he lives. He is down near the walls. He sent me to see if you were safe and to find out if the keep was breached."

Elana released the breath she had been holding, relief flooding through her. "Thank you. The keep was not breached, but it was close. Please, take me to the king."

Exhausted soldiers walked among the bodies of the slain, looking for wounded, calling out for aid when someone was found alive. Elana finally saw Cerebus, standing with General Preven, among a knot of soldiers and horses near the city gates. She almost didn't recognize him. He looked dead on his feet – covered in blood with his armour gone.

The battered city gates stood open, and along a path cleared through the debris streamed the Klyssen cavalry and Taborian infantry.

Captain Kreagan stepped forward from the knot of soldiers surrounding Cerebus and hailed the Klyssen officer riding at the front of the column of cavalry. The man smiled widely at his kinsman as he dismounted. He clasped forearms with Kreagan and then moved forward to speak with Cerebus.

Elana threaded her way through the gathering crowd of soldiers towards her husband. The men fell back respectfully when they saw her and some murmured honorariums. Most, though, simply looked on in utter exhaustion.

She reached Cerebus's side and slipped her arm through his. He turned at the touch and his eyes flooded with relief at the sight of her; he reached over and squeezed her hand, smearing blood on her skin.

Captain Kreagan stopped in front of them. He bowed to Elana and introduced them to the man beside him. "King Cerebus, Queen Elana, may I present Captain Welan of the Royal Klyssen Cavalry."

Cerebus reached out and shook the man's hand. "We thank you, Captain Welan, for responding to our call for aid. You arrived when our need was dire. We are most grateful to you and your riders."

Welan nodded. He was a stern looking soldier, much like Kreagan in bearing, but with age and experience tempering that stiff Klyssen demeanour.

"King Cerebus, on behalf of Klyssen and King Andeus in Wyborn, I commanded fifteen hundred cavalry, to come to your aid. We lost many good men and horses today against the Raken beasts. I hope their deaths were not in vain and that Pellar's hard-won freedom is not taken for granted."

Elana watched Cerebus's face carefully. He closed his eyes briefly and she squeezed his hand in reassurance – she no idea how he was still standing on his feet. Cerebus opened his eyes again. "The people of Pellar are thankful for the sacrifice of the brave people of Klyssen. Rest assured they will not be forgotten, nor will Pellar squander its freedom."

Welan appraised Cerebus for a moment and then bowed low. They were a proud people, the Klyssen.

Cerebus turned to another man who had dismounted and stepped forward. The man was shorter than the Klyssen officers were but his bearing was just as proud. He wore the golden of Tabor and his silver overlapping armour was covered in spiralling scrollwork. He looked up at Cerebus, passing a hand over the short reddish beard that jutted from his chin. He bowed smartly with a clicking of heels. The Taborian ignored Captain Welan completely and received little more recognition in return, but Kreagan nodded respectfully to the man. The Taborian's eyes widened in surprise and he frowned at the greeting – he had probably never received such an honour from a Klyssen.

"Captain Feryell, at you service, your Majesty," the Taborian said with a flourish.

Cerebus clasped the man's hand as well. "Welcome to Pellaris, Captain. You brought us hope when the battle seemed lost."

Feryell gave a curt nod. "We met with the Klyssen just to the south and knew our best strategy would be to combine our forces. It appears that we were just in time."

"Indeed." Cerebus replied. "It is well that your two kingdoms set aside your disagreements in order to meet a common threat. These Raken and the one controlling them would not have left the rest of Eryos unmolested once they were finished with Pellar."

A huge man, wearing a bearskin cloak, his red leather armour creaking, stepped past Welan and Feryell. His small grey eyes cast a hard look over Cerebus and Elana. "Where is the swordswoman from the island of Myris Dar?" he asked gruffly. "I have a message for her."

Cerebus blinked in surprise. "Rowan Mor Lanyar is not here, but I believe this battle was truly won by her and a small group of warriors that left fifteen days ago to venture into Krang to confront the Black Rith Miroth. It was he who controlled the Raken and commanded them to attack. The reason that Pellaris was not lost this night was because the Raken were released from Miroth's spell. That could only have happened if they made it to Lok Myrr and stopped or killed Miroth."

Welan's blue eyes sharpened. "I remember them. Rowan was not easily forgotten, with her sword and her odd band of mercenary friends."

"You met Rowan and Torrin?" asked Elana.

Welan stroked his mustache, lost in a memory. "I did indeed. They make quite an impression. You say they went into Krang to assault Lok Myrr? To kill a black Rith?"

Cerebus nodded, then turned back to the large man in the bearskin. “Forgive me, you are?”

The man turned his head and whistled. Mounted Horse Clansmen trotted forward adorned with red leather armour and bows across their backs, spears couched in the stirrups of their saddles. The big man turned and mounted. “My name is Brynar, Clan Chief of Shorna.” he said as he settled himself. “The horse clans did not come to fight for Pellar; we came to fight for Clan. Many great horses were lost this night and the men who rode them fought bravely. Rowan of Myris Dar was the reason the Horse Clans came, for the Mora’Taith saw her path shadowed in darkness.”

“We can only hope that she and her companions will return to us safely,” said Cerebus. Everyone bowed their heads respectfully, murmuring agreement.

The big Chief pointed up at the moons. All eyes followed his gesture and Elana gasped when she realized what she was looking at.

“It is an omen,” said Brynar. “A sign of the great deeds that have taken place this night. Rowan of Myris Dar is welcome among the Clans. You tell her that if ever you see her again.” He turned his horse and with a clatter of hooves the Horse Clansmen filed back out the gate.

“The message, from the Seers of Danum,” whispered Cerebus as he gazed up at the two moons melded as one.

Cerebus sagged and Elana tried to steady her exhausted husband. She turned to the nearest soldier. “Find a horse for the king, we will return to the keep to see to the damage there.”

Cerebus nodded wearily, the deepest sorrow in his eyes. The city had survived, barely; it would be a long time before Pellaris recovered from the struggle. There was still the Priesthood and its treacherous leadership to contend with.

For now, Elana was content that Cerebus was safe and the people of the city could finally, truly rest without constant fear of impending doom.

Epilogue

A New Beginning

Torrin took the steps two at a time up through the hatch to the deck of the rolling ship. He glanced around at the activity in the bright sunlight. The white sails snapped in the brisk wind and nimble sailors ran across the scrubbed planks to tighten ropes and trim the canvas sheets.

He searched for his wife – found her at the rail, long, loose golden hair draped over her back, the wind lifting it in waves. He watched her for a moment, enjoying the sight of her lean figure, the curve of cheekbone. Her hand upon the wooden rail looked delicate, but he knew how strong and capable it was. She was looking down at the water next to the prow of the sleek ship, a smile lighting her features – watching the dolphins swim. Ever since they had entered these southern waters the fast, playful creatures had been escorting them.

A laugh sounded behind him and he turned toward it expecting to see Nathel. It wasn't him, though, only a sailor joking with his mates. Torrin's chest tightened, he swallowed hard as fresh grief washed over him. It was like that these days, caught in the happiness of the present only to be pulled back suddenly into the pain of loss.

Nathel.

All his years, his younger brother had been a constant in his life. They had been as close as brothers could be. They had fought together, laughed together, slept together in the cold mud to keep from freezing. They had grieved the loss of their parents together and hauled each other out of trouble. Nathel had saved Torrin's life countless times and Torrin had saved Nathel's as many.

But not this time.

Torrin looked at Rowan again, moving across the deck toward her. They were so far away from Pellar and Eryos now – it seemed another life.

As he leaned against the ship's railing and wrapped his arm around her, Rowan turned and smiled up at him. He brushed back strands of her loose hair; she wore it down most of the time now. It was a Myrian custom, she told him – a symbol of new beginnings.

There were new beginnings of many kinds. The passing of Miroth from the world coincided with a transformation taking place in Eryos. Tabor and Klyssen had finally opened treaty negotiations and a tentative truce had been agreed upon. Thaius, the young priest Torrin had met in Pellaris was leading the Priesthood of Erys through the Restoration – had begun moving the teachings out of the political arena and back into the province of spiritual pursuit. The companionship had split, each moving toward new endeavours. With Nathel's death something had been lost – when the mortar that binds a stone wall fails, the rocks fall and scatter.

Torrin and Rowan stood together for a while and looked out over the sparkling water.

Rowan leaned into Torrin, her hair caressed his cheek. "Do you think Dalemar and Hathunor will manage to find all the Raken?" she asked.

Torrin shrugged. "They will certainly learn a lot from each other while they search."

Rowan smiled. "I imagine Dalemar will be very powerful when next we see him. I miss them already."

"So do I." Torrin hoped they were successful for Hathunor's sake.

"Arynilas and Borlin must be very near Dan Tynell by now too," said Rowan.

Torrin nodded and reached into the inside pocket of his tunic, withdrawing a slim leather-bound folder. He opened the cover to reveal an intricate ink drawing of Eryos done in Dalemar's precise hand. Together they looked at the map the Rith had given them for a wedding gift. It detailed the journey the companions had taken together. There were tiny drawings of places they had seen, people they had met and battles they had fought.

Torrin traced his finger down the page to where Ren and the Black Hills were outlined in black ink. "Borlin will have a way to travel once he leaves Dan Tynell, but Arynilas promised to provide and escort to get him through the War Lord territories. His real work will begin once he reaches the Black Hills and his father – it is never easy to bury old family grievances."

Rowan turned and faced him. “Do you regret not taking the commission from Cerebus?”

Torrin sighed and tucked the map away. “A part of me wanted to take it. To live up to the expectations of my king and return to the life that I lost, but I have existed in the midst of war long enough. I need there to be more, for the first time in years, I *want* more. I will not let my sword rust, but for now I am content to spend my days with the woman I love.”

Rowan hugged him. She looked up and grinned. “You will not manage three days without a weapon in your hand, even if it is a practice sword.”

“Is that a challenge?” Torrin laughed.

Rowan’s green eyes sparkled in the sunlight. “Your warrior’s heart will always rise to a challenge, my love,” she whispered.

Torrin hugged her to him and bent down to kiss her. She felt good in his arms, complete. The air was warm this far south, the winter’s chill only a memory and the blue water of the Eryos Ocean was pure and deep.

Somewhere out there on the distant horizon was Myris Dar.

The End

The Adventure Continues...

BOOK TWO
OF
THE STONE GUARDIANS

To find info on the release of Book Two visit:
http://www.thestoneguardians.com/

Remembering
Book II of the Stone Guardians
A novel
by
Kindrie Grove

The Ren Warlord

Torrin's broadsword sang as he pulled it from the scabbard. With a sweep of his arm, its tip was at the man's throat. "Do not touch my wife."

The soldier, swallowed and lifted his hands in surrender. "No offence, no offence. I was only testing the waters. She does not wear the mark."

"We are not from Ren. Back off." Torrin pushed until his sword nicked the man's neck.

Rowan released the grip on her own dagger and stepped between them. "We need to speak with your warlord." She turned to Torrin and raised her eyebrows.

Torrin lowered his sword. "Bartholimus. He and I are – old friends."

The soldier blinked and looked from one to the other. "Well why didn't you just say so!" He turned and motioned for the other soldiers to stand down. "Follow me."

Torrin and Rowan shared a glance as they stepped after the man. "Let me do the talking. We know what kind of an impression you have made so far," whispered Torrin.

Rowan scowled. "I would almost welcome the challenge."

"You may get your wish. I don't even know if he will remember me."

They were led through the squalid camp to a large conglomeration of tents. Light glowed within, flooding from the entrance as servants scurried in and out. Torrin eyed the guards outside and their weaponry as they approached, noting those that looked battle hardened and those that did not.

"Wait here." The soldier ducked through the entrance.

Rowan nudged Torrin, pointing with her glance at the warriors that had subtly surrounded them as they had made their way through the camp. Either to serve as guards or simply because they were bored and curious, Torrin wasn't sure.

He folded his arms across his chest and waited with Rowan. "If this works we will get safe passage through the southern Ren tip," he said quietly.

"If it doesn't?"

"Then we will be taking a hostage."

Rowan raised her eyebrows. "Let us hope he remembers you." She turned to face the entrance to the tent as their escort came back out.

The man smiled obsequiously. "Come, come, Bartholimus is always happy to greet *old friends*." Torrin felt the hair stand up on the back of his neck. He and Rowan took a step towards the entrance but the man raised a hand. "No weapons. If you are old friends, then you know what Ren is like."

Torrin frowned – he was afraid of this. Reluctantly he pulled his sword from its scabbard and handed it over to the guard next to the entrance.

"The lady too."

Rowan sighed and reached up to pull out her sword as well. The dagger on her hip did not go unnoticed either.

Feeling decidedly exposed, Torrin followed the man into the tent. He reached out for Rowan's hand as they went through, but there was nothing there. He spun.

She was gone.

"Rowan!" Torrin charged back outside and saw her being dragged away by a group of soldiers.

He launched himself after her, but was pulled up short by spears levelled at him by the guards. He grabbed the closest one and yanked the soldier off his feet as the man tried to hold on. Jabbing as hard as he could, he struck the soldier in the chest and sent him flying. He spun the spear as the rest came for him.

"Stop! Or she will be killed. I have but to give the order." The man who had led them here called from behind. "She is feisty but cannot hope to stand against the four men who hold her."

You don't know my wife. Torrin smiled grimly as he thought of the small daggers they had each hidden upon themselves before approaching the camp.

Torrin dropped the spear and turned, glowering at the man. "If she comes to any harm, I will kill *you* first."

"You have my word. She will not be touched, as long as you *are* who you say you are."

Torrin took a last look at Rowan, who was standing now in the midst of the soldiers. She nodded to him and lifted a clenched fist to her heart. Torrin closed his eyes and took a deep breath. "Take me to Bartholimus. Let's get this over with."

About the Author

Kindrie Grove is a Canadian-born artist and author. Her works convey the honest truth of animals and legendary subjects with passion, respect and iconic artistic resonance.

Formal training at the Alberta College of Art and Design in Canada has led to her successful career as a professional artist. Kindrie is the author/illustrator of A Field Guide to Horses (Lone Pine Publishing), and has illustrated two children's books: Little Oolly the Garden Gnome (Dravida Publishing) and Claire's Bear (Dragonfly Media Publishing).

She is best known for her large, original oil paintings of wildlife and horses, and bronze sculpture. Studies of wildlife in natural habitats throughout North America, southern Africa and Europe have informed Kindrie's extensive portfolio. Her work is currently featured in galleries across Canada, and in numerous international private and corporate collections including the Toronto Congress Centre's Kindrie Grove Lobby.

Her most recent works in the *Legend Art Collection* depict the essence and spirit of the characters in the books of her newly released fantasy series – The Stone Guardians.

She lives with her husband, Michael, and son, Kellen, in the Okanagan valley of British Columbia, Canada.

To learn more about the Stone Guardian Books and the Legend Art Collection, visit:

www.thestoneguardians.com

To learn more about Kindrie's sculpture and paintings, visit:

www.kindriegrove.com

CPSIA information can be obtained
at www.ICGtesting.com
Printed in the USA
LVHW04s1318101018
593098LV00003B/94/P

9 781549 945472